THE MAGEFIRE

THE MAGEFIRE

First Book of the Amulets of Darkness Cycle

Alexander Baliol

HEADLINE

Copyright © 1990 Alexander Baliol

The right of Alexander Baliol to be identified as the Author of the Work has been asserted by him in accordance with the Copyright, Designs and Patents Act 1988.

First published in 1990
by HEADLINE BOOK PUBLISHING PLC

10 9 8 7 6 5 4 3 2 1

All rights reserved. No part of this publication may be reproduced, stored in a retrieval system, or transmitted, in any form or by any means without the prior written permission of the publisher, nor be otherwise circulated in any form of binding or cover other than that in which it is published and without a similar condition being imposed on the subsequent purchaser.

All characters in this publication are fictitious and any resemblance to real persons, living or dead, is purely coincidental.

British Library Cataloguing in Publication Data

Baliol, Alexander
The magefire.
I. Title
823'.914 [F]

Hardback ISBN 0-7472-0241-9

Royal Paperback ISBN 0 7472 7980 2

Typeset in 11/11 pt Plantin
by Colset Private Limited, Singapore

Printed and bound in Great Britain by
Richard Clay Ltd, Bungay, Suffolk

HEADLINE BOOK PUBLISHING PLC
Headline House
79 Great Titchfield Street
London W1P 7FN

For Martha Jessie

CONTENTS

PART ONE: SIELDER — 1
1. A Summons — 3
2. Outlaw — 13
3. The Way to Istlass — 26
4. Ravenshald — 39
5. The Sea Islands — 52

PART TWO: THE CHOOSING OF THE PATH — 69
6. A New Companion — 71
7. Bracken Heath and Pine — 89
8. Githrim's Tower — 99
9. Hurkling Edge — 115
10. The Keep upon Silentwater — 126
11. Lord Fralcel's Bane — 139

PART THREE: HATHANWILD — 151
12. Argonan Vale — 153
13. The Grey Fortress — 165
14. Goblin Trails — 182
15. Hirda's Garden — 200
16. Stormday Tiding — 218
17. The Cauldron of Embor-Horeoth — 231
18. The Inn at the Bridge — 245
19. Silith Race — 263
20. Valmaalina — 276

PART FOUR: CITADEL — 287
21. The Wall with no Way — 289
22. The Hall of the Stormgiant King — 305
23. The Stratagems of Karadas Ulgar — 316
24. Fair Weather North — 332
25. Darien — 341
26. Hoethan — 352
27. The Ride for the River — 367

PART FIVE: THE GREY SWORD 377
28. Helietrim 379
29. White Death 391
30. The Testing of King Arminor 407
31. The Lee of Clanamel 422

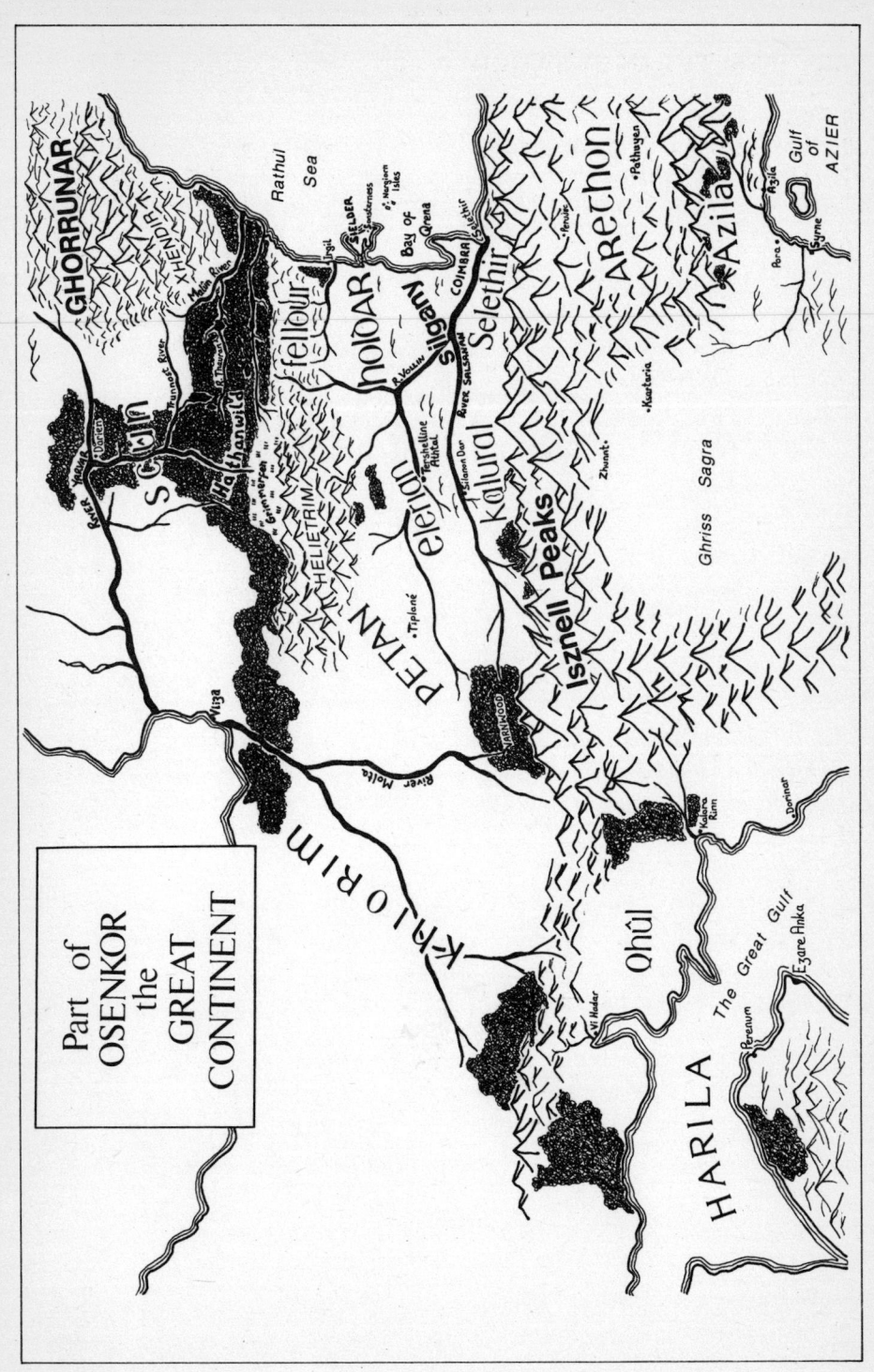

Part One
SIELDER

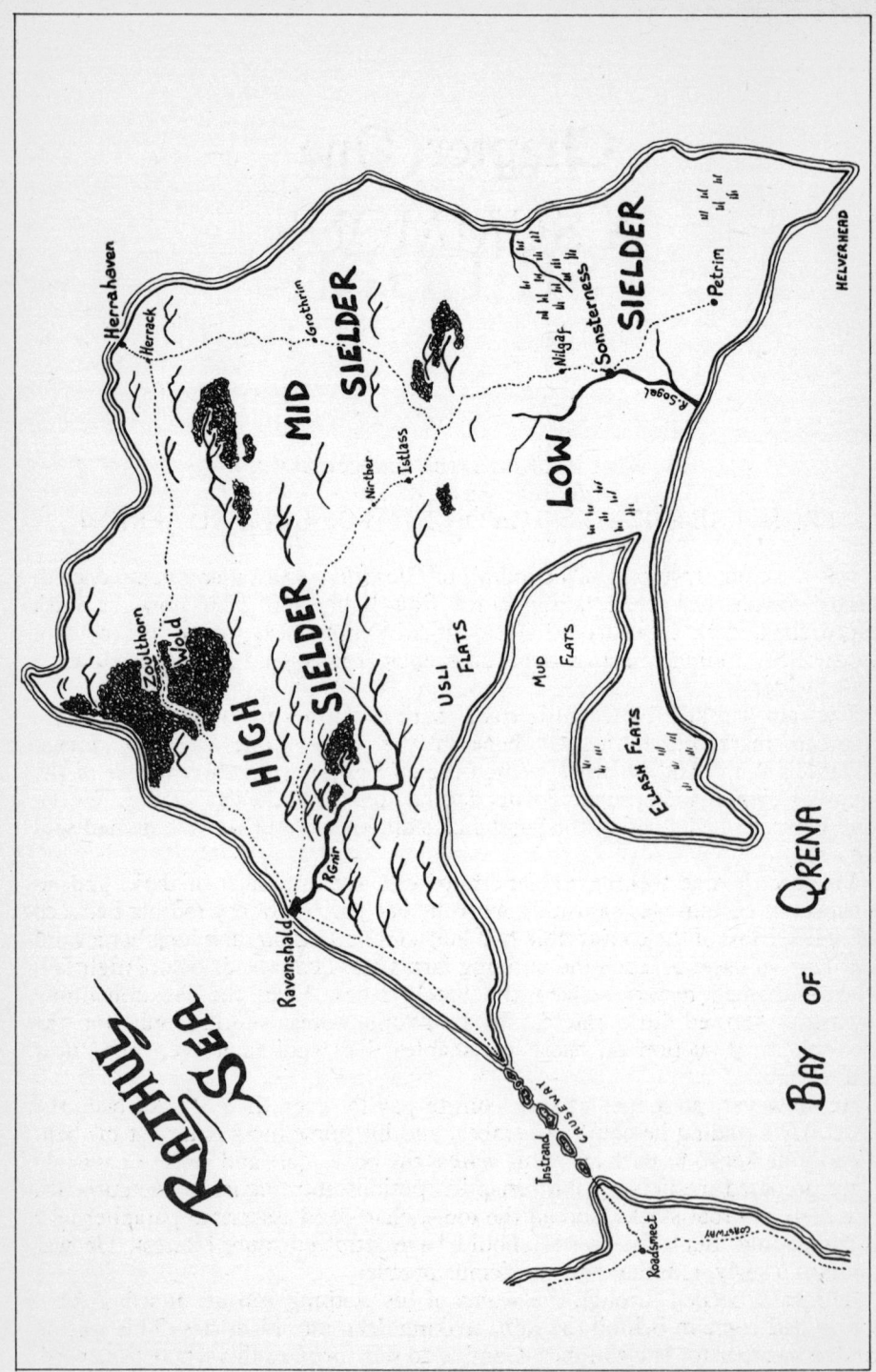

Chapter One
A SUMMONS

Q. What is the one, true and eternal ward?
A. The Circle of Time.
FROM THE INITIATE'S CATECHISM OF HELIARD AERION

It was the eighteenth day of the month of *Gurnithun* and a market day. A cold, steady drizzle had been falling since first light, and even now, as dusk approached, dark moisture-laden clouds still hung heavy over the town of Sonsterness, rolling in across the mud-drenched fields and empty meadows of Low Sielder.

The rain had killed what little trade there might normally have been in the cramped marketplace crushed beneath the squat stone walls of Thegn Hiyarde's keep. And, in what seemed the farthest and muddiest corner of the square, Leighor, sometime of Syrne, had had his fill of the day's trade. For ten long hours he had stood at this wretched stall, and in all that time he had sold nothing.

The drizzle was turning to hard rain with the approach of dark, and all prospect of custom was vanishing with the last patches of dry footing between the stalls. Most of the countryfolk had long since set off on their long homeward journeys, in haste to reach the outlying farms and homesteads before nightfall, when unnamed terrors stalked the lonely lanes. Even the few remaining townsfolk showed little interest in Leighor's wares, waiting only for the food-sellers to auction off those perishables that would not keep until next market day.

He, however, no longer had the coin to pay for even these. It had been the worst day's trading he could remember, and his purse hung empty at his belt. Wearily he began to pack away his wares: the boxes, jars and vials of painstakingly prepared medicines, philtres, pills, potions and unguents; the cure-alls, rare herb and root stocks, and all the tools, charts and associated paraphernalia of his calling. Such fine wares should have attracted more interest. He was amongst a surly, ignorant and suspicious people.

Rainwater seeped through the seams of his clothing and he cursed. A chill breeze had come in behind the rain, striking deep into his bones. This was no kind of weather for late summer. Coming to this town, to this whole backward, forgotten province, had been a mistake. He had hoped to find eager patrons here, clamouring for his cures; perhaps even a rich and powerful sponsor who might provide him with the basis of a settled living. But those were vain dreams. The Holdar Traders had badly misled him. There was scant profit to be gained in the Sielders; and if there were few healers here, it was for good reason. He had gone entirely unnoticed, even by whatever oafish nobility chose to dwell in such a place at this.

A curfew bell tolled from the watchtower above. The town gates would soon be closed, and the streets empty. But where was he to go? Paying the rent on his stall had taken his last remaining coins. And it would be most unwise to return to the Blue Gryphon Inn without the wherewithal to pay his past week's board: payment he had promised to make from this day's profit.

The rain came on harder as he heaved the heavy weight of his trunk onto a rickety handcart. Despite himself he smiled as he read for the thousandth time the old and faded legend etched upon its lid. The letters, once painted in bright greens and golds, were now dull and weatherworn, but still clearly decipherable to any who had the learning and cared to read them: LEIGHOR OF SYRNE – APOTHECARY, PHYSICIAN & HERBALIST – STUDENT OF MIRIUME OF CARNOLIS. The great Miriume would turn in his grave if he but knew how his name was now used, here, so far north of the golden city of Syrne – a thousand leagues away, beyond the cold and mighty Isznell Mountains.

'But who here has ever heard of Miriume of Carnolis?' Leighor muttered to himself, drawing down the cowl of his cloak against the rain as he heaved the barrow into motion. Spots of mud spun up from the wheels.

'Watch out for my linens, you drunken pill-pedlar!' a harsh voice berated from beneath an awning. 'I have sold little enough today for you to be ruining my wares with your southron mud!'

Leighor ignored him and pressed deliberately on out of the square. His face had been enough to betray him an outlander. His dark southron colouring stood out sharply from that of the pale local folk. His height too marked him out, for he was certainly taller than the average, although his sparse build made him no heavier than most of the northron men. Wry and clean shaven, his face yet bore evidence that its owner was not of great age, the only lines being those about the eyes – smile lines he told himself, but more likely gained by reading too long by the light of too cheap a candle.

He passed now between low, grey stone houses, letting his feet carry him where they willed through the maze of twisting streets. All the buildings of this town were low and squat, huddled tight together against the harsh rain-winds that tore in constantly from the surrounding sea. No fine stone guildhalls, no rich palaces, none of the high-gabled mansions of proud merchants towered here. This was a dead end.

Coming at last to an opening in the tight tangle of streets and alleyways, he found himself once again at the house of Cervas, commonly called the Blue Gryphon Inn. For some moments he hesitated, the rain lashing down all about him. He could not sleep outdoors on a night like this, and no other inn would take him in without ready coin. Cervas, however, was not celebrated for his softness of heart, if he threw himself upon the innkeeper's mercy, he knew that he could expect little. Yet if he did not return, the watch would only be roused against him all the sooner – and he could expect the same harsh justice for seven nights' unpaid lodging as for eight . . .

Yes, he was resolved: he would go back to the Blue Gryphon, eat well, sleep well, and try to avoid payment for as long as he could. Perhaps then something might turn up to save him before retribution fell. After all, he smiled grimly, it was almost worth a whipping and a night in the stocks to be out of a night like this.

Pushing open the inn door, he found the tavern unexpectedly full. This was a rare occurrence indeed, for the province of Low Sielder was seldom visited. Surrounded on three sides by the stormy waters of the Rathul Sea, it was on the road to nowhere else. No one came here unless on business, and few had business here, for the Sielders possessed little in the way of natural wealth and could boast few inhabitants of great skill.

'Aha, southron!' Cervas stood at once before him, three mugs of ale gathered into one large fist. 'You have done well, I hope?'

'Indeed!' Leighor forced his face into a grin. A bold front would most likely forestall an immediate demand for payment. 'They were queueing nine deep for my remedies this forenoon! This night I think I shall have a fine roast, and one of your best ales!'

Cervas snorted, on the point of saying something further when a cry from the kitchens summoned him away. Leighor sighed deeply, squeezing himself into a place at one of the long tables. The loud babble of talk slowly resumed, mostly in the homely Durian Sielder-speech, but a few words of the more courtly Varroain of the conquerors, and even of the lilting merchant Giellin, could occasionally be heard alongside the rest.

Cervas reappeared. Yet he seemed now in better mood, cheered by the unexpected plenty the downpour had brought him.

'It should always rain on market day, my friend,' he grinned, passing the southron a bowl of watery soup along with a hunk of dark rye bread. 'I have a good fowl roasting for you. Eat well. We shall settle our business when it is quieter.'

As he ate, Leighor got his first glimpse of Cervas' most recent acquisitions. Two Kobolds from the westlands who had, Cervas told his patrons, bound themselves in service to him for a year and a day for some undisclosed sum. The creatures themselves barely came past the burly innkeeper's knee. Looking neither to left nor to right, they passed through the throng, filling proffered mugs with warm ale in return for coins. Yet still they proved a great success. The Small Folk had become an uncommon sight in these eastern lands. Seldom now did they venture so deep into the realms of men, and that they had ever once done so had now been forgotten by most. There must be some deep trouble in the dark westron hills that were their home, to have brought these two so far. Cervas had made a good bargain.

The innkeeper added to the enjoyment by planting one broad foot firmly in the middle of the nearest Kobold's back and giving a mighty shove. Delighted cries rang out from the audience as the creature hurtled forward, trying to steady itself and its cargo of ale as it slewed to a ragged halt.

'See. Not a drop spilled!' Cervas declared, taking the flagon in his hand and displaying its contents to the cheering patrons, many of whom chose to continue the merriment in like manner by attempting to jar and trip the passing Kobolds where and when they could.

Leighor, however, chose to take more of an interest in his fellow customers. They were mostly farmers and petty merchants, here for the market like himself. But there were several others of a less commonplace sort scattered about the inn: a scarlet-robed Heliard priest who sat alone over a bowl of stewed legumes at one end of the table; two half-armoured men, who looked to be mercenaries, talking quietly in a far corner of the room; and a well-dressed man in a green velvet cloak, who might have been a minor official. The man seemed half to catch Leighor's eye, looking at him strangely, nervously, and then turning away.

But even as Leighor began to wonder who this stranger might be, his attention was drawn away. The main door burst abruptly open to admit a tall man in a grey travelling cloak, stained with the mud and dirt of the road. He waited, seeming to linger deliberately in the doorway until all eyes were turned to him.

'For the sake of Thall, shut that door!' someone shouted.

'Have you not heard the news?' The newcomer's voice cut sharply through the room. 'It is all about the town.'

'What news?'

The stranger seemed about to speak, but then halted, holding up one hand for silence. For some reason all obeyed. And at once they could all hear the long low notes of a distant horn above the sound of the falling rain.

'The Bale Horn!' one of the farmers hissed. 'What new evil has befallen us?'

'The horn announces the death of Galdan, High King and Overlord of all the Varroain dominions.' The stranger closed the door and turned back to face the assembly. 'He has been dead these past ten days, and his nephew Misan will stand regent until a new High King is chosen. The news has only just come from Tershelline!'

A strange sense of dullness and shock fell upon the room at the newcomer's words. It was unlikely that a single person present had ever actually seen the great overlord under whose nominal rule they all lived, let alone known enough of him to feel any personal loss or sadness. Yet Galdan had been High King for longer than most of them had been alive, his invisible presence a pillar of all their lives: the final judge, the ultimate arbiter, the defender of a delicate and all too short-lived peace in these disparate lands of the slowly weakening Varroain dominion. No, it was not sorrow, but more a sense of emptiness, of fear for an uncertain future, that held the patrons of the Blue Gryphon Inn of Sonsterness in solemn silence that night.

The tall man shook his head, taking off his sodden grey cloak to ask for ale, and the spell was broken; all the inn suddenly a-babble with the news, and people debating what changes it might bring for good or ill. Galdan's reign had been long and peaceable, unlike the troubled reigns of Riladar and Imran which had preceded it; and although the High King could exercise few real powers over such a vast and widespread dominion, in which lords like Hiyarde and Eridar more truly ruled, the fears were real. Some could still remember the time when feuds and civil strife had allowed Riever hordes to come down to the very gates of Harnkrath. That had been in the year 737 as the Varroain reckoned, less than fifty years before this current year of 784 . . .

Leighor felt a furtive tap on his shoulder. 'Physician, I think you are the one I seek.' It was the self-same man in green who had been staring at him across the chamber. 'Are you Leighor, physician of Syrne?'

Leighor acknowledged the charge.

'My name is Raiyde,' the other continued. 'I have been commanded by my master, Thegn Hiyarde, to bring you to the keep.'

The southron stood at once, hope rising in his heart. When great opportunity came to one such as he, this was often the way of it. Just being called to the keep was an honour that could bring a hundred new patrons flocking to his stall, all anxious to share a physician with the Thegn of Low Sielder. And if he were successful . . . Who knew what might not follow?

'Well, what is your answer?' Raiyde asked.

'Of course, yes,' Leighor gasped. 'I will come at once!'

The rain had all but ceased by the time they left the inn. Yet throughout the long walk back to the keep, Raiyde said nothing, and could be persuaded to divulge no further information regarding the identity of the patient. But this Leighor took with good heart. After all, if his patient were merely a servant or low functionary there would be no need for such secrecy.

It was fully dark when they reached the castle. Dim yellow lights flickered eerily from the narrow tower windows above them. A lone sentry let them pass without challenge, and Raiyde led the way briskly upward, via several dimly lit passages and stairways, to a reed-strewn corridor high in the main tower. Here, beneath a single guttering torch, stood four men, all nobly dressed in rich damasks and velvets. Three were of middle years, one considerably older. It was this man who beckoned them impatiently forward.

Raiyde bowed. Leighor followed suit.

'My lords, I present the physician, Leighor of Syrne.' His guide spoke now in the courtly Varroain tongue of the rulers, rather than the common Sielder-speech of tavern and marketplace.

'Kneel, fellow!' one of the younger men snarled. 'You stand before Hiyarde, Thegn of Low Sielder.'

Leighor knelt.

'Be not so harsh, Girvan. He knows not to whom he speaks.' The older man motioned Leighor to his feet. 'We have need of your skills, healer. My guest, the noble Eridar, Archbaron of the Sielders, is newly arrived from Ravenshald, and has this day been taken ill. None of his own physicians are here to attend him. My own healing woman seems not to agree with him, and he will trust none of the local leeches . . .' He paused. 'They tell me that you are a pupil of Miriume, the great southland healer?'

Leighor nodded, irrationally fearful that his deception might be uncovered. But that was foolishness. The only people who knew that he had not in fact studied under Miriume long enough to learn more than a few choice curses and a method for cheating at cards, lay at least a thousand leagues away, in the distant city of Syrne.

'Good. Good.' The other smiled. 'This is most fortunate. Please go to my lord now, and do what your skills allow.' He nodded to Raiyde, who at once opened the door to a nearby chamber, indicating that Leighor should enter.

Bowing once more to the four nobles, he did so, hearing the door click to behind him as he walked into the darkness. Raiyde did not follow. He was alone. The only light in the room came from a low-burning log fire at its far end. Making a silent prayer to Shereor, god of healers, Leighor ventured a few steps forward, trying not to trip over the furniture as his eyes gradually accustomed themselves to the lack of light. A large canopied bed towered out of the gloom in front of him, and he moved towards it, not at first noticing the two figures standing, still and silent, upon the far side. Their movement startled him, and timorously he announced himself.

'I am the physician, Leighor of Syrne. I am here to attend upon my lord Eridar . . .'

He could see the two figures more clearly now. One was large and cowled, probably a cultish priest of some sort, the other a tall youth in the dandified tunic of a nobleman.

The cowled figure spoke, but not to him. He said softly, 'Awake, my lord Eridar, it is the physician from the town.'

And then another voice came from within the dark confines of the bed; one which did not, to Leighor, seem to indicate great infirmity.

'Who? Who is there?' The shadow figure tried to sit up in bed. 'Let us have some light! Even a devil out of Qhilmun could not see in this darkness!'

At once a third attendant, a wimpled servant, whom Leighor – to his surprise – had not noticed before, rose from a darkened corner to move silently across the room. Lighting two smoking torches from the fire, she set them into iron rings on either side of the bed, and withdrew. The brighter light enabled Leighor to examine his two other companions more closely.

The youth was tall, two or three inches taller than Leighor himself, with the lean grace that still occasionally surfaced amongst the Varroain nobility. Leighor guessed him to be perhaps seventeen or eighteen, yet already with the careless hauteur of one accustomed to giving orders and seeing them obeyed. Yet there was a strength about him that his height only partly disguised. Broad of shoulder and narrow of waist, he possessed the tense, barely restrained energy of a coiled spring. The face too was Varroain, with fine-drawn arrogant features as yet unmoulded by the pressures of responsibility or ambition, topped by a shock of dark brown hair which would have tended to curl were it not cut short to the nape of the neck in the style currently fashionable amongst young noblemen of his years.

The cowled man was a head shorter, yet probably bore the more weight, being thickset and stout of build. His ample frame was clearly visible beneath the light brown robes and darker cowled mantle that Leighor immediately recognised as being of the Mallenian cult – a small unfashionable faith, certainly not held openly by many of the nobility in these days. And this man's face bore no marks of high birth, being broad, ill-shaven and plain. He was of later middle years, with a generally dour look, although Leighor guessed that there were traces of humour buried somewhere within that heavy face which might be revealed if its owner chose.

'I am Leighor of Syrne, my lord,' the southron repeated, hoping his nervousness was not betrayed in his voice, which to him seemed very thin and shaky.

Now, for the first time, he could look directly down into the face of Archbaron Eridar, the feudal lord of all the Sielders: a man who owed fealty of service only to the High King himself. The face he saw was broad and strong, with short brown hair, a brief, rough-trimmed beard and deep calculating eyes. It was the strong, unyielding visage of a man who had ruled these three provinces with a firm hand for over a quarter of a century.

'I am the physician summoned to attend you,' he added to fill the silence.

'I need no physician, fool!' Eridar spluttered with sudden anger. 'I know well enough what ails me. Did I not tell Hiyarde and Darvir both, only to let me rest?'

'Yes, my lord,' the monk murmured softly. 'Yet they claim to be concerned for your health . . .'

Eridar laughed darkly. 'What, Darvir? He waits upon my death like a hungered vulture! When I go, he will have my crown upon his head before it has had time to grow cold.' With a painful heave, he pulled himself erect, resting back against thick velvet bolsters, his searching eyes fastening once more upon Leighor. 'Who are you, dark one?' he asked sharply. 'Some market quack sent here to finish me off?'

The words stung, taking away much of Leighor's remaining confidence. How much could this man possibly have learned of his true origins, he wondered? 'No, my lord,' he managed to croak. 'I am a physician of Syrne. I have studied long in the southlands under such as Miriume of Carnolis . . .'

'Indeed. Indeed.' The archbaron seem unimpressed. 'No doubt you have as much learning as any who ply your trade. Yet that is little enough in these dark days. Why should I permit you to paw your pocky hands all over me?'

'I have heard of Miriume, sire,' the priest intervened unexpectedly. 'He was reputed to be one of the greatest physicians of the south. If this man truly comes from Syrne it would be small harm to let him examine you; and it might satisfy my lord Darvir.'

'Very well,' Eridar nodded with little enthusiasm. 'In order to rid me of my brother's attentions, you may examine me; but be brief.'

Leighor prepared himself nervously, removing the small satchel of potions and instruments that he always carried with him on such occasions, while the monk readied his patient.

'What is the nature of your illness, my lord?' he asked briskly, realising at once that this was a mistake.

'Surely that is for you to tell me, good physician,' Eridar growled.

'Yes, my lord.' Much depended on this. He must be careful. Keep calm. Begin the routine patter of his examination.

'But what are your symptoms? How do they afflict you?'

'I have pain,' Eridar grunted irritably. 'Pain that runs through all the joints of my body. It comes on worse and worse with the passing years. My ankles and legs are swollen with it and I am sore afflicted. Yon priest says that it is all due to eating meat in surfeit – which is a good enough tale for the peasant folk, but does little good to me.'

'I will have to examine you now, my lord,' Leighor told him.

Eridar protested, but it was soon done. A clear case of the *bone-harrow*. There was little Leighor could do, and reluctantly he told Eridar so. 'There is a salve that will reduce the pain,' he offered, 'but I have not brought it with me. If you will permit, I will go back to my lodging and return with some immediately.'

'There is no need to bother yourself,' Eridar grunted. 'The morning will do.

I have seen more than enough of purulent salves to last me a lifetime! Have you nothing else to give me, no pills, no elixirs?'

Leighor shook his head. 'No, your grace – unless you would like a draught to make you sleep, or a herbal tea to invigorate your vital organs?'

Eridar held up his hand. 'The gods forbid! But you are a strange physician. The first I have met in forty years who has not tried to ply me with four score kinds of medicine. What is your name again, healer? I have misheard it.'

'Leighor, Leighor of Syrne, sire.'

'Hmm.' Eridar thought for a moment. 'Good, I may have need of your services again. You may return in the morning with your salve.'

Leighor bowed low. 'Very good, my lord.'

Eridar smiled. 'And if you were wondering, these two glum gentlemen,' – he nodded towards the other side of the canopied bed – 'are my young nephew Yeon and his new tutor Uhlendof – a Mallenian, but a good scribe and tutor nevertheless.'

Leighor bowed again, but met with only the curtest of acknowledgements from across the bed.

'It is not a common thing for a young nobleman to study the philosophies and the histories in these days,' Eridar went on, to the youth's evident displeasure at being discussed so before a common stranger. 'But that is the unusual opportunity I am about to give to my youngest nephew. Our noblemen in these days spend too much time learning the arts of war, and of their own honour; too little learning of their duty and the arts of peace. That is where both my brothers, Darvir and Girvan, have gone so sadly astray: do you not think so, physician?'

'That I cannot say, my lord.' Leighor chose his words carefully. He was on very dangerous ground. To criticise a noble in another's hearing could mean a flogging, imprisonment, or worse. Perhaps Eridar was playing with him – or testing him.

Now was the time to withdraw.

'You must sleep now, sire,' he added quickly, hurriedly donning his satchel. 'I shall return at dawn with the salve, and to see how you progress.' He bowed again and backed away.

In the corridor outside the lords still waited. Thegn Hiyarde asked a question or two regarding Eridar's illness and, seeming satisfied with the answers, thanked the southron and dismissed him. Raiyde walked with him from the keep. But on drawing near to the gate, his guide halted and withdrew a small leather purse from his doublet.

'I have here your fee, physician,' he said softly, handing the purse to him. 'Payment for the good work you have done this night. Now go.'

The purse held three small gold talents, each bearing a crude representation of King Galdan's head.

'But I have done little yet,' Leighor protested. 'My task is not yet completed. The fee is not yet due!'

'These are my instructions.' Raiyde's face was expressionless. 'If my lord needs your services again he will send for you.'

'You don't understand . . .' Leighor began, but Raiyde had already turned away.

Leighor shrugged. It was late. He would return in the morning to sort things out. He jingled the coins in his hand and pocketed them. At least he had gold now to show to Cervas; and if he were to become one of Eridar's personal physicians, this was but the beginning . . .

Smiling, he strode jauntily from the keep, hearing the great iron gate slam shut behind him and the heavy bolts crash to. Suddenly alone in the blackness of the deserted marketplace, he realised how late it must be. Not a light showed through all the dark city. The whole town must be abed. He began to make more haste towards the maze of alleyways that would eventually bring him back to the inn.

The night was chill and he looked warily about him, hoping that Cervas had left somebody awake to admit him. The alleyways seemed narrower and less familiar now, and full of hidden obstacles to trip over or bump into. There was no moon, not even a glimmer of starlight to brighten his way, for the sky was still overcast. He cursed – and then he drew up, suddenly alert. He could have sworn he heard footsteps on the cobblestones behind him! But now there was no sound. He moved on a little farther, and again he felt that he heard something behind him – something more than just the echo of his own footsteps. He halted again. This time there was no doubt. Not one, but two pairs of footfalls sounded briefly behind him and then halted.

Someone followed! Probably robbers waiting to corner him, strip him and leave him for dead upon the empty street. And he could expect little help from the townsfolk, safely abed behind their stout shutters. He must get back to the inn before they caught up with him. Casting caution to the winds, he ran; hearing the footfalls behind him quicken as his unknown pursuers gave chase. Now he ran the harder, crashing blindly into signs, barrels, everything in his path, in his desperation to escape them.

Yet despite his greatest efforts, he was not succeeding. He could still hear the running footsteps closing behind him, and soon he must slow. He was nearly out of breath, he could hear his own heart drumming in his ears almost above the sound of his fast-closing pursuers. Again he stumbled. They were almost upon him.

'Hold, friend!' A rough voice grated without amity, and a leather-gloved hand closed upon his trailing arm. They had him!

Instinctively, Leighor dipped into his pocket with his free hand and threw his precious three gold talents straight into his assailant's face. The coins scattered, clattering down on to the hard cobblestones. But his stratagem did the trick. The hand released him, whether from shock or greed he never knew, but he was free once again to race off into the darkness as the two dark shadows reeled behind him.

But he suspected that the sight of gold would only whet their appetites for more, they would be on his trail again in moments. He must find some means of escape! He turned left into an alleyway that must surely take him straight back to the inn. It could not be very far now . . . But no! The alley turned sharp right again, and he found himself facing a blank stone wall. A dead end! He had lost his way, and now he was trapped, cornered, with no way forward or back!

He thought of hammering upon one of the bolted doors that opened on to the alley, but no one would open at this hour – at least not in time to save him. He heard running feet and whispered oaths behind him. He had but one chance . . .

Turning, he ran at the barrier wall, making a desperate lunge for the top, grasping and clinging to the rough stone. Fear giving him strength, Leighor hauled his body up until he lay astride the wall, but the ledge was narrower than he expected and he lost his balance, crashing heavily to the ground on the other side. His head struck hard stone, and he lost consciousness.

Chapter Two
OUTLAW

Harsh light tore into his senses. Leighor screwed up his eyes, trying to blot it out – but it would not go away. He felt something hard and cold against the back of his neck.

Where was he?

Slowly he forced his eyes open, quickly shutting them again as bright sunlight flooded into them. His head was splitting, and every part of his body seemed to hurt. He began to remember his fall ... Surely every bone in his body must be broken? No, that was nonsense, his hands and feet protested but they obeyed his commands. There could not be too much amiss there.

With a major effort of will, he forced himself into a sitting position – the movement was painful but not impossible. No, he seemed to have no broken bones after all, but plenty of bruises in their stead. His satchel lay where it had fallen, a few feet away, it contents scattered across the muddy stones. With a silent oath, he gathered them together, refastening the satchel across his back. Using the nearby wall for support, he managed at last to scramble back to his feet. Gasping for breath, he rested, the events of the previous night slowly coming back to him.

What time was it? From the height of the sun it must be near noon. He had lost his pursuers. That must have been hours ago. But what had happened since then? And what of Lord Eridar? His patient had expected to see him again at dawn! Why must disaster ever befall him when he had the most to lose by it? Did Vuhna's curse still follow him, even now? But whatever the cause, he must get back to the keep ... must explain ...

Shading his eyes from the sun, he looked around him. Where in Gehenna was he? He seemed to be standing in a small enclosed courtyard, high walls surrounding him on three sides, and a low timber and daub building on the fourth. This last seemed to offer the only means of egress, and so he picked his way unsteadily through the piles of rubbish and firewood that littered the courtyard, towards the small wooden door.

He knocked, but there was no response, and the door was firmly bolted. There was a small grimy window to the right of the door, so dark and filthy that he could see nothing through it. In desperation he hammered on the door again, making enough noise, he thought, to raise the whole city; and to his surprise there at once came the sound of someone pulling back the bolt from the inside.

Slowly, timorously, the door crept open, and the frightened face of an old woman peered out through the gap.

As soon as she saw the stranger in her courtyard, she gave a startled scream and made to slam the door again. But Leighor was too fast for her; placing his body firmly between door and jamb, he forced it back open.

'What are you doing here? Who are you?' The woman's voice trembled as she spoke.

'I mean you no harm, good lady,' Leighor tried to reassure her. 'I have had an accident and fallen into your courtyard. I think I must have lain here all night . . .'

'All night! You've been here all night?'

'Yes, yes!' Leighor was flustered and irritated by her alarm. 'I was pursued by thieves and tried to escape over your wall – but I must have slipped. All I need is to pass through your house and be on my way.'

'Pa . . . pass . . .' the woman stuttered incoherently before finally managing to compose herself. 'How . . . How do I know you're telling the truth?'

'Look,' Leighor replied patiently, removing his small satchel of potions and implements to show her. 'I am physician. I need to get to Lord Eridar at once! I am his personal physician. I was with him last night!'

The effect of these few words on the old woman was entirely unexpected; her face transforming itself immediately into a mask of terror – as if she had just recognised a demon from the pit.

'You!' she exhaled hoarsely. 'It was you! With Lord Eridar . . .' Her eyes widened in horror.

'Yes, I am his physician.' Leighor lost patience with the woman. Her brain must be addled! He made to push past her, and so cut short this pointless conversation. But even as he moved forward, the old woman let forth a loud, piercing scream, which must surely have been heard for miles. She prepared to scream again.

Leighor leapt forward to silence her; and she cowered back in genuine terror. 'Come not near me, dark murderer!'

'Murderer?' Leighor gasped. His head was beginning to spin.

'Aye.' The woman's eyes stared. 'You admit it yourself. You are Eridar's physician. You are his murderer, then! Come no closer!'

She made to scream again, but this time Leighor caught her and held her firm, his hand tight across her mouth so that she could not.

'Tell me, woman,' he gasped. 'Tell me true and I shall not harm you: why do you name me Lord Eridar's murderer? Is he dead since yesternight?'

The woman trembled as he released her mouth, but she did not scream. Sobbing, she spoke haltingly: 'The news has been throughout the city, sir, since dawn . . .' She shuddered, '. . . when Lord Eridar was found poisoned in his bed! The guard now search high and low for Lord Eridar's southron physician – you!'

'Me?' Now it was Leighor's turn to shudder.

'Maybe it wasn't you, sir . . .' the woman quavered fearfully, but even as she spoke the words they caught in her throat. Leighor was without doubt the only southron of any description she had seen for many a long month. There was no mistake.

'Who . . . who says it was me?' Leighor demanded, still unbelieving. 'When I saw him last he was alive and well.'

The woman still sobbed, near paralysed with fear: but he had to have an answer. He shook her violently. 'Who says this? Answer me!'

'Lord Darvir,' she choked. 'The Archbaron's own brother. He it is who gives evidence against you! Saying that after taking a draught you gave him, he sickened and died!'

Leighor released her, a sickening chill spreading through his body. 'But I gave him no draught . . .' His own voice faded as the woman backed away. 'How can this be . . . ?'

'Perhaps there is some mistake . . .' the woman gabbled feverishly – yet it was plain to see that she believed no such thing. 'You should surrender yourself to the guard and explain . . .'

Leighor's mind was in turmoil. This was all happening far too quickly! He must get away . . . Must have time to think, before he did anything foolish – like giving himself up! The death of the Archbaron would have the whole city hunting for him. He could remain here no longer. At any moment someone might come to investigate the cause of this disturbance. He must get away quickly: before the woman started screaming again.

Drawing the hood of his cloak down across his face, he turned abruptly away, crashing through the shambles of the downstairs room towards the street door. He drew it cautiously open to see what lay beyond. Yet all seemed normal enough: the street was thronging with all the bustle of a normal weekday. He took a deep breath and crept out onto the cobbled way.

Trying to attract as little attention to himself as possible, he strode briskly away from the house. Yet still he felt the whole world watching him as he forced a path through the crowds. If someone had killed the Archbaron, he thought with bitterness, how clever to cast the blame an itinerant like himself; scarcely known in the city, with no friends and no family. What's more, a southron, so easily recognised, so easy for all to believe the assassin!

Then he heard it. The sound he had dreaded but had known must surely come. The loud harsh scream of vented terror from the house behind him. 'The murderer! The southron! He is here . . . Stop him!' The old woman had found her voice again.

All heads turned. But for now they looked past him, towards the origin of the screaming. For the moment he was safe, but the pursuit would not be long in starting. He tried to inch his way forward, away from the excitable throng now gathering outside the old woman's dwelling. He dared not run; he must force himself to move slowly, innocently, without drawing attention to himself. There was a small alley a little farther on, leading off to the right. If only he could reach it before he were noticed . . . He was almost there: just a few steps more, past tables loaded with pots, pans, knives and trinkets . . .

At last, gratefully, he turned into the alley and ran. He could hear the sounds of the hue and cry rising behind him, but this alley was empty and deserted. He was away.

But where? Where could he go? No one would give him shelter. Certainly not Cervas at the Blue Gryphon – that was the first place they would look for him. So where in all this grey shambles of a town could he hide?

He glimpsed a high wall ahead. His heart missed a beat. Surely not another blind alley? But no: he breathed again. There was an open gateway on his left. The rear entrance to a large inn. He kept close to the wall and peered into the courtyard. The main building was directly in front of him, to either side were the stables and outbuildings. Half a dozen wine-barrels were in the process of being unloaded from a small ox-cart, but otherwise the courtyard was empty. Everyone must be at their midday meal. Excellent. He made quickly for the cover of some heavy farm waggons that stood in the far corner of the stables, letting out a deep sigh once safe in their shadow. But his immediate sense of relief quickly subsided. He could not stay here either, for he would be discovered the moment the liverymen returned. There must be somewhere he could hide for at least long enough to come to a decision as to what he was to do. Then he saw the open hatchway leading down to the cellars beneath the inn. Of course! It had been left open for the loading of the new wine. Once in those dark cellars, he could remain hidden almost as long as he pleased.

He crept slowly around the side of the courtyard, moving cautiously from shadow to shadow, and running the last few feet down the sloping ramp into the gloomy cellar below. He drew a deep breath. No one had called out. Hopefully he was unseen.

The cellar was large, cool and dark, piled high with ale casks and vast barrels of Giellin wine. Finding a path through the jumble to a corner hidden from the entrance ramp by a pile of sour-smelling barrels, he made a makeshift seat out of an upturned wooden crate, and rested. For the first time since he had left the safety of the Blue Gryphon Inn the night before, he felt that he could relax. The cellar was cool, the darkness restful, and at last he could think.

Aye, he could think. And if Lord Eridar were truly dead, he had much thinking to do. Yet in truth he had but two options. Either to give himself up and try to prove his innocence, or else to remain fugitive and try to escape from Sonsterness. There was – there could be – no middle way.

What would an innocent man do? Give himself up, of course. Prove his innocence. He had not done the deed, he *was* innocent. Why then could he not come forward and say so? After all, he had given Eridar no potion or philtre of any kind. He could not have poisoned him, and the priest and the boy should be witnesses to that . . .

But there was a major flaw in that argument. If what the old woman had told him was true, no less a person than Lord Darvir himself, Eridar's own brother and presumed successor, had let it be known that he had poisoned the Archbaron. And who was he, Leighor the southron, travelling apothecary, to challenge the word of such a noble lord? To save his life he would have to prove Darvir mistaken, or worse still, a liar; and no court in the Sielders would take his word over that of the next ruler of the Sielders. Under such circumstances he would receive little more than a mockery of a trial followed by a speedy execution. That was, if he were lucky, and not put to the torture first to gain a confession. He shivered. And no doubt he would confess, given time.

No, if he was to give himself up, he must first have incontrovertible proof of his own innocence – and to gain that he would have to discover who truly had killed Lord Eridar . . . Yet surely that was what Darvir and Hiyarde wanted too? They would need to know the truth, to discover the traitor in their midst, simply in order to protect themselves. Certainly they could not be satisfied with the death of one itinerant southerner.

That was . . . the thought came suddenly and broke over Leighor like a thunderflash . . . That was, unless they already knew the truth. Unless they knew only too well who had killed Eridar; because they had done it themselves!

The idea horrified him. But the more he thought about it, the stronger hold it took. After all, was it not Darvir and Hiyarde, not Eridar himself, who had summoned him? Summoned him when all that Eridar had wrong with him was a resurgence of his old bone-harrow – a condition that was probably well known and long remarked. Certainly not dangerous enough to call in an untried and untested physician so urgently from the marketplace.

Yes, everything now fell neatly into place: the call, the implied urgency, the fact that Raiyde had insisted on paying him off, and even the witnesses standing by. He had probably been picked out as the victim of this plot from the moment he had first appeared in the marketplace.

A sharp chill ran down the length of his spine. His apparent good fortune had in fact been a marker for death. His real good luck had been the two footpads who had pursued him and driven him out of his way, to lie unconscious yet undetected in the old woman's courtyard. Were it not for them he would have been waiting at the inn, all unknowing when Darvir's guards came for him the next morning. He shivered: suddenly the cellar seemed intensely cold. If any of this was even partly true, then he could trust no one. He was entirely alone.

Yet now, at least, he had no decision to make. There was only one option left open to him, the second; to stay free as long as he could, to escape. He could not hope to expose Eridar's true murderer. He was far too low in station to intervene in the intrigues of the nobility. He had but one duty, to get himself away.

But how was that to be accomplished? He was utterly alone, in a well guarded, walled city, with every man's hand turned against him. If he could but get beyond the walls he might have a chance, but within the city he would certainly be caught sooner or later. He could not even remain here for more than a few hours, for if this cellar had not already been searched, it soon would be. For the moment, though, he would just have to take his chances; he was too weary and confused to move again until after nightfall.

Leighor stayed awake, watchful and brooding, for the rest of the afternoon, hiding low in the shadows whenever anyone entered the cellar – which was a fairly frequent occurrence, for boys came down regularly from the tavern above to fetch ale and wine. Leighor felt a little more secure once the unloading of the wine from the courtyard had been completed, and the great double doors leading down from above were finally shut and bolted. Even so, he dared not let himself sleep, and his hours in the cellar were a cold, cramped and hungry misery.

The growing sounds of revelry from above seemed to mock him in his wretchedness as the night drew on. Yet despite his resolve Leighor now slept in short bursts, to snap suddenly awake at any small sound. Most often this was the trapdoor opening to admit two more youths for wine or ale. Then he might hear garbled snatches of conversation, quite often upon the subject of the previous night's murder.

'It was an evil crime,' said one. 'And 'tis enough to make the flesh creep that the southron still lurks within the city. I hope they catch him quickly so we can watch him burn in Black Swan square.'

'Aye,' said another, 'though I reckon it be a bad omen that High King and Archbaron are both struck dead upon the same night. They say that a teller of the White Oracle predicted it all not three months since, and worse to follow . . .' The trapdoor closed and Leighor fell back into his fractured doze.

At length the inn above grew quieter, and the visits from the ale-lads less and less frequent, until eventually no one came, and there was silence.

Dark silence.

There was a sudden high-pitched squeak from Leighor's right. He felt something move against his leg, something else scurrying behind him. Leaping up in horror he heard a dozen small scrabbling movements and then silence. Rats. The cellar must be infested with them, and this was their hour. That settled it. It was time to leave. He edged his way warily towards the narrow stair that led up into the main body of the inn, having to feel his way through the darkness. There might be food and wine above also, and not having eaten or drunk for more than a day, he began to imagine that that alone might be well worth the risk of discovery.

The rats had begun to move again. He could hear their squeals and chatterings all around him. They did not fear him now, alone and quiet with them in their darkness. Hurriedly he climbed the narrow stair, edging the wooden trapdoor partially open with his shoulders to peer out. Seeing nothing but blackness, and hearing nothing but a dull, distant snoring, he raised the trapdoor a little further and scrambled out.

There was some light here, a broad stream of moonlight that flooded in from the unshuttered window overlooking the inner courtyard. And by this he could tell that he was behind the long counting-board of the tavern. Behind him were shelves and an open doorway: in front, a wide hall filled with benches and forms. These were of most interest to Leighor at this moment, strewn as they were with mugs, goblets and pewter tankards, wooden platters, empty wine pitchers and stone ale-jugs. Most of the clearing and cleaning in a place like this was generally left until the morning, and there would be many useful pickings to be had from those tables. He made his way silently across the room, scouring the tables until he had found a half-eaten plate of cold meats and the remains of a small loaf. Sitting down at the nearest bench, he ate. Ravenously. He had almost forgotten how hungry he could be. The food was delicious. No wonder the rats prospered here.

Suddenly he heard a heavy padding behind him. At once he swung about, to find himself staring straight into the eyes of a large, gleaming mastiff. The beast growled low and threatening, slowly advancing upon him, fangs bared. Leighor's heart skipped a beat. What was he to do now? He tried speaking softly to the dog to calm it, but his voice was too furtive to achieve the desired effect, and the dog only growled louder. In panic, he seized a ham bone from a nearby platter and hurled it. The dog leapt, catching it neatly between its teeth, and ran off with it to some secret corner of its own. Despite himself, Leighor smiled. Stupid dog.

Hurriedly finishing his meal, he sought out something to drink, sniffing all the wine jugs in turn until he found one with a pleasant smelling liquid in it. This he downed in one draught. The inn was turning out to be very propitious after all. Quietly he rose and tiptoed away, pausing only to gather up scraps of meat and cheese and placing them in his satchel for later on, as well as a small bottle chosen at random from the pile behind the main counter. He thought of searching for money, but decided not to risk it. He must leave now and find somewhere safe to rest – but how? He dared not leave by the main door, that would indeed raise the dogs. And besides, he might walk straight into the arms of the watch.

At least he knew where he was now. He recognised the layout of the inn. This was the Dove, the largest inn of Sonsterness, which lay close to the South Gate. If only he could be out of that gate and on the open road, he would have some chance of gaining his freedom. But that goal lay as distant now as the snows of the Isznells. He would have to concentrate upon more immediate matters. He remembered a little of the geography of the inn from previous visits, and, not quite knowing what he intended, made his way up the great flight of oaken stairs that were the pride of the establishment, to the upper gallery that looked down upon the main hall. Many private chambers opened on to this balcony, but these did not now interest him. He sought only the sturdy wooden ladder that led up to the loft, where the communal sleeping quarters lay.

Here the floor was laid with straw and snoring patrons, most covered only by their cloaks, their weapons at their sides. A large man lurched out of the darkness, on his way down the ladder, presumably in search of the jakes, but he paid Leighor no attention and passed on by. The temptation to lie down and join the sleeping patrons was overwhelming, but Leighor resisted it, stepping over the snoring bodies to one of the small, shuttered casements that opened out on to the sloping roof. These were the only means of egress, and these he must now use if ever he intended to escape this place. Perhaps thus he might find his way to an unguarded stretch of wall, or at least a warm attic in which to hide. The shutter creaked slowly open at his touch, admitting a broad band of moonlight to the chamber as he stepped out onto the roof.

Seeing the drop beneath him he almost lost his nerve, but forced himself to pull the shutters to behind him and begin the dangerous ascent of the tiled roof. He had seen this done many times before, by children and roofers, but until this moment he had not realised the full terror of the experience. His booted feet tended far too often to slip on the loose tiles as he scrambled upwards, threatening to send him cannoning down into the dark courtyard below. And he was in constant fear that the whole creaking roof might suddenly give way beneath him. But at last he made it, to sit triumphantly astride the summit, resting awhile in relative safety.

In the brilliant moonlight he could just see the dark walls surrounding the city of Sonsterness – walls that were low and crumbling, but still well enough guarded to prevent his escape. In front of him, at the end of a winding street, were the twin grey towers of the South Gate. Turning to look behind him, he found that he could see across a sea of steeply-pitched rooftops to the distant keep, where a few flickering yellow lights still burned, even at this hour. What must Darvir and Hiyarde be doing now, he wondered; what plans did they make for his capture, for the control and plunder of all the Sielders?

He very nearly found out, for only then did he see the cluster of bright lights approaching on the darkened street below. It was Thegn Hiyarde's watch, patrolling the streets with considerably more diligence than was usual for their sort. Eight or nine shabbily liveried men shuffled torpidly up the roadway bearing flaming pitch torches to light their way, their ancient halberds drooped carelessly across their shoulders. Leighor kept low and still, trying to merge with the dark slope of the roof. Yet still he felt utterly vulnerable, exposed to the searching light of their torches, which seemed to rise with a malevolent will of its own to seek him out. Surely one of them must glance upward and see him here? Yet although they poked their torches into every arch and alley they passed, not one of the watch chanced to look up; and slowly, interminably slowly, they went by.

Leighor breathed again. They were gone. But what now? He looked along the line of buildings towards the South Gate. The houses were joined one to another in a higgledy-piggledy terrace, their rooftops all at slightly different heights and angles, culminating in the broad flat roof and high flame tower of a Heliard temple. His spirits rose a little at the sight. He was no flame-worshipping Heliard, nor overly religious in any form, yet the temple suddenly became connected in his mind with sanctuary, and so his immediate goal. He had an objective.

Crawling unsteadily along the rooftops, balancing precariously on the steep ridges, he clambered haltingly from housetop to housetop. Some roofs were in a better state than others, and he had several heart-stopping moments, clinging grimly to rotting slate and crumbling mortar. Once a handhold gave way, two tiles crashing noisily down the sloping roof to shatter on the cobblestones below. He froze, waiting for any sign of a raised alarm, but after a long period of silence he forced himself to move on once more.

It was only when he had reached the last of the intervening houses that he saw the gap; the deep dark chasm some four yards wide that separated him from the temple. His heart sank as he stared down into the dirty alleyway three storeys below. There was no possible way down. He must either turn, and go back the way he had come, or else try to leap the chasm. Near certain discovery, or sudden death: neither prospect pleased. Yet in truth the gap between the angled roof to which he now clung, and the flat roof of the temple, was not great. Given a flat surface to stand upon he could have leapt it easily. Why not try? He would have to take a considerable risk anyway, just to turn around.

Screwing up all his courage, he managed to draw himself slowly to his feet, swaying uncertainly, one foot on either side of the roof ridge, his ankles twisted awkwardly inward. No. It was no use. He was never going to make the jump this way. He must be bolder. He must take a run at it, whatever the footing. Crouching down once more, he inched his way several feet backward before attempting to stand again. There was a coping of curved tiles on the ridge of this roof, just broad enough for one foot to balance rather unsteadily. If he ran, he could probably keep his balance for just long enough to launch himself over the gap. He stood, placing the weight of his right foot on the coping. He nearly lost his balance. He felt himself beginning to slip. It was now or never.

Holding his arms outstretched, he ran. One, two, three paces. His foot slipped. But he had just enough purchase to launch himself out over the chasm . . .

His arms flailed wildly, at last catching on the low brick parapet that surrounded the temple roof; and there he hung, his heart pounding in his ears, his legs swinging over a thirty foot drop. He had made it! He had feared he was going to plummet into the black void between the buildings, that he was going to die. But now, as he scrambled up on to the flat roof of the temple, he was filled with a wild surge of elation. He had survived even this mad escapade. Surely now anything was possible? Bless these Heliard priests for their uncompromising architecture. Even the stormlashed Sielders could not persuade them to abandon the flat roofs and open flame towers of their desert forebears.

The Heliards served a new faith, yet a powerful one. In barely three centuries they had spread from their heartland, deep in the southron wastes, to overwhelm most of the neighbouring Samaran kingdoms. Even as far north as this they seemed to prosper. They sought only belief, obedience, and ultimate union with their returning Sun God in the fires of a final cataclysmic cleansing; and this simple, absolutist creed seemed steadily to be attracting converts from the fading older faiths.

Despite his southern origins, however, Leighor was not of their number. His religion, as far as it existed, was of a more pragmatic, self-interested sort. He saw no reason not to propitiate the many local gods he met upon his way, especially when there was little to be lost, and perhaps a great deal to be gained. But the single-minded fanaticism of the Heliards, and their constant prayer for the long-awaited, world-ending destruction, made him uneasy. He had learned enough of their ways, however, to know that somewhere on this roof would lie a trapdoor that led up from the temple below. This the acolytes would use when they came to tend the eternal flame at dawn, midday and dusk. He would be safe until then within the flame tower.

A small door at the base of the tower opened on to a narrow stairway that climbed steeply to the high platform where burned the lantern of the faithful, its undying flame fed a constant repast of rich and scented oils. A lazy temple dragon, chained beneath the lantern, belched out a startled puff of flame before returning to its small hopper of marsh grass. Wingless, fire-eyed, and barely two yards long, this was but a modest reminder of the fearsome monsters still said to roam the distant corners of the earth. Even its fabled flame would not come, if it were not regularly fed on certain foul-smelling grasses from its native marshlands. Now it curled up beneath its flame to sleep as Leighor crept by.

Above his head, a broad latticework of wooden rafters provided support for several hanging censers beneath the tiled roof. He looked up into the dark space between tiles and timbers with interest. This might well offer a more promising retreat even than he had hoped for.

Using the heavy bronze lantern as a stepping stone, he clambered up into the rafters, finding the dark space above dry and warm, if cramped and far from comfortable. The beams were broad enough, but there was little security to lie down or sleep unless he crammed himself into the confined space of the overhanging eaves. Here, however, he found an unexpected bonus. For he could now see right down on to the temple roof below. And if he moved into the right position he could even see part of the narrow street that ran alongside the temple and much of the small square that lay before the South Gate. Here he decided to remain. Here at last was sanctuary. Wedging himself tightly between tiles and rafters, he slept.

When he awoke it was daylight. In fact it must be well past noon, from the way the sun's rays slanted down into the quiet street beneath. The day was nearly over! How long had he slept? Below him occasional worshippers came and went through the temple gates, bearing small gifts. Otherwise the street was largely empty – apart, that was, from the small group of workmen driving long staves into the cobblestone roadway. Staves which bore the ceremonial black Varroain death flags in mourning for Eridar.

Leighor rolled painfully onto his side, opening his satchel to eat a little of the food he had brought from the inn, and to try some of the wine. The liquid was hot and spicy, a distilled wine from Silgany – not exactly what he would have chosen to quench his thirst just now, but better than nothing at all. There was little to do for the rest of the day other than to try and rest.

Once, late on, he imagined that he heard harsh military voices close by below. Yet if they were indeed guards searching for him, they soon departed, not daring to take too many liberties with the powerful Heliard cult. And so he passed another long night of cramped and comfortless sleep.

Throughout the second day too, Leighor remained hidden. His limbs cut and bruised from his rooftop journey, and his cramps so painful now that even sleep would not come, he had long since finished the last of his meagre supply of food, and the pangs of hunger gnawed him. His only diversion was to watch and take careful note of the cycle of events in the street and square below.

At dawn the great wooden gates were unbarred and swung back into place beneath the twin towers of the South Gate. Half a dozen new guards replaced the night watch, rigorously checking everyone who passed in or out. First to leave were the men of the town, setting out for their long day's labour in the fields. And then, as the morning drew on, there followed the many artisans and petty merchants leaving Sonsterness for the next town on their travels. All of these were carefully searched and scrutinised by the guard, with many sent back protesting to obtain further identification or permission to leave.

The streets grew busier towards mid-morning as bakers, potters and hawkers displayed their wares, and farmers and homesteaders started to come in from the surrounding hamlets to do business. Knights and landholders arrived now, in ones and twos with their retainers, assembling for the funeral of Eridar and his last long journey north. At midday the guard on the gate was changed again. A gentle straggle of worshippers started to visit the temple, and a dull, creaking chant could be heard from below. Children played in the streets.

The season of harvest was drawing to a close, and as the afternoon wore on great ox-wains began rumbling and scraping their way through the narrow streets, bearing in their loads of turnips and other root crops from the fields; splattering the roadways near the gate with thick Sielder mud.

Then Leighor noticed a sudden change in the pattern of activity below. Silent crowds began to gather in the street, and the road slowly cleared of horses, wains and traders. Some ceremony was about to begin. Indeed, within moments the deep throbbing of drums could be heard, echoing dully through the city from the direction of the keep. The crowd stirred. The sound drew slowly nearer over the next quarter of an hour until it was almost beneath him. People below were craning their necks to see what he as yet could not: the funeral cortège of Eridar, twenty-third Archbaron of the Sielders.

And now it was beneath him, led by two liveried drummers whose task it was to beat out the slow, repetitive pace of the march. Behind came four standard-bearers, wielding the fluttering golden arms of Eridar on silken flags of black. Mounted guards followed, attired in dark chain-mail and bearing black-pennoned lances. These rode escort to the great gilded bier of the Archlord, drawn by six black horses. Upon it lay the open coffin of Lord Eridar. Unnervingly, the face of the dead Archbaron seemed to stare directly up into Leighor's own – almost as if the great lord's eyes truly saw, as if he might rise up from his coffin at any moment to denounce the lurking fugitive in the flame tower above ... But Eridar lay still and silent in his shimmering armour of steel and burnished gold; forever lifeless amid the shields and silks and flowers piled high about his coffin.

And then he was gone.

More mounted men followed. And behind, in rich black robes of heavy damask and shimmering silk, walked the chief mourners. Leighor recognised Darvir at their head, already wearing the jewelled double crown of the Archlords of the Sielders, Girvan and Hiyarde at his side. Many others followed, some of whom Leighor recognised – including the boy, Yeon, and the monkish priest, who must surely have betrayed him. But all passed with never a glance upward on their way. Last of all came a rearguard of local knights and seigneurs, mounted and in full armour, each preceded by his own personal standard: a dozen or more of the chief landholders of Low Sielder riding silently through the subdued crowd. Each attempted the stern, proud aspect of a noble of a warrior race in his little-used armour, yet each was somewhat less than he pretended to be. Little remained of the raw Varroain warriors who had overrun so much of this north-eastern corner of Osenkor, the great World-Continent, over five centuries before. Generations of somnolence and rural isolation had tamed them. Now virtually indistinguishable from the plain Durian Sielder-folk they ruled, the twin columns of dull provincial landholders passed slowly on their way towards the South Gate.

It was over. The crowds were beginning to break up and return home. It had not been a great affair for one such as Eridar, but probably as great as a place like Sonsterness could manage at such short notice. Much of the procession, Leighor knew, would soon return to the city; but the knights and seigneurs and many of the high lords must accompany Eridar's coffin on the slow, four-day journey to the ancient burial place of the Lords of the Sielders within the great stone-girt fortress of Istlass.

As night fell once more, Leighor finished the last dregs of the Giellin wine from the tavern.

He was still thirsty.

He had not eaten for a day or more and would soon begin to grow weaker. Whatever small chance there was of his making a successful escape from the city would quickly evaporate with his departing strength. If he remained where he was, he would have to take greater and greater risks merely to stay alive. His eventual capture would become inevitable. The time had come. He must move tonight. Perhaps with Darvir and Hiyarde gone, and after the excitement of the day, the guard would be laxer, the thought of dark assassins farther from their minds. Anyway he hoped so.

This decided, he tried to sleep, to conserve his strength until the night was deeper and all was quiet. Only then, for the first time in two days, did he dare to lower himself out of his small attic, and down on to the floor of the flame tower. All seemed exactly as it had been when he had first entered. The small dragon hardly even bothered to open its eyes as he passed on down the stair to the temple roof. He found the trapdoor with little difficulty and made his way down through a succession of dark passages to a vast, dimly-lit hall, its ceiling vaulting high into the gloom. This was the sanctuary of the temple. High above him, the giant, six-pointed golden sunburst symbol of the Heliards hung in splendour. Beneath it, a great bronze brazier burned upon a circular altar, its fires a strange, unnatural ember-scarlet. These dark flames provided the sole illumination for the sanctuary, causing a thousand black shadows to dance and flicker across the walls, and breathing quivering life into each silent statue.

Behind the altar he detected the sleeping form of a robed acolyte. He moved on, almost running right into a startled red-robed priest. For an instant he stared straight into the harsh eyes of the *patrarch*; then, lowering his head, he hurried, almost ran, for the door. In the darkness of the street beyond, he quickly sought out a narrow alley in which to secrete himself and waited, hoping desperately that the priest had not recognised him for a southron. He could still see the looming shadow of the flame tower, darker yet against an obsidian sky. From his place in that tower he had watched every movement in these grimy streets beneath. He had seen everything, yet still he had not gleaned a single idea for a plan of escape.

Had he really seen everything? Suddenly he noticed the rows of covered buckets that waited outside the doors of many of the houses. No! There was one thing he had not seen – at least not in daylight. He had slept through the passage of the one vehicle for which the city gates would be opened before the break of day; the one waggon that no one would wish to investigate too closely. The nightsoil cart. It must pass this way on its journey towards the South Gate. All he had to do was wait for it.

He crouched shivering in the alleyway, waiting, listening, for what seemed an eternity before he finally heard the welcome sound of the heavy, iron-rimmed wheels grinding across the cobblestones towards him. He rose, picking up a heavy wooden stave from the litter of the alleyway, and stepped out into the road. The driver, cowled and masked against the smell, looked down from his seat in mild surprise that anyone should approach him. The stench from the waggon was overpowering, yet Leighor was thankful for the excuse to cover his face.

'Carter!' His voice sounded thin and shaky. Would the man suspect him? 'Carter, I need your help.'

'What help do you want of me?' The driver's voice was harsh and suspicious. 'Who are you?'

Leighor said nothing, but drew closer.

'What do you want?' The carter was beginning to rise from his seat, his hand reaching for the whip that lay across his knees.

This was the moment.

Leighor made a lunge for him, seizing hold of one end of the whip whilst its owner was still unbalanced, to pull backward with all his strength. The carter fell forward at once, losing his balance to crash down heavily on to the cobblestones below. His loud groan was muffled by the thick facemask he wore, yet still it echoed horrendously through the empty streets. Overcome with panic, Leighor silenced him with a heavy blow of his stave. Yet the man still lay groaning in the roadway for several moments more before the southron had the wit to drag him back into the darkness of the alleyway, and bind him with strips torn from his own clothing.

Taking his victim's robe and linen facemask, he donned them, climbing up into the driving seat of the waggon, behind its two placid oxen. They knew the way forward far better than he did, and needed little urging to pull the cart along its familiar route towards the darkened South Gate. The guards, crouched around their smoking brazier, stood and stretched at his approach, the familiar herald of the ending of their watch. Wordlessly removing the iron bars from the great wooden gates, they swung them open, just wide enough for the nightsoil cart to pass, and stood well back.

Leighor decided that his safest course was to say nothing, and to make no sign or acknowledgement bar a cursory nod as he passed. It was dark, the soldiers should notice nothing amiss. He hunched himself up in his seat, keeping his hood well down, and his mask firmly in place.

In fact the guards seemed to expect nothing more of him, making no attempt to stop him or to probe the secrets of his stinking waggon. Leighor held his breath, looking neither to right nor to left as he passed slowly out beneath the great arch. Out, into the cool fresh air and the flat levels of Low Sielder.

Chapter Three
THE WAY TO ISTLASS

The road was rutted and potholed, so thick with mud that it took all the strength of the two oxen to keep the heavy wain moving. And even as he finally began to draw away from the city, Leighor's heart sank to see the dim grey line of dawn on the horizon ahead. It was too soon. He was still within clear sight of the city walls, and suspicions would quickly be aroused if the cart were to be seen diverging from its normal route. No. The time had come to abandon the nightsoil cart and to rely upon his own two feet. There was a waist-high mud embankment just ahead, separating two recently-ploughed fields. He pulled sharply on the reins, managing at length to make the oxen change direction sufficiently to drag the waggon off the road. Here, behind the embankment, it would remain hidden from the town walls for some time.

Leaving the sweating oxen behind him, breathing clouds of white vapour into the clear morning air, he doffed his stolen robe and facemask, and ran; making his way roughly northward along the line of the embankment. He kept to the water-clogged drainage ditches where he could, hoping that these would hide his tracks. He headed north because it was the only direction he could go. He knew that, and so would his pursuers. Sonsterness was near the southern tip of the Sielder peninsula, and the road south went on for only a few more leagues, to the small town of Petrim, and thence to the windblown sand-dunes of lonely Helverhead. There was no escape for him there. To the west, Ellash Flats sloped muddily into the bay of Qrena; and to the east, the wilder shoreline of the Rathul Sea was less than a dozen leagues distant. Both were barren, empty coasts, bereft of all help or habitation.

No. The only way out of the Sielders lay to the north, either by sea, as he had come, via the ports of Herrahaven or Ravenshald; or else across the long narrow causeway from Instrand – the only land-link between the Sielders and the mainland of Osenkor, the great World-Continent. He would have to move quickly, for the pursuit would begin the moment the real carter was found, bound and gagged, in the alleyway beside the temple. He did not have much of a start.

That was if they bothered to hunt for him . . . Perhaps Darvir and Hiyarde would just let him escape quietly, and not risk the complications that would arise from his capture? But no, he must not allow himself such dangerous hopes. Those who had truly murdered Lord Eridar could not afford to appear lax in the pursuit of their chosen substitute. They must hunt him down with all due vigour and endeavour. They need not worry about what he would say when they caught him. His word was of no account, and he would very soon be dead . . .

Mud was already oozing through his boots; the soft leather was not made for this sort of treatment. But whatever the conditions, he must stay off the road. Pursuers on horseback would ride him down on any road inside the hour. His pace had by now fallen to a slow jog, but he had made some progress. The dark shadow of Sonsterness had diminished to an inky smudge against the brightening sky behind him. So far there had been no alarm or clamour from the walls. For the moment he seemed to be safe. For no reason at all he began to recall a silly walking song from his childhood, how did it go now:

*On country paths I like to roam,
In dappled greenwood is my home,
And high above the race below,
Through merry meadows I shall go.*

Yes, that was it. It was not very appropriate to his present situation, but it cheered him up and seemed to make the running easier.

The edge of the sun, bright and orange, appeared above the eastern horizon. Dawn! His brief respite would not last much longer. He was far too exposed in these open fields. He must find some cover – but where?

There was a long line of tall aspen trees some distance away to the east; they stood upon a low earthen dyke and seemed to have been planted as a windbreak across the flat landscape. Leighor made his way towards them as the daylight strengthened, wading stagnant drainage canals and clambering muddy embankments with singleminded purpose. The main embankment rose some six to eight feet above the level of the surrounding fields, running in a straight line from north to south. It would be the ideal path to follow.

His immediate goal achieved, he slumped against the trunk of one of the great trees and rested, staring up into the crown of whispering leaves, just beginning to change colour at the first approach of autumn. A faint mist had risen with the dawn: a damp, cloying haze which drew a gentle veil across all things more than half a league distant. Looking round him, Leighor found that he could no longer see even the dim outline of the towers of Sonsterness. He smiled. Now at last he was truly free.

Perhaps he ought to see what resources he had with him for his new life as a fugitive. He was travelling light, by necessity. Most of his possessions – the tools of his trade, his herbs and philtres and potions, so many irreplaceable things – were lost to him forever with his old wooden chest back in Sonsterness. All he had left was his satchel, the clothes he stood up in, and the parcel of food he had taken from the carter.

In the satchel were his surgical knives and some of his more basic tools: a pill press, pestle and mortar, cauterising iron, vessel and burner, lint and linen. There were a few small sachets of dry herbs, rootstocks and powders, and, most precious of all, a small wooden box that held five small glass vials. These contained costly medicinal oils, his own wound cream, and the precious smoke-salve of Miriume. Leighor sighed. These were valuable items, yet but a pitiful fraction of what had been lost. Besides his physician's tools, the only other contents of his satchel were two leatherbound books and a small brown velvet bag. The thick, well-thumbed book was *Hallur's Herbal Notes*, the aged tome from which he had in fact gained much of his medical learning, the other was the key book for the ivory *Rudäis* pieces that lay within the velvet bag. And that was all. No money. Not much food.

Thinking of food made him remember his hunger, and he drew out the nightsoil carrier's small packet of provisions. These he divided in two; one half of the dark rye bread and coarse Sielder cheese he replaced in his tunic, and the rest he ate at once. It was the first food he had eaten for a day and a half, and even though the bread was dry and crusty, and the cheese had a harsh tang that lingered on the tongue, it took a major effort of will not to consume the reserve as soon as he had finished.

Instead he took up the battered book of the *Rudäis*. In the breakneck course of events since his call to Eridar's bedside he had had no time to perform a consultation, and now, in spite of the delay it would cause, he felt an urgent need to do so. Hurriedly he emptied the ivory pieces into his left hand, placing the other on top of them as he silently recited the invocation to the oracle. He concentrated hard upon his question, and then dropped the pieces randomly to the ground, checking immediately to see how they had fallen. Each of the pieces of the *Rudäis* bore two symbols, one on either side, and these could fall in any combination or order. How they fell was governed by the oracle, and was his pronouncement on the question asked. There were literally thousands of combinations possible, and all were learned by heart by the *Rudäis* priests, but his own book gave most of these interpretations in a shortened form, suitable for the untrained novice. Most of the symbols he knew already: the seeing eye was a warning of danger. *Ilethon* meant hardship for the future. The sun was a hopeful sign, but this might be negated by the baleful effects of dark *Qorib*. Air could indicate a need for movement – or discard nothing. What did the whole mean? He thumbed through the tissue-thin pages of the key. Yet as with all such readings it was a couplet that could probably itself be interpreted in many ways:

> *The wise man takes a higher road,*
> *The fool in danger sheds his load.*

Well, it seemed to apply to him in some manner, but he had for the moment no real idea of how the advice of the oracle could be used to his benefit. This ridge was the higher road perhaps? But somehow he did not think that the oracle intended itself to be taken quite so literally. No doubt when the right time came, things would fall into place. So thinking, he packed up his few possessions once more and prepared to move on. He would keep to the line of trees and follow their course north along the embankment. That would provide him with shelter, and have the added benefit of complying with the directions of the oracle.

He made better time on the firmer footing of the embankment, and from his height above the surrounding country he could see every movement in the flat, open fields around him. Yet barring the odd hare and the occasional wheeling swallow, nothing moved. There seemed to be no sign of human life anywhere in this empty landscape. A soft, gentle rain began to fall, barely noticeable at first except as a quiet rustling in the treetops and a smooth whispering into the earth – a gentle wall of sound that made the silence and his sense of isolation complete.

Eventually the long line of trees ran out and, not wanting to walk any farther along the exposed embankment, he was forced to turn off on to a rutted cart track which ran roughly north-westwards across the empty fields. He trudged onward. Each of the huge, square fields seemed to take hours to cross, and beyond each straggly dividing hedge or low dyke there were several more exactly the same. To Leighor's despair the track seemed to be leading nowhere, wandering purposelessly across a featureless landscape. Occasionally a simple wooden bridge would echo across a muddy stream, and once or twice Leighor thought he heard distant voices across the fields, but he saw nothing. He passed two low timber and daub farmsteads in the course of the long afternoon: both ramshackle, windowless and apparently deserted. Yet he dared not take the risk of someone remaining within – not so close to Sonsterness – and he passed on by. Moving mechanically, instinctively, numbing out all pain and weariness, he stumbled, tired and filthy, ever northwards.

Now he passed through fields that were already flooded and useless with the autumn rains – as they would remain throughout the wet Sielder winter. He was slowly passing from cultivated fields into deserted fenland, and leaving all trace of human habitation behind him. Here there were none but swampland creatures for company, the only sounds the soft plipping of frogs and water-lizards in their brackish pools and the quiet whisper of the marsh grass. A skein of geese flew past overhead and a few lonely grebe and heron sulked in the small cold ponds that dotted the fen.

Leighor recognised no feature in all this bleak landscape. In his previous travels he had never had cause to pass down this benighted little track before. But perhaps that would save him. Once he crossed the path of a lonely tinker, tools and pots upon his back and stout staff in hand. But Leighor had seen him well in advance and had time to adopt the cowering, crouching gait of an itinerant beggar, and the tinker passed without a second glance. Yet he was the only human soul that Leighor had seen all day, and as darkness gathered the southron began to wonder where – or even how – he was going to spend the night. The drizzle had not slackened with the ending of the day and he had come upon no prospect of shelter.

A few bobbing lights appeared suddenly, some distance away from the road, on his left. Leighor stared out at them intently. They seemed to be small hand-lanterns from the way they moved, gently swaying through the deepening darkness in unseen hands. Perhaps they were coming closer, and would meet up with the road ahead of him. Yet in fact they seemed to be moving slowly away – farther out into the marshes. Who could these people be, he wondered? Perhaps friendly reed-cutters, who would know nothing of the death of Eridar out here in the fen, and might take him in and give him food and shelter. They were still not too far distant. Perhaps he could find some way across to them, even though it would mean leaving the road. The lights seemed to pause and flicker, as if beckoning him on. There was what looked like the beginning of a dry path ahead. It must be the path the travellers had taken. Why not follow it?

He was just about to set foot on the narrow pathway when sudden realisation struck him. If these travellers had indeed come from the road, why had he not seen them earlier? The land was flat and the way was clear. And where those encouraging lights now bobbed so enticingly, there seemed to be nothing but deep marsh and waving reed-beds. He paused, remembering an oft-told tale. Were those truly lanterns he saw – or siren fenlights, the malign, dancing phantoms that had led many a tired, unwary traveller to his doom in the deep bogs of the Sielders?

The thought gave him pause, and he decided to ignore the beckoning pathway and keep to the road he knew. He walked on for several minutes, half angered by his own peasant fear and credulity. Then, suddenly, the distant, bobbing lights rose up as one, and scattered like a dozen darting fireflies above the marshes. Leighor gasped, staring in wonder as a small cluster of the tiny fire-globes swarmed angrily towards him. They circled him at a distance of several feet, never coming within arm's reach, but buzzing furiously about his head in the growing darkness, as if annoyed by his failure to follow their traitorous summons. And then, seeming suddenly to tire of their play, they sped away across the marshes, gleaming fleetingly above the dull landscape. And then they were gone, leaving him completely alone on the darkening roadway once more.

For many minutes Leighor stood still, wondering at what he had seen, hardly able to believe it. But full darkness fast approached, and tonight there would be no moon or stars. He must move on.

The road still coiled on endlessly, once passing a broad silent river, full to overflowing, which oozed ominously through the landscape, lapping level with its shoreline as if but one more drop of water would be enough to make it burst its banks and flood the entire country.

He would meet with no more travellers now, for few people in these times journeyed abroad at night. There was much talk of bandits and night horrors that stalked the lonely byways. Abruptly he halted. Had he heard something – the snap of a dry twig behind him? He held his breath, listening for any sound. But he heard nothing more, and his eyes could detect no movement in the open country around. It had been nothing at all. He was frightening himself with all these peasant tales. Yet here in the lonely darkness there seemed far more substance to such stories. He moved on as swiftly as possible, hoping now to find some human habitation where he might rest the night in safety.

Yet for several hours more the road ran on through featureless fenland with no sign of any settlement. There might have been dwellings near the road, but if there were, they were well hidden, or else showed no light, and Leighor did not see them. It was only when he was beginning to believe that this empty, wandering road would never end, that he at last caught sight of the dark huddle of buildings ahead.

His pace quickened as he drew near, coming first upon a few low, close-shuttered homesteads. But these he ignored, making his way cautiously on to the centre of the village. Here the houses huddled close together against the darkness, with not a glimmer of light nor a reassuring sound from any one of them. He walked on in silence. At the very centre of the village another, broader roadway crossed his own. The crossroads were marked by a stone well and a tall inn, now as silent and dark-shuttered as the rest of the settlement. A creaking sign swayed above the door, and Leighor could just discern the painting of a dark, tusked animal upon it. Sudden realisation hit him. This was the Black Boar Inn! The discovery brought a dull sinking feeling to the pit of his stomach. He at last knew where he was, and the knowledge gave him no pleasure.

This was the village of Nilgaf, on the main road north from Sonsterness, and part of the demesne of Sarnuil – one of the knights who even now rode north with the bier of Eridar. To the west lay Great Tholon Hold, with its cluster of attendant farm buildings and its great kitchen, where, on his way to the city, he had spent a profitable day tending to the minor ailments of the farm folk. But that was of little moment now, for Nilgaf was but an easy morning's ride out from Sonsterness: from the upper windows of the Hold – on a clear day – the walls of the city could quite clearly be seen. He had come all this way, walked all these long hours, for nothing. He had followed a roundabout trail that had returned him almost to his start. Curse his ill-fortune! Now he could neither stop nor rest. Instead of being, as he had thought, in some forgotten backwater miles from anywhere, he was exactly where his pursuers would most expect to find him. Cold, tired, and wet as he was, he must move on again: now, before dawn made his capture inevitable. Suddenly nervous, he looked about him warily, fearing immediate discovery. But there was no movement, no sound. If any of Darvir's guards were billeted here, they must be sleeping, like the rest of the village folk.

Leighor slid as quickly and silently as he could out of Nilgaf, crossing the stream of Ornil onto the dark and lonely road north. A dark shape loomed suddenly out of the murk ahead, and for a fearful instant he imagined that it was indeed one of the sinister night-walkers waiting to fall upon him. But it was only some poor wretch hanging creaking in the gallows, as sombre warning to any who thought to evade the full penalty of Varroain justice. The sight unsettled him greatly, for he knew that, all too soon, it might be his body hanging there above the dark roadway. He must take greater care. This road was too dangerous, even at night. He must leave it, and make his way across country.

So decided, he scrambled off the road into the blackness of the surrounding fields. He stumbled and fell more often now on the uneven ground, but somehow he felt more secure away from the road. Here in the open fields the darkness was his friend, protecting him from the eyes of those who sought him, rather than concealing his foes.

Yet he was incredibly weary. He would not be able to keep going for much longer. He must find somewhere to rest. His eyes having grown used to the near-total darkness, he discerned the faint glimmer of a light somewhere in the distance ahead. He made for it, trying to clear his swimming head. He should have some idea where he was now. He had been here not two weeks ago . . .

As he drew closer, he began to recognise the shapes of familiar buildings. Clustered around a central courtyard in an almost perfect defensive square, their high outer walls rose windowless into the dark night sky, to make the whole seem like a small fortress set amid the fields.

This was surely the hold of Uriyen, a welcoming place where he had recently tended to the needs of the freeholder and his retainers. Uriyen enjoyed talking of the distant world beyond his own quiet lands, for he had travelled much in his youth and now took every opportunity to glean news and opinions from passing travellers. An intelligent man, with a broad, enquiring mind: Leighor and he had conversed long into the night while the fires burned low and the servants slept. If there was anywhere in the Sielders he would receive a fair hearing, it would be here, from Uriyen. He strode towards the high wooden gates with renewed hope.

But even as he approached the gateway, he heard a low rumbling behind him, somewhat like distant thunder. He spun round. A column of blazing yellow lights was moving swiftly towards him from the south – flickering torches borne by mounted men! They would reach him within minutes.

There was no time to seek refuge within the farmstead. In any event, there would be no sanctuary for him there now. Urging his tired limbs into motion once more, he stumbled away into the dark countryside, not looking back until the thunder of hoofbeats drowned out all else behind him.

Looking back, he saw clusters of flaring orange lights fanning out across the open fields. He smiled grimly. They were fools to search for him with blazing torches. As long as those torches remained lit, he knew exactly where his pursuers were – and provided he kept low and moved sensibly and quietly, he could evade them with relative ease.

So it proved, and although he came near to discovery several times, as the riders passed within yards of him in the darkness, by first light he was well away from Uriyen's hold and seeking out the shelter of a wood or small spinney where he might spend the coming day. With men searching for him afoot and on horseback, he must travel only by night, for the immediate future at least.

There was a small piece of coppiced woodland ahead. He made for that. It turned out to be the rooting ground for a large number of brown pigs that crashed noisily through the undergrowth, churning up the earth between the trees. But these, he supposed, would serve to cover his tracks, and the woods themselves would give him much protection.

With the coming of dark Leighor finally dared to move again, sitting up in a makeshift hide to eat the last of the carter's bread and cheese, before setting off once more. This night the going was easier, for he now caught brief glimpses of the stars between the scurrying clouds, guiding his true way north.

That night, and the next, he continued roughly northward, keeping his distance from the road and from all human habitation. By day he took advantage of whatever coarse shelter he could find – whether a thorny hedge or a rough bed of bracken on the edge of woodland – to lie low and sleep.

As dawn broke on the third day following his narrow escape near Uriyen's farmstead, Leighor was encouraged to see that the land was at last beginning to rise. There were now green rolling hills all around him, with thick patches of woodland carpeting their upper slopes. Slowly but surely, he was beginning to leave the appalling mud-flats of Low Sielder behind.

Dusk found him deep in the rolling, wooded country of Mid Sielder. He had chanced journeying by day again now that he had rich woodlands to give him cover. He had not seen one of Darvir's riders for more than a day, and was beginning to feel that he might now be beyond pursuit. He decided to chance a break across open country towards the next wooded hillcrest. There he might find shelter for the night, and would be able to see what lay ahead of him for the morrow.

But what he saw when he finally reached his goal nearly paralysed him with dismay. For there, not sixty yards beneath him, lay the north roadway; and beside it a great encampment, with four blazing campfires, scores of horses, and at least a dozen tents pitched between the trees. Bright coloured awnings snapped and fluttered in the breeze, as did a dozen emblazoned banners. Men-at-arms, squires and servants passed to and fro between the tents.

For a moment or two Leighor was thrown into confusion. This was no ordinary camp of merchants or fair-folk. Nor was it a guard camp or search party; there were too many noble banners here for that.

Then, at once, the truth dawned on him. This was the funeral cortège of Eridar. The weather and the state of the roads must have slowed its progress to less than walking pace all the way from Sonsterness. And now he had caught up with it – packed with the noblest lords and the best fighting men in all the Sielders! A chill ran down his spine. Trust him to fall upon the one gathering he most wished to avoid; the one thing he most desired never to set eyes on again. Quickly he shrank away from the crest, fearful of being seen, stepping back into the shadow of the trees.

Yet even as he turned, a pair of strong arms circled him from behind, pinning his elbows tightly to his sides. A large hand fastened itself firmly across his mouth, cutting off all air.

'Murdering dog!' a voice hissed sharply in his ear. 'We have you now!'

Sheer panic gave Leighor the strength to break his right arm free and jerk it down and back into the stomach of his assailant. There was a gasp of pain, and the grip slackened enough for the southron to twist away. But Leighor had not time to turn to face his attacker before a hard fist crashed into the side of his head. A second, more painful still, exploded into the small of his back to send him spinning to the ground. Before he could move or attempt to rise, the full weight of his assailant came down upon him. His head struck against hard stone and he lost consciousness.

He came round to the sound of hushed voices approaching from below. One was his attacker. There were two others.

'It was there I saw him running across the meadow,' whispered the first. 'I followed, and waited here for him.'

Leighor listened as the footsteps drew closer, at last managing to twist his head round sufficiently to see the three figures approaching through the dark. He found to his surprise that he recognised two of them. The first, the one who had attacked him, was Yeon, the young nephew of Eridar, whom he had last seen close to on the night of the Archbaron's death.

'Did you have much trouble with him?' A second whispered voice cut through the silence. It was the Mallenian priest, Uhlendof, the only other witness at Eridar's bedside upon that fateful night.

'None at all,' Yeon said contemptuously. 'He is no fighter.'

'So I see.' The third figure stooped to examine him dispassionately. A tall, dark-bearded man of middle years, hair close-cropped about his face in workmanlike style, he was arrayed in rich travelling attire of damask and brocade. 'Unbind him now, and let us speak.'

Monk and youth raised him unsteadily to his feet, removing the dirty linen gag from his mouth. Leighor swallowed hard, trying to banish the harsh dryness that clung to his mouth and throat.

'Southron,' the bearded man spoke again, yet more softly, as if he feared to be overheard. 'What part had you in the death of my lord Eridar?'

'None, my lord,' Leighor stumbled, wondering why his questioner spoke in such hushed and secretive tones. 'None at all – as these two men know well. They were with me all the while. They cannot deny that I gave your lord neither pills nor potion, nor left him anything. I could not have poisoned him.'

'There are many ways that a poison may be administered by skilful hands,' the priest said coldly. 'A dust breathed in while the victim sleeps, an ointment smeared upon the skin, a concealed needle, or even a drop of fluid in a bedside drink. Any of these, you could have used without our knowledge.'

Leighor stared up at the monk in horror, his one line of defence crumbling into ruins before him. 'No,' he shook his head desperately. 'I swear that is not true! Why should I wish to kill your lord? I have no reason to hate him . . .'

'We are not such fools, dog!' The bearded man raised a gloved hand in warning. 'We know that you could not have planned this murder on your own. You are in the pay of someone! What we would learn is his name – is it Darvir?'

'I am in no one's pay!' Leighor insisted. 'I have harmed nobody! If I had worked for Darvir, why does he now hunt me?'

'But does he truly hunt you, southron?' the monk snorted. 'Or does he but put on a show of it for the world to see?'

'Aye,' Yeon nodded. 'You seemed free enough just now! How did you escape Sonsterness without Darvir's aid, tell us that? And why did you fly into hiding the moment you left Lord Eridar's bedside – unless you knew aforehand that he would soon lie dead?'

'I did not hide . . .' Leighor stammered, 'I was waylaid . . .

'It is true, my lords!' he added, seeing the contemptuous looks that passed between his captors. 'I can tell you no more . . . It seems that you are determined to disbelieve me, whatever I say.'

'Your whole tale rings false as goblin gold!' the bearded man spat with vehemence. 'Yet we have not the time to tarry here.' He stood abruptly, turning to face his two companions. 'If our good fortune in taking this man is to be turned to advantage, we must get him away from here at once! He must be kept out of Darvir's hands at all costs!'

'But why?' Yeon asked.

'Because if Darvir and his allies truly paid this southron to slay Lord Eridar, then he can expose them all. They dare not let him speak! That is why we can trust no one in all this camp – and none in Hiyarde's city of Sonsterness either.' The deep voice paused momentarily. 'Only in Ravenshald, Eridar's fief-city, may there yet be a few men of rank who remain loyal to their former lord. There we shall obtain the means to extract the truth from this southron dog! But we must be careful. Should Darvir's men find us with him now, they would gladly slit all our throats before they let him betray their master.'

'Aye, my lord Halaron,' the monk nodded grimly. 'We must be swift. You had best go down at once and order the horses made ready. The men are less likely to question your orders, even now. We shall meet you where the grey stream crosses the roadway, to the north of the camp.'

A gag was once more pressed into Leighor's mouth, Yeon bending to take him up across one bony shoulder. They passed along the hillcrest under cover of the high trees, Uhlendof striding ahead to force a way down the wooded eastern slope towards the road.

In time the path grew level again, and they came out of the trees into the moonlight. Yet they did not halt until they reached the dark earthen gash of the road.

'Make haste!' Halaron's agitated voice hissed from the shadow of the trees. 'I have three horses, but we must ride quickly. I cut the tethers of the rest to give us a start, but I have been seen!'

Momentarily lowered from his uncomfortable perch, Leighor found himself lifted in strong arms and thrown, face down, across the back of one of the waiting horses. Yet even as his hands and feet were trussed beneath the beast's belly, there came a sudden great commotion from behind. Several dozen armoured men, bearing pikes and halberds, issued hurriedly from the trees some two hundred paces behind them. At their head stood the unmistakable gaunt figure of Darvir.

'My lord Halaron!' Darvir's voice rang out sharp and clear across the clearing. 'Why do you flee my lord Eridar's funeral train, setting all the mounts of this noble company to the four winds? What rank evils do you plot here?'

'We plot nothing, sire,' Halaron spoke. 'But we have urgent business in Ravenshald this night, and no time to forewarn you of our parting.'

'So I see,' Darvir nodded scornfully, the line of pikemen advancing slowly as he spoke. 'Yet ere you depart, perhaps you will show us the dark-faced companion you try to hide . . . Who is he, pray? Is he not the southron assassin? The very same who slew my brother, Lord Eridar?' The new Archlord shook his head sorrowfully. 'I am saddened to find such old and trusted friends involved in this great treason.'

'Look elsewhere for your treasons, my lord!' Halaron burst out with sudden anger. 'You will find none here!'

Darvir smiled thinly, turning away. 'Do you not see?' he demanded of the growing number of knights and men-at-arms now gathering behind him. 'There lies the southron! There lie the traitors! The assassins! The murderers of Eridar! Seize them!'

'It is not true!' Yeon's voice broke the sudden silence that followed. 'We only take the southron to R—'

But his words were cut off as the gathered multitude came to their own conclusions, and with a united roar of fury began to race towards the three riders, weapons drawn.

'For the sake of Thall, flee!' Halaron shouted, clambering up on to his mount and spurring it northward. Uhlendof and Yeon quickly followed, the youth's mount bearing the double burden. Slowly, painfully slowly, they gathered speed; first cantering, and then at last galloping into the darkness of the north.

Darvir's followers howled with frustrated fury as they were left behind on the open roadway, hurling pikes, spears and lances impotently after the fleeing riders. Darvir alone stood back, biding his time, apparently unconcerned, as the rest of the mob surged forward. And only Leighor, from where he lay behind the saddle of Yeon's horse, saw the Archbaron slowly raise one long thin hand above his head to reveal a slender metal bracelet gleaming on the wrist beneath. A curious amulet which, even at this distance, seemed to glow with a strange inner light – a deep steely-purple incandescence that grew steadily brighter as the southron stared.

Then, without warning, it seemed to explode with light, emitting a burst so bright, so brilliant, that for an instant it lit up the whole of the country like day. Leighor buried his eyes, fearing himself struck blind.

A terrible hissing, a sound of pure power, tore viciously through the air above them. There was a fearsome explosion just ahead – as if a dozen bolts of lightning had struck all at once, only feet away. And in the midst of this maelstrom there came the fearsome shriek of man and beast in terrible short-lived unison. Then darkness and silence once more.

Yeon's horse reared in terror, and it took a prodigious effort on the part of its rider to bring it back under control. Leighor could still see nothing at all, for the night had become again utterly black. Desperately he blinked his eyes, trying to accustom them once more to the smothering darkness. The horse swerved suddenly from its path, as if to avoid some obstacle on the roadway, before returning once more to its former course, and only then did Leighor see the smouldering, blackened remains of the first horse and its rider. Halaron's body lay stretched out on the road, barely recognisable but for the tattered remnants of his clothing, the whole of his upper body black, as if scorched by some terrible fire. Frantically, Yeon spurred on his horse, racing for the shelter of the dark line of trees that swept down from the hills ahead to swallow up the road.

After a league or so of hard riding they drew their horses slowly to a halt. There was a deep silence on the road behind them, and a deeper stillness in the country all around.

'How long do you think it will take them to come after us?' Yeon asked.

'They will have to catch the horses first,' the monk gasped, breathless. 'But they will not be far behind!'

'And what of Lord Halaron? How . . . ?' The youth stumbled for words.

'I do not know,' Uhlendof's voice answered bleakly. 'It seemed a thunderbolt from the heavens. I have never seen its like before . . . But whatever it was, good Lord Halaron now lies dead because of it. May his soul rise now to greater honour than it has suffered here.'

The monk fell silent for a moment. And then a new determination seemed suddenly to grow in him. 'We must ride now,' he said firmly. 'Ride fast and without halt for Ravenshald. There to inform my lord Careil of what has happened. He alone can we now trust, in all of the Sielders!'

'And the southron?'

'He is now more important than ever. Come!' Uhlendof spurred on his horse and the youth followed his lead, gaining speed until they were both galloping fast and wild, northward through the cold dark night of Mid Sielder. Tightly bound as he was, Leighor sank into unconsciousness several times through the long night, only to come to once more and find himself still in the same cramped position, galloping steadily on through the darkness.

At dawn, a change in the rhythm of the ride brought Leighor back once again to his senses. The horses slowed, and they halted to barter for fresh mounts at a roadside farmstead. High above them rose the grey, dark bulk of the great castle of Istlass: strongest fortress of the Sielders and the final destination of Eridar's cortège. Cold and empty now, only a single small light flickered behind one of the high windows to bear evidence that any humans yet dwelt within.

Uhlendof obtained three snorting beasts in exchange for their two more noble mounts. But when he and the youth attempted once more to tie Leighor down across the back of one, the physician chose to rebel: twisting, kicking and struggling in their grasp, defying all their efforts, grimly determined not to permit himself to be so trussed up again.

Furiously they lowered him to the ground, Leighor finally managing to struggle free of the loosened gag as they did so. 'Release me,' he called, out, his words emerging weakly from between parched lips. 'Release me and I will ride with you.'

The monk and the youth stared at one another in silence.

'You will move faster with a willing rider at your side,' the southron continued, 'and if you release me, I swear that for as long as you believe me guilty I shall not try to escape.'

'No!' Yeon said quickly. 'We cannot trust him.'

'You have no choice,' Leighor said. 'We are all fugitives now. If I wish, I can delay you, both here and on the road. Perhaps even until Darvir's men catch up with us. After all, what care I which of you holds me prisoner?'

There was a moment's silence.

'He has us,' the monk acknowledged grimly. 'Swear all you say, and we shall release you.' He sighed. 'It seems that we three now ride together.'

'Can you ride at speed?' Yeon asked acidly.

'We have horses in the southlands too,' Leighor retorted, 'and faster by far than these clumsy northron nags.' He sincerely hoped that he could make good his boast as he hauled himself up into the broad country saddle and urged his mount reluctantly forward.

The sun shone warmly down upon them as they slowly picked up speed. The three rode in earnest silence, and by noon they were riding hard through the flat, upland country of High Sielder: a land of broad meadows and ripening corn. Villages were few and far between on the white chalkstone road, and where they did occur they were small and silent, passed through in a brief moment of hooves echoing on dusty cobblestones. Even here, in the part of the Sielder peninsula closest to the mainland, the roads were empty.

Leighor did not take in much of the passing scene, despite his partially regained freedom. His head throbbed with sleeplessness, there was a nagging pain in his side where he had fallen, and even the heat of the sun could not drive out the terrible cold that lay deep in his bones. Despite the mountain of troubles that now faced him, he could not think. The whole range and scope of his problems confounded him. All he could do now was to concentrate on staying in the saddle and remaining conscious. He did not know what the two men wanted with him, nor what their plans were once they reached Ravenshald. But they were enemies of Darvir, and for the moment that would have to be enough.

Later on, most of the events of that long day's journey would be beyond Leighor's recall. He would only remember once; having reached the top of a long steady climb, looking back to see the distant glint of armour-clad pursuers on the road several leagues behind, riding, as it seemed to him then, imperceptibly slowly across the open country far below.

After this, their own pace increased, and there were no more stops. The journey seemed to go on and on: an eternal ride with neither beginning nor end, proceeding wearisomely, without respite, until Leighor could almost bring himself to believe that he had been riding this horse for half his life. And still they rode; ever onwards, into the north.

Only when the sun was declining, orange and bloated, into the west, did the travellers at last catch sight of the iron-grey Rathul Sea ahead of them, over miles of brown heath. And there, hazy in the distance, the dark huddle of Ravenshald sheltered beside its steep estuary.

Journey's end.

Chapter Four
RAVENSHALD

The town of Ravenshald clung to the steeply sloping banks of the River Gnir, where it broadened into a sheltered estuary, protected by towering cliffs from the stormy waters of the Rathul Sea. The narrow streets were crowded with petty merchants, hawkers and townsfolk: the riders' pace slowed to a crawl as they passed between rows of tall, high-gabled artisans' houses and clamorous workshops.

A thousand seagulls circled above the bowl of the river, their cries echoing through the streets like harsh challenges or baleful warnings of attack. There were also the duller, deeper croaks of the many jet-black ravens that lurked upon every rooftop like dark conspirators, watching and brooding over the seaport town to which they gave their name.

Yeon leaned forward to make himself heard above the noise. 'What are we to do now? Do we go straight to the keep?'

'No,' Uhlendof shouted back. 'That would be unwise. We will bide at the house of Careil. From there we may more quickly escape if the need arises.'

They rode on, down to the river Gnir, and past the dozens of small boatyards that lined its timber-palisaded banks. The seven-arched Ravensbridge spanned the river on their left, lined with buildings that towered up to five storeys high, arching high above the roadway and leaning far out over the busy river. The travellers did not cross, but passed on, following the river towards the sea and into an area of grander stone houses. These were tall and dark, decked with intricate stone carvings of arms, flowers and heraldic beasts above gabled doors and leaded windows. Here dwelt the richer merchants of the city, and those of higher rank. It was into the enclosed courtyard of one of these houses, on a quiet street some way from the river, that Yeon and Uhlendof finally led the horses.

A small man with thinly greying hair emerged hurriedly from a rear door. He seemed to recognise the new arrivals at once, and whistled for a boy to take their horses before engaging in a brief whispered conversation with Uhlendof – one which entailed much pointing and gesturing. When it was finished, the little man, looking considerably agitated, beckoned them hurriedly into the house.

'This is Delleris,' Uhlendof introduced the slight figure as they entered the main hall, securely bolting the door behind them, 'Major-domo to my lord Careil. I have told him that our arrival here must remain a close secret.'

Delleris looked at the newcomers uneasily. 'My master sits in council at present,' he said; 'at the high keep. But I shall send one of the lads with a message for him. Even so, I cannot say when he will return.'

'Is there anywhere we can rest while we wait?' asked Uhlendof. 'For we have ridden long and hard this day, too hard for my old bones.'

Delleris nodded, leading them through a maze of quiet corridors to a large airy room where several long couches lay prepared.

Exhausted, Leighor sank into the nearest of them. He felt the damp cloak being removed from his shoulders and the boots pulled from his feet: and then nothing.

He awoke to the feel of the midday sun flooding down on to his face though diamond leaded windows. A small, leafy tree rustled somewhere outside, and someone was shaking his shoulder. There was a voice:

'Awake, southron! We have left you as long as we may, but you must arise now and dress. We can delay no longer.'

Leighor opened his eyes to see that it was Uhlendof.

'Do you feel rested now?' the monk asked.

Leighor nodded, although within himself he was not so sure. He felt that he had slept for but a few minutes, instead of a whole night and half a day besides – as he must have done. Slowly he forced himself to sit up and take in his surroundings, wincing as he felt the large bruises on the side of his face and the nagging pain in the small of his back, where Yeon had fallen upon him.

'There is food on the table,' Uhlendof told him. 'Warm water for washing and clean clothes by the fire. Prepare yourself and join us in the upper chamber. What is said there will concern you.'

Leighor nodded uneasily. He did not know exactly what lay ahead, but whatever it was he suspected it would be unpleasant. Yet at least he was no longer bound and gagged, and there seemed to be no guards on the door. As soon as he was alone he hurriedly consumed the small bowl of oatmeal porridge and the plate of cold meats that awaited him and, with his hunger still largely unsatisfied, he rose and crossed the wood-panelled room to the pile of clean dry clothes by the fire.

A new tunic had been provided for him, roughly similar in style to the old, and his outer clothes and boots had been carefully cleaned and dried. The new tunic was of warm light wool and fitted well, falling straight to his feet, with long pockets and straight-cut sleeves. Over this went his apothecary's surcoat – worn tabard-fashion over the head and belted at the waist – and then his satchel and rough cloak. Sitting once more to pull on his boots, he was fully dressed, and as ready as he would ever be to face whatever fate lay beyond the door.

A small boy awaited him in the gloomy corridor outside, nodding briefly in encouragement before leading Leighor silently up several flights of stairs to a large double doorway. Nodding again, the boy indicated that he should enter. Pushing the twin doors gently open, he found himself in a large empty room at the very top of the house. Doors opened on to a cool balcony, overlooking the river and the rooftops of the city. Leighor was drawn to it by the sheer magnificence of the vista beyond. Below him, the dark waters of the Gnir ran out between high cliffs into a sea choppy and grey with the brisk north-easterly wind. Herring cobles and other small boats were drawn up on a small riverside beach far below, nestling beneath the humble dwellings of the fisherfolk. On the far bank were salt-stained wooden wharves and piers, where three large merchant cogs lay berthed against a backdrop of boatyards and warehouses. The river itself teemed with craft, from poled ferries, hawker skiffs and lobster boats, to large, sea-going trading vessels riding at anchor in the low water. Over all, row upon row of houses rose up from the waterside to the high south wall, its tall Lee Bar marking the limits of the city. Everywhere he looked sails rose and fell, hundreds of people thronged and jostled along the riverside, and seagulls, terns and gannets in their tens of hundreds soared and wheeled overhead. The whole panorama was so full of movement and interest that Leighor could have easily stood staring out at the city for the rest of the day. But a voice from behind him abruptly interrupted his contemplation.

'So you are the southron for whom the whole countryside has been turned upside down, eh?'

Leighor spun around, to face the short man, bald and unimposing, who advanced towards him across the room. He was dressed entirely in black, in heavy robes that would have been well-suited to a rich merchant were it not for their sombre colour. 'I am Careil,' he introduced himself gravely. 'High Chancellor, Counsellor in Chief to my lord Eridar. The view is pleasant, is it not?'

Leighor nodded.

His host smiled thinly. 'From here one can see all the commerce of this great city, and the wealth that it creates. Were it not for this, the Sielders would be a poor place indeed.' Careil turned suddenly to look the southron full in the face. 'But that is not what we are here to discuss, is it? Ours are higher matters: of treason and regicide . . .'

So here it was.

'My lord,' Leighor replied. 'I am an honest man. A physician of Syrne. A stranger in your land. I had no part in the murder of your lord.'

'Of course not.' Careil smiled as Leighor's jaw fell open. 'I would not be so foolish as to imagine that anything Lord Darvir chooses to announce bears any relation to the truth. I know Darvir well – and he prefers to leave no loose ends . . .' The counsellor turned abruptly from him as Yeon and Uhlendof entered the chamber. He nodded silently, acknowledging their presence, and motioned them to sit at a large darkwood table in the middle of the room.

'We have little time for long debate,' he began briskly as soon as they were all seated. 'My servants tell me that Lord Darvir even now enters the city by the Lower Gate, and that he receives a warm welcome from the people. We must make our decisions quickly.'

Yeon was appalled. 'The people welcome him? How so? Surely they know of my uncle's corruptions, his many crimes . . . What he will do to this land?'

Careil shook his head. 'Few have yet had the misfortune to learn what his rule truly means. And now that he is Archbaron, many will cheer him who did not before. His servants will have spent much time, and more gold, upon this welcome. It means little.'

'But can you do nothing to stop him?' The youth rose, grey eyes blazing as he leant across the table, Leighor for the moment forgotten. 'You are still High Chancellor. Can you not act – arrest Darvir's allies before they seize all power? Or will you just sit here, and do nothing to bring Eridar's murderers to justice!'

'Yeon, Yeon,' the other frowned. 'As ever, you are foolhardy and overhasty. You must understand that most of my authority died with Lord Eridar, and what little remains dwindles almost by the hour. Outright opposition to Darvir now, without firm proof of his guilt, would be disastrous. The southron does not begin to provide that proof, his presence here serves only to incriminate us all! You should know this. After Girvan, you now lie third in line to the throne of the Sielders. You should long ago have developed the wisdom to think and act with circumspection. For goodness sake act your age, boy!'

Yeon glowered, slumping sulkily back into his seat.

'Yet you have had no proof,' Uhlendof said. 'Why then do you believe Darvir to be guilty of Lord Eridar's murder?' The monk looked tired, the heavy lines of his face seeming to deepen as he spoke.

'Because there is no one else who would benefit from that murder,' Careil stated flatly. 'Darvir has planned two other attempts on his brother's life before this. Each was without success. But Darvir was careful to leave no living witness to either of his failures, and without such proof, Eridar could not be persuaded to act against his own brother. No,' he shook his head sadly, 'this has been a crude plot, yet one which seems to have succeeded all too well.'

'But if we know Darvir to be guilty,' Yeon objected, 'surely others must know as well? If we were to speak out, with you beside us, perhaps we might convince more?'

Careil shook his head vigorously. 'Darvir is Archbaron now. He controls the courts, the guard and the inquisitors. In these lands you are now outlaws and no man may help you. Certainly none will take your word against that of Darvir and his followers; and his followers are many.'

'What then of the southron?' Yeon demanded. 'He could provide proof of Darvir's guilt! How can we be sure that he had no part in this?'

'We may not be totally sure, but it is unlikely.' Careil smiled. 'You were with him at the time and saw nothing. He has no gold nor any other means of payment on his person, no lethal dusts or poisons, no weapons more deadly than a surgeon's knife. If he is truly an assassin, then he is a very incompetent one. No, I doubt not that the poison was administered by Darvir's own hand, or by that of someone truly in his employ. The southron, I think, is as innocent as you – who now also stand accused of this same treason!'

'That is the truth, my lords,' Leighor added swiftly. 'If I were truly in this plot, would I not now have good reason to betray my employer, as he has betrayed me? To tell you all I knew, in order to bring Darvir down?'

'That is what we had hoped . . .' Uhlendof growled.

'Yet it seems that it is not to be,' Careil said shortly.

'But surely,' Yeon persisted, 'if we could come out openly, and obtain a public trial, all those who know of Darvir's crimes would have a chance to speak out, and the people would learn the truth.'

Uhlendof shook his head. But again it was Careil who spoke first.

'Once you had come forward and placed yourselves in Darvir's power, you would never appear in open court. He would have better use for you than that. After several hours with my lord's inquisitors you would sign any document that Darvir wanted you to sign. You would implicate all Darvir's enemies in your treason. And then you would die, quietly in some dark dungeon. That would serve no purpose at all. None but Darvir's. The Sielders are no safe place for any of you now. If Galdan were yet alive, we might appeal to him, but now . . .' he shook his head.

'Then what are we to do?' Leighor asked bleakly.

'As I have said, you must leave the Sielders.' Careil held up one hand to forestall any interruption. 'It is the only way. Here, you are a danger to all of us who yet remain to oppose Darvir. He cannot act against us without some pretext, he is not yet secure enough in his power. You, however, provide just the pretext he needs to destroy all who oppose him. You have performed a useful service in keeping the southron out of his hands, but now you must leave.'

'Where for?' Uhlendof asked quickly.

'Of your final destination I am as yet unsure,' Careil admitted. 'But I know where your first port of call must be. That must be Irgil, where Lord Eridar's last testament is held by the Durian Knights. It is important that this be retrieved at once, before Darvir can get his hands on it and destroy it.'

'Why?' Leighor asked. 'What is this testament?'

'It is the last will of Eridar,' the High Counsellor explained. 'I know not exactly what it contains – my Lord Halaron had a better idea than I of its full contents – but it is a document of great importance. The Archbaron may not have the power to choose his successor, but there will be many other important bequests, of lands and of titles, which may limit Darvir's power somewhat. It may also bear references to Eridar's fears of his brother's ambition, and that too may help us greatly. But most important of all, it contains the proxy vote of the Sielders.'

'What is that?' Yeon asked.

'If you had paid more attention to the few lessons that I and Lord Halaron have tried to give you, you would not need to ask.' Careil sighed, drawing a deep breath before continuing. 'As you know, Galdan, the High King of the Varroain, is dead. A new High King must now be chosen by the electors, the rulers of the central Varroain realms. Normally such an election would be no more than a formality, for there would be an obvious successor. But Galdan has left no heirs, and this time the election will be disputed. One vote – of the thirteen that are needed to elect the new High King – is held by the Archbaron of the Sielders. And since my lord Eridar was still alive at the time of Galdan's death, it is his vote, if it still exists, that must count. It cannot be altered or changed by his successor.'

'Are you sure of this?' Uhlendof asked. 'There is no way of setting Eridar's choice aside?'

'None.' Careil ruffled through some of his papers. 'I have been through both precedent and law in these matters many times. The High King of the Varroain is like no other king. In times of peace he has few powers beyond his own realm of Elerian. But in time of danger or crisis, all the kings of the eleven Varroain realms must defer to his will, and follow his call to battle. Within the person of the High King is said to reside the spirit, the essence of the whole Varroain race. This must pass to the High King upon the instant of his predecessor's death, and therefore the new High King exists already in theory, his existence waiting only to be revealed at the actual Diet, the conclave of electors. That is why there can be no possibility of a change of mind once the decision of the elector has been made. And at the time of Galdan's death that elector was Eridar, not Darvir.'

'I do not understand any of this,' Yeon said, much to Leighor's relief. 'What has all this to do with our present strait?'

'A very great deal,' Careil answered slowly. 'But to answer your question fully would take time that we do not have at present. Let me just say that of recent years there have grown up two factions amongst the nobility of these lands: those who have followed the older ways of rule, like Galdan and Eridar; and those like Darvir, and many others, who follow new and less generous ways. Who see themselves not as servants and guardians, holding their lands in trust, but as true lords of the earth and wielders of power absolute, before whom all men must bow the knee and tremble, and whose will is law. From such beginnings have many great evils been brought upon the world in times past. And it was ever Eridar's fear that the greatest ills that might afflict these lands would come not from without, but from our own midst. I think in this he has already been proved all too correct.'

'But there is no evil in these lands to compare with what lies beyond,' Yeon protested. 'The Riever hordes and vile Tarintarmen that harry the north and swarm upon the westron plains. The hordes of fouler creatures that lurk in the dark places of the earth: goblins, haroodin, the fell Khiorim riders who pillage and plunder the westron marches . . . Surely these are a greater threat than our own petty feudings?'

'Perhaps, perhaps,' Careil admitted. 'But sometimes we must fight the evils that lie closest to us. And the rule of Darvir will be evil indeed. He is a dangerous man, vicious and intemperate, a lover of violence and bloodshed. He would quickly squander all the wealth of these lands in ruin and war. Nor does he stand alone, for his mentor is Misan, King of Petan, and a candidate for the High Kingship itself. Darvir's rise to power here will be of great benefit to Misan, and to all who think as he does. Mayhap it is somewhat more than coincidence that Lord Eridar's murder should take place so immediately upon High King Galdan's death . . .' He sighed, turning to look out at the teeming harbour. 'In truth we know but little of the world in which we dwell. The great continent of Osenkor itself is vast beyond our knowing of it. Yet it is here, in the heart of our own small land, that evil first chooses to show its hand. And if that evil should conquer the mighty Varroain realms, then nowhere in the world is there power great enough to withstand its force. Not in the scattered kingdoms of the south, not in the merchant cities of the Bay of Qrena, nor in the beleaguered settlements of the northern wastes.'

'You speak with force,' Leighor said. 'But does the vote of Eridar truly hold the key to all this?'

'In a small way, perhaps,' Careil nodded, 'but one that may yet prove decisive. It depends upon how the votes fall when they are finally cast at the Kingmaking in Tershelline. King Misan of Petan, is candidate of the royal house of Arnan. If he is chosen High King, the position for which he now stands regent, then there will be such a reckoning as has not been seen for a hundred years. None who have dared oppose him, in all the eleven kingdoms, will be safe. He will lead us down into war and strife. Aye, and into a hundred other horrors unseen in these lands since the interregnum of Riladar.'

'Then what is the alternative?' Leighor asked.

'The only other candidate is Arminor, of the house of Urendor: the King of Helietrim, the Mountain King.' Careil looked up sombrely. 'Arminor is no great king. Many doubt that he has all of the qualities that a High King of the Varroain must needs possess in these troubled times. But he follows the older ways, his heart is sound, and he is a man of peace. He was Eridar's choice, and a thousand times preferable to the rule of Misan.'

'It is said that the vote is evenly balanced,' Uhlendof murmured.

Careil shook his head. 'Not quite. To my knowledge Misan has the more votes promised, although not yet a majority. Many of the electors will keep their vote secret until the spring when the election is held, in the hope of extracting favours from the winning candidate. It would be bitterest gall for Darvir now to learn that he had no vote to give to Misan. It would certainly be enough to speed his fall from favour with his mentor and protector.'

'How do we obtain Eridar's testament?' Yeon cut in sharply. 'I think we should act quickly.'

'Indeed.' Careil smiled. 'You must leave Ravenshald tonight. We have so far managed to keep the existence of the testament a secret, even from Darvir, and that gives us our sole advantage. You must hurry therefore, and make your way as best you can to Irgil. Once there, you will present certain documents, that I shall give you, to the Master of the Durian Knights in that city.'

'The Durian Knights?' Yeon objected. 'But why do you leave these things with foreigners? Were there no good Varroain knights or nobles you could have entrusted with the task?'

'It is always better to leave a document one does not wish opened with someone who has no interest in opening it,' Careil replied gently. 'There are very few in all the Varroain dominions who could be trusted with a confidence of such import, not even the Giellin bankers themselves.'

'Nor even the Knights of Imsild?'

'Especially not the Knights of Imsild. They are powerful, I grant you, and they perform a worthy task in warding the wilderlands and the northron marches. But they are no longer the selfless, independent order of which the ballads sing – the last true flower of Varroain chivalry. They hold numberless alliances throughout the Eastern Realms, and have gained great wealth and power thereby. They have a finger in every pie and an interest in every matter, large or small. The Durian Knights may be lax and uncouth northerners, but at least they are genuinely independent. If we had given the testament to the Knights of Imsild, the seals would not have lain unlifted a week!'

'The Knights would never break an oath!' Yeon was outraged. 'How can you speak so of them, even as they protect us all from the Riever hordes – and who knows what other evils beyond our borders!'

'We have no time to argue the point,' Careil said abruptly. 'Someday you will learn that all things are not as they appear on the surface. Eridar's testament is with the Knights of Dur, and there is an end to it! Many things must be quickly arranged – and time passes! If we are all finished . . .' He prepared to rise.

'There is one thing that still troubles me greatly, my lord,' Leighor forced himself to speak. 'And that is the manner of the death of Lord Halaron.'

'Aye.' Careil seated himself once more. 'The story in the city is that he was struck by a thunderbolt from out of a clear sky. Retribution from the gods, Darvir's supporters say.'

'There was no thunderbolt,' Leighor said quietly.

'You could see nothing,' Uhlendof cut in with impatience. 'You were bound across the horse's back. But it was clear enough to all who witnessed it. I myself saw it strike just ahead of me.'

'I had view enough to see the source of your thunderbolt,' Leighor insisted. 'And that it was Darvir himself!'

'How is this?' Careil sat bolt upright in his chair. 'You speak in riddles. Whatever else he may be, Darvir is no sorcerer, and it would take as great a sorcerer as ever lived in the days of the Qhilmun Kings to call down such a thunderbolt.'

'But I saw it.' Leighor refused to be moved. 'Darvir stood back from the chase when we fled the camp. He raised one arm, and upon it was a heavy amulet – not of gold or silver but of a dull colour, akin to steel. Although somehow it seemed to burn from within, with a purple fire, just before the blast came from Darvir's fingers.'

'*Harrunor*!' Uhlendof exclaimed in horror.

'You know of this?' Careil asked.

'Only from the histories,' the monk spoke slowly. 'And from a few of the dustier texts that lurk still in corners of the old libraries. Yet all speak of *harrunor* with fear and awe: a metal of great power, a bane to corrupt both high and low, a stealer of souls. It was thought lost forever with the fall of Qhilmun. If such is again abroad in the world, all may have cause to fear.'

Leighor shivered. An ominously cold wind had blown in from the sea beyond, and thick banks of grey cloud began to sprawl across the sky. The day had changed, and even the black ravens sitting silent upon the roof-tops seemed now to be watching their every movement, and listening to every word spoken in this small upper chamber. With an effort of will he dismissed the foolish thought.

'What could it do, this metal?' he asked.

The monk was silent for a moment, as if having to decide within himself whether or not to speak. '*Harrunor* was once known as the Mage Metal,' he said at last. 'And was reputed to have many sorcerous properties. It is said that it had the power to produce Magefire such as you claim to have witnessed. That, and much more. For some say that it had the power to enslave minds, to increase the strength of its bearer, even to lengthen a man's days if he knew its secrets ... Yet ever was there very little of it, and it was prized above all else and bloodily fought over. It is thought by some that *harrunor* brought about the fall of the Great Age, the ruin of the Westron Wastes, and the long dark age since.'

'And thus did all great sorcery come to an end,' Careil added.

'Not entirely,' Uhlendof corrected. 'There are still many sorceries and magicks pratised of a lesser sort. But nothing to compare with this – until now. Truly this seems a Demon's Gift.'

'A what?'

'A Demon's Gift,' Uhlendof repeated, 'designed to bring about the fall of man. We of the Mallenians teach that the One God, when he began to build the world we know from the chaos of the first creation, made first Angelic and Spirit beings to serve him. These were noble and beautiful, the firstborn of all living things, and all later creatures were but pale shadows of them. The One's last work, however, was man. And man he planned to be his final creation, the summit of all his work; and ruler, beneath him, of all else.' He paused. 'Yet when the mighty Prince of Angels learned of this plan to raise so high an upstart new creation, he rebelled, and with many of his angels was flung down into utter darkness, where now he rules as Lord of Demons. Man too was tricked into disobedience, and so did he fall into his present state. And, in their bitterness and fury, the Lord of Evil and his demons have tried ever since to lead and tempt mankind into further evils, that we too should be given into their power and they might have their final revenge upon us in the pit.'

'This is all well and good,' Careil said. 'And no doubt your Mallenian tales are as true as any others. But what we need to know in a more practical sense, is how exactly Darvir has come by this thing?'

Uhlendof shook his head. 'If I knew that, I would sleep far sounder this night. Perhaps he has rediscovered some ancient artefact and now makes use of it for his own purposes. I would rather it were that than any other source: for then we may hope that there is only one such amulet, and that it may quickly weaken and decay. But if someone has discovered the power of *harrunor* anew, we may truly tremble.'

'All this old women's talk is fruitless!' Yeon broke in impatiently. 'Let us hope these magicks are long done with.'

'I fear that this may be but the beginning,' Uhlendof said grimly.

'But for now Yeon is right,' Careil shrugged. 'There is little we can hope to do about these things. For the moment we must follow other paths. Let us go down now, you should prepare for your journey to Irgil. It grows cold here and we have tarried too long.'

It was late into the evening before Careil returned from his second visit to the keep, and the long intervening hours were filled with anxieties and fears. Light travel packs were speedily filled with clothes, utensils and food for the journey. All other arrangements were to be made by Careil, so there was little else for the travellers to do but sit in their chamber and wait.

Leighor brooded restlessly. Once again, events seemed to be running fast out of his control. He would have preferred to have struck out on his own if he could: Ravenshald was quickly becoming even more of a prison than Sonsterness had been. But with none of Careil's contacts or local knowledge, he had virtually no chance of escaping from the city alive, let alone of ever getting out of the Sielders. His only real hope of eventual freedom was to remain with the monk and the youth until they reached Irgil. Once he was safely out of Darvir's lands he would decide what he was going to do, until then, he would just have to go along with the High Counsellor's plan.

As the hours dragged on, servants brought worrying rumours: of guards being set upon all important crossroads, or of house-to-house searches taking place in various parts of the city. Eventually a flustered Delleris advised them to take refuge in a secret room beneath one of the large wine cellars, lest even this high house be searched by Darvir's men. And there, amid the dusty furnishings of the grimy under-chamber, Uhlendof, Yeon and Leighor nervously awaited Careil's return.

'Darvir has already been acknowledged by the Council,' Careil announced grimly, as he pushed fretfully into their chamber several hours later. 'You must leave at once.' He paused to wipe the beads of perspiration from his forehead. 'Many of those whom I had supposed our friends and allies have turned overnight to support Darvir, and he was able to note well all who called for delay or spoke against him. Your continued presence here becomes increasingly dangerous for us all!' He handed a sheaf of papers to Uhlendof. 'These are your authorities to obtain Eridar's possessions from the Durian Knights, and letters of credit redeemable upon the Giellin bankers of Irgil. Guard them well. They are the only means by which we may yet save something from this disaster!'

'And when we have the testament, what then?' Uhlendof asked, securing the documents within his robes.

'Do not attempt to return,' Careil said sharply. 'These things must not fall into Darvir's hands! If Galdan were still alive, I would have advised you to bear them to Tershelline Athtal, and present them there. Now you must travel to King Arminor in Helietrim, he will know how to use them to best advantage.'

'And how shall we leave?' Leighor asked.

'I had hoped to gain you berths in one of the ships now at anchor in the river but once Darvir was acknowledged Archbaron he was able to bring his own men into the city, and now they guard all places of importance. Even the smallest lobster boat cannot leave the river without being thoroughly searched.'

'Then what do you propose?' Yeon demanded.

'We shall deal with that in a moment,' Careil replied. 'But first I have something to give to each of you.' From his belt he produced two small leather pouches, giving one each to the youth and the priest. 'There are forty gold talents in each bag. That should be ample to cover your expenses between here and Irgil.' Turning to Leighor, he presented him with a flat wooden case. 'On this journey you may have need of a weapon, and so I thought to bring you one that needs little in the way of training to master, or to use to good effect.'

Within the box was a fine crossbow of yew and tempered steel. It was perfect in every detail and easily worth a hundred talents on its own. Any slight resentment he had felt at not being trusted with a share of the journey gold vanished at once.

'It is superb,' Yeon said, eyeing it enviously. 'Where did you get such a weapon?'

'It seems to bear the mark of Northwright hands,' Uhlendof observed quietly.

'Indeed,' Careil nodded. 'I bought it many years ago from a northron trader – for its beauty alone, for I am no shot. But it is better that such a noble weapon should see service in a good cause, than rust away in some damp corner of my hall.' He turned back to the southron. 'Take good care of it, and hang it at your belt. There are a dozen quarrels only, so you must retrieve them wherever possible. As for the box, leave it here, you will have little need of it.'

'It is indeed a goodly weapon,' Leighor said. 'I hope that I may use it as nobly as it was given.'

Careil gave a thin smile in acknowledgement of the compliment. 'Now we must leave,' he told them briskly. 'Take up your packs and follow me. We have an appointment to keep.'

They passed out of the house through a series of low passageways, to emerge in a dark and narrow alley.

'Follow me in silence,' Careil ordered, drawing up his hood against the smoky light of the wall-torches that flickered from every street corner. 'We shall keep to the byways. But take care. If we pass anyone, you must act as normal revellers celebrating Darvir's accession.' He turned away, to lead them down the narrow alleyway towards the river.

To Leighor's relief the journey passed without event. They had to cross only a few main streets, all of which were nearly empty at this hour. And none of Darvir's guards were to be seen upon the quieter ways through which Careil mostly led them. At length Careil halted before an oaken door, one of many that led directly off the street, carved into it were ravens, bears, and other creatures dear to the hearts of the engravers of Ravenshald, framed amid dark vines and coiling tendrils. He knocked softly. After a few moments the door opened and a small woman nodded in silent greeting. She turned, to lead them wordlessly through several long halls and passages to a small kitchen. Here she left them.

Yet as soon as they were alone, a large, dark-robed figure emerged from the shadows of the great fireplace.

'You are lucky I am still here,' he growled. 'I have been stood waiting an hour or more! I feared something had happened to you.'

'I apologise,' Careil stepped forward to greet the stranger. 'But there is no keeping to time in these days.'

'Who is this?' Yeon's voice cut through their guide's brittle apologies. 'I do not know him!'

'This is Master Telsyan,' Careil whispered reprovingly, standing back to introduce the large stranger. 'He has agreed to accompany you on your journey.'

Telsyan was a big man, both broad and tall, with a square, no-nonsense face, and he wore the rich capacious robes of a Giellin merchant. The cloth was damask of deepest mauve, belted tight at the waist with a length of thin white calf leather, the trailing end of which hung fashionably down to the hem of his robe. Hidden beneath were more practical breeches and stout leather boots. But the rest of his costume seemed designed more to impress the observer with the wealth and status of its owner than to bear the vicissitudes of travel. From the puff cap that adorned his plain features, to the fine kid gloves that covered his strong stubby hands, the impression was of a thin veneer of refinement confining the hardened energy within.

'We need no more strangers to accompany us to Irgil!' Yeon insisted with a surly glance towards Leighor. 'There is enough risk in this venture already.'

'Ssh!' Careil hissed sharply, holding a finger to his lips. He looked around quickly to see whether anyone approached. 'We must not be heard! This is not a safe house, but was chosen for another reason. In any case, I assure you that Master Telsyan is well known to me and has served my lord Eridar well in his time. That is why I have requested him to do me the great favour of journeying with you to Irgil and beyond. He has travelled much in the north, and knows the ways of Irgil as do few others. His presence will greatly increase your chances of success in your task—' He stared straight at Yeon – 'which I hope is what we all desire?'

'Of course,' the youth admitted unwillingly, turning to hold out his hand to the merchant. 'I apologise, good Master Telsyan, for doubting you.'

'It is forgotten,' the merchant grunted, taking his hand to shake it firmly. 'I have been thought far worse of in my time, by friend and foe alike. I am a plain man and appreciate honest speaking. Indeed I think it best that all such matters are settled at the start. So if there is anyone else here who doubts me, or would prefer it that I had no further part in this enterprise, let him speak now, and I shall be happy to return at once to my lodgings.' He looked about him at the gathered company, but there was no response.

'Good,' Uhlendof sighed. 'We shall have time for fuller introductions later, but for now I am sure we are all glad to have your aid and company upon this journey.'

'And now it is time to begin that journey,' Careil stepped forward. 'As I have said, I have brought you all to this house for a reason, and that is because a way leads from here beneath the walls and out of the city.'

'Where?' Yeon looked about him with new interest.

'It is one of the secret ways of the old guilds,' Careil replied, turning his back on them to duck beneath the heavy stone mantel of the great fireplace. He stood erect in the centre of the cavernous hearth and beckoned them to follow, waiting until they were all gathered in the confined space to point to a narrow break in the stonework on the right-hand side of the hearth. The gap was dark, and little more than a foot and a half in width, yet it extended from floor to ceiling, and was so positioned that it was totally hidden from the sight of anyone not standing beneath the chimney breast. 'That is your way,' the counsellor nodded.

'I hope it is not that narrow all along,' Uhlendof muttered. 'When you spoke of a passage I presumed it would be one of fit size for a man.'

'The passage will be of normal size once you are through the gap,' Careil assured him. 'It is quite safe and sufficient for your needs. In fact a man has been through this afternoon to prepare your way. The tunnel will take you beneath the river and out to the base of the West Cliff beyond the walls. There you shall find horses waiting. Now go.' He ducked back beneath the mantel to fetch them two smouldering torches, one for Telsyan, who was to lead, and the other for Yeon who would bring up the rear. Embracing them all before they parted, he wished them godspeed and safe journey, watching as they filed slowly into the darkness of the tunnel.

After the first yard or so the passageway widened, so much so that two persons might walk abreast with little difficulty. Yet there was little headroom, and as the four fugitives made their way onward, the roof came lower still, until all but the monk were forced either to stoop or bow their heads. After a few minutes of this, every forward step became a torment, and the dankness of the air and the sense of confinement became ever more oppressive. Few words were spoken, for the travellers now needed all their energy and breath to negotiate a passage through the cramped, uneven tunnel. The walls grew wet with slime as they progressed, and the floor beneath their feet became slick with mud and running water. Telsyan lifted his finger to the ceiling where a stone had fallen from the arching roof. A stream of water ran down his arm.

'We must be beneath the river,' he murmured. 'We are halfway.'

'That is good,' Uhlendof muttered grimly. 'For from the state of this tunnel, I do not think it will endure for many years longer.'

'So long as it sees us through I'll be happy,' Telsyan grunted, moving on.

It seemed an age before the merchant next called a halt. And all the while Leighor toiled on in silence, head bowed against the low roof, constantly imagining the terrible weight of water that must lie above them. All the travellers were now breathing hard, their faces red and sweaty in the torchlight.

'There is a wooden stair here, leading up,' Telsyan announced. 'I shall go up first to take a look. You wait here.' He passed his torch back to Leighor and began to climb purposefully.

Reaching the top of the stairway, he put his back to the trapdoor, raising it easily. He stared silently out into the darkness for several moments before venturing up and out . . .

A wave of cool fresh air swept down into the tunnel, and for the first time Leighor realised just how foul and dank the air in the passageway had become.

It was several more minutes before Telsyan's head appeared again in the opening, and this was to announce their release. 'All seems to be well,' he whispered hurriedly. 'Come on up.'

'We seem to be at the back of a small cave,' Telsyan told them as they emerged. The air was unbelievably sweet and cold, and the sound of the sea came from somewhere beyond the cave mouth. Thankfully, the travellers wiped the sticky tunnel mud from their feet and, closing the wooden trapdoor behind them, prepared to leave.

'Where are the horses?' Leighor whispered.

The merchant nodded briskly towards the cave mouth. 'Farther down. Come!' He motioned them all forward.

The horses were safely tethered just inside the cave mouth, yet they seemed nervous, pulling sharply at their tethers as the travellers approached.

'They are fearful of the tide,' Uhlendof said, selecting the nearest mount for his own and attempting to calm it. 'Yet they are well provided, just as Careil said.'

'Good.' Telsyan led one of the larger horses out of the cave and swung himself expertly into the saddle. 'We shall have to ride long and hard if we are to be across the causeway by first light.'

'Cross the causeway?' Uhlendof objected. 'But the tide is rising!'

'It will not be full till after dawn,' Telsyan snapped quickly. 'If we make good time we shall be across long before then. There are ten good leagues of flat sand between here and the causeway, so we shall cover the distance sooner this way than we could on the road. And once we are on the mainland, and the tide has closed behind us, we shall be safe from pursuit for the rest of the day.'

The others were all now mounted and waiting, Leighor upon a broad, snorting beast of speckled black, and Yeon upon a slighter, more elegant steed which he had made for at once. Needing no further signal, Telsyan reined in his circling mount and led the way out across the sands.

The moon was just beginning to set, sinking slowly into the sea directly ahead, along the line of the beach. Behind them, the high cliffs of Ravenshald towered above the narrow estuary of the Gnir, the red braziers of the watch-towers burning like fiery embers upon the city walls. Leighor shivered. This felt far too much like the leaving of Sonsterness.

Chapter Five
THE SEA ISLANDS

They rode slowly and silently at first, beneath the shadow of the dark cliffs. Only when they were well away from the last of the city towers that crowned the high cliffs above them did they chance urging their horses into a gallop across the flat hard-packed sands. They rode in single file, keeping only close enough together to ensure that each was in plain sight of the next. The steady pace ate up the miles quickly, but it seemed that they rode for hours through the velvet darkness, along the long straight line between the cliffs and the sea, watching the last dim crescent of the moon vanish into the waters ahead of them.

Leighor had little to concentrate upon other than keeping the rounded form of Uhlendof, next in line, always in sight, and he had time to think. The cool breeze from the sea had been stiff enough when they had started out, yet as time passed it seemed to be growing even stronger. The thought worried him. He had not made use of the causeway to reach the Sielders, having journeyed here by ferry skiff from southern Holdar. But he knew it well enough by repute. It was little more than a succession of small sandswept islands, joined for several hours each day by the causeway road that ran across the sands and rockbeds at low tide, linking the Sielders with the mainland of Holdar. At high tide, however, the sea swept in over the road from both sides, isolating the individual islands and cutting off all travel between. He had no wish to be on the road when that happened.

The sea seemed to be advancing too steadily up the beach for his ease of mind, and he had less confidence than Master Telsyan in the Ravenshald Tide Tables. Even the breaking of the waves sounded louder and nearer than it had before. He could hear the crashing of each individual breaker now, even above the drumming of the horses' hooves on the hard sand. He raised a hand to shield his eyes from the wind, and tried to look out to sea. Heavy clouds churned in across the skies, and in the fast-fleeting rays of moonlight he saw what he feared: a thousand white horses glinting beyond the breakers, whipped up by the rising north-east wind. A stormwind. Leighor shivered and tried to urge his horse on the faster, but it seemed that their present pace was all his mount could maintain for more than a short burst, and he soon dropped back.

And so the four travellers continued to ride steadily westward through the night, the pace as unvarying as the scenery of sand and sea and high-towering cliffs; until at last the steep cliffs that had marked their passage throughout the journey began to fall away, and the hard sand of the beach changed to a rounded shingle that suited the horses less and slowed their passage to a trot. In a few minutes they had reached the point where the last of the cliffs slumped wearily into the shingle, and all that could be seen on their left was impenetrable blackness. In unspoken agreement the fugitives drew their mounts to a halt.

'We approach the causeway!' Telsyan announced, having to shout loud to make himself heard against the wind. 'We shall have to turn here, and ride south until we meet the road from Ravenshald. It will take us to Roadsmeet on the mainland. There will be no travellers at this hour, but there may be guards, so be careful!'

The others nodded and followed as the merchant led them around the last crumbling outcrop of grey rock on to the southward-running beach. Looking eastwards now, Leighor could just detect the thin white line of the chalk road winding down towards them from the bare Sielder hills. A quarter of a league farther and they came to it, its course clearly marked by the pairs of large white boulders that had been set upon either side, every hundred paces or so along its length. The twinned lines of stones ran straight as a die, westward across the beach, and then out beyond the reach of their vision into the velvet darkness of the sea.

Leighor did not like the look of it at all. 'How can we tell if the road is clear?' he asked.

'It is clear,' Telsyan assured him. 'There are no lights, and the moon has only just set. That gives us three good hours to be across. I have done it in half that.' He turned away and spurred his horse across the sands.

But for the paired white chalkstones that marked its passage across the beach, it would have been impossible to tell the course of the roadway from the rest of the flat sands around them, and this gave the southron no extra confidence as the small company formed up in single file behind Telsyan to begin the crossing.

Almost as soon as they were out of the shelter of the cliffs they felt the full force of the north-east wind upon them, fiercer and stronger than before. Blazing unfettered across the open wastes of the Rathul Sea, it tore through the travellers' clothing, chilling them to the bone. Leighor felt the hint of rain in the wind as well – unless perhaps it was spray torn from the waves that broke somewhere beyond his vision to the north? Even though he could not see those breakers now, he could still hear them all too well, thundering against the screaming shingle at what seemed disconcertingly close range. Looking forward and behind, he found that he could see nothing but the long lines of ghostly white stones that marked out the line of the causeway, receding grimly into the darkness in both directions. With the dark shadows of his three companions ahead of him, the whole effect was dreamlike and eerie, filling him with bleak foreboding. They seemed to travel a phantom path, suspended somehow in time and space amidst a raging sea.

To his relief they soon came upon a small island. But this turned out to be little more than a glorified sandbank that rose a few feet above the level of the causeway, enduring for only a few dozen yards – long enough to support a sparse vegetation of tussocky sea grasses – before slipping back into the flat sameness of the causeway once more. For what seemed another hour they rode across barren, featureless sands, occasionally coming upon a similar small islet or windcarved sandbank, but meeting nothing else to disturb the bleak forgotten dominion of the exiled sea. Not until suddenly a darker shadow, high and broad, loomed out of the darkness ahead of them. Land!

'Are we across?' Yeon rode forward eagerly, screaming the words against the wind.

'No,' Telsyan shook his head firmly as the others drew level with him, 'it is only the isle of Nefarn, almost halfway across. There is first this island, then five leagues on Helfarn, where there is a small settlement of fisherfolk called Instrand, and after that naught but sandbanks and an hour's ride to the mainland.'

Leighor's heart sank at this news. For a moment he had thought the crossing over, and their long, tense travail at an end. 'Why should we not spend the night upon this island?' he ventured. 'The seas are high, it may storm; and we could then continue in the daylight.'

Again the merchant shook his head. 'If we stay here we shall be trapped half a day by the tide, easy meat for Darvir's men if they pursue us. We must go on. If we keep up our present pace we shall be safe on the mainland before dawn breaks.'

'To my ears the sea sounds close,' Uhlendof warned, 'and our pace may be slower than we think. Perhaps there are some fisherfolk here who could ferry us to the mainland at daybreak?'

'No,' Telsyan said firmly, pulling down his hood against the gathering rain. 'No one lives on Nefarn but half-wild hermits and gatherers of shellfish. The only way off this isle is by road. The wind is high and we are on the causeway's narrowest part; but the tide will not change its appointed course just to entrap us.'

Resignedly priest and southron nodded; and Telsyan spurred on his horse to lead them up on to the lonely isle of Nefarn. Here the road bent and twisted for the first time since leaving the Sielder shore, climbing slowly upward through towering thick-set trees. The dark trees gave them more protection from the cutting wind than they had had on the causeway, although curiously they made it sound far worse – for the trees creaked and shuddered with every gust, sending showers of twigs, leaves and broken branches hurtling downward into their path. Soon even Leighor began to have second thoughts about spending the night here, and to wonder why even the hermits and shellfish-gatherers chose to remain. And then the ground stopped rising and the forest fell away, to leave them unprotected on the exposed western hillside where the road sloped down towards the sea flats once more.

Leighor shuddered inwardly when he saw the lines of white marker stones appear again ahead of them, but he knew that he had no choice but to follow until they reached the mainland. The wind did not seem quite so strong as it had been, but Leighor supposed that this might only be due to the sheltering effects of the island, and his spirits did not rise. Now there was less sand, for the roadway passed across great exposed sheets of barnacled rock, strewn with limpets and flaccid sea-wrack. The white guidestones grew fewer and farther apart. The road was no longer straight, beginning to twist and turn to follow the most level course across the shattered broken surface left by the departed sea. Jagged edges and deep rockpools lurked in the darkness just off the path to trap the unwary rider; and the stone, even on the roadway itself, was often slippery with strewn weed. Ominously, their pace slowed. Leighor now had to guide every footfall of his heavy mount, peering down into the murky dullness beneath, to seek out the light-coloured patches of barnacle and the dark mussel beds that made the surest footing.

Again the journey began to seem endless, as the constant strain of the ride continued without break. Every now and again Leighor would look up apprehensively to search the eastern skies for any sign of the coming dawn; relieved each time to see nothing. The imagined length of their crossing must be no more than an illusion conjured up out of a tired mind. Yet when Leighor next looked back down, his eyes widened with horror. For some time the road had been rising gently, the ground sloping sharply away beneath them to the right. But now, even as he watched, he could see the small rockpools to his right slowly filling up and linking, replenishing themselves with water from some unseen source – gradually merging to cover the surrounding patches of dry rock. Cold terror struck through him like a lance. Here were his darkest fears being realised . . . The sea was coming back!

For long moments he sat still, almost hypnotised by the sight, which none of the others seemed yet to have noticed; watching with a terrible fascination as the water streamed in. A stumble from his mount brought him sharply back to reality. He steadied his horse, screaming out to the others ahead. 'The sea!' he pointed wildly towards the rockpools, 'The sea is coming in!'

The others turned to stare at him, then followed his pointing finger to stare out into the advancing sea instead, surprise turning to horror as they began to take in the full import of what they saw.

'This cannot be!' Telsyan stammered, staring now behind him into the east. 'It is still an hour till the dawn . . .'

'Yet the tide is here now!' Yeon accused angrily. 'What do your tables say to that?'

'The tables cannot be wrong,' the merchant gasped, shaking his head in perplexity, 'it must be the wind. This ungodly north-easter is pushing the tide in early.'

'Then we shall be overrun!' Leighor said, horrified. 'Can we not get quickly back to Nefarn?'

For the first time Telsyan began to look uncertain. 'I am not sure,' he said at last. 'I think we are about halfway between the two islands. Ahead lies Helfarn, behind its sister. I do not know which we might hope to reach first. We know the road behind was clear – but that was the lowest section of the causeway. It might be better to keep going forward.'

Uhlendof shook his head. 'No, let us go back! We do not know what lies ahead. We know what lies behind.'

'Either way let us decide quickly,' Leighor warned. 'The tide is coming in too fast for my liking.'

'Back then.' Telsyan said, looking around at the other faces. One by one they nodded.

Riding back Leighor, who had been last, was now in the lead, and it was he who must make their pace. Journeying west the road had been slowly rising, now it sloped back down across the flats to Nefarn. He tried to make good use of the slope to increase their pace, but his mount was not keen and refused to be hurried. As they retraced their steps Leighor's fears grew, he did not like going downwards and his eye was constantly upon the close-lapping waters to the north.

Suddenly the horse stopped dead. Leighor staring ahead of him in his horror, saw that the whole road in front of him had disappeared! Where only a short while before they had ridden across a plain of all-too-solid rock, there was now nothing but a wide expanse of choppy water, across which the first small wavelets were beginning to roll. It could not be very deep. Yet, in the darkness, Leighor could see no farther shore, and the waters continued unbroken and fearsome into the unknown. A few short minutes ago he had been dreading any sign of the dawn; now he longed for it, to show them some way of escape, and he knew it would not come.

'It is not possible!' Uhlendof said, drawing up beside him. 'We were here but minutes ago!'

'It is all too possible,' Telsyan spoke urgently, 'the sea bed here is flat. When the tide comes, it comes quickly! We must turn again at once, take the upward path. We cannot risk trying to cross this way; it will get yet deeper! Westward. Hurry!' His voice was agitated, barely able to suppress the first sharp edges of panic, as he turned his horse.

For a while it seemed reassuring to be rising again, if only very gradually, and Leighor began to hope that they might continue in this manner until they came upon the good dry land of Helfarn. But as soon as he came to the spot where he had first noticed the advancing waters his hopes left him, for there was no longer any ground visible to the north. The right side of the roadway just sloped gently down into the oily waters of the Rathul Sea. As one, the travellers drew to a halt, struck dumb as they watched the choppy waters rise and fall. Gently, yet to the same chilling rhythm as the great breakers crashing against unseen rocks somewhere out in the darkness.

'Ride on!' Telsyan shouted suddenly from in front. 'Whatever rocks protect us now, they will not stop the waves forever, as we dawdle here.'

The company spurred their horses on now with renewed urgency, white-rimmed eyes staring out from beneath dark cowls, constantly upon the ever-rising waters to the north. Always with them as they rode were the too-familiar white marker-stones which Leighor knew would follow him through his future nightmares – if they survived this crossing. Now the ground to the south of them began to fall away, leaving only the thin line of the road itself above the vast deep bowl of the sea bed. Then Leighor saw the first glimpse of water to his left, several dozen yards away and at the limit of his vision, but the white surf of the wavecaps was unmistakable. This time he did not rush to draw the discovery to the attention of his companions. They would know soon enough.

The horses were tiring now, and despite the strongest urgings of their riders they had slowed. Nothing was going right; and still the wind continued pitilessly from the north-east. Even so, the first wave came as a shock. A sudden rush from behind, followed by the heavy crash of a wall of water breaking over the north edge of the roadway. The wave was not large, but the shock of it was enough to make their horses leap and forget their tiredness; the spray rained down upon them, drenching their clothes, and bringing the sharp taste of salt to their mouths.

Leighor saw Uhlendof turn a dark-cowled face back to stare at something behind him. Swinging sharply round, he followed the monk's gaze, to see a long dim line of grey-white fast approaching from the north – another wave! He saw it strike the causeway, breaking up and over the path as it bore down upon them. This was larger than the first, and this time its waters crashed right across the roadway, the sudden force almost sweeping his horse from its feet as the wave broke about its ankles. And then it was past, and the sea drained slowly away again, seeping back through a hundred cracks and crevices in the basestone, to leave the road exposed once more. Yet the sea was all about them now, and only the narrow strip of road was clear.

Leighor swore and spurred on his horse, almost colliding with Uhlendof in his sudden panic to escape. 'Hurry!' he screamed, reining in his horse to give the monk room to manoeuvre his bulky mount in the right direction.

Eventually, mercifully, Uhlendof got his mount moving forward at a fair speed, and Leighor followed; wanting to race ahead even faster but knowing the wisdom of the monk's careful pace. A further two large waves had broken over them before Telsyan and Yeon came into sight ahead. These were less violent, than the first, yet their waters seemed to remain longer on the road, and to slip away less freely, leaving it partly clear. The tide was rising fast.

'Where were you?' Yeon shouted above the waves, his horse ankle-deep in water, 'We thought you lost . . .'

'No time!' Telsyan seized the youth's bridle, pulling him forward urgently. 'There is no time for questions now, ride on!' He spurred on his own horse in example, and for the first time Leighor found himself taking the side of the brusque merchant, urging his own horse onward. Yet much as the travellers wished to hurry, the horses were now too tired to move very fast; and the water, rising around their feet, only slowed them further. Within minutes the causeway was permanently covered, and in place of the waves came large, smooth rollers, which passed across the road as if it did not exist before sweeping southwards to leave it for a few seconds tantalisingly clear. Leighor prayed each time that the waters would finally part to reveal the solid rock beneath, but always the water flooded back still higher than before.

Suddenly Leighor's horse stumbled. Fearful, it screamed, rearing wildly as Leighor clung on for dear life. Then sickeningly, heart-stoppingly, he felt the beast's rear feet begin to slip from the edge of the roadway. Impotently Leighor hung on tight as the terrified horse struggled for its footing. He had just time to cry out before the water hit him, covering him to his waist. He clung desperately to the horse's neck, seeing the other riders gather in front of him as a great swell washed over him. Yet that swell may well have saved them both, lifting the horse enough for it to scramble back up on to the roadway again. Shakily the horse staggered back to firm footing, and Leighor was borne clear of the water once more. Only his feet were now touched by the rising swells, although his entire body was drenched with cold salt water.

'Are you all right?' Uhlendof asked, taking hold of his bridle.

Weakly Leighor nodded, although he was frozen cold and still half in shock. His heart raced as if he had run a pair of leagues, but he had not been swept away, he still lived.

A sudden urgent cry from Yeon brought him instantly back to full awareness: 'Telsyan, Uhlendof! Where are the stones? I cannot see them!'

Leighor sat up and looked ahead, looked all around him, but he could see nothing. Nothing but the white caps of a thousand fleeting wavelets, themselves borne on the backs of larger swells, sweeping across the dark sea. A chill crept over him. The marker stones had sunk beneath the waves. Now they were surely lost.

Yeon too stared blankly into the darkness. 'Which way lies Helfarn now? All ways look the same . . .'

'We still know the direction of the wind.' Telsyan's voice sounded a deal less certain than he meant it to. 'If we keep it behind us and to our right . . .'

'No!' Uhlendof moved his horse to block the merchant's intended path. 'Don't act like a fool! You've just seen how easy it is to fall from the road, and that was when we had the stones to follow. By guesswork alone we wouldn't get ten paces!'

'Then what do you suggest?' Telsyan rounded on the monk angrily. 'That we just sit here until we are swept away?'

'Stop!' Yeon screamed urgently, pointing away into the darkness. 'I see something! A light, far ahead. Can you see it?'

'Where?' Telsyan span around to look. 'I see nothing.'

'There, above the waves! A small light. It's moving!'

'I see it.' Telsyan seemed almost irritated by the discovery, or at least the means of it. 'It must be land, or someone else on the road. Either way we had best make towards it quickly before we lose that as well.'

The onward passage was hard, for the horses were weak and the swells strong, yet the light was true and they did not stray from the causeway as they made towards it. In fact almost immediately the road began to rise. Imperceptibly at first, but after some time unmistakably so. Slowly but surely the level of the water was falling, until soon only the larger swells washed up above their mounts' knees. And still the flickering light shone true ahead, just above the wavetops. Yet although they rode as hard as they could, they did not seem to draw any closer to their guiding light or to whoever it was who carried it: it seemed to stay always just over a half league ahead of them.

'Whoever it is must be moving to the shore like us.' Telsyan's voice carried back to them.

'Yet how do they find their way?' Uhlendof wondered.

'Perhaps they have a lodestone, or know the road better than we . . .'

'I think I can see a figure!' Yeon squinted into the darkness. 'A man beneath the lantern, a figure wading . . .'

'You dream, boy!' Telsyan snorted after staring intently ahead for some moments. 'I see no one. And who could walk unaided through such waters? Whoever they are, they must ride.'

Without warning, the light vanished ahead of them.

'It's gone!' Alarm crept rapidly into the merchant's voice as he scanned the horizon for the vanished light. 'Keep on in the same direction! Do not stop even once or we are lost!'

'It's all right!' Uhlendof sighed rapidly, pointing ahead. 'There are the marker stones!'

Indeed the tips of two of the familiar paired white stones pointed out of the water not a dozen yards ahead of them, and there were more beyond, emerging from the choppy sea to greet them like old friends, each receding pair a little clearer of the water than the last. Within minutes the water was streaming rapidly away from the roadway as it rose gently out of the sea; and shortly thereafter they came up on to the dark dry land of Helfarn.

Immediately the travellers tumbled from their stricken horses to slump gratefully to the warm soft earth. Thus they lay for many minutes in the partial shelter of a line of low, straggling pines that grew close to the shore, hardly even noticing the wind and the rain as they rested.

'Come,' Telsyan said after a while, standing, 'we cannot stay here. We must find shelter, or else exposure will kill us as surely as the sea would have done. Perhaps if we move quickly we may catch up with the owners of that light.'

Reluctantly the others pulled themselves to their feet once more, even Leighor recognising the truth in the merchant's words. However cold and tired they felt, they must find shelter. Slowly they trudged inland, away from the sound of the sea, leading horses that were too exhausted to bear them. The way ran on featurelessly through the low scrubby vegetation of the island as the dim grey quarter-light of the approaching dawn crept slowly up behind them. Leighor was numb with weariness; he could feel nothing at all now, neither cold nor pain, nothing but the intense desire to lie down and rest. He stumbled on, trying as hard as he could to remain on his feet; for he knew that if he allowed himself to fall it would be a long time before he rose again.

There was a light somewhere ahead, glimmering through the grey middle-distance ahead of them. They all saw it at once, yet none of them were able to make out its source; it might be a house, a settlement, or even their fortuitous guide from the flooded causeway. Yet despite their weariness their feet gathered speed as they drew towards it.

Yeon reached its source first: a single tallowfat lantern suspended from the eaves of a wooden hut. Beneath it sat a man, a thin, drawn figure, working at his pile of wicker lobster-pots. He looked sharply up at the strangers, yet with little interest, as they gathered round him out of the morning gloom.

'Where are we?' Yeon demanded. 'Is this Instrand?'

'No sirs,' the man spoke with aggravating slowness. 'Not Instrand. This place is called by name Harstensond.'

'Are we not then on Helfarn Isle?' Telsyan broke in.

'Aye, but Instrand lies two leagues to the west, upon the farther shore – not far, if that's where you're going. Here we are few, just one or two poor fisherfolk who try to grub a living from the sea.' He looked up again, and for the first time seemed to take full note of the wet, bedraggled travellers who stood in front of him, and wonder at their origin. 'You have not been out on the causeway,' he gasped, 'in this!'

'Aye,' Telsyan grunted, 'we have been caught by the tide and nearly perished. Is there somewhere hereabouts we may rest awhile and get ourselves dry and warm?'

'Nowhere here, my good sirs. Yet it is but a step to the dwelling of Garshan, where lie what small comforts are to be found in Harstensond.' The man rose. 'I will lead you.'

Taking down the smoking lantern from where it hung in the eaves, the fisherman led them away from the road, down a narrow muddy track towards the north shore of Helfarn isle. Leighor's eyes were drawn to the flickering light their guide carried, the yellow flame guttering and smoking in the strong breeze, yet refusing to be extinguished. It gave out only the dimmest and most vapid of lights. Could this have been the light that had shone ahead of them on the causeway and shown them the way to land? He decided to ask.

The fisherman stopped and turned at the question, looking back at him sharply. 'Who shines lights upon the water? Who indeed? Not I, nor any who dwell here; for it is deemed ill-luck to do so. Perhaps you saw a light that was not there . . .'

'How so?'

There was no answer, and the fisherman continued on his way.

'Did no other traveller pass on the road before we came?' Uhlendof persisted.

'None have passed me, and I have been at my work an hour or more.'

'Then could it have been someone who dwells apart from your folk?'

'There are none but we seven who still fish out of old Harstensond.' The fisherman seemed irritated at the repeated questioning. 'None other on all the eastern side of Helfarn Isle. No. There is no one else to light your lights!'

The path ended suddenly upon a long stony beach. Here their guide paused to stare out at the sea in the grey eastern light of the foredawn. Foaming white horses topped the long rollers as they stormed into the lonely beach.

'No,' he suddenly spoke again, his voice soft against the background of the sea. 'This is a night for the sea folk. Seldom do they return now to the grey shores of Helfarn. It is a good omen indeed if they chose to intervene in your favour.'

'Sea folk?' Yeon hissed, incredulous. 'You cannot believe in such tales!'

The fisherman turned. 'Have ye never walked a lonely beach when the grey mists fall . . . ? Have ye never heard the distant song of the sea folk upon the waters . . . ? I have – many times.' He sighed. And now his voice became barely audible – almost as if his words were not truly meant for them at all. 'I saw them once, long ago; when I was a boy. Saw them for but a moment, sporting upon a distant shore. Like men they were, but not like men, tall and beautiful, arrayed in all the colours of the sea, laughing like children among the breakers . . .' His voice faded into the wind. For a few moments he stood in silence, then he turned away, to lead them briskly on down the beach.

In minutes they came upon a small wooden dwelling, set on piles, some way back from the beach, its rear leaning against the rising sand-dunes behind. A fair-sized boat was drawn up on the sand before it, and wooden steps led up to the only door. This must be the home of Garshan.

When roused, its owner came down to welcome them; instructing their guide to tether the four horses where they might graze on the tussocky sand grasses before conducting the strangers up into his house. A long wooden bench, which ran along one wall, provided the only comfort in the small inner room. Yet the travellers sat together gratefully on this, thankful at last for the rest and the shelter. If Garshan was truly the richest man of Harstensond, the community must indeed be a poor one. Yet he made the travellers as welcome as he was able, piling driftwood on the smouldering central fire whilst his wife served them warm fish soup from an iron pan that hung above the flames.

Garshan was quite a tall man, strongly built, yet thinner than he might have been. He was forty, perhaps fifty, with the tight, drawn features that bespoke constant hardship and uncertainty. His wife said little, keeping herself withdrawn in a far corner of the room as the travellers told something of their story.

Yet Leighor noticed that she avoided the strangers' gaze, keeping her head bowed and partially hidden beneath a long grey shawl. Even so, from what glimpses Leighor could catch of her face, she appeared to be more youthful than her husband – although she too bore the strained and haunted look of all these fisherfolk.

'. . . I see that you have a fair boat outside.' Telsyan's voice rolled dimly back into Leighor's consciousness. 'Would you be prepared to sail her for us in these seas?'

Garshan looked to the shuttered window doubtfully and shook his head. 'Irgil is a long crossing in the best of weathers, sirs. And even though the storm is abating, there will still be high seas for many hours. Could your journey not wait until tomorrow, when the sea will be calmer?'

'No.' Telsyan's voice was firm. 'It is of the utmost urgency that we go now. We will pay you well, but we must leave at once.'

Again Garshan shook his head. 'It will be very dangerous, and I have but one boat . . .'

'Look. It is worth fifty talents to me if you will make the crossing at full light, carrying all four of us across to Irgil. Aye, and the horses too, they are yours.'

The others were aghast at the amount of money Telsyan was offering for their passage. Garshan would normally be fortunate to see even twenty talents in a whole year. Yet to Leighor's astonishment, once more he declined.

'You are most generous, my lords. And upon any day but this, it would be hard indeed to refuse such an offer. But this has been a special night, such as comes not twice in a sevenyear. A night of dark songs upon the waters, and of bitter ill-omen for men of the sea. A time when I can do no other than remain with my wife, and ward her safe upon the shore.'

'We understand your reluctance, my friend,' Uhlendof rose to face the fisherman. 'But this matter is more urgent than you know. For in truth all four of us flee for our very lives this night!'

'For your lives?'

'Aye.' Uhlendof told their story quickly, and when he had finished, Garshan nodded.

'Your tale is a most disturbing one,' he said softly. 'Yet we have had rumours, even here, of good Lord Eridar's murder, and few of us bear any love for Darvir. But what you ask is greater than you guess. I must think a while.'

Walking across to the doorway, he looked out once more at the sea, remaining there several minutes before turning at last to face the travellers again. 'I will take you across,' he told them gravely, 'but only on condition that you pay the agreed amount to my wife Zeiar before we depart – in case I do not return from this voyage.'

Telsyan nodded, but even as he gave his assent, Zeiar stood.

'No,' she said simply, her voice as soft and as calm as the heart of the ocean itself, yet somehow managing to fill the whole room. 'You will have need of me if you are to sail the sea today.'

Garshan turned sharply to stare at his wife. Their eyes met, and some message unseen seemed to pass between them; their eyes holding until at last Garshan turned away, defeated. 'We shall both go,' he sighed wearily.

In the short half hour before full light, the travellers made ready for the voyage, transferring their packs and possessions to the belly of the open boat while Garshan prepared it to sail. Their former guide watched in silence from the shore, but made no attempt to approach or give assistance. When the time came to leave, it was Zeiar who summoned the travellers to help push out the boat. And now, for the first time, Leighor caught a glimpse of her face full on. It was not beautiful, but looked as though it must once have been, very. Now it was only weatherworn and sad.

'You are unwell,' she said, looking at him long and hard. 'If you will, I shall prepare a place for you to lie in the centre of the boat, for the journey will be hard and long.'

He said nothing, but turned away to help the others with the waiting fishing boat. But the way Zeiar had looked at him unsettled him; it was as if she could see deep within him, deeper than he cared to contemplate; and suddenly he indeed felt weary, feeling the full burden of the day's travels and misfortunes falling upon him at once. The sea was still rough, the pounding surf making it difficult to get the boat out into deep water. Yet at last the task was done, waves crashing in all around them as one by one the travellers managed to drag themselves, or were dragged, into the wildly bobbing fishing boat. Garshan hauled up the single triangular sail, catching the wind to pull the boat sharply away from the shore. Zeiar sat silent in the stern, her arms firmly clasped about the tiller as she strove to hold the course steady against the incoming swells.

The travellers huddled out of Garshan's way on the centre cross-thwarts as he moved briskly about the swaying boat, trimming the sail, tightening and readjusting the many ropes and stays, until they were set entirely in accord with his wishes. Then, suddenly, they were out of the shelter of the headland and the full force of the wind and the waves began to hit them. The boat pitched and yawed wildly, dwarfed by the high seas that rose up all about them, like roaring hills suddenly set in motion. Hills upon which they bobbed like a rose-leaf in a maelstrom. Such a small frail craft, Leighor thought, how could it long survive the awesome force of these wild elements?

'This will be a hard crossing!' Garshan shouted to them at last, as he made his way back to take the tiller from Zeiar. Then suddenly he seemed to relent, grinning as he saw their anxious faces turned to follow his. 'But I have seen worse,' he growled. 'The storm is dying.'

Even so, his voice was barely audible against the crashing of the seas, and the gusting squalls that slammed the sail drum-taut, before releasing it once more for a moment or two of noisy, edge-flapping freedom. The rigging whined and shrieked in the wild wind as it strained to hold the small craft together, and the soft timbers groaned deeply beneath them. Leighor half-expected the boat to break apart with each new wave that struck, feeling sure that it was only a matter of time before the small boat was breached, and they all perished. It seemed that they were all fated to die by water this day, one way or another.

Zeiar struggled forward, having been relieved at the tiller by Garshan. Steadying herself against the side of the hull, she looked past the seated travellers for a moment into the grey light of the dawn. 'We are fortunate,' she whispered, 'that the wind has veered to the east and we can run across its edge. If it had stayed as it was last night, the crossing would have been impossible.' She did not wait for a reply but turned to make her way back to the stern. Then, as an afterthought, she halted and spoke again, 'If your companion feels the need, he may rest in the prow. Beneath the awning of oilskins there is room for one to sleep. Take what rest you may, sirs; for it will be a long journey.'

'Aye, you do look pale, southron.' The merchant inspected him closely. 'You shiver. Do you feel the cold?'

Leighor grunted.

'He has a fever,' Uhlendof said crisply. 'Little wonder, considering what he has been through these past days. We had best do as the lady suggests.'

Together they helped Leighor forward to a makeshift bed on the dry planking, beneath an awning that normally sheltered only a few poor nets and lobster pots. There was barely room for one in the confined space of the prow, and the rest of the travellers could only draw their cloaks even closer about them. Yet the damp cloaks provided scant protection from the cutting wind and the stinging clouds of spray that swept across the deck each time a wave broke over the prow.

As he lay beneath the flimsy oilskin awning, Leighor felt a pang of guilt for his companions, huddled outside in the teeth of the raging elements. Yet despite his comparative comfort, he could not rest. He was wet, cold, his fever was rising, and he felt that if he took his eyes off the roaring waves about them for even a moment, one might rise up to swallow their little pea-pod of a boat like a minnow. Stiffly, he twisted round to see Zeiar sitting beside her husband at the tiller. Yeon clung tightly to the side of the hull, his face blanched and tight set. They came briefly into the shelter of a rocky island that rose from the waves like a stormlashed leviathan, and for precious moments, the waters about them calmed. Yeon seized the opportunity to rise and stumble aft.

Garshan looked up from his labour, displeased. 'I am sore pressed, my lord. How may I aid you?'

'Is there some way that I can help?' the youth asked.

'You may help best by remaining seated.'

Yeon shook his head. 'I would have some task to perform, however small. I cannot be still.'

'There is nothing you can do, you have not the craft.'

'Then let him bale,' Zeiar smiled. 'It requires little knowledge of ships or the sea – other than where lies its proper place.'

Garshan nodded and pointed to a leather bucket rolling about in the bottom of the boat. 'You may use that, if the task is not repellent to you, my lord. That would be useful work.'

Yeon nodded and took up the bucket, clinging to one of the wooden thwarts, and baling unsteadily with his free arm. The period of calm was brief, and the waves soon rose again all about them, even higher than before. And so the day drifted on, Yeon sometimes baling, at other times huddled with the other travellers in the belly of the boat. Leighor dozed fitfully, constantly awoken by the discomfort of his position and the wild lurching of the boat. The sun never managed to break through the heavy sheets of iron-grey cloud that swept past overhead. Occasionally fresh spatters of rain would blow down in the wind, and for a time the gusts would seem to increase in fervour, but these times were short, and gradually the force of the storm did indeed seem to be abating. No conversation was now possible against the roar of the elements, and all either worked or sat in silence, isolated in their own private worlds of howling wind and raging water. How Garshan kept his course, Leighor could not guess, but in all the time that he watched him, the wiry fisherman never once released his grip on the tiller. Only Zeiar managed to move about the boat, and when she was not at her partner's side her nimble fingers were constantly at work; in the belly of the boat, in the rigging, or making rapid adjustments to the trim of the sail. This last had to be done often, as their path seemed to require many sudden tacks and sharp changes of course. Sometimes they ran before the wind and the waters swept in on them from behind as they raced the roaring waves. At other times they would have to alter course to steer right into the eye of the wind, and then the elements would seem to redouble in force, and clouds of water swept into the boat far faster than any could bale it out.

Yet through all this Zeiar worked on unaffected, never seeming to fear the great seas all about them, never seeming to stumble or lose her balance; and wherever she went a curious calmness seemed to follow her. Snags, knots and tangles seemed to disappear at her touch, strained lines to ease, and even the old creaking timbers of the vessel to breathe in new strength and youth. Late in the day she came astern with a small oilcloth bundle containing dry dusty strips of something dark and brown.

'Smoked fish,' she explained. 'Eat. It will give you strength. It is all we have.'

It was pleasant enough after its own fashion, although Leighor could swallow no more than a mouthful. It had a sharp flavour that brought the senses back to life and in some way managed to keep at bay the numbing sensations of cold and damp. Again Leighor dozed.

When he awoke it was dark, and the sea had calmed a little. The wind had dropped a deal since morning, yet there was no sign of any break in the cloud. The night would be black and starless. There was more smoked fish for those who could eat it, and then nothing to do but try to sleep. The others lay down where they could on the bare boards of the foredeck, while Garshan and Zeiar remained in the stern, taking the tiller in turn whilst the other slept. But however much he tried, Leighor was unable to get back to sleep for long, and for long hours he could only hover uncomfortably on the dim verges of consciousness, ever aware of the steady pitching and yawing of the boat and the wild roaring of the sea.

A sudden change in the sound of the sea made him snap instantly awake. It was louder now, and more violent, as if waves were breaking over solid rock nearby. He rose startled from his flimsy shelter. Was this land? But no – there was no land in view, nothing but waves and . . . His heart missed a beat. Long ranks of jagged rocks rose grimly out of the sea like shattered teeth barely a dozen yards off the port bow. And to the right there were more; farther in the distance, but more than enough to drag a whole armada of merchantmen to their doom. And only Zeiar was awake and at the helm.

Leighor fought his way desperately aft, burdened with anxious demands; but Zeiar held up her hand to silence him before he could begin to speak.

'Do not wake my husband,' she whispered hoarsely. 'We are in no danger.' Intently she stared down once more into a rough sheet of oval crystal balanced upon her knees. In fact, to Leighor's surprise, she did not look out at the sea at all, but seemed to steer her course entirely by what she saw in her glass. He edged closer, his fears for their safety momentarily forgotten as he tried to see for himself what was in the milk-white crystal. Yet as he stared down, he could see only a dim reflection of the sea around them. Or was it a reflection? The waves were small yet astonishingly distinct, too distinct and over too wide an area for a normal reflection. It was almost as if it were a scene of the storm seen from somewhere high above: a clifftop perhaps – condensed somehow into this milky crystal.

Enthralled, he bent closer. Could he discern a small brown speck bobbing in the middle of that wild maelstrom? A small boat? Surely it was? But no; that was not possible. Yet as his eyes adjusted, he began to make out long lines of jagged rocks, and a single channel between them, through which the boat passed. Could this – he almost feared to ask himself the question – could this somehow be their own boat that he saw, even as it sailed between those selfsame rocks? The idea ensorcelled him. Could he – if he looked close enough – make out the people who moved and breathed upon that tiny boat in the glass? Would he be able to make out himself?

'Do not!' Zeiar hissed with a mixture of anger and terror, shying fearfully away from him as she tried to shield the crystal with one hand. 'Do not try to look through the scrying glass! Lest great ill befall us all!' She looked flustered and fearful now, almost letting slip the tiller in her anxiety to keep Leighor away from the crystal.

'So this is how you navigate with no stars,' Leighor murmured. 'Some sorcery . . .'

Suddenly the boat pitched wildly; he stumbled backwards, losing his footing, and it was some moments before Zeiar once again had the vessel under control.

'Stay where you are and say no more!' Her stare was a warning which Leighor obeyed, staying well back against the side of the hull as Zeiar continued to speak; softly now, almost as though she feared someone might overhear her. 'To use such tools as these there are payments that must be made, forfeits that must be given. For another to look, to see those things he should not see, must destroy the bargain . . . must destroy all if it were overlong.' She looked back down into the glass and shrouded it with her shawl before speaking again. 'Return to your friends,' she commanded at last, 'sleep, and if you are wise you shall forget all you have seen.'

To his own surprise Leighor found himself obeying her instruction, retreating backward down the boat as Zeiar returned her full concentration to the steering. He felt strangely guilty, as if he had committed some dark crime, had stolen something that was more precious than he knew. He had broken in upon a secret he had no right to uncover, perhaps disturbing some benificence dearly bought, which he and all those upon this small vessel now relied upon for their lives.

Slowly the reefs fell away behind them, and Leighor sank back on to his hard bed in the prow. He looked up at the dark shape of their sail as it flapped against a stone-dark sky. He felt the rhythmic movement of the boat as it crested the deep, sea rollers, and slept.

He awoke at daybreak to a gentler wind and a calmer sea. A brilliant yellow sun was rising out of the green waters to starboard. The skies were clear. Sitting up, he saw that the others were already up and about. Garshan was now at the tiller, with Zeiar, still awake, by his side.

'There is land!' Uhlendof pointed westward as soon as he realised Leighor was awake.

And indeed there was a thin pale line just discernible far off to the west, that could just be a line of white cliffs reflecting the morning sun, with darker hills rising up behind. Yes, there was no mistaking, it was land; their journey was nearly over.

'Probably the mainland coast of Holdar,' Telsyan's voice came from close behind him, 'or Felldur. Either way we are close enough to Irgil.'

'If it is Felldur then we are too far north,' Uhlendof said quickly. 'Yet I do not think that likely, the coast of Felldur is rougher and more indented than this. But no matter, the sooner we are back on dry land the better. However far we have to walk.'

'There will be no need for walking,' Garshan's voice cut across to them with surprising clarity through the clear morning air, 'for I will take you to the very Mouths of Irgil themselves. It is our bargain.'

Leighor tried to drive the sleep from his head with cold salt water from the Rathul Sea, watching, bleary-eyed, as the others shared the last remains of the saltfish while the autumn sun climbed into the eastern sky. It was an hour more before they drew appreciably closer to the rocky coastline. And what they saw then did nothing to raise their spirits. The coast along which they now sailed seemed as wild and inhospitable as any of them had ever seen. High granite cliffs formed an impenetrable barrier between the sea and the land, dropping sheer and precipitate from the bleak heights above into the churning waters below. Here the sea broke upon hidden reefs and jagged masses of rock to send great geysers of spray sweeping upward on the wind. There was no sign of a spot where any vessel, even one as small and fleet as their own, might attempt to put ashore in safety. The coast seemed utterly barren of life, and devoid of all human settlement. Only a few harsh-crying seabirds wheeled overhead.

'It is a bleak and cruel coast,' Telsyan commented.

'Indeed it is, my lord,' Garshan nodded from the tiller. 'There are few landing places on this shore, and even the fish seem to spurn these waters.'

'Yet that is the fortune of Irgil,' Uhlendof added, 'for theirs is the only haven for large ships upon this coast.'

'But where is Irgil?' Yeon demanded.

'There ahead!' Garshan pointed forward, north along the line of high cliffs, to a spot where a tall section of the cliff wall seemed to jut out oddly into the sea.

'I see no city,' said Yeon, 'nor any harbour.'

'You will,' Garshan told him.

And slowly, as they drew closer, the hidden features of Irgil became clear. The section of cliff that jutted out into the sea was larger than it had first appeared; a mighty triangular pillar of rock – almost a small island – that touched the main line of cliffs only at a single point. Its broad base faced out into the sea, its narrowest point only brushing against the land. Its surface was not flat but nearly so, a strange irregular jumble of changing levels and sharp geometric edges. It was only with a start that Leighor suddenly realised that he was looking at buildings. Raised out of the same grey stone as the cliff itself, they were built into it as if they had grown up naturally from its roots. Tall and close-set, they lined the clifftops like a curtain wall, with only their dark windows and sloping rooftops to betray their true nature. Built as they were, Leighor thought, it was no wonder that the city could not be distinguished from afar. While from here, near to, it seemed as daunting and imposing, as ageless and impassive, as the rugged cliffs themselves.

All eyes were drawn to the great city as it loomed high above them on its stone eyrie. All eyes but those of Zeiar, who now sat alone on the far side of the boat, her face cupped in her hands as she stared in melancholy out to sea. He did not know whether it was a symptom of his fever, yet to Leighor, Zeiar appeared curiously fresher – even younger – than she had ever seemed before. The long hard voyage which had so drained and wearied them all, Garshan not least, seemed to have had no ill-effect upon her. In fact the contrary was the case. She looked almost youthful; the lost beauty of years gone by somehow restored by the grey sea mists which had left Garshan still drawn and haggard, to bear the full weight of his years.

But now they were close to the city and there was no time to spare for such thoughts. The boat was rocked and buffeted by great sea swells as Garshan guided it about the southernmost point of the high cliff wall, to run beneath the long east-facing outer cliff. Yeon gasped to see two great sea caverns yawning above them, piercing the sheer cliff face beneath the city: dark and empty maws, each easily large enough to take two fully-rigged trading galleons sailing abreast. Leighor too was staggered by the sheer enormity of these high sea caves, whose roofs vaulted hundreds of feet above them.

'These are the Mouths of Irgil,' Uhlendof smiled. 'You have seen something this day that you will long remember.'

All stood silent as Garshan manoeuvred their small craft into the blackness of the first of these awesome caverns. The moment they sailed beneath the cliff the wind fell away from the sail and they began to drift.

'Take the oars!' Garshan shouted urgently. 'Or we may yet run aground.'

By the time the boat was again under control, Leighor's eyes had grown accustomed to the dim light, and he could see a little of what lay around him. A man-made breakwater stretched across much of the natural mouth of the cavern, and this had to be negotiated. But once within, in the calm of its inner harbour, Leighor had time to marvel at the vastness of this natural haven. Stone jetties, large enough for half a dozen ships and scores of smaller craft, jutted into the oily waters. The skeletal masts of great trading vessels filled the gloom all around them, although the harbour was no more than a quarter full. And everywhere there were lights: ships' lights, hand torches, smoking flambeaus and vast swinging braziers on chains that hung from unseen supports somewhere high on the dark cavern roof. This was surely one of the wonders of the earth.

They drew slowly up to one of the great stone piers and berthed, tying up next to a Giellin cog from Coimbra, from which heavy barrels of wine were being unloaded.

'You are now in Irgil,' Garshan declared flatly. 'Our bargain is complete, and it is time for us to part.'

'Will you not bide with us this one night at least?' Uhlendof protested. 'You cannot return today, after such a voyage!'

'We can and we must. There can be no rest for us in the city of Irgil. We must return at once or miss the tide.'

From this Garshan could not be dissuaded, and so they unloaded their few remaining possessions on to the harbour steps before returning to make their farewells. To Leighor's dismay Zeiar seemed no longer even to notice their presence, her eyes fixed only upon the mouth of the cavern and the sea beyond. She sat close to the stern, huddled against the side of the boat, and could not be brought to speak.

'Are you sure she is not unwell?' Uhlendof asked in concern. 'For her sake you must remain. Come ashore and stay with us until she recovers.'

Garshan smiled sadly and shook his head. 'That which will heal her lies not here, not in any of the lands of men. She has been borne once more across the waves, and heard again the songs of her people; for that sickness there is no cure upon this earth, and I will return alone to Harstensond.'

And so they took their last farewells of Garshan and Zeiar, though whether she heard them or not they could not tell. For Leighor had now to be supported up on to the high stone pier, and the travellers hardly noticed Garshan slip the boat free of its moorings and take up the oars to row silently yet steadily for the cavern mouth.

And so did the four travellers from Sielder go up into the city of Irgil.

Part Two
THE CHOOSING OF THE PATH

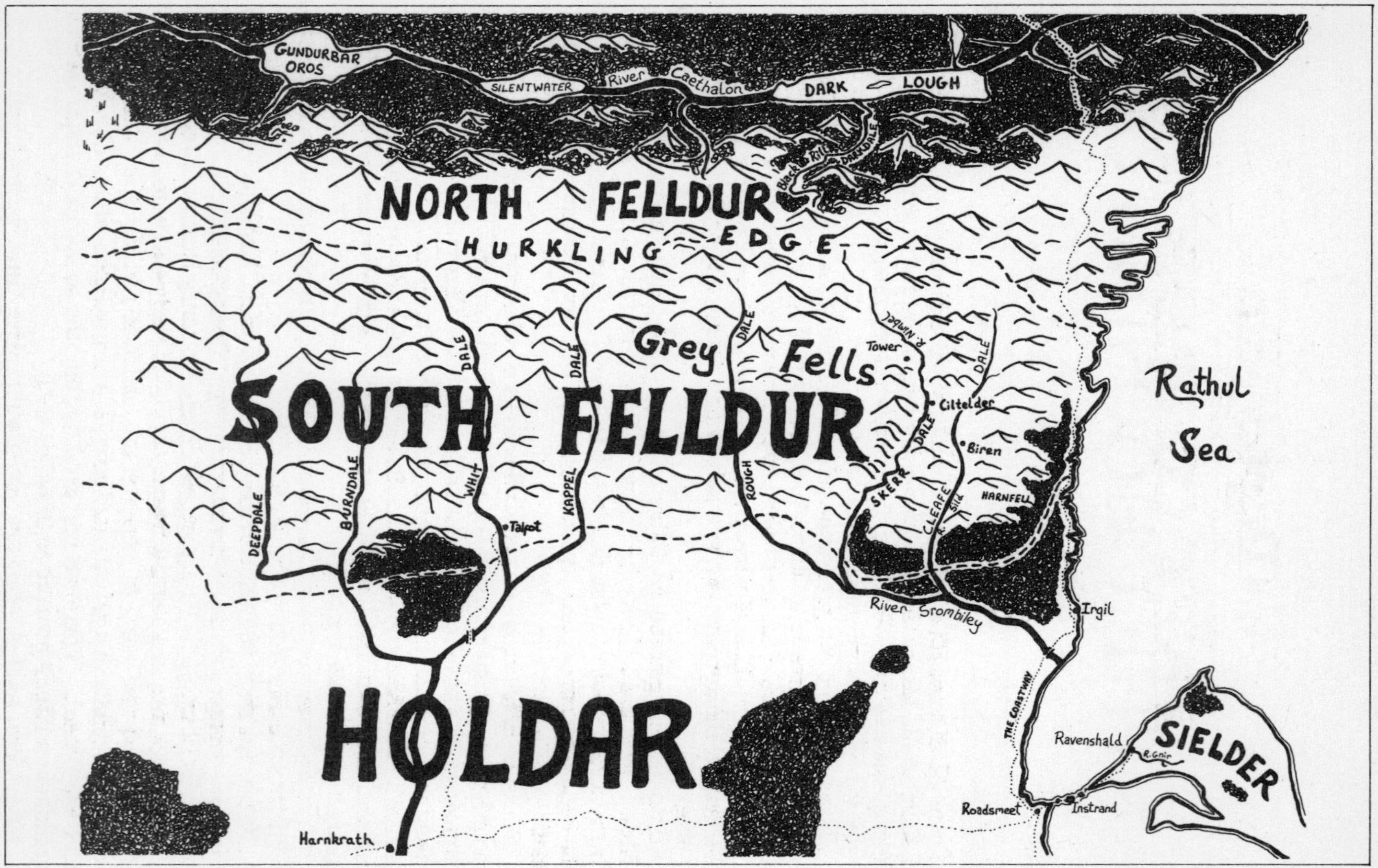
GUNDURBAR OROS
SILENTWATER
River Caethalon
DARK LOUGH
Black Rill
DARKDALE
NORTH FELLDUR
HURKLING EDGE
Grey Fells
SOUTH FELLDUR
DEEPDALE
BURNDALE
WHIT DALE
Talpot
KAPPEL DALE
ROUGH DALE
R. Nimbel
Tower
SKERR DALE
Ciltelder
CLEAFE DALE
Biren
R. Silk
HARNFELL
River Srombiley
Irgil
Rathul Sea
HOLDAR
THE COASTWAY
Ravenshald
R. Gnir
SIELDER
Roadsmeet
Instrand
Harnkrath

Chapter Six
A NEW COMPANION

The muffled sound of waves came from beyond high windows. Through them Leighor could see neither land nor buildings, nothing but a vast panorama of stormy sea and sky – almost as if he were in some magical vessel that floated hundreds of feet above the roaring breakers.

The main hall of the guildhouse of the Giellin Merchants in Irgil was all but deserted. Rich carpets lay beneath tall clifftop windows. Leather books lined oak-panelled walls. Scattered about were dozens of high-backed chairs, large and comfortable. A low-burning fire of sea-coals glowed warmly in the grate. Yet despite the apparent warmth and comfort of his surroundings, Leighor felt uneasy.

Two days had passed since their arrival in the echoing harbour far beneath. Most of that time he had spent alone, without news, recovering from his fever in the nearby house of the Samaran Guild of Physicians. Only today had he managed to escape their attentions, evading both wardens and a gate porter to make good his getaway.

He scanned the chamber quickly for any sign of his three companions. A few people muttered quietly to one another around a nearby table. A man and a woman laughed over some joke in a distant corner. Nearby, close to the fire, sat Yeon and Uhlendof. Both seemed genuinely glad to see him, showing great concern for his health and welfare. Uhlendof sat him down between them and ordered some food and a mug of warm ale before beginning to tell him what had passed while he slept.

'It is a pity we could not have bided together,' Leighor said quickly. 'And with those we seek rather than in this place.'

'It was best that you remained with the physicians,' Uhlendof assured him. 'Irgil is a strange city, and it has its own ways. It was raised here, in this barren and deserted spot, to be a place of refuge – a lonely fortress upon the wild Holdar coast, where goods and money could be safely sent in time of trouble. A place beyond the reach of petty tyrants and local princes. The bankers and merchants guilds that raised it still guard their privileges well, and visitors are not encouraged. There are no inns within the walls, and those with a guildhouse of their own are expected to use it.'

'Aye,' Yeon added. 'And we had trouble when first we took you to the

Physicians' Hall. The Keeper could not find your Guild Badge. He said that all Guild physicians should bear one – yet you had none.'

The southron cursed inwardly, trying to stifle the sudden surge of resentment that boiled up within him. The Samaran Guild of Physicians . . . Always they endeavoured to complicate his life. It had been they who had driven him north in the first place, into these cold and frozen lands. And now, even here, they reappeared to torment him!

'The badge . . .' he felt about his neck, thinking quickly. 'I must have lost it . . . Aye . . . Lost it upon the causeway . . .' He breathed deeply. 'Yet that is of little matter now. Do you have any news? What has been happening since we were parted? Where is Master Telsyan?'

'That we would all like to know,' the youth grumbled. 'We have waited here two whole days while Telsyan takes off on his own to parley with the knights and guildmasters. Or so he says, but we have had no word from him since he left us to rot in this place!'

'We have spoken enough on that score,' Uhlendof sighed. 'Telsyan knows these people and their ways as we do not. He can deal with them to best advantage on his own.'

'So there is no news?' Leighor asked.

'Little indeed,' the monk acknowledged. 'Irgil is alive with rumours, but there are none of Eridar's murder, and there have been no emissaries yet from Darvir. Even so, I do not think it will be safe to stay here much longer.'

'How well do you know this city?' Leighor asked, hoping to keep the conversation away from himself and his missing guild badge.

'Not at all,' Uhlendof smiled, pausing to fill a clay pipe with tobacco. 'Although I have had cause to journey far and wide in Lord Eridar's service, this, curiously enough, is one place to which duty has not brought me.'

'And have you served Lord Eridar long?'

'For a good many years now.' Uhlendof sighed. 'Longer than I care to remember.' He indicated that Leighor should light a straw for him from the fire, and continued. 'I met him first when on an errand from Father Abbot. It had become my task to bear messages to other houses of our order and to kings and princes friendly to our cause. Eridar was one such; and soon I was bearing messages of his along with my others. He was an easy man to begin to work for.'

'So of recent years you have been less the monk and more the statesman?' Leighor passed him the lighted straw.

'It may sometimes seem that way.' Uhlendof took the straw and attempted to ignite the dark mixture in his pipe-bowl. 'Yet I shall always be first a monk.' A dark cloud of smoke emerged from the pipe, and he sat back in his chair with a sigh. 'My father was a poor man, a leatherworker of Harnkrath, the chief city of Holdar. But at the age of fifteen I ran away to make my fortune in the rich cities of the Bay of Qrena. It was the Brothers who took me in, hungry and destitute, when I had nowhere else to go. I chose to stay with them and learn their faith. Once in vows, I was sent to the Nargiorn Isles – little more than specks of grassy rock scattered amongst the breakers of the Rathul Sea. There is barely room on the largest for more than half a dozen houses and a few goats. But it was there, in the cold library of Celid Isle, that I became a scholar. I read many books and copied more – astrologies, histories, religious works – in all the tongues of the Eastern Realms . . .'

'So, my friends, I find you all together!' Telsyan's voice boomed unexpectedly loudly across the now empty chamber. 'A cosy sight indeed!'

'Where have you been?' Uhlendof rose from his seat with some vigour. 'What have you been doing all this while? Have you gained what we seek?'

'I have been to the mission of the Durian Knights and thence to many others in the city,' the merchant sighed, slumping into a nearby seat. He paused to catch his breath, wiping beads of perspiration from his forehead. 'But I am afraid that there is no one here who will admit to any knowledge of Lord Eridar's testament.'

'What?'

'How is this possible?'

'The Knights . . .' They all spoke at once.

'The Knights have left the city.' Telsyan shook his head. 'They are gone out of Irgil and have taken everything of value north with them to Darien. I have gained even this knowledge only with great difficulty. Irgil is full of wild rumours. Much gold and silver has flooded into the city since Galdan's death, and there is talk of civil strife and war if the succession is not quickly settled. This, I think, is what has driven the Durians north, to the safety of their own territories. The Knights of Dur are well known for their excess of caution, but they are not the only ones seeking to protect their fortunes in these unpredictable times.' He drew a deep breath. 'No, I fear that we must now either follow the knights north to Darien, or else give up all hope of obtaining what we seek. We have no other choices open to us.'

'To Darien?' Uhlendof exclaimed, horrified. 'But that is near a thousand leagues into the northlands! We have no protection, no provisions, no gold for so long and dangerous a journey! In but a few short months it will be winter. You cannot propose this seriously!'

Telsyan shrugged. 'I cannot see what else we can do if we intend to fulfil our commission.' He delved into a pocket in his robes. 'Yet with regard to money and provisions, we may not be as badly off as you think. I have letters of credit from my lord Careil to the value of several hundred talents, which I carry against just such an eventuality as this.'

'Indeed?' Yeon said dangerously. 'I like this not! You are far too easy with this matter for my liking. It is almost as if you knew all along that there would be nothing here for us.'

'You know not of what you speak!' Telsyan snorted with impatience.

'Then why were we not told these things?' Yeon demanded, rising to stare directly down into Telsyan's face, his eyes cold and hostile. 'What other matters have you hidden from us? What other lies have you to tell?'

'Use not such rash words with me, boy.' Telsyan rose angrily. 'I have my trust from Lord Careil, and will not be made to answer to you!' He spun quickly on his heel. 'Think well upon your future course, and inform me when you have decided what you wish to do.'

'Oh no,' Yeon lunged forward to seize the merchant roughly by the arm, jerking him furiously back round to face them. 'You will give us full account now for once, of all your knowledge of this errand of ours, and all else that you have withheld from us so far!'

'Nay!' Telsyan twisted his arm violently free and made to turn away again.

But he had not time to complete the movement before Yeon's body slammed solidly into his, the full force of the youth's frame driving the larger man heavily back into the near wall. Taken by surprise, the merchant struggled to tear himself free. But although Telsyan clearly bore the more weight, to Leighor's surprise it was Yeon who proved the stronger; and with a sudden sweep of his arms he wrenched the larger man from his feet to hurl him heavily down on to one of the old, studded benches. With a cavernous crack, the legs gave way, and it collapsed in a cloud of dust.

'Stop this at once!' Uhlendof leapt urgently forward.

But Yeon was not to be halted now; brushing the monk aside, he made to haul the merchant back to his feet.

'Enough!' Telsyan gasped, holding up a hand to ward off the youth. 'I am too old now for this sort of thing. If you wish the whole story, I will tell it to you.'

'The truth,' Yeon warned, his hands clenching once more into large bony fists.

'Yes,' the merchant responded wearily. 'Although there is little you do not already know. Careil feared that you might refuse to leave Ravenshald if you knew the whole truth from the start. He was already virtually certain, before we set off, that the Durian Knights had left Irgil. That being so, a far longer and more dangerous journey would be required to retrieve the documents we seek: one which you might not have been prepared to undertake. Careil wished you out of the Sielders at all costs, to keep you out of Darvir's hands. This errand was one way to ensure your co-operation.'

'Then this whole story of Eridar's testament, and of its great value to our cause, is untrue?' Uhlendof said starkly.

'Careil did not lie to you,' Telsyan insisted. 'All that he told you of the testament of Eridar, and of its importance, was true. It is held by the Durian Knights and will remain so until we, or some other, collect it. The decision you have to make is the same now as it was then. So what is that decision going to be?'

'It's not quite as simple as that,' Uhlendof shook his head firmly. 'Even assuming that you have now told us the whole truth, I am still forced to ask what purpose would be served by our proceeding upon this wild trek into the northlands? A journey to Irgil, and even to Helietrim, upon safe roads through well-ordered country, is a different matter altogether to venturing alone into the wilderness of the north – a long journey in pursuit of assorted documents that might be lost, stolen, separated or destroyed long before we ever caught up with them . . .'

'That will not be so,' Telsyan broke in. 'The Knights of Dur are sworn to preserve and protect Lord Eridar's testament, and that they will do. They still have so much honour – in a matter of this importance at least.'

'Yet even so,' Uhlendof continued, 'it is a dangerous and foolish quest.'

'If you wish now to withdraw,' Telsyan shrugged, 'I cannot stay you. You did not promise to journey to Darien. I cannot make you do so against your will. You may stay here in Irgil, or else return to Darvir's mercies, as you please. Yet I at least shall keep faith with my promise, and try to see that Eridar's wishes are carried out and his murderers exposed.'

'And how come you to such sudden devotion to Eridar's cause?' Yeon asked sharply.

'It is not sudden. I have run errands and made reports, both for Lord Eridar and for his Chancellor, Careil, for many years. I am a merchant, yes: but that does not make me blind to all that passes in the world. I am a man of Selethir, the greatest of all the Giellin merchant cities, and a kingdom of the Empire in its own right. We of the merchant states may not be of the noblest blood in the world, nor always act with the purest motives, but we prize our independence and our freedom of action above all things. Aye, and some of us fear the rule of Misan as much as any of you! I fear not this journey into the northlands, and I shall proceed alone if I must.'

'There is no need for that,' Yeon said quickly. 'If all that you say is true, I will journey with you.'

'I too,' Uhlendof sighed. 'If we are to remain here, it can only be as fugitives. I was entrusted to stay at the boy's side and keep him out of trouble. That I will do, for I too will not forget my duty to Lord Eridar. Yet in my heart of hearts I do not believe that our task will be anywhere near so easy as you suggest.'

'And what of you, good physician?' Telsyan asked, turning back to him at last. 'Will you join us upon this mad journey north?'

Now that he had to make a definite choice, Leighor was more than a little nonplussed. He had come with these three so far, more or less unwillingly: a fugitive, fleeing the near-certain death that awaited him in the Sielders. Now, for a day or two at least – perhaps long enough to get clear – he was out of immediate danger. And now he must choose. He could try to lose himself, and resume his former life as an itinerant pedlar among the towns and villages of the mainland, or he could join these three in a dangerous quest that was truly little concern of his.

Until now he had been a purposeless wanderer, easygoing, letting the road bear him where it willed, quite enjoying the freedom from responsibility, even as he complained at the uncertainty and inconvenience. Simply in order to survive, he had had to scrape himself out of perilous situations many times. Perhaps, if he left these three now, he could do so again. That was what cold logic told him. Was that cowardice or was it prudence? He had an uncomfortable feeling that it was the former. But then, why get mixed up in this lunatic venture? It was a fatal error for any lowborn wanderer to become involved in the power struggles of the great . . .

Yet he *was* involved. He had been involved since that fatal night in Sonsterness when Darvir had marked him for death. He had asked himself 'Why me?' a thousand times since then, and had found no satisfactory answer. Fate itself seemed to have placed him upon this path. And if that was what fate decreed, who was he to argue? No. This was one matter he must see through. And so, in spite of all his deepest instincts and all that he counted as wisdom, he heard his voice saying, 'Yes, I will go with you. I have reason enough to hate Darvir, and anything that I may do to aid the cause of Lord Eridar, I shall do.'

'Well spoken, southron!' The merchant clapped him firmly on the back. 'Together, even with no one else in the world to aid us, we may yet prevail.'

'If the Durians are gone,' Yeon said suddenly, 'what of the Knights of Imsild? Could we not seek their aid?'

'Indeed not!' the merchant scowled. 'The less the Knights of Imsild know of our quest, the better I like it.'

'Why must you oppose the knights so?' Yeon's voice was pained. 'They are good, they are strong, they know all that passes in the northlands. They could give us much help.'

'No!' Telsyan said vehemently. 'When will you understand that the Knights of Imsild are neutral in nothing? If Darvir has taken power in the Sielders then the knights will have a policy on it, and seeing that they have not chosen to make it known to me, I suspect that that policy may not be a favourable one!'

'You see conspiracy everywhere,' said Yeon. 'I will not listen.'

'When shall we leave?' Leighor asked quickly, hoping to bring the conversation back on to more useful lines.

'As soon as possible,' Telsyan said briskly, producing a tattered sheaf of parchment from his robes and laying it out upon a nearby table. 'Tongues wag, and Irgil is fast becoming too dangerous for us.' The map was of Felldur and Northern Holdar, yet it did not extend into the true Northlands, which began where the northern dales of Felldur ran out, and few mapmakers ventured. 'I suggest we leave at dawn tomorrow and take the Coastway north – for a day or two, at least.' He indicated the thin black line with his finger. 'It is the safest route into the northlands in normal times, and still served by one or two fair hostelries. That is until one leaves the Varroain realms and enters the wilder regions.'

'And then?' Leighor asked.

'Then we must fend for ourselves.'

At first light the following morning, four dark-cloaked figures emerged from the Landgates of Irgil to step out on to the brief isthmus that connected the silent city with the mainland of Holdar.

Fearsome precipices fell sharply away on either side of them, and for several dozen paces the travellers walked a crumbling, windblown path that seemed to balance only precariously above the churning ocean. Powerful squalls threatened constantly to hurl them down on to the jagged rocks far beneath. And only once safe upon the high cliffs of the Holdar shore did Leighor dare to look back.

They had left Irgil hurriedly, for rumours of Eridar's death had already begun to be heard in the city. And once this was so, the bankers could not be persuaded to redeem Careil's letters of credit for much more than half of their face value. One hundred and eighty gold talents was all they had to see them all the way to Darien.

The surface of the northbound road was of ground chalkstone, making a firm hard way that was better by far than any of the vile sloughs of the Sielders. The road itself looked as if it had been much broader of old, but now tall grass and dense thickets of gorse had overgrown all but the few central feet of its width.

'This is one of the old imperial roads from the age of Qhilmun,' the priest told them as they walked. 'One could follow this road due south to Selethir and beyond if one wished; or, as we are doing, north to King Culvar's Road and Scûn. In the Great Age this road would have been thronged with soldiers and merchants going north and south, but now,' he pointed to the empty road ahead, 'it is almost unused.'

They talked for a while, as they walked, of the age when this road had been made, and of the pity of its decay in the long centuries of Varroain rule. As they spoke, the sun dispelled the last lingering mists to reveal the rolling wooded landscape of Northern Holdar in all its glory; the road seeming to hang precariously between forested hills and a precipitous drop into the sea far below.

The road was excellently engineered, running always at the same height, but following every spur and promontory of the coastline, so that they quickly lost sight of the town of Irgil behind them.

They walked now in silence, and it was mid-morning before they met anyone else upon the road – then all at once there came a host.

Two mounted heralds preceded a much larger group of riders, spurring on their horses as soon as they saw the travellers ahead.

Their words when they drew level were curt: 'Off the road! Our party would pass!'

Yeon did not take kindly to this, but Uhlendof shook his head. 'These are the knights,' he whispered. 'The knights of Imsild.'

Yeon turned to look, and sure enough here was a full cohort of the knights going south, the main party almost upon them. No fewer than eighteen knights, the flower of Varroain nobility, riding together in loose formation – some abreast and talking, some alone – each accompanied on foot by a lance-bearing squire, each wearing the finest raiment of silk and velvet, their breastplates gleaming brightly in the morning sun. Two mounted minstrels played upon lute and lyre to entertain their journey.

'They are a noble sight,' Yeon said, having quite forgotten his earlier anger at being pushed off the road.

None of the knights deigned to acknowledge the presence of the four lowly travellers. They might have been invisible to the exalted ones who rode so high above them, laughing and talking or engaged in their own lonely thoughts.

'They are haughty and vain,' said Telsyan when they were safely past, and only the long baggage train behind them occupied the road.

Leighor counted seventy mules, each laden with baggage, tents, valuables and possessions – and thirty muleteers to guard them. Eventually the slow train was past and the travellers were free to use the empty road once more. Yeon was clearly irked by the merchant's disrespect, and told him so. But Telsyan was unmoved.

'Haughty and vain, I say,' he repeated, 'and that is the truth! They may be sworn to protect the wilderlands, yet in these days they are mostly the second sons of middling lords, landless men, more concerned with gaining wealth and power than lonely battles in the borderlands. Why else are they travelling south? And for a long stay, by the size of their baggage train.'

The quarrel went on, but Leighor did not listen; he had something else to think about. As they passed, he had noticed a curious orb-like amulet hanging about the neck of one of the leading knights. It was of neither silver nor gold, but of a brilliant purple metal that drew the eye to it like a living flame, flashing and glinting in the sunlight. Yet the sight made Leighor shiver inexplicably, sending a fleeting spear of pure ice down his spine . . .

They journeyed on a league further before they again stopped for rest. It was not quite noon, but the sun was high and it had grown hot, too hot to walk comfortably, attired as they were. A grassy promontory thrust out into the sea to their right. Yeon flung himself to the ground near the clifftop and the others gratefully followed his example, setting down their full packs and sprawling out upon the warm grass.

'I am not used to this walking!' Yeon sighed, wiping the sweat from his brow and then drinking deep from a bottle of light red wine taken from his satchel.

'Then you will soon learn,' Telsyan frowned, tying his heavy cloak into swathed folds across the top of his pack. 'This is not a pleasure trip, as you shall soon discover; our supplies, our food and our clothes must all be borne many a league upon our backs alone.'

But no one paid much attention to Telsyan's strictures. The sun was far too warm, the air was clean and fresh and the sea beyond was deepest blue in the sharp sunlight. They drank wine and passed around thin slices of Holdar spice-sausage, as seagulls and kittiwakes dived and wheeled along the cliffs.

'How far have we travelled?' asked Yeon at last.

'About four or five leagues, no more,' Telsyan replied tersely. 'If we still had our horses we could have covered a score! And there is little chance of our obtaining more now. Four good mounts would cost us more money than we have for our whole journey! A good horse is a rare beast in the northlands.'

Uhlendof stood to look out over the forested hills. 'One might travel through this country faster afoot than on horseback if one left the road,' he observed thoughtfully. 'Indeed where we are headed, a horse might easily prove as much a hindrance as a help. And we shall not catch up with the Durians now, either on foot or on horseback; so let us not pine for lost treasures.'

'But what if Darvir has sent riders north in pursuit of us, or that which we seek?' Yeon asked.

'Darvir knows nothing of Eridar's testament,' Uhlendof replied, refastening his pack, 'so he has no reason to suspect that we have taken this road.'

'Mayhap,' Telsyan grunted, mopping the sweat from his face. 'But he may soon learn of our presence in Irgil. He is likely to send riders that far to announce his succession and to collect gold. So we must prepare to hide ourselves quickly should we hear riders from the south, and build our fires well out of sight of the road – at least until we are out of easy riding range of Irgil.'

The sun shone hot throughout the afternoon, yet the sky was hazy and there was no breeze. Even without their heavy cloaks, the heat soon became stifling and tempers began to fray. Uhlendof grew more and more irritable as the day wore on, and all conversation ceased. They made slower pace now, trudging along beneath the heavy burden of their full packs.

'How many more days walking like this will there be?' Yeon asked once, and got a short answer from Telsyan for his pains.

Even at sundown the heat lingered in the air, and the travellers were glad indeed when a suitable camp site came into view. A clear rivulet splashed down on to the roadway from a narrow cleft in the hillside. Here there were few trees, and with only a scattering of thin gorse bushes to bar their path, they were soon able to climb away from the road to a dry upland dell whose hills sloped gently down towards the streambed. Uhlendof directed the company in the proper gathering of dry bracken to make a mattress, assuring them that there was no better bed on a calm night.

'How safe is the country hereabouts?' Leighor asked quickly. 'Could we not be set upon by raiders out of the forest?'

The merchant shook his head. 'We are too far south yet to worry about Rievers, or even goblins. Despite their wild look, these lands are fairly law-abiding, and we are quite safe here. There will be plenty of time for night watches when we are north of Felldur.'

Telsyan took first turn at making their meal: a hot stew from Silgany, prepared with meat he had bought in Irgil that morning. The travellers were hungry and the meal tasted better than anything they had eaten for a long while. The pot was scraped clean and the food washed down with the one skin of wine they had brought.

'We shall be drinking only water from now on,' Telsyan said, turning to lie back and stare up into the starlit sky. 'It is clearer now. The haze has gone. Perhaps the weather will improve.'

The others looked upward in their turn. Relaxed, and with full bellies, they lay contentedly around the fire.

'All the constellations of harvest show well tonight,' Uhlendof said after a time, beginning to point out each one in turn. 'There is Keimos the reaper climbing to the heights, and beneath him Surida the boar, the first herald of autumn. Over there, shaped like a hammer, is Forgan the ruler of summer, and next is Kal the anvil.'

'You are too fast,' said Yeon. 'I cannot make them out!'

'Their shapes are clear if you follow the lines of the stars, one to another, trace them with your eye and see the forms, the images of the old gods.' He sat up and pointed. 'There now is Ultan the hunter, his legs are the stars Erimur and Nultur to the left and Ara, Miresis and Imlis to the right. The row of stars from Maatol to Quimbar form his great spear, which points towards the boar.'

'Yes!' said Yeon suddenly, 'I see him now; but what is that bright star to the north?'

'That is the north star itself,' Telsyan now spoke, 'the true star, the only one that keeps its place in the firmament. Follow that and you are always heading north, wherever in the world you might be.'

'Her true name is Ginara,' added Uhlendof softly, 'and she is the tip of the constellation of Ginara, the lady, queen of the north. There are many legends of Ginara and mayhap when there is time I will tell you of them.'

'The constellations have different names in the south,' said Leighor, 'and some we do not see at all, but we have others to replace them brighter and more beautiful than any you can see here.'

'So say all men of their homeland,' Telsyan nodded, 'and I suppose in a way it is true.'

There was silence again for several minutes, and Yeon sat up. 'They are all very pretty, but what is their use, why are they set there so?'

'Some say they are there to remind men of their gods,' Uhlendof spoke softly still. 'Each has its own legends. But we of the Mallenians believe that their main purpose is to mark the passing of the seasons as they run their circle. There above you is the living picture of the circle of time.'

'That is a curious notion,' Leighor said stiffly. 'Surely time must always go forward, and cannot repeat itself?'

'It is no curious notion. It is revealed truth,' Uhlendof pronounced slowly and somewhat dangerously, as if he defied anyone to contradict him. 'Time is a wheel, so vast that we can see neither beginning nor end, nor where they join and are one – and so simple folk pronounce it a straight line.'

'That is not strictly logical,' Leighor insisted.

'It is perfectly logical. If we were not on a wheel of time, upon the whole of which the deity may glance at any moment – how could he be all-seeing? In what can time itself exist but the void of eternity? How far can we see back in history? Four, five thousand years? That is nothing to a circle of time that could be twenty, thirty times as great.'

'And what would occupy the rest of this cycle?' Telsyan asked.

'Ah! Other kingdoms, civilisations, worlds that we do not even dream of. After all, could the deity be satisfied with but one order, but one single pattern for the occupation of this great world? No, there must be a whole string of histories, each thinking that it is the beginning and end of time. Yet each sharing the same earth.'

'Then why have we not known of them, the ones that precede us at least?' Leighor asked.

'Each segment cannot be known to the next; that would offend the purpose. All are separated by disasters so great, so terrible, that no memories of the times preceding them survive in the memory of man. What do we know of history before the founding of Urza, the first city? Nothing. But something came before.'

'The Heliards teach that this was when the Eternal Fire left the world to rule the heavens,' said Telsyan sleepily, 'leaving all else behind for mere mortals. Before, there was nothing; or so we were told as children.'

'It is a pleasing enough tale,' Uhlendof said. 'But I do not believe it is truth. There can only be one truth.'

Telsyan sighed. 'It is too late to debate such matters now. I am tired, and we must rise before dawn to get the best of the day. Let us sleep.'

Only Uhlendof did not retire at once, but lingered to say his evening devotions quietly by the fading light of the fire. Leighor found his bed surprisingly comfortable. He listened for a few minutes to the night cries and sounds of the forest, and slept.

They rose the next morning far later than they intended, and an irritated Telsyan led them at an unrelenting pace northwards. The sun still shone bright, but the sky was not so clear as they had hoped. Clouds loomed on the far horizon and, as the morning wore on, a heat haze again began to rise when the early morning breeze stilled.

The country around them grew grander and more rugged as they journeyed north, the cliffs now sheering away in vertical drops straight into the roiling sea hundreds of feet below. Great rocky bluffs rose up to separate the swathes of trees that still clung to the steep slopes, leaving the roadway itself the one isolated ribbon of flatness and order suspended precariously and unnaturally on the edge of this wild coast.

Occasionally there would be a sea inlet, a river, or some other break in the sheer line of cliffs, and then the Coastway would be borne across the gap upon one of many wondrous stone bridges. Noble and truly beautiful works of the master masons of old, they arched elegantly over the widest chasms in single spans of precise masonry.

'Look,' Uhlendof stabbed enthusiastically at the stones as they stood poised high above a broad inlet of the sea. 'Every stone still as smooth as the day it was first cut. Such were the skills of the ancients that they could forge a road where none could dream of in these poor days.'

'It feels unsafe to me,' said Yeon, looking uneasily over the edge. 'Let us be across before it crumbles away entirely.'

'This bridge has stood for two millennia,' Uhlendof smiled, 'and I have a good guess it will be here long after we are all forgotten.'

From now on their way sloped gently downward, the cliff upon which their road was set steadily diminishing until at last it approached sea level, running for a while along a broad sandy beach, beneath craggy bluffs and vertiginous forests.

After some time the road turned inland and upwards again. Here there was a small stonebuilt tavern, entered by a stairway to its upper storey. Above the door swung a small sign bearing upon it the red representation of a lobster. They dined upon fresh lobster and sour Holdar wine. They were the only patrons, although the innkeeper assured them that he had more customers for the evening trade.

'Ah yes, people do dwell hereabouts,' he told them, 'though you wouldn't guess it from the roadway, passing by. Folk in these parts don't like to bide too close to the road, for many reasons.'

'But why do you dwell on the top floor?' Yeon asked, 'and leave the bottom empty?'

The innkeeper began clearing away the wooden plates and bowls. 'That is another custom of these parts, young sir. If there is a high tide, we are dry, and only my nets and lobster-pots below. And they are used to the water anyhow! And should a band of Rievers come a-knocking at my door, why they've got to come up the stairs, and we can take 'em one by one!' He laughed.

They all laughed. It seemed a relief to be here in this pleasant tavern in such beautiful country, away from all the plotting and intrigue of the city.

'Do you get many Riever raids here, then?' Uhlendof asked more seriously.

'Oh no, sir,' the innkeeper smiled. 'The last time we had Rievers round here was in my grandfather's time; yes, back in 692 I think, or was it '93? Anyways, over ninety years ago.'

Uhlendof was relieved, and with reluctance they paid their reckoning and prepared to depart, stepping once more down the narrow tavern steps to the roadway. It was then, to their surprise, that they noticed a small hunched figure walking, or rather scuttling, towards them from the south. The man at first seemed old, for he bore a stout stick upon which he placed much weight, but despite this he moved surprisingly swiftly and was soon nearly upon them.

Despite the heat he wore several layers of clothing, and these were old and ragged and caked with dust and dirt. A grimy grey undershirt was only partly hidden by a tight, horn-buttoned jerkin of torn leather that itself passed beneath a thin leather belt, in which three sharp stiletto knives gleamed. Beneath this, the stranger wore a pair of knee-length britches of indeterminate rough cloth. He wore no shoes, but instead bore the badge of the poorest and most destitute of men, his feet and lower limbs being covered only with thin bindings made from strips of torn rag-cloth, knotted together, filthy, and several layers thick. Over all he wore a long dark coat of buttoned leather, old enough to have seen far better days; this hung open to the breeze as sole concession to the heat of the day.

Panting harshly, he drew level with them, staring them straight in the face for the first time.

'Good day, my noble lords.' He gave a low, slightly mocking, bow. His voice was sibilant, with an irritating whine of the sort that could easily turn either pleading or contemptuous. A thin smile passed across his face as he spoke, reminding Leighor disconcertingly of the humourless grin of a serpent. The reptilian impression was accentuated by the stranger's shiny white forehead and crown, which bore no trace of hair. Yet although he was entirely bald on top, to the back and sides of his head there was hair in abundance – growing long and lank in greasy brown rat-tails to hang down well below his frayed and tattered collar. A musty smell blew towards them on the breeze.

Leighor could not guess at the man's age, only that he was neither very young nor very old: he could have seen anything from thirty to fifty winters.

'What do you want?' Yeon demanded sharply, all good humour vanishing at the sight of the interloper.

The hunched figure cowered away from the words like a blow. 'Nothing good sirs, but to beg your pardon. It is a lonely road and dangerous for one travelling alone. I saw you ahead on the road and I wondered if I might catch up with you . . .' He paused to study the faces of the travellers with a quick and shifting eye.

'What is your business with us?' Telsyan demanded, before the crookback could speak further.

'My name is Inanys, my lord. I am but a humble trader in fortunes and charms . . .'

'We need none of your charms! Be on your way!' Yeon stepped forward purposefully, and the stranger took two steps back.

'No, your honour,' he cowered away. 'I come not to sell or tell fortunes – unless you wish. I am only a poor man who desires to walk with you awhile along the road, if our paths should match, as any lone traveller might in these wild places; for the safety of numbers.' He smiled again.

'We do not wish your company!' Uhlendof spat vehemently.

A wave of fury and wild malevolence seemed to flash across the newcomer's face for an instant – and then was gone, to be replaced by the same ingratiating smile as before. 'But surely my lord would not allow a poor lone traveller to be abandoned in this dangerous place, when such a small favour might save his life? Or are you not a holy man – a man of god?'

'I . . . I . . .' Uhlendof struggled unsuccessfully for words.

Telsyan was not so handicapped. 'Who bade you travel alone on this road?' he demanded. 'We did not. So what you began alone you may finish alone. We have private business, and require no company! This is a good tavern, if you need assistance.'

'No, my lords. I need to journey onwards, like yourselves. I have just parted company with my last travelling companions, for their business lay to the west, and mine upon this road.'

'Who would travel with such as he?' Yeon whispered. 'He is filthy!'

'If my appearance offends your eyes, my lords, I will walk behind. Ten paces, forty paces, even a hundred paces if you wish; just so that I may be permitted to remain within sight, and under the protection of your noble selves.'

'No!' Yeon said, angry at being overheard. 'Go now, and and do not trouble us further!'

'Is that your answer, noble lords?' Inanys said, no longer smiling. 'Mayhap I have news that will make you change your mind.'

'What news?' Telsyan snorted.

The crookback shuffled forward, 'There are strange stories from out of the Sielders; of the murder of the Archbaron, and of four fugitives fleeing from justice; a dark southron, a priest, a boy, and . . . some other . . .' he stared up into the eyes of the four of them in turn.

'Where did you hear this, stranger?' Telsyan moved forward angrily. 'Tell me quickly, for you speak dangerous words.'

Inanys scuttled hastily backwards, out of the larger man's reach. 'These things were much spoken of at the great inn at Roadsmeet, when I lay there three nights past. I am surprised that the tale has not reached you before this . . . But then again my lords, I am surprised to find you still so close to the Sielders.'

'Curb your tongue!' Telsyan hissed.

'As you wish, my lord,' the crookback smiled.

'We are unjustly accused,' said Yeon after a pause.

'Of course,' Inanys smiled again. Yeon's eyes flamed with anger, but Telsyan spoke first.

'What do you want?' he asked.

'Nothing, my lords, I am a humble man, with no interest in matters so high above my own poor station. I desire only your word that I may journey with you for as long as I wish.'

'Why?' Yeon demanded.

'That is my concern.' Inanys smiled thinly.

'I like this not!' Yeon spat. 'I do not trust this vile creature; let us drive him away.'

'That might not be wise,' Uhlendof said quietly. 'He would undoubtedly repay us by setting Darvir's men on our trail.'

'You pain me, my lords,' Inanys croaked. 'I am, after all, an honourable man. Surely, if any, it is *your* honour that is in doubt?'

'You stinking toad!' Yeon leapt forward to grasp the crookback by the lapels of his coat, dragging him roughly forward.

Immediately Leighor saw a small dark thing dart from within the smaller man's clothing and run quickly up Yeon's arm. Yeon released Inanys in horror, stumbling backwards as he tried to brush the scurrying spider off. He was not quite quick enough; the startled spider bit him before receiving its death blow.

Yeon cursed loudly and drew his sword from its sheath. The crookback clutched his staff before him as if to ward off a blow.

'Hold!' Telsyan intervened, seizing the youth's arm. 'This goes too far!'

Leighor quickly grabbed Yeon's other arm to hold him back, as Inanys retired a few paces; re-ordering his clothing, yet still bearing a satisfied smile. Only Uhlendof took no part in this, standing quite still and staring blankly at the stranger.

'*Xgarathûl*,' he hissed.

'What?' Telsyan scowled impatiently.

'*Xgarathûl*,' Uhlendof repeated, 'the spider god. He is an acolyte!'

'What does that mean?' Yeon asked.

'It means that he serves a Dark One!' Uhlendof growled, quickly making the sign to ward off the evil eye. 'He cannot travel with us!'

'*Xgarathûl* is not dark, my lords,' Inanys quickly recovered his composure, 'he is many-coloured, all the hues of the cosmos are in him.'

'Nay,' Uhlendof said loudly, 'he is abhorrence itself, an abomination from the pit! He must away!' He held up his own stout staff as if to ward the stranger off, but Telsyan stepped between them.

'I have met with cultists before,' the merchant said calmly. 'I admit that they may be strange in many ways, but they are not entirely evil.'

Uhlendof snorted and turned away. 'Do as you wish,' he snapped, 'so long as he comes not near me.'

'Well?' Inanys said. 'Are you decided? May I accompany you, or must I turn back and hope to find better company in Irgil?'

'You may come with us,' Telsyan sighed at last, 'so long as you do not pry into our business, or hinder us in any way. Make but one mistake, and you will be on your own. Do you so swear?'

'Indeed sirs, I give you my oath,' Inanys tripped lightly. 'I will be the most dutiful companion.' He stared cunningly up into the travellers' faces once more. 'So do you now swear, upon your honour, upon your holiest oaths, that I may travel with you for as long as I wish?'

'Yes,' Telsyan and Leighor grunted in turn. Yeon nodded half-heartedly.

'And you, my lord,' Inanys turned upon the monk. 'Do you give me your oath as well? I know I may trust the word of a man of prayer like yourself.'

'No,' Uhlendof shook his head. 'This oath binds us to too much. Greatest ill fortune would fall upon us should we break such an oath as this. We make ourselves his prisoners. I will not swear!'

'Then I must return to Irgil with my news.' The crookback turned on his heel as if to journey back the way he had come. But he had taken few steps before Telsyan called him back.

'You must swear!' he hissed to Uhlendof. 'You cannot risk our whole venture over so small a matter!'

Uhlendof sighed. 'Under duress, unwillingly, I will swear.'

'Upon your holiest oath . . .' the crookback pressed, '. . . to the One?'

'Yes!'

'Then it is settled.' Inanys gave another mocking bow. 'I will be pleased to join your company.'

'Mark my words,' Uhlendof growled lowly. 'We shall have cause to regret these hastily given oaths.'

'Hypocrite!' Inanys spat, his mood violently changed in an instant. 'You shall burn in all the seven hells, holy man!'

'Cease!' Telsyan turned on the crookback angrily. 'Is this how you keep your oath! If so, it is soon broken, and we shall consider ourselves free.'

'No, no,' Inanys said quickly. 'I was provoked by harsh words. But I shall not permit myself to be so provoked in future, my lords, however harshly you may speak of me. Surely my place can only be to bear all and say nothing, to do my noble lords' bidding in all things . . .'

'Come!' Telsyan turned from him impatiently. 'We must be on our way. We have already wasted too much time.' Rearranging his pack on his shoulders, he began to make his way back on to the road.

'Hold,' Inanys called. 'Continue along the beach and you save half a day and much climbing of hills. Then there is the added benefit of not meeting old friends on the road.'

'Would that we had left it sooner,' the monk muttered.

'He has a point though,' said Telsyan. 'We need to make good speed, and now that it seems our descriptions have become the talk of Holdar, it might be best to keep off the main road.'

'Let us not rush to place our destiny into the hands of this stranger,' Uhlendof objected, turning to Yeon. 'At least check his tale with the tavernkeeper to see if he tells the truth.'

Yeon ran back to the small tavern and quickly returned with confirmation. 'Yes.' He pointed along the beach. 'The coastway returns to the shore further north, in about a day's march. He says the beach is often used by local folk instead of the road, and that there are caves in which to sleep.'

Grudgingly Uhlendof accepted this verdict, and followed on behind the others as they made their way down on to the dry sands. Some way behind these four, muttering quietly to himself, trailed Inanys. The travellers made no attempt to converse with him; merely glad that, for the moment, he chose to keep himself to himself.

The day was still warm and the sea calm, and they soon lost sight of the tavern and the coast road. Sheer cliffs now rose up high upon their left, blocking off all way of escape should the tide come in suddenly upon them; but the strand was broad, and there seemed no prospect of a repeat of their recent sea peril. Even between the four, few words were spoken; yet as the afternoon bore on, the travellers made their way by mutual consent down to the sea, taking off boots and sandals to let the cool wavelets wash over their tired feet as they walked. So refreshed, they made good time along the beach, soon leaving the struggling figure of Inanys far behind them.

It was late afternoon when they felt the first chill breeze from the east, and turned to see the towering thunderclouds now nearly upon them, speeding in rapidly from the sea.

'Hurry, we must find shelter!' Uhlendof called. He turned to Yeon. 'Where are these caves?'

'Just ahead, I think.' He pointed to where several darker patches could be dimly made out against the grey limestone.

They hurried onwards as the sun was rapidly overtaken, and then submerged, beneath the advancing banks of grey cloud, the temperature dropping rapidly all around them. A few heavy spots of rain cratered the dry sand ahead. But now they could see the welcome shape of a large cavemouth nearby, and most of the party managed to gain its shelter before they got too wet.

'Where is Inanys?' Telsyan asked, removing his pack to shake the rainwater from his clothing, as the downpour redoubled in fury outside.

'Why do you care?' Yeon shrugged. 'Perhaps he will find shelter elsewhere, and if not mayhap the rain will wash him a little cleaner!'

Uhlendof ignored them both, staring out wordlessly into the dark rainstorm and the unyielding banks of cloud that rolled in from the far horizon. 'I do not think we shall be going any farther today,' he finally adjudged. 'We had best prepare to spend the night here.'

'That is no bad thing,' Telsyan grunted. 'Had we taken the road we should have been caught in the open when this came upon us.'

At that moment Inanys hobbled into the cave, dripping wet, having been thoroughly sodden by the cloudburst. He sneezed violently and huddled himself into a dark corner, saying no word. And there he sat motionless, still fully dressed in his rain-soaked clothing.

The others too sat in depressed silence for a while, staring out at the driving rain, shuddering as brilliant flashes of lightning tore through the sky, and dark thunder crashed like the ending of the world. They were all damp and miserable. With no wood for a fire, and no fresh water, there was no cooking to be done; and so they passed around dry journey biscuits and drank only what little water they had brought with them. Uhlendof produced a small piece of honeycake that he had purchased in Irgil, to cheer up their meal, but the travellers were so cold and tired that even this small delicacy did little to revive their spirits.

Inanys did not attempt to eat with them, but nibbled at something brown and unidentifiable that he produced from his coat. He said no word, curling up to sleep when he had finished, in his own dark corner.

'We had best do the same,' Telsyan observed. 'There is no point our sitting up in the dark.'

'Shall we set no watch?' Uhlendof objected. 'Our new companion might easily slit all our throats this night!'

'Then you may stand watch if you wish,' Telsyan grunted. 'I shall lose no sleep over such as he! Besides, there is little to fear from brigands yet awhile. We are still a long way from the true wilderlands. There are most likely several villages within a fivemile of this coast!' And setting his outer clothes to dry on the nearby rocks, he dug a blanket from his pack and settled down upon a ridge of dry sand to sleep.

Reluctantly, the others did the same, but Yeon and Uhlendof made certain to lie facing the disconcerting stranger, and kept their weapons close to hand. The storm seemed to be abating when at last Leighor slept.

The morning dawned bright and clear, as if there had never been a storm the night before. Yet the travellers rose chill and cramped, to swallow a few morsels of dry biscuit before setting off on their long trek once more. The storm had cleared the air, and a fresh breeze blew in from the sea to banish all traces of mist and mugginess. The day would be perfect for walking. As their clothes and packs dried out, the travellers' morale improved, and it seemed no time at all before the sun was directly above them and the end of the long beach finally came into sight.

It finished suddenly, a solid wall of perpendicular cliffs blocking the way ahead. A great grey barrier ran eastwards, far beyond the beach, to form a huge, finger-like promontory pointing out into the sea.

'We can go no farther this way.' Telsyan halted, watching the deep sea rollers shatter into great clouds of spray against the jagged rocks of the point. 'But where is the road?'

'It must run along the top of those cliffs.' Leighor pointed upward. 'There must be a way up somewhere.'

The travellers' eyes scoured the long line of vertical cliffs behind them, but could find no trace of any possible path.

'We must have passed it,' Uhlendof said at last. 'We shall have to go back.'

'Aye, and we had best move quickly.' Telsyan pointed northward along the beach, to the point where it ended beneath the high promontory no more than a quarter of a mile away. 'There. Look! We have company!'

Leighor's eyes followed his pointing finger, just able to make out the small manlike shapes moving beneath the cliff. Small grey figures, that emerged from the many caves beneath the headland to watch them silently. He guessed that there must be forty or fifty of them at least; perhaps more within the caves. Near-naked, their leathery skin exposed to the elements, they stood upon two legs like men. Yet men they were not. Their gait was crouched and unsteady, but they moved with the sinuous, disconcerting speed of the hunter.

'What are they?' he hissed at last.

'Sand goblins,' Telsyan answered at once. 'Scavengers on many a lonely shore. In ones and twos they are no danger; yet in such numbers they could slay us at their ease, should they gather up the courage to attack. We had best move quietly backward, and hope they do not follow. But whatever you do, do not run – that would be fatal.'

Cautiously the travellers turned, and began to retrace their steps; looking backward every dozen paces or so to see what effect their actions were having on the sand goblins behind them.

Yet for a while the creatures just stood and watched the retreating humans; some pointing, or exchanging sharp, screeching cries, but doing nothing to offer any serious threat. It was minutes later that the first small groups began to move forward, following after them in the shadow of the cliffs. In their hands they bore sharp stones and angular makeshift clubs.

'I think they mean to attack us!' Yeon said sharply.

'Perhaps,' Telsyan said. 'Perhaps not. They may only wish to ensure their own safety, and see what we intend. After all, they will not want to start a feud with any humans who might dwell nearby.'

'I hope that we can depend on that,' Uhlendof grunted, walking a little faster. 'And anyway, where is our companion Inanys?'

Now, for the first time that morning, Leighor too noticed the crookback's absence. 'He was behind us when I last saw him,' he said, looking southwards down the beach. 'Now I see him not at all!'

Suddenly Yeon gave a loud shout and pointed forward. 'There! I see it! The way up!'

'Where?' Uhlendof asked. 'I see no path.'

'Not a path,' Yeon corrected quickly. 'A stair. A stone stair running up the cliff face!'

And then they all saw it, a thin line of steps cut into a narrow cleft in the sheer cliff wall; yet so unobtrusive that it could easily have been missed by anyone not deliberately seeking it out. So relieved were they to see salvation near at hand that now indeed they did run, racing towards the base of the narrow stair as if it might somehow be enchanted away before they could reach it.

There came a series of loud shrieks from behind them, and Leighor looked back to see the goblins who followed break suddenly into a run to pursue them across the open sands. They were still several hundred yards away, but despite the shortness of their stride they seemed to be gaining quickly.

Leighor redoubled his efforts. Now the stairway was only yards away. Gasping for breath, the travellers rounded a last stony ridge to see the start of the stair before them. And there, sitting unconcerned upon the bottom step, was Inanys.

'I have been waiting for you for some time, my lords,' he leered.

'Why did you not tell us the stairway was here?' Telsyan demanded furiously.

'Did you not know?' The crookback feigned surprise. 'I apologise most humbly, my lords. But I feared your visit to the sand goblins might be on your own private business – and I did not wish to interfere . . .'

Impatiently the merchant pushed past him to climb the stair, and the others followed, leaving the crookback once more to bring up the rear. The steps were steep and narrow, being rough-hewn from the living rock, and it was a long, precarious climb. There were steep drops now, as the stair zig-zagged up the cliff-face, and many times their feet slid and scrabbled on the slippery stone. Only Inanys seemed to take the steps in his stride, trotting up apparently without effort, his short, crooked staff tap, tap, tapping against the stone.

For the moment, however, the sand goblins did not attempt to follow, seeming content merely to gather about the foot of the stair and hurl a few ill-aimed rocks and stones up at them as they climbed, screeching insults and encouragement to one another in their own harsh tongue.

Lungs bursting and bodies damp with sweat, the travellers finally gained the clifftop, to be rewarded with the sight of the familiar chalkstone road running away before them into the north.

'It is good to see the old road again,' Yeon breathed after a while.

'Perhaps,' Telsyan said. 'But I do not think it wise long to remain upon it. The goblins may yet follow us after dark, when they think it safe; and I also fear pursuit from Irgil.' He reached into his robes and withdrew his map, unfurling it before them. 'Here we are very close to the border with Felldur; which runs inland, to the west. Farther north along the coast, one comes to the Black Fjords, which are beset by dark fogs and riptides. And there we may meet with more sand goblins, or worse. I have been thinking that it might now suit us better to make our way inland, and into Felldur. There we may pose as ordinary travellers making our way north along one of the minor roads that run up the great dales . . . And I have also heard of a great alchemist who dwells in Felldur, one with great knowledge of metal lore of all kinds. Should we meet, he might perhaps be able to help us with . . .' he took a sidelong look at Inanys, '. . . our other matter.'

'Aye,' Uhlendof nodded. 'And inland we could travel with far less notice. This road is no longer safe for us.'

The others nodded.

'Then we are decided,' Telsyan said briskly, scrolling his map once more. 'We shall turn off to the west upon the first track or footpath we find, and make our way over the Grey Fells into Felldur.'

Chapter Seven
BRACKEN HEATH AND PINE

Within the hour they came upon a wide grassy track that led away from the Coastway, coiling enticingly westward through a narrow gap between wooded hills.

Telsyan halted. 'This looks a promising way, better than I had hoped. Shall this be our path?'

Yeon looked uncertain, but Leighor and the monk both nodded.

They made good time along the westward-leading track, and in minutes they were a world away from the Coastway. Leaves rustled gently overhead and birds sang in the overhanging branches. The travellers were thankful for the shelter of the steep, tree-clad hills as they walked in the dappled shade beneath. Soon, however, they came out from between the hills to enter a broad, open valley that climbed gently into the north-west. A gleaming silver stream danced through its lush glades and verdant meadows. For an hour or more they toiled up through the long valley, climbing beside the stream until at last the sun began to set. And here, in the shelter of a great linden tree, they made camp for the night. Uhlendof found a small eddy-pool in the stream and set out a line of sharp hooks, baited with the remains of that morning's breakfast; by full dark he had caught half a dozen small silvery fish. These he cleaned and grilled over a low fire in a crisp herb batter. Inanys looked on hungrily as the travellers prepared to eat.

'Go and find your own meal!' Yeon said, angered by the crookback's stare. 'Our bargain did not include feeding you!'

'I ask for nothing,' Inanys responded reproachfully. But still his eyes clung to the hot food.

'This is no use!' Uhlendof said at last. 'We shall have to give him something!' He produced a fifth platter and set about re-dividing the meagre fare.

Yet the crookback seemed less than full of gratitude. 'If it is given freely I will accept,' he rasped. 'I cannot eat food that is grudged.'

'Be that on your own head,' Uhlendof shrugged. 'The food is there.'

But Inanys refused to touch it, again watching while the others ate. Uhlendof bore this in silence for some minutes, then finally snapped.

'By all that's holy!' he roared. 'It is given freely! Eat it or depart!'

His lip curling into a sly smile, the crookback nodded and took up the plate.

Finishing their meal as the last fading embers of the sun retreated behind the dark western hills, the travellers prepared for sleep, rising early from their makeshift beds the next morning. Bleary-eyed and aching, they swallowed a little dry journey biscuit as the grey mists rose slowly above the valley floor. Then they set off once more, Telsyan leading them at a brisk pace north by west up the valley, beside the racing stream.

Narrow and little-used now, the path was overgrown with weeds, and scattered with the nodding, blood-red poppies of late summer. Hundreds of tiny seeds, borne on threads of gossamer, drifted gently about them as they forced a way through the rank vegetation. Sharp, straggling brambles, showing the first signs of the fruitfulness soon to come, had to be manoeuvred out of their path with sticks or gingerly placed fingers. The sun grew stronger as they climbed, attracting all forms of buzzing and fluttering life: from the giant bumblebees, laden with pollen, that blundered clumsily across their path, to the myriad many-coloured butterflies – wings glinting with blues and oranges, reds and whites – that seemed to congregate over every flowering plant in the valley. Less pleasingly, the fair weather also brought out hundreds of darting black flies to buzz annoyingly about their ears, alighting constantly on faces, arms and packs to make life as miserable as possible for the sweating travellers. By midday the valley was rising steeply, and the path finally left the stream to make its own way up the hillside. Here, where the water cascaded coolingly down a sheer precipice of mossy rock, they stopped to refill their flasks, and to rest awhile in the pleasant cool before moving on.

Now, as they climbed still higher, the vegetation began to change. The path grew clearer and easier to follow as much of the tall, straggling plant-life of the valley fell away, to be replaced by open meadows of delicate, feather-headed hill grasses, spotted with dainty yellow cinquefoils, pink campions and purple clover. Here and there grew small wild rose bushes bearing fragrant hips, which Leighor would have liked to stop and pick, and simple flowers of red or white. Now and then a gentle breeze might waft traces of their delicate scent towards the travellers, to refresh their senses as they climbed. Stretches of broom and gorse once more appeared, only to vanish again as they finally rose out of the valley and on to the bare, open crest of the high ridge above.

The travellers sank to the ground amid the soft grass, thankful that the long hard climb was over. Leighor looked back down the long valley they had spent most of the day following, catching faint glimpses of their stream amid the dark greens of its floor. He turned to see what lay ahead.

'These must be the Grey Fells,' Uhlendof's voice came from his right. 'If so, they stretch for nigh on half a dozen leagues before falling down into Cleafedale, the first of the seven great dales of Felldur which cut northward into the wilderness.'

The fells stretched out in front of them for as far as the eye could see: a high, boggy plateau that rolled bleakly away to north and south and west. Many low hills rose above the general level of the undulating terrain, but even these were scoured smooth by some great weathering force, and bore upon them the same low, treeless vegetation as the rest of these uplands. Leighor could see at once why these were termed the Grey Fells, for apart from the dull greys of the bare rock and the many lichen-covered boulders, the very grasses and low, ground-clinging plants that grew here seemed dull and sombre. At least compared to the riot of light greens, dark greens, limes and emeralds of the valley below. The plants were grey, like the mists which hung still on the shadowed hillsides even on this warm afternoon, quenching the very colour of the skies.

'This is a dismal place,' said Yeon, giving voice to all their thoughts.

'We shall not be here long.' Telsyan responded, taking a long deep draught from his waterflask. 'Even so, we shall not reach Cleafedale tonight.'

'Do you mean that we shall have to sleep here?' Leighor asked, dismayed.

'There are worse places to spend a night,' Telsyan said briefly. 'Here there is at least clean water and little chance of disturbance.'

'But it will be cold,' Yeon protested, 'and wet.'

'Not if we select the right site. Tomorrow we shall sleep in the warm beds of a goodly hostelry in Cleafedale, so what matters it if tonight we sleep in less comfort? But come!' the merchant rose. 'We can still make several more miles today, before daylight fails.'

Groaning, the others rose to follow him up on to the plateau itself. Yet now the little path they had followed all day betrayed them, dividing first into two and then three, with each branch they took running out and finally fading away into nothing amid the thick hummocky grass and damp bog moss of the fell.

'What now, merchant?' Yeon asked scornfully. 'Are we lost?'

'It is impossible to lose oneself here,' Telsyan snapped. 'If we move westwards we are sure to come upon Cleafedale sooner or later. I suggest we head due west, finding what route we can. If we keep the sun slightly to our left as we walk, we shall be in broadly the right direction.'

They kept as far as they could to the high ground and the flanks of the steeply rounded hills. Although inconvenient, this soon proved the only way of avoiding the many deep bogs that lurked in the flats between – where one could be walking upon firm ground one minute, and shin-deep in muddy ooze the next. With only a few half-wild mountain sheep for company, the travellers journeyed on.

Shortly thereafter they passed across a wide plain between the hills. Yet even here the ground was far from flat, being strewn with hundreds of small tussocky mounds, round hillocks and raised barrows, all covered with clumps of thick springy moor grass of a type that made them trip and tumble constantly if they attempted to walk too fast.

'Do you recognise this land?' Telsyan asked Uhlendof after some minutes of picking their way in silence across the plain.

'No. Why should I?'

'I thought you a historian,' Telsyan chided. 'Yet I recognised this place at once, and you do not. Do you not see the four hills that surround us at the four compass points, and the cairn of piled stones ahead?'

'Yes, of course!' said Uhlendof suddenly. 'Strike me for a fool! This can be none other than Harnfell, that which was known to the ancients as *Duranoêl*. For are these not the four great hills that marked the battlefield; Cumon, Heraphon, Adlas and Mornimhos? And that the cairn that marks the resting place of Utigeln? I little thought that ever I should see this place.'

'A battlefield?' asked Yeon curiously. 'Up here?'

'Yes,' said Uhlendof with enthusiasm, 'there were two great battles fought on this ground. The most recent was over two hundred years ago, when Utigeln and his men fought their last battle against the combined Varroain overlords of Felldur and Holdar.'

'Do you speak of Utigeln the rebel?' Yeon demanded.

'Yes,' Uhlendof nodded gravely, 'to the Varroain nobility he was both rebel and traitor, but to many of his own Durian folk he was a hero; that is why they built that great stone cairn above the spot where he fell. Let us go over to it.'

They approached the cairn, which was constructed of boulders carefully fitted together without mortar, rising close on a dozen feet above the marshy ground. Carved on one of the base stones was a single rune.

'What does it read?' Telsyan asked, examining the carving.

'It is a rune in the old Durian script,' the monk answered slowly. 'It says simply, Utigeln Triumphant! or something near to that, it does not translate well.'

'That is a strange thing to write of one who lost the battle,' Yeon said.

'Perhaps,' Uhlendof nodded, 'but that is the way a conquered people often think. After all, he had won several great battles before this; he only retreated up here once he had grown weak and the Varroain overlords had raised up a great army against him. Here his forces hid all winter of the year 565, finally to battle half-starved against the forces of the overlords, the Imsild Knights and even horsemen from far Khiorim. It is said that ten thousand men died here upon that single day.'

For a moment they all stood in silence, staring out over the tussocked heathland where so many had died in a past still not too distant for the remembrance of local folk.

'All men are fools!' said Inanys suddenly, and walked away.

'You spoke of another battle,' Leighor said after a while, 'and another name.'

'Yes, *Duranoêl*,' Uhlendof whispered. 'That is how this place was known before the Varroain came, before even the Durians renamed it Harnfell. For it was through *Duranoêl* that the ancient Durians first came into Felldur and down on to the Holdar plains, long before the histories were written, at the dawning of the age of the Spellbinder Kings. Here they fought and won their first great battle with the original inhabitants of this land. And so this site became the place of burial for the Durian kings of Holdar and Felldur for nearly two thousand years – until the Durian kingdoms finally fell to the armies of the Varroain in the year 297.' He stretched his arm out to the horizon. 'That is why Utigeln brought his tired warriors here for their last stand. All these mounds and barrows you can see mark the burial places of heroes, and dug deep into those mountains are the tombs of forty generations of the kings of Holdar and Felldur. I only wish that we had the time to spend a few days exploring the tombs.'

'Well I am glad we do not!' Telsyan said with a shiver. 'Let us leave this baleful place. We cannot sleep here!'

They passed on across the broad plain, walking steadily. But dusk was almost upon them before they had finally left its wide bleakness behind them, climbing up into a shallow valley between two rounded hills. Leighor looked back to see the shadows gathering on the plain behind. A ground-clinging mist had risen out of the earth with the fall of the sun, and strange shapes seemed to be gathered within it. Whether it was the eddying of the mist combined with the dark shadows of the silent barrows, or whether it was just his overworked imagination, he could not tell – but for a moment he was sure that he could discern the grey spirits of long-dead warriors moving silently across the plain behind them. He shivered and turned away, glad that they did not have to cross the plain of *Duranoêl* at night.

Shortly after this, the narrow vale they followed broadened out, and the party found themselves by the shore of a small, reed-skirted lake that filled most of the valley. The surface of the lake was completely still and shrouded in mist, and no living thing seemed to move upon it. No bird swam upon its waters, nor did any fish seem to stir in its still depths. It too seemed somehow haunted with the tragedy of the plain behind them, and its misty silence thoroughly depressed the travellers.

'Where shall we spend the night?' Yeon asked at last, through the gathering darkness.

'There, I think,' Telsyan answered at once, pointing to a tiny windowless hut on the lake's far side. 'There are many such on these fells, built for the use of shepherds, or of any traveller who finds himself in need, out of reach of one of the dales. The dalesfolk are a hospitable people.'

It took some time for them to skirt the lake and its marshy edges to reach the small timber hut. But once there, the door opened easily, to reveal a not unpleasant interior, with wooden benches set around the walls, and a tiny fireplace at its far end, complete with a small pile of neatly chopped wood.

'We must be sparing with the firewood,' Telsyan warned, 'for it has all to be carried up on someone's back.'

'Then we shall leave a silver mark to pay for what we use.' Yeon produced one from his pouch to lay it prominently by the fireplace.

'There will be food here somewhere,' Telsyan added, looking around. 'But that we must not touch, for we have our own.' He lit a small fire in the grate. 'Choose your sleeping places carefully, for it will be a cramped night with the five of us here.'

It was Leighor's turn to prepare their meal, but as provisions were short he finally had to settle for making a thick broth with the remaining cooking herbs, dried meat, peas and beans.

'How far must we travel tomorrow?' Yeon asked as they ate.

'Not far,' Telsyan grunted. 'We should soon be out of this high country, and down in the shelter of Cleafedale. Then we shall have a few quiet days journeying up the dales of Felldur before we must leave the Varroain realms for the northlands proper, and cross into the Kingdom of Scûn.'

'Scûn?' Leighor repeated. 'I have not heard that name before.'

'Scûn is the kingdom that rules the northlands,' the merchant told him. 'Or more precisely, it is the kingdom that lays claim to the greater part of the northern wastes. It is an ancient kingdom, but even at its height the claim was a tenuous one. And in these poor days the King of Scûn rules little beyond his own cold fortress of Vliza. All else is anarchy. What little order truly exists lies only around the few small settlements of the Imsild and Durian Knights. Elsewhere there are only mountains, forests and endless plains: bare, wild and uninhabited.'

'You do not make it sound pleasant,' Leighor said.

'No,' Telsyan sipped his soup. 'It is not pleasant. The northlands hold many hardships and dangers, and we must be prepared for them. There are wolves and snow tigers that will fall upon travellers in a bad winter. Goblins and hill tribesmen swarm through the land. But most fearsome of all, should we ever have the misfortune to come upon them, are the Rievers.'

'Rievers!' Uhlendof shuddered as a gust of wind rattled the door. 'What chance have we of meeting them?'

'Little enough, in normal times.' The merchant frowned. 'They are murderous brigands that prey upon all things living. But their numbers rise and fall unpredictably. Normally they run in small bands, for the northland forests cannot support great numbers for very long. But occasionally the bands will join together for a span, forming a horde strong enough to plunder a major settlement or to raid deep into the northern dales.'

'But who are they?' Leighor asked, 'and where do they come from?'

Telsyan shook his head. 'I do not know. They gather from all corners of the north, sometimes simply to slay and to steal at random, at others it seems almost as if they are being wielded as one great club, to batter down the defences of the Eastern Realms. They are men and less than men: men, goblins and demonspawn Tarintarmen from the westron wastes; any who will gather beneath the banners of the Riever chieftains.'

There fell a brief silence, the bright flames flickering in the grate.

'But what of you, southron?' Uhlendof asked suddenly. 'We have not yet heard your whole story. How came you to these lands?'

Leighor hesitated, not quite knowing what to say. He had lied about being a qualified physician, a student of Miriume, and he knew that he must now either admit his lie or continue with it, expand upon it.

Yet what would be the benefit of admitting the truth now? It would only create distrust, and further reduce his standing in the eyes of his companions. Anyway, he was now at least as good a physician as any of Miriume's high-born apprentices – and that was all that truly mattered.

He kept, therefore, to the well-rehearsed tale of his birth as the son of a lowly apothecary in the far city of Syrne, of his hard childhood in the city streets and herb markets, and of his growing interest in the uses rather than the preparation of the herbs he handled. That part was true enough, but what came next was less so: the tale of his apprenticeship and lengthy studies at the Hospitarion of the Flame . . .

'Was this when you studied under Miriume of Carnolis?' the monk asked.

'Yes,' Leighor answered briskly, hoping that this would dispose of the matter without the need for further explanation. 'But when I finished my apprenticeship, there was no place for me, and so I decided to come north.'

'Why was this?' Inanys stirred unexpectedly in the congealing darkness at the end of the hut. 'Were you not good enough at your craft?'

'No,' Leighor responded stiffly. 'I wished to seek new patrons and new cures undiscovered in the south.'

'And were there no fit patrons in your homeland?' the crookback flashed a serpentine smile, 'no places to perfect your cures?'

'It is not as simple as that,' Leighor stammered. 'There are in the southlands certain ancient laws, known as the Codes of Virien, that forbid a man from following any trade other than that of his fathers before him. I was the son merely of an apothecary. I could not aspire to be a physician.'

'Yes. Yes indeed,' Inanys nodded, as if suddenly recalling the fact. 'I have heard of these laws. And yet,' he paused, 'there are those who have escaped the effect of the Codes of Virien simply by moving to the next city. Why have you chosen to come here, a thousand leagues to the north? There must be some other reason . . .'

'Enough of your questioning!' Telsyan broke in, to Leighor's immense relief. 'We have not yet heard from you, Spider Friend. It is high time you gave some accounting of yourself.'

'Me?' Inanys feigned surprise. 'I have no story to tell that would interest such noble ones as you. I am Inanys the wanderer, that is all.'

'That is not enough,' the merchant said bluntly. 'Whence came you, and what is your purpose here with us?'

'Whence came I?' Inanys chuckled. 'I come from all places and see all things: Inanys of the hundred eyes, to see the foul corruption that lurks within men's souls. Wherever pride and folly, braggartry and boastfulness are to be found, there too may you find Inanys. What is my purpose?' He paused and then smiled. 'What is the purpose of the full moon or of the mists that crawl upon the sea? Why do toads eat the spawn of their own kind, and the bats fly sightless in the night?' He laughed again. 'Answer me these riddles, merchant, and I shall answer thine!'

Telsyan turned from the crookback impatiently. 'We shall get no sense out of him! To talk to such is a waste of time far better spent on sleeping! It is late; let us take what rest we can.'

Yet despite the shelter which the little hut offered, the travellers spent an uncomfortable and unquiet night. There was little room for five people to sleep on the narrow wall benches, and so Inanys curled up alone upon the floor. The crookback soon seemed to fall into a peaceful slumber, but for the others the night was long, cramped and comfortless. Finally they slept, but their sleep was fitful and troubled, filled with dark dreams of slaughter and death. It was as if some pain and darkness, long past, still lingered here to haunt their slumbers.

Leighor felt a dark spectre, ageless and relentless, hovering over them, feeding on the darkness, awaiting only some brief lapsing of their guard to fall upon them and engulf them in its inner soullessness – its utter, unimaginable evil. He awoke sweating in the close darkness, filled with dread. He slept no more that night, listening only to the howling wind which seemed to have crept up on them, and which now shook and buffeted their frail wooden shelter like the hand of a giant, whistling through each tiny crevice, and gusting hard against the barred doorway.

Eventually Leighor saw the dull grey edges of the dawn seeping in through the cracks beneath the door and gratefully slid from his hard bench, glad of the excuse to rise at last. The others still slept, and he decided to let them lie for a while longer while he went down to the lake alone to wash the tiredness from his eyes and fetch water for breakfast. Silently he unbarred the door and, with the soup-pot in his hand, stepped out into the cold morning air. The east wind hit him full in the face as he emerged, cutting through his thin tunic like a knife and causing him for a moment to regret his decision to leave the warm hut. The high fells brooded darkly all around him, solid black against the slowly lightening sky. Leighor shivered, moving quickly down to the lakeside.

High reeds bordered the lake, but there was a firm path that led through them right to the water's edge. Here Leighor knelt, now entirely hidden from the hut by a sea of swaying reeds, whipped up by the wind into an undulating waveswept ocean. Waves of a smaller, choppier sort covered the surface of the lake, violating the terrible stillness of the evening before, yet somehow not making it any the less sombre and forbidding. Leighor dipped his hands into the water and shuddered, shocked by its icy coldness; this was late summer and all water should now be at its warmest, yet he had never felt such cold. He pulled his hands from the lake – it seemed to take a great effort – and splashed the cold water over his face. At once he felt awake and refreshed, more alive than he had been for days, the aches and tiredness of the long night washed away. He plunged his arms deeper into the water – it seemed less cold now, tingling refreshingly against his skin.

He suddenly felt an irresistible urge to bathe, to swim in this cool clear water. Almost unconsciously he pulled himself forward, his hands touching the cold lake bottom, until his whole body was in the water. He floated easily, borne up almost without effort by the water itself. And then he swam, using the steady frog-stroke of his Syrne boyhood. Only then did he realise that he still wore his long woollen tunic. How could he have been so careless? The heavy cloth would take an age to dry out now, he would either have to delay the whole party or else risk a serious chill by travelling in wet clothing. He remembered the cold east wind – somehow forgotten while he wallowed in the enveloping lake waters – and turned.

He was surprised by how far he had come from the lakeshore in so short a time. The land seemed a very long way away, and now that he had turned he was swimming against the run of the wavelets. Dozens of small waves slapped gently into his face as he swam onward, soft and warm, yet blurring his vision even when his face was free of the water. He quickly found that he was only able to breathe if he managed to seize each breath at just the right moment between the waves. The air seemed raw and cold now, choking him and making his lungs scream out in pain. How stark the contrast to the sweet, pleasing warmth of the water.

He tried to stand, but deep as he stretched his feet he could not find the bottom. He began to flounder, panic-stricken, as his head sank beneath the surface, vainly trying to make his legs and arms obey. But his limbs felt heavy, useless, and he could not raise them. In his head a gentle voice – a female voice – seemed to speak softly, only to him. *Relax, Leighor of Syrne, be still. Do not struggle against what is inevitable. Stay here with me. Always.* The voice seemed so warm, so comforting, so restful. Was it his imagination or did he see, somewhere in these murky depths, the misty form of . . . who? What? Yes . . . The Maiden. The Lake Maiden! The idea pleased Leighor. There, in the dark gloom just beyond his vision, there she was, beckoning, ever beckoning him, deeper and darker.

Or was it she? Surely there was something else deep down in the heart of the lake? He felt the nearness, the hungry nearness – undisguisable now – of something dark and ancient, dread and loathsome; like . . . What was it? What shape had haunted his dreams in the night, that seemed so long, so long ago? Suddenly the same fearful dread hit Leighor like a blow. The waters swirled. And he saw bones. Tens . . . Hundreds! Bare white human bones littering the bottom of the lake!

He choked. He could not breathe. He must get to the surface. Straining every limb, every muscle, he rose. Slowly, so slowly. It seemed as if he were bearing a weight of many tons upon each arm, each leg. It was too late. He would never reach the surface! His lungs were close to bursting . . .

There came a terrible howling, a fearsome screaming in his ears. Was it rage, anguish, or his own fast-darkening blood screaming through his tortured arteries? He broke the surface, gulping down frenzied lungfuls of raw, sharp air. Yet still the water held him. He felt the pull from below, the clutching wavelets as they tried to smother him. He tried to raise his head to call out; to raise his arms, but they could not be dragged free of the water. He had overtaxed himself; again he began to sink.

His hands brushed against a piece of rounded wood. He clung to it desperately, feeling a slight movement in it, pulling him forward. A strong hand gripped the back of his tunic. Others grasped his arms and shoulders, pulling him upwards, straining against the insistent downward pull of the lake. Then, suddenly, the waters seemed to release him, and he was out in the ice-cold air, sprawled across the damp grass of the landing.

'Are you all right?' asked a distant voice.

'He is breathing,' came another. 'He will survive.'

'What on earth were you doing out there?' Telsyan asked him somewhat later, when he had recovered a little. 'We thought we had seen the last of you, my friend, when you sank beneath the water for so long. What possessed you to try to swim with your clothes on?'

Uhlendof nodded. 'We shouted and called out to you, but you didn't answer. You didn't even seem to hear us.'

Yeon knelt by the lakeside, rippling his fingers idly through the water. 'It is so cold!' he shivered.

'Don't do that!' Leighor sat up with a start to grip the boy's hand. 'That is how it starts!'

Uhlendof began to look concerned once more. 'Let us get him away from this place. Now!' His voice was sharp and urgent. 'And do not touch the water again!'

He and Telsyan helped Leighor to his feet, supporting him back to the comparative warmth of the hut. There Leighor sat, wrapped in his own dry cloak whilst his tunic dried before the fire, and told his tale.

'I should have guessed as much,' Uhlendof said grimly once he had finished. 'I should have seen the signs. The lake is unclean, accursed, it bears the slain and murdered of long centuries. It is the natural abode of a *Roegannaith*, a deep-lurker.'

'What?' Telsyan said, smiling. 'Do not read too many dark magicks into this simple misfortune. It is the cold water that is responsible for this, no more, it gives the cramp to swimmers. A drowning man often hears voices.'

'Did you not yourself dream the same dark dreams as the rest of us this night?' Uhlendof asked sharply. 'How do you explain that?'

'Dreams have nothing to do with the matter,' Telsyan said, somewhat defensively. 'I am a commonsense man and I look for commonsense explanations, that is all.'

'Then perhaps you would like to take a swim in the lake?' Inanys grinned.

'I do not swim,' Telsyan replied shortly.

Yeon was sent off to find water from a clear stream which did not run from the lake. When he returned Uhlendof prepared a thick, lumpy porridge from the remaining oatmeal. This they all ate gratefully, for it was heavy and warming, and made them feel full of something substantial before their day's walk. The pots and bowls were rinsed, Leighor replaced his by now dry tunic, and they were ready to leave. Carefully bolting the door to the tiny wooden hut, they turned away at last to take up their journey into the west. Behind them the east winds continued to moan softly above the surface of the still, reed-skirted lake, in whose dark waters no birds paddled and no fish swam.

Chapter Eight
GITHRIM'S TOWER

The spirits of the company began to lighten only when they had put a good league between themselves and the lake – which Uhlendof now insisted upon calling the Lake of the Lurker. They continued across grassy moorland for a further hour, their backs to the east wind yet warmed by the sun whenever it managed to peep out between the scurrying clouds that raced on ahead of them, and then they came suddenly upon the edge of Cleafedale, the moorland tumbling away before them into a broad, steep-sided valley of fields and pastures, dotted here and there with small farmhouses and stone-built homesteads. A thin white road coiled northward along the valley floor, upon the eastern side of a strong, fast-flowing river which Telsyan named the Sild. Yet only a league or so to the west, across the valley, the bleak high wastes of the Grey Fells rose up once again.

Gladly the travellers hurried down the steep slope into the shelter of the great dale, and once down on the firm, dry chalkstone roadway they seemed to be in a different country. The east wind had far less force here, the sun shone warmly; and ferns, ivies and flowering plants grew in profusion.

'The summer has not quite left this place,' Yeon said happily, 'as it has forsaken those dark fells above.'

'Yet today is the first day of *Faestan* month,' Leighor worked the dates out on his fingers. 'By most reckonings the autumn has begun.'

'Aye,' Uhlendof added, looking around him. 'The harvest is done in these fields, and it looks to have been gathered in for some while.'

'So must we hurry,' Telsyan glanced up towards the fleeting clouds, 'if we are to get to Darien and return before winter.'

'What is your plan now, Master Telsyan?' Leighor asked. 'Shall we journey north, or are we to seek out this alchemist of yours?'

'Both,' Telsyan said shortly. 'This is Cleafedale.' He pointed to the west. 'Over those fells lies Skerrdale, which is the home of the Alchemist Githrim; to get there we must take the road from Biren, which lies farther up the valley to the north, I am not certain how far.'

The party journeyed north for the rest of the day. They bought fresh milk, bread and cheese from an old woman whose tiny farmyard verged on to the road. She told them that it was still more than a day's journey north to Biren on foot.

'But the road is straight and fair,' she added, 'and there are four good inns between there and here, so you will not lose your way.'

The day was warm, and occasionally fish could be seen darting in the shadows beneath one or another of the many low humpback bridges that carried their path to and fro across the southward-rushing river. They saw only a few people on the road, mainly shepherds, farm labourers or journeymen; all of whom seemed friendly enough, wishing them the best of the day as they passed on by.

The company spent the night at the Chained Eagle inn, just outside the small village of Enselt, the second of the four inns they had been promised. By force of habit they rose early, taking a brisk breakfast before setting off northward once more.

The new day was as pleasant as the last, and by late afternoon, with the sun still high in the sky, they had reached the outskirts of Biren. Leighor was surprised to see that despite its size, the town of Biren had no walls, rising like any small village, higgledy-piggledy from out of the fields – though a large walled castle rose up to the west of the town.

The whole town was built of fine grey stone, and seemed prosperous indeed after the poverty of the Sielders. The gilded signs of the masters of a score of trades hung over the close-set houses and workshops of the high street, and the town was thronged with people. Mules, ox-carts and horse wains clattered through the streets, and everywhere was bustle. Leighor began to think that this province might have made a better place to ply his trade than the Sielders.

After some searching, they found an inn with a single room they could share. Inanys however, soon departed, and his litter in their cramped room remained empty throughout the night. He reappeared outside the inn the next morning bearing all the signs of having slept rough amongst the leaves and refuse of an alley. Yet on his feet he now wore two brand new leather shoes in place of his tattered leggings, with a bright silver buckle on each.

'Good morrow, my lords.' He made them a florid obeisance. 'The pauper Inanys at your service. And now he has coin to pay his way.' Smiling thinly, he withdrew a large leather purse from his coat, opening it before them to display a minor treasury of gold and silver coins.

'Where did you get this?' Uhlendof asked sharply. 'Is it stolen?'

'Of course he stole it,' Yeon spat with contempt. 'How else could he have come by it? He is a thief.'

'Gold was set in the earth for all men,' Inanys grinned. 'Why should some have all and many nothing?'

'Because—' the monk paused for a moment, stumped. 'Because it is so set!' he finished at last.

'That is very convenient for those who have the gold.'

'Yes, but it is nevertheless so.'

'Well now I have the gold!' Inanys chuckled gleefully to himself and danced ahead of them, clicking the cobblestones with his new shoes.

Uhlendof would have taken the matter further, but was restrained by a Telsyan anxious now to be away. 'Do not cause trouble,' he whispered, 'or we could be kept here for months! Let us buy our food quickly and go.'

The last low cottages of Biren fell away behind them as the road began to curve gently up the western slope of Cleafedale, sweeping around and back on itself in great loops to lessen the gradient. So it was that the travellers found the climb fairly easy, soon overtaking a lone peasant farmer who was driving an empty ox-wain up the hill.

'Ho there!' he greeted them. 'Good morning, my lords.' He looked to be in his late thirties with hair the colour of fresh carrots. 'It is a long climb over into Skerrdale and my waggon is empty. If you wish you may place your packs in it and walk free alongside.'

Gratefully they accepted his offer, stretching to relieve their sore muscles.

'I am Vistien,' their benefactor introduced himself, climbing off the waggon now to lead the oxen. 'I farm a few acres in Skerrdale, but have had to come here to Cleafedale to sell my corn.'

'Why is that?' asked Leighor.

'The people of Skerrdale are grown poor of recent years, and poor folk eat little wheatbread and fewer cakes.'

'These dales look prosperous enough to me,' Telsyan commented.

'Aye, perhaps,' Vistien nodded, 'for you have seen but Cleafedale, which has a noble lord in Ingal, one who follows the older ways. Our lord is Qiaren, and he is the ruin of many good men.' The farmer walked on quietly for a few moments, guiding his oxen around a tight bend in the road before speaking again. 'But what of yourselves, good sirs?' he asked. 'There can be little enough reason to leave Cleafedale for poor Skerrdale in these days. Unless you seek my lord Qiaren?'

'No,' Leighor said quickly. 'That is not who we seek.' He caught a warning look from Telsyan and said no more, merely introducing his companions by their first names.

Vistien nodded to each in turn. 'If you do not seek my lord,' he ventured after a further silence. 'Perhaps it is the great Githrim who draws you to Skerrdale?' The travellers looked at one another, and the farmer smiled. 'I see by your countenance that I am correct. Githrim draws many men to our dale, so if it was not one it must be the other. He is a great man, Master Githrim, although feared by many. His reputation spreads through Felldur and Holdar and beyond.'

Almost without noticing it, the travellers had come to the summit of the climb, at the top of the western edge of Cleafedale. They could look back for the last time to see the town of Biren set like a child's toy beneath them, and the river Sild gleaming silver in the reflected sunlight as it snaked down the valley towards the plains of Holdar. Ahead of them, the road dwindled to little more than a humble cart track across the rolling moorland fells. Vistien stopped to rest the oxen, and the men shared a flask of wine that Uhlendof had bought in Biren before moving on. The journey across these fells proved much shorter than their previous crossing to reach Cleafedale, and it was only just past midday when the small party reached the eastern edge of Skerrdale.

Here the farmer stopped and pointed up the valley to the north. 'There lies the town of Ciltelder, and beyond – do you see that smoke there?' Leighor made out a dark smudge on the horizon far away in the north. 'That is the tower of Githrim.'

'How long do you think it will take us to reach it?' Telsyan asked.

'No more than a day or two, the road is good, and you cannot get lost with that plume of smoke to guide you, it hangs always over his abode.'

They sat on the warm grass to share their midday meal, looking out upon the broad dale before them. To their surprise, after having listened to Vistien, Skerrdale looked every bit as broad and rich as Cleafedale had done, and Yeon said so.

'It is rich enough,' replied the farmer sadly. 'The best soil of all the great dales, so my father used to say. In older days this land kept seven fat barons and all their retainers, and kept them well. Now it is not enough for one man. It is Qiaren's greed that makes men poor. He farms sheep on his lands instead of turnips or flax. The wool and the meat bring him more silver in the markets of the south, but there is less work here for the men. Many are evicted and left to begging and charity for their livelihood. And so do all suffer. Even honest artisans have no custom for their wares, for the dalesfolk have no money, and Qiaren prefers to buy fancier goods from the south with his new gold.'

'So the vale is richer, yet its people poorer,' Leighor mused. 'It is a curious paradox.'

'It is the very misuse of power and stewardship that Eridar warned against!' Uhlendof snapped. 'For what reason does a lord hold his lands, except to protect his people – to order all to the benefit of all? That is his trust, not the serving of his own self-interest!'

'Is it selfishness to want the best from your lands?' Telsyan asked, 'Surely you would not halt all progress?'

'Such as this is not progress,' said Uhlendof firmly. 'It happens now in all too many lands where the old ways are dying: commons ripped up and fenced in, rents demanded in full whether there be a good harvest or no. The lust for gold is becoming a disease of all in power. One that may soon lead to far worse ills.'

The travellers parted from Vistien in the small village which lay at the bottom of the pass from Biren. Here the houses were indeed shabbier and more ill-kempt than those of Cleafedale: many abandoned, with glassless windows and shuttered doors; the rest in poor condition, with windows boarded up and repairs not made. A few men stood in a small group outside one of the houses; they looked pale, sullen and underfed. The company made their farewells and watched for a while as the ox-cart made its way slowly down the road to the south, and out of their vision.

'I feel sorry for him,' said Leighor. 'There is little hope of things getting any better here.'

'I see no need,' said Yeon sharply. 'He is full of self-pity. The people here are not too badly off; they do not starve, many have good clothes and shoes, and fat bellies besides!'

'Is it not ever the same, my lord?' Inanys croaked sharply. 'However much they strive, the poor can never get quite poor enough to suit the rich.'

Yeon looked at him stonily but said nothing.

They reached Ciltelder just before dark. Little more than a large village, it seemed a sad and empty place. Here there were few visitors, and the travellers found it easy enough to obtain rooms for the night at the only inn.

'This is the last town we shall see for many weeks,' Telsyan told them as they purchased provisions in the small market the next morning. 'We had best buy as much food as we can carry, for who knows where we shall find more?'

The day was windy and dull, and each cold gust that blew in from the east bore upon it the taste of rain soon to come. They travelled now in silence, cloaks wrapped tight about them for warmth, making their way slowly towards the thin column of black smoke that rose up to the north-west. The road north followed the banks of the River Nimbel, but this stream was not clear and bright as the Sild had been. Its waters ran a dirty reddish black, splashing rust-coloured droplets on to barren banks as it cascaded along its rockstrewn path. Small polluted waterfalls poured into malodorous pools whose surfaces ran adrift with scum. It took little wisdom to guess that this fouled stream most probably shared its source with the black smoke ahead of them. The travellers walked on joylessly.

The dale had narrowed a great deal since Ciltelder, and now it began to twist and turn between great outcrops of rock that rolled down in vast sweeps from the high fells. The road was climbing steeply now, and it seemed to take more and more effort to cover each successive league. They walked all day with only brief pauses for rest, meeting with only two other travellers upon the road, and it was not until dusk that the company first caught sight of the tower of Githrim.

Coming around a high limestone spur, they suddenly gained a sweeping view up the dale to the north. And no more than two leagues away, built into the steep western cliffs of the valley wall, was Githrim's Tower. It grew out of the dark mountainside like some misshapen extrusion of the living rock, belching forth great quantities of black smoke and roaring with all the thunder of a raging dragon. There were twin towers, high and dark and square, like grim guardians to the fortress of some fierce mountain king. The travellers halted in their tracks, staring in silence at the scene.

'It is an impressive home for an alchemist,' Telsyan admitted at last. 'Let us hope that he can help us.'

It was too late now to reach the tower before dark, so they camped where they were, making up their beds on the soft dry ground in the shelter of a tangled mass of broom and hawthorn. They were out of sight of the tower here, yet constantly reminded of its presence by the unceasing booming roar that it produced, a sound that echoed and re-echoed around the narrow dale. Dim yellow lights glimmered in the tower's upper windows as they slept.

The tower seemed to grow still higher and more forbidding as they approached it the next morning: a grim bastion poised several hundreds of feet above the valley floor. A rushing stream of dark, evil-smelling water burst forth from its foot to cascade down into the River Nimbel, polluting its crystal clarity forever.

There was but one doorway, set into the base of the northernmost tower, yet this was of solid iron and fully broad enough for a horse and cart to pass through unhindered. Telsyan knocked. They waited still for some minutes, but there was no response from within. Losing patience, Uhlendof stepped forward, raising his staff to thunder heavily against the great iron door – producing a surprisingly loud and cavernous noise. Eventually a small grille opened in the door, just above eye level.

'Who disturbs the peace of the tower of Githrim?' came a harsh voice.

'Five travellers, seeking aid,' Telsyan answered in a voice equally loud. 'We wish to speak with the alchemist Githrim . . .'

'Wait here!' The grille slammed shut.

The travellers waited for several minutes in silence, as the wind blew harder and the first large drops of rain began to fall. Then they heard the sound of a giant bolt crashing free behind the great door which stood so high before them, and, slowly, the door shuddered open, halting when there was a gap just wide enough to allow the travellers to squeeze through one by one.

Leighor was next to last passing into the tower, and a wave of intense heat hit him as he entered. As his eyes adjusted to the dark, he found that he stood with the others in one corner of a cavernous hall which occupied the whole interior space, vaulting in fire-blackened stonework to a height of three or four storeys, the whole lit by the infernal red glow of two huge furnaces, scarlet flames roaring hungrily from their gaping mouths to send a rusty flickering light into the four corners of the hall. The space was so vast that for long minutes it held the travellers speechless. Half a dozen men hauled handcarts of wood and charcoal towards the furnaces, other smaller figures slunk amid piles of stony rubble that littered the hall from end to end. High above them three pigeons flew between the high rafter beams, circling half-blind in the dim light of a dozen small ventilation holes.

A stout figure appeared suddenly from out of the smoke of the furnaces to stride hurriedly towards them. Large, clean-shaven and about fifty years of age, he wore robes of rich wine-crimson, over which he was hastily arranging an expensively embroidered surcoat. A small skullcap sat loosely on his head. Beckoning the five travellers to follow, he led them across to a far corner where a broad wooden platform stood. A long, oiled chain swung tautly up into the darkness.

Mounting the platform, they were at once jerked from the ground, the wooden dais rocking and swaying beneath them as it clattered upward to the call of some great hidden engine. The travellers huddled to the centre, Leighor hardly daring to look down at the scuttling figures already so far below. Within moments they were rising through the solid stone vault of the ceiling to come at last to a halt in a spacious upper room.

Two large bottle-glazed windows penetrated the far walls. The larger of these overlooked a fine stone balcony, which now seemed more a part of the rainlashed dale beyond the tower than of all that stood within.

'Welcome,' said their guide, at last, 'to the home of Githrim the Wise.'

The room was filled with rich furnishings: a large table and carved oaken chairs out of Coimbra, curtains of rich Tershelline cloth, cases of the finest alchemist's instruments, cups and plates of solid silver, and a cabinet of some thirty books, a great number for a single man to own.

Their guide acknowledged their admiring glances. 'I try to keep myself comfortable here,' he said, 'even in these unfortunate climes.' He gave a brusque nod towards the window. 'I of course am Githrim . . . And you . . . ?'

'We are travellers,' Uhlendof said quickly.

'Travellers?' Githrim's eyebrows rose. 'I had heard that you were rather more. You answer the description of the fugitives from Sielder if I recall it aright. Yes,' he recited the list, 'a Mallenian monk of evil countenance; a dark southron, apothecary and poisoner; a young nobleman, nephew to the departed one; and a fat merchant, probably from Selethir. The other I do not know, but all sought by Archbaron Darvir for the foul murder of Eridar, Archlord of the Sielders . . .'

'What treachery is this?' Yeon snarled, drawing his sword. Telsyan swiftly followed his example, and even Leighor began to feel for the stock of his crossbow.

'No treachery,' said Githrim hastily, holding up his hands. 'We are all friends here. Put your swords away. This is my tower which I name Sanctuary, sanctuary from the ills of the world. And once here you are my guests. No more, no less. If I had wished I could have had you seized at my gates when you announced yourselves. So you see, you are in no danger here, put away your swords.'

Warily the travellers looked at one another, then Telsyan, seeming to accept their position, gave a brief nod and sheathed his weapon. Reluctantly Ycon followed his lead.

'Who else knows we are here?' Telsyan asked quickly.

'None but I,' Githrim answered. 'I doubt if the news of Eridar's death has yet reached the common folk of Felldur.'

'Then how come you to know of this?' Yeon asked.

'Little that occurs in the Varroain kingdoms escapes the notice of Githrim. Yet I care little for the concerns of the outer world as long as it contents itself to leave me in peace.' The alchemist indicated the books and instruments about him. 'This is the world of Githrim, and here you are welcome.' He clapped his hands once, and a small man immediately emerged from a doorway to his left. 'Fetch wine for my guests.' Githrim commanded, and the retainer was gone, reappearing a moment or so later with a silver tray bearing the traditional welcoming fare of red wine and curdcakes.

'I see you follow the Giellin ways,' said Telsyan. 'Do you perhaps come from Selethir or Coimbra?'

'That was long ago,' said the alchemist absently, seating himself in his own great chair to watch them, 'much has passed since then.' He began to drum his fingers upon the arms of his chair as they sipped their wine. 'But to more pressing matters.' he said at last. 'The moment I heard your descriptions, I was consumed with curiosity as to why you should wish to come here to call on me. Perhaps you could tell me something of yourselves, and of how it is you come to be here; and not least, what exactly it is you require?'

Telsyan quickly told him much of their story up to the present, leaving out only those details that lay closest to the core of their quest. Through all this Githrim sat silent with his chin resting lightly upon his steepled fingertips and, as far as this position permitted, nodding sagely at appropriate intervals during the discourse. When the tale was finished he sat back in his seat, viewing his visitors pensively from beneath hooded eyelids. 'It is an interesting story you have to tell,' he said, 'yet still I am unsure how it is that you expect me to help you.'

'We have heard that you were learned in the ways of alchemy and metalcraft,' Telsyan responded.

Githrim nodded wordlessly.

'Well then,' Telsyan went on, 'we are here to see if you can tell us anything at all of the purple metal called *harrunor*, sometimes called the Mage Metal, which seems to have reappeared in these eastern lands.'

Githrim's grey eyes hardened and he looked at the merchant sharply. 'How come you to know of *harrunor*?'

'The blast I told you of,' said Telsyan, 'that struck down Lord Halaron from his horse – we have been given reason to believe that *harrunor* might be the cause.'

'Ah!' said Githrim, relaxing a little. 'I cannot think so. The history of the Mage Metal is long indeed, yet in all that time rarely has more than an ounce or two of the metal ever been held in any one place. *Harrunor* is without doubt the rarest stuff of the earth. If your Lord Darvir has found enough of it to form a bangle, then he wastes his time in Ravenshald, for he has on his arm enough wealth to buy the Sielders five times over!' He smiled a little at this thought, and then as an afterthought turned to Yeon. 'Is your uncle a man of great wealth?'

'Only moderately so,' Yeon answered hesitantly. 'He had his holds and his retainers, a fine company of minstrels, and many horses and falcons, yet he had no large sums in gold or in jewels as far as I know.'

'There, you see!' Githrim spread his hands wide, displaying a fine collection of jewelled rings. 'You would need halls of gold to buy so much *harrunor*. It seems that Lord Darvir lives well; such men have little gold to spare. What you saw cannot have been *harrunor*. You must look to more natural explanations for your thunderbolt.'

'But if it were *harrunor*,' Leighor insisted, 'could it have produced fire enough to kill a man?'

Githrim hummed and hawed for a moment, scratching his stubbled chin with one finger, and then shook his head. 'There are tales of such events from ancient times. But just to possess the raw metal was never enough. To make use of it, one must have the power and skill of a sorcerer. It would take as great a mage as ever lived in the days of the Qhilmun Kings to master the purple metal, to empower it and draw out its fire. Many dusty centuries have passed since such men last walked the earth. Your Darvir is no sorcerer surely, and unless he has found some great mage to construct for him a working talisman, such as could be used by an ordinary man like him, then what you think you saw is impossible. And what sorcerer, great or small, having gained the power to master the Mage Metal itself, would be foolish enough to give it to a man like Darvir?'

'Perhaps some amulet of old might have been discovered on an ancient site,' Uhlendof suggested, 'and somehow fallen into Darvir's hands?'

'Mayhap,' Githrim shrugged, 'but it is unlikely. All such things have been lost to men for millennia, and have been sought for as long by seekers after the ancient powers. The few scraps we have in these days are but remnants discovered long ago from sites combed over many times since.'

'Do you, then, have such a remnant?' Uhlendof broke in.

'A very little,' Githrim nodded, 'and it cost me a hundred times its weight in gold to purchase.' He rose. 'I am sure you will wish to see it; let me show you.' Without waiting for their assent he led them briskly through into a large dark room lined with hundreds of jars and bottles – most cracked with age, and shrouded in cobwebs and dust, their contents indeterminable. In the centre of the room stood three lines of heavy oaken tables, bearing large ceramic dishes filled with various coloured liquids. Here and there elaborate wooden supports bore thin traceries of fine glass tubing which conducted other liquids from one bubbling pot to another; small copper braziers, such as Leighor had seen often used in Syrne, burned with a low, quiet flame beneath. Yeon halted to look into a dish containing a clear yellow liquid. Beneath its surface was an exquisite jewel cut in such a wondrous way that even beneath the surface of the liquid light gleamed from a score of delicate facets; the others, too, paused to gaze upon its beauty.

'I have never seen a stone so cut,' Yeon whispered. 'Normally they are round and dimpled and dull; this one has fire!' He extended one hand towards the jewel, as if to touch it.

'No!' the alchemist turned swiftly to seize the youth's hand before it could come into contact with the still yellow liquid, his cold grey eyes flashing with sudden anger. 'That is purest *ilminath*!'

'The stone is so beautiful,' Yeon said stubbornly. 'I just wanted to touch it.'

'Then perhaps I should have let the liquid burn your fingers to the bone!' Githrim glowered. 'The stone is but one sapphire of many; the liquid is as useful to me, for it tempers steel and burns away false gold, valueless gems and prying fingers. But I thought you wished to see the *harrunor*?'

They left the gemstone soaking in its cold-hot bath of *ilminath*, following Githrim to the end of the long room where stood row upon row of shelves bearing dozens of small crystal bottles, each of which contained a tiny amount of some different substance.

'All the minerals known to the skill of man,' Githrim nodded, 'and among them . . .' he took down a small bottle and emptied it casually onto a space on the table, '*harrunor*!'

They crowded around.

'Do not breathe too hard!' Githrim said sharply. 'You will blow it away!'

The travellers craned their necks to see the small piece of gleaming metal before them, burnished and shining like gold, yet in colour purest mauve. But that too was false; in fact, like true gold, the *harrunor* bore not one brassy shade but a thousand subtler hues of mauve and purple, red and blue, deep within it to entrance the eye. Yet it was the tiniest scrap of metal which they now beheld, a fingernail clipping of Sorcerers' Gold – of a size such as jewellers might use in the daintiest of filigree work. This was what had cost a hundred times its weight in gold? Yet it seemed to have a certain power; they could not draw their eyes from it, the bright jewel of moments before forgotten, each of them now wanting to possess only this merest flake of *harrunor*.

Suddenly Leighor remembered. This was the metal he had seen upon the neck of the knight on the Coastway. But it could not be! From what Githrim had just told them, there could not possibly be more than one *harrunor* amulet anywhere in these lands. Yet here was a second, set about the throat of an ordinary Varroain knight! Either what he had seen on the Coastway had been no more than a trick of the light, or else there was something very wrong with Githrim's story . . .

'True *harrunor* has a drawing power that makes all desire it,' Githrim smiled, 'yet that is not its only property. See!' He passed a beringed hand above the metal shard, seeming as he did so to draw forth a shimmer of power which made the air tremble about it. Then suddenly there arose from its heart a sheet of flame, dark purple-red, and evil to look upon, though no more than a few inches high. Swiftly it spread, running in a straight line for a foot or so across the table before slowly fading to nothingness once more. Githrim sighed and closed his hand, picking up the scrap of *harrunor* and putting it away. There was a thin line of blackened wood running across the table where the flame had been.

'So, you have seen a little of the raw power that lies within the metal,' he said at last, 'yet in such small quantities it gathers slowly and exhausts itself quickly, and can be turned to no practical purpose. A curiosity, no more.'

'And this is what is termed the Magefire?' Leighor ventured.

The alchemist nodded. 'Yet the true secrets that gave it power and purpose are lost, and none in these lands could have re-discovered them, not without my knowledge. I am the foremost in metalcraft, none could have surpassed me.' He paused thoughtfully. 'Yet it is rumoured that far to the west, beyond even the boundless wastes of Khiorim, there still dwell great philosophers who hold many ancient secrets, and dabble in mysteries we know not . . .' He fell into silence for a moment or two before speaking again. 'But I forget myself. You will be tired and journey-soiled. You must remain here this one night before you set off again on the morrow. I shall arrange it.'

The five travellers were taken by one of Githrim's servants to the small chamber where they would spend the night. It seemed to be little more than a tiny guardroom, with narrow bunks for eight set against the bare, windowless walls, and few other furnishings. Here they had hardly time to set down their packs and to wash the dirt of the road from their arms and faces before they were summoned for the evening meal.

They were led this time not, as they had expected, to the entrance chamber, but up several flights of stairs to a long narrow upper room with a great oaken dining table that ran its entire length. They seemed to be at the very top of the tower. A strong wind blew, tearing with iron fingers at the roof above and hurling a hundred thousand raindrops against leaded windows that shuddered and rattled fearfully with each new gust. Smoking flamboys hung from great brackets along the walls, while tall flickering candles gave illumination to the table. The chamber might have seemed cold and desolate under different circumstances, but now the travellers were more than happy not to be spending a wild night like this out of doors. A silent servant directed them to several high oaken seats, each carved into the shape of a winged dragon, set along the mid-section of the table. At the head sat Githrim. The foot of the table was left empty, but three others of Githrim's household sat on the far side, facing the travellers.

One was Savart, a tall, mean-looking man, introduced as Githrim's high steward. The other two – a youngish woman called Deovar and an older, stout man named Guron – Githrim termed his guests; although they both seemed to have an air of permanence here, and to slightly resent the intrusion of the five strangers.

'Normally the four of us dine alone,' Githrim told them. 'We have our own quiet needs, and require little in the way of conversation. But for tonight we shall try to be more hospitable.'

Two servants bore in their supper on solid silver platters. The cooking was spicy and Giellin in provenance, the flavour of the original game still just detectable beneath the heavy sauces. Yet despite Githrim's declaration, most of the meal passed in silence.

'What work do you do here,' Yeon asked abruptly towards the end of the meal, 'that causes so much smoke and foulness?'

The alchemist stiffened, although he did not look up from his plate. The three opposite seemed shocked at the temerity of the stranger's question, and there was a long moment of embarrassed silence before Githrim spoke:

'Some of it you have seen already,' he said slowly. 'The tempering of metals for swords and armour for many noble lords; who come to me also for gold that is pure and to find whether the gem merchants have defrauded them. Below . . .' he paused, 'I make metal, fine metal and strong, the best in the eastern lands: perhaps for a stiletto slender enough to slip through the finest mail, or a sword with an edge keen enough to break an iron chain. And then I have other projects of many kinds – which are my own, and need not concern you at this moment. I study all things of the earth, and my helpers do likewise, that is why we stay in this desolate place.'

'The wilds of Felldur,' Guron added sharply from across the table, 'are one of the few remaining places in this world of prying eyes and small vision where a man may study the ancient arts without persecution!' He spoke bitterly, and seemingly more for his own benefit than that of the rest of them.

'That is true enough,' Githrim added gravely. 'The world is still fearful of those who adopt uncommon ways; of visionaries and seekers after truth. Guron and Deovar, like myself, have known the harsh edge of intolerance in their own lands. One can work nowhere in the Varroain kingdoms in these days without the protection of some great prince – and then one is naught but servitor. Here we may dwell in peace as we please, for as long as we can keep Lord Qiaren supplied with revenues. There are some benefits in having a lord who thinks only of gold.'

'And this tower,' Yeon asked, 'did you raise it yourself?'

'Oh no.' Githrim laughed for the first time. 'This was a tower of the old Hill-folk, raised up many centuries ago, long before all such were driven from the Varroain lands. In the tunnels beneath this tower they mined the black earth-coal for their furnaces, and those workings I use still. A tower such as this could not be raised so strong now by the overlord himself. Why then should I build anew, when a few simple repairs to this excellent structure sufficed for my needs? As Kalmandur says:

> Stir not the temple of the earth,
> Nor break the soil that gave thee birth,
> On vain and idle ground.'

'You have studied the ancient poets?' Uhlendof asked in mild surprise.

'Why should I not?' Githrim asked in turn. 'I have had much time to study all things, old and new. The poets of Qhilmun were profound, their songs carried deep thoughts and philosophies long gone from the world.'

'Ah, yes,' said Uhlendof, 'although the ancients clearly did not practise what they preached.'

'The ancients were unwise,' said Githrim calmly. 'They were corrupted by their own power and lost all. If that power is to be regained, it must be by those who know how to master it.'

A gust of wind blasted noisily into the windows. A cold draught swept through the chamber and a candle fell. The torches guttered wildly as if their light too might soon fail. There was silence for a moment as a servant rushed to re-light the fallen candle and pour more wine for Githrim's guests.

'Perhaps,' said Uhlendof, 'the true lesson of the ancients is that such power should not be regained.'

'So it begins!' Guron's voice cut through the hall even above the crashing of the wind, his anger growing as he spoke. 'So speak all canting and interfering priests. Hypocrites who would limit men's minds, the better to enslave them to the dictates of their own cruel gods! Do not tell me you seek aught but greater power for yourselves! A curse upon you all!'

'This must cease!' Githrim rose angrily to still him in full flow. 'I must apologise for the inhospitable words of my friend Guron,' he said stonily, his eyes still fixed firmly upon the other. 'He has suffered greatly in the past, so you must excuse his bitterness.'

Guron stared angrily back at the alchemist for a moment, then rose quickly, and with a last malevolent glance at the priest, strode out of the room without a word, the great door slamming shut behind him. Silently, and with a reproachful look at the travellers, the lady Deovar rose and followed him.

'Let us speak of less contentious matters,' Githrim said quickly, before silence could settle upon them once more. 'You journey into the northlands, do you not? Perhaps I may advise you upon your road?'

'We had merely intended passing over Hurkling Edge and then down into Darkdale,' Telsyan said, 'and from there we shall make our way on to King Culvar's Road as soon as we may.'

'No.' Githrim shook his head. 'The road is most unsafe at the best of times. But now, with so many of the Knights of Imsild riding south for the spring Diet and the election of the new High King, even the strongest parties would be ill-advised to be seen upon the open road.'

'Will the Knights then leave the roads abandoned?' Yeon demanded.

'The Knights keep regular watch only as it suits them, these days,' Githrim nodded, 'and as numbers allow. And north of the line of the Thauran and Malûn rivers, they do not venture at all. That is the domain of the Durian Knights, and they will provide scant escort.'

'Then which way do you advise?' Telsyan asked.

'Follow the road down Darkdale until you reach the River Caethalon, and then turn west upriver two or three days journey until you reach the mines of Zumir, where some lead and copper are still mined for King Arminor. I know the miners well and they have safe paths of their own that will take you northward.'

'Will your way be faster than if we stayed with King Culvar's Road,' Yeon asked, 'or will it waste yet more time?'

'King Culvar's Road might save you a day or two,' Githrim shrugged, 'but it twists and turns greatly to stay on the high ground, above the forests. I do not advise it. If you would reach your destination whole, take the lower roads.' Suddenly he rose. 'I have many tasks for the morning and must rise before the dawn, so you will pardon me if I bid you goodnight.' He nodded in the direction of his seated steward. 'Savart will show you back to your chamber. I will wish you safe journey now as well, for I doubt I shall see you again before you leave.'

'Farewell then, my lord Githrim,' Telsyan said formally, rising in his turn. 'We thank you for the hospitality of your house and for the wisdom of your counsel.'

Githrim nodded briefly in absent-minded acknowledgement and was gone.

'What is your true opinion of this Githrim and his counsel?' Telsyan asked when the travellers were once again alone in their small chamber.

'I do not know if I completely trust him,' said Leighor, 'He has told us much of the *harrunor*, yet I have the feeling that he knows far more than he is prepared to say.'

'Indeed,' Uhlendof nodded. 'There is much to this Githrim that lies hidden . . . Yet he has shown us more than he had need to, and I sense little evil here. I feel no dark shadow over this pla—'

'What do you know, priestling?' Inanys cut scornfully through his words. 'What know ye of the Dark Shadow? Look to your own doorway if you would see what lingers here!'

At once Telsyan leapt to his feet, striding to the door and flinging it open wide. The startled figure of Guron was crouched there. He dropped a small piece of charcoal to the floor and ran off down the hallway. There was a strange, half-completed marking upon the outside of their door.

'It is a rune of summoning!' Uhlendof gasped. 'If he had completed it . . .' His voice trailed off into silence.

'Catch him, for goodness sake!' Telsyan shouted, leading on.

Yeon and Leighor quickly outdistanced the merchant as they pursued the fleeing Guron along the dark passage and thence up several winding flights of stairs. Guron was clearly not much used to such exercise, and they could hear his laboured breathing growing closer and closer ahead of them. Yeon was in front as they came out on to another narrow passage, and with a final spurt he managed to grasp hold of the trailing left arm of their quarry, hauling him roughly about to hit him hard beneath the ribs. Guron groaned as the force of the blow slammed him into the stone wall of the corridor. There was a dull moan, and Guron slid silently to the ground. It was all over by the time Leighor reached the scene, their quarry lying unconscious and bleeding on the cold stone floor.

'If you had been less violent we might have questioned him!' Leighor said angrily. 'Now we shall not have the time!'

'Let us rather explore his lair,' Yeon grinned. 'His chamber may be along the passage, since he was fleeing this way. I am sure that that will be of far more interest than anything he would have told us.' He bent to lift Guron's unconscious form smoothly up across his shoulders, and then led the way onward without a further word. Reluctantly Leighor followed.

'I was right,' Yeon hissed triumphantly as they came to a dead end at a closed door. 'This must be it.'

Leighor tried the handle and shook his head. 'It's locked.'

'Our friend will have the key,' Yeon said. 'Search his pockets.'

Leighor did so as Yeon held the body steady on his shoulders, at last finding a large key in one of the pockets of Guron's robes. It turned easily in the lock, and they entered. This room was far larger and better furnished than the one which all five of them shared below. Leighor secured the door behind them, turning to see Yeon fling Guron's body casually down on to the broad, silken-sheeted bed. Two ravens croaked hoarsely in a small cage by the window.

There was a locked cabinet in one corner of the chamber, and again Leighor sought through Guron's clothes for a key, eventually finding a ring of them in an inner pocket of his tunic, along with a strange scroll – just small enough to be borne by one of the waiting birds. It bore a written message of some sort, in a strange tongue that he could not decipher. Slipping it into his pocket for future reference, he rejoined Yeon, who was attempting to open the locked cabinet. When at last they found the right key, the door folded back silently to reveal three lines of ancient leatherbound books and several small glass vials containing potions. Leighor drew a deep breath. The potions were rare enough, expensive beyond most people's means, but the books were singular tomes indeed: volumes of summonings and old dark magicks, the mere possession of which would be enough to merit a stoning in most lands. They gave off an unsettling chill, a distinctive cold aura of evil, that even he could feel – and he was not usually sensitive to such things.

'Do not touch them!' he hissed urgently to Yeon. 'They are dangerous!'

'The books?' Yeon asked in surprise.

'Yes.'

'Then I shall examine the rest.' Yeon rifled quickly through the three small drawers below, but found nothing except a few crude sketches of strange runes and symbols, and copious notes on various aspects of higher alchemy. There was also a small silver mirror, hidden at the bottom of the drawer. He seemed disappointed.

'We have discovered very little,' he said gloomily.

'Enough,' said Leighor. 'We know that Guron practices dark magicks, whether with or without the approval of Githrim. Let us be content with that. Who knows what else we may stir up in this viper's nest.'

Guron groaned behind them, coming round.

'What shall we do?' Yeon asked. 'Shall we question him?'

'No,' Leighor shook his head quickly. 'We want no noise to alert the house.' He took a small vial from one of the cabinet shelves, examined it for a moment, and smiled. 'This will silence him for a while.'

'What is it?'

'A sleeping draught. Efficient and long lasting.' Leighor raised the half-conscious man's head slightly, forcing Guron to swallow a large part of the contents of the bottle. 'There,' he said, satisfied, letting Guron's head fall once more to the pillow. 'That should keep him in the land of shadows for many hours.' He replaced the bottle on the shelf and looked at the others wistfully. 'If only we had space to carry them, they might prove worth their weight in gold.' Finally he gave into temptation and selected a couple of the smaller vials, placing them in the pocket of his tunic.

'Leave everything else as it is,' he said at last. 'We shall lock the door from without. Let us depart.'

'It confirms my own suspicions,' said Uhlendof when they had returned and told their story. 'The rune, if successfully completed, might have drawn some pit demon down upon us as we slept.' He turned once more to Leighor. 'Where is this unreadable note you found?'

Leighor produced it from his pocket and handed it to the monk, who studied it closely for some minutes.

'It is very strange,' he announced finally. 'I thought that I knew all the forms of the ancient Qhilmun tongue, but this variant is new to me. It seems based on a lesser westron dialect; but it contains many odd constructions and words unknown to me.'

'Can you read it?' Telsyan demanded impatiently.

'Yes, to a certain extent; but I cannot derive the exact meaning of every word. It is a message of some sort, and it says either; "At full of moon", or "At dark of moon", I can't tell which. But anyway, at that time, "the friends of Korgul will empty" or is it "purify"? "Will purify the lands of . . ." he paused, holding the parchment up to the light of their single flickering oil lamp, and continued slowly, "the lands of *Gorzinosc* and – and renew? . . . Regain. Regain the ancient rights across the shores of *Uberezeg Ingur* from the taker"; or I suppose it could be "from the usurper." It finishes, "send news" and is signed "Master of the North".'

'What does it mean?' Yeon asked slowly.

'I do not know,' Uhlendof said. 'But the reference to a Master of the North might help explain it. It has long been known for the western nomads and the disparate Riever bands to unite occasionally around some great war leader. The Master of the North may be one such, and if that is so I would guess that this message refers in some way to a Riever raid; but as to where and when, I have no idea, the names referred to are unknown to me.'

'Then what is Guron's part in this?' Leighor asked, 'And Githrim's?'

'Guron at least must be in league with the Rievers,' Telsyan said bluntly. 'Whether Githrim is also, I cannot say; but this would be a very good place for one who trades with Rievers, buys the produce of their raids, supplies them with information and weapons.'

'We must leave at once!' Uhlendof said.

'There is nowhere we can go until daybreak,' Telsyan told them. 'This tower makes a good prison, one that we could not easily escape if Githrim did not wish it. And we know not whether the master knows of his pupil's works. Therefore we have a choice: we may either inform our host, Githrim, of all that has occurred, and trust to his innocence; or else we can try to leave at first light tomorrow as if nothing had happened – and hope to be well away from here before any of this night's work is uncovered.'

'I think we should adopt the latter course,' Leighor said quickly. 'I know not whether we can trust Githrim, or what he would do if he knew what we had learned this night.'

'You are right,' Uhlendof nodded. 'The risk is too great. Let Githrim think that we know nothing of Guron or his works until we are well away from here.'

The travellers found little rest for the remainder of the night, keeping constant vigil for the coming of daybreak as they talked in low voices of the tower and its secrets. When dawn came it was icy cold, as only the first hours before the sunrise can be cold. A freezing draught swept ominously through the stone corridors as the five finally emerged from their chamber.

It seemed, however, that nothing had yet been found amiss. Githrim's servants welcomed them cordially enough, serving them a generous breakfast before finally conducting them back down, via the swinging chain-lift, to the furnace hall below. Even so, Leighor did not breathe freely again until the great iron gate of the tower slammed firmly behind them, and they were out on the open, windswept flanks of Skerrdale once more.

Chapter Nine
HURKLING EDGE

It was noon before the five travellers were finally out of sight of Githrim's tower. Only then, having found a spot where they could keep watch on the road both before and behind, did they pause for the first time to rest.

'Do you think we are pursued?' Leighor asked, once he had regained his breath.

'I do not think so,' Telsyan replied thoughtfully. 'Even if he wished it, I doubt whether Githrim has the horses or the men to send chasing after us. I have more fears for the intentions of his friends.'

'You mean the "Friends of Korgul",' Leighor said.

'In part, though if Githrim truly wishes us harm, he may have other allies than the Riever bands. We must be on our guard.'

'Even so,' Uhlendof panted. 'I think we can afford to walk at a slightly slower pace now. We have a long way to go, and we cannot race all the way to Darien and back.'

'Slower?' Yeon grinned. 'I thought we had been dawdling all morning to let you watch the daisies grow!'

'You may laugh,' the monk snorted. 'But we'll see what happens when you grow to be my age! If you can walk as fast then as I do now, I'll be very surprised!'

'If you gave up that foul pipe of yours, it might help,' Telsyan smiled. 'Githrim's Tower is nothing to the stench caused by that thing! I thought a monk was not permitted such worldly pleasures.'

'If I did not count you a sinner beyond all hope of redemption,' Uhlendof countered, 'I might explain to you what it truly means to be a monk. But . . .'

At that moment a great black raven glided over the crest of a low hill to the south of them. It began to circle overhead, giving out an occasional hoarse caw as it eyed them cannily.

'Is it one of Guron's?' Yeon asked anxiously.

'What if it is?' said Telsyan, dismissing the question with a shrug.

'Shoot it in any case!' Uhlendof spoke more urgently. 'You yourself have just said that we know not what allies Githrim may have.'

'But a bird?'

'Don't argue!' The monk turned sharply to Leighor. 'Use your bow, and shoot quickly, before it has time to escape!'

Wordlessly Leighor obeyed. But the mechanism of the crossbow was still unfamiliar to him, and it was several moments before he managed to get the bolt home, the tension wound, and the weapon aimed. By this time the bird had gained height until it seemed little more than a fleeting speck against the grey clouds sweeping by above. Leighor steadied his aim and fired. The bolt whistled up towards its quarry, seeming on target – yet it missed. It was a near miss, but not close enough to do the bird any visible harm. It gave a startled squawk, then flapped its wings lazily to wheel away once again into the south. The bolt too was lost; he would never recover it amid the sea of rock and stones far below.

'Another failure, southlander,' Inanys' voice rose scathingly beside him. 'Surely there must be some small thing you can do well?'

'It was an easy shot!' Yeon stared after the vanishing bird in disgust. 'How could you miss?'

'That is of no moment now,' said Telsyan, stepping between them. 'Though I would advise you to keep your bow better primed in future.'

'The bird has surely seen us.' Uhlendof stared after it grimly.

'What difference does that make?' Telsyan shrugged. 'I doubt if even Githrim can talk to birds.'

'Speech is not necessary. It is quite possible for a trained adept to see through eyes other than his own – the eyes perhaps of a familiar.'

'Pah!' Telsyan made no effort to hide his scorn. 'These are child's tales! If we are to fear every blackbird that passes, we shall never leave this valley.'

'These things are more important than you know,' Uhlendof snapped. 'In time you will learn, and then you will cease to laugh.' The monk swung angrily away, to stride determinedly north along the stony roadway.

'I fear this is going to be a long journey,' Telsyan sighed, readjusting his heavy pack before turning to follow.

They did not halt again for many hours, finding it more advisable to eat and drink what little they bore with them while still on the move. The last of the sweet cakes bought in Ciltelder were shared out as they climbed steadily into the grim hills of the Uthrun Chain. The dale narrowed quickly as they rose, becoming steep and V-shaped, all trace of the lush lowland vegetation fast departing, to be replaced by scrawny upland plants more suited to the stony soil. The road, now little more than a track, clung precariously to the sheer eastern wall of Skerrdale, several hundred feet above the torrent that was the young River Nimbel. Leighor shivered. The plains of the Sielders had seemed cold and barren enough, but now they entered lands of utter desolation.

As the sun withdrew behind the western ranges, the travellers were still climbing into the folds of the darkening hills. The road coiled and twisted like a fallen ribbon upon the steep hillside, but now it showed clear signs of decay and disrepair, large falls of boulders and loose scree blocking the way and having to be edged around with care. The fells had been entirely deserted for some hours, and the travellers began to despair of ever finding shelter in this bare, desolate hill-country.

A light spattering of rain began to fall, quickly turning into a steady downpour: a continuous, debilitating rain that soaked the travellers through, turning the gritty soil of the hillside into a sodden sponge that precluded all thought of sleeping out in the open, even if the downpour ceased.

'What are we to do?' Yeon demanded at last. 'I'm soaked, frozen and tired. Is there nowhere we can rest?'

'Where do you suggest?' Telsyan snapped, pointing to the darkening hills all around. 'There is not shelter here even for a sparrow! We will just have to keep going, whether it be dark or no, until we find a suitable place to halt.'

'At least we can get no wetter than we are,' Uhlendof added. 'If we stop now to huddle behind some rock, we might half of us be dead of cold by morning.'

And so the party proceeded: in single file, and close enough together to guide one another through the dark. Yet it was a miserable journey, for the rainclouds blotted out the friendly light of moon and stars, and with no lamp to guide them they stumbled constantly over fallen rocks or the loose piles of scree and clinker that lay tumbled across the road.

Relief of a sort came much deeper into the night, when the rain finally ceased, and the heavy clouds rolled silently away into the west, leaving behind a thin crescent moon to light the scene. It shone dimly, with a pale, blue-white wanness that only made Leighor feel the colder. And still no hut, no cave, nor any other possible shelter came into view. The five travellers climbed steadily and mechanically, their conscious minds no longer heeding the pleading calls of their aching bodies, their very thoughts numbed with weariness. And so they passed on through the dark hours of the early morning. Dawn, when it finally came, found them still in territory very similar to that in which night had met them. Only the hills seemed higher, bleaker and stonier than before, and the road itself more like a presumptuous goat-trail than anything ever made by the hand of man.

Wearily the travellers continued northward, a red sun rising slowly above the gaunt ridges to their right. No words were spoken and none required as they toiled onward. They stopped but once, where a small stream cascaded down the steep hillside, to wash the sleep from their faces and to drink the cold fresh water. Only when the sun was high in the sky did they halt again, pausing to prepare a brief meal for themselves by the side of the road before moving on. By late afternoon their climb had carried them high above the ravine of the Nimbel, to bring them on to the softer, drier ground of the hilltops. And while there was little enough shelter even here, they were at least able when night came to make up fairly comfortable beds from the sun-dried bracken that grew all around them, and they slept well.

There were only a few poor journey biscuits left for their breakfast the following morning, and they ate in glum silence. It was bitterly cold; for even though the sun shone down from a clear blue sky, it was too late in the year for it to do much to temper the cutting north wind that scoured these heights. The travellers had no wish to linger here any longer than was necessary, and were soon once again on their way northward.

'It is hard to imagine,' Telsyan said as he picked his way through a tangle of trailing briar and loose scree, 'that this was once a well kept and busy trading route.'

'That is certainly hard to believe,' Leighor agreed. 'How long ago was all this?'

'But two centuries ago, no more: when North Felldur was still a productive and populated land.'

'And how come you to know of this?' asked Yeon.

Telsyan smiled. 'The merchants' guilds of Selethir have long records, which any aspirant to a Mastery of the Brotherhood did well to study. They record the profitable trade routes over many centuries past, the most beneficial dates for travel, the markets, and the prices achieved over every year since the founding of the guilds. North Felldur was once a very profitable place to do business, but it has not been so for many long years.'

'Do you have records for everywhere?' Yeon asked.

'As far north as Vliza, as far south as Mount Aerion, west to the tent cities of the Khiorim tribes, and east to the rim of the mountains, and great Oleiyor itself; everywhere the merchants from the guild have ever journeyed. It is information that many kings would give half their wealth for,' Telsyan told them with satisfaction.

'It is rumoured that most already have,' Inanys added.

'But what has caused the ruin of these lands?' Leighor asked. 'All this destruction?'

'Proximity to the northlands,' the merchant said briefly. 'All that we now term Felldur, from Hurkling Edge south to Holdar, was once only South Felldur. The dales of North Felldur run down to the Caethalon river and beyond, but these lie now abandoned. They proved too vulnerable to Riever attack and brigand raids. Many of their people were slain, and the rest fled to the safer lands of the south. Eventually the Varroain King of Holdar ran out of gold to pay his troops and, receiving no help from High King Shelasil in Tershelline, and only quarrels from the Imsild Knights, he recalled his levies in the Varroain year 588. You will shortly see what is left of North Felldur as a result, for we approach Hurkling Edge.'

Leighor looked up from the path to see that this was indeed so. They were now almost level with the bare hilltops, and had completely lost sight of the headwaters of the Nimbel far below. Ahead, the last trace of Skerrdale ended where the hills melded together to form a single high ridge that barred their way northward; his eyes could just pick out the track that snaked uneasily across the windblown moor. Dense banks of heather grew rankly to waist height and beyond, crowding in upon the narrow way, the dry tendrils of their roots gradually colonising the hard-packed earth and broken stone of the road. Yet these hardy plants now provided a heartening blaze of colour: a rich purple that belied the lateness of the season, sowing seeds of hope and optimism anew in the weary company.

In less than an hour they had reached the ridge. A small cairn stood, half-ruined, beside the road, a tiny shrine set to receive the votive offerings to some local wayfarers' deity. A single small vessel lay within, worked from thin, cracked pottery, any contents long since swept away by wind, sun and rain. The travellers passed without obeisance, and came at last upon Hurkling Edge.

It was as if a great chasm in the world had suddenly opened out before them. And where formerly their view had been limited to the few neighbouring hillsides, they now enjoyed a prospect so vast that it took their breath away, stretching unbroken for scores of leagues into the far blue distances of the north. Beneath them, the ground fell steeply away into a series of minor ridges and narrow, wooded valleys that ran northwards from the ridge. Their own road coiled down into the nearest of these, in a series of precipitous falls and sharp bends. Beyond lay an awe-inspiring vista of mile upon mile of thick, unbroken forest, shrouding the land in every direction as far as the eye could see. It smothered all in its path: plains, valleys, and ridge upon ridge of hills, flowing forever northward, it seemed. The only breaks that Leighor could see were the shimmering silver surfaces of lakes; some surely greater than any he had ever seen. For long minutes they could do nothing but stare in silence at the awesome sight before them.

'That is Hathanwild,' said Telsyan after some while. 'It has long since reclaimed North Felldur of the older days. Yet once one is within its fold, it is not perhaps as daunting as it first seems.'

'That I do not know,' said Leighor. 'But such a sight makes one wish only to turn back for civilised lands.'

'Aye,' Uhlendof nodded. 'Whole armies could be marching unseen through those dark forests.'

'Indeed they could,' answered the merchant. 'But that which would hide them, will hide us from prying eyes just as well.'

Inanys picked his way to a small boulder and sat down upon it, facing the party, his crooked stick clasped to his knees. 'This place is called Wiseman's Turning,' he informed them. 'For only men without hope enter the northlands – or fools!'

'We are not without hope,' Telsyan said firmly. 'And if you think us fools, you are free to leave our company whenever you wish – nothing holds you. We have good cause to travel here, although yours we know not. And for all that you caw like a hooded crow, I have been into the northlands more than once, and have returned safely.'

'Cocks crow, crows caw,' Inanys sang mockingly. 'The northlands stir, and he who once ruled would rule once more.'

'What does that mean?' Uhlendof asked sharply. 'What do you know of stirrings in the northlands?'

'Naught, my lords. Naught but the whispers of the north wind and the mutterings of the treetops.'

'Listen to him no more!' Telsyan turned away impatiently, beginning the descent. 'He babbles meaningless nonsense to deceive us all! Let him know that if he speaks again without my leave I shall personally toss him over this precipice, oath or no.'

Inanys bowed submissively, following on behind the rest of the company as they took the downward road.

'If one had good eyes,' Yeon began as they descended, 'one could surely see the whole way to Darien from here, I have no doubt.'

'You are wrong in that, my lad,' Uhlendof interrupted. 'For the world is round, and one cannot see more than a certain portion of it, however high one may be.'

'Do not lead your charge astray, Master Uhlendof,' Telsyan stepped in swiftly. 'That is an old fallacy, long discarded by men of intellect. The world is clearly flat. Why, even your compatriots, the Heliard priests, have recognised that. Why else do they build their citadel atop Mount Aerion, that from there they may see what passes in all the lands of the world?'

'The world is spherical in form,' Uhlendof repeated the Mallenian dogma precisely. 'It is the one pure shape. The living spark of the creator. That is truth absolute. Holy writ. Incontrovertible.'

Leighor shook his head. 'If that is so, why do we not all slide off as we journey northward?' Telsyan and Yeon smiled. 'And all the water run away to the bottom?'

'Because the creator wills it otherwise!' the monk said sharply. 'Look, here is your proof.' He halted, to point away into the north. 'If the world is flat, why can we not see Darien from here, and the seas to the east, and the islands beyond?'

'Ah!' Leighor pounced eagerly. 'That is your mistake. Among the learned of the south the explanation is well known, for it is the human eye itself that is at fault. It distorts the world so that a distant tree may look no larger than one's own thumbnail, if that thumbnail is held close to. It is all the more so with more distant things, so that they disappear from view entirely.'

Telsyan held one finger up to his eye and gazed at the surrounding hillsides. 'It is a convincing argument,' he admitted.

'It is stuff and nonsense!' said the priest angrily. Yet not knowing what else to say, he strode off down the hill on his own, leaving the others to make the rest of the way down into the dale in silence.

'This my map shows as Darkdale,' Telsyan announced as they approached the glowering line of forest that grew up to meet them from the valley floor. 'The stream that passes through it is known as Black Rill, and runs down into Lake Lan, or the Dark Lough, as it is better called, which lies upon the Caethalon, the river that we seek.'

'Why seek we the Caethalon?' Yeon demanded, 'Unless we follow Githrim's path! We have no reason to trust his word. Rather the opposite. Let us take the straight road north as we planned.'

'There is no straight road from this point,' Telsyan said wearily. 'King Culvar's Road is many leagues from here, and to reach it we must first find a crossing of the Caethalon. Even then, I grow increasing wary of the road. The northland roads are too open and exposed for lonely travellers in these lawless times. In that at least Githrim was correct. I would not like to travel such a road in time of trouble without a mounted escort at my back.'

'Could we not join with some protected caravan?' Leighor suggested.

The merchant shook his head. 'All trade to and from Darien is controlled by the Durian Knights, and there are few free caravans journeying north of Felldur in these days. We could go east and wait at Imball, which is a none too pleasant frontier village on the road, but that is many days out of our way, and we might have to wait until the spring for a party of knights going north. Even then the Knights of Dur will charge between five hundred and a thousand gold talents for their services – and such sums we do not have.'

'Then it seems we must travel alone,' said Uhlendof.

'And I would far rather we did that off the Great Way,' Telsyan responded.

They soon came down into the shade of the great trees at the valley bottom, their path wandering beside the gurgling brown waters of Black Rill. Tall stands of thick-boled pines clung to the valley walls, their branches meeting to form a high canopy that cut out the greater part of the daylight. So dense was the canopy that it seemed near to dusk even though it could actually be little past the second hour of the afternoon.

Now twenty yards appeared a goodly view – and there was little to see even then but the trail ahead, and occasionally the bubbling waters of Black Rill as it wended its way through the rooty forest floor. There was little undergrowth, and for a time the travellers trod a soft carpet of pine needles – thankful as much for the absence of the cutting winds of the high moor as for the ease to their feet. The scene was unchanging for the rest of the day, and they met nothing more threatening than the odd chattering squirrel. With their anxieties somewhat eased, the company made their first night's camp within the woods of Darkdale, building a small fire of fallen timbers, and sleeping on soft beds of pine needles beneath the sheltering trees.

They woke late, long after dawn, to discover that their camp had been visited during the night. Their well-ordered packs had been torn open and the contents scattered across the clearing. Clothes, pans, bowls and eating utensils lay everywhere. Someone had clearly gone through all their possessions in a great hurry.

'Many knives are gone,' said Uhlendof, making a quick tally of what had been lost. 'My small wood-axe, a leather belt, and much food.'

'This is all my fault.' Telsyan shook his head ruefully. 'I had fallen under the spell of this quiet dale and neglected to insist on proper precautions. I had not expected to have to set a watch on our first night out of Felldur. I shall not be so lax again.'

'The damage is already done!' Yeon snorted. 'Nearly all our remaining journey biscuits are gone. And had we not kept our weapons by us as we slept, we might have lost those as well!'

'Aye,' Uhlendof agreed. 'Who could it have been, to have come so close, yet left us all snoring and unharmed?'

'Goblins,' said Telsyan shortly, poking about the camp with a long stick. 'This bears all their signs, look!' He pointed. 'Here are their tracks, leading off into the forest. There can only have been two or three of them. They must have crept about the outskirts of our camp, afraid to waken us. These woods must be full of them! I would guess they have been following us since we came into the forest yesterday.'

The others drew about him in the exposed mud by the stream, to examine the tracks for themselves. They were of narrow bare feet: half the width, but almost all the length, of Leighor's own. A thin claw had indented the mud at the end of each long, bony toe.

'Shall we follow their trail?' Yeon asked eagerly.

'It would be of little use,' Telsyan shook his head. 'Forest goblins are a slippery lot, and these will be many leagues away by now, most likely over the hills and in the next dale. We could waste many days fruitlessly chasing after them. They were probably just scavengers, like most of their kind: stealing where they can, begging where they can't. I know goblins well. They are cowardly creatures, and will only attack if they are in far greater number. Even so, we have been very fortunate. Far worse can happen to the unwary in these northlands.'

The travellers set about re-ordering their scattered possessions in a depressed, watchful silence, conscious now of every slight movement and rustle in the forest around them. Leighor was glad only that although many of his medicines had been scattered, none seemed to be missing, the goblins clearly having found little they valued amongst his baggage.

Once all was ready, the somewhat demoralised group set off once again down the valley, with only a single small journey biscuit each to allay their hunger. Uhlendof estimated that they had but two days worth of journey biscuit left, which could be stretched to perhaps three or four days with judicious economy. Even with the aid of Leighor's bow and the monk's few fishhooks, living off the land would not be easy. They would have to conserve the little food they had for as long as they could.

The travellers journeyed for two days more through the hushed forests of Darkdale, keeping silent now, but for a few brief whispered words as they walked. Two of the party must now stand watch each night, dividing the hours of darkness between them. Yet all the while they remained within the valley, they met with no other living being.

It was late on the second day when they came finally out of Darkdale, the forest slowly beginning to thin as light poured into its depths from the north. In moments Black Rill was tumbling out of the dale before them, racing down through steeply sloping meadows to run into the vastest lake Leighor had ever seen. The warm light of the failing sun glinted off its surface in a million dazzling ripples of silver and gold, to dance with painful brilliance before their forest-dimmed eyes.

On the far side of the lake, a good three leagues distant, there rose a range of high, forested hills, now tinted red and gold by the autumnal sun. The trail they had followed thus far spilled down the slope to join a narrow, rutted track that ran along the lakeshore; to east and west the lake seemed to run on and on without limit.

'By my map,' Telsyan announced, 'this is termed Dark Lough, although it does not live up to its name today.'

'It will be dark enough by nightfall,' Inanys said cheerily.

'Shall we go down?' Leighor suggested, learning now to ignore the remarks of their stunted companion.

'No,' the merchant paused to remove his cap and scratch his balding head. 'On reflection I think it best to remain within the confines of the wood. A fire lit upon that lakeshore would be seen for a dozen leagues around come nightfall – and who knows what eyes lurk in these forests?'

They did as he said, building their small campfire within the shelter of the dark pines and setting watches as before. The following day they set off early, with rumbling bellies and complaining feet, to follow the shore of Dark Lough westwards. For much of the time they kept to the narrow, stony track that skirted the lake, but sometimes they would walk upon the long sandbanks at the lake's edge, which proved far softer on their feet. There was less need to keep silent now, since they were already in clear sight of any who might watch from the surrounding forests.

Somewhat after noon Uhlendof issued them all with a little more dry biscuit, to general groans of dismay.

'It is the only thing the goblins have left us,' he told them.

'Even they did not think it worth carrying such stale, hard biscuit over the mountains,' Yeon said bitterly.

Leighor asked for a little more, but Uhlendof shook his head. 'We must conserve our supplies to the limit, or we will end up going hungry. It is the best way.'

'But I have looked at Telsyan's map,' Leighor insisted, 'and it is only two days journey, maybe less, to the mines of Zumir.'

The monk was unmoved. 'And who knows what welcome we shall find there?' he demanded, re-securing the small pack which now held all their food. 'What if there is no one there, or if we are hastening to meet an army of goblins or Tarintarmen? No, let us keep our food until we know exactly what our prospects are.'

It was an argument that brooked no objection, and the travellers set off again hungry, reaching the western edge of the great lake by sundown. Here the dull waters of the River Caethalon eased their way gently eastward, to spill into the vast expanse of Dark Lough. The Caethalon was broad, at least a quarter of a mile across, flowing black and sluggish between thickly forested banks. The travellers traced its course westward, sleeping the night beneath a broad canopy of pines close to the water's edge. Again they set a watch, but the night passed undisturbed.

For most of the next day the track guided them westward along the southern bank of the Dark River. Occasionally it would turn inland for a while, to cut across a loop of the river or to avoid a patch of marshy ground. And it was during one of these brief detours that the travellers first came upon a party of goblins.

It was Leighor who saw them first. He had been walking somewhat ahead of the main group, and on rounding a gentle curve he was not surprised to see the broad sweep of the Caethalon once more before him. But there, just ahead, in the shadow of a great pine, was a party of goblins, busy at some unseen task at the water's edge. He turned swiftly to silence the others.

'What is it?' Telsyan whispered as they drew level.

The southron pointed.

'Goblins!' Uhlendof hissed. 'Do you suppose these are the same ones who . . .'

'I doubt it,' Telsyan whispered, drawing his sword. 'But let us approach quietly. Perhaps we may surprise them.'

The goblins seemed to be involved in some minor squabble of their own, not noticing the advancing company until it was almost too late. Leighor studied them with interest. Thin and spindly, yet unnervingly human, the tallest of them scarce came higher than his waist. They seemed half-starved, with small pot-bellies such as he had seen on hungry peasant children, and long, bony limbs that ended in tapering clawed fingers and toes. Their clothes, if they wore any at all, were tattered scraps of sacking and animal skins; ragged, torn, and caked with filth. Unlike the pale sand goblins, their warty skins were of many shades of green and yellow, running from sallow tan to olive green. This, combined with their large angular ears, splayed feet, and their total lack of head or body hair, gave them an amphibian air.

'Do not be misled by their size,' Telsyan hissed. 'They can be very dangerous.'

One of the goblins heard his voice and started up in surprise, hissing like a snake. His fellows turned as one, forgetting their quarrel to stand transfixed, staring in panic-stricken horror at the advancing group.

Yeon counted eight of them, gathered about the remains of a large river fish that looked to have been dead for many days. And suddenly the spell broke. As one, the goblins scrambled for their weapons, picking up staves, rocks and stone clubs from the ground beside them. Two or three of them had iron knives, and splintered and rusted as these were, they were wielded with a certain pride of possession. Yet they swiftly realised that the travellers were better armed.

Yeon and Telsyan stood ready with swords drawn, while Leighor clicked a quarrel into his crossbow. Even Uhlendof and Inanys bore heavy, workmanlike staves. The goblins looked slyly at one another, seeming to recognise that outright attack was a poor proposition, and that their line of escape was cut off.

'Humanss,' one of their number began. He spoke in a broken form of north Durian which could just be understood by most of the company. Yet his voice was slimy and sibilant: as slippery, Yeon thought, as he probably was. 'There iss no need fighting be. We are poor goblin men. Hungry goblin men. You have food, yess? Much food?'

'No.' Telsyan spoke loudly in the southern Durian of the Sielders. 'We have no food to give away! We have none for ourselves.'

'No food?' the other repeated disbelievingly. He turned to his fellows, speaking several words to them in an unknown tongue. They seemed to grow more agitated. 'Humanss musst not be sselfish,' he spoke to them again. 'You have no tasty meatss, no ssweet breadss? No appless?'

'No,' said Yeon. 'All we had was stolen – by goblins like you!'

'Why don't you tell them that we keep no watch, as well?' Telsyan hissed furiously.

'Poor goblin men do not ssteal!' the goblin shrieked in outrage. 'Goblin men ask for help, assk nicely. But you refuse. Call us thieffss! Perhaps now we become thieffss!' He shifted his jagged dagger threateningly in his hand, and the others began to move forward. 'If you have no food, give uss gold, ssilver, to buy food.'

For a moment Leighor thought they would have to fight, and then an idea came to him. 'I have something for you,' he said, slowly removing his pack and sorting through the contents.

The goblins lowered their weapons in renewed interest, while his own companions simply stood staring at him in something close to dumbfounded amazement. Quickly, so as not to lose their attention, Leighor ferreted out a small vial of iron-grey powder from amongst the several other items he had taken from Guron's chamber, pouring its contents deftly into the rear chamber of his tinderbox. Then, rapidly striking the flint, he turned and hurled the box into the midst of the assembled goblins.

There was a loud hissing sound as clouds of dark smoke billowed upward. Alarmed, the goblins scurried hurriedly back. But when nothing further seemed to happen, they began to inch forward once more towards the smoking metal object, harsh cries of anger rising in their throats. Leighor began to fear that his ruse had gone badly wrong. Then suddenly, with a blinding flash and two great explosive bangs, the powder ignited. The tinder box was blown apart in a shower of white sparks, and red hot shrapnel that shot through the clearing, burning and singeing every goblin it touched.

The goblins screamed – shrill and loud with pain and terror – dropping everything, even their precious weapons, in their panic-stricken flight from the clearing. Their cries could still be heard minutes later, as they fled southward into the depths of the forest.

'What in heaven was that?' Telsyan asked, his eyes wide with amazement.

'Just a Samaran flashpowder,' Leighor said dismissively. 'It has little known use, but it makes a loud bang when lit. It is a pity that that was the last of it. I had to use it all to be sure the noise was effective enough.'

'Aye, it was effective!' Yeon laughed. 'See how they ran!'

'In a way I feel a little sorry for them,' Uhlendof said.

'What?' Yeon's jaw dropped.

'It is hard for a goblin to lead a goodly life,' the monk said thoughtfully. 'If a goblin ever comes by anything of worth, there is always someone stronger to take it from him and drive him away. So do they exist, despised and friendless, on the edges of civilisation. Are you truly surprised they behave so?'

'I am surprised at you,' Telsyan said shortly, 'for giving voice to such witterings! Let us make haste to find some shelter before they gather the courage to attack us again!'

Chapter Ten
THE KEEP UPON SILENTWATER

Regretting only the loss of his precious tinderbox, Leighor re-ordered his possessions and secured his somewhat lightened pack across his back. His companions, meanwhile, set about the task of hurling the assorted clubs and knives dropped by the fleeing goblins into the murky waters of the Caethalon. Yeon was about to do the same with the fish when Uhlendof halted him.

'If that can give those creatures some sustenance,' he said, 'they are welcome.'

'Aye,' said Telsyan. 'If they are fed they will have less cause to follow us, or alert others to our presence. Without their weapons I do not think they will dare attack us.'

The travellers continued westward at a brisk pace, the road soon taking them once more away from the river and into dense pine forest, through which they journeyed for several leagues.

'We are a long way from the river,' said Uhlendof at length. 'Are you sure that we are on the right road?'

'There is none other,' the merchant said briskly. 'Yet we are right enough. If we could but glimpse beyond those trees we would see the land rising all around us. We will soon come upon the lake called Silentwater, and thus to the mines.'

'You do not know this,' Yeon said. 'You only follow Githrim's word.'

Telsyan made no reply, remaining silent until they had covered a further half league, and then pointing wordlessly to the right.

Here there was a break in the trees, where many had been cut down in times past, and the travellers saw now that for quite some time they had been walking close to the shore of another large lake. This was fully as broad as Dark Lough had been, but nowhere near so long from east to west. Its eastern shore was hidden by the inward curve of the lake, but it was clear from the convergence of the forested western hills that the far end of the lake in that direction could be no more than four or five miles distant. Nowhere could Leighor see where the waters of the Caethalon flowed into or out of this still, silent lake. There was not a single ripple on all its broad surface to mar the perfect reflection of the high hills and thick forests that skirted its waters.

The forest closed in on them again as they moved west, shielding the lake once more from their eyes. Now dark hills began to rise steeply to the south, hemming them in against the invisible lakeshore. Old rock-spills and piles of rotting timbers bore witness to the presence of disused mineworkings nearby and occasionally thin overgrown trails would branch off from their narrow track to climb into the hills.

The sun was failing fast, and the towering pines were already beginning to cast their cold shadows across the path. Telsyan shivered. They had been walking all day without rest, and had still to come upon human habitation. Perhaps Githrim had indeed misled them, and all the mineworkings lay long-abandoned . . . Yet he did not choose to share his worries with the others, who now seemed to be resigning themselves to spending another cold and hungry night in the open.

Then, without warning, the dense wall of forest broke once more, to reveal the apparent end to all their travails.

Leighor drew a sharp breath. There before them, in the middle of a large open clearing, stood a secure, civilised, stonebuilt castle. Not large and grand like those of Istlass and Biren, capable of holding off an entire army for many months: this was in fact little more than a keep raised up in the northern style, a fortified hall built across its own thick outer walls, which formed two large defended courtyards, before and behind. A single gateway penetrated the roadward wall of the southern courtyard, the northern court extending a fair distance out into the lake. The whinnying of horses and the sounds of working men carried across to them. A large yellow flag fluttered lazily behind thin columns of smoke, making stark contrast with the iron-grey slate of the keep roof.

'What banner is that?' Yeon asked anxiously.

Uhlendof studied it for a moment. 'It is the banner of the kings of Helietrim,' he answered at last. 'The banner of King Arminor. Again Githrim has spoken true.'

'Aye,' said Telsyan impassively, as Yeon started forward. 'But hold! Do not run towards the gates. This is hostile country and we must move slowly and openly, to show that we mean no harm – else we are as like as not to be welcomed with a hail of arrows.'

They did as the merchant advised, yet heard no challenge as they approached. Iron-studded gates lay casually ajar to reveal the open courtyard beyond. It was only when Telsyan made to step through into the courtyard itself that a loud voice rang out.

'Who dares approach the keep of Silentwater?' A stout, greying figure emerged from the gatehouse at the base of the guard tower to stand before them, broad arms folded across a broader chest.

'None but five weary travellers,' Telsyan replied, 'seeking the shelter of your hall and the hospitality of your most noble lord.'

'Few honest travellers journey these regions,' the gatekeeper snorted. 'What is your business here?'

'We are from the south, and bear important messages to Darien upon the safest route – which we are told is no longer the Great Road.'

'Aye, I suppose that is true enough,' the other admitted. 'But if you are to rest here, you must first speak with my lord.'

He turned to lead them through the courtyard. Here were stables, workshops and storerooms in abundance: low, makeshift buildings, set into the outer walls, their upper storeys occupied by long dormitories for the guards, grooms and serving men. Across the northern side of the courtyard rose the main hall: of greater age than the rest, and built to a far grander scale. Like the surrounding buildings, it had only two storeys, yet these raised it to nearly twice their height. Great dark windows glowered beneath a sloping roof, above which floated the yellow banner of King Arminor. Two stumpy refuge towers rose up to east and west.

The company waited in the dusty courtyard, enduring the stares of the grooms and servants until the Hall Steward finally appeared. He was tall and of middle years, bearing upon his face the full burden of his weighty responsibility for the smooth running of the keep and its lands. He wore rich robes of black and green, his silver chain of office displayed prominently against them.

'I am Nalmuth,' he announced briskly. 'You are the strangers who seek the hospitality of my lord Fralcel?' It was a question.

'That is so.' Telsyan nodded.

'Then you must have audience.' Nalmuth began to turn away. 'I shall make arrangements for my lord to receive you in the main hall . . .'

'There is no need,' a cultured voice rang down from above. The travellers looked up at once. The courtly figure of a man in his mid thirties stood upon the small stone balcony that overlooked the outer courtyard. Beside him stood a lady much shorter than he, and some years younger. Both were dressed richly, in red and grey damasks of the latest fashion.

'My Lord Fralcel?' Telsyan asked, bowing.

The other travellers deemed it wise to follow suit.

'I am Lord Fralcel, yes. And this is my lady, Gwildé. What do you wish of me?'

'We seek only shelter for a night or two,' Telsyan answered. 'And perhaps to purchase some provisions for our onward journey.'

'You seek my hospitality then.' Fralcel turned quickly to his wife and whispered in a voice that all could hear: 'Why must every vagrant who walks the roads expect bed and board at my expense?'

'It is the custom,' Gwildé said gently.

'Like many that must soon change,' Fralcel hissed. He turned back to the travellers once more. 'Yet I suppose I must do my duty, and bid you welcome to my house and table.' He turned and swept briskly into the inner chamber. Gwildé followed.

'He treats us like beggars!' Yeon hissed with fury. 'He dishonours us . . .'

'Be silent!' Telsyan growled at once. 'We are Lord Fralcel's guests now, even if it was done with bad grace.'

'There is much on my lord's mind,' Nalmuth apologised. 'I shall conduct you to your lodgings.'

They were taken from the outer courtyard to the inner by means of a broad passage that ran through the main building. The northern court was far quieter than the other, for this was where dwelt the higher retainers of the keep. Here too were the guest chambers located, in low cottages built into the far wall, facing the main hall. A walkway ran along the outer walls above the level of these lodging houses, and above this rose two squat corner towers that overlooked the invisible waters of the lake.

Nalmuth bade two servants conduct the travellers to rooms in the guesthouse. Leighor and Uhlendof shared one of the lower rooms, Telsyan and

Yeon were lodged on the upper floor, while Inanys had the honour of a chamber to himself. All the rooms were identical; small and clean with two narrow beds each and a large chest for their possessions. But otherwise they were completely bare, and extremely cold.

Leighor unpacked his possessions, looking hopefully at the empty fireplace set into one wall. But no one appeared with fuel or kindling to light it, and he soon recognised that no one would. A rusting iron shutter closed off an opening in the outer wall. Curious, Leighor prised it open to reveal a small arrow-slit window that looked out over the darkening waters of the lake. It was too narrow for anyone – even a goblin – to pass through, but admitted a surprisingly chill night breeze. He slammed the shutter and fastened it securely, suddenly reminded of his experience beside another still, dark lake, up on the Grey Fells between Cleafedale and the sea.

There were near forty people seated within the great hall when the travellers entered. Seydal, the Hall Marshal, stepped forward at once to conduct the newcomers to seats at the high table, where Lord Fralcel and his lady, Gwildé, presided over the company. The seating was rigidly ordered, although all ranks still seemed to eat together after the old fashion. To the right sat the grooms, craftsmen, and those servants not actually engaged in the cooking or the serving of the meal. To the left, the squires, mercenary guards and craft-masters sat together.

'You are somewhat late,' Fralcel rose to greet them as they approached. And as he rose, so too did the whole company, creating a scene of tense silence as the five were ushered to their places.

'Be seated,' Fralcel commanded. 'You have missed little. The main part of the meal is yet to come.'

As they took their seats, Gwildé introduced them to their other companions at the high table: Birash, Almanar and Uldain, the three knights in Fralcel's service; Claighar, commander of the mercenaries; Duruldun, a priest of Thall, the Varroain warrior god; the Steward, Nalmuth; and finally Kereg Indur, master of the mines.

Seydal tapped his wand of office on the floor, and at once a large roast was borne in by two straining scullions. Three servants waited upon the needs of Fralcel and Gwildé alone. The remaining diners were attended to after a fashion by various other yellow-liveried servitors who stood about the hall.

A great iron brazier burned with ferocious heat between the tables, its smoke swirling up twenty or thirty feet into the great dark vault of the roof, where it lurked broodingly amongst the rafters. Even so, the air beneath was a haze of wisping, curling smoke, augmented constantly by the dozens of smouldering torches and flickering candles that lit the great hall. The murk made it hard to discern the galleries above, or even the devices upon the many old and faded banners that hung over the long tables, each bearing the emblem of a previous governor of Silentwater.

Gwildé was speaking again: '. . . this is one of my serving women: Keran is her name, and she will wait upon you whilst you are in the hall.'

Leighor looked around, to see a tall, big-boned girl standing uneasily behind him, bearing a jug of wine for the travellers' goblets. She seemed rather shy and withdrawn, and could not have been much beyond her twentieth year, although Leighor guessed her to be almost as tall as he. Her hair was thick and dark, constrained to shoulder height by a loose, spidery hairnet; she wore a simple skirt and a long-sleeved bodice of the same dull yellow sported by the rest of the servitors at the high table.

'Well, strangers, what news do you bring with you from the south?' Fralcel asked amiably.

'There is much that you may not have heard, my lord,' Telsyan answered. 'There is the grave news of the death of Archbaron Eridar of the Sielders. News that we now bear north to Darien.'

'Lord Eridar is dead?' Fralcel's knife stopped halfway to his mouth. 'That is ill news indeed. We have only recently heard news of the death of the High King himself – and now this! Tell me: how came Lord Eridar to die?'

Telsyan explained in some detail the story of Eridar's death and the suspicion that it had been murder, although he did not choose to reveal the present company's role in those events, going on to speak of the rise of Darvir to power in the Sielders.

'Darvir,' Fralcel said, without inflection, looking first to the three knights and then to his wife. 'I fear that this will not be good news for my liege, King Arminor, for it is well known that Darvir is a supporter of King Misan of Petan, and so will cast the Sielder vote for his master.'

Leighor wondered whether any of the company would take the chance of revealing the true secret of their errand, and what they bore to Darien. But if that thought passed through any of their minds, none acted upon it, and there was silence.

'If this news is true,' Uldain pondered thoughtfully from behind a goblet of wine, 'then the election is over, and Misan will be High King.'

'There are still the votes of Selethir unaccounted for,' Gwildé suggested.

'They will fall to the strongest party, as always,' Fralcel snorted. 'I fear that we must resign ourselves to the stewardship of Misan. Yet that mayhap need not be all for ill. King Misan would be a powerful overlord, and might unite all the scattered kingdoms into something stronger than they have ever been. If so, he has oft stated that he will not cling to the old ways; the ancient restrictions which Arminor, though he be a goodly king, still holds to out of excessive love for the past.'

'What restrictions are these?' Yeon asked.

'Oho, my lad,' Fralcel laughed. 'You would have me talk till cockcrow were I to number them all! I hold a few lands in the Lee of Clanamel, as do many of the noblemen of Helietrim. Rich and fruitful they are, but I have little profit from them, for more than half are tilled by thieves and idlers, who possess them in perpetuity in return for a few days labour, or a bushel or two of grain. They could be better ordered, better farmed, but Arminor forbids it. I may not farm them myself, nor fence in my own commons, but must leave them fallow for every idler within twenty leagues who pleases to graze his pigs and goats. Yet when there is a poor harvest I am expected to feed the entire vale at my expense.'

'But surely,' Uhlendof said, 'the ownership of land carries with it duties as well as benefits?'

'You talk just like Arminor and old King Galdan,' Fralcel sighed. 'Yet why can a man not do as he pleases with his own lands? I hold the title to much rich land, but for all the use it is to me I might burn the deeds tomorrow with little loss. These are new times, and things must be ordered in new ways – as they are now in Holdar and much of Felldur.'

'But we have passed through many of these lands on our journey north,' Uhlendof said, 'and have seen much poverty and bitterness there.'

'I too have heard of this,' said Gwildé. 'There are many abroad now with no lands and no ties. Do you not fear they may turn to ill works, or take up arms against us?'

'It will go hard with them if they do,' Fralcel growled. 'It is not my business to find a living for all men. There is much new land to be settled in the north, armies needed in the west. People are needed for many tasks – not just to lie idle in the central kingdoms.'

'Must men then leave their homes, their families, the countries of their birth – ' Uhlendof began.

Fralcel laughed, 'Like all your kind, you overdramatise, priest. No. In this matter Misan is right. Progress can be held back no longer. A landholder must regain authority over all he owns; and men must learn to obey their lords, not give them cares and quarrels.'

'That is very fine,' Inanys's sibilant voice rang out across the table, and Leighor shuddered, expecting trouble. 'Yet you seem not too greatly discomforted in your present beggary, my lord.' The crookback waved a scrawny hand across the fine plate and furnishings of the table. 'Could any man desire more than this?'

'Do you dare judge me?' A hard edge of anger cut through Fralcel's voice. 'I need not justify myself to you, nor to anyone! I will have only what is rightfully mine under the law: the freedom to do as I will in my own lands!'

'Certainly,' Inanys said pleasantly. 'For did not the first thief invent the law, to protect the fruits of his labours from others of like mind?'

Fralcel's face froze, and an awful silence descended upon the hall. The distant shouts and curses of the kitchen scullions across the way seemed now to dominate the whole chamber.

'I apologise for our companion, my lord,' Telsyan said, breaking the silence abruptly. 'His mind is run somewhat astray and turned to spite. He takes pleasure in angering his betters. We keep him with us only out of pity.'

'Take care then, that your pity does not soon give you cause for regret,' Fralcel snapped. 'If your friend were not protected by the rules of hospitality, he would swiftly learn the reward of one who names me thief within my own hall! Even so, the more I think upon it, the more these words seem a slur against all law and all nobility – a matter more perhaps of treason than of etiquette—'

'Nay, my lord,' Gwildé said quickly. 'If his brain is addled, he is a fool; and you cannot hold a fool's words against him.'

'Perhaps so – but I suspect there is more than the fool to that one. There is something evil about him, which I like not!'

'I think it might be better if we withdrew,' Uhlendof said, rising. 'If, by our conduct, we have angered you . . .'

'No, no,' Fralcel waved him back to his seat. 'Let no one doubt the hospitality of Lord Fralcel and his lady. The crookback must go – it is not fitting that a man of rank should sup with such – but you may stay.'

Telsyan nodded. Inanys gave a low and solemn bow as he was conducted from the hall.

'This has put me in an evil humour,' Fralcel grunted. 'Let there be music!' He clapped his hands twice, and at once three musicians appeared on the main gallery above. Barely visible through the thick smoke, they set to playing pretty melodies on the lute and pipes. One man sang in a high clear voice that carried to every corner of the hall; songs of the hunt and of battles long past, of lost loves and errant knights, so that soon the whole hall was lost in thrall to the music.

When the singer could sing no more, the musicians still played, but more softly; and the hall returned to talk. But neither Fralcel nor Gwildé were in much mood for further conversation that night. Fralcel soon rose, and wishing his guests a cold goodnight, turned to leave the hall with Gwildé on his arm.

'I am afraid our welcome here will be very short,' Uhlendof whispered as the travellers too prepared to leave. 'We had best seek what aid and information we can tomorrow, and then depart.'

But Telsyan shook his head. 'That is too soon. If we are to prepare properly we will not be ready before midday, and that will be too late to start out. We must stay one night further. Even in his present mood, Fralcel will not be able to deny us that.'

The dark castle stones seemed to retain and concentrate the cold, so that to Leighor, the night in their small guest chamber felt colder than many he had spent out of doors. He was not sorry, therefore, when first light finally came, and it was time to rise. Unbarring the tiny shutter, he looked out across the lake through the slim gap of the arrowslit. The morning mist was just beginning to rise, and a butter-coloured sun cast its first weak rays on to the still water. Three white swans passed slowly by, close to the castle wall, and in the distance the awakening forests sang with life.

'These northlands do not seem quite so terrible once one is within them,' he noted at last.

'These forests may look beautiful when the sun shines upon them,' Uhlendof said grimly. 'But it is all illusion. There are few places in this world I would sooner avoid.' He shook his head bitterly. 'These lands stink of death.' He too had now risen, and was preparing to step out of their small chamber when Telsyan and Yeon burst in.

'Our friend is missing!' the merchant announced with irritation.

'Inanys?' Uhlendof looked concerned.

'Aye, he is gone from his chamber, and no one in the keep seems to have seen hide nor hair of him since he left the banquet.'

'He will be about somewhere,' Leighor shrugged.

'I am not so sure,' Uhlendof said thoughtfully. 'Perhaps he was fearful after last night's harsh words, and has fled the castle.'

Yeon snorted. 'If so, then good riddance! He cared little enough for our safety. Let him travel his own road.'

'Perhaps,' Telsyan agreed. 'Yet questions could be asked were we to arrive as five and depart but four. If he does not reappear by this evening, we must inform Nalmuth at least. Meanwhile, let us see what we can do about some breakfast.'

They soon discovered that warm gruel and cold meats were available to all from the kitchens, along with mulled ale or cider to wash it down. Once they had satisfied their hunger, however, the travellers had little else to do but set about preparing themselves for their onward venture. Uhlendof sought out the steward, to negotiate the purchase of provisions and such additional equipment as could be spared. The others attended to their packs and possessions before seeking aid and information from the keep's less exalted inhabitants.

They quickly discovered that most of Fralcel's servants and fighting men had come with him from the south, and that none could tell them of paths to the north, or of what they could expect to find beyond the far edges of Silentwater.

'You must speak to the men of the mines,' Joephar the armourer told them. 'Only they know of these things. Here in the keep there are only two such: Kereg Indur, Master of the Mines, who came north only a few months before my lord Fralcel; and one who I think is named Haflas, who brings the weekly tally of the workings – but he is not due from the western mines until tomorrow eve.'

'I think we shall have to go west to the mines tomorrow anyway,' Telsyan admitted as midday approached. 'It seems that much of our time here has been wasted.'

'Not entirely wasted,' said Uhlendof. 'We have much good food, and have gained a much-needed rest. And if we cannot cross the lake, we will have to go west or return east. Why not west to the mines?'

'I had preferred that we take a boat across the lake from here,' said Telsyan. 'The lake is broad, but at least it is calm and smooth. The river Caethalon may be much harder to cross farther upstream, even with a good boat. There may be strong currents that will sweep us far from where we wish to go.'

Most of the men of the keep were now busy at their respective tasks; some moving stores and ale barrels, others engaged in cleaning and minor repairs. Two of the mercenaries stood guard above the main gate, watching the rest engage in some half-hearted weapons drill upon the open grass outside. Neither Fralcel, Gwildé, nor any of their knights, were in evidence; and since the travellers had not been invited into the great hall, they decided to go out and eat their midday bread and cheese by the lakeshore. Here they sat in the warm sun, sharing the open meadow with a cow, two tethered goats and some scratching chickens. They lay back, idly watching the women tending the kitchen garden beneath the walls. Unused to the luxury of such a long respite from the rigours of the march, the four companions lingered by the water until the chill evening breeze began to make their sojourn there unpleasant.

They were met on their way back to the gate by Duruldun, the dark-robed priest of Thall, who had been gathering fungi in the forest. He seemed more inclined to conversation now than he had been the night before, and he looked worried.

'The forest disturbs me today,' he told them briskly. 'I have seldom seen it so silent and lifeless as it has been this afternoon. It is almost as if something has frightened all the animals and birds away. I quite fear for Lord Fralcel.'

'Why? Is he out in the forest?' Leighor asked.

'Yes. He rode out at daybreak with two of his knights. I know not for what purpose.'

'Perhaps it was to hunt,' Yeon suggested.

'Nay, my lord likes to make his hunting a merry affair, with many horns and beaters, and a pavilion for meat and wine at midday. No, this was no hunting party. He has ridden out in this manner several times over the past few weeks. There are rumours among the men that he rides out to meet with someone in the forest, but that is just keep tattle. He most likely goes out just to take the air, or to talk with his knights in private.'

'And what are the mushrooms for?' Yeon asked suddenly.

'These are no mushrooms,' the cleric smiled. 'They are quite deadly. I use them for the making of incense and holy oil.'

'Do they have any medicinal properties?' Leighor asked.

'None.' Duruldun shook his head. 'None that I know of, anyway. They are extremely dangerous and reserved to Thall.' They had now reached the southern courtyard, and the cleric bade them a distracted farewell as he hurried off to his small chapel set into the outer wall.

Lord Fralcel returned some minutes later, while the travellers were still in the outer courtyard. He gave no sign of having seen them, dismounting with his two knights to stride briskly up into the hall without the slightest acknowledgement of their presence. Yet apart from this, he seemed not ill at ease, and fairly cheerful.

It was some time later when Lady Gwildé's fief maid, Keran, came to summon them to their evening meal. She no longer wore the yellow livery of the previous night, but a simpler dress of deep wine red. Her hair, now unbound, was long, straight, and darkest brown. 'My lord and lady will not be dining in the hall this night,' she announced with a nervous smile. Her face, seen now clearly, unshrouded by the brazier's smoke, was strong yet quite fetching; faintly freckled, with deep green eyes. 'On days when custom does not require their presence, they prefer to take their meals in their private apartments. Folk say it is the new fashion in the south to dine alone, so please do not think yourselves slighted.'

'You are not of the south?' Telsyan asked.

'Nay, my lord. I am from Darien, to the north.'

'Darien!' Telsyan said in surprise. 'That is where we are bound, and we need a safe route north through the forests. Can you perhaps tell us the best way from here that is both quick and safe?'

'I am sorry, my lord,' she shook her head. 'I know no more than these others. From Darien I was taken direct to Helietrim, by way of the Ormul River, and across the mountains. I came here from the south, in the train of my lady Gwildé.'

'And could we get to Darien that way?' the merchant asked quickly. 'If we followed the Caethalon far enough west, could we not perhaps reach the source of the Ormul, and sail down it to Darien?'

'No,' Keran shook her head once more. 'One cannot reach the Ormul from here. There are no roads west of the mines, and no boat could survive the rapids of the Caethalon. There are hundreds of miles of trackless forest between here and the river's source, and even after that, you would still have to find a way across the great swamp of Grimmerfen before you came to the Ormul.'

'Ah well, no matter,' Telsyan said, disappointed. 'We will find a way.'

The girl seated them this time at one of the lower tables, amongst the squires and mercenaries. 'The high table is not used unless my lord is present,' she explained hurriedly. But even Yeon appeared not to notice the slight.

The hall was noisier and less organised now, in its informal state, without Steward or Hall Marshal. No musicians played from the gallery, and liveries were not worn. Salt beef was served with boiled tubers, or else cold venison if this was more to the diners' taste; and to drink, only mulled ale, from goblets of pewter.

The girl, Keran, brought the travellers their meat and ale. 'It is a strange time to be travelling north, my lords,' she ventured. 'In one month, maybe two, winter will be here, and none will dare to travel. The northern winters are hard indeed – deadly to those who have no experience of them. Surely, sirs, you would do better to save your business until the spring?'

'Our business is most urgent, girl,' said Uhlendof softly. 'It cannot wait. We must be in Darien and back again before winter falls.'

She shook her head. 'Such a double journey cannot be made so late in the year. It may seem mild and pleasant now – that is how the northland deceives strangers. But winter strikes suddenly, like a serpent, as many an unwary traveller has found to his cost.'

'It is all right, lass,' Telsyan said swiftly. 'I am a merchant, and have travelled these northlands for many years. Do not worry yourself on our account. Go now. You have done enough for us this night. The hall grows rowdy, and you should be away to your chamber. We shall ourselves retire soon.'

'Thank you, my lords,' Keran made a half curtsey and withdrew, leaving the hall to climb the steps to the gallery above.

The gallery ran along two sides of the hall, connecting Fralcel's apartments to the west with those of Lady Gwildé that lay in the eastern half of the building. She looked down from its shadows to see again the mysterious strangers below. Already they were the talk of the keep, but none had so far been able to divine their true business here so late in the year. And now they were leaving on the morrow. A pity. She doubted that they would make their two way journey before the snows came. Yet, barring accidents, these strangers would now see Darien before her, and they would probably be disappointed with what they found. For her, Darien held little enough in real terms, but it was the only place she had ever known a home; and there still dwelt her father and her sister . . .

There was a sudden rustle of silks beside her. Someone had drawn near without her realising it, and now stood at her side.

She looked up irritably to see that it was Claighar, captain of the mercenary guard. She shuddered. She did not know why – by all accounts she should be flattered by his attentions – but she was repelled by him in a way she did not fully understand.

'So I have caught you at last,' he began. 'And in such a pleasant spot. Dark and quiet, so we need not be disturbed.'

Keran tried to edge her way past him, but he blocked her movement, crowding her against the wall. 'Please, my lord,' she said, straining to keep her voice level. 'I must attend my lady!'

'She can wait on you awhile, my girl,' Claighar smiled. 'She has two other fine ladies to attend her, and that is enough. Let us speak of other things. The winter nights will be long and cold; shall we not share a few of them together? There will be many changes here shortly. Aye, very shortly; and I may then have need of my own lady – so you would do well to be a little friendlier towards me now.' His arms encircled her.

'Nay, my lord!' Keran's mind raced uncertainly, searching for an inoffensive way out of his embrace. 'I am promised . . .' she lied.

'To whom, girl?' Claighar's voice grew suddenly cold and angry, and his arms tightened about her body, the iron-grey amulet he always wore pressing hard into her chest. 'Lie not to me, lass! To whom would you be promised, a common beggar whelp out of the northlands? I do you honour, girl. I am the best that you will ever get!'

Keran tried to call out, but the mercenary captain's lips were hard against hers, smothering her cries. She felt herself forced tight into a dark corner of the gallery, the muffled sounds of their struggle completely unheard by the noisy throng upon the floor of the hall below. Claighar's strong fingers began to tear away her linen dress, ripping the shoulder from the bodice. Only then was she finally able to wrench her right arm free, dashing it to her waist to grasp the hilt of the sharp knife that she always kept hidden there, beneath the folds of her skirt. In an instant she had it free of its leather sheath, edging it slowly to the base of Claighar's neck, pressing the point home until it drew a thin trickle of blood.

The captain's head drew back in shock, all ardour vanishing instantly.

'Move not a muscle,' she whispered, 'or I drive the point home.' She held the blade firm and steady now, resolute. She believed she had the will to attempt the deed if she had to.

'Damn you, girl!' Claighar hissed. 'There is no need for that. It is only harmless merriment I want with you.' But his lip trembled, and Keran knew that he was uncertain what she was capable of.

Slowly she forced him away to arm's length, keeping his chin high as she had been taught. 'Keep your arms to your side,' she ordered. And Claighar obeyed. She held him thus for some moments before releasing him, yet still she held her dagger ready before her. 'Go now,' she commanded suddenly, 'and come no closer to me, or I shall scream and shall not cease until the whole castle is here!'

Claighar wiped the thin streak of blood from his neck with the back of his hand. 'I shall go now,' he said grimly. 'I have more urgent business elsewhere. But there will be time enough to resume our business later on: and then there shall be full reckoning.' He spat, turning on his heel to stride away along the gallery and down the stair.

Keran let out a deep sigh of relief, breathing out, it seemed, for the first time since she had drawn the dagger. She crouched, shivering, in her dark corner. Why had she not cried out and roused the castle as soon as she was free? She did not know. In some way it would all have been too shaming: to have called out, and let all see her humiliation. But what was she to do now? Complain to Gwildé? Yet these were serious charges, and Claighar would surely deny them, or plead enticement. Who then would believe her? Either way there would be great trouble. How had Claighar dared? Perhaps it was the ale . . . But she had smelt none on his breath. He must have little fear of retribution to threaten her so. What if he had done this many times? Again she shuddered.

Slowly, she rose, to make her way down the small passage that led to Gwildé apartments, pausing outside the door in an agony of indecision. Should she knock and enter, or pass on? A sudden movement in the passage behind decided her. She ran on, up the narrow stair, to the chamber in the east tower that she shared with Gwildé's two other women. She would stay here and rest and think, and then decide. Yes, perhaps tomorrow she would decide what to do.

Few now remained in the hall below, although the travellers still lingered, discussing the morrow's journey. Two huntsmen and five serving men played cards at the next table and, along from where the travellers sat, the four remaining mercenaries were engaged in a tournament of arm wrestling. Yeon, growing bored with his companions' talk, crossed over to them and engaged in their contest – with much success. Silver changed hands and a small crowd began to gather. By the time the last mercenary fist had been forced down into the hard oak of the table by a perspiring Yeon, he had amassed quite a substantial sum in silver coin, which the guardsmen were loath to lose.

'You have not yet met our champion,' one of them said, as Yeon prepared to rise.

'And who may he be?' Yeon demanded.

'One Zindur, who stands guard now at the gate. We shall send someone at once to fetch him.'

'There is no need,' a deep voice boomed from the doorway behind them. 'I am already here. Captain Claighar has just relieved me. He says he cannot sleep, and wishes to stand watch himself awhile.'

The man who spoke was easily the largest of the mercenaries, standing nearly as tall as Yeon himself, but much broader. He bore a battered iron helmet in one hand, and a large axe across his back. A heavy coat of chainmail covered a short-sleeved leather jerkin and dark breeches. His limbs were heavy and muscular, a wide grin passing across his broad, red-bearded face when he saw his opponent.

Yet the contest proved less easy that he expected. Yeon's arm held rock steady against the larger man's initial onslaught; and Zindur's smile froze quickly into a fierce grimace of effort, his arm shuddering and shaking as he strained to end the contest. Beads of perspiration broke upon the brows of both combatants, and their breath began to come in deep, raking gasps.

After a month in the boy's company, Leighor was no longer surprised that Yeon was able to survive for so long against the much larger man. The fierce intensity that Yeon put into even this small contest was daunting. It was as if the sheer force of his will, of his single-minded determination not to be defeated, was enough of itself against the mercenary's greater strength. His face contorting itself into a fearful grimace, Yeon summoned up one last great surge of effort; and to gasps of astonishment from about the table, his arm began incredibly to inch its way forward, driving Zindur's before it. But it was not to be. Slowly but surely the larger man began to prevail, and Yeon's wrist swayed slowly back towards the table; he resisting with all his force until the last, inevitable, moment.

'If I had been fresh I might have beaten you!' Yeon accepted his defeat with a minimum of grace.

Zindur smiled. 'You did well indeed, lad. Few men full grown have held me so long. Where did you get such strength?'

Yeon said nothing, but drew back the sleeve of his tunic to display an impressively muscular arm.

'To bear a stout blade,' he stated, 'one needs a strong arm. Such is the duty of a warrior of the Varroain.'

'Aye,' Zindur nodded, looking about him. 'That is true enough. But come. The hour grows late. What say I use these few coins to treat you all to some decent ale?'

The travellers could not avoid his invitation, and soon found themselves crossing the outer courtyard in the company of Zindur and the other four mercenaries, towards the small brewhouse built into the eastern wall. The cellarer, Geltan, did not seem overjoyed to see them all at this late hour, but his attitude changed when he saw the pile of coins Zindur bore, and he sat them down at a long table between the ale-barrels.

'The court is pitch black this night,' he said, shutting and bolting the outer door. 'I like not these moonless nights.'

'Is it dark of moon already?' Uhlendof said, somewhat strangely. 'I had not noticed.'

'Aye,' Geltan nodded. 'No moon this night, or the next.'

The priest looked up suddenly. 'This lake,' he asked, 'is it called only Silentwater? It has no other name?'

Leighor wondered what Uhlendof was talking about. Perhaps the monk had less capacity for ale than he had imagined.

'I know not,' said Zindur. 'To me this lake is only Silentwater. What of you, Master Geltan, have you heard of any other names for this stretch of water?'

'All these northron lakes have many names,' the cellarer replied, 'given by the *Ghrormun* or other such dark folk, but they are little used nowadays.'

'Can you remember another name for *this* lake?' Uhlendof insisted, with more urgency in his voice. 'It is very important!'

The cellarer scratched his head. 'I used to know one,' he said, 'but it seems to have slipped my mind. No. I don't know – though it was long and began with a "U", Ubas or the like.' He shook his head. 'What is this all about anyway?'

'Was the name *Uberezeg Ingur*?' Uhlendof asked sharply; and Leighor began to remember.

'Aye, that was it!' said Geltan at once. '*Uberezeg Ingur*, the old name of Silentwater from the Hillmen tongue. How on earth did you know that? It is an old secret of the mineworkers.'

Uhlendof leapt abruptly to his feet. 'We must speak with my lord Fralcel at once! It may already be too late. Let someone rouse the guard, for we are in most fearful danger!'

'What?' Yeon grunted.

'Guron's message!' Uhlendof said. 'Do you not remember what it said in Guron's message? This is *Uberezeg Ingur*, it is dark of moon, and the Rievers will soon be upon us!'

Chapter Eleven
LORD FRALCEL'S BANE

In the small room in the east turret that she shared with Gwildé's two other ladies, Keran lay alone in the darkness. Mireal and Ithren would still be attending upon their mistress below, and for once she had the room to herself. She had thought to sleep, and so escape her troubles, but sleep had refused to come, and she still lay dwelling on the events of the evening, tossing and turning upon her lumpy horsehair mattress.

One of the things that frightened her most was that Claighar did not seem to fear her reporting his attack. In fact he had even threatened her with worse to come . . .

Would he make good his threat? Keran shuddered. There was something in the confidence with which the guard commander had spoken that made her believe that he had every intention of doing just that. He seemed to fear no one, not even Lord Fralcel. What was it he had said about changes soon to come . . . ? She did not know exactly what he had meant, but she feared anything that would bring increase in Claighar's authority.

She hated this place, with its cavernous halls and cold dark rooms in which no fires burned. So unlike her father's warm timber house in Darien . . . Yes, those had indeed been happier days – happier than she had realised at the time. She recalled her father: so strong and comforting, with his warm smile and weatherbeaten face, half-hidden beneath a deep grey beard. He had seemed so much in control of the little world he had created for them all. Yet in the end it had all collapsed so quickly. Then, of course, there was Kerel: not like an elder sister at all, but always full of mischief, plotting and merrymaking. She had been the extrovert, the ringleader. They had run somewhat wild after their mother's death, sharing secrets, alone with the servants in the big old house, or journeying with their trader father around the outer settlements. The northlands were hard lands, but they could be most beautiful in summer . . .

Here she had no friends in whom she could confide. Ithren affected to despise her, and called her a gawky northern savage, whilst Mireal could not be trusted with a confidence, spreading any little secret far and wide among the women of the keep, to the general amusement of all. Even when Ithren could not find some laborious task to fill Keran's idle hours, she tended to discourage too close a contact with those she termed the 'lower servants', so there was little other opportunity for companionship. There seemed to be neither hope nor friendship for her here. She swallowed hard, weeping until she was again dry of tears, and then lay still.

Something – she knew not what – made her turn to lie face up on the bed. She stared into the silence of the opposite wall. There was no moon tonight, only starlight crept in through the narrow tower window. Yet for no reason at all Keran suddenly experienced an overwhelming surge of terror. An almost physical wave of intense, gut-churning dread flooded through her. This had nothing to do with Claighar – or so she presumed. This was of a different order altogether. Just once before in her life had she felt anything like this: on the fateful day of the brigand ambush in which her mother had died. She shuddered. Her terror, then, had been a premonition, a fearsome forewarning of catastrophe. And that same absolute dread overwhelmed her now. Every nerve of her body screamed disaster. Something utterly evil and malignant threatened every living thing in this castle. That she knew.

Almost paralysed with terror, she forced herself to her feet. Stumbling across the chamber, she crept to the narrow turret window, peering down into the outer courtyard far below. And what she saw there filled her with new horror.

Dozens of pale, grey-clad shapes were swarming over the western wall and dropping silently on to the stable roof. Even as she watched, the main gate pushed slowly open to admit more of the gaunt figures into the courtyard. The scene was almost dreamlike. There was no alarm, no guard, no sentry on the gate . . .

A breeze rustled through the thin curtain beside her; the movement broke her trance. She tried to scream, but all the breath seemed to have left her. She realised suddenly how utterly alone she was in this dark tower. Pausing for nothing, she fled the chamber, scrambling panic-stricken down the winding stair. At last reaching the sought-for door, she burst into Gwildé's well-lit chamber, turning at once to lock and bar the door behind her.

'What is it?' Ithren exclaimed angrily, looking up. 'What are you doing in my lady's chamber in your nightgown?'

Gwildé lay in her bed with Mireal beside her, brushing her hair. Mireal's mouth hung open.

'We are attacked!' Keran gasped. 'I have seen them . . . The Curséd Ones!'

Mireal giggled and Ithren seemed hard put to restrain her anger. Gwildé merely looked bewildered.

'What sort of lunatic raving is this, girl?' Ithren said sharply. 'Have you been at the ale bucket with the strangers in yon hall?'

'No!' Keran tried mightily to compose herself, to bring her panicked mind back under control. 'It is true! We are under attack from the Curséd Ones: the Rievers! The gates are open!'

Gwildé sat up sharply in her bed. 'What? How do you know this, girl? There has been no alarm . . .'

'I saw from my window,' Keran gasped, pointing towards the curtain. 'Look! Out in the courtyard!'

Ithren strode to the narrow window and pulled back the curtain. 'There is nothing there, my lady!' she snorted. 'It is all foolishness. The courtyard is empty!'

'No!' Keran raced to the window in disbelief. But the outer courtyard lay as Ithren had said: still, dark and empty. All seemed quiet. Nothing moved. Yet from that silent court there emanated a malevolence even stronger and more evil than before. The whole castle seemed to reek of blood.

'The girl is nothing but a liar!' Ithren turned away. 'She shall be well punished for this.'

'It is true . . . !' Keran began, but was interrupted by a fierce knocking upon the locked door behind her, and a rattling of its handle. She could feel the threat, the malevolence, through inches of solid wood. 'Do not open it!' she cried. 'It is they!'

'Who is it who knocks?' Ithren demanded loudly. Dimly, in the distance, a horn blew.

'It is only I. I seek your safety!' It was Claighar's voice; and the ladies – all but one – relaxed.

'Admit him,' Gwildé said quickly. 'He shall give us the truth of this.'

'No!' Keran screamed, her terror returning as she moved to stand in front of the door. 'He is with them!' She knew it now, instinctively, undeniably. She also knew that he was not alone out there in the hallway as he pretended. Someone else – some*thing* else – lurked out there with him. Faint sounds of shouting and fighting began to echo up from below through the thick stones. Several screams – distant but piercing and filled with agony. Death screams.

'Hurry!' Claighar's agitated voice came from without. 'We are attacked!' His fist hammered against the door.

'Open it,' Gwildé commanded, rising from her bed to step into her slippers. 'Open it at once!'

To Keran this all began to seemed more than ever like some dreadful nightmare, which moved inexorably towards its inevitable, fated conclusion. 'No!' she said again, hardly able to speak; her voice quaking with terror. 'You do not know what is out there!'

'It is Claighar, commander of the guard and our only hope, you stupid girl!' Ithren said angrily. She too was now beginning to panic, and as she spoke she rushed forward, pushing Keran aside.

For an instant Keran watched the older woman's hand reaching for the bolt, and then she acted. This she could not permit; it was madness! Her restraint snapped, she seized Ithren by arm and shoulder and hurled her back across the chamber with all her not inconsiderable force. Ithren did not halt until she crashed into the hard edge of Gwildé's dressing table on the other side of the chamber, where she gave out a sharp cry of pain and fell to the floor.

'She is gone mad. Stop her!'

There came another loud battering at the door. 'What is the trouble, my lady? Why do you not open? My lord Fralcel would have you go to him.' The sound of conflict from below intensified.

'Keran,' Gwildé spoke coldly, approaching her with a reluctant Mireal alongside. 'I order you to stand aside. Obey me now, or else you shall be soundly whipped and sent from here.'

But Keran was beyond all obedience; she knew what lay beyond that door, and she was determined that it would not be opened while she lived. Why would they not listen to her? A white hot anger burned within her. Did they trust her so little?

Mireal suddenly tried to take her arm, while Gwildé moved towards the door on her other side. But Keran was faster, evading Mireal's grasp with ease to drive her right fist hard into the smaller girl's stomach; there was a gasp of pain mixed with shock as she doubled up and staggered backwards, clasping her belly. Now there was only Gwildé to deal with. Gwildé was easy, she was slight and could be easily pushed back from the door into the far wall, where perhaps she would listen. Gwildé struggled hard, but Keran was much stronger, and soon had her prisoned in the far corner of the room.

'Listen, my lady,' she said quickly, breathing hard. 'That beyond the door is not what it seems. It is evil. Claighar is with the attackers! I *know*.'

A loud crash came from the door. Claighar and whoever was with him were trying to break in! Yet the door had been built to withstand just such an attack, and it would take some time.

'Claighar?' Gwildé questioned. She seemed totally bewildered. 'I cannot believe it.' But she looked now a little more uneasily towards the doorway, where the crashing grew still louder.

'The secret way, my lady!' Keran begged desperately. 'Can we not use the secret way; or at least hide there until we know who is without?'

'Yes, yes, perhaps that is best,' Gwildé admitted hesitantly, beginning slowly to feel for the hidden lever amongst the carvings on the oaken panelling beside her bed; leaving Keran free for the moment to look behind her.

Mireal was seated upon the end of the great bed, nursing her stomach and looking up at Keran reproachfully. But Ithren, unfortunately, was more active; she had limped most of the way across the room and was now only two paces from the door. Keran would not be able to reach her in time.

'No!' she shouted, stepping forward, but Ithren took no notice.

The crashing against the door had stopped. 'It is no use!' came Claighar's voice.

'Then use the amulet!' another hissed.

'It can be used but once,' Claighar spoke again, 'and then it is done for many hours.'

'Use it,' said the other.

Ithren drew back the first bolt. And in that selfsame instant the whole door seemed to fly apart in front of her as the chamber filled with a bright, ever so bright, smouldering purple light.

Keran screamed. Ithren had not time, as a thousand shards of shattered wood from the door tore into her body. Keran turned despairingly to face Gwildé, seeing that she had at last managed to pry the narrow secret doorway open. Keran made for it and then, suddenly remembering Mireal, turned back for her. The smaller girl was on her feet but stumbling aimlessly. Quickly Keran caught her hand and dragged her towards the secret door.

Claighar stepped through the other, shattered doorway, the amulet upon his chest smouldering and glowing like a red hot poker. He looked down at Ithren's shattered body, and then up towards Keran. Their eyes met. He smiled, but his smile contained no mirth; grim and hideous, it was the smile of the snow tiger sighting its prey. Keran turned and ran. Suddenly Claighar saw the danger.

'Hold!' he cried. And others followed him into the room.

Gwildé screamed, but Keran only dared look round once she had pushed Mireal into the shelter of the dark passage behind the narrow stone door.

Rievers! Grey Tarintarmen! She recognised them instantly: an old, half-forgotten terror returned. Several now hurtled into the room, a newly severed head bobbing on a long pike behind them. She squeezed through the narrow opening in the wall, attempting to drag Gwildé bodily in after her. But Gwildé suddenly broke away to gather up the small jewel casket that lay at her bedside. Keran despaired. She saw Claighar rushing forward, even as Gwildé at last managed to duck beneath her arm into the tunnel. Feverishly Keran gripped the inner bar, trying to drag the heavy door to; but it had been little used and the hinges were rusted near solid with age. Slowly it started to close, but too late. Claighar was there, seizing the outer edge of the narrow door and trying to haul it back open. There was pandemonium without, screaming and harsh orders shouted in some unknown but hateful tongue.

'Help me!' Keran screamed, her urgency and fear giving her the audacity to shout orders at her mistress.

And Gwildé helped, hauling at the inner handle of the door with all her meagre strength. Mireal, however, did not aid them in their struggle but sat on a lower step of the passageway moaning quietly to herself. Even so, Claighar alone did not have strength enough to defeat the two women, and the door began slowly to close. Then another hand fastened upon the outer edge of the door: a thin hand, narrow and sinuous, pale as death – a *tarintar* hand! The door stopped moving.

A second hand snaked suddenly inwards to grasp Gwildé's wrist in a demon grip: long milky-white nails, sharp as talons, sinking into the soft skin and drawing a thin line of rose-red blood. Gwildé screamed; her free hand letting loose the door. In desperation Keran braced herself against the stone of the passage wall. Releasing the door for a single instant, she drew the knife at her waist, plunging it deep into the pale, shrouded arm that held her mistress . . .

There was a fearsome scream as Keran ripped the sharp hunter's knife down the entire length of the Riever arm. A warm sticky fluid clung to her hand. It burned slightly. Howling in agony, the Riever snatched its injured arm away, releasing both Gwildé and the door at the same time.

Instantly Keran dropped the knife, and using every atom of her remaining strength, helped Gwildé to haul the heavy door firmly shut. At last she managed to slam the twin bolts home into the comforting thickness of the stone. And for a moment she and Gwildé just stood, hugging each other, relieved to be still alive.

Bending to pick up her bloodied knife, Keran urged Mireal to her feet, pleased for the moment to follow Gwildé as she led them down the pitch dark stairway. The tunnel came finally to an end in a small darkened chamber which opened on to the dimly-lit inner courtyard.

At once the clamour and mayhem became intense. The castle was thoroughly roused, and although there was no fighting yet in this cramped inner courtyard, there were the sounds of a fierce battle in the main hall. Wild cries came from the kitchens and from the outer courtyard beyond. As the women paused, two grey figures forced their way into the inner court, bloodstained sabres glinting in their hands. Keran glimpsed the fallen figure of one of the guards at their feet.

A gloved hand clasped Gwildé's arm. 'This way, my lady!' It was Seydal, the Hall Marshal, with one other: Tavolir, one of the musicians. 'We must move quickly or we are lost!' He dragged rather than led Gwildé to the north-eastern Water Tower, and through the small door there. Keran and Mireal followed as quickly as they could; the musician, sword in hand, brought up the rear.

They were almost through the door before the two Tarintarmen saw them. At once they hurtled screaming across the courtyard. Tavolir turned to ward off the first of them, managing to hold him the vital few seconds to enable the others to gain the safety of the tower, but a sabre cut deep into his left arm as he turned to follow. He cried out in pain, almost dropping his sword as Keran dragged him inward and Seydal bolted the door behind. Blows and curses rained down on the door from without. Once again they were trapped.

'What has happened?' Gwildé gasped. 'Who has attacked us? Where is my lord?'

'Patience, my lady,' Seydal pleaded, trying to calm her. 'There are Rievers, Tarintarmen and who knows what else! Somehow they have gained entry to the keep. There is great confusion. The dark creatures appeared from out of nowhere, forced the gates and poured over the western wall. We were totally unprepared. I have seen many slain.'

'What of my husband?' Gwildé demanded urgently.

'I am afraid I do not know. Perhaps he has found some other means of escape . . .'

'We are not escaped yet!' Keran broke in sharply. She tightened a strip of cloth as hard as she could about the musician's upper arm in an attempt to staunch the bleeding. 'The door will not hold for much longer, we have little time!'

'Perhaps if we climbed the tower,' Mireal suggested, 'we could hold out until rescue comes.'

'No!' Gwildé shook her head firmly. 'We must leave this place. I know the Rievers, they will leave none alive!'

'How can we leave?' Seydal asked bleakly. 'Even if we could get out of the keep we would only be hacked to pieces in the darkness beyond!'

'The lake!' Keran cried suddenly. 'It is said the Cursèd Ones dislike water! It is our only chance . . .' Without waiting for approval, she ran across the room to the heavy iron shutter bolted to the outer wall. Tugging at the rusted bolts until they came free, she wrenched the shutter partly open. After a moment Seydal came to her aid, and together they forced it wide enough to reveal the lapping waters of Silentwater beyond. A cold night breeze flooded the room. Keran raised herself on to the sill and peered out through the two-yard thickness of the stone wall. The lake waters lapped the base of the tower a few feet beneath her, and there, a few yards to the right, bobbed an old wooden boat, tethered to the unseen lakeshore.

'A boat!' she cried out joyously; and, unable to restrain herself, forced her way through the narrow opening to plunge into the ice-cold waters of the lake.

Slowly, unbearably slowly, the others began to follow. Keran found that she could just about stand in four feet of muddy water, and was able to help Gwildé, Mireal and the musician down, before Seydal made his noisier descent. The Hall Marshal was first to haul himself into the small boat, and with his weight balanced in the centre, the others managed to struggle aboard, Keran and Tavolir remaining to the last.

Only after the wounded musician was helped up into the boat did Keran at last cut the frayed mooring-line and scramble aboard herself.

'There are no oars!' Mireal realised suddenly.

'Then paddle with your hands!' Keran hissed, desperate to be away.

This they did: and slowly, painfully slowly, the overloaded boat pulled away from the castle walls.

Even as they drew away, there came a great shudder from the heart of the Water Tower, followed by a loud crash as the door gave way. Soon gaunt shadows could be seen in the half-open window, staring out after them into the darkness. Furious howls of rage echoed over the water. There was a shimmer as a lithe figure slipped into the lake, and a tremor of fear passed down Keran's spine. Hopefully the water ran too deep and cold for anyone to reach them.

Flaming torches appeared suddenly on the open greensward beside the castle, and hissing arrows began to lance into the water all about them. Yet the trajectories were ill-judged, and within moments the fugitives were out of range. Still they did not slacken in their efforts, paddling desperately northward until a bright golden light began to rise up behind them.

At once they ceased paddling and turned to look back. Horrorstruck, they saw high, flickering tongues of flame licking up the walls of the great hall. Other fires burned and spread along the outer walls of the keep, the whole slowly melding and joining into one great sheet of blood-red flame that seemed to feed upon and consume everything it touched. Somehow this, more than anything else, etched the whole nightmare of the past hour into grim reality. The destruction of Silentwater Keep was complete. The place they had come to think of as the cornerstone of their existence, their bastion against the unspoken horrors of these dark brooding forests, was gone forever, utterly destroyed. They were completely alone, and surrounded by enemies.

'My lord Fralcel!' Gwildé suddenly screamed. 'He is in there! We must go back!' She leapt wildly to her feet, rocking the boat as she tried to break free of the many hands that restrained her.

Eventually they managed to subdue her and the boat was steadied. Keran held her mistress close. Yet still Gwildé sobbed with a bitter heart-rending despair that would not be comforted.

'It will be all right,' Keran spoke softly, knowing in her heart that she lied. 'Lord Fralcel will have escaped just as we have done, and will surely find some way to meet us on the other side.'

The boat had begun to drift directionlessly. Keran felt Gwildé shivering against her, and realised for the first time that she too was frozen to the marrow. She and Gwildé were the only ones in the boat with nothing on but their flimsy linen nightdresses.

'Look!' A terrified scream from Mireal jerked her back to full awareness.

'What is it?' Seydal demanded.

'There!' Mireal sobbed, pointing ahead. 'Another boat: coming straight for us!'

Keran turned, and shuddered to the depths of her soul.

Even as Uhlendof pulled open the brewhouse door he knew that it was already too late. Although everything looked as quiet and peaceful in the darkness of the courtyard as it had done moments earlier, all of the priest's senses screamed out to him that something was terribly wrong.

'What are you waiting for?' Yeon's voice came startlingly loud from behind him.

'Ssh!' Uhlendof hissed sharply. 'Something is amiss!' He stepped cautiously out into the courtyard. From his right there came the normal reassuring sounds of clattering dishes and bickering voices in the great kitchens beyond. The last revels in the hall were breaking up, and small lights flickered from many of the keep's upper windows. Yet elsewhere, to his left, from the other buildings clustered around the courtyard and from the main gate, there came an ominous silence – broken only by the terrified whinnying of several horses in the stable opposite.

It was Zindur who first noticed something tangible. 'There!' he hissed, pointing suddenly up into the gloom.

The others followed his finger to see two thick ropes trailing down from the top of the western wall to the stable roof beneath. But before any of them could take in the full significance of this, they were halted by a shower of arrows, both from the gate and from the stable roof. One of the guardsmen fell at once, an arrow through his neck. The rest of the company fled for the dark shelter of the eastern wall. A number of grey figures moved in the shadows of the far side of the courtyard and the gateway. A second flurry of arrows rattled down; but these were less effective than the first, for the hidden archers were now unsighted.

'Treachery!' Zindur bellowed with all his force – attempting to raise the alarm, to rouse the whole of the sleeping castle. 'Treachery! We are attacked! Rievers! The Rievers are upon us!' A stray arrow glanced off his mail coat and he retreated back into the shadow of the wall.

Scores of pale, leather-clad figures now swarmed on the walkway above the stables. Others began to scurry silently into the courtyard from the grooms' quarters below. Now, for the first time, Leighor saw the tall gaunt Tarintarmen of the northron wastes: grisly visages hidden beneath dark cowls and ragged bindings as they melted through the shadows. True men ran with them too: grim northron warriors in gleaming warpaint, and shorter, darker figures out of the west. All moved in dread silence, blood dripping from keen-edged swords. A muffled scream, quickly stifled, came from one of the buildings.

Startled cries rang out now from various parts of the main keep. Yet it seemed not that the castle had roused to Zindur's call, but that some form of scattered conflict had already commenced within the keep. Leighor would now have made for the hall, where their only aid would lie, but the main force of the assembled raiders seemed to be gathering between them and the inner gateway. The courtyard was full of them – their number easily enough to overwhelm the small group by the eastern wall if they chose. Yet they held back, seeming to await some signal. A signal that was not long in coming.

A single figure forced his way to the head of the Riever throng. He seemed shorter than the rest, and ruddier of countenance, although his face bore a terrible scar that ran from the corner of one eye diagonally across to the bottom of his farther cheekbone, cutting through both nose and lips upon its way. He wore a dark jerkin of grease-drenched leather and bore a cruel hooked shortsword. A double-headed axe ran with blood. Overall he wore a circular cap of deep red leather that alone would have marked him out from his gaunter fellows. But it was only after staring at it for some moments that Leighor saw what gave it its colour, the dye which ran down across its wearer's forehead and trickled along his short dark rat-tails of hair ... The whole cap was soaked in fresh blood. Other unspeakable objects of human hair and skin hung from thongs at his belt.

All eyes were on him now. Yet he looked neither to them nor to the lighted keep above, but turned to stare deep into the shadows where the travellers stood – almost as if he could see them as clearly there in the pitch darkness as when the broad light of day shone upon them. Leighor shuddered. But the Redcap turned away.

Taking a carven horn from his waist and raising it to his lips, he blew. One long note: wild and harsh as the iron winds of Khiorim and the cries of the winter wolves on the northern plains. And it drew an answering cry from the serried ranks of the host. All stealth forsaken now, they turned as one to storm the open doors of the hall.

There was no resistance. Those few within who had had time to rouse themselves were swiftly overwhelmed beneath the surging wave of raiders, bursting through undefended doors and windows to pour into the keep from the courtyard and the western wall.

Drawing his great broadsword, Zindur suddenly found his voice. 'Attack them!' he roared to the three remaining mercenaries, launching himself upon the intruders' rear. But even as the others moved to support him, they realised that any rearguard action would be hopeless. Howls of victory and screams of terror now rose from every corner of the keep, the raiders sweeping through halls, kitchens and private chambers; killing, looting and burning as they went. Gaunt figures seemed to swarm everywhere. It was a massacre.

There came a low creaking rumble from behind; Leighor spun about to see the outer gates swinging slowly open. And through the ever-widening gap now swept the *Khorlûn* – the rabble and detritus of the Riever band. Here were the crooked-men, the old, the small, the weak; the ones whose shapes were too deformed or too far askew to scale the walls. Here too were goblins, singly and in small groups, scurrying ahead and around the edges of the larger throng, bearing only sharpened knives and rusting daggers for weapons, but hungry – as hungry as all the rest – for the blood and the booty of the sacking. The travellers were surrounded.

Leighor looked urgently about him. Who of all their small company was still alive? Telsyan, Yeon, Uhlendof, the cellarer, and perhaps three guardsmen, plus Zindur. So few – and all now realised their peril.

'Back into the cellar!' Geltan screamed. 'We can bolt ourselves in there!'

'No,' Zindur made his decision instantly. 'We will be sealing ourselves into a trap. We must fight our way out! Back through the rabble.'

The others looked appalled. Were they to abandon all the others? Abandon the relative shelter of the keep for whatever might lie in the darkness beyond? This was all happening too fast . . .

But Zindur was already on his way, racing for the outer gates, his great sword raised to bite deeply into the first of the unsuspecting *Khorlûn* rabble. With a sudden great war-whoop, Yeon charged after him; bright longsword sweeping wildly through the night. It tore with equal fury through air, leather and bone as Yeon began to hack a two-handed path through the ranks of the intruders. Reluctantly, Leighor and the others followed on.

The fight was easier than they had any right to expect. Most of the rag-tag army of followers were unprepared for a fight of any sort, least of all with what they took to be a desperate rearguard. They were here for the scavenging, the easy pickings, hoping to find only half-dead survivors and wounded captives for the stripping and the slaughter. The desperate party managed to cut their way through them with little difficulty, at last to gain the main gates and the freedom of the dark greensward without.

Leighor was almost the last to break free. Armed now with a shattered stave picked up from the litter of the courtyard, he knocked a last restraining hand from his arm, feeling the thin burn of pain as a knife-blade cut across his left thigh. The cut was painful yet not deep, and he half ran, half hobbled away from the gate, following the others eastward into the darkness. He was struggling for breath now, and turned to look behind him constantly as he ran. But after a few half-hearted attempts at pursuit, none of the *Khorlûn* who crowded the open gateway attempted to follow. There was little to gain from chasing after fleeing madmen; far more to be won at less risk within the confines of the castle – before the quickly rising flames took it all.

The travellers were free. Yet they did not stop running until they had reached the dark line of forest at the eastern edge of the castle clearing. Only here did they halt to catch their breath and stare back at the burning keep.

Leighor was horrified to see how far the flames had spread. They rose now from the very rooftops of the great hall, burning through a dozen glassless windows. The entire mid-section of the keep was aflame – although the lesser buildings around the outer courtyard seemed for the moment to have been spared. The flames burned a terrible crimson-red, illumining the open greensward about the castle and reflecting on the lake until the waters seemed to run with blood. And still the fires burned higher.

'We must move away,' Zindur said urgently. 'Get as far from here as we can – before they remember us!'

'Are they all dead?' Geltan the cellarer asked vacantly, hardly able to believe what he saw with his own eyes.

'Aye,' Zindur said brusquely. 'Let us go quickly.'

'We cannot just run wildly into the forest!' Telsyan objected. 'Where are we headed? What is your plan?'

'There is a hunting lodge on the lakeshore farther east. Perhaps we may find a boat there and get across the lake.'

Pausing for no further debate, Zindur turned away into the darkness of the forest, crashing noisily through the undergrowth as he set off at a jogging run through the trees. Leighor, with his injured leg, found it hard to keep up with the others, following more by sound than by vision in the intense blackness. But fear was a better spur than most, and each time he felt himself losing contact, the thought of what lay behind drove him on to greater effort.

After some time the run slowed to a brisk walk. Shortly thereafter, Zindur led them down out of the denser forest and on to a lakeside path that ran eastward along the wooded shore of Silentwater.

A thousand stars stared impassively down upon them – just as they looked down upon the fearsome scene of slaughter and destruction so close behind. Yet apart from a few startled forest animals, the company met with no further hindrance for the remaining hours of their flight. It was shortly before dawn, when the dark sky ahead had at last begun to reveal its dim grey underbelly, that they finally came upon the hunters' lodge.

It was disappointingly small, a single storeyed pinewood house built on the lakeshore. A small wooden jetty ran out into the lake, but there was no boat of any kind moored there. Zindur approached first, to check that the building was safe. Only when satisfied that it was empty did he signal them to follow.

'What are we to do now?' Yeon asked grimly once they were all inside.

'I do not know,' Zindur admitted, worry clouding his features as he paced the bare floor. 'I had hoped to have found a boat here, or at least some food and weapons; but this place has been stripped bare. It should not be so!'

Exhausted, the others began to slump on to the narrow wooden benches that lined the walls.

'How secure are we here?' Telsyan asked. 'I fear we are still too near the castle for safety.'

'Aye, we cannot stay here long,' Zindur acknowledged. 'This place is too easy to find. It marks us out and is quickly surrounded. It is said that Rievers do not like to travel by daylight – but I would not like to trust my life to the truth of that tale.'

'Even at midday these forests are as black as night,' another of the guardsmen said. 'Dark enough to stay the sun from the backs of a thousand Tarintarmen!'

'But we have nowhere else to go,' Geltan said. 'Let us remain here and rest for a while, until sunrise at least.'

There was silence. Most of the others soon slept or half slept. Leighor's leg, however, still provided pain enough to prevent him from sitting still for any length of time, and so he alternated between resting it along the wooden bench and standing up to shuffle up and down the floor. From time to time he would look out through one of the two small windows, either at the lake or the forest beyond.

There was a heavy morning mist upon the lake, and little could be seen. The forest, too, provided little comfort. It was still as black as night beneath its evergreen mantle, and Leighor could not have told if a thousand Rievers watched them from its depths. He crossed the room to look out at the lake again. He was not sure, perhaps it was his imagination, but was that really the far shore he could see, dark against the paleness of the mist? Or was it an island – or perhaps a boat? He stared out of the window with new intent, his leg for the moment forgotten. Yes, something was indeed bobbing perhaps half a thousand paces out into the lake. It could only be a boat: a hulk of some sort, with a thin straight mast but no sail. There was no movement. If there was anyone aboard, they either slept or were lying low. The thought made Leighor uneasy. He decided to wake the others.

'Whose is it?' Uhlendof asked anxiously, moments later, peering bleary-eyed through the window. 'Does it belong to the Rievers?'

'The Rievers dislike water and rarely navigate it voluntarily,' Zindur frowned. 'Yet some of them may have conquered their dislike. There were men and goblins running with this band, and it may be they who lie out there now, waiting for us to show ourselves.'

'So how do we tell?' Telsyan asked impatiently.

'Let us wait a little longer and see what happens,' Zindur grunted. 'If there is no movement after full sunrise, then we shall show ourselves.'

Part Three
HATHANWILD

VIRN DEEP
GRAZ ESCH VILI
XHENDIR
UROZ DIRR
Malûn River
R. Trimsil
Valmaalina
Silith Race
Bare Hills
Vhori Bridge
ESCH ERMON
Hith Giber
OROUDN HULAN
Ahockul Crest
SOLON'S LOUGH
R. Berend
Greenlog Marshes
Great Xhendir Road
Furthka
Ford
River Thauran
IRNPOOL
Hathanwild
R. Thauran
DAGOR'S LAKE
WOTLÉ LOUGH
BRAD LOUGH
ESCH TUARN
Hallad's Keep
Heights of Du'ath
King Culvar's Way
ORODUN UBAS
DUNKERWATER
Whilstone Dell
GUNDURBAR UBAS
SILENT WATER Keep
River Coethalon
DARK LOUGH
Imball
Rathul Sea

Chapter Twelve
ARGONAN VALE

They waited for what seemed an eternity as the deep golden eye of the sun dragged itself clear of the surrounding hills, driving the soft lake mists before it, to leave the boat clearly visible upon the mirror-smooth surface of Silentwater.

'I recognise it,' said one of the men at last. 'It is the ore boat from the mine!'

'Aye,' said the cellarer. 'But that is far to the west of here, and will have fallen to the Rievers even before the keep.'

Still there was no sign of movement aboard the high-sided boat. Yet there were unsettling noises from the forest behind. A slight breeze had risen with the dawn, and the tall pines swayed and whispered in its thrall, their whipping branches producing sounds unpleasantly akin to clumsy footfalls upon the brittle twigs of the forest floor.

'It is time,' said Zindur suddenly. 'I have had enough of waiting. Let us show ourselves!' He turned abruptly from them, to stride out on to the old wooden jetty. 'Keep your weapons to hand,' he warned the others. 'Stay close together, and be prepared to run for the forest at any sign of a trap.'

Leighor was beginning to warm to the careful prudence of the warrior, who appeared, for the moment, to have assumed command. Yet for some minutes there was no reaction at all to their presence on the jetty, and it began to seem that the boat was indeed abandoned and that they would have to swim out to it. But just then a small figure stood up, high in the stern. He looked across at them for a moment or two and waved.

'It is Haflas!' the cellarer shouted at once. 'Haflas from the mines! We are saved!'

It took some time for the small figure to work the boat in towards the jetty; and it quickly became clear that the craft already carried several passengers.

'There are other survivors!' Geltan sighed with relief. 'Thank the gods we are not the only ones. My lady Gwildé is there, and Seydal; Sire Uldain, and Jemel, his young squire; and Armon the huntsman and . . .' but the cellarer's words slowed to a halt when he saw the stricken faces of those within – who, like him, were now beginning to number the many friends and companions who were not in either small party. And so the little boat moored in silence, the tired survivors acknowledging each other only with grim nods as the small steersman, whom the cellarer had named Haflas, let down the long gangplank to allow the party from the lodge to climb aboard.

Gwildé studied them all as they boarded, looking into their faces with searching eyes, as if she sought news of her husband in each. Only when Telsyan, the last of their number, had made his way down into the broad, flat hull of the boat, and Haflas had begun once more to raise the gangplank, did she finally break the silence.

'Is that all?' she asked despairingly. 'Are you the only survivors?'

'Aye, my lady,' Zindur nodded. 'We managed to fight our way out of the gate, but I think none could have followed us, for the main force of the Rievers lay between us and the hall.'

'And what of my husband, your lord? Have you no news of him?'

Zindur shook his head.

Gwildé stared at him for a moment; a hard stare that filled slowly with cold contempt. Zindur shrank visibly beneath that intense accusal, and looked away, shamefaced.

'Fine guardsman!' Gwildé spat bitterly. 'To have fled and left your master to die!'

And then she fell to weeping, sobbing uncontrollably before the embarrassed throng as her two women tried vainly to comfort her.

To Leighor she seemed a piteous sight, dressed no longer in robes of silk and velvet, but in a damp and tattered nightgown, with the heavy cloak of Sire Uldain about her shoulders to warm her; alone and weeping for her lord.

'We must move from the shore,' the knight said quickly. 'We are far too open to attack here.'

Haflas nodded, making his way swiftly back to the high boatswain's platform. He was short of stature, although stocky and powerfully built, with close-shorn dark hair, and a broad, sombre face, marked by many small burns and scars, most probably gained before the smelting furnace. A longer, tighter scar stretched beneath his left eye. He turned to cradle the shaft of the long paddle-shaped stern oar in both arms. 'We shall need one other to help row, if we are to make best speed.'

Zindur worked his way swiftly astern, only too pleased to be freed from the presence of his lady. The warrior worked under the direction of the smaller man, for a stern oar must be swung with a steady, rhythmic stroke to keep the boat on an even keel, and this took much practice. Yet even with both of them straining on the heavy oar, their progress from the shore was painfully slow.

'Are there no simpler oars on this craft?' Telsyan asked eventually. 'That we may all share in the rowing, and move the swifter?'

Seydal shook his head. 'These boats were built to bear heavy cargo: ore and metal from the mines, or pine logs downstream to the workings. Goods that need only be ferried slowly, and by a small crew.'

'So this is indeed the mine boat?' Leighor said.

'Yes,' Seydal replied grimly. 'The Rievers came out of the west, as ever; and the mines were the first to fall – many hours before the raiders ever reached the keep. Haflas himself only escaped by great good fortune, having set out in this very craft, with the weekly cargo of lead ingots, only an hour before . . .'

Grimly he told how Haflas had seen the dark flames rise up from the mineworkings behind him, turning the laden boat to find naught but burning timbers and a hail of furious arrows from the Riever stragglers – the main force having already passed on to assault the keep. Haflas had then striven to reach the keep and raise the alarm before the raiders could make their way there overland. But in that too he had failed, arriving only in time to rescue a small boatload of survivors from the main attack. Only upon dumping the cargo and proceeding farther eastwards did he finally succeed in forestalling the Rievers, and rescuing Sire Uldain, Jemel his squire, and Armon, one of Fralcel's huntsmen. They had stripped the lodge of axes, traps, longbows, ropes, food, and anything else they had thought might be useful, and then rowed out into the middle of the lake, where they had thought it safest to spend the night.

'You were lucky we saw you,' said Uldain, 'for we had intended crossing to the northern shore at daybreak . . .'

A sudden appalled gasp from the rest of the passengers interrupted him, as Silentwater Keep came into view to the south-west. Until this moment a low, wooded promontory had hidden the castle from their sight, and the full force of the dread scene of devastation and destruction came upon them all at once.

The fire-blackened remains of Silentwater Keep smouldered still, little more than a quarter of a mile from where they lay. Thin columns of dark smoke rose sullenly from isolated fires along the walls, yet these still remained more or less intact. Of the great hall, however, nothing was left but a gutted, fired-blackened shell, the ruined walls rising up broken and roofless to meet the sky. Two great campfires had been built upon the open greensward of the castle clearing, and a heavy pall of smoke hung over the scene. Many in the boat who had shown little emotion before now wept openly. Fortunately little evidence of the human carnage that had occurred remained visible.

Even as the travellers watched, gaunt grey figures arose from about the great campfires to point and gesticulate out towards them. More Rievers poured from the shattered gates of the keep. Others began to emerge from the woodlands beyond the clearing. Masses of figures, large and small, crowded down to the water's edge: above them was raised a simple, tattered banner, bearing the device of a grey skull upon a field of white.

A flurry of arrows, spears and smaller missiles began to whistle across the lake towards the boat. But even the best aimed of these splashed harmlessly into the water far short of the boat, though the furious screams of the Rievers carried clearly out to them over the still water.

'Will they follow us?' Mireal asked fearfully, from the corner where she sat huddled with Gwildé and Keran.

'They have no boats,' Uldain reassured her. 'And the lake is too deep to wade and too broad to swim. We are quite safe for the moment . . .'

Even as he spoke, a score of straining figures dragged a large wooden machine out on to the greensward from where it had lain hidden behind the keep; and began cranking it into position.

'A ballista!' Zindur cried in dismay. 'They did not have one last night . . .'

'Or they did not need to use it!' Uldain barked. 'There was treachery enough last night for there to be no need of siege-engines!'

Before the words were fully out of his mouth the ballista arm was released, crashing forward to send a huge boulder arcing high into the clear blue sky straight towards them. Mireal screamed.

The boulder hurtled down, seeming for long seconds as if it were about to land right on top of them; but actually splashing into the lake on the far side of the boat, drenching them with spray.

'Pull harder!' Uldain shouted. 'For the north shore!' And the two oarsmen bent to with a will.

Other large stones crashed into the water near them, but although there were two more near misses before they were finally out of range, none hit the boat. The rain of missiles ceased. They were safe.

Then, without warning, a bright dagger of light flared beneath the great banner: a baleful, deathly colour that Leighor recognised only too well – the purple fire of *harrunor*. A line of fire raced out across the lake: smoking, flaring, faster than a horse could run. It speared erratically yet inexorably towards them, as if guided by some phantom hand – a smouldering finger of flame, whose name was death. Leighor stared at it, transfixed by fear. But as it drew nearer it seemed to die: the flames fading as they came, breaking up and dissipating as they lost their force in the cold morning air. An instant later, a wave of intense heat struck them: a sudden searing blast, as if a furnace door had been opened beside them. Then, as quickly as it had come, it was gone, leaving them apparently unharmed.

'What was that?' Seydal gasped.

Leighor pointed. Half-way up the stern of the boat, the wooden hull was scorched and blackened over an area a yard or so in circumference.

'It was *harrunor*!' he exclaimed. 'They hold the Magefire!'

'What do you know of this?' Uldain demanded with sudden suspicion. 'What is *harrunor*?'

'Something very dangerous and powerful,' said Uhlendof; 'that should not exist in such quantity as it has seemed to of late.'

'It is what we saw!' Keran burst out. 'Some magick that belongs to Claighar! With it he burst down the door to our chamber, and slew Ithren.'

Gwildé now was showing interest. 'That—' she said in open disbelief. 'That was *harrunor*?'

'Aye, milady, it would seem so,' Uhlendof answered, looking at her strangely.

But Gwildé merely shook her head, and rested back between her ladies, muttering inaudibly to herself.

'There will be no more attacks,' Keran comforted. 'The force is spent.'

'How do you know that?' Uhlendof asked sharply.

Keran was flustered. 'That is what Claighar said. He could not use his amulet-eye a second time, to break the door to the inner passage. That was how we escaped.'

'We have no time now to debate such matters,' Uldain broke in irritably. 'We must get away quickly – before they find some other infernal device to reach us.'

'But how do we know that the north shore is any safer than the south?' Leighor asked.

'All their force will have been needed to take the keep,' Uldain said quickly. 'And by any means, the north cannot be worse than this!'

Parties of grey figures now began to separate from the main body of the Riever force to run along the shore, passing into the forests to both east and west. Others quickly gathered up weapons and supplies and followed them.

'They are circling the lake,' Uldain said matter-of-factly. 'If they truly intend to follow us, we will have but a day's advantage, even when we get to the far shore. We must lose no time!'

The boat fell silent then, but for the steady splash and creak of the single oar. The survivors stared back wordlessly at the forested shoreline to the south, imagining the many faceless raiders, the hordes of men and not-quite-men, who pursued them relentlessly and singlemindedly through those dark forests.

All too slowly the northern shore drew closer.

There was some smoke-dried venison in the boat, rescued from the hunting lodge, and strips of this were shared amongst the passengers. 'It is all the food we have,' Seydal told them. 'So be sparing of it.'

Leighor found this an easy task, for it was like leather, and almost unchewable. He gnawed on the hard, charcoal-flavoured meat for a few minutes, and then set it aside.

By noon they were upon the north shore. There was a decayed landing-stage here, beneath the tall pines, with a crumbling wooden jetty and a small, overgrown path that ran inland, into the hills. The forest here was quiet, but not utterly silent as it had been upon the southern shore; and the gentle sounds of birdsong, and of buzzing and flying insects, began to fill them with new confidence.

'This is the north landing,' Haflas told them as he stepped down on to the rickety jetty. 'From here a path leads north, two days' march, to the great castle of the Knights of Imsild at Hallad's Keep.'

'What if that castle too has fallen?' Leighor asked.

'Hallad's Keep is impregnable,' Uldain snorted. 'It would take far more than one malodorous Riever band to breach those walls.'

'Then let us not delay.' Seydal glanced back at the thin column of smoke that still rose from the southern shore.

'Do you fear for your life?' Gwildé asked mildly. 'You are fortunate. I fear not. My life is over.'

'Your life is hardly yet begun, my lady,' Keran chided. 'You must preserve yourself, to have revenge upon your lord's murderers.'

Gwildé said nothing, but shook her head sadly. Yet when Uldain had marshalled the party, she allowed herself to be led between her ladies at the centre of the column. They could march no more than two abreast along the narrow forest trail; Sire Uldain in the lead, with Zindur, Haflas, and the huntsman, Armon. Then followed Gwildé and her two ladies, Seydal, Tavolir and the four travellers, and last of all, the three remaining guardsmen and Geltan.

And so the small party of survivors walked away from the lake, and up into the dark pine-clad hills to the north of Silentwater. They halted often, for Gwildé and the others to rest and regain their strength. Leighor and Tavolir, in particular, still nursed the wounds they had gained in the previous night's battle – a disaster from which few of them had saved more than the clothes they stood up in. Fortunately the last dinner at Silentwater had been an informal one, and they had been permitted to retain a few weapons, along with Leighor's small satchel of medicaments, that would otherwise have been lost. Gwildé and her ladies, however, had fared worst of all, and despite thick cloaks borrowed from the men, they still shivered in flimsy dresses and dainty indoor shoes totally unsuited to the rugged terrain. Consequently their pace was much slower than either Uldain or Zindur would have liked. The terrain too was hard, their path rising and falling as it crested the flanks of the steeply forested hills. Sometimes trees would part on a hilltop to reveal a sweeping vista of the forest below, or else of Silentwater, still disconcertingly close behind.

'Where exactly are we heading?' Telsyan asked as dark began to fall. 'We cannot walk all night. These paths are slippery and treacherous, and the women at least will need some rest.'

'But dare we stop?' Geltan asked nervously. 'If the Rievers follow close behind . . . ?'

'Unless they have found some means of crossing Silentwater,' Uldain answered, 'they will still be a good day behind us. We have time for a little rest.'

'Rest, yes. But where?' Telsyan demanded. 'We cannot just camp out in the forest, open to all eyes.'

Haflas nodded. 'There is a place close by where we may rest for a while. No more than half a league away – an old place of the Hillfolk called Whitestone Delf.'

'A Hillman place?' said Uldain sharply. 'I like not the sound of that.'

'It is long abandoned,' Haflas reassured him, 'and quite safe. There are few of the Dark Hillfolk these days west of the land of Xhendir. Come,' he beckoned them onward. 'You shall see.'

When finally they came upon the high ridge of Whitestone Delf, most of the company were close to exhaustion; and the sight that greeted them did little to raise their spirits. A low but massive octagonal tower stood rooted to a huge outcrop of white rock. Its ruined stump pointed up into the sky like the shattered finger of some giant hand.

'This is your place of refuge?' Yeon asked in disbelief, looking up into its crenellated, bat-haunted heights.

'It looks naught so much as a nest of goblins!' Uldain snorted.

'Few goblins come up on this ridge,' Haflas explained as he unworked a complex knot holding the iron door-latch in place; 'for the old workings still hold much fear for them. This is one of the safe places of our people. All are protected by such knots as these, which only we can make and unloose.'

'This might be as much of a trap as was the keep at Silentwater,' Telsyan commented bluntly. 'The tower must stand out clearly for many leagues.'

Haflas shook his head. 'The trees are tall. The forests hide it well from eyes below. We are quite safe here.'

The stone floor had been fairly recently furnished with supplies of dry bracken, arranged about a central stone hearth. Within moments the flickering light of a small fire illumined the rough stone walls.

'My lady,' Uhlendof sat down next to Gwildé. 'You will pardon me if I ask you one small question, but it is important. Do you know of any reason at all why Rievers should suddenly fall upon Silentwater?'

Gwildé looked across at him sharply. 'What do you suppose that I should know, Mallenian? I presume they came to rob and plunder. What else should I know of these things?'

'Naught, my lady,' Uhlendof said quickly. 'It is only that we have happened to obtain some forewarning of this.' Producing the small scrap of parchment they had obtained in Githrim's tower, he explained how they had come into possession of it, and its presumed significance. 'Unfortunately,' he went on, 'we did not realise exactly what it referred to until it was too late – an unpleasant truth with most prophecies – but undoubtedly it is a forewarning of the attack upon Silentwater Keep.'

'I have heard of this "Master of the North",' said Uldain. 'It is an old legend of the goblins and their allies: a great war-leader who will return to have dominion over all the northlanders, exterminating the hated humans and all who do not kneel to his banner.'

'Then there is your answer!' Gwildé said coldly, turning back to the priest. 'Someone seeks to rouse and unite the Riever bands – and we are his first victims.'

'Yet why,' Uhlendof persisted, 'does the King of Helietrim choose to keep such a large establishment in these northern wilds, so far from his own kingdom? Surely not merely to oversee a few declining lead mines? I know little of the value of metals, but I cannot think that what you mine here can be worth the cost of such an enterprise. Surely there is lead and copper to be found closer to Helietrim?'

'The mines of Zumir have belonged to the kings of Helietrim for centuries,' Gwildé answered flatly. 'Why should we give them up now?'

'My lady grows weary of such questioning,' Uldain broke in. 'Let it cease! Your own role in this affair is not beyond question.'

'There is but one thing further I would ask,' the monk insisted. 'It is quite simple, but nonetheless important.' He leaned forward to look hard into Gwildé's face, much to the consternation of her ladies. 'When the word *harrunor* was mentioned in the boat this morning, you reacted strangely, my lady. Why?'

'*Harrunor*.' Gwildé repeated the word slowly. 'You say that *harrunor* was what produced the heat? The burn upon our boat? And' – she turned to look at Keran— 'the door. The shattering of my chamber door, that killed Ithren . . .' She paused. 'How is this possible?'

'*Harrunor* is a very rare and powerful metal, my lady,' Uhlendof told her gravely. 'The Mage Metal of the ancients. One that has been almost unknown since the time of the Qhilmun Kings. Yet now it has reappeared in new quantities, and in new and dangerous hands, to do work of great evil. And I fear that there is greater evil yet to come. Do you know anything of this? Anything at all?'

Gwildé sat strangely silent for several moments; and when she at last spoke it was to ask another question: 'This *harrunor* of which you speak – is it a dull, purple-grey metal?'

'Yes,' said Leighor eagerly, 'but sometimes it can burn with an inner fire.'

'I have never seen it so,' Gwildé said; 'but I have seen the metal.'

'My lady!' Sire Uldain broke in. But Gwildé ignored him.

'Of recent years we have produced a metal so called, in the mines,' she continued, 'a metal just such as you describe. Only a very little, perhaps only a single ingot in a six-month; but all that we produced was sent down to Helietrim in the greatest of secrecy. Even the miners themselves were told naught of the strange metal they found with the lead, and which took so long to refine. We sent it south in the ordinary shipments, with the lead and copper, so that it would not attract undue attention.'

'And you knew not what it was used for?'

'No, that was kept close secret.'

'As that which you have just divulged to this quartet of strangers should have been kept!' Uldain glowered. 'You have broken a great trust, my lady.'

'It grows clear to me, good Sire Uldain,' Gwildé's voice bore a hard edge, 'that there are already far too many in these northlands who know more of our secrets than we seem to ourselves! Perhaps if we had known a little more of the value of what we mined, we would not have been so unprepared for attack!'

'Aye, milady,' Uldain nodded weakly.

'So you have been sending two large ingots of this metal south to King Arminor every year?' Uhlendof asked. 'For how long?'

'Two or three years, no more,' Gwildé answered. 'My lord Fralcel replaced Lord Aameril, who began the shipments when the metal was first discovered.'

'Then Arminor must have close on half a hundredweight of the metal by now,' Telsyan calculated quickly. 'Do you have any idea what is done with it?'

Gwildé shook her head. 'None at all. I only know that it is sent south into the hands of the king's seer, Ariscel. What he does with it I do not know.' She glanced around her, at the intent faces of the assembled company, noting their expressions. 'Every ounce of the metal is accounted for. I cannot believe that he uses it for ill.'

'Not our king perhaps,' Uldain said grimly, 'but what if he is betrayed? Seers and wizards are vile and deceitful creatures, ambitious and untrustworthy all. Claighar could well have wormed his amulet from any such. I trust them not!'

'Nor I,' said Yeon. 'I say that we should look to this seer's door for the cause of our betrayal!'

'Aye,' Zindur grunted loudly in agreement.

'But what would Ariscel have to gain from an attack on Silentwater?' Gwildé frowned. 'All the *harrunor* from the mines already goes to him. If the attack was truly to seize this purple metal, then it must have been planned by someone else.'

'It could well have been,' Uhlendof nodded, leaning forward. 'The four of us witnessed Lord Fralcel returning from a ride into the forest yesterday. Do you know, my lady, whether he went to meet anyone?'

'He did ride out that morning,' Gwildé nodded. 'But it was for no meeting that I had knowledge of. He often rode out so, just to take the air. Though, I admit, there have been times when he would ride into the forest to meet with some knight or emissary who preferred his business to be private.'

'And were there any such who seemed unduly interested in the purple metal or the mines?'

Gwildé fell silent for a moment as if in thought. 'There was one, some months ago,' she said at last. 'A merchant, or so he claimed to be. More than once he offered gold to my lord if he could have metal from the mines in return. He did not specify *harrunor*, he just seemed interested in lead and copper. He even offered to supply labourers so that the King would notice no difference in the amount of metal reaching Helietrim. Many lords would have agreed to such a bargain. But Fralcel would do nothing to betray King Arminor.'

'Did this man offer no violence,' Uhlendof asked. 'No threats?'

'None.'

'And you have no idea who he was?'

Gwildé shook her head. 'He gave only a name: Naurlek I think it was. We did not think there was anything strange in his request.' She halted. 'You do not think it was he who . . . ?'

'I do not know,' the monk shrugged. 'But it seems to have been an early attempt to probe the availability of the metal. If so, then this attack has been planned for a long while.'

The travellers fell silent after this, each interred in his own gloomy thoughts. Gradually they drifted into a restless and uneasy sleep.

The travellers slept for only a few short hours, waking gritty-eyed and yawning to stumble through the icy pre-dawn dark. When the first dim light of dawn finally appeared in the eastern sky they were cold, aching and weary. Then suddenly, they emerged on to the eastern shore of another large lake, whose misty reaches ran away into the west as far as the eye could see.

'Is this where Hallad's Keep lies?' asked Yeon hopefully.

Haflas shook his head. 'That is a day's march yet. There is a castle upon the farther shore, but that, like Whitestone Delf, is long forsaken by its builders. This lake has no human name but still bears its old Hillman title of *Orodun Ubas*, though none of the Dark Hillfolk dwell here now.'

'Does that name have any meaning?' Uhlendof asked.

'All the names of the Hillfolk have meaning, my lord,' said Haflas softly.

The morning light revealed large flocks of crane and grey geese floating serenely on the still waters. They seemed still half-asleep in the early quarter-light.

'Would that one of those fine fat birds would come a little closer,' Zindur said with feeling. 'I can just see one of them turning on an open spit.'

Only then did the travellers begin to realise how hungry they were, and Leighor did not thank the warrior for this reminder. They had eaten next to nothing for a day and a half, and the thought of freshly roasted goose was almost unbearable.

'We could surely shoot one from here,' Yeon said eagerly.

'It would be a waste of time and a waste of good arrows,' Uldain grunted. 'Even if we chanced to hit one of them, who would swim out and bring it back? No,' he shook his head regretfully, 'we have no time to waste upon chasing wild geese.'

Fording a broad, fast-flowing river that tumbled down into *Orodun Ubas* from the eastern hills, they journeyed beside the lake for some hours. By late morning they had reached its north-easternmost corner. And here another great river rolled down from the north, deeper and more powerful than the first, its constricted waters surging powerfully into the lake, its banks deep-scoured and steep.

'We shall never cross this,' Uldain said at once. 'Not even a mastodon could brave such a current!'

'We shall not have to,' Haflas acknowledged to everyone's relief. 'This river is the Argonan, which flows down from the lake of Esch Tuarn, upon which lies Hallad's Keep. Yet it passes through many steep gorges between there and here, so we will do best to journey through the hills.'

Noon came and went as they climbed away from the river and up into the low, wooded hills. This was Argonan Vale, and a country quite different from that which they had passed through so far. Instead of dark, towering pines, the travellers now walked between tall stands of white and silver birch, in drier, well drained soils. Most of the leaves had already fallen from these trees, and a flood of unaccustomed daylight brightened their path. Occasionally they caught glimpses of the twisting valley floor, where the Argonan River roared and thundered through deep chasms in the ancient rock.

The travellers made good time through this pleasing country. And as the afternoon passed, the feeling so long common to them all, that they were unlikely to survive this perilous journey, at last began to fade. It came as a shock, therefore, to hear a human voice crying out in alarm some distance ahead of them.

The company froze. There was silence. And then again the plaintive voice rang out form somewhere close ahead. Uldain crept forward to investigate, reappearing moments later to beckon them forward. They approached cautiously, finding themselves on the edge of a small clearing.

'Have you found anything?' Zindur whispered.

Uldain pointed across the clearing to three large trees that stood together beside the path. Beneath the second of these, half hidden amongst its branches, a clumsy birchpole cage huge from a rope of knotted vines. Leighor could not see clearly, but there seemed to be someone imprisoned inside. No one else was visible anywhere around.

Weapons drawn, they crept cautiously about the edge of the clearing, keeping always to the shadow of the trees. Leighor kept a firm grip upon the stock of his crossbow, eyes constantly scanning the surrounding forest for any sign of the ambush they all feared. As he drew closer to the swaying cage, however, a startling realisation impressed itself upon him.

The form huddled within that birchpole cage was gut-wrenchingly familiar. It could not be . . . But yes . . . He was sure it was . . .

'Inanys!' he blurted out, running ahead of the others to stand beneath the suspended cage, staring up at the dishevelled form within. 'It is him!' he shouted. 'The crookback!'

'Be silent!' Uldain hissed angrily, drawing closer. 'Would you waken the whole forest?' He looked up sharply into the cage. 'Aye, it is your companion of late,' he observed coldly. 'It is strange indeed that we should chance upon him so. A happenstance that would seem to make your number once again complete . . .'

But the knight was prevented from saying more by a loud cry from above: 'My friends! Release me! I have been hung here two long days. I have the cramp. My bones are bent and twisted. I am wracked with pain! Can you do nothing there below but talk?'

'It is the evil crooked one!' Geltan declared, arriving late upon the scene. 'He who was cast out by my lord Fralcel.'

Inanys lashed out at him in sudden fury: rattling the thin wooden slats as if he would break free and tear the unfortunate cellarer to pieces.

'Set me free!' he demanded. 'Why do you linger?'

Uldain snorted. 'First I would like a good few answers from you. Aye, and from your friends also!' He looked up once more into the wildly swinging cage. 'How came you to this plight?' he demanded. 'And moreover, how came you here, set right upon our route – through lands filled with raiders, Rievers and Tarintarmen – unless you be one of them yourself!'

'Nay, my lords!' Inanys shrank back from the bars, his face now stricken with terror – or so it seemed, although Leighor thought he saw more of artifice in the crookback's gaze. 'I fled because I feared the wrath of my lord Fralcel. That is the truth, I swear it! I feared for my life, my lords, and so I took a small boat and crossed the lake, hoping to meet with my companions later, on the road. But I was waylaid here by more than three score goblins; and tormented and beaten, and wretchedly hung here for their amusement – tied up in this foul cage and poked with sharp sticks, until they tired of my poor screams and abandoned me, to go in search of new sport!'

'He may speak the truth,' Uhlendof said slowly. 'It is a tale which has grains of likelihood within it . . .'

'It is a pack of lies!' Uldain spat. 'I would not credit one word that rolls from his evil tongue! I say leave him in his cage to rot, and if his four stormcrow companions wish to remain here with him, then all the better!'

'I bid you guard your tongue!' Telsyan bridled at once. 'If you have any accusations to bring against our company, let us have them out in the open, and at once!'

'Aye,' Yeon nodded. 'If there were any treason at Silentwater it was well established long before we came. Charge us not with your own failings!'

There was a tense silence.

'Well?' Gwildé demanded at last, holding Uldain's gaze tight with her own. 'Have you any proofs to bring against these our former guests, with whom we have shared all of our late sorrows and privations?'

Uldain hesitated, scratching his beard. 'No, my lady, I have no proofs,' he admitted at last. 'But with greatest respect, I must advise . . .'

'Save your advice, my lord, until we have greater need of it!' Gwildé turned sharply away from him. 'And for mercy's sake, cut this man down, and let us go! Then, perhaps, we may end our journey before nightfall.'

Uldain was visibly angered by this open rebuke from his lady, but must perforce swallow it; and with a nod to Zindur and the other guardsmen he ordered the captive's release.

Zindur's sword made short work of the wattle bindings that held the cage together; and the familiar crumpled form of Inanys soon stood erect within the wreckage, for all his travails still bearing the familiar crooked stick and wearing the bright, silver-buckled shoes he had obtained in Biren. He stretched, rubbing his joints to restore their circulation, and was soon hobbling briskly about the clearing with the aid of his stick. Telsyan, Yeon, Uhlendof and Leighor he greeted as long lost friends; clasping their hands firmly in his clammy, unpleasant grip, his narrow eyes revealing no iota of his true feelings. He then made his way towards the lady Gwildé to render his over-profuse thanks, lank hair falling across his face as he seized her hand and bent to kiss it.

Just in time, Gwildé snatched her hand away, and giving him a cold smile, bade the march continue. Leighor hung back a little as the now quite large party straggled onward; pausing to examine the wreckage of Inanys's cage. There seemed little unusual about it, but for one curious thing which the others seemed to have missed. For although the soil about the cage bore the footmarks of Inanys, and of the rest of their company; there was nowhere upon it any trace of the footprints of even one goblin – let alone three score. As they journeyed onward, Leighor thought long and hard upon that.

Chapter Thirteen
THE GREY FORTRESS

They arrived at Hallad's Keep shortly before dark, having followed the narrow path out of the hills and down on to the dark shores of Esch Tuarn, into whose waters jutted this mighty citadel of the Knights of Imsild. The island fortress was connected to the shore only by a single fortified bridge; otherwise the grey ancient walls fell away directly into the lake, leaving not the smallest pinpoint of undefended land upon which an enemy might gain a toehold. Above it, the white and gold banners of the Knights of Imsild floated from every turret and bastion. The travellers' spirits soared at the sight. Here at last, after all the fears and terrors of the past few days, was safety.

The gatekeeper of the fortress first heard their tale, and then bade them enter. They must however, leave all their weapons at the gate. This only Inanys refused to do, choosing to remain at the gatehouse while the others passed on across the narrow causeway.

To Leighor's surprise, behind its granite facings the bridge was built entirely of wood. For a moment this puzzled him, until he realised that this could only be to allow for its speedy demolition it time of siege. Then, passing beneath a second high barbican, they came into a gigantic fortified courtyard, easily the largest enclosed court he had ever seen. High outer walls towered up on three sides, and ahead rose the main bastion and rambling living quarters of the fortress.

A small party of merchants unloaded their mules in one corner, dwarfed by the great buildings and the sheer immensity of the courtyard around them – easily large enough, Leighor thought, for two fair-sized battles to be fought side by side, neither interfering with the other. And all around it, at regular intervals, stood massive defensive towers of grey stone, each bearing its own great white and gold banner.

'This is where we should have made for from the start,' Yeon said, looking about with pride. 'To seek the aid of these most noble knights.'

They entered the central bastion through another great portcullised door, guarded by two unflinching sentries. Both raised gleaming halberds in salute as the strangers passed – almost as if instructions of their coming had already been given, although none had run ahead of them from the gates to bear the news. In moments the travellers found themselves within a great, white-bannered hall, whose walls were lined with the shields, swords and armour of many knights long departed. At the head of the hall stood a single empty chair beneath a silken canopy of white and gold – or rather it was an empty throne, for it was so huge and mighty as to be fittingly called such. And so, ragged and dishevelled as they were, they drew wordlessly to a halt and waited.

'The fortress seems quite empty,' Leighor whispered quietly to Uhlendof. His words echoed strangely around the hall. 'This place seems fitted for many thousands.'

'Alas, the Knights of Imsild are far fewer than they were,' an incisive voice cut through the gloom behind them. The startled travellers swung about as one to face the newcomer.

A tall man of noble lineage strode briskly towards them from a side doorway. His face was strong and handsome, belying the wisps of iron-grey that streaked the temples of his otherwise dark hair. A shining hauberk of glittering mail lay beneath a simple white linen tabard, which bore upon it the golden star insignia of the knights. His boots were of gleaming silver and polished white leather. Yet beneath these spartan outer garments he wore comfortable silks and kidskin, in colours of darkest blue and black.

'Welcome to Hallad's Keep, my friends,' he said. 'Here there is welcome for all who seek refuge, and here you may remain as long as you please. I am Thunant, Master of the Knights of the Northern Marches – in the absence of my noble lord Sayardein in the south.' He held out his hand, but Gwildé ignored it, stepping forward angrily to confront him.

'Where were the knights?' she demanded bitterly. 'Where were the knights who were sworn to defend us? Where were they when our keep was overrun by foul hordes of vile Rievers, my lord murdered, and countless other good men slain? All while you rested safe here behind these walls!'

Thunant's face whitened. 'My lady, our numbers are not limitless! We cannot know all the plans of the dark hordes, and be ever there in time to stay them. The task is impossible, my lady; especially when your own liege, King Arminor, does not choose to keep us informed of his dealings in these lands!'

'What has that to do with the matter?' Gwildé said coldly. 'Is it not your duty to keep close watch upon the Riever bands, to follow their movements, to prevent just such an attack as this? How then could such a vast horde have evaded your notice?'

'My lady,' Thunant took her arm gently. 'All things are not as we might prefer them to be. We are fewer in number than in former days, and errors can be made, large bands can be missed by even the most expert of trackers. Our intelligence is by no means perfect, and the northlands grow more dangerous month by month.' He shook his head. 'I am sorry if we have failed in our duty towards you, madam; and that the knights were unable to come to your aid. Yet now I can do no more than offer you the hospitality of Hallad's Keep, and of the knights, and give you my promise that this outrage will be avenged.' He turned to Uldain. 'You, I see, are a man of war, and will recognise the many difficulties we face here. I hope that you will eventually be able to persuade your lady that we are not wholly to blame for this tragic happenstance.'

Uldain nodded, leading Gwildé gently away.

Dinner, at one of the great tables of Hallad's Keep, was not a cheerful affair. Too much had passed recently, too much had been lost, for there to be anything other than a dull relief in the travellers' hearts; and Gwildé, dining for the first time for many years without her lord, was in the depths of despair. Thunant and two other of the Knight Commanders of Hallad's Keep, Veresun and Skalanduir, tried to explain their situation over the several rich courses of the meal.

'Our forces in the north are very much reduced,' Thunant repeated. 'Few knights wish to spend much time in these dour lands, and our Grand Master, Usialdun, sees little point in sending knights where there are so few folk left to protect. Centuries of Riever raids and Varroain neglect have done their work well, and these lands are now all but empty. Consequently only Hallad's Keep remains to the Knights of Imsild of all our former fortresses north of the Caethalon River. And even here we have not our full complement this season, for many of the greatest among us have ridden south for the choosing of the new High King in Tershelline, and will not return before the spring.'

'So this is why the Rievers murder and pillage throughout the north as they please!' Seydal said bitterly.

Veresun shook his head. 'That is not the case, by your leave, sir. We still have a strong force here, a force more than capable of matching any Riever band that ventures abroad. Even those of Foln or Korgûl Slainhand, the Redcap brothers, one of whom we are sure led the attack upon your keep at Silentwater. The cap dipped in the blood of their victims: that is their hallmark alone.'

'So there are two of them?' Leighor said, surprised.

'Aye,' Thunant nodded. 'Both are vicious murderers and perpetrators of countless outrages. We know the location of one brother, Foln, who was seen camped with the remnant of his forces at Virn Deep, some twenty days march to the north-west of here.'

Uldain sat forward. 'So the one who attacked us must have been the other: Korgûl Slainhand. It is good to know his name. So do we come one step closer to his destruction.'

'You can be sure we shall seek him out,' Thunant nodded. 'Such an outrage cannot be left unpunished. No keep the size of Silentwater has fallen to Rievers in living memory. It is a fearsome crime.'

'We think there is a plan afoot,' Yeon said, 'to unite all the Rievers of the northlands in a great rising, led by one who is termed "Master of the North".'

Thunant and the other knights exchanged smiles. 'You have been listening to too many goblins' tales, lad,' the Knight Master said. 'Such stories have been common amongst the goblins of the north since before this castle was raised – and that was many centuries ago!' He shook his head. 'Sometimes a Riever band may take up the legend as an excuse for their robbing and pillaging, but no more than that. No man could ever unite all the Rievers of the northlands. Even a band of the size that sacked Silentwater Keep will generally break up and melt into the forests as soon as the booty has been divided.'

'But if such a situation were to arise,' Telsyan asked. 'Would you have the force to deal with it?'

Thunant nodded. 'A well-armed, mounted knight is worth ten of these Rievers. We would not even need to recall all the knights from the south to defeat such scum, if they would stand and fight like men!'

'And what of the Durian Knights?' Leighor asked. 'Would they come to your assistance?'

Skalanduir laughed, but Veresun spoke with anger, 'We need no assistance from such as they! The order of Durian Knights is naught but a jest amongst honest men. They are lax and corrupt, concerned only with keeping tight hold on the wealth of the northlands, and the broad lands they have extracted from the King of Scûn! There is not one good fighting soldier among them; nor one nobleman.'

'Aye,' Thunant nodded. 'They are unworthy of their sacred trust. They were never of our mettle, but a lesser order, founded long ago to colonise the northlands and protect the few scattered settlements that yet remain. That mission was long ago forgotten. It is even rumoured that they now pay tribute to the Riever bands to keep their lands secure! I would as soon seek assistance from the King of the Goblins as from the Knights of Dur – though there is no need to do either on the basis of your goblin tales.'

'But we have more than goblin tales!' Yeon insisted angrily. 'Uhlendof,' he ordered. 'Show them the paper – the writings that forecast the attack upon Silentwater and the mines!'

Somewhat reluctantly the monk rose and handed the parchment to Thunant. 'We had this several days before the attack, at the tower of the alchemist Githrim, which lies in Skerrdale.'

The Knight Master studied the scroll and shook his head. 'It is meaningless,' he said. 'Written in no known language. A scrawl.'

Patiently Uhlendof translated. Yet Thunant still did not seem convinced. 'If it reads as you say, it is some form of threat – common enough in these times. No doubt it was meant for my lord Fralcel, to frighten him into paying tribute.'

'But why should it come into Githrim's hands?' Yeon demanded.

Thunant shrugged his shoulders. 'I do not know. But we believe Githrim to be one of those who buy the goods the Rievers steal and cannot use themselves. There are many in the borderlands who turn a good profit by that means.'

'Then it is a crime punishable by death!' said Uldain angrily.

'The matter will be investigated,' Thunant said calmly.

There was more talk that night: of Riever bands, of past skirmishes, and the lay of the land to north and south. But Gwildé was clearly too exhausted for further conversation, and the travellers retired early to their beds.

The following morning Keran woke at daybreak, despite having spent most of the previous two nights without sleep. For a few minutes she enjoyed the luxury of lying still in her warm soft bed, between fine sheets of smooth crisp linen. The knights certainly did themselves well, she thought, glancing about the well-furnished room she shared with Mireal, her eyes catching upon the glowing tapestries of hunting scenes, great feasts, and men in battle that lined the walls. The sun was risen behind her, and the sound of merry cries rang up from without. Curious, she rose and tiptoed across the room. A delicate latticed window opened over the western aspect of the lake and the forested hills beyond.

Four young men were fishing the calm waters from two small boats, with but a single net between them. They laughed and joked with one another in a manner so carefree that it made her heart lurch and filled her with sudden melancholy. For a moment she felt the strong desire to be one with them, happy and untroubled in the water on a fine sunny morning. But how was she to know their troubles and their hardships? Perhaps they just bore their cares better than most, and would think her quite the fool for ever envying them. She turned away, deciding to leave Mireal to sleep a few moments longer while she went to attend upon her lady, drawing back the heavy curtains of her chamber to admit the morning sun.

Gwildé stirred. 'Is that you, Keran?' she mumbled sleepily.

'Aye, my lady,' Keran answered, with as much lightness in her voice as she could muster. 'It is a fine morning, but cold. I thought I might go down to the kitchens and find us some breakfast.'

'If you wish,' Gwildé murmured, 'but send in Mireal and let her attend to my hair and my dressing while you are gone.'

Keran bobbed a quick curtsey and departed, giving Mireal a determined shake upon the way. She came out into a long, cavernous hallway, with a stairway leading down. This she followed, and almost immediately – by lucky happenstance – fell upon the kitchens.

The High Kitchen of Hallad's Keep formed the greater part of an enormous vaulted hall. One whole side of it was occupied by three great stone hearths, flanked by numerous glowing ovens and cluttered with cauldrons and slowly turning spits. Squires, bondsmen and estate workers broke their fast at rows of wooden tables at the far end of the hall. The rest of the kitchen stood in a state of teeming chaos, with skivvies, cooks and servitors scurrying everywhere, seemingly in the course of preparing a hundred different meals at once.

Keran pushed her way through a maze of tables, pots, pans, piles of firewood, turnips, tubers, and even baskets of fowl, which clucked angrily at her as she passed; trying to find someone who might be in charge.

She got in the way of a large man mixing something in a vast ironclay bowl. He cursed, pushing her aside so roughly that she staggered back into his preparing table, dislodging many of the small pots of herbs and spices that were balanced there.

'Look what you've done, you great clumsy wench!' he bellowed, slamming his bowl furiously down upon the table. For an instant Keran feared that he would strike her, and she tried to make a hasty escape between the tables. But the fat man was a deal faster than he looked, and his arm shot out to grasp her firmly about the wrist.

'Oh no, my lass!' he gasped, dragging her back towards him. 'First you shall tell me the name of your master, that he may make full restitution for your clumsiness. Either that, or I shall take the worth of the goods out of your hide! Look!' he quivered, pointing at the mess of shattered potsherds and their contents, now mingling with the waste peelings and other refuse on the kitchen floor. 'Some of the rarest spices in the Eleven Kingdoms – and all ruined!'

A small pig appeared beneath the table, and sniffed dismissively at the pile of condiments before moving on.

Disconcerted by the sudden turn of events, Keran attempted to regain her composure. 'I serve the Lady Gwildé,' she said at once, 'and she cares naught for your vile herbs and spices! She is an honoured guest in this place, and will have you well whipped for your insolence if you do not at once release me and inform me where I may find breakfast for her.'

The fat man was temporarily taken aback. 'What?' he bellowed. 'You dare speak to me of whippings? I, who am personal cook to Sire Nombarel! I shall give you whippings, my girl—' He raised one hand as if to strike her – but even as he did so, Keran managed to twist herself free of his grip and take several quick steps backward . . . bumping unexpectedly into the plump form of the Mallenian priest, Uhlendof, who had drawn up behind her, along with the dark southron herbalist, Leighor.

'What is this?' the monk asked sharply. 'Do you threaten one of our company?'

'No, your honour,' the cook rushed to explain. 'The girl provoked me. She has destroyed all my finest herbs and sp—'

'That is small matter,' Uhlendof broke in swiftly. 'We have far more pressing concerns than these kitchen trifles. If you have any complaints, pray take them up with Master General Thunant.'

He turned to go.

'That is not sufficient—' the cook began. But before he could say anything further, he was interrupted by a small wiry man bearing a heavy pail of fresh milk.

'Come,' said Leighor, tugging at Keran's arm. 'Let us go while we may.'

But Keran was loath to follow her two rescuers at once, hanging back for a moment to watch her would-be assailant haggle with the dairyman, before bending to sample a little of the new milk.

She was decided.

She stared hard at the dull copper ladle as it rose slowly towards the fat cook's lips. She concentrated, focusing her mind on the ladle and the fresh milk within; and then with a single surge of effort, willed the change.

For a moment Keran hovered anxiously, not sure whether she had accomplished the deed or not. But then, as the cook took his first deep draught, she knew. Half choking on the foul liquid, he spat it out on to the floor, retching uncontrollably as he stared in rank disbelief at the fallen ladle, now spilling out sour, malodorous milk. Oaths and curses rang out across the hall.

Keran allowed herself a brief smile of satisfaction, and turned away, curdling the milk in the bucket for good measure as she did so. But to her surprise the monk had halted too, and now stared at her intently. For an instant their eyes met. She lowered her head quickly. But the priest said nothing, turning away from her to follow Leighor across the floor of the kitchen.

Remaining with her rescuers only long enough to gather up a platter of cold meats, bread and wine for her lady, Keran made her way briskly back through the maze of corridors. Yet even now, she could not suppress a thrill of elation at what she had done. No longer did the curious power she seemed to possess frighten her, as it had when she had first discovered it in her last days at Darien. Now she felt sure that whatever small talent she had was hers alone, and not something dark and evil from without. But it was the darkness and the evil that most people would concentrate upon; and that was why she kept her secret well.

Yet for all that, her power seemed of little practical use. She could play a few small childish tricks with it, and that was all. It seemed, too, that she could only do negative things. She had more than once tried uncurdling milk, but that never seemed to work. Certainly her talent was of no help to her in a dangerous situation like the Riever attack upon Silentwater, or even in trouble of less immediacy, such as her father's fall . . .

It had been hard indeed to watch the slow ruin of her father at the hands of the Durian Knights, and be able to do nothing to help. The Durians barely tolerated independent traders like her father at the best of times. But when he had quarrelled with Iruldas, one of the Knight Commanders, over the branding of a servant, all doors had suddenly closed.

The Knights had said nothing directly. That was not their way. But sources of supply abruptly dried up, markets ceased to exist, and punitive fines were levied for minor infringements. Demands for payment mounted, and her father's health declined. He was still just able to eke out an impoverished, hand-to-mouth existence, but the burden of two grown daughters was too great. Her sister, Kerel, had the prospect of an early marriage, but she, Keran, had been too young, and in any event there was no dowry for her. It had seemed an act of kindness then, when a merchant friend of her father's had offered to take her south with him, to be schooled as a lady, in service to one of the lesser barons of Helietrim. And so had she come to her current situation.

Gwildé was up and dressed when Keran finally regained their chambers. But despite the best urgings of herself and Mireal, Gwildé could be persuaded to take no more than the tiniest morsel of food, and would have spent the whole of the day in grieving and melancholy had there not been a summons from Thunant halfway through the morning to join him in the great courtyard, where he had news of the attack on Silentwater.

Only this was enough to drag Gwildé from her chamber, and she followed reluctantly as Thunant led the assembled travellers down into a lower chamber of vaulted stone. Vast as the great audience hall above, this was cold and dark, its low roof supported by a forest of thick stone pillars, each barely an arm's length apart from its neighbour. Keran shivered. Yet there was a dim light somewhere ahead.

Set beneath two flickering torches stood three men: one of the knights, an armoured guardsman, and another, larger figure, scarred of face and large of limb, who wore dark leathers and heavy iron arm-bands.

Thunant nodded briefly in greeting, and halted. 'Here is your news of Silentwater,' he frowned. 'A small company of knights met with some goblin stragglers on the Great Road yesternight. They slew all but one, whom they brought back for questioning. It took time,' he continued. 'Most of the night. But at last it admitted that it had been part of the band of Korgûl Slainhand: the same band that sacked Silentwater Keep. It claims to have split from Korgûl's band the night before.'

'Can we see the goblin ourselves?' Gwildé asked.

Thunant looked a little surprised. 'Are you sure that you wish to, my lady? It will not be—'

'I would know all that I am able of those who slew my lord,' she said firmly, 'whatever the discomfiture.'

Thunant nodded to the large, leather-clad figure, who at once turned to descend a small flight of steps that had lain unseen behind him in the darkness. There was the dull boom and groan of a heavy iron door being opened somewhere deep below, and then a plaintive wail. Moments later the gaoler reappeared, dragging a small, slight, almost naked figure behind him. The goblin gave out a low continuous moan as it was dragged along. It halted, to stand cowering before them, gibbering in terror, its thin, leathery legs bound together with iron chains. Keran could see many marks upon its warty, sallow skin; one of its arms bled profusely and was twisted back at an unnatural angle.

Thunant glowered at the cringing figure. 'Goblin,' he said harshly. 'Here is a lady who wishes you to answer her questions. You will speak the truth to her, and tell her all she wishes to know. Do you understand?'

'No more hurt . . . No more hurt for Vashnur!' the creature screamed wretchedly, trying to twist itself free of the gaoler's fierce grip.

Thunant snorted. 'There will be no more pain . . . if you answer our questions truthfully. If you lie, you shall be taken to the wheel.' He turned back to Gwildé, reverting to the courtly Varroain speech, 'The creature only understands the peasant Durian, and its own dark tongue.'

'I can speak a little Durian,' said Gwildé, over the goblin's whimpering. 'I have lived close on two years in these northlands now. But has this creature been tortured? It seems half mad with fear.'

'Some things are regrettable necessities.' Thunant spoke in an offhand manner. 'I tried to warn you, madam, that this sight might not be a pleasant one.'

'But is it necessary to torture any creature so?' Gwildé persisted. 'For it would seem to make us little better than they.'

'That is an unexpected judgement, my lady,' Thunant's voice darkened with disapproval, 'especially after all that you have so recently suffered at their hands!' He looked harshly down at the goblin. 'Have you any questions to ask of this creature – or shall it be returned to the cells below?'

'I will question it,' Sire Uldain said at once, stepping forward to stare directly down at the captive. At a signal from Thunant, the gaoler grasped the small head of the goblin in one massive hand, forcing its face upward until its large eyes gazed, oily and unblinking, into those of the knight from Silentwater. 'Were you a part of the Riever band of one Korgûl Slainhand?' Uldain asked.

The goblin tried to nod.

'Answer!' the gaoler jerked the creature's neck brutally backward.

It screamed in pain: 'Mercy masters. Mercy! Not hurt Vashnur. Vashnur tell all; but not hurt!'

'No hurt if you answer my questions,' Uldain said firmly. 'Do you know why Korgûl wished to attack Silentwater?'

'Vashnur not at Ssilentwater!' the creature moaned desperately. 'Vashnur not killer. Vashnur good goblin. Not sslay humanss, not take cattle or sheep . . .'

'If that is so,' Uldain said, 'you have nothing to fear. Yet I speak not of you, but the others, those who followed Korgûl: why did they attack a strong keep like Silentwater?'

The goblin's eyes flashed cunningly from side to side, and Keran perceived that despite its pain and terror it still held something back. Perhaps it spoke the truth, but not the whole truth.

'Korgûl say Ssilentwater rich, very rich,' the creature mumbled. 'Much gold in mines, much food, many horses, boots, weaponss. He say sservants of the Masster will open gates for uss. Make capture easy. But I say no. Thiss is bad thing. I . . .'

'Who is the "Master"?' Uldain cut in sharply.

The goblin abruptly stopped speaking and began to seek rapidly about him, as if he feared some hand might strike him out of the dark. 'He is master of all,' he hissed. 'All in the northlandss. He is everywhere! All must obey.'

'And Korgûl obeys the Master?'

'All must obey.'

'And who is he?' Uldain repeated. 'Where does he dwell? What is his purpose?'

The goblin seemed to grow increasingly agitated as Uldain's voice rose. 'Vashnur cannot know,' he stammered, shaking his head wildly. 'Vashnur cannot say. It is death . . .' His voice trailed away into nothingness, and it seemed that he was suddenly in the utmost terror. His whole body squirmed in the gaoler's grasp as he tried to roll himself up into a tight ball, gibbering madly.

'You will get no more from the creature now,' Thunant said, turning away. 'Its wits are gone.' He gave an abrupt signal to the gaoler, and the goblin was dragged away once more to the cells below.

'What will you do with him now?' Uhlendof asked. 'Will you release him?'

Thunant turned to stare at the monk for a moment before speaking. 'You are a Mallenian, are you not?' he asked.

'Yes, my lord. That is my faith.'

'You worship the One then, the all-father who holds small interest, it is said, in earthly affairs. And that is fitting for one of your sort, with few worldly responsibilities and much time to spend upon moral debates and fair philosophies. Here we worship Thall, an active god who knows well the true ways of the world. An honest god, who shows no mercy to the servants of the Evil One, and who will suffer no dealings with them. Do not interfere with our ways, outsider; for it is we who fight, we who stand watch upon the wilderlands, who give you the freedom to follow your own practices in safety and to sleep easy in your bed.'

'The goblin has done no wrong,' Uhlendof insisted. 'He has told you what you wish to know; is it justice to ill-treat him further?'

'Who knows what evils he has not committed in his foul life?' Thunant said grimly. 'Doubtless his past holds many deeds to blanch your fair complexions and make all of you shudder to the marrow of your bones. He will get no more than his deserts.' He turned upon his heel. 'But now I have no further time for talk. The hour of vigil draws near, and your midday meal awaits. I would advise you all to consider your futures. You are welcome if you wish to remain here until the spring, when it should again be safe for travel, and the caravans will come down from the lands of Scûn. If you wish to journey south before then, a small escort of knights will be available to conduct you as far as Imball. But you must inform me of your decision today so that arrangements may be made.' He bowed. 'I bid you good day, good sirs, my lady.' He and the other knight strode away, leaving the travellers to find their own way upward.

'What do you think of your knights now?' Telsyan turned to Yeon once they were gone.

'They are fine men,' the youth answered defiantly. 'There are none nobler in all the Eastern Realms. I spoke with many of their number this morning. They fight with honour; not just for their own lands, but here in the north, where no one else will stand against the dark.'

'Well said, lad!' Uldain grunted his approval.

'They have their reasons for what they do,' Telsyan growled. 'For every knight in the borderlands, there are ten in richer pickings farther south. Most of these knights fight as do all other men – for their own wealth and power.'

'I will not listen to you!' Yeon turned from him. 'You cannot understand men with nobler motives than your own!'

'And what of the goblin?' Uhlendof asked. 'Was his treatment fair and noble?'

Yeon hesitated. 'The knights had no choice,' he said haltingly at last. 'Set against the good they do, it is so small a matter . . .'

The monk shook his head sadly. 'The ways of the Dark One are cunning indeed. For even as men believe they fight for good, so their ways turn to evil. And in the end one might find it hard to tell one apart from the other.'

'What mean you by that?' Uldain demanded. 'These are goodly men!'

'I mean that there is more to good than wearing a white tabard and killing goblins!' Uhlendof snapped. 'To use the means of evil to counter evil is to let evil conquer all!'

'Pah!' the knight exclaimed impatiently, turning to stride back up towards the courtyard.

'Well?' Seydal demanded after they had eaten in silence for a time. 'What are we to do?'

'As for ourselves,' Telsyan said, indicating the three other travellers as well as himself; 'we are bound upon a set course. We can neither remain here, nor return south, but must continue our journey to Darien before the winter snows.'

Gwildé's eyebrows rose. 'What goal could possibly make you persist so, upon so dangerous a course?'

There was silence for a moment before Telsyan spoke: 'We are bound upon an important errand, my lady. One that might easily have effect upon the outcome of the election of the new High King in Tershelline, in the spring; and which therefore cannot be delayed.'

The revelation evoked a surprised ripple of interest around the table, and the other diners fell silent.

'And has this also to do with the sudden death of Archbaron Eridar?' Gwildé asked succinctly.

'Aye, my lady,' the merchant frowned. 'It has much to do with his death, and with the overhasty succession of one Darvir to his lands and title.'

'You are opposed to Darvir then?' Gwildé said.

Telsyan nodded. 'That is true, my lady. All four of us have served Lord Eridar in the past, in various capacities; and would not see all that he worked and strived for in his life, undone now at Darvir's hand.'

'And what right have you, as subjects, to quarrel with your lawful lord?' Uldain asked sharply. 'And to act against his will? Many would term such conduct treasonous – disloyal at least!'

'Peace, my lord.' Gwildé said firmly, yet with a sudden deep weariness in her voice. 'We are in no position yet to judge these men or their actions. Darvir is no friend of our liege, King Arminor, as was good Lord Eridar. So let us not be overhasty to rush to his defence.'

The knight's face hardened. 'I urge caution in dealing with these strangers, madam. It seems to me that the more we learn of them, the greater cause we have for misgivings.'

'I have been given no cause yet to doubt these gentlemen,' Gwildé said quickly, to forestall any quarrel. 'All that they have told us has been disclosed freely enough, and there is much they could have kept secret had they so chosen . . . Yet still,' she turned back to the four companions across the table, 'I would know more of your reasons for this journey, and of your quarrel with Darvir.'

Uhlendof answered slowly. 'We oppose Darvir because he has gained his crown through treachery and murder. We have not told you this before, my lady, but he, like Claighar, bears one of the amulets of *harrunor*, and most likely he had it from the same source. We travel north now with warrants to obtain the last testament of my lord Eridar, which may help us to prove some of Darvir's treasons, and ensure that the proxy vote of the Sielders is truly cast in accordance with Eridar's wishes.' He withdrew the papers from his robe and handed them to Gwildé for her inspection.

'Your errand seems genuine enough,' she said at last. 'And in truth, a great deal seems to fall into place with this. A conspiracy against King Arminor, and in favour of Misan, would explain much. And if this magick metal, *harrunor*, plays some part in these affairs, then even the attack upon Silentwater seems no longer such a mystery . . .'

'Perhaps, my lady,' said Uldain. 'Yet if so, then these are matters of great importance – clearly too great to be left in the hands of these . . .' he paused, 'wanderers. I feel the recovery of this testament of Eridar's would be far better left to the knights.'

'No!' both Telsyan and Uhlendof exclaimed at once.

'The knights must not be brought into this!' Uhlendof rose from his seat sharply. 'They are far from impartial, even in small matters. And in a matter of such importance as the succession to Galdan, they cannot be trusted!'

'You are a fine one to speak of trust!' Uldain spat. 'You ask us to take you on naught but your own recognisance, and then dare to suggest that the knights themselves are unworthy!'

'Sire Uldain,' Gwildé said gently. 'You know as well as I that the knights now dabble in politics more than any. The monk is right, they cannot be trusted with documents as delicate as these.'

'But in all honour, my lady,' Uldain said, rising. 'We cannot accept the knights' hospitality whilst we keep them ignorant of such matters! Even they would not dare to interfere with Lord Eridar's own testament.'

'Of that I am not as certain as you, my lord,' Gwildé shook her head. 'And as for these travellers, I consider them good men, upon a worthy errand, and I will help them as much as remains in my power.'

'Very good, my lady,' Seydal nodded. 'But the most immediate question we must face is whether or not to accept Lord Thunant's offer of escort south to the borderlands.'

'Far better that, than to spend the whole of the winter in this bleak place,' Uldain said with feeling.

'But there are many dangers on that course,' Geltan said nervously. 'Even a full cohort of knights could not save us if we again ran across a great horde of Rievers. Would it not be better to wait until spring?'

'There is risk in all things, Master Cellarer,' Gwildé admonished. 'But I would still far rather go south now than remain here all winter in these cold halls, thinking each night of the enemy hordes without. Who is to say that this castle too has not its Claighar, waiting in darkness to admit the Riever hordes?'

'Then I shall so inform Lord Thunant,' Seydal rose briskly. 'He will not be sorry to see us depart, I think.'

'Perhaps so,' Gwildé said, 'but as a knight he is sworn to give sanctuary to all in need of it. There will be little enough for me now in the lands of Helietrim, and I shall have small need for such retinue as I have had here. Therefore I will release any here who wish to follow their own path, from my service.'

It was Haflas who spoke first. 'I do not wish to go south, milady. Those are not my lands, nor my folk; but neither would I remain here in these great halls. My people are slain, my friends scattered and gone. But if these four are bound upon some errand that may somehow aid in the defeat of those who fell upon us at Silentwater, then in that cause, these tragedies may perhaps attain some meaning, and our travails shall have served some purpose. I know the northlands and the ways of forest and hill. Perhaps in this wise I may be of use to them.'

'And you would be most welcome,' said Telsyan warmly.

'And I,' said Zindur suddenly, rising. 'I have no longing for the peace of the southlands. I would far rather face a dozen rogues such as this Korgûl Slainhand than a single spade or ploughshare. Do you release me, my lady?'

Gwildé nodded. 'Is there anyone else?'

'I too would journey north.' Tavolir the musician rose.

Keran was surprised. She had never considered the slender, fair-haired young minstrel at all adventurous. From the little she had known of him at the keep, he had always seemed to be merry enough, if somewhat mercurial, with sudden swift enthusiasms and changes of mood. Perhaps it was one of these that had led to his abrupt decision? At any rate his choice had made the announcement of her own resolution a little easier.

The chamber fell silent as she forced herself self-consciously to her feet. 'I too, my lady,' she said quietly.

'What?' Gwildé looked up at her in open astonishment. 'You cannot mean this, Keran? What would you do alone in these wild northlands?'

'I will not be alone,' Keran said; 'and you forget that the northlands are my home. I was born in Darien, and journeyed much with my father between the settlements of the north. I would go home, my lady; back to Darien, where these men are headed. I still have some family there, my father and one sister; and as you have said, you will need a lesser retinue from now on: perhaps but one fiefmaid, and Mireal is truly better suited to that task than I.'

'That may be so,' Gwildé nodded; 'but I had not thought to lose you yet awhile. I little imagined that you should be one of those who chose to remain here . . .' she looked about her with distaste at the thick stone walls, and at the cold, grey skies that boiled beyond the single window, 'in this dismal land.'

'It is not that I do not love you well, my lady,' Keran stumbled. 'But I have been away from my home long enough now to know that I wish to return, and that I have no wish to travel farther to the south.'

Gwildé nodded. 'But what if these fine men do not wish your company?'

'It is a good point, my lady,' Telsyan said grimly. 'The journey we make will be hard and dangerous enough, without this additional burden. I would advise the girl to think again before embarking upon such a rash course.'

'I have thought all I need!' Keran said firmly. 'If these men will not have me, I shall remain here until the spring – when the first caravans go north.'

'Oh, let her come with us if she pleases,' Uhlendof said. 'She can do us little harm. And who knows, she may prove useful in some manner.'

'I am surprised at you for supporting such foolishness!' Telsyan rounded on him irritably. 'There are a dozen good reasons why we should not drag this silly girl with us across the northlands: she could delay us, get lost or injured, cause endless trouble. I say no!'

'I was born in these northlands,' Keran said coldly, feeling a wave of sharp anger rising up within her. 'I probably know more of this country than any of you, barring Haflas. Certainly more than you, man of Selethir!' She stared hard at the merchant, hoping to make him squirm beneath her gaze. But he looked back at her unflinchingly.

'No,' he repeated.

'I agree,' said Yeon firmly. 'We need no serving wenches with us on this journey!'

'Come now,' Uhlendof said at once. 'You are both being unreasonable. I do not think that the girl will be more of a burden than any other member of our party. She knows the dangers: she travels at her own risk. If she is prepared to accept that, I see no reason to oppose her.'

'That seems fair enough to me,' Zindur grunted.

Leighor nodded, as did Haflas and Tavolir.

'All right!' said Telsyan suddenly. 'If it is the wish of the majority, then she may come with us. But let it be known for later that I was against it. And,' he pointed a warning finger in her direction, 'she must not expect to be mollycoddled, nor delay or hinder us for any reason.'

'I shall endeavour not,' Keran said meekly.

'Then it is settled,' said the priest. 'Let us have no more argument.'

Gwildé nodded, standing. 'Were it not for Keran,' she began quietly, 'I am sure that I would not now be here speaking to you all, but would have been lost with so many others at Silentwater. For that I owe her more than I can repay. But I promise her, and all of you who journey northwards, my blessing, and all the help and assistance I may give.' She turned to the merchant. 'How much gold do you have to equip and re-provision yourselves for this journey?'

Telsyan hesitated. 'I should say a hundred and fifty talents, my lady; perhaps a little more.'

'Little enough for such a journey.' Gwildé produced a small, golden casket from the pocket of her kirtle, setting it upon the table in front of her. 'Here,' she said, 'are those rings and jewels of mine that I was able to save from Silentwater. With one or two of these, I may perhaps be able to purchase new arms and sturdier clothing for your journey northward. It will not be much, but it is all that I in my present circumstances can give.

'Nay madam, nay,' Telsyan said, shaking his head. 'It is too much. We cannot permit you to do such a thing for our sakes. I could not sleep at night thinking you had sold your last remaining possessions for our comfort. We have come so far fitly. We are well enough equipped to go farther.'

Gwildé smiled. 'Your reticence does you credit, merchant; but I cannot allow it. Your few gold coins are barely half enough to purchase what you will need to see you to Darien and back. You must allow me to do this one small thing in furtherance of your errand. Think not of my few jewels; for those I have left will mostly be taken for my dower. Accept these things as my free gift to you.'

Telsyan bowed. 'Bidden in such a wise I can do no other, noble lady. You have done us great service this day which shall be long remembered.'

The following morning those travellers who were to go north gathered in the knights' armoury to select the equipment that Seydal had bargained for them in exchange for two of Gwildé's finest jewelled rings. They were permitted one new weapon apiece, but as some carried more than one weapon already and others had none, these were divided unevenly. Zindur wished for nothing more than his familiar mace, sword and heavy war-axe. Leighor also elected to keep his own crossbow, receiving a fine, light southron rapier, much like that borne by Telsyan, for closer in-fighting. To match things up the merchant was issued with a crossbow, although this was of slightly lesser quality than Leighor's.

Likewise Tavolir kept the shortsword he had taken up at Silentwater, and, expressing more knowledge of bowmanship, was given a yew longbow and a quiver of arrows. Yeon had his own heavy broadsword, and selected a fine shortbow, more normally used for fighting from horseback, disdaining the stouter, peasant longbow which Zindur pressed upon him. Uhlendof refused any weapon bar his own stout quarterstaff, but was eventually persuaded to accept one of Zindur's own sharp handknives, 'for hunting'.

This left only Haflas and Keran, with four weapons to divide between them. Neither had any knowledge of swordsmanship, but Zindur insisted that each should carry a heavy medium-length broadsword, primarily for defence, promising to drill them in the necessary moves later on. In addition, Haflas selected a short but heavy warhammer to carry with him, weighing it in his hands and swinging it briefly about his head before settling on it as his final choice. Keran meanwhile had made her way to a rank of mid-length longbows and was fingering through them.

'Not there,' Zindur ordered. 'Those require a fair amount of skill, and are not quickly learned.'

Keran smiled, removing one from its rack. 'I know these well of old, master warrior. In the north, archery is considered a fitting amusement for ladies, and I venture to say I am quite good at it.'

Zindur shrugged. So far, the choosing of the weapons had worked out fairly well, but there was now little else the knights were willing to provide them with in return for Gwildé's few rings, and the travellers were loath to ask her to sacrifice more for their sake. Telsyan insisted that what gold they had must be spent on tents and supplies, and so they had to settle for very little in the way of new clothing, choosing instead several rolls of stout thread and some assorted bronze needles to repair the old. The only exception to this frugality had to be Keran, who definitely needed new clothing. A long heavy tunic of thick brown wool was eventually found for her, thick and stout enough for a winter's journey. In addition she managed to obtain a long-sleeved jerkin in soft brown leather, with a strong belt at her waist for sword and knife; and with the addition of a pair of stout, calf-length boots her attire was complete.

Telsyan gained a brown leather hat with a broad brim, to replace his bedraggled felt cap. Seven thick cloaks of iron-grey wool completed their purchases. For Leighor, however, the merchant produced a long, dark robe of midnight black, with a heavy cowl and broad sleeves that hung loosely from the wrists. There was also a thin ashwood staff.

'What is this?' Leighor's mouth fell open. 'Surely you do not expect me to wear that?'

'It is a form of disguise, no more,' Telsyan placated. 'These once belonged to Erchoron, an alchemist and mage, who dwelt here for a time, a century or more ago. They seemed to be of about your size and so I bribed the launderwoman to let me have them, thinking that one in such attire might discourage any motley band of goblins, or others who might espy our number, from attacking.'

Leighor looked at the costume doubtfully. 'I am ill-fitted to play the part of mage, Master Telsyan. I have no spells and few potions, and even the flash-powder with which I dispersed the goblins is now gone. I fear that I would make a poor wizard, and besides,' he fingered the dusty robes with some distaste, 'I dislike wearing dead men's clothes.'

'Perhaps this Erchoron is not yet dead,' Yeon grinned. 'They say some mages live for many hundred years. Mayhap he still walks the earth—'

'Enough of that!' said Telsyan quickly. 'I would have worn the robes myself had they been of the proper size. Northron folk are simple and superstitious. I am sure that it would take little more than your appearance in these robes to frighten off the untutored. Your dark face will be fearful enough to many here already, and in these robes you may perhaps need to cast no more than a black look or two to turn a party of goblins upon their heels.'

Reluctantly Leighor drew the heavy robes on, over his own light tunic, finding to his surprise that they fitted him near perfectly; the smooth feel of the inner silks, and the unaccustomed warmth, quickly banishing much of his aversion to wearing this strange costume. 'It certainly feels well,' he admitted.

'And it looks well,' Telsyan complimented him, smiling and standing back to admire the full effect. The others nodded encouragingly.

It seemed to Leighor that he was trapped, and that he might as well concede gracefully. 'All right,' he sighed. 'I shall do it, but do not cast the blame on me if this all goes somehow astray.'

'Good!' Telsyan smiled. 'From now on it seems that you are Leighor the Mage, the mighty wizard of Syrne, with whom all may trifle at their peril . . .'

'Now you go too far!' Uhlendof shook his head. 'Let us not seek out trouble. Leighor of Syrne will do quite well enough; folk will just have to draw their own conclusions.'

Later that day Thunant repeated that he could provide no escort for any party going north. Yet they would not be entirely alone, for the party of merchants they had seen in the courtyard on their arrival were journeying north too. They would depart in two days for Vliza, and would most probably welcome the company of the eight travellers.

Throughout the following day Zindur kept the small company working on their sword drill and target practice. Haflas and Keran presented the greatest problem. Both had hardly even held a sword in their hands before, and had to be taught the defensive rudiments from scratch. Mainly they practised a few basic sweeps and parries; simple moves that might keep an enemy at a distance, and perhaps prevent their heads being shorn from their shoulders in the first few blows of any combat.

'That will have to do for the moment,' Zindur sighed grimly after a long succession of faltering blows and wild swings. 'Perhaps there will be more time for practice as we travel.' But his face quite clearly betrayed that he doubted it would do much good.

Keran did far better in the use of the bow, surprising even Yeon and Zindur with the accuracy of her shot. She drew the bow well and held it steady, surpassing in her average score all of the other bow-and crossbowmen of the company.

'She does well,' said Zindur in surprise, giving her a comradely clap on the back that almost knocked her over. 'And her swordplay progresses too. After this day she might easily hold her own, for a few minutes, with a fair-sized goblin – providing, perhaps, he was a little unwell.'

There was general laughter; which displeased her more than a little. But his comments were good-natured enough, and it was generally in good heart that the eight left their weapons at the gatehouse to re-enter the fortress for what was probably the last night before their departure.

Telsyan spent most of the time left before their evening meal bargaining with the Master Reeve for the purchase of two mules and two large weatherproof tents of oxhide. After that struggle, very little of the gold they had brought with them from Irgil remained, and most of that would have to be used immediately to purchase provisions for the morrow.

'Even with what Uhlendof holds,' he told Leighor later in the knights' great dusty library; 'we will have less than a dozen gold talents left when we leave here tomorrow. I have never set out on a major journey with so little money to my name. Unless Eridar has left us some gold in Darien, or the Durian Knights prove far more hospitable than they are reputed to be of late, we are going to have a very hard time of it.'

'But surely we have little need of money now?' Leighor said. 'We are well away from civilised lands. Surely we can barter for what we need, or live off the country if we have to?'

'Perhaps,' Telsyan admitted with little conviction. 'Yet a well filled bag of gold is never a hindrance upon any enterprise, while the lack of one can often prove fatal.'

There was silence for some minutes, as the merchant's eyes scanned the dusty rows of leatherbound tomes that lined the four walls of the ill-lit, vaulted hall. Suddenly, he reached out to pull down a heavy volume, brushing away its coat of dust and cobwebs with growing excitement.

'Well I'll be—!' he exclaimed. 'I never expected to find one of these so far from Selethir. How did these rogues lay their hands upon a copy?'

'What is it?' Uhlendof asked quickly, drawing closer to get a better view of the merchant's find.

'It is a copy of the journeybook of the Ethimathe Merchants' Guild of Great Selethir,' Telsyan said absently. 'It is the book I told you of, in which the merchants of the guild set down a report of the distant places they have visited. This volume will be a century or so out of date, but it may still contain much of interest.'

'What?' Yeon asked.

'Well, the safest and best routes for travel, for one thing; for my own maps do not run this far north.' Telsyan scanned through the pages quickly. 'Then perhaps something of the welcome strangers might expect, or the things not to say or do if one wishes to remain in good health. There are many useful things a merchant might tell you of the places he visits, and many things that you will learn truthfully from no one else.' He pointed to an entry on one of the pages. 'Here, look;' he began to read:

'King Culvar's road, commonly called the Great Road. A great trading route in the warmer days of the Second Millennium; it has since lost much of its former importance, due in part to the steady decline in the peoples and wealth of the northlands, and also to the increasing dangers and uncertainty of the region. The road now, in the first years of the Fourth Millennium, is used by few travellers other than those who by urgent necessity are forced to make the arduous journey north. Even so, the rewards of such a journey for the intrepid traveller can still be great.

As to condition, the greater part of the roadway is badly decayed and unmaintained, with several bridges down, the great Trunnost Bridge being the major gap. The River Trunnost is thus a major obstacle when not frozen over, being both broad and fast-flowing. All goods and beasts must needs be ferried across, at great expense of time and labour.

Upon average stretches of the road a large train can expect to achieve a pace of no more than five leagues a day, due to the broken and treacherous nature of the surface. The route is lawless, and only nominally protected by the two orders of knights under whose jurisdiction it lies. Attacks in strength by large, well-armed bands of brigands and Rievers must be guarded against along its entire length. Any guild member wishing to survive the journey would be best advised to employ a large company of mercenaries or other seasoned troops before venturing on to the road, and to deploy reliable scouts half a day's march to front and rear. Even so, the cost of these measures will certainly come cheaper than would paying the large fees normally demanded for escort by the Durian Knights of Vliza, under whose protection the central and northern sections of the road nominally resides.'

'That sounds discouraging enough,' said Uhlendof. 'Has your little book no better news for us?'

'Little in the way of cheerful news at all, I fear,' the merchant responded; 'although there is an entry for Darien itself.' He read:

'DARIEN. A small northland town lying at the confluence of the rivers Ormul and Yarvar; upon King Culvar's Road, roughly half the distance between the outpost of Imball to the south and the seaport town of Vliza to the north and west.

'Darien is a poor-looking wooden township, wholly owned by the Durian Knights, and subject to their rule. There is little in the way of general trade in food, cheap cloths or trinkets, but for those who turn their attention to the needs of the wealthier personages, a surprisingly great deal of money can be gained here . . .'

Telsyan paused. 'There is little more of note. The rest is just a list of commodities and prices; furs, skins, metals and suchlike; along with the names of important personages long dead.' He slammed the book shut and replaced it on its shelf. 'Let us to bed,' he said wearily; 'for it seems we have much to face in the morning.'

Chapter Fourteen
GOBLIN TRAILS

For Keran, the final parting from Gwildé and all those she had known in Lord Fralcel's service proved far more painful than she had expected. For close upon two years these had been her only friends and companions, and there were several times during that long morning of preparation and farewells when she had come very close to announcing that she had abandoned the whole scatter-brained idea of returning to Darien with these strangers. But pride, if nothing else, maintained her hold upon her tongue, and with an empty feeling of foreboding she had kissed her lady Gwildé on the cheek for the last time and followed the rest of their small party out across the windswept courtyard towards the outer bailey.

Here they met with the larger group of Elerian merchants who were to lead the company. Filoral stood at their head, conversing quietly with Thelnir, his second in command. Seven other merchants oversaw the work of a dozen hired men, whose duties were to guard the train, attend to the heavier physical labour and watch over the twenty-five mules that bore their supplies and trading goods. Behind these, Zindur and Telsyan led the smaller company bound for Darien. Yeon and Leighor followed on, then came Haflas and Tavolir, each leading one of the two laden mules, at whose pace they would all have to travel. Keran found herself rather uncomfortably bringing up the rear, alongside the disconcerting priest, Uhlendof. For the first part of their journey, until they reached the Great Road, they were to be escorted by two of the knights. These rode ostentatiously ahead of the main group, white pennons fluttering from their silvered lances in the cold autumn breeze.

Crossing the narrow bridge to the shore, they halted before the gates to buckle on their weapons. At once the grey figure of Inanys emerged from the shadow of one of the twin guard-towers to tag along behind the party.

'Why do you still follow us?' Uhlendof demanded.

'Do I not but journey north like yourselves?' the crookback answered slyly. 'Would you have me travel alone through these dark forests? I had hoped for a better welcome after four long days of waiting. Have you so soon forgotten your solemn oath that I might accompany you for as long as I wished?'

'The oath that you extorted from us!' the monk snorted. 'But what is done is done. Follow if you must, but stir no trouble.'

Inanys bowed low. 'As you command, my lord.'

Not for the first time Keran felt a shudder of revulsion for the scuttling creature; yet in a nagging way she felt more than a little guilty about this. What must it be like, she wondered, to be such a wretched thing, scorned and despised by all men? Most like it was the fair and high-born of this world, with their taunts and jibes, their thoughtless, sniggering cruelty that had warped him and made him so sour and bitter . . .

But all further thought along these lines was interrupted by the sudden movement of the loaded mules ahead, as they jerked reluctantly back into motion. The company at last set off up the well-trodden trackway that led northwards along the sunlit shores of Esch Tuarn.

The lakeshore curved away slightly to the east as it ran northward, and so it was not long before they had lost all sight of the great emblazoned towers of Hallad's Keep behind them. These lay hidden now behind a wall of forest, which in places crowded right down upon the lakeshore itself. Here the woodland was mixed; and as well as the white birch and pine they had passed through in Argonan Vale, there were also bright, red-berried rowan trees, and thick stands of almost leafless beech and linden; all battling for space upon the steep hillsides. Esch Tuarn itself looked strikingly beautiful in the dappled sunlight, its myriad wavelets spirited into life by the steady north-west breeze – a sparkling of silver beneath the gold of the autumn trees. Yet that breeze was cold, Keran noted: icy cold, with the taste of winter upon it. It would quickly chill her to the bone if she paused for too long in the open, despite the thick grey cloak she wore. She drew it tighter about her, and walked on.

Here and there along the lakeshore, small clearings had been cut into the forest – anywhere where a small piece of relatively flat ground could be found, and a half-hearted attempt made at farming. Small, thinly-furrowed fields lay stripped and bare now against the high ramparts of forest and hill; with perhaps a small stone or timber hovel, to house the impoverished folk who laboured there. In few of these small farmsteads was there any sign of life or enterprise. Nothing moved. They seemed already half-abandoned: and the travellers passed on in silence.

By afternoon, however, they had come to the end of Esch Tuarn, and begun to climb the gently rising track that wound its way up into the hills of the north-east, past a single, nameless tributary lake surrounded by silent forest, before finally reaching the Great Road.

It was mid-afternoon when they emerged from their sheltered track to find themselves on the high, open ridge across which King Culvar's Road ran in noble solitude. The knights called a halt, reining in their horses to survey the scene. The road was, as the Selethir Merchants' Journeybook had said, in a very bad state of repair. The great stones, out of which the imperial way had been raised long centuries before, still stood a good six to seven feet above the surrounding country, separated by deep drainage ditches from the marshy ground to either side. An earth and rubble ramp had been constructed at a more recent date to join the rough trail from Hallad's Keep with the higher road. But now the surface of the ancient way was cracked and broken, shattered by numberless frozen winters into an uneven twisted mass; or else fallen away entirely, to expose a rough core of hard-packed rubble. The travellers would have to pick their way with care.

One of their two mounted escorts drew up to the leaders of the main party ahead, speaking with them in hushed tones for several minutes before riding back down the line to say some words to those of the lesser company.

'There lies your way, my lords. To the north and west.' The knight raised a mailed hand to point left along the road. 'As I have told your companions, we can accompany you no further that way, for the dominion of the Knights of Imsild ends upon the southern bank of the River Thauran, which you should meet before nightfall. From there onward you come under the suzerainty of the North King, who rules at Vliza; and of the Durian Knights, who have ways of their own.' He paused for a moment and then drew a breath: 'I am reluctant to leave you to travel alone upon this road, good sirs. It is still not too late to change your minds and return.'

Telsyan shook his head: 'I thank you, but we know the dangers. We are bound and determined upon our course.'

'Very well,' the knight's face was unreadable. 'I can but give you my advice, and tell you a little of what you face. The old roadway passes down now from the Heights of Du'oth, and then for nine days journey through the lower forests of *Orodun Hulan*, before coming out on to the great wastes of the plain of Scûn. It is only once you have crossed these, which should take you a further eighteen to twenty days, if all goes well, that you will come to Darien. I advise you to keep either to the road or to the hills to the east of the road. Do not on any account venture off into the western forests, with Rievers abroad in such number.' He nodded, as if in dismissal. 'May the gods be with you!' Abruptly he swung his horse about, and with his companion in tow, he was gone once more into the forest, a fleeting shimmer of white and silver and gold. Then, suddenly, the travellers were alone.

They seemed high here, higher than they truly were above the surrounding country. Zindur looked about him warily, paying close attention to the leafless forest on either side.

'I like this not,' he said grimly at last. 'This road was built for times of peace, not for days like these; of anarchy and war. We are far too exposed here. No good general would lead anything less than an army along this road if he feared attack. And even an army could be cut to pieces by a hundred good bowmen from out of these forests.'

Keran shivered in the cutting breeze, beginning once more to wish that she had had the sense to remain safe with the rest of her company at Hallad's Keep. She liked not this road. She could not say why, only that it gave her an inexplicable sense of deep foreboding.

'I did not much like the look our escort gave us as they left,' Tavolir announced. 'I would chance that neither of them would wager much coin on our survival.'

'We can but do what we must,' Uhlendof said firmly, 'and hope that providence guides our path.'

Zindur snorted, but said nothing.

The going was far worse than any of them had imagined. Over the long centuries the great square paving stones of former days had been reduced to a shattered causeway of crumbling rock and ill-sorted rubble. Even those few stones that remained whole were loose, ill-balanced, or covered with a thick mantle of slippery moss.

'Frankly, this Great Road seems far worse than any other we have chanced upon in these northlands,' Uhlendof observed irritably, after what seemed several hours of limb-wearying travel, but had probably been closer to one.

'Perhaps the road will improve later on,' Leighor said, halting.

Haflas shook his head. 'My folk know these roads well, and make little use of them. They were here long before our time, and have lasted well for the handiwork of men. But nowadays this is about as good a wayfaring as you will get.'

'Why do you halt?' Thelnir shouted suddenly from somewhere ahead. 'Do you not know that it is unwise to linger in the open like this?'

'We find the road difficult!' Uhlendof retorted. 'I am unused to such ill-favoured ways!'

'You may rest at the day's end. But we must keep up our pace or we shall not reach the river before dark.'

'I do not like this road,' Zindur said bluntly. 'I have been keeping watch these past few miles, and have noticed movements in the trees as we have passed. Most likely only some disturbed animal, a deer or boar perhaps – but it would be all the same if it were a band of Rievers preparing an ambush. We would have little chance to defend ourselves up here.'

'Cease such talk!' Filoral said sharply. 'Our journey is hardly yet begun, and already you prattle of unseen dangers! We cannot turn back because you see shadows beneath the trees!'

'More than shadows,' Zindur growled. 'Besides, the way is bad. Is there no better road?'

Thelnir shook his head.

'There is another way, good sirs,' Haflas said at once. 'It may not run exactly parallel to this, but it should serve almost as well – a track that runs north-east of this way, not more than a league distant as we travel now.'

'But will it get us to Darien?' Telsyan broke in.

'Oh yes, my lord,' Haflas nodded. 'One might journey where one willed throughout these northlands using only the lesser paths. There will also be small settlements of friendly folk to the east of the Great Way, which may be of great help to us should we chance upon misfortune. We will find no such villages upon this road, for none in these days dares dwell upon the ancient way. And I too feel ill-suited to this open road.'

'Your feelings do not concern me, northron,' Filoral broke in with impatience. 'There is but one road north, and it is this. I will not lead my caravan off into the wild woods just because you fear shades by the roadside!' At these words, most of the other merchants either nodded or grunted their assent. 'You, of course, are free to do as you please. But make your decision quickly, because we cannot linger here much longer!' He turned away, leaving the nine travellers to face one another in silence.

'Well?' Telsyan asked sourly. 'What are we to do? Do we remain of this number, or do we follow Haflas' advice, break company with our fellow venturers, and follow forest trails?'

'Stay,' Yeon said firmly. 'Why break such a strong company? It is foolishness.'

Zindur shook his head. 'Thirty is no strong company. Not in the northlands. Such a number can be destroyed as easily and as quickly as nine. It is only good fortune and sound judgement that will preserve us. I am for leaving.'

Yeon snorted. 'Is it sound judgement to run off into the forest, where all the dangers lie?'

'We are in the forest now,' Haflas said plainly. 'That you imagine we are not is much of our danger. Here we share all the forest's dangers but none of its protection. There is nothing here to hide us from unfriendly eyes. We have nowhere to flee. Let us go!'

'How do we know we shall not walk straight into the danger we are fleeing?' Tavolir shook his head. 'I like it not. Let us remain here, where we can at least see what we face!'

'Enough!' Telsyan held up his hand to still the rising chorus of voices. 'We have had time enough for argument. Now is the time to decide. We have had four votes. What do the others say?'

'I would do anything to get off this vile road,' Uhlendof announced. 'I am with Master Haflas.'

'And you?' Telsyan nodded towards Leighor.

'I am not sure,' the southron admitted hesitantly. 'I do not like this road, but I do not like the forest either.' He shook his head. 'I will go with the majority.'

'I too am in two minds,' Telsyan nodded; 'but on balance I suppose I must cast my vote for remaining with the larger group. So that makes it three upon either side: we are evenly divided.'

'What of the crookback?' Tavolir asked. 'And Keran, you have not asked either of them.'

Inanys lowered his head in pretended gratitude. 'It is my pleasure always to bow to the wisdom of my noble lords.' His smile was as sly and ingratiating as ever.

'And you, girl?'

'I say we go,' Keran announced firmly. 'The road is not safe.'

'That makes it four to three,' said Zindur. 'We go.'

'No!' Yeon protested, pushing forward angrily. 'You cannot count her vote as equal to ours!'

'Why not?' Keran felt her anger rising.

'Because you are but a girl. You have no knowledge . . .'

'And you are but a runt, boy,' Zindur flashed back. 'Why should we count yours?'

'I shall show you why, if you have the courage!' Yeon came forward belligerently, his hands drawing themselves into heavy fists.

'Enough!' Uhlendof snapped irritably, pushing the two apart. 'The matter is decided: we go.'

Reluctantly Telsyan nodded. 'I had better inform Master Filoral.'

The merchants from Elerian showed little surprise when Telsyan told them of their decision, almost as if they had never expected the motley group of travellers who tagged along behind them to last the course for long. And so it was that the travellers journeyed with the larger party for less than a league more – until they came to Haflas's path.

It was a grave disappointment, little more than an overgrown deer-track between the trees.

'Are you sure?' Uhlendof asked in dismay. 'Is this the trail that will carry us to Darien?'

'Our folk have little need for broad ways,' Haflas nodded shortly. 'That is the way right enough.'

'But this path runs north-eastward,' Telsyan said. 'By all accounts, Darien lies to the north-west. Will not this backland way be longer?'

'No,' Haflas shook his head. 'To avoid the northern lakes, the Great Road itself must curve deep into the western forests. This way may run a little to the east before it turns northward once more, but in the end it will be shorter. Besides, we shall make far better time with the mules upon a good soft trail – if you still wish to take it.'

Uhlendof looked back at the others, and nodded.

A few shattered stones, piled up seemingly at random against the roadway, provided a rough and ready stair down into the ancient drainage ditch, and thence up on to the tussocky open ground beyond. Yet whatever the arguments in theory, the actual act of breaking with the larger party in this empty wilderness was traumatic, and despite her fears Keran began to worry whether they had indeed made the right decision. For, at the last, as she had never wanted it to be, the final choice had been hers. It was as Yeon had said; for an instant she had had the power to decide the fate of the entire company, and now in a way she bore full responsibility for whatever happened.

Filoral's party watched them dispassionately until they were all gathered on the open ground beneath the road. Then, with no more than a single word of farewell, they took up their steady march again into the north. The travellers watched them in silence for several minutes before turning towards the waiting forest. A hundred paces or so of spongy tussock grass separated them from the dark line of brooding trees where the forest trail began.

'How is it that no trees have ever grown between road and forest over the years?' Leighor asked.

'The stories tell that the land to either side of the Great Road was blighted with dark magicks, upon the orders of the Elder Kings of Scûn,' Haflas answered; 'that the old south way might be kept open when none were left to tend it. And since those days naught but coarse grass has grown here.'

'Then it is a great pity they did not cast some stronger spells, and so keep the forest out of bowshot!' Zindur snorted. 'The road might then have been a little safer for travellers.'

'Once I think it was so,' said Haflas, pushing aside the trailing briars that blocked the entrance to the path; 'yet the power fades, and the forest grows a little closer to the road each year.'

The forest trail seemed very hushed and enclosed after the road, and there were far fewer brambles and nettles to hinder their passage once they were beneath the dark autumn trees. The fallen leaves made a soft carpet of golds and reds and browns for them to walk upon, although there was still only room for them to travel in single file. Within minutes, they were out of sight of the Great Road; the boles of the forest trees, hung with moss and decked with grey lichens, hemming them in. The great wood seemed to cloak them benevolently with the same dark mantle of stillness that it had offered to deer and wolf, goblin and Riever, woodsman and hill-dweller before them. The forest, at least, took no sides, offering its shelter and protection impartially to all who cared to learn its ways.

Semboron was displeased at the sudden parting with the ill-sorted company of travellers from Silentwater. He was far younger than most of the others who shared this late, unseasonal journey north; and their company had been dour and joyless of late. He feared it would only grow worse over the long, unbroken distances that yet remained before they got to Vliza. He had hoped that the new travellers would provide a little brighter company about the campfire, and new tales and songs to lighten the long cold evenings; but that pleasing prospect had now vanished, leaving him trapped with these sour merchants and their sullen, grumbling hirelings.

The travellers had had some secret reason for wanting to reach Darien so urgently, and that had intrigued him; as it had intrigued Thelnir, his father, and most of the other merchants of their company. Whatever that reason, it was bound to be far more interesting than their own long-delayed venture, the tight-packed consignments of oils and winter spices, the many minor luxuries and the scores of dreary letters from merchants and local potentates, which they carried north. But whatever the travellers' business, they were foolish to leave the road. Semboron shuddered even to look too long into the dark, silent woods that bordered this one great ribbon of civilisation that still traversed the northern wilderness. He, for one, had no desire to venture off the road and into those fearful forests.

The force of the wind diminished a little as they began the long descent into the wooded vale of the River Thauran. He could see the river below them now, flowing dark and murky into the east where it fed the broad, gleaming reaches of Irnpool, just visible against a backdrop of high hills. The view disappeared gradually as they descended, the trees closing in on them once more. Only the river remained visible ahead of them, and the ancient stone bridge that carried the road across. Despite the delays they had made good time.

The sun was just beginning to dip beneath the western horizon when they reached the river. The forest grew back some yards from the water's edge, and it was in this open space that Filoral ordered them to make camp.

Semboron could not help but marvel at the great bridge. It was old beyond measure, its parapets grey, its arches crumbling, yet still holding firm against the immense power of the river. Older than a score of centuries, it looked as though it might yet stand a good many more before it fell . . .

Suddenly his heart missed a beat. Something had moved upon the bridge. He stared up hard into the gathering dusk, but saw nothing. Had he imagined it? But no . . . There it was again! A small grey face peered over the parapet for an instant, and then was gone. A goblin.

Semboron turned to shout a warning, and saw immediately that he was too late. A small group of goblins, perhaps a dozen or more, were clambering openly down from the roadway towards them. All work on the campsite abruptly ceased: merchants and men drawing together, swords unsheathed.

Filoral moved to the fore. 'Come no closer, manlings!' His voice was loud and strong – but did Semboron detect a note of uncertainty, of fear? 'What business have you with us? State it and depart!'

A goblin stepped forward. Somewhat larger than the rest, his mottled skin was draped in tattered rags of sackcloth, held loosely together by a small, silvered brooch. The long, rusting remnant of what must once have been a fine sword was wielded proudly in one hand. 'Have no fear, humanss.' He made a misshapen attempt at a smile. 'We mean you no harm. We only seek your charity . . .'

'You will get nothing from us!' Thelnir stabbed the air angrily with his sword. 'We are well armed and can defend all we have. Your thieving hands shall touch none of it!'

'Thiefss!' the goblin turned sharply to his companions. 'They call us thiefss!' There was an angry murmuring among the goblins, and weapons lifted. 'Ignorant ssons of men call all goblinss thief!' He stepped a pace back towards his followers. 'Let us ssee who they call thiefss!'

These last words were shouted in a rising voice, almost as a signal; and they had scarcely left his throat when goblins began to pour out of the surrounding forest, from the roadway, and even from the bridge itself, to hem the travellers tight in against the river. Semboron numbered twenty, forty, sixty of them before he lost count: all bearing sticks, staves, knives and other makeshift weapons in addition to their sharp, milky talons.

The goblin chieftain saw the fear in the eyes of the merchants and their men, and smiled. 'Perhapss you will give uss something now, noble ssons of men? What iss it you carry upon your fat muless? Gold? Weaponss? Ssilkss?'

Filoral shook his head. 'We have little.' He gave a nervous smile. 'We bear naught but spices and letters, and a little food. You may share some of that if you wish.'

'Spicess? Letterss?' The goblin gave a long, high-pitched squawk of a laugh. 'Do you think uss sso foolish, humanss?' His voice became suddenly hard and cruel. 'Open your packss, humanss, and let uss ssee!'

'No!' Thelnir hissed urgently. 'When they have what they want, they will slay us anyway! Let us fight! They are cowardly and ill-armed. We may yet drive them off.'

Filoral ignored him, stepping forward to produce a small leather pouch from within his robes, which he held out towards the chieftain. 'Here, I have gold! All that we carry. Take it, as a gift of goodwill, and go; before the knights come. They are only an hour behind us. They will soon be here – and will destroy you utterly if you are still in this place!'

There was a nervous stirring amongst the goblins at these words – at once stilled by their chieftain's sharp voice.

'Liar!' he screamed. 'There will be no knightss! Knightss safe and warm inside their big sstrong castle. Dzoraszch know thiss. Dzoraszch hass been told! Liar!' He snatched the bag of gold coins from the merchant's hands and hurled it contemptuously to the ground. 'You lie to Dzoraszch for the lasst time, human!' His sword darted forward, twisting cruelly as it entered the merchant's body. Filoral's mouth opened. He gave a sharp gasp of surprise and pain, and slumped forward on to the blade.

With a wild chorus of screams the goblins fell upon the startled travellers in a savage blood-frenzy that Semboron had thought beyond such feeble creatures. Shocked, the party fell back. A sea of goblins now surrounded them: small spindly shapes that merged into the gathering dark. Many fell beneath the keen swords and axes of merchants and guardsmen, but for each that fell it seemed three more rose up to replace him. Knives, staves, spears and flaming firebrands soon began to take their toll of the defenders too. Cut, injured and bleeding, the smallest mistake, the slightest hesitation, was fatal. A knife between the ribs felled a second victim. A severed hamstring, and another collapsed beneath the throng. The merchants' line shortened and fell back further towards the river. Even for Semboron at the rear there was no respite: sharp stones rained down on him from above, and flaming brands began to set the tents ablaze.

A mule panicked and burst out through the line. At once a wave of goblins fell upon it, rending it limb from limb. But more importantly, the line itself was now broken. Goblins poured through the gap before the defenders could react. More men died. Others broke in panic. Semboron suddenly knew that all was lost. He did not see his father fall, but no more than half a dozen of all their company now remained standing.

Sharp claws raked along his arm. His sword flashed desperately backward, and there was a sharp howl of pain. Two men threw themselves, panic-stricken, into the surging waters of the Thauran. Neither could swim, and both were swept away like scraps of flotsam. But Semboron was decided: better the river than certain death here where he stood. He had learnt to swim only in the slow, eddying waters of the Gierend, but he would take his chances.

Avoiding a leaping goblin, he ducked beneath one of the tethered mules to emerge only a yard from the water's edge. He made a single desperate lunge for the river; but something held him! A clawed hand on his ankle; another on his shoulder. He twisted free to see the thin, grey, inhuman figure beside him; the cold yellow eyes, with their black slits of pupils. He raised his sword. Yet even as he did so he felt the cold, hard metal of a rusty knife pierce his backbone. Another ... There was another goblin behind him. Such pain! Surely it was impossible to hurt so much? He tried to move his legs, his arms; but his body refused to obey his commands. His vision darkened. The last thing he saw was the grinning face of a goblin close above his own, and the flames of the burning tents.

Haflas finally called a halt at a small clearing, where their trail dipped down into a gentle dell watered by a swift, clear stream.

'I think we should set up our camp there.' He pointed to the edge of the clearing. 'Up from the water's edge, where the ground is dry and we will be under the shadow of the trees.'

It took some time to unload the mules and erect the two large circular tents on the sloping ground. The dark leather blended well with the dull browns of the forest, and possibly helped to hide the campsite from above. Yet the penalty was the great heaviness of the fabric, which needed many stout wooden poles, long staves and strong guy ropes to hold it up. Haflas oversaw this arduous task, giving his orders with a natural authority that made even Yeon momentarily forget the miner's lowly station and accept his instructions without demur.

It was dark before the task of setting up camp was finally completed to Haflas' satisfaction, and a small, dampened fire at last flickered between the tents. The travellers ate their evening meal in silence, seated outside upon the short grass. Basking in the dim light of a thin new moon, they watched the tethered mules nibble gently at the long grass beside the stream. The night was not yet frosty, and there was still warmth in the fire. There seemed no need yet to retreat into the dark shelter of the tents, and so they talked, recalling past journeys through difficult lands and fair. Telsyan and Leighor told of their various travels through the countries of the south and the east, of the dry mountains and hot, dusty plains, and the pretty lands along the Azier Sea.

Uhlendof spoke of the dark shores of eastern Xhendir, where the ice-winds blasted unimpeded across the bare cliffs and barren hills, and also of the softer lands of Holdar where he was born and travelling was a merry affair between well-stocked taverns and friendly inns. And even Haflas was called upon to tell of his younger days, when he had journeyed far and wide along the hill trails, and to the cold settlements of Vliza and Scuné-ev upon the distant shores of the Sea of Ice.

They retired late to their tents, Uhlendof remaining without to stand the first watch. Wolves howled somewhere far away in the depths of the forest – a cold and fearful sound. Keran, wakeful, felt how isolated they were in this vast wilderness. She shivered; and turning over to wrap herself tighter in her trailing cloak, at last, unexpectedly, found sleep.

Keran was used to waking early, but even so she found Haflas up before her. The tent flap was open, admitting a flood of cold air along with the dank, grey almost-light of the pre-dawn. Silently, she rose and stepped outside. Only Zindur was visible, standing the tail end of his watch, crouched over the newly built-up fire, warming his hands before the flames. The sweet smell of woodsmoke hung in the air.

The warrior smiled and beckoned her over to the fire. 'A fine morning!'

She nodded. 'Has the night passed well?'

'As well as can be expected,' Zindur shrugged. 'It is bitter cold in these forests at night, and I fancied I saw a red glow far to the north-west, as if a great fire burned there. But nothing came near us – if that's what you mean.'

The others were soon risen: all but Inanys. No one seemed to have seen the crookback at all that morning – none but Zindur, who had caught sight of him making his way into the woods above the camp at least an hour before dawn. The travellers were not unduly worried, however, until their breakfast was long over and they were almost ready to leave. Their only tinderbox was missing, and Inanys had still not returned.

After a brief search, Haflas found a trail of footprints leading up into the trees. With growing irritation the travellers followed, leaving Zindur and Tavolir behind to finish striking camp. The trail did not lead far, ending at a low, exposed rockface split by a narrow cleft, just wide and high enough for a stooping man to squeeze his way through. Shouting into the narrow opening several times without response, they reluctantly entered, Telsyan bearing their single lantern. The passage was pitch dark, and Keran was able to catch only occasional glimpses of Telsyan's glinting light far ahead. She tripped and stumbled constantly as the passage wound its way steadily downward, into the very heart of the old mountain. What on earth could have possessed anyone, even the verminous crookback, to enter here? And indeed who – or what – had made this dismal way?

A sudden exclamation of surprise came from Haflas and Telsyan ahead. Yet still Keran could see nothing. She pushed forward, fearful of what they might have found; to emerge seconds later into a vast underground chamber, laboriously hewn from the living rock. The dim lanternlight struck cumbrous walls and ceilings, crudely daubed with painted images of men and birds and beasts. Rough stone plinths lined the walls, supporting heavy bowls of dark earthenware. A huge stone altar stood facing them across the chamber.

'It is a temple to the Earth Goddess of old,' Uhlendof's voice echoed and rumbled around the cavernous hall as his staff drew a skein of cobwebs from one of the plinths, 'long abandoned.'

'Look here!' Telsyan held the flickering lantern aloft, casting its light upon a huge, almost formless statue that stood in a niche above the brown-stained altar.

'I like it not.' Leighor shook his head briskly. 'Let us finish our search and be gone as soon as we may.'

Keran, however, no longer felt fearful. Instead she felt strangely elated, electrified. It was as if this old dark place, where a simple forest people had crept to worship millennia ago, were still a source of power. The source of a humming, aching power that she was somehow in tune with, yet at the same time incredibly – painfully – distant from: whatever force dwelt here had been too long lost to the realms of mankind.

The others finished their brief search.

'He is not here!' Uhlendof snapped. 'Let us depart this evil place!'

'It is not evil!' Keran found herself saying. 'There is naught but peace and gentleness here – a warmth that still lingers.'

The others looked at her as if she had gone out of her mind, and suddenly she felt very foolish. Why had she felt bound to defend this old, forgotten place? She could not now have said. Slowly her companions turned away, to make their way back out of the chamber. Keran was about to follow when a sudden glint caught her eye. A tiny sparkle near the floor. Intrigued, she made her way across and stooped to investigate.

A small, coloured stone, no bigger than the nail of her middle finger, lay hidden in a small crevice at the base of the altar. She felt somehow drawn to it. An insistent voice within her urged her to touch it, to pick it up. She watched the others filing into the passageway, and then, surreptitiously, bent forward to take it between her fingers, wondering even as she did so whether this might be considered a sacrilege by the forces that ruled here. But there was no alteration to her sense of well-being, and she stood, holding the tiny gem balanced in the palm of her hand. Was it her imagination, or did it truly seem to glow for a second with a dim inner fire? It seemed so to her, yet it was probably just a trick of the light, a stray reflection from Telsyan's lantern. She clenched her fingers over the stone and turned to follow the fast-vanishing men, pausing only to leave a single silver coin upon the rough-hewn altar. The jewel was hers, that she knew . . . It was somehow a gift from this place and its lonely goddess. But she knew enough of temple lore not to take only, and leave nothing in exchange.

The way out of the temple seemed to Keran friendlier and shorter than their coming in, although this did not seem to appear so to her companions, who muttered and stumbled their way ill-temperedly through the darkness ahead. To her surprise, waiting for them outside were Zindur and Haflas, along with the two loaded mules – and Inanys.

'Where have you been!' Telsyan strode furiously towards the crookback. 'Leading us on such a fool's errand!'

Inanys backed away.

'He appeared shortly after you left in search for him,' Tavolir explained. 'He gave us some story of a cave and a lost temple.'

'Aye,' Uhlendof nodded. 'That is what we found. Though we knew not that he had been and gone, or we would never have entered.' He brushed thick dust from his robes. 'It was a poor and primitive place!'

'We shall waste no time searching for you in future,' Telsyan announced briskly, moving on. 'If you get yourself lost again it will be your own affair, and no concern of ours!'

'What were you doing there?' Uhlendof asked curtly. 'Do you rob forsaken temples, in addition to your other mischiefs?'

'Nay, my lord,' the crookback's voice rolled sibilantly. 'I seek only the habitations of my friends.'

Nobody knew what to make of this, since Inanys could hardly be termed a devotee of the Mother Goddess. But such thoughts were quickly forgotten on the difficult journey onward.

As they walked, Keran chanced another glance at the tiny jewel in her hand. She opened her fingers slowly to see it lying there, balanced in the centre of her palm: still, bright, and glinting in the dappled sunlight. She could see its true colour now, a delicate shade of pink such as she had never seen before, even amongst the many jewels of her lady Gwildé. And equally surprisingly, even though rough and uncut, it still seemed to possess a peculiar inner radiance all its own.

'What is that?'

Uhlendof had caught sight of the stone.

Her fingers closed like a trap. 'It is mine!'

'Is it, girl?' The monk caught her wrist. 'Let me see it.'

'No!' Keran twisted her hand roughly free; but Uhlendof caught her by the shoulder and spun her around to face him.

The rest of the caravan drew to a halt, the whole company turning to discover the cause of the commotion.

'What is it now?' Telsyan shouted back impatiently, his harsh voice stilling a background of birdsong that none of them had noticed until it abruptly ceased.

'The girl has a jewel!' Uhlendof pointed to Keran's tightly clenched fist. 'She must have taken it from the temple.' The others crowded round.

'All right.' Keran gave in, holding out her open hand to display the stone. 'There it is!'

Telsyan smiled. 'A rose stone! Very pretty, but not very valuable.'

'It does not look much,' Yeon eyed the squarish chip caustically; 'it is very small and rough.'

'Nonetheless they are prized by many,' Uhlendof said, taking it up to examine it more closely. 'They are quite rare, being especially sought after by the Heliards and the followers of Ginara; amongst whom they are called Ginara Stones. Larger stones are often used by seers, but smaller ones like this are generally used to decorate the temples.'

'Ah, Ginara Stones!' Tavolir exclaimed, as if suddenly remembering. 'There is a pretty legend about them, is there not?'

Uhlendof nodded. 'Yes indeed. It is part of the story of the creation of the world as told by the Heliards, and in slightly different forms by many of the lesser cults.'

'Yes?' Keran prodded.

'Well,' the monk began, 'at the beginning of time – well before the Golden Age, as the Heliards have it – the world was a formless place: hot and fiery and uninhabitable. For all the elements, Earth, Air, Fire and Water, dwelt together;

and the four Elder Gods – the children of the Great One, and the rulers of the four elements – lived in constant war and enmity. The elements ever strove and fought, and were nowhere stable upon the earth. Conditions that persisted for untold ages; until at last there came a time when Helior, the god of fire, and Ginara, the goddess of water, chanced to meet – as was forbidden to them – and upon seeing each other's great beauty, fell instantly in love one with the other.

'Yet, as I have said, this was against the fixed and determined laws of being; which none may alter, even the gods themselves. And so the All Highest, the one supreme god, whom the Heliards foolishly believe takes no interest in the day to day affairs of the world, was forced to intervene. And when he learned how Helior and Ginara had broken the supreme law, his wrath was great against them both, and they were given the punishment of perpetual banishment from the earth. Yet Helior it was who was considered the greater transgressor; for it had been he who had first entered upon the forbidden domain of Ginara. Therefore he and all that was his, save for those fires that burned in the protection of the high mountains of the earth, or forked downwards from the firmament of the sky, were banished utterly from the world. To separate, to rise, and to become the living sun that we see now in the sky. Whilst all the substance that was left, freed at last of the flames of Helior, cooled and settled to become the earth we know, and all the mortal creatures that dwell upon it. For, as the Heliards say, we are all formed of naught but earth, water and air.'

'But what of the Ginara Stones?' Keran insisted.

'I am coming to that,' Uhlendof said stiffly. 'For when Helior was banished, so too was Ginara, to become the constellation that now bears her name. But, as I have said, her punishment was the lesser; and all her works were allowed to remain upon the earth. Yet when she and her lover parted for the last time, she wept bitterly; and as her tears fell towards the earth, it is said that they turned instantly to purest gemstone, so that each might remain forever a memory upon the face of the earth. Three thousand tears she shed, and each one a rare and beautiful jewel: a Ginara Stone.'

'It is indeed a pretty story,' said Leighor; 'and a fine way to explain how Helior became the sun, and Ginara the Pole Star. But what of the two other gods; what happened to them?'

'They remain upon the earth somewhere,' the monk shrugged; 'or upon their own planes of being. The followers of Ethimathé say that she too departed, to become the moon. I do not know; the legend is very vague upon that point. But both Ethimathé the Earth Goddess, and Arul the god of the air, are still worshipped by many, under different names. Yet, I think, the worship of Ginara has almost vanished from the world. But for some scattered desert dwellers, and a few score sailors and fishermen upon the eastern seas, her cult is forgotten. The Heliards, however, are great in number; and still work unceasingly for the return of Helior to rule the world.'

'You spoke of war between the elements,' Yeon cut in. 'Yet if there were no living creatures alive, then who fought the war?'

'Such a war does not need men to fight it,' Uhlendof smiled. 'The elements of themselves have power enough to make a pretty commotion if they please, as anyone who has seen a storm at sea or a mountain afire will testify. Yet it is said that there are also living servants of the elements. Elementals: sprites, imps, salamanders and their like; all created long before men and the world that we know. They were the first things that god made after the angels, while he was still practising for the making of man. Most are long since destroyed, or banished from this world; but perhaps some still do remain.'

'I do not believe in such things,' Yeon stated flatly.

The monk shrugged and made to move on.

'What shall we do about the jewel?' Telsyan asked, halting him.

Uhlendof paused for a moment in thought. 'Throw it away! That is best. To keep such things from old temples only brings ill-fortune.'

'No!' Keran cried out at once. 'It is mine! There shall be no ill-luck, for it was given; and I have left a small coin in payment for it!'

'Nevertheless,' Uhlendof insisted firmly, 'it must go.' Without a further word, he turned and hurled the tiny gemstone out into the thick undergrowth.

Keran gasped. She had not dreamt that even the monk would dare do such a thing, and she had not realised how much it would hurt her to see it go. Something like panic rose up within her as her bright jewel vanished into the distant undergrowth. She crashed through the straggling briars after it.

'Leave it!' Uhlendof ordered. 'Do not waste any more time upon that bauble. Come. We must go on!'

At that moment Keran truly hated the fat monk, so arrogant and self-satisfied as he led the rest of the party away along the trail. He knew that she would soon have to leave her search and follow; that she had little or no chance of finding her jewel again amid the confusion of roots, leaves and tangled vinery.

Suddenly she stopped searching and stood, a new resolution forming within her. She would have her gemstone back whatever they wanted, whatever they thought. There was a way. She shut her eyes and tried to picture the pink gemstone in her mind. The image came surprisingly easily and clearly. She trapped it and held it firm.

At once she felt a pinprick of warmth in the palm of her left hand as it passed near to a low clump of bushes. Intrigued, she repeated the movement – with precisely the same result.

Stepping forward, she drew the heavy sword at her side, the metal cold and grey. She smiled: at least it would be this much use to her. With a few deft sweeps she cut away the nettles and trailing briars, to be rewarded by the sight of her precious Ginara Stone half-hidden in a nest of fallen leaves no more than a yard to the right of where her hand had been. The jewel still glinted and sparkled in the dappled light, almost as if glad to be with her again.

As she caught her breath she paused to consider what she had done. Was it magick? Witchcraft? Yet if it was magick, it was – like her ability to turn milk – of little practical use. It could not protect her, enrich her, or alter matters of import. It was too slow even for a show of conjuring.

Perhaps somewhere there was someone who could teach her the true uses of magick. Perhaps there were even books on the subject? She suspected that the priest knew something of these matters. He was a learned man. But his sort rarely approved of magicks.

Her train of thought abruptly snapped. She could no longer hear the rest of the company ahead – she had lingered here too long! Hurriedly secreting the jewel in her jerkin, she turned on her heel and began to run down the track after the others.

The travellers spent the night upon a steep hillside overlooking the still waters of Irnpool, Leighor and Yeon keeping an uneventful watch throughout the dark night hours. The next day was a Starday, the twenty-third of *Faestan* month, and the day of the week once held sacred to *Ginara,* as Sunday was to *Helior,* Moonday to *Ethimathé,* and Stormday to *Arul,* Lord of the Air. And it was on this day that, after an early start, the travellers finally came down to the River Thauran in the late afternoon. The river was broad and strong, presenting a truly daunting prospect, and they were content to set up camp and leave the crossing for the morrow.

When cold morning came the prospect looked bleak. The crossing was still a few leagues to the east, and as the travellers walked, the roar of an unseen cataract grew steadily louder and more fearsome, until its great fury seemed to cower the whole forest. Then, with surprisingly little warning, they were upon it. The river broadened, its far bank retreating behind a number of tree-scattered islands. Leighor's eyes followed the flow of the river until it reached a point, not a thousand paces distant, where everything suddenly vanished. One moment the river was there, where it should be, roiling and coursing over the flat stones; the next it had disappeared, its place taken by a thick haze of swirling grey mist. The cataract! He had not imagined it so close. How much closer to that fearsome edge must they go before they found the crossing?

His answer was almost immediate. 'Here!' Haflas cried, holding up one hand to bring the small caravan to a halt. 'This is where we cross.'

'How do you know?' Yeon asked, staring out across the swirling waters.

Haflas pointed to a tall linden tree on the nearest island. It bore a thin white score half way up its trunk. A large, rounded boulder lay at their feet, with a similar mark etched into its rough surface. 'Between these two lies our way. The secret ford of Loron.'

The first stage of the crossing was waded with little difficulty, the travellers emerging on to the nearest island to follow Haflas along an overgrown track that led towards the falls. The deafening roar of the cataract now drowned out all else, even shouted conversation – so that they could only make signs to one another and pull faces as they drew nearer to the torrent. Suddenly the trees parted in front of them – and immediately Leighor wished they had not: the rocky island fell away beneath their feet to reveal its true nature as but one shattered, rocky pinnacle on the mid-point of a huge series of falls. The whole mighty Thauran River roared its life away upon either side of them, falling straight down, three hundred feet or more, into its rocky gorge. As it fell it created an impenetrable mist – so dense that nothing at all could be seen of the country beneath or round about.

'What have you brought us to?' Telsyan asked, aghast. 'You say we can cross this? Are you mad?'

'There is a bridge.' Haflas pointed to a rickety rope and plank construction that hung suspended from the trees of their tiny islet, connecting it precariously with another similar isle to the north. It was a bridge which the herbalist would not normally have trusted over a muddy creek. But here, swaying in the breeze, its mid-point only a few short feet above the impossibly powerful, surging waters of the Thauran, it seemed sheer madness.

'Are you sure it is safe?' he bellowed desperately.

Haflas smiled and nodded. None of the others seemed overly convinced.

'We shall go one . . .' the rest of the words were lost against the roar of the falls.
'What?'
'One by one!' Haflas pointed to them each in turn and then to the swaying bridge. The travellers nodded grimly.

Telsyan was the first to step on to the bridge. It seemed to take an age for him to cross. And all the while Leighor's eyes were constantly scanning the creaking ropes and knots that held the bridge together, convinced that any moment the whole structure would suddenly unravel, sending the merchant tumbling to his doom.

But Telsyan made it across, to slump down exhausted on to a small patch of grass amid the jumbled rocks of the far bank. Now it was Leighor's turn: and this was far worse than ever watching the merchant had been. The bridge seemed to have a dozen different modes of movement all its own: rolling, twisting, rocking and swaying; up and down, and from side to side; bucking unpredictably with every slight move he made. He teetered constantly upon the edge of destruction, his heart in his mouth.

Each step on the green slippery timbers became a torture as the roiling waters rose higher and higher beneath him. He was almost at the lowest point of the bridge. The waters hurtled by less than a yard beneath his feet. He looked ahead. The far bank seemed incredibly high up and far away.

Suddenly there was a dull crack, and with a sickening snap of rotten timber, the plank he had just set most of his weight upon, fell apart beneath him. Slowly, so slowly, the jagged pieces tumbled into the surging waters below, and for terror-stricken seconds Leighor dangled from the handropes. At last he managed to regain his footing on the next rung, watching in horror as the shattered remnants of the plank were hurled over the edge of the precipice and immediately drowned in thousands of tons of falling water. His head spun. He heard the others urging him onward, but their voices sounded like plaintive despairing cries against the roar of the cataract, and it was a full minute before he could force his limbs to move again – somehow managing to crawl up on to the far bank.

There he sat next to the merchant, gasping for breath as he watched the musician, Tavolir, follow his path gingerly but safely across. Next came Yeon, Keran, Uhlendof, and then Inanys. Now only Zindur and Haflas were left, with the two laden mules.

Haflas went first, gently coaxing his mule on to the swaying bridge. It showed no liking for the creaking structure, but somehow Haflas managed to urge it across and up on to the far bank and safety. Now came Zindur with the second mule. The warrior tried to steady his charge as Haflas had done, but from the beginning things did not look well. Rearing in terror at the sight of the raging torrent beneath it, the fearstricken mule tore itself suddenly free of Zindur's grip in a vain attempt to get back to the island. Yet there was no room on the narrow walkway for it to turn, and as the horrified company watched, its hooves crashed down once more into the frail bridge. Several timbers broke away, splintering as they splashed down into the torrent below. Zindur began to back fearfully away. Then, slowly, terribly, the whole bridge began to break up. The taut ropes snapped one by one, the structure tearing itself apart, to plummet piece by piece into the river. And Zindur and the mule followed, their screams almost inaudible against the thunder of the falls.

Leighor sprang, horror-struck, to his feet. Pieces of the bridge were already being swept over the falls, and the last sight he caught of the mule was of its panic-stricken face staring up out of the roiling waters as it too was carried over.

But of Zindur there was no sign.

'There! There!' Yeon screamed suddenly beside him, pointing into the water halfway between themselves and the precipice.

And there Zindur floated, clinging tenaciously to one of the two trailing ropes still attached to the bank. There was no shelter for him there, no respite from the terrible pull of the waters as they raced for the cataract. Desperately the travellers tried to haul the mercenary back upstream towards them; but only the surviving mule was finally able to draw him, shuddering and gasping, to the shore.

Frozen to the marrow and soaked to the skin, the travellers quickly set about building a fire of bracken and fallen branches. Both tents, along with their ropes and poles, had been borne by the first mule, and so were safe. But the second mule had been carrying most of their other equipment, and their dearly-purchased supplies of food. All of this was now lost. Only a single pot and a few small bags of flour and herbs remained. For all practical purposes they were completely without food.

'Can we live off the land as we travel?' Leighor asked.

Haflas nodded uncertainly. 'There is much that can be gleaned from the forest. If we have the time we may hunt or set traps, and we may eat roots, mushrooms and berries. But to survive for long we shall have to have a few basic provisions: flour, fat, dry beans . . .' He ticked the various items off on his fingers.

'Aye, much as we had!' Yeon broke in bitterly. 'But which, thanks to your crossing, are now floating down the Thauran!'

'Enough!' Uhlendof rebuked wearily. 'What is done is done. Haflas was not to know how the bridge had rotted: and further quarrelling will get us nowhere.'

Telsyan snorted. 'One thing is certain: none of this would have happened upon the Great Way! We are alive now only by greatest good fortune. We could all have perished in these waters. The whole company could have been separated when the bridge fell; half on one bank, half on the other. What would we have done then? Mayhap in future you will all give less credence to fears and foolish fantasies?'

There was silence.

'Well, we cannot go back now,' he admitted finally, 'so we must go on. But remember this day. Remember it well!'

'That we shall,' Inanys croaked suddenly. 'We shall name it "The Day of the Wisdom of Master Telsyan"; and in years to come it shall be set aside solely for the contemplation of your works!'

Keran bit her lip to suppress an involuntary smile. The crookback might be a spite-filled, venomous creature, but he knew well enough how to puncture an inflated ego.

Telsyan's face went beetroot red, but he said nothing.

There was now another wide ford to traverse. But the arm of the Thauran that still separated them from the mainland ran not nearly so full nor so wild as had the first crossing. And when the travellers finally clambered up on to the gently rising north bank of the Thauran, they still had half the afternoon in front of them.

'I hope there are not many more such rivers to cross on our journey,' Tavolir gasped, trying to catch his breath. 'The waters of civilised lands are wont to run in a far gentler manner!'

'There are many great rivers in the north,' Haflas replied flatly. 'But I think that from now on you will find the crossings a little more to your liking.'

'I certainly hope so,' Telsyan grunted. And slowly they began to trudge across the broad swathe of muddy grassland that separated them from the waiting forest.

Chapter Fifteen
HIRDA'S GARDEN

There was no longer any definite trail as such; and Haflas appeared to lead them more by intuition than anything else as they made their way steadily northward. The power of the great dark trees pressed them all into silence as they toiled upwards through the grey dappled shade. They seemed to travel outside of time, beneath a distant and overcast sky. Only when the light finally began to fade, and murky pools of darkness spread beneath the trees, was the silence at last broken.

Zindur cursed, tripping over a tree root half-hidden by the fallen leaves. 'It grows too dark for travel!' he complained loudly. 'Are we never to halt?'

'Keep your voice down!' Telsyan hissed. 'We shall make camp when we find fresh water!'

'I fear that we shall find little of that for some while,' Uhlendof observed. 'We travel now through chalkland. There will be no pools or surface streams until we find a valley that cuts beneath the chalk.'

'Let us camp here then,' Yeon pointed out a nearby glade. 'I have seen more than enough of water for one day!'

Telsyan shook his head. 'We need water for cooking and for the mule. We cannot halt until we find some.'

Groans rose from many of the party, but they took up the march all the same, seeking through the gathering dark for a vale that might conceal a stream, a spring or any other kind of water. Yet their search was without success.

'We shall have to stop soon whether we find water or not,' Uhlendof declared at last. 'It is madness to keep going like this!'

And then Leighor noticed a dim glimmer through the trees below. It was faint but steady, and he wondered why he hadn't seen it before. 'Look!' he hissed in warning. 'Down there! A light!'

'Where?' Telsyan asked sharply.

Leighor pointed it out, some way to the west, near the bottom of what appeared to be a broad, fertile valley. Soon they had all seen it, a tiny pinpoint of light, small and dim and yellow in the distance, a single flickering dot against the vast, blue-green darkness of vale and forest.

'Do you know of any settlement in these parts?' the merchant demanded of Haflas.

'No, my lord,' the smaller man replied, concerned. 'I cannot think what it could be, for it is no campfire to be sure. It seems more a candle, or a lamp of some sort.'

'Then it is likely to be friendly,' Yeon said optimistically. 'Let us go down!'

'Nay, let us not be overhasty,' Zindur warned. 'There is many a foul trap baited with a friendly lantern. We must descend silently and with caution.'

Dense patches of bramble and briar clawed and tore at their clothing, clutching desperately at feet and ankles as if seeking actively to hinder their passage. Once down upon the broad valley floor, however, the going became easier. But the strange yellow light seemed now to have vanished; and for some minutes the travellers stumbled about in the near-total darkness. Then, as they moved slowly on, the light reappeared once more, emerging from the shadow of a great stand of trees. Leighor could just make out the dim outline of a small, low building.

'A cabin!' Uhlendof whispered.

Yet as they drew closer it became clear that they in fact approached a tiny stone cottage, with a steeply pitched roof of dark slate. A pair of thick red curtains hung slightly apart in the nearest window; and through these a gentle, flickering light beckoned.

Seeing this, it was all the travellers could do to prevent themselves breaking into a run straight for the door. But hard-learned caution made them circle the cottage first, noting the well-tended garden that seemed to merge almost naturally into the surrounding meadow and forest. The cottage itself was entirely silent. If anyone within guessed at their presence, they gave no sign.

'It seems that no one lies in ambush,' Haflas whispered. 'Shall we knock?'

'Aye,' Zindur grunted. 'I think we shall outnumber any within; let us make ourselves known.' He put his hand to his sword.

Uhlendof caught his arm. 'We are not brigands!' he hissed angrily. 'We shall beg hospitality from those within, but if that is refused we shall leave peacefully to build our own camp across the valley.'

'What else?' Zindur shrugged, grinning gently. 'I had no other intention.'

'Indeed!' Uhlendof snorted. 'Yet you had best stay well to the rear. We do not want to frighten these poor folk out of their wits.'

In the end Uhlendof and Haflas went forward to knock upon the stout oaken door, while the rest of the party remained some paces behind. The monk's light tap cut through the silence like a cleaver; but for some minutes there was no answer, nor any sound of movement from within. Uhlendof was just about to knock again when there came an abrupt grating, as if of a large bolt being shifted. And slowly the door creaked open; just wide enough for a large round face to peer suspiciously out at them.

'Well, what do you want?' It was a woman; she spoke sharply, fearfully. Leighor could see that she was quite old – well past her middle years – and that she appeared extremely nervous.

'We intend you no harm,' Uhlendof said quickly, 'We are a small party of travellers who have become lost in these forests and, seeing the light from your window, have made our way here.'

'You saw the light?' the woman frowned. 'Which of you?'

'Master Leighor here,' Uhlendof pointed back.

The woman nodded. 'Let me look at you. Come closer!'

Leighor came forward, and the others followed.

'That is all of us,' Uhlendof stated. 'We are nine.'

'Where are you from?' The door opened a little wider.

'From Hallad's Keep by way of the Thauran,' the monk explained; 'where we have this day lost one of our mules and most of our food.'

'There are a great many of you,' the old woman's eyes scanned the small group hurriedly; 'and I . . .' She hesitated.

'Do you live alone?' Telsyan asked.

The woman seemed hard put to decide. 'No,' she said at last.

Telsyan smiled. 'Truly we mean you no harm, good lady. We only seek water, somewhere to raise our tents, and perhaps we may buy some food?'

'No tents!' the woman said hurriedly, seeming now even more fearful. 'No,' she shook her head with haste; 'I cannot have tents here!' She seemed almost about to slam the door, and then thought better of it, opening it wider instead. She poked her head out briefly to stare past the travellers into the darkness beyond, her eyes darting apprehensively across the dark landscape. As if she were fearful of something, Leighor thought, something she knew to be out there, and which worried her more even than the motley group of strangers at her door.

She withdrew into the shelter of the doorway, and her small sharp eyes examined them again. 'You'd better come in,' she said quickly. 'It is not safe to be out of doors at night.' She stood back from the door and waved them hurriedly inward, as if she could not wait to slam and bar it firmly behind them.

The nine found themselves crowded into a small, bare-boarded room, with a low peat fire smouldering in one corner. A tall oaken chair stood before the fire, but apart from this, and a huge dark dresser set against one wall, the room was unfurnished. The rest of the wallspace was hung with plain, country tapestries sewn in simple yarns of bright colours; depicting trees, flowers and pleasant landscapes.

'Sit down before the fire.' The woman pointed to some cushions piled up in one corner. 'You may use those if you wish; and then you may tell me your business.'

Telsyan blinked; turning to pass the cushions to the other members of the party. The cushions, like the tapestries, were neatly and painstakingly sewn; yet to Leighor's surprise were filled only with coarse straw. Surely something better could be found, even here? He sat cross-legged on the floor, studying the features of their hostess as she sat facing them in the only chair. She was short and dumpy, and even when standing must come no higher than his chest. She wore simple homespun clothes of dappled browns and dull yellows; her dark-brown hair was draped in a dark shawl, which she did not attempt to remove, even here at her own fireside. She took up her needlework.

'I am Hirda,' she said; 'and this is my dwelling. Mine and . . .' she paused, some secret lurking in the darkness beyond her eyes; '. . . my husband's.'

'And is he here now?' Telsyan asked.

'No,' the woman's eyes shifted uneasily again. 'But he is nearby. He may be home this night, or on the morrow . . .' She stared at them. 'If he returns you must leave. Leave at once!'

'But surely—' Telsyan began.

'At once!' the woman insisted. 'My husband is a quick-tempered man who likes no strangers!'

Telsyan's eyebrows rose, but he let the matter drop. Introducing each member of the company in turn, he told the woman that they were traders, come to buy skins and pelts from the hunters and trappers of the northern settlements. 'Does your husband perhaps have skins to sell?' he asked.

The woman chuckled. 'None that he would sell to such as thee! Be glad of the shelter, and be on your way before sunrise tomorrow!'

'My lady—' Inanys began. He sat crouched on his heels in a dark corner of the room, his crooked staff propped upright against his knees as if to ward off some expected danger.

'Why do you call me that?' Hirda turned on him sharply.

'Mere politeness,' the crookback flashed a deceitful smile. 'But what would you rather I call you?'

'Goodwife will do for such as ye,' she frowned. 'Hirda, if you will. I have small time for such conceits. Now what do you want of me?'

'I wished only to ask you one question. How long have you dwelt here, goodwife, in these old dark woods . . . ?'

The woman's eyes narrowed as she studied the crookback long and hard. It could have been Leighor's imagination, but Inanys seemed curiously uneasy under that stare, appearing to relax again only when it had at last relented. A thin smile of triumph momentarily escaped the crookback's lips.

'You think you are wise,' Hirda said darkly. 'But it is only fools who probe too deeply into matters of which they understand nothing.' She rose. 'I suppose I must find you all a bite to eat. But it will not be much, for I am a poor woman.' She nodded to Zindur. 'While I do this, you had best get your mule under shelter. I shall show you where!' She hurried out of the room with Zindur in tow.

'This is a very curious place,' Leighor noted, as soon as they were alone; 'and she a curious lady.'

Uhlendof nodded. 'And what form of man is her husband, to frighten her so? It seems that she has not even a chair to herself to sit upon, when he is at home.'

Haflas frowned. 'What business would take a man out of doors alone and at night in country such as this?'

'Perhaps he sets his traps,' Keran suggested.

'Perhaps,' the merchant said drily; 'perhaps not.'

'Do you think he is allied with the Rievers?' Tavolir ventured. 'If so, we are indeed unsafe here.'

'It would explain many things,' Telsyan agreed; 'including how they remain secure enough in lands such as these to show a light. I . . .'

Just then the door opened to re-admit Zindur, with the old woman, Hirda, close behind.

'We have placed the mule in a stall behind the house,' the warrior announced. 'He has hay; though he would have fed just as well tethered outside.'

Hirda shook her head briskly. 'I want no mules trampling my garden. He and you must stay inside!' She peered at them closely. 'Whatever happens, you are not to leave this house before daybreak – unless at my order.' She swept out of the room once more, to return within minutes carrying a large tray which bore nine small bowls of steaming soup.

The bowls were of smoothest aspenwood, each with its own slender wooden spoon, carved with entwining leaves and branches. The soup itself came as something of a disappointment, being thin, tasteless and barely warm. Yet surprisingly, once finished, it seemed to allay their hunger.

Hirda had stood watching whilst they ate, and now collected their empty bowls to take them from the chamber. But as she turned to leave, another entered the room: a slight, barefoot girl dressed in a simple homespun shift, fair hair flowing in thin straggles down her shoulders. Simple doe-eyes shone as she smiled.

'Who is this?' Telsyan asked quickly, before Hirda could push her back out again.

The older woman stiffened. 'This,' she told them slowly, 'is Ardri, my sister.'

'Your sister?' Leighor asked in surprise, for the girl could not have been more than fifteen years of age, and her face might have been that of a girl much younger.

'Aye, Ardri is my sister,' Hirda admitted; but gave no further explanation. She turned back to the girl. 'Go!' she ordered, making a sharp forward movement to grasp her.

But Ardri ducked quickly beneath her arm, squeezing past into the centre of the room. She grinned triumphantly.

Hirda took two steps towards her and then sighed, her anger seeming to melt into weary resignation. Wordlessly she turned and strode from the room.

The girl smiled nervously at the seated travellers but said nothing.

'You are very young,' Uhlendof said.

Ardri giggled.

'It is unusual to find such a difference in ages between two sisters . . .' the priest probed gently. But Ardri merely shrugged her shoulders and continued to grin.

'She is a little . . .' Telsyan shook his head.

Uhlendof nodded, turning back to the girl. 'What do you do here all day, Ardri?' he asked, trying a new approach. 'It must be very lonely for you here.'

'Lonely?' the girl spoke for the first time. Her voice was high and childlike, and filled with wonder. 'What is lonely?'

Uhlendof sighed. 'Do you have no friends, no one to talk to, apart from your sister?'

Ardri shook her head. 'Only cousin Uirass.'

'And is he the other who lives here?' Telsyan broke in.

'Yes,' Ardri nodded; 'though he's not here now. Now he hunts.' She pointed out of the window into the dark beyond.

'Is that how you all live?' Uhlendof asked. 'Hunting?'

'No,' the girl giggled again. 'Only Uirass hunts. We must stay here and tend the garden for the other.'

'Other?' Uhlendof stiffened. 'What other?'

Ardri frowned. 'That is a secret Hirda knows. Not for strangers' ears.'

'And do many strangers come here?' the monk asked quickly.

The girl shook her head, 'No one comes here now; none but the lost.'

'Like us, you mean?'

Ardri nodded. 'Perhaps.'

The monk sighed, and seemed about to give up his questioning when Tavolir suddenly leaned forward:

'So then, Ardri; perhaps you will tell us what it is you do all day here? What it is you most like to do?'

'Me?' the girl seemed surprised that he should show an interest.

The musician nodded.

Ardri suddenly beamed, as if some deep wellspring had been released within her. 'Well,' she began enthusiastically; 'what I like best is to run in the forest all alone; to watch the lilies grow and the toadstools bloom, to sing with the streams, and to dance with the Fair Ones down in the marshy hollow . . .'

'Fair Ones?' Uhlendof asked, surprised.

'Yes,' Ardri nodded, starting to spin gracefully across the confined space, her arms outstretched. 'Dance beneath the trees, between the moonbeams.' She came to a sudden halt against the far wall, and turned back instantly to face Tavolir, her mind already on another subject. 'Sometimes I go to the old elm of Blacksthorn Top and listen to his stories. He is old. Older than all the trees but the grey yew – and *he* has forgotten how to speak long since!'

'Do all the trees speak then?' Tavolir asked, entranced.

'Of course they do!' Ardri laughed – a distant bell-like sound. 'All the forest speaks if you know how to listen, but only the old elm tells stories. The birches are very young and will say nothing to strangers but "It's cold," or "It's too windy," or "I'm losing my leaves." The old oaks say more, but they only want to talk about their rheumatism or the rot in their roots, or what tricks the squirrels have been playing in their hair.'

'Oh,' nodded Tavolir. The rest of the room listened in spellbound silence.

'Yes,' Ardri nodded again, revelling in the attention she was getting. 'The pines talk too. They tell you who has passed by recently, but they forget. They think only of growing taller.' She laughed. 'But best of all I like to watch – and make things grow.'

'How do you do that?'

'Like this!' She darted suddenly forward to snatch up Uhlendof's staff from where it lay on the floor beside him, running back with it to a corner of the room where she turned back to face them all, holding it upright in her outstretched hands. She stared hard at the dry, gnarled wood. Minutes passed in total silence, and then a huge beaming smile appeared upon her face.

A tiny green dot had appeared near the tip of the staff; and slowly, as the spellbound travellers watched, the dot grew, forming itself into a clearly recognisable bud which swelled and began to open before their eyes. A small green shoot appeared, and two tiny leaves which grew longer and broader as the shoot extended. Below Ardri's fingers two more small shoots had appeared, both growing equally – impossibly – fast.

Leighor watched open-mouthed, hardly daring to believe his eyes, as the stems lengthened and the leaves grew, and finally circlets of young white flowers decorated the new green branches. All from one dry old hawthorn staff! It was impossible: but there it was, still growing and flowering in the simple girl's hands.

'Ardri!' A scream of anger, mixed with what – fear? – broke the spell. Ardri turned, letting the staff fall from her hands in startled terror, to run, cowering, for the far corner of the chamber, as Hirda hurtled into the room.

But there was to be no escape. Hirda ignored the dumbstruck travellers, storming across the room to seize the younger girl roughly by arm and shoulder, hauling her furiously towards the door.

'You are never to do that!' she hissed. 'Never before strangers! That work – the Making – is long ago finished!'

Ardri tried desperately to cling to the trailing curtains, but Hirda dragged her ruthlessly away; her feet crushing the new young shoots that adorned Uhlendof's staff as she did so.

'I am sorry, sister,' the girl whimpered. 'I was just . . .'

'I know well what you were just, girl,' the elder broke in harshly, 'and I will see you well whipped for this night's work!'

Ardri wailed, scratched and struggled like a wild thing, but she could not resist the determined strength of the older woman.

'Madam,' Uhlendof rose. 'Whatever the girl has done, it was on our account. Pray do no punish her for it.'

'This is none of your concern!' Hirda spat out the words. 'You would do well to forget all that you have seen here this night. All!' With a loud grunt she hauled the whimpering girl a little further towards the door. 'Now sleep, and sleep well, for you must rise early on the morrow!' With a final protesting heave she dragged Ardri fully out of the room and slammed the heavy door behind her. The flames in the hearth gave a last resentful flicker, and faded into the hot embers.

Almost as if commanded by Hirda's parting words, a feeling of overwhelming tiredness fell suddenly upon them all.

'I think . . . I think we have been drugged,' Leighor warned, stifling a yawn. 'It must have been . . . the soup . . .'

'Drugged?' Uhlendof slumped down beside him. 'Drugged?' He seemed quite unable to grasp the concept. 'Then there is nothing we can do . . . Nothing but . . .' he yawned loudly, '. . . sleep it off.'

'That's what they want . . .' Leighor started to protest, but he could find neither the words nor the coherent thought to finish the sentence. The room was so warm, his pillow so near . . . There was something he had wanted to talk about . . . something he had wanted to do . . . But no, that could wait . . . whatever it was. Without even troubling to cover himself with his cloak, he fell back against the bare boards: and sleep came instantly.

Yet the travellers' sleep brought them little rest. It was troubled and fitful and filled with dreams – or at least they supposed them dreams, for each of them seemed in some way to remain semi-conscious throughout the long night. Whether what they heard, or thought they heard, were dream or no, none of them could later have sworn; but all night through, the house was oppressive and unquiet – as if alive, with a will and a purpose of its own; casting sombre, baleful images into the minds of them all.

All would later agree that there had been a constant roaring and heavy growling beyond the window, as if some great beast lurked beneath and thirsted for their blood. The beast had stayed near for several hours; sometimes snuffling outside the chamber, sometimes roaring in terrible, frustrated anger, at other times trying to break in – the heavy pounding and tearing of its great claws at the stones and timbers filling them all with dread.

Yet throughout this onslaught the travellers remained prisoners, able to hear all that look place, able to recognise the terrible sounds and their full ominous portent, yet unable to free themselves from the iron bonds of sleep that held them motionless and defenceless upon the bare chamber floor.

Full awakening, when it finally came, was a blessed relief from the fearful torture of their sleeping. It was Hirda who woke them, bursting through the stout square door, and bringing with her a chilling rush of cool air from the dark morning beyond.

'It is time,' she said sharply. 'Time for you to be up and on your way!' She turned on her heel and swept out of the room.

Leighor stretched, wincing at the aches and cramps that now screamed through his body.

'It must have been a nightmare,' he ventured at last; somehow sensing, without the need to ask, that the others had all shared his dream.

'I think not.' Uhlendof shook his head grimly, as he too staggered to his feet. 'That was no natural sleep we slept, and our dreams no proper dreams. I fear that there was indeed something solid and tangible without these walls last night.'

'Well, whatever it was,' Tavolir stifled a yawn; 'we took no harm from it. So let us away, with the light!'

One by one the others rose and gathered up their scattered possessions. Uhlendof's staff lay in the middle of the room, as dry and lifeless as it had always been. It bore no sign that it had ever once blossomed into life at Ardri's touch, and Leighor wondered whether that too had not been but a part of the night's tormented dreams. The monk picked it up with slightly more hesitancy than usual, but after examining it closely for a second or two, he shrugged and turned away, following the others as they filed out through the single narrow passage that led to the garden.

Here a long wooden trough of cold water awaited them. But even the icy freshness of its touch upon their faces could do nothing to dispel the persistent, eyepricking, dull, yawning tiredness that beset them all – so that even the slowly-brightening landscape all around them appeared distant and grey, as if half-seen through the eyes of a dream.

Hirda appeared once more, standing on the step at the cottage doorway. She watched them grimly for a moment or so before she spoke.

'Your mule awaits you in the outhouse.' She nodded towards a small wooden lean-to hard against the rear wall. 'Load him up and be on your way!'

'But my lady,' Telsyan protested, drying his face on the hem of his cloak; 'can we not buy some provisions from you, and perhaps a bite or two to eat before we go?'

The woman shook her head vigorously. 'No. No! You must go now. Without delay!' Much of the fearfulness of the evening before had returned to her voice, and she scanned the fast-paling skyline of the eastern hills as if dreading the first glimpse of the returning sun. 'You must be gone before sunrise. That was the bargain.'

'We cannot go far on an empty stomach, lady,' Zindur objected. 'Show some hospitality.'

Hirda strode towards him angrily. 'You have had hospitality enough from a poor lonely woman; all nine of you!' She glared up furiously into the face of the large mercenary, who towered high above her. 'Now begone! And trouble me no more.'

'Why are you so anxious to see us depart?' Uhlendof asked. 'What secret do you hide in this small house of yours?'

Her bearing changed. 'That you are better off not knowing, little man.'

'I am a priest. If evil lurks here it may be exorcised. You seem fearful indeed of something that lies in this vale. What evils beset you here?'

The woman laughed out loud: a harsh unpleasant sound. 'None you would like to meet, Mallenian! Bide with those simple things you know and understand.' Her eyes returned once more to the eastern sky. 'Now go. Before you bring down yet more trouble upon us!' She turned away.

'Where is Ardri?' Keran asked suddenly. 'What have you done with her?'

Hirda halted and turned back once more to face the travellers. 'Ardri is safe.' She stared at them strangely, her voice softer now. 'It is not fitting that you see her again, nor she you. Worry more for your own selves, if you are wise.' She turned away again towards the cottage. 'I shall see what food I can find for you. It will not be much, but it should see you as far as the settlement of men.' She was gone.

'This is a strange place indeed,' Haflas said, staring about him at the broad, wooded vale, the open meadows and the high, lonely hills above; all part of a great primaeval forest whose spur came down to the very edge of the cottage garden, not two score paces from where they stood. A forest that seemed unsullied by the hand of man; its trees high and dark and ancient, yet still crowned in the full verdant foliage of high summer. There was no trace here of autumn browns or winter greys to mar the regal splendour of these forest kings. Haflas shook his head. 'In all my life I have not seen the like of this before. It is beautiful, too beautiful to exist in these sad days. Let us go, as the woman says.'

Telsyan nodded, and wordlessly he, Haflas and Zindur made their way across the garden to free the mule and begin the loading.

'Here!' Uhlendof called suddenly from beneath the window of the room in which they had spent the night. 'Come and look at this.'

Leighor and the others crowded round, to see several large paw prints in the soft ground beneath the window.

'Bear!' Zindur hissed.

'Aye, those are bear sure enough,' Haflas nodded. 'And a big one, by the look of him. Look at the size of those claws! No wonder the lady is afeared to go out at nights.'

'And see here!' Tavolir pointed up towards several fresh claws marks scored deep into the thick green layers of moss and lichen that decked the cottage wall, some cutting into the very stone itself. He shivered. 'I would not want to meet any creature with claws like that. We have been very lucky to have been safe indoors this night.'

Telsyan scratched the stubble on his chin. 'I wonder.' He paused for a moment in thought. 'Where do the prints lead?'

Haflas was already following them across the thick beds of herbs and greenery that made up Hirda's garden. 'It seems to have gone off north into the forest,' he told them on his return; 'but it may not be very far away. We had better keep good watch as we go.'

'Are you not finished yet?' Hirda's sharp voice cut across the short distance from her cottage door. 'I had hoped you all packed and ready to go by now!'

'We are sorry, ma'am,' Haflas apologised, hurrying back to the mule to finish the loading.

'Sorry gets no pumpkins picked,' Hirda scolded. 'Sorry fills no ladles! Get on with you, and be away!'

Hirda clucked and tutted impatiently until the packing was at last completed, handing Telsyan a small bag of rough-ground meal when they were finally ready to depart. 'You may make oatcakes out of that,' she told them shortly. 'They will sustain you for today. But do not – I warn you – stop to cook them until you are well out of this vale: now go.'

Leighor looked round to see if everything was ready. But once again it appeared that Inanys had vanished.

'Here, my lady.' Telsyan drew a few silver coins from his purse. 'I hope that we may recompense you in some small way for your trouble.'

'What use have I for those?' Hirda asked scornfully, dashing the proffered coins aside. 'Save your coin until you reach Furthka: there you shall have more need of it!'

'Furthka?' Telsyan repeated.

'Aye, the settlement of men that lies . . .' she paused, '. . . eastward, a day's journey. Is that not where you are bound?' She pointed up towards the distant hilltops; and as she did so the words caught in her throat. A tiny chink of orange sunlight had appeared between the tree-clad eastern hills. 'Sunrise!' she shuddered visibly. 'Hurry! You must go. Please – go now!' She seemed to want to push the travellers physically away from the house, so great was her desire to see them depart.

'What is all this, goodwife?' An old, gentle voice came suddenly from behind them; from the direction of the forest. Hirda froze at the sound.

Leighor turned sharply, now almost as fearful as the old woman herself of what the sunrise would bring. Yet the owner of the voice did not seem at first of threatening mien – a tall, elderly man who might perhaps once, long ago, have made quite a commanding figure. He still held himself ramrod straight, his bearing proud and erect. He wore a long gown of silver-grey, but his feet were bare. His hair too was grey, iron grey, strong and straight cropped, yet his face was thin and lined with years. Only his eyes, dark, brown and piercing, gave any indication of the strength within.

'Who are these strangers?' he asked again, his voice gentle yet imperative, demanding an answer.

Hirda stepped forward, placing herself between him and the travellers, almost as if trying to protect them. 'No, Uirass, my husband,' she began quickly; 'it is not as you think. They were lost. Somehow one of them must have seen the light, and they came down out of the hills for shelter.'

'They saw the light?' the old man asked, surprised. 'In what manner could such as these see a Limning Light?'

'One of them is a wizard,' the woman explained hurriedly, pointing to Leighor. 'It was he who saw!'

'A wizard?' Uirass glanced at the dark-robed southron for an instant; his eyes penetrating, searching, holding Leighor's gaze, seeming to have the power to seek out his closest secrets, his innermost thoughts. And then it was over. Uirass smiled. 'I see no wizard before me – though mayhap a wizard's garb.'

'But he saw the light!' Hirda pleaded.

'So you say.' The old man shook his head. 'Yet you know the law as well as I. What is done may not be undone. Not by your hand nor mine, nor by any save the master.'

'No!' Hirda shook her head fearfully. 'Let them depart. This house and this garden are yet mine. Cause no harm to these wayfarers here!'

The old man shook his head sadly and stepped past her.

'My lord,' Telsyan began, stepping forward. 'We mean you no ill. We are, as your lady says, only travellers . . .'

Uirass' eyes caught his; held his; and the merchant was still. He raised his left hand towards the forest; and as if in answer, three great bears appeared at the forest's edge, not a hundred paces from where they stood.

'What means this?' Zindur bellowed, drawing his sword. 'What sort of demon are you that has power over wild beasts?'

Uirass made a sign in the air with one hand, and the mercenary let out a sudden howl of pain, dropping his sword to the ground as if it had burnt him.

The old man smiled thinly. 'Beware: I have power over much, both within this vale and without. All Hathanwild is my domain – yet this is the vessel of power. All else may be defiled, but this alone must remain pure; else we are no more, and the touch of our hand will no longer be felt beneath the skies of the great forest.' He turned on the party accusingly. 'You have taken from the vale. Do you think I could not feel it, though I were a thousand leagues distant? You have eaten of its fruit, you have filled it with your filth and your ordure!' The old man's voice began to tremble with emotion. 'It cannot be endured!'

Hirda appeared again behind her husband, her voice filled with pain. 'Let it pass. Let it pass. They know nothing of what they do. They have done little damage; and what if they had? Is it not time our work was finished? I grow weary, I have not been beyond the vale for so long . . . so many distant summers . . .' her voice faded. 'Our time is past, husband, and our master long forgotten. If he still dwells upon the earth he has ceased to remember our existence . . .'

'No!' Uirass shouted out loud, casting her aside with surprising force, to send her sprawling amid the herbs of her garden. 'The task is not yet done! The work not yet complete; and will not be until he shall return!' He turned again to face the awestruck travellers. 'You – You shall remain! Your journey over. Your cares done!' He held his hands outstretched above the ground; and before the stunned travellers could attempt to react, their feet were gripped tight to the ground.

Leighor cried out in horror as long dark roots snaked out of the soil like thick, obscene worms to coil about their feet and legs, binding them tight to the living earth. In moments all the travellers were held immobile, bound in the grip of innumerable roots and tendrils that thickened and hardened about them.

Uirass nodded grimly and lowered his hands. 'Become one with the vale,' he ordered. 'Add life where you have taken.'

'Release us!' Uhlendof called angrily, 'You have no right—'

'Pray!' the old man sneered; 'and see if the High One chooses to aid you!' He prepared to turn away.

Leighor was already beginning to feel weaker. As if the living roots were in some way drawing away his strength, draining his life-essence, to replenish the hungry soil beneath. Where was Inanys? He must be somewhere close by, surely? In his heart the southron felt only deepest despair. 'You cannot do this!' he screamed our urgently, knowing that this was his last and only chance to affect matters. 'We nine are upon an errand, a great and urgent errand; one that might yet help to save these lands from great evils that arise in the south. That might save your forests from the Riever hordes, the *tarintari*, and from one who uses *harrunor* and usurps the title "Master of the North".'

Uirass turned. 'What care I for your errands?' He advanced on Leighor angrily. 'For your Rievers and usurpers? What care I what they name themselves? Are Rievers worse enemies of mine than the sons of men? Have they less right here than your own folk, who come north only to destroy those few lands still left undefiled!' He spat in the southron's face. 'That for your quests and your noble errands! Be still.'

The old man was about to turn away once more, when his eyes caught upon the slender ashen staff that Leighor had dropped, in his horror, when the tendrils had first coiled about his feet. Uirass studied it for a moment.

'Never seen such a thing,' he muttered to himself.' Limber ashwood ... seems plain; but isn't ... There is some magic there ...' He shook his head. 'But what?' He made an absent-minded sign above the staff, and it gently floated upward into his hand.

Yet the instant that he touched it, Uirass' arm began to shake and tremble uncontrollably – almost as if the staff itself were trying to break free. His jaw fell open and his eyes widened in horror for one brief moment, one dark instant, before his whole face began to dissolve into grey formlessness.

'Noooo ...' His strangled cry faded away into an echoing void. The Uirass they had known no longer stood before them. Instead a great, grey, intangible shapelessness rose above them, seeming to change even as it grew. Its dim shadows took on the semblance of many fleeting forms, each melting one into the other before the travellers could fully grasp what they had seen. One moment a great grey wolf lowered over them; then a mighty bird of prey, fierce eyed and razor taloned; a young man in the fullness of his strength who bore passing resemblance to Uirass; a great brown bear, fur mottled with dull streaks of grey and white. And then finally a tall, terrible figure; human yet inhuman, with two great stag antlers growing from its head. It stared down at them, stern and unrelenting, awesome and ageless; a spirit-lord from a time before memory. And then, suddenly, even this figure appeared to dissolve from within, consumed by an inner fire. Absorbed into a single brilliant flare of light, bright beyond enduring. Like a thuderbolt, yet utterly silent; an intense, burning radiance that threatened to blind all who dared look upon it.

And then nothing.

Darkness.

Silence.

It took several seconds for Leighor's eyes to accustom themselves once more to the dim light of early dawn. And only then did he see the old man lying, still and silent, sprawled dead or unconscious – he knew not which – in the exact spot where he had first taken up the staff. The wand itself lay still beside him, looking no more than the plain ashen rod it was, free in his outstretched hand.

The woman, Hirda, crawled forward to kneel weeping at his side. Leighor looked on in stunned silence. He struggled to move his shoulder – surprisingly his bonds felt easier, looser. He moved his arms and hands, trying to free them. Indeed, the bonds *were* growing weaker. The roots seemed to be losing their cohesion, crumbling, falling into dust, even as he fought against them. Dust? No, earth. The roots that had grown and bound him so tightly were nothing but mouldings of dry earth, that now fell clodlike to the ground around him.

In moments, all the travellers were free; shaking the dry, caked soil from their clothing as they watched Hirda try to revive the fallen Uirass. Of the forest bears there was now no sign.

'Is he . . . is he badly hurt?' Leighor gasped, feeling somehow, foolishly, to blame for all that had happened.

The woman looked up sharply. 'Take your foul stick, dark one! Remove it from his hand! Now!'

Leighor hesitated.

'He will not harm you,' she sneered. 'You have done your work well; he is sorely hurt. Yet none may grant Uirass rest but the master. It is the change; it should never happen in the daylight! Now take your stick!' she commanded.

Hesitantly Leighor bent to take up the staff. It looked harmless and commonplace enough now; yet having seen its effect upon Uirass, he was wary.

'Go on!' Hirda spat. 'How can it harm you? Take it!'

Holding his breath Leighor grasped the staff, but he felt nothing. There was no reaction. No movement. No warmth. No feel of power – nothing to indicate that the staff he held was any more than an ordinary piece of common ash-wood.

Yet the old woman shrank away from him fearfully now that he held the staff; turning to look at the other travellers, who stood unsteadily behind her. 'You have seen,' she hissed. 'You have survived. Now go! Before Uirass awakens. For when he does, none of your tricks will save you!'

'Will you be all right?' Telsyan asked, shaken.

'Aye,' Hirda said bitterly. 'Little thanks to you. Now go, and take your magic stick with you!'

'You are ever the most generous hostess, my lady.' The crookback's voice came suddenly from behind them.

'Where have you been?' Telsyan swung furiously round upon him. 'Where were you hiding when Uirass had us in his power and would have slain us?'

'I had to return to the cottage,' Inanys held his crooked wand up before him, 'for my stick. I would have returned to aid you sooner, but I too was prisoned by the spell . . .'

'Pah!' the merchant turned from him in disgust. 'You are worse than useless for any purpose! Come.' He waved the others onward. 'Let us do as the lady says, and go quickly!'

The travellers needed no further urging. With the laden mule ahead of them to make a path through the long grass, they made their way from the cottage with all the speed they could muster, heading eastward across the vale. They travelled too fast for any speech, not that Leighor could yet form any appropriate words to utter about their experience, had he the breath to do so. His main thought now was merely to place as much distance as he could, as quickly as he could, between himself and Hirda's garden.

As far as possible the travellers kept their distance from the forested portions of the vale, keeping instead to the open meadows of tall, waist-high grass – half dead now, and streaked with the dry yellows and browns of approaching winter. The sound of a lone bear, or perhaps more than one, would occasionally echo out of a nearby tract of forest as they passed; low angry growls that chilled the blood with the promise of vengeance. But for the present the bears were leaderless, and let them pass.

In little more than an hour the travellers were approaching the steeply wooded hills to the east of the vale. Here a clear mountain brook tumbled out of the heights, and many of the party would have paused for rest. But Haflas urged them onward. 'We are not yet out,' he gasped. 'Remember what the old woman told us: to halt only when completely beyond the limits of the vale. I would not ignore her counsel a second time.'

Leighor nodded, and prepared for the hot, steep climb ahead.

In that instant, a fearsome, animal howl of fury tore down the length of the vale behind them, echoing and re-echoing along the high lines of the surrounding hills. Leighor's heart turned to ice, and he spun about to see what came behind them. But there was nothing: only the still forest and the gently swaying meadow grass. All was once more silent.

'What was that?' Keran gasped.

'I fear that Uirass has awakened,' Uhlendof answered quietly. 'Let us make haste!'

The company obeyed with alacrity, racing for the cover of the steep woods that clothed the hillside. Once beneath the trees the going was hard; there was no path to follow, and the travellers had to force their way upward through waist-high undergrowth. Dense thickets of thorn and briar barred their way, whilst long trailing brambles tore at their limbs and cut through their clothing. New sounds now rose up out of the vale behind them: the howls of distant wolves, and the deeper, throatier roars of bears, or other, more fearsome, creatures. Leighor tried to persuade himself that the noises below were in no way related to their flight. But Yeon swiftly confirmed his worst fears.

'They are coming closer!' he shouted urgently. 'The woman! She knows which way we are headed! They can follow!'

'Then hurry!' Zindur roared. 'Or the whole vale will be upon us!'

But it was no use. The undergrowth only seemed to grow thicker and more impassable as they made their way upwards, and the slope of the hill became so steep that it was near impossible to climb. Several times the travellers had to turn and make their way back downwards, retracing their steps to find a more passable route; all the while the fearsome howls from below growing still closer.

'Not that way,' a familiar voice called out suddenly from their left. 'Follow me!'

It was Ardri. Her face was more serious than Leighor had yet seen it; yet even so still full of mischief.

Telsyan halted, appraising her suspiciously. 'Where would you lead us, girl?'

'Upward. To the top!' Ardri grinned. 'I know the paths.'

The travellers hesitated.

'What if this is a trap?' Zindur hissed.

There was no answer.

'Hurry,' the girl called, pointing downward. 'Uirass's children come!' She began to dart away between the trees.

'It seems we have no choice,' Uhlendof sighed.

Reluctantly the travellers followed.

Yet Ardri indeed led them on to easier paths. The dense undergrowth seemed to part and give way before her as they climbed, previously unseen paths appearing as if by magic through the close-set trees. All the while the girl led them merrily onward, dancing ahead of them like a small ragged sprite, her green linen shift billowing softly about her slender form.

Even the steep climb went easier with Ardri ahead of them, the sheltering canopy of broad, dark trees arching high above their path. Autumn seemed not yet to have touched this place, and the birds still sang gaily above their heads, as though it were still high summer. The small girl's merriment was surprisingly infectious, and soon the travellers began to feel that they had indeed left all their troubles far behind them in the vale below. But of this notion they were swiftly disabused.

There came a sudden thunderous crashing through the trees behind them, and a single giant bear lurched out of the undergrowth not fifty paces to their rear. The mule screamed, and broke free of Haflas's hold to bolt away up the pathway. Zindur drew his sword, just as a second giant bear appeared on the path a little way behind the first.

'What shall we do?' Keran cried.

'Draw your swords!' Zindur ordered; 'and move backward slowly. Don't let them get behind us! You who have them, use your bows. Mayhap with luck we can drive them off.'

Keran and Tavolir drew their bows behind a makeshift line formed by Yeon, Zindur, Haflas and Uhlendof – the latter having only his stout staff to protect him. Telsyan fumbled with his crossbow, while Leighor hesitated; undecided as to whether to use his bow, or rely upon the undefined powers of his disconcerting ashen staff. The first bear advanced slowly upon them, growling deep in its throat. There was no time now to fumble beneath his robes for the crossbow. Leighor tightened his grip on the staff.

'Loose your arrows!' Zindur screamed as the bears drew closer.

Keran and Tavolir let fly. The musician's shot missed entirely, to whirr uselessly into the undergrowth; but Keran's arrow flew straight and true, striking deep into the neck of the first advancing animal. It gave out a fearsome howl. But the pain only seemed to anger it the more; and it charged furiously towards the line of its tormentors, maddened with rage.

The line broke before it, Zindur, Haflas and the monk hurling themselves into the undergrowth on either side of the path. But Yeon stood rooted to the spot, sword in hand. Fortunately Telsyan got off a single shot from his crossbow, before he too dived into the undergrowth. The quarrel stung the creature in the flank, slowing its charge, and giving Keran, Tavolir and Yeon just time enough to leap aside.

Now only Leighor still stood in the path of the lumbering bear. Inanys and Ardri were nowhere to be seen. The creature's full attention now fell upon the dark southron; its eyes following him, dark and unblinking, as he backed away up the path. The great bear was clearly hurt, yet it still retained the ability, and the temper, to kill. Despairingly Leighor tried to ward off the creature with his staff, half-hoping that it might prove as devastating here as it had against Uirass.

The staff struck. Yet in the same instant the bear reared: the staff bouncing harmlessly off its shoulder like the thin scrap of wood it truly was. Nothing happened. There was no spark, no feel of power, no reaction of any kind. The wand was swept harmlessly from Leighor's grasp to fall frail and useless to the ground. For a few seconds Leighor stared death in the face, rooted to the spot as the great creature towered over him, its razor-taloned paws less than two yards from his face.

But before the bear could strike, two more arrows embedded themselves in its back. It screamed and turned furiously, falling back to all fours to seek out its new attacker. A quarrel from Telsyan's crossbow whistled past its ear; and the bloodied beast finally decided it had had enough, spinning about on its heels to take off back down the path towards the vale. Its companion retreated before it.

'Come on! Quickly! Run!' Zindur ordered, scrambling out of the undergrowth back on to the pathway.

'Aye, you seem very good at that!' Yeon said bitterly, crawling to his feet beside him.

'There is no time for that now!' Uhlendof snapped. 'Do as he says!'

Leighor retrieved his fallen staff and turned to follow the others, who had set off at a fair pace along the pathway. Several minutes of hard uphill running brought them finally to a gentle sloping clearing, where both Ardri and Inanys stood waiting for them with the mule.

'Come,' the girl beckoned, turning once more to lead the travellers out of the clearing into a deep stony gully that ran steeply upward. A small stream clattered down towards them over a rising sea of flat rocks and smooth boulders. The going would be hard.

'This is a death trap!' Zindur protested, grasping the girl's arm.

Yet Ardri spun out of his grip, quickly, easily; as if the warrior's huge hand held as little substance as a brook rainbow. She giggled at Zindur's stunned look as he stared down at his clenched fist, wondering just how she had managed to escape him.

'Come here girl!' he stormed. But Ardri ran ahead of him, clambering even higher up the stony gully, to halt only when she was a safe distance ahead of him, pointing upwards.

'Safe at the top! Safe at the top!' she repeated happily, before turning again to continue her climb.

Telsyan shrugged. 'Do we have any choice?' He spoke to no one in particular; waiting only a moment for an answer before he too began to follow Zindur up the gully.

The climb turned out to be less difficult than it had looked at first, and within the hour the company finally found themselves clambering out on to the open hilltop above Uirass's vale. They slumped gratefully down on to the short meadow grass, letting the fresh autumn breeze cool and revive them, as the warm, pale sun of Faestan month beat gently down upon their upturned faces.

'Do you think we are safe here?' Leighor spoke hoarsely, trying to catch his breath.

'Safe as safe!' Ardri sang, apparently not at all tired by the climb. 'Safer and safer!' She began to spin around on the tips of her toes, with her arms outstretched, singing all the while in a high delicate voice:

> He hunts below,
> But not on high.
> He hunts below,
> With hue and cry.
> He hunts below,

> *With wolf and deer.*
> *He hunts below,*
> *He hunts not here.*

She sat down on the grass in front of them with a broad grin. 'Safest,' she said.

'But will you be safe?' Tavolir asked with some concern. 'Will not Uirass harm you when he finds out what you've done?'

Ardri shook her head. 'He will forget before sunfall. He is old. He always forgets.'

'How old?' Telsyan asked. 'How old is he?'

'Old,' she shrugged, bored. 'Older than old; older than the hills, older than the stars . . .'

'Who are you, girl; you and your sister?' Uhlendof asked firmly. 'Where do you come from?'

'I am Ardri,' the girl replied simply. 'I come from the vale.'

The monk sighed. 'But where originally? Who were your parents?'

Ardri began to look puzzled . . . 'I've always been here; for ever and ever and . . . and . . .' she paused suddenly. 'What are parents?'

Uhlendof drew a deep breath; but before he could speak again Tavolir had cut in. 'Do you know any more songs?' he asked.

The girl nodded.

'Then sing us one, a longer one; one about the vale, or about you and your sister.'

Ardri smiled once more, and looking around to the others for approval, began once more to sing in her high, piping voice:

> *When world was young*
> *And days were old,*
> *And long before the story told,*
> *Of Qhil-mûn-il,*
> *And Gho-ro-nar,*
> *And other lands that shone afar,*
> *Did Ardri dwell,*
> *And fashion well,*
> *The glades of Du-ran-dar.*
>
> *When spring was done,*
> *A sister fair,*
> *The braids of summer in her hair,*
> *Descended on the Elder plane,*
> *Bore gifts of sunrise in her train,*
> *Her arms enfold,*
> *In autumn gold,*
> *And Hirthé was her name.*
>
> *In winter bare,*
> *When man did rise,*
> *The flame of Geltan in his eyes,*
> *Did Eirass walk,*

Upon the earth,
To ward the land that gave him birth,
'Til Hathanwold,
Lies dark and cold,
And few shall grieve the dearth.

In the end it was a sad song, with a melancholy, haunting tune that seemed to hang wistfully in the air. Yet when she had finished, Ardri laughed gaily and rose to her feet, preparing to turn away.

'That was a beautiful song,' Uhlendof said quickly, 'Do you know what it means?'

'Sometimes.' The girl looked at him strangely, her deep grey eyes holding his uncertainly for a moment, before she span suddenly away to perform a series of cartwheels on the grass. She turned back to the party, now a good dozen yards away. 'But not now. Now I must go. Goodbye!' Ardri gave them a last nervous smile, and then was gone, back into the vale, before any of the travellers could lift a hand to prevent her.

Uhlendof rose, following her path to the crest of the hill, to stare down after her into the broad valley below. He shook his head, his face expressionless. 'She is gone: but look!' he beckoned them all to rise and join him. 'It is much as I expected.'

To the travellers astonishment the valley below now seemed utterly different to that which they had just spent the best part of the morning in crossing. Below them was little more than a steep and narrow ravine, filled with scrawny, stunted pines. There was no stream, no gully; no broad wooded vale beneath; no wide, swaying meadows; and no sign of Ardri.

'This cannot be!' Zindur declared almost angrily. 'We have just . . .' his voice trailed away in disbelief.

'I think we have chanced to trespass upon an ancient place,' Uhlendof said quietly. 'One, perhaps, that we were never meant to enter. Let us ask no further questions, and be glad that we have escaped so lightly.'

'But what were they?' Yeon asked. 'Witches, sprites, enchanters?'

The monk shook his head. 'I doubt in any manner you might mean. I believe that they are guardians. Guardians, perhaps in a small way creators, of a world whose time is long past. Lost souls.' He looked away.

'Let us be gone from here,' Zindur said grimly. 'I like this place not. I shall rejoice only when we are well out of it!'

'I do not think we shall be entirely out of it for some time,' Uhlendof smiled softly. 'Do you not see? Hirthanwold . . . Hirthanwild . . . Hathanwild . . .' he ticked off the names on his fingers. 'The whole of this great forest was once Hirthé's! It was all once Hirda's garden.'

Chapter Sixteen
STORMDAY TIDING

'But what of your staff?' Tavolir asked, pointing to the thin, ashen wand in Leighor's hand. 'I had all but forgotten it in the excitement. But it surely holds some great power.'

'Aye,' Zindur nodded, stepping back a little. 'We all saw what it did to the old man!'

Leighor too had tended to dismiss the strange power so recently displayed by his staff; and now, on being reminded of it, he let the wand fall from his fingers as if it had burnt him.

'Indeed,' Uhlendof observed thoughtfully. 'I begin to doubt that we would ever have fallen upon yon vale without the benefit of Leighor's staff. It was he who first saw the light, I remember.'

'But you all saw it,' Leighor objected. 'It had nothing to do with me!'

'None of us saw the light until you pointed it out,' Telsyan corrected him. 'Even at the time I wondered how I could have missed it, being ahead of you all.'

'No.' Leighor shook his head briskly. 'You make too much of a small thing! The staff had no effect upon the bear in the forest. which nearly killed me – and that was when I had most need of it.' He bent to pick up the slim grey staff once more, re-examining it closely. Yet it lay still in his hands, as dead and lifeless as ever. 'I feel nothing,' he said, shaking his head once more. 'If any power lies within this wand, I have neither the wit nor the knowledge to divine its presence; let alone make use of it. What happened to Uirass, I cannot explain.'

'There has been far too much this day that cannot be explained,' Zindur cut in shortly. 'Let us make now for Furthka and be away from here!'

There was no dissent. And, pausing only to make and swallow a lukewarm gruel of Hirda's oatmeal, the travellers took up the long march eastward, passing between two great oaks to come again beneath the dark forest. Soon thereafter they fell upon a narrow trail, whether made by men or beasts they could not guess, but it served its purpose, leading them roughly north-east across the rolling hills.

Away from the vale the forests once again took on their more normal autumnal aspect, the tall trees stripped almost bare by stark northron winds, their leaves strewn in an amber carpet across the ground beneath. Gradually the hills steepened and rose higher all around them, even as the nature of the forest itself began to alter. The ranks of bare-stripped elm, birch and linden fell away, to be replaced by tall evergreens: spruce, fir and glowering darkwood pine. Grim, close-set trees whose dense foliage cut most of the light from the forest floor.

At about the fourth hour of the afternoon the trail came out on to a broad greenway that ran down from the north-west, and here turned eastward with their path along a steep-walled valley.

'This will certainly have been an ancient road,' Telsyan told them as they walked; 'one of the old ways into Xhendir from the west, in the days when that land was a powerful kingdom of rich mines and great armies. But that was many centuries ago, and it has been longer yet since the great caravans of gold, silver and gemstones last took this road to reach the lost cities of the west.'

'Is all the gold now gone?' Yeon asked with interest.

The merchant nodded. 'The hills of Xhendir have long since been mined bare. If anyone yet ventures there, their fate goes unrecorded in the world beyond.'

The old road wound on along the dark valley, shaded by the high-towering ranks of spruce and fir upon either side. After some time the closeness of the forest became oppressive, so that it seemed they were hemmed in by dark, living walls of green, whose cold shadow leaked out to touch them all, leaving only a thin line of clear sky above their heads.

It came as a relief therefore, when, just before dusk, the greenway finally opened out into a narrow clearing. This was coarse and newly cut, still littered with the stumps of several score new-felled trees, whose knotted roots clung grimly to the bare earth.

'Settled folk must dwell nearby,' Haflas said. 'Most likely the village that Hirda told us of.'

'Do you not know?' Inanys asked. 'You are a fine guide!'

'I should know, yes,' the miner looked around him, seeming more than a little flustered. 'But the land has been all wrong somehow since we left the vale. If we are close to Furthka, then we are many leagues farther east than we should be.'

'Where is Furthka?' Yeon asked. 'Have you been there?'

Haflas shook his head. 'No, but I know of it. It is one of the forest hamlets under the rule of the Durian Knights.'

'Yes, it has the feel,' Keran spoke in a low cool voice. 'There is a feel to all the lands of the Knights. I know it well.'

'A welcome feel?' Leighor asked.

'No!' Keran shuddered. 'I have grown to hate the Knights and all their works!' As they walked onward, Keran retold the story of her father's ruin, and of her subsequent journey south to enter Lord Fralcel's service. 'Since then I have neither seen nor heard from any of my family,' she concluded. 'I know not how my father is, nor what has happened to him.' She halted, her eyes suddenly brimming with tears. 'It is all the fault of the overmighty Durians!'

'Have you had no letters or messages?' Haflas asked.

Keran shook her head. 'Few travellers came to Silentwater, and none going as far north as Darien. I managed to put one letter into the hands of a minor merchant, but I do not think it ever reached its goal.'

'Come lass,' Leighor comforted. 'You shall see them all again soon.' For no reason at all, the memory suddenly came to him of the burning sands upon the beach at Syrne on the day of his exile. The day that the curse of the wanderer had finally been pronounced upon him for daring to try to rise above his preordained condition . . . He quickly blanked the scene from his mind.

'I too have had to bear long separations from my friends and family,' Telsyan was saying 'Why, I have a wife and four children at home in Selethir whom I have not set eyes on for more than a twelvemonth. But do not take on so! Come now, girl . . . It will soon be dark.'

'Aye.' Keran smiled weakly and began to walk on.

The clearing broadened slowly, beginning to look more permanent and settled. Then at last there came first sight of the settlement itself ahead of them. It seemed little more than a thin line of straggling, single-storeyed cabins, raised of crude logs and rough-hewn timbers, with ragged, unkempt roofs of turf and mottled straw. There were no more than a dozen dwellings, scattered between the northern edge of the forest and the road; each with its own small vegetable plot or pig-sty, haphazardly fenced in with wicker hurdles. Muddy tracks linked the buildings, and uneven piles of turf, firewood and edible tubers lay scattered between. On a thin pole above the settlement, the tattered crimson and gold banner of the Durian Knights fluttered in the rising breeze. In all, the settlement of Furthka seemed a poor, run-down and depressing place.

The few settlers, too, seemed at first unwelcoming and suspicious, and it took some time for the travellers to persuade them that their intentions were entirely peaceful and that they had silver in their purses to pay their way. Most of the villagers seemed to be either simple peasant farmers or herdsmen, trying to eke a meagre living from the hard northern soil. There were no craftsmen apart from Gerthar, who served as village blacksmith and carpenter in the time he could spare from tending his own few acres.

'We must do many things in order to survive here,' Vorig, the village headman, told them in the great barn somewhat later, when they had all gathered for a communal meal. 'We have a few forest goblins, who work for us when they will, in return for a little grain. Our only luxuries are those we buy from the knights. They sell dear and they buy cheap, but that is part of the price we must pay for their protection.'

'I see little sign here of their protection,' Leighor frowned. 'Where are the knights? How do they protect you?'

'The knights are many leagues away,' Gerthar answered softly. 'They come here but thrice a year to collect the rents and tithes. There is a bailiff at Hith-Gibor, fifty leagues to the north, but otherwise their protection comes in less tangible forms.'

'How so?' Yeon demanded.

'As is well known,' Vorig answered, 'the Durian Knights are no longer noted for their skill at arms, and have not been for many a long year. They prefer in these days to pay tribute to the Riever chieftains; and thus are their settlements protected, and no others.'

'They pay tributes to the Rievers?' Yeon was aghast.

The headman nodded. 'That you may believe, my lords. They find such arrangements far more profitable than open conflict. For in this wise no one else may set up settlements with any safety in these northlands; and the gold to pay for all comes from our pockets!'

'But can you trust the Rievers to keep such agreements?' Tavolir asked disbelievingly.

'They have no reason not to,' Vorig shrugged. 'There is little enough in these settlements worth the bother of looting. It is far easier for the Riever Lords to let the Knights do their collecting for them – and that they do well enough. No matter to them that we go hungry half the winter.'

'Then why do you stay here?' Yeon asked. 'Why not go south to the Varroain lands, or live under the Knights of Imsild, who pay no such tributes?'

Vorig shook his head. 'This is our home, young one. Here lies all that most of us know, all that we can call our own. Here we know the ways of the land and of the passing seasons. What is there for us elsewhere? There is little land free to poor peasant folk in the south. And the Knights of Imsild, we are told, charge tithes just as heavy as those of the Durians. No, life is at least quiet and predictable here, which it may not be elsewhere.'

'Now come,' he settled back in his seat. 'Tell us your story and let us hear what news you bear from far parts. Leave out nothing, for we learn little indeed here of what passes in the world beyond.'

The travellers' story took long to tell, and warm rye bread, game stew and hot bramble pies came and went as the tale progressed.

'It is grave and troubling news you bring to us,' Vorig said once they had finished. 'If Rievers do now move abroad in such numbers then there is much to fear. Yet we are far here from the great crossways of the world. Perhaps these troubles will pass us by.'

There were nods of agreement from about the long table.

'Perhaps,' Zindur said grimly. 'But I would not trust my life to it. If I were you I would set watchers in the hills to raise alarm if Rievers are seen, and give you time to flee to some place of safety. As you sit now, a whole army could fall upon you unsuspected from out of these dark forests.'

'But it is the duty of the Durian Knights to protect us,' another villager protested. 'That is what we pay them for!'

'And when you have all been slain by Rievers,' Inanys sneered, 'which of you will go to the Knights to demand your money back?'

There was a long silence.

The gathering broke up soon after, the travellers being separated amongst the various village dwellings where they would sleep. Leighor was billeted in Gerthar's narrow cabin, sleeping the night in a cramped box-bed set into the kitchen wall. There was little room for his long legs, and only a gaily coloured curtain to offer any privacy, but the bed was soft and warm, and he slept better than he had for many nights.

Catching a glimpse of the world outside the next morning, through the half-open kitchen shutters, he shivered. It was raining. Not heavily, but a thin, steady drizzle that made everything out of doors look cold, wet and unencouraging.

'It is poor weather for travel,' Gerthar agreed, following the southron's gaze out across the sodden pasture to the dripping forest beyond. 'Perhaps the day will improve.' He looked out again at the dark clouds drifting overhead. 'Yet I doubt it.'

'What is the best road north?' Leighor asked as he watched Gerthar's wife, Semmerle, ready their brief breakfast, their tiny four year old playing merrily with his wooden blocks beneath the kitchen table. 'Will this greenway we follow, bring us any closer to Darien?'

The smith shook his head. 'Not if you remain on it too long. The greenway, as you call it, is more properly known as the Great Xhendir Road, for in older days it ran due east from here to the Malûn River and thence across into the land of Xhendir. But no bridge remains now across the great river, even if you wished to make the journey. To the west, the way has fallen into ruin at the Greenlag Marshes, and none may pass. The only way north in these days is a newer trail that cuts up from the road, some three leagues to the east of here. It is not like the roads of the ancients, yet it is quite a broad way, much used by the Knights of Dur and their servants. It will bring you safely to Hith-Gibor in three or four days. From there run other ways to Darien.'

Leighor was displeased at the thought of leaving the greenway so soon, and his face must have shown it, for at once Gerthar made pains to reassure him:

'It is a good trail, stranger, easy on the feet and well marked. There is truly no chance of your losing your way, for the path to Hith-Gibor is broad and well-beaten.'

In the end none of the villagers accompanied the nine travellers as they followed the greenway eastward through the drizzle, and out of the small settlement. And the travellers left Furthka much as they had found it: still and silent beneath the glowering hills.

Leighor looked back briefly as they left the cleared land to enter once more into the forest. But the little huddle of buildings had already vanished into the mists behind them. Only the hanging smoke of its low wood fires was still visible, drifting gently up to merge with the grey clouds that brushed the hilltops.

In just under an hour the travellers came upon a rutted earthen track that curved away northward into the hills. This was clearly the path they were intended to follow. Yet it was with great reluctance that they finally inured themselves to abandoning the grassy smoothness of the older way for the muddier uncertainties of the ill-kempt, bumpy track before them.

'The art of road making has declined much since the great age,' Uhlendof sniffed darkly, as he took his first step on to the furrowed surface of the new way.

'Nothing is as it was in the great age,' Telsyan sighed; 'nor do I think shall ever be so again.'

The drizzle did not slacken as the day wore on. Neither did it turn to full rain – although in steady persistence it more than made up for its lack of force, soaking the travellers through before they had covered a further league.

They paused awhile at midday, in the shelter of a giant fir, to eat the few morsels of brown bread and goat cheese they had been given by the villagers. But there was little comfort in the rest, and they moved on quickly.

The trail curled steadily higher into the hills, the travellers catching brief glimpses of the country around them through occasional breaks in the forest. Yet they saw only still higher ranges of forested hills ahead of them: silent, brooding and ominous.

Late in the afternoon they came down into a long, deep valley through which their track ran lazily. One or two smaller trails now branched off into the hills to east and west; but who had made them, and for what purpose, they could not guess. The main way itself seemed clear enough, however, leading them constantly up the valley into the north.

Evening came early beneath the dark sea of cloud, and the company drew to a grateful halt beside a hurrying stream that tumbled down out of the hills to cross their trail. Yet there was no dry ground to be found for their tents, and the camp proved a chill and waterlogged place. With no fire possible, they chewed glumly upon their last crusts of dry, village bread, spending a cramped, confined and comfortless night.

The following day's journey proved as much of a misery as the first. Little rested from their cramped night in the tents, the nine travellers were now cold and hungry into the bargain. The rain hurtled down as relentlessly as before, a strong north-east wind hurling it sharply into their faces. Wherever the trail ran steeply up or downhill, it quickly became a streaming watercourse, bearing a gritty burden of rainwater down into the valleys below. Keran began to fear that she might never be warm and dry again, numb with cold as she slipped and skittered along the water-logged trackway in her squelching boots.

'We shall have to halt!' Tavolir gasped at last. 'We cannot go on like this!'

'We can and we must,' Telsyan glowered grimly. 'We can afford no more delay! I have been through far worse than this in my time.'

No one else took up the argument or spoke in favour of halting, and much as she would have liked to have done so, Keran decided, perhaps wisely, to hold her tongue.

They journeyed north all day, the country growing grander and wilder as they did so. High, forested hills tumbled into steep-sided valleys through which nameless torrents roared, their road seeming ever after each fall to rise still higher than before. The travellers were still climbing steadily when darkness fell.

It took them much longer than usual to set up camp, for the leather tents were heavy with water, and their fingers numb with cold. While the others struggled with this task, Keran began to gather firewood from the dripping forest, piling it between the tents.

'What are you wasting time on that for?' Telsyan paused irritably from driving tent pegs into the soft ground. 'None of it will ever burn!'

'If we keep some in the tents tonight, it may burn tomorrow,' she retorted. 'I would have thought such a great traveller as yourself would have known that!'

'It might work,' the merchant conceded. 'But we cannot have too many wet branches in the tents.'

Again there was little sleep for anyone in the icy dampness of the tents. There was thunder in the night, and harder rain that might have been hail. This passed, but the steadier rain continued, and at dawn it still came down as heavily as ever from an obstinately leaden sky. No one, not even Zindur, felt much like venturing out; and in the end it was Telsyan who came in from the tent he shared with the original party.

'There will be no fire today,' he announced grimly, nodding towards the still damp heap of wood piled in the middle of the tent. 'So the sooner we are up and on the road the better. Let us have these tents down quickly, and with luck we shall be in Hith-Gibor before dark.'

'Before dark?' Inanys' voice rose mockingly from beneath hooded eyes. 'Then we shall need luck indeed, Master merchant.'

'All the more important that we lose no more time!' Telsyan scowled. 'Come, let's have you all up, and the tents down!'

Keran was cold, hungry and wet, and beginning to feel somewhat mutinous. She did not relish another endless day of marching through this downpour. Yet that was precisely what the merchant proposed: and in moments they would all be following him obediently back out on to the rain-lashed road again. This would be her only chance to object.

'No,' she said firmly, just as Telsyan turned to leave. 'This is foolishness. If we keep on like this we shall all be dead of cold long before we ever get to Darien. None of us has eaten properly for two days. We have not had a fire. We must halt this day at least, or we shall all come down with fever. I fear some of us may have it already.'

Telsyan stopped dead for an instant at the mouth of the tent. Then he swung sharply round upon her, his face flushed with fury. 'I warned you this would be no pleasure jaunt, girl. Yet you insisted upon coming – none could dissuade you! Now you must journey as men journey; and you may like it or lump it as you will, I care not. But one thing is certain: I will tolerate none of your whining or whimpering, and I will not delay this errand for you; not for one day, not for one morning, not for one hour! Do you understand?'

Keran's eyes smarted. 'You are a stubborn, blind fool!' she spat, trying all the while to suppress the quiver in her voice. 'You would march us all till we drop for no purpose! Just to satisfy your own vanity!'

Telsyan snorted, and would have turned away again were it not for Zindur's sudden intervention.

'The maid has a point,' he said. 'I too feel the cold in my bones, and the touch of the fever in my throat. One may march through weather such as this if one has a dry bed each night and a full belly, but we have neither. What good will it do us to get to Hith-Gibor a day early if we are laid up for two weeks with fever as soon as we get there?'

There was silence. Telsyan's hard eyes burning furiously into the faces of girl and warrior. Both stared back unflinching.

'Is this how you all feel?' he growled at last.

Haflas and Tavolir nodded. Only Inanys, as usual, gave no indication of his feelings.

The merchant studied their faces irritably. 'Very well, then,' he conceded. 'We shall stay. But for one day only, to dry ourselves out. Tomorrow at first light we depart: rain or shine!' He turned and made his way back to his own tent to inform the others.

'You make a good mutineer, girl,' Zindur grinned. 'If I were your commander I would promote you quick to keep you out of trouble.'

'Or else hang you.' Inanys smiled pleasantly.

The decision to stay having been made, the travellers' spirits began to rise noticeably. The leather side-walls of the tents, where they bordered upon one another, were lifted and raised together on poles to link the tents by making a small, covered space between them. Here, where the smoke could most easily escape, they finally managed to get a small fire going with some of the drier wood from the tents. Once this was burning evenly, wet branches could be piled on top, smouldering greenly before eventually catching alight. Slowly their clothes began to dry; and by mid-morning they all had bowls of Leighor's herbal tea to warm them through, and simple brown pancakes which Keran and Uhlendof made between them from the small amount of flour and goat butter they had been able to purchase in Furthka.

Beginning to feel warm at last, and with food in their bellies, tempers cooled, and even the unceasing rain that poured down all about them began to seem less oppressive.

'I shouldn't wonder if it were raining all over the world,' Haflas declared, staring out into the streaming forest.

'There are many places where it never rains,' Leighor corrected. 'In the south, in the great barren lands between the Gulf of Azier and the World Rim mountains, there is no rain. Only the sun, which beats endlessly down upon burning rocks and shifting sands. There nothing can live – nothing grows – there is no shade, and a man would be dead of heat and thirst inside a day unless he carried his own drink and shelter with him.'

'Can this be true?' Haflas asked in wonder. 'I cannot imagine such a thing as a land without rain. Are there no lakes, rivers and suchlike?'

Leighor shook his head. 'None, except near the coast where the winter rains sometimes bring enough water. My own city, Syrne, possesses just such a river, which flows but six or seven months a year, and at other times is completely dry. Farther inland nothing lives but lizards, scorpions and sand devils. Though it was not ever so; for there are many wonders and lost cities that lie abandoned and forgotten in the empty lands.'

'Some day I would like to visit these lands,' Haflas announced. 'That would indeed be a thing to tell to one's grandchildren.'

'There are greater wonders in the world than those,' Telsyan rejoined quickly, leaning back against a stout tentpole to tell his story. 'In Arethon there are rivers of living fire, in which the many-coloured salamanders leap and dance; and in the lands of the Southern Sea dwell wondrous creatures beyond number . . .'

Normally Keran liked nothing better than to sit back and listen to just such travellers' tales as these. But now she felt strangely impelled to withdraw, to separate herself from the others, to find some secret corner where she could retreat and look upon her Ginara Stone once more. Silently she inched her way back towards the rear of the tent; then, surreptitiously, she drew the small stone from the hidden pocket of her leather jerkin where it lay secreted.

A sudden squall of wind and rain drummed hard against the tent roof. She glanced quickly up at the rest of the group, huddled around the small fire at the mouth of the tent. For the moment they paid her no heed, listening to Telsyan's tales, but at any time one of them might look up or wonder where she was. Perhaps she could lessen the chances of that somewhat – or so she hoped. She stared at the small group briefly, concentrating all her will upon them. Trying to veil herself in the deep darkness at the back of the tent, she willed them not to notice her, for a brief while to forget her very presence in this small tent. To forget her, and her forbidden jewel.

She was not sure whether she had any true power to alter their perceiving. Perhaps the only one she deluded was herself. Yet the act comforted her and made her feel more secure. Many times as a child she had seemed able to hide small objects from the eyes of others, quite often for long periods. She felt the fine gold chain about her neck. It, along with with the small, plain pendant it bore, had been a gift from her father many years ago. For the past two years she had been in the service of Lord Fralcel and his lady. Such a chain was an unusual possession for a girl in her position, yet in all that time none had ever noticed it or chanced to comment upon it. Perhaps she could achieve the same for her jewel. The act of will required was small; and having satisfied herself that she had done all she could, she sat cross-legged in the three-quarter dark to examine her find.

She was delighted to discover that even here in the darkness the tiny Ginara Stone still seemed to glow; burning with a rose-pink inner fire that could not now be a refraction – it could only come from within the jewel itself. Then, unexpectedly, a tiny flare of light shot upward from the heart of the gemstone, rising like the spark of an exploding firework to make brief contact with her forehead. Keran just managed to stay herself from crying out aloud; but in her alarm she dropped the jewel. It fell, and its fire died. She trembled, looking fearfully up at the others. But none of them seemed to have noticed what had happened – all still apparently engrossed in Telsyan's tales.

It was several long minutes before Keran managed to gather up courage enough to pick up the stone again. Her hand crept slowly forward to touch it, fearful of some other disconcerting reaction. But this time there was nothing. The jewel seemed to brighten slightly as she touched it; it felt warm and comforting against her skin; but that was all. Yet as she studied it, it again seemed to draw her eyes deeper into its rose-coloured heart. Lying cupped in the palm of her hand like the entrance to another world, it called to her. Called her to share its secret.

In that same instant her eyes seemed to burn down through its depths and out into a world beyond . . . She was flying, soaring, high above the dark forest. Her long wings seeking out the warm air currents. She was there, but somehow not in control, a passenger. Present, yet beyond the perception of the consciousness that bore her. A simple consciousness, a mind that sparked with few thoughts: food, home, balance, weariness and fear. Her eyes . . . the bird's eyes . . . kept constant fearful watch for the shadow of the hawk above, and on the lie of the land below. It seemed she could see forever, the whole world laid out beneath her like a map of a thousand colours; nameless lakes, mountains and valleys approached and then receded again as she – they? – swept ever onward into the west. How swiftly they could be in Darien if they but had the power of this small bird! She drank in the dizzying sensation, half-wishing that this flight might endure for ever.

But almost as soon as the thought had crossed her mind, the vision faded, to be replaced by another, very different in form. She was fleeing, blundering, cold, tired and panic-stricken through the forest. Yet again the eyes she saw with were not her own, the feelings she felt those of some other: a man, who ran in fear and exhaustion through the dark forest. Briars tore at his feet, stray branches whipped across his face, but he paid no heed, still running onward, impervious to cold and rain. Fear was the one emotion that coursed through his awareness. Fear of something that pursued him. Fear of what would happen if it . . . they? . . . caught him. He ran onward, the roaring of his lungs, the pounding of his heart, filling Keran's brain until she could take in no more.

Now she wished for the vision to end . . . And again the contact – the dream? – abruptly broke.

She was still seated where she always had been, in the gloomy safety of the enclosed tent. Yet now she found herself gasping for breath, almost as if it had indeed been she fleeing panic-stricken through the trees. She let out an audible sigh of relief, but the next instant caught her breath once more at the sight of Inanys sitting across the tent from her. He stared at her boldly, rocking on his heels as if highly amused. She snatched the stone at once to her chest. But it was too late. He'd seen it – that she knew – and what else besides?

'What do you want?' she demanded hoarsely, trying to sound angry, but coming out weak and uncertain.

'You play a dangerous game, little maid,' Inanys whispered furtively, edging still closer in the darkness. 'You may befuddle the rest of them perhaps, but not I. From Inanys you may hide nothing.'

'Hide?' Keran quavered. 'I have nothing to hide.'

'Then it is hidden well,' the crookback sneered, studying her closely. Suddenly he smiled, his teeth glinting in the dark. 'Perhaps we are more alike than you imagine, you and I; for do we not both have our little secrets?' He seemed to take a perverse pleasure in the way his words made her involuntarily shudder and draw back from him.

'I have naught in common with you!' she hissed coldly.

Inanys smiled his most snakelike smile. 'Think you not, my dear?' He leaned forward. 'Advice from one who knows: babes had best beware bright baubles!' He chuckled quietly to himself, as if at some great secret jest, and turned away.

Keran had but an instant to digest all this, before there came a sudden heavy crashing through the undergrowth outside the tent. The small group at the entrance leapt to their feet in alarm, reaching urgently for their scattered weapons.

Were they under attack?

Keran felt desperately about her in the darkness for her sword, wondering as she did so whether she would actually be able to use it to any effect. The jewel in her right hand burned brighter, brushing against her plain gold pendant as she tried to put it away. There was a sudden pinprick of heat against her palm: the stone seeming to stick and fuse with the gold of her pendant. She glanced down to see the pink jewel embedded firmly in the centre of the plain gold disc, set right and firm as if it had always been there: as if it was always meant to have been there . . .

'It is a wounded man!' Haflas called out from the tentmouth, lowering his weapon. 'He is unarmed.'

'Beware!' Zindur warned sharply, running forward out of Keran's line of sight. 'It may be a trap!'

'No, trap,' a low voice rang out in strange, heavily-accented Durian. A creaking voice: deep, yet somehow distant. 'I mean you no harm . . . Help me!' There was a heavy crump, as if of a man falling.

'Bring him inside,' Uhlendof's voice ordered. 'He looks badly hurt!'

'Aye, if you like,' Keran heard the warrior grunt agreement. 'But we shall keep watch still, in case he has friends.'

Before she had time to emerge, Leighor and Tavolir had dragged the stocky figure into the tent; Haflas and the monk entered close on their heels. The man was short yet powerfully built, and dressed only in coarse sackcloth, rent and torn. His feet were bare, cut and bruised; his face scarred and bleeding. Yet the instant she saw him, Keran knew beyond doubting that this was the man whose flight she had shared just moments before.

'He does not seem too badly hurt,' Leighor said, after quickly examining the new arrival. 'The cuts and bruises are not deep. He suffers from exposure and underfeeding, little else.'

Uhlendof nodded. 'He seems to be coming round.'

'He is a strange figure of a man, to be sure,' Tavolir noted. 'All out of proportion somehow. Were it not for his face and stoutness I'd have taken him for a goblin.'

'Yes,' Haflas smiled. 'You are right. If he'd only had a beard I'd have noticed sooner, but now I'm sure. This is one of the Dark Hillfolk, they who raised the great towers that dot these northlands. Yet even I have not seen one beardless before.'

'No *mazgroll* goes beardless by choice,' the new arrival gasped bitterly. 'It has been torn out by the root!'

'By whom?' Telsyan asked sharply, joining the group within the tent. 'Does someone follow you?'

'I do not think they still follow,' the newcomer answered the last question first.

'Who?' Telsyan repeated. 'Rievers?' Goblins?'

The stocky figure nodded. 'Many such.'

The travellers exchanged anxious glances.

'Where? Where are they now?' Yeon demanded.

'Ahockûl Crest. There lie Curséd Ones without number. There was I taken when I was captured many months ago – by the lake which our folk call *Esch Ermon*, and theirs *Korlag Ul-Imshu*. Taken to the Shattered Mountain where rules Embor Horeoth, the lord of that place; and there have I lain these many months.' He fell silent.

'And you have escaped . . .' Uhlendof prodded.

The Hillman nodded slowly. 'I escaped, and have been two days in the forest since, with neither food nor rest, until I found you here. That is my story.' He closed his eyes.

'You may rest in a little while,' Telsyan said firmly; 'and you shall have some food, what little we can provide. But first you must tell us more of these dangers. Where is Ahockûl Crest? How far? And what kind of evil abides there?'

With some difficulty the stunted Hillman forced himself awake. 'I am sorry . . . My mind wanders. But you are in little danger here. We are far from the lair of Embor Horeoth and those he rules. You are safe. Yet if you would remain so, avoid Ahockûl Crest at all costs!' He paused. 'Which way do you travel?'

'We go north,' Uhlendof answered; 'towards Hith-Gibor.' Telsyan flashed him an angry look.

The newcomer lay silent for a moment. 'That is well. I make my way there also. Ahockûl Crest lies to the east, two days march. We shall be in Hith-Gibor before then.' He closed his eyes once more.

'But who is this Embor-Horeoth?' Telsyan demanded. 'A common brigand, or something more? What are his plans? With whom does he align? Why does he gather these great forces so far north?'

But there was no answer, the Hillman's breath coming now in deep irregular gasps.

'No more questions,' Leighor ordered. 'He is too ill now. Make up a bed for him by the fire. He can talk again when he is rested.'

Telsyan turned impatiently away. 'Do you know of this crest?' he demanded of Haflas. 'Does the Hillman speak the truth?'

'I cannot tell.' Haflas shook his head. 'We are in broad lands that I do not know well. There are many crests and strangely named mountains in these northern hills. I could not know them all.'

'We *must* learn more than this!' Telsyan smote the palm of his hand impatiently, and made for the tent mouth.

The Hillman slept for most of the rest of the day. The worried travellers sat in a tense, watchful huddle nearby, quietly discussing the ill news that he had brought.

'Is there no end to the Rievers that swarm through these northlands?' Uhlendof asked sourly. 'These forests seem to crawl with them like maggots!'

'I have never known Rievers abroad in such numbers,' Haflas frowned. 'I cannot say from where they come.'

'Who can?' Telsyan sighed. But if the stranger speaks true, we know that those who camp at Ahockûl Crest obey the command of a great lord. That worries me more than all the rest. We have already heard tales of a "Master of the North" who controls the Riever bands: perhaps this is he?'

'All the more reason to keep our distance,' Uhlendof warned, 'that we may survive to warn the folk of Hith-Gibor, and of Darien, of these things!'

'Do we truly know ourselves exactly what we face?' Telsyan asked sharply. 'I begin to think that we do not even begin to comprehend the forces now in motion in these lands and beyond: the *harrunor*; the power it bears; the Rievers without number; Darvir; Misan; Claighar; the Master of the North; the fall of Silentwater. All are linked somehow, and the Mage Metal is the key. I fear that all who dwell in these Eastern Realms are in far greater danger than they realise – a danger we seem helpless to avert.'

'We can but do what we must,' Uhlendof insisted. 'We have our small part to play, and that may yet tip the balance.'

'I cannot see it.' Telsyan shook his head and stared out into the blanketing rain. 'How can our small errand affect such mighty forces? The armies that move through these forests care not a fig which way falls the vote of the Sielders at the spring conclave, nor whether Arminor or Misan rules in High Tershelline. They are set to crush this land like a rotten fruit; and when they are finished here, will they not move south? And who will then stand against them?'

'Arminor,' Yeon said firmly. 'That is our goal: to install Arminor upon the Iron Throne, whence he shall lead the armies of the Varroain north to slay these spawn of evil, and root them out wherever they may hide!'

'Would that it were so simple,' Uhlendof smiled thinly. 'But in this I fear Master Telsyan is correct. All who hold the *harrunor* work towards the same end: and in truth the Mage Metal seems spread wide indeed – as much amongst the lords of the Varroain as among the northern tribes.'

'But why?' Leighor asked. 'By whom, and towards what end?'

'That we do not yet know,' Uhlendof repeated. 'But I suspect that that knowledge would be of more worth than all the votes of the electors of the High College put together.'

'And this stranger, this Hillman,' Yeon asked suddenly. 'Can he be trusted?'

Haflas shrugged. 'He seems to speak the truth, but he is a *mazgroll*, one of the Dark Hillfolk, and our people trust them little.'

'Why so?' Leighor queried.

'The *maezgrull* are lesser men.' Haflas nodded towards the sleeping figure. 'The men of the hills, they are named, or the Dark Mountain Folk. They are an elder race, a folk apart: few in number now, yet strong and cunning, with many skills. Once all these lands were theirs; but in these days their sort and ours rarely bide together. They keep to their own clans in the high and wild places, and shun the works of men. There is little trust between the peoples.'

'But which way do they run?' Telsyan asked impatiently. 'Are they friend or foe?'

'That depends upon much,' Haflas shrugged. 'They have fought goblins and Rievers in the past, but others of their kin have joined with them – or so the tales go. The *ghrornan*, who dwell in the western ranges, are friendlier folk and oft engage in trade; the *mhorrimmon* are herders and woodcrafters, but devious and never to be trusted. As for the *maezgrull*, they are known chiefly as bladesmiths and warriors; it is said there is some honour among them, but few are met with by true men.'

With the news of Rievers nearby, it became necessary to keep a watch once more, and it fell to Haflas and Tavolir to spend most of the long night in the scant shelter of the tentmouths, trying to keep the small, flickering fire alight.

By morning, however, the rain had all but ceased; and the dark clouds that had ruled the skies for the past three days were at last beginning to break.

Chapter Seventeen
THE CAULDRON OF EMBOR-HOREOTH

The Hillman's name was Korzhlin, and he seemed much recovered after his day and night of sleep. But even so, he could tell them very little of further use about either Embor-Horeoth or the road ahead.

'Embor-Horeoth is a great lord,' Korzhlin told them briefly. 'He rules many men, and practises great magicks. Who his allies are, I know not. But he is cruel indeed, and enslaves many. As for the road, it is as good and straight as the northlands will allow. It will take us little more than a day and a half to reach the knights' township on the Rohrdri: the place you call Hith-Gibor.'

'Longer than I thought,' Telsyan sighed. 'But all the more reason to get started now.'

The travellers journeyed north all day, through hill and thick forest, with Telsyan and the almost fully recovered *mazgroll* at their head. During the march Haflas told the rest of the company a little more of Korzhlin's folk who, legend told, had once ruled all these great northlands before the coming of true men.

'That is why so many lakes, hills and rivers are yet named in their tongue, there being no mannish name for them,' the miner informed Leighor as they passed across a small stream. '*Uberezeg Ingur*, the Malûn River, *Orodun Ubas*; these are all Hillfolk names. Their name for themselves is *Zumur*, their term for true humankind being *Zumir*, only a little different from their own.'

'So the name, "Mines of Zumir", means only "the mines of men",' Yeon noted, quite pleased to have worked this out for himself.

Haflas nodded. 'The workings at Silentwater were always those of humankind, ever since the days when Boru Ironmaster ventured north from Felldur with two dogs and a mule, and found veins of dark silver in the pebbles of Swirlwater Brook. I suppose that is why your 'Mage Metal' was never discovered or used earlier than it was. Men, you see, were only ever interested in the lead and the silver. We had no use for dull slivers of purple metal that could not even be used to forge a decent spoon!'

Uhlendof gave a faint smile. 'Perhaps it would have been better had it remained so.'

Haflas nodded. 'It was the King's Seer, Ariscel, who first saw value in the purple metal of Silentwater. But when we started to seek it out and form it into ingots, many said that it was a change for the worse. The metal seemed to bring ill-fortune to all who worked with it, and even the lake itself seemed to darken. The bright shoals of fish that once filled its waters departed, and with them went many of the fair waterfowl of old. Silentwater was ever a quiet and tranquil place, but in past years it has seemed to grow grimmer and more shadowed – and I have no doubt now that the *harrunor* was the cause.'

Evening brought the company to the shores of yet another great lake, which spread its shimmering surface out into the unseen distances of north and west and to the shores of the mist-shrouded mountains beyond.

'Is there no end to this country?' Tavolir asked, staring out across a vista of glinting wavelets in the fading sunlight. 'If it were not that the hills grow steeper and the lakes wider as we march, I would think we were walking in circles!'

'The lake country will end,' Haflas assured him, 'and the forests too, as we journey north. Soon we must either come out on to the plains of Scûn, or else pass into the eastern mountains. Either way, we shall soon leave these lakes and forests far behind us.'

Leighor was first to rise the next morning, joining Uhlendof upon his lonely watch outside. The monk had caught a few fish during the night, and these the travellers ate for their breakfast before setting off once more. The day's journey began easily enough, the company following the narrow trackway eastward along the southern shore of the lake. Yet when they came to its eastern end, their road turned northward once more.

The travellers were not pleased to learn from Korzhlin that another great river, the Berend, must soon be crossed. Yet when they approached, they saw that a stout timber bridge had recently been built to the far shore, its trestled arches bearing them safely across.

Once over the Berend, the trail curled steeply up into the high country, and soon both lake and river were lost to their sight behind high ridges of forested hills. Somewhat after noon, there being no sign of any change in the immediate prospect, the travellers began to grow uneasy.

'How far is Hith-Gibor?' Telsyan demanded of their *mazgroll* guide at last. 'It seems to me that if we are to reach the settlement before dark, we should soon be coming out of these hills!'

'Aye,' Haflas agreed. 'I know not this road, but I know well enough that Hith-Gibor lies upon the River Rohrdri, and has good farming land around.'

'So it has,' Korzhlin nodded. 'The river you speak of passes through these very hills.' He pointed northward. 'There are few lowlands to this country, so we are closer than you think. It will not be another hour.'

The trail now climbed a sharp ridge, to fall into a narrow, steep-sided valley, which broadened only a little as it sank gently into the north-east. Wearily the travellers stumbled down the precipitous way; a tiny, tumbling stream soon appearing alongside it to accompany them northward. Farther on, the valley veered sharply to the left, a high ridge of vertiginous rock barring their way north. Korzhlin called a halt.

'Are we near?' Leighor asked.

'Yes,' the Hillman whispered, raising a warning finger to his lips. 'Yon stream runs into the River Rohrdri at the bottom of this valley, and there lies Hith-Gibor. And yet . . .' he paused for a moment to listen to the stillness of the forest and the faint sounds carried southward on the breeze, 'I am troubled. There is something not right. It is too silent. I feel danger . . .'

'Danger?' Tavolir hissed.

'Wait here!' Korzhlin ordered sharply. 'I shall take a look ahead. I know these woods and shall not be seen. You had best remain here.'

'I shall come with you.' Zindur stepped forward.

The barefoot figure shook his head. 'I will be safer alone.' He turned quickly away, and in an instant was swallowed by the forest.

The rest of the company waited anxiously beneath the trees, their worries growing greater and their imaginings wilder as time went by. In the still silence it was only too easy to believe that they heard all sorts of disconcerting sounds borne across the high ridges by the wind: moans or cries, the distant echo of what could have been many harsh, guttural voices; an occasional high-pitched shout or scream.

'Do you think Hith-Gibor has fallen?' Keran put all their fears into words.

'I don't know what to think!' Telsyan replied irritably. I only hope that our *mazgroll* friend has kept himself safe enough to return and tell us what's happening.'

'If ever he intends to return,' Yeon added.

'Why do you say that?' Telsyan asked sharply.

'I do not trust the hill-dweller.' The youth's eyes narrowed. 'What do we know of him, other than what he himself has told us? He could all too easily be selling our hides now, to save his own skin!'

'I too have had such thoughts,' the merchant agreed reluctantly. 'But we have little choice now but to trust him.'

'Can we not at least send someone after him?' Yeon demanded.

Telsyan shook his head. 'If there were any trap, they would just walk straight into it. Besides, I do not think it wise to divide the party further.'

'Then what?' said Yeon.

'Let us go back up the valley,' Zindur suggested. 'There we shall at least be able to see all that comes, and have a ready retreat.'

'But what if Korzhlin is no traitor,' Haflas asked, 'and returns, seeking our aid?'

There was silence.

'This is foolishness!' Yeon declared with impatience. He stepped down on to the roadway and pointed upward. 'Yon ridge must overlook the town, and it is easily climbed. Let us go up it, and then we shall be able to see the truth for ourselves.'

At once he began to scramble steadily up between the boulders, quickly vanishing into the straggly conifers that crowded the lower slopes. The others stared after him for a moment, and then reluctantly, one by one, began to follow, leaving the mule loose-tethered beneath.

Yeon was first to reach the crest, some dozen yards ahead of the others, swiftly disappearing from view. It was several weary, shin-grazing minutes before the rest of the party caught up with him. Yet when they did so, and gained the narrow windswept ridge, they saw a sight to take their breath away.

Hith-Gibor was nowhere to be seen. What they saw instead from their high eyrie was nothing more than a continuation of their own zig-zagging valley, hemmed in tight to north and west. Yet now it was far broader and more immense as it twisted sharply back on itself once more. There was no river, no township, no girdle of small, furrowed fields. But where these should have lain, a quarter of a mile distant, there rose up a great shattered mountain – a savage scarp of rock and jagged stone that reared its shoulders hundreds of feet above them. Half a league to the east, the crest ended abruptly – as if it had been cut away by some giant cleaver – its highest point a sheer, rocky crag that dominated the entire valley, and from whose summit rose a narrow goblin tower.

The cliff face itself was pitted with great dark holes, which stared out like monstrous empty eye sockets from the bare rock. Beneath yawned dark, measureless caverns, from which an inky blackness seemed to ooze like gore into the valley below. Yet worst of all, the caves, the cliff face, and the entire valley floor crawled with life – for directly beneath them burned the smoking pyres of a great encampment of Rievers.

Dark leathern tents and squalid, makeshift structures of wicker and rough timbers covered the western end of the vale. Grey shapes moved between the tents and about the fires, gathering around several long timber hurdles upon which flayed skins and thick strips of meat hung out to dry. Nearer to the cliff wall, and around the gaping cavern mouths, a dozen large pens had been constructed. Some of these held swine, goats and other animals, while others held scores of huddled goblins. Farther on, beneath the crooked tower, more goblins were encamped, and dull shapes moved upon the high ridge opposite. What lay beyond the crest, beneath the all-seeing eye of the goblin tower, none could imagine.

Even the pleasant stream that they had followed down the valley now ran black with foulness, and the whole of the vale was stripped bare. There was not a blade of grass, nor any other living thing, that did not cling to some high, inaccessible ridge.

For long minutes the travellers lay still upon their stomachs, staring down in awestruck silence at the terrible scene below.

'Ahockûl Crest!' Leighor gasped at last. 'The Shattered Mountain.'

'Aye,' Telsyan nodded grimly. 'It seems our *mazgroll* friend knew all along where he was leading us.'

'But the road . . .' Tavolir began to object.

'We must have been on the wrong road since our first day out from Furthka,' Uhlendof said at once. 'Remember the many partings of the way? And it was we who told the Hillman that we were bound for Hith-Gibor. He but chose to agree with us.'

'But why?' Haflas gasped. 'Why do such a thing?'

'Perhaps to buy favour with whoever rules here,' the merchant said drily. 'I cannot say.'

'But he had escaped,' Leighor objected. 'Why risk returning to this dread place – even to buy favour?'

'Perhaps more than just one Hillman was captured by your Embor-Horeoth,' Inanys suggested.

'You mean he might have had friends . . . family . . . imprisoned here?' The implication took a moment to strike home.

'Aye.' Inanys's smile was cruel. 'More than one noble lord of the Varroain holds hostages against the behaviour of his servants. Mayhap these Rievers have learned a few tricks from their betters.'

'All this is of little concern to us now,' Telsyan broke in. 'The immediate question is: what do we do?'

'Escape,' Leighor said at once. 'Make our way back down, and fly back the way we have come!'

Zindur shook his head. 'If Korzhlin has betrayed us to the Rievers, that is just where they will expect to find us. They will be only steps behind – if they do not already lie below. How long do you think we could stay ahead of that number in such a narrow vale with nowhere to turn?'

'Then what else can we do?' Uhlendof asked.

'The unexpected,' Zindur replied at once, resolve hardening in his voice as he spoke. 'We must pass north, through the camp, and beneath the shadow of the goblin tower.'

'What!'

'Are you mad?' Voices rose all around him.

The soldier raised his hand to silence them. 'Not as mad as you might think. There are only two ways we can go: south, back up the vale, which is what the Rievers will expect of us; or north, and through their own camp, which they will not.'

'But how . . .' the monk began.

'We wait here until dark, and then make our way down this side of the ridge into the camp. It will be full of men, half-men and goblins, as well as the *tarintari*. A few more cowled figures passing in the dark will attract little notice.'

There was dead silence, the cold wind riffling through their clothes as they lay crouched among the stones.

'I do not much like this idea,' Telsyan grunted at last. 'Yet it has courage. And if we are indeed to face death this day, it can at least be in a manner of our own choosing.' He nodded his head slowly. 'I am with you.'

'And I!' said Yeon.

Keran said nothing. The sight below filled her with fear and loathing, bringing back all the dread and terror of the fall of Silentwater. She much preferred the idea of retracing their steps. Despite the danger. Despite the probability of pursuit. Almost anything rather than endure that horror again . . .

But one by one all of her companions nodded their agreement. She was trapped. And however she felt, she would have to follow – follow them down into the heart of the Riever horde. A cold lance of fear worked its way slowly in towards her heart.

The wait for nightfall seemed endless, the daylight stubbornly lingering, the dark refusing to come. Exposed as they were upon the open ridge, the travellers felt every eye below and every eye that lay hidden within the hollow mountain above to be upon them. And they lay still, trusting to their grey cloaks and the high distances to shield them from any who might watch.

The sun at last began to sink, scarlet and bloody, into the western hills. And the camp below began to stir and rouse itself. The great fires burned higher as fresh fuel was piled upon them, leaving a thick pall of smoke hanging above the teeming shelters. The figures that moved below now seemed almost beyond numbering – yet of Korzhlin, who had betrayed them, they saw no sign.

Suddenly, the goblin drums began to beat; their low throbbing quickly taken up and magnified in the harsher, fiercer crash of the great war drums of the Tarintarmen. High cries and shrieks began to rise from amongst the tents, as vast numbers of the Riever host gathered about the great bonfires, waiting expectantly.

Almost at once, five gaunt figures appeared in their midst, performing strange, whirling dances between the pyres. Upon their heads they bore circled crowns of ox-horns or standing antlers. Skulls dangled at their waists and decorated their short, hand-held staffs. Faces fearfully mutilated and tatooed, hair braided with dank and obscene things, they struck fear and terror even into the hearts of those amongst whom they passed. Spaces opened up before them through the tightest throng, only to close up once more in a cautious semicircle behind.

'Shamans!' Haflas hissed. 'They make their foul magicks!'

And indeed, bright flashes of colour began to glint and sparkle in the fires as they passed. And clouds of dense smoke erupted in cannonades of sound as small missiles were hurled at the feet of the crowd. Leighor knew that these were no true magicks. He could accomplish the same himself had he but the correct ingredients for the smokeballs and fireflashes.

Yet still it made a fearsome and awe-inspiring sight: the tribal shamans spinning to the frenzied pulse of the drums, whirling and dancing beneath the fires . . . The wild shrieks of the multitude, their baleful shapes silhouetted against the crimson flames; spears, axes and great curved sabres swaying and glinting in the firelight. It was a sight of barbaric splendour, the stuff of dark dreams. Perhaps enough to shake the confidence of a legion – and it was no legion that watched from the high ridgetop that night.

Then, abruptly, as if on some secret signal, the dancing ceased, the drums stilled, and a different wail could be heard from the distant pens – a fearful howl of anguish and terror. And now the travellers could see from whence it came. A huddled mass of figures began slowly to emerge from out of the shadows of one of the great caverns in the cliff wall, moving steadily towards the central bonfire. They appeared to be dragging with them something large and clumsy, but none of the watching travellers could yet determine what it was. Only slowly did they at last begin to recognise what they saw. It was a giant wooden hurdle, such as they had seen meat and skins nailed to, to dry in the sun; but this hurdle bore other burdens – men!

There were three writhing figures, bound hand and foot to the stout timber laths. They struggled ineffectually to free themselves as a hundred waiting hands joined to raise the hurdle erect between the central bonfires. Now all but the shamans hurriedly retreated, forming a broad circle, a hundred paces across, around the central actors in the drama about to unfold. There was no sound whatsoever now in all the broad valley but the fearful wailings of the bound captives. And even that was swiftly stilled as the shamans began once again, silently, to dance.

Leighor watched in horrified fascination as the shamans swayed and wove their subtle patterns of entrancement before the terrified captives. Sometimes darting forward, to touch a bound prisoner with long sinuous fingers or skull-decked wands; then darting back once more to spin and sway about the edges of the great circle, as if in an attempt to mesmerise the fearsome host itself. The southron was glad only that he was too far distant to be able to discern anything of the faces of the three tormented captives – although it struck him that one of them could just have been short and squat enough to be a *mazgroll*.

From somewhere in the crowd the dancing shamans had obtained what looked to be large leathern wineskins or water bags – yet these smoked and smouldered at their ends, as if some fire were held within. The crowd stirred, and the drums began once more to beat. Slowly, the horned shamans manoeuvred themselves into a rough semicircle in front of the captives. There was a sudden shrill scream of terror; as one of the captives suddenly guessed what was going to happen. And at once – as if he had been waiting upon just such a signal – the leading shaman took two swift paces forward to hurl his smouldering leather bag directly at the body of the shrieking captive.

The bag burst on impact, to release a ball of screaming fire that clung and spread instantly, to envelop its hapless victim. A fearsome howl broke forth from the throats of the whole assembly as the flames rose. And in quick succession the four remaining bags were hurled at the writhing bodies, to consume men and hurdles alike in sheets of crimson flame.

The travellers averted their eyes from the wall of fire, which seemed to rise and flare in great hungry bursts, as if driven and fed by the frenzied shrieks of the Riever horde.

The burning and the screaming seemed to go on for ever.

Then, abruptly, it was all over. The flames died, and all that was left were the charred and broken remains – but of wooden hurdle or of human body, none could tell which. Leighor shuddered, and let out a loud, soul-draining sigh of relief. Surely now the nightmare was at an end.

Yet almost immediately the drums rose again. It seemed that this was not the last of the horrors the night held in store.

'No more!' Uhlendof hissed fiercely. 'Surely there can be no more?'

'I do not think they intend more killings,' Telsyan whispered quickly. 'Something else is prepared. Look!' His fingers rose, pointing to the mouth of one of the great caverns, where scores of spindly figures now moved in the reflected light of the flames. As they came farther out from beneath the shadow of the mountain, the travellers could see that these were goblins – or mostly goblins, for there were men and other races among them. Prisoners, who dragged and hauled for dear life upon six giant chains, encouraged by tall guardsmen whose coiling whips licked tenderly across their backs. What they strained to bring out into the open could not yet be seen. But slowly, ever so slowly, a looming shape began to emerge.

The travellers gave an involuntary gasp at the sheer size and weight of the thing that now trundled out of the cavern. A vast, hollow square of stone, somehow hewn from the living rock of the mountain itself, and hauled forth upon a dozen great rollers of solid iron. The very earth seemed to tremble beneath it as it shuddered inexorably forward. Leighor guessed that it must be fully the height of three men from foot to rim, and the length of twenty from end to end. But what on earth could its purpose be?

It seemed to be some sort of monstrous vat: its outer walls rough and crudely shaped; its inner surface laboriously polished to a sheer, crystal smoothness. A dark, fuming liquid, viscous and impenetrable, slopped greasily within the bowl. Yet Leighor felt rather than saw the dark and formless *something* that seemed to slither within.

There was a harsh command, and the slaves fell exhausted to their knees, the juggernaut behind juddering to a ponderous halt beneath the high cliff. And all around, the frenzied figures of moments before had fallen still, watching and waiting again in utter silence. Only the low goblin drums still beat in the distance: and soon even these were stilled. All eyes now stared upward, towards the highest of the great sightless eyesockets in the towering cliff above. A low fire burned there, hot crimson against the darkness. And there beside it, appeared the tall, gaunt figure of a man, his features wholly hidden in the deep shadow. Yet the instant they caught sight of him, the whole Riever horde gave out a low rumble of acknowledgement.

'Embor-Horeoth!' Telsyan whispered. 'It must be he.'

Even as he spoke, a flare of sharp scarlet light rose up in the small fire to illumine the tall figure sharply from below. The strange disposition of the shadows adding to his sinister aspect. The lord of the Shattered Mountain was thin, wiry and gaunt. Even at this distance his face seemed drawn and shrunken – not so much by age as by the terrible inner intensity of the soul-essence that burned within. His hair was strong and dark, yet like his close-cropped beard, already streaked with grey. A cowled gown of mauve and gold fell in a straight line from his neck to his heels, its silken stuff shimmering in the firelight. The billowing sleeves parted as his arm rose, to reveal the bony hand beneath; its long, white-taloned fingers clenched tightly about a slim wand. A purple wand.

Harrunor.

They could hear his voice now, high and sharp as he spoke to the assembled multitude; but although the sound carried faintly up to the watching travellers, his actual words were lost and indecipherable, broken on the wind to a meaningless echo, quickly swallowed by the night. Yet now there was renewed movement below, as the lines of chained slaves were led away into the caverns, the shamans returning to stand in a wide circle about the great vat.

Again Embor-Horeoth spoke. Yet this time his voice seemed no longer directed towards his followers, but rose and fell in a high, sing-song chant: words of power forming upon his lips, to be given voice in some corrupt, forgotten tongue whose very syllables seemed to taint and soil the air through which they passed. Majestically, he stretched out his arms across the valley.

'What does he do?' Keran whispered.

'The form is unknown to me,' Uhlendof shook his head. 'But I suspect that he intends some rite of summoning . . .'

The words had hardly left the monk's lips before the air was rent by a savage bolt of purple fire. Impossibly bright, incredibly loud, it struck down from the Riever lord's wand to shatter like a dark thunderbolt against the polished stone of the open vat below. The nearest of the Rievers screamed out in terror, shying away from the crackling explosion: its echoes still ringing and reverberating about the enclosed mountainside long moments afterwards. Yet the glow that now hung above the great cauldron did not so easily die. And the waters began to boil and shudder, as if trying physically to spew out some dark thing that slowly grew and gathered form beneath.

Again the wand-bearer's wrath harrowed the boiling vat, the light of its fires reaching up even to the high ridgetop from which the nine fugitive travellers watched. But there was no need now to fear discovery, for all eyes below were unwaveringly fixed upon the churning waters of the vat.

Leighor's breath caught in his throat as a great clawed hand suddenly broke the surface of the smouldering liquid, grasping the rough edge of the great cauldron to haul an unhallowed body upward into the night.

Men and goblins fled howling into the darkness, and even the stauncher ranks of the *tarintari* shrank away.

Not even the light from the great bonfires seemed able to penetrate the dark-shadowed formlessness of the towering thing that emerged from the waters. Darker yet against the clinging blackness of the night, it rose at least fifteen – perhaps twenty – feet above the valley floor. Leighor could make out nothing at all of its true form. Only brief glimmerings of great white talons caught his sight, and of blazing embers of eyes that seemed created of living fire; and these but filled him with dread and the longing never to look upon their like again.

The creature exhaled an aura of sheer power; of inviolable, unutterable evil. A force that could be felt almost physically, even from where the travellers lay on their lonely ridgetop.

With a roar of heartstopping fury, the creature tried suddenly to break free of the vast stone vat that had given it birth – striking out with great taloned limbs as if intent upon rending and destroying all about it.

Embor-Horeoth's voice rose sharply, fearfully – as if he too now trembled at the power and the destructiveness of that which his own dark magicks had called forth. And another torrent of purple fire leapt from his wand to strike down at the feet of the raging fiend.

For a moment Leighor feared that even the mage himself would be unable to control the creature; that it would indeed break free from whatever constraints still bound it, to turn upon them all: invincible, irresistible, unstoppable.

Yet from where the bolt of *harrunor* flame had struck home, there now sprang a high wall of scarlet fire to encircle and encompass the summoned nightmare-thing. It screamed – its fury echoing across the vale as the flames wrapped it tight about. And for moments the fires did indeed seem to restrain the awesome creature, and its roars were stilled. Again Embor-Horeoth spoke, his words seeming now to entreat rather than to command. But even as his voice rose it was torn apart upon the wind, and the ring of fire began once more to collapse, the flames trembling, beginning inexorably to diminish and break asunder. And with a fearsome cry that seemed to make the very mountains shrink, the creature broke free of them; one great taloned limb tearing through the fading curtain of flame to hook into the harrowed soil beneath.

The Riever ranks broke before it, hundreds of their number fleeing howling into the darkness. But some were too slow. A taloned hand caught two in its grip, raising them a dozen feet above the ground to hurl them, screaming, into the stark rock face. Within seconds the creature would be entirely free. And Leighor knew instinctively that, once free of the confines of its birthing vat, no power on earth could then restrain it.

A last bolt of fire struck down from Embor-Horeoth's wand. Pale and slight, its force seemed to diminish even as it descended to strike the monster. Yet still it bore power enough to shatter the near wall of the vat.

Dark and glutinous, the boiling inner fluid now poured from the rent in the side of the great cauldron, spreading crimson flame wherever it flowed. The fiend screamed out in sudden anguish; seeming to Leighor's eyes at once to dissipate, to tear itself apart from within, even as it was once more consumed in a tower of hungry flame.

The fire died as quickly as it had arisen, to leave behind it nothing. Blackness. Utter silence. The creature – whatever it had been – was gone: back to whatever dark plane had spawned it, leaving no trace that it had ever been – apart from the two mangled corpses at the bases of the high cliff. The Riever lord glowered down upon the scene for a moment; and then, with a sweep of his shimmering robes, was gone, back to whatever secret lair he inhabited within the heart of the mountain.

And then, as if a trigger had suddenly been released, the waiting ranks of warriors and Tarintarmen swept forward to swarm across the ruined circle.

'What . . . What was it?' Yeon hissed.

'Some form of lesser demon, or pit fiend – I know not.' Uhlendof shook his head briskly. 'Enormous power can be gained if such can be summoned and successfully bound to the caller's will. But the dangers of releasing such a thing upon the world are immeasurable.' He fell silent.

'But what of the wand?' Telsyan asked. 'That seemed to hold power enough for any man.'

'The wand is a thing of great power, sure enough,' the monk grunted. 'It must be purest *harrunor*. Yet believe me that the power of the creature the sorcerer tried to summon would have been far the greater – had he been able to control it. We must be thankful that he seems not yet to have such knowledge. One other matter worries me, however.' He turned to Keran. 'You told us that the Mage Metal could be used but once, yet this artefact produced several blasts before its power failed.'

'I told you only what I heard Claighar say at the keep,' Keran answered, concerned. 'Perhaps the greater amulets do not have such a limit. I cannot say . . .'

'No time for talk!' Zindur said sharply. 'This is our chance. We must go down now, while they're still distracted.'

The travellers looked at one another, but in their hearts they knew the mercenary was right. And reluctantly they bestirred themselves to stand erect and follow Zindur down the steep-sloping ridge towards the camp.

The going was loose and treacherous. Stretches of flaky, furrowed stone gave way without warning to unstable banks of gravel and scree that slipped away beneath their feet to clatter noisily into the darkness below. Yet none of the fearsome multitude beneath appeared to glance upward. No one, it seemed, had yet noticed the nine shadowy figures who clambered down the dark ridge towards them.

Nine? Leighor looked quickly around, counting only seven others beside himself. Eight! Someone was missing! A quick check of the shadowed shapes confirmed his suspicions. It was the crookback who was absent. Inanys had abandoned them once more. The knowledge did nothing to bolster the southron's confidence. The little crookback had a nose for trouble. And if Inanys was not with them, then Leighor was prepared to wager that danger lay ahead.

'Come! We cannot linger here!' Telsyan's brawny arm pushed him forward. 'We are perfect silhouettes against the slope!'

Leighor stumbled downward. Yet the sharpest part of the descent soon came to an end. A tussocky slope, riven by dry gullies and scattered with short, twisted pines, swept gently down to the camp beneath. He breathed a sigh of relief at the welcome cover. But that relief was short-lived.

There came a sudden sharp hissing from out of the gloom ahead, and a voice rose in anger. Leighor and Telsyan rushed forward, hearts racing, to discover Zindur and Haflas facing two crouching goblins, a small pile of half-gnawed roots at their side.

'Who are you?' one croaked in sharp, harshly accented Durian.

'Men of the West,' Zindur replied edgily, '—for all that it concerns you!'

'Have not seen such as you before . . .' Goblin eyes narrowed into thin, suspicious slits. 'Of whose company?'

'None but our own!' Yeon answered, his Durian weak and halting.

Leighor's hand felt beneath his robes for his crossbow. This feeble charade would convince no one, not even two goblin scavengers.

'Are not of our band!' the second goblin hissed sharply, backing away. 'Are sspies.' It drew breath to scream louder. 'Sspies!'

There was a flicker of steel through the air, and Zindur's great double-headed axe embedded itself deep in the goblin's neck, cleaving the writhing creature near in two.

The other gave out a loud shriek of terror and tried to make off into the trees, splayed feet skittering on the hard ground. But Yeon and Haflas were faster, intercepting the fleeing goblin and holding him tightly.

'Foolss!'' the goblin spat, thrashing about wildly as they began to truss him up. 'You will die! No man livess who harms a sservant of the Lord Embor-Horeoth! Did you not ssee his power? He callss Dark Oness from the night – to desstroy his enemiess.'

'They will destroy *him* first,' Zindur snarled.

'No!' The goblin fought with new vigour to bite through restraining hands and bonds. 'It iss you who will die! They will find you, hunt you to the endss of the earth—' Peace came at last, as his mouth was gagged.

'Quick! Hurry!' Zindur gasped. 'We must be gone at once!'

They left their captive bound in a nearby gully, moving hurriedly on. Some moments later, Telsyan again halted, instructing them to smear their faces with dust and the thick grey mud from a nearby ravine.

'It will make our faces less obvious,' he told them. 'Streak the marks from ear to cheek like I do – in the manner of their own war marks.' He raised a stubby finger from his face to show them the effect, waiting a moment or so for them to do the same. 'Now come!' he waved them forward impatiently. 'Stay together and say nothing. If anyone must speak, let it be Zindur or Haflas, who know the northron dialects. No others!'

Hoping that these hurried attempts at disguise would prove effective, Leighor found himself following Zindur and Haflas out into the disconcertingly sharp light of the great pyres.

For a few moments the travellers stood in silence, taking in the anarchic scene before them. To their left lay the ramshackle tents and shanties of the main Riever encampment. Between these and the looming caverns of the cliff-face burned several great fires, each surrounded by milling groups of men, goblins and grey-swathed Tarintarmen: gaunt and dark-shadowed as they toasted great hunks of bleeding meat above the flames. Here also were new forms of men, such as Leighor had never seen before; gathering in twos and threes about the dark cavemouths opposite. They towered a foot or so above even the tall Tarintarmen, seeming almost as if carved out of the solid rock. Hairless and massive, stolid and slow moving, they cringed from even the fitful light of the great fires. He recalled dark childhood tales of fearsome beings that cowered out of sight of the sun, in the deep bowels of the earth, and shivered, hoping he would need come no closer to them than this.

Zindur pointed away to the right, where the great cauldron of Embor-Horeoth had recently stood, and was now departed: drawn away once more into one of the great caverns. 'That is our way.'

Leighor nodded. Eastward: beneath the great mountain crest that now towered so high above them. Then north, around the base of that final crag which bore upon it the crooked goblin tower, and then hopefully, away, undetected, into the hills. It would be a long trek.

At first they seemed to attract no notice. A group of men – barbarians out of the west by their rasping Khiorim voices – passed by laughing, aleskins in hand. The travellers walked in tense silence, allowing them to pass as quickly as they would, in constant dread of challenge or discovery. Rievers clustered about the great fires like flies about dead meat, carousing loudly from one to another.

Many now came discomfitingly close – close enough to stare straight into the strangers' faces if they wished. But still the eight cowled figures occasioned no comment. Leighor caught brief glimpses of many faces as they passed, sharp flashes of personality hidden beneath shadowed hoods and visored helmets. The broad, scarred faces of barbarian tribesmen: cold gimlet eyes, hardened to sights that he could not even conceive of. The grey-green furtive faces of the goblins: running between the feet of the others, hooked fingers grasping for fallen scraps of food, scrawny bodies gleaming as they darted out of the way of promised kicks and blows, ever trying to steal some choice tit-bit or vessel of ale. Yet worst by far were the dread faces of the *tarintari*, the true Rievers of the west. Swathed in crude wrappings to protect the festering flesh from sun and wind, these faces did not laugh or smile, even in the depraved manner of the goblins and men. These were creatures that knew only hatred and the lust for vengeance. Vengeance for all the ills that the centuries had heaped upon them. Vengeance for their own malformed and rotting bodies. Vengeance against all who dwelt in peace and plenty where they could not. Their faces white as bone; their skin hanging in a maggotlike profusion of loose folds; their eyes dark and sunken – glinting bloodstones in hollow sockets – red and soulless as the night: Leighor feared these more than any.

Now the line of fires gave way, and there was nothing between them and the dark, gaping cavemouths of the cliff face. There were fewer people here, beneath the eastern edge of the mountain. Fewer to offer challenge, perhaps, but also fewer to hide themselves amongst. A small group of goblins came towards them, chattering excitedly, passing on by without even acknowledging the strangers' existence. Yet Leighor now felt himself sweating beneath his robes, wishing beyond all else that this interminable journey would end. His heart began to beat faster as the end of the vast cliff at last came in sight. Only a little farther now, and the worst of their passage would be over. In moments they would be beneath the last great horn of rock where the crest ran out.

Like all goblin works, the tower that stood upon the peak was crooked and ill-made, dwarfed by the massive crag it crouched upon: a slender broken pencil against the baleful disc of the full moon. No lights shone within it, no sound or movement rang down from its walls. To all intents it looked abandoned still, standing its lonely watch above the vale.

Suddenly a voice called out, harsh and commanding. A man's voice, and, although Leighor could not understand the speech, a voice that clearly demanded a response. His blood froze. They were almost beyond the crest: why now? Just behind them, in the shadows beneath the tower, stood two armed men. A dark passage behind them, leading down into the mountain, promised that there might all too soon be many more.

'What speech is that?' Telsyan whispered urgently.

'Khiorim, the westron tongue,' Zindur growled. 'He calls on us to halt: to state our business.'

'Do not!' Telsyan hissed. 'Keep moving, as though we had not heard. But slowly! Do not run. We shall soon be out of their sight.'

'*Viáthniich! Viáthniich! Kur Qhamchâr!*' the call came again. But the travellers ignored it, pressing onward in huddled silence around the base of the towering crag.

A large group of goblins appeared suddenly from the tents ahead. They surged noisily westward between guardsmen and travellers – and for a few precious moments they could feel themselves safe. Now, for the first time, Leighor could see what lay to the north of the great crest: and the sight that met his eyes was of surpassing enormity.

The Shattered Mountain rose up just as sharply on its northern flank as upon the south, declining only as it ran away into the hills of the north-west. The broad valley now twisted sharply westward once more. And here, between Ahockûl Crest and the surrounding hills, lay an encampment of goblins so vast as to dwarf even the great Riever camp through which they had just passed. This was scattered and less ordered, perhaps, but the numbers that dwelt here must be beyond counting.

'By the One! What have we come upon!' Uhlendof gasped.

'No more than we have already come through,' Zindur said flatly. 'Let us make haste and be out of this place!'

The goblins had passed on behind them, but the travellers were now almost out of sight of the two guards beneath the crest. They hurried on into the haphazard mass of rough, lean-to shelters that made up the goblin camp. Filth and sewage lay ankle deep between the shanties. The stench was appalling. Great angry clouds of flies rose up all about them with every onward step. Goblin faces looked up from half-chewed roots and bony hanks of meat. Small rodents turned on spits above flickering fires, and pots of greasy, foul-smelling broth bubbled quietly. It was clear that the best of whatever provisions were to be had in this vast encampment went to those who dwelt higher up the vale.

Yet despite the fact that they passed through unbidden, the goblins seemed to accept the travellers' presence in their camp without question. Evidently it was not wise for these small folk to be too curious about the affairs of those they assumed to be the greater servants of Embor-Horeoth. Leighor chanced a last quick glance behind him, to see one of the guardsmen staring anxiously after them into the encampment. But even as the southron caught sight of him, the tall figure turned away, perhaps not reckoning his duty to question the eight travellers worth the bother of venturing into the foul sump of the goblin camp. It seemed they were home free.

Yet the goblin encampment appeared to go on for ever, an endless succession of squalid shelters of mud and wicker, tattered tents and low turf round-houses. The paths through this maze of smoking, verminous dwellings twisted and turned to such an extent that it was impossible to keep going in any one direction for more than a dozen paces at a time. Even so, Telsyan managed to keep them heading roughly north-eastward, away from the high crest, until even that fearsome landmark had vanished into the gloom and smoke behind them.

There seemed to be no definite border to the camp, no ditch or line of staves to mark its frontier. The goblin shelters merely grew fewer and farther apart as the ground slowly rose and the great dark hills crept down to meet them – pine-clad silhouettes against a starsplashed sky. Clearly Embor-Horeoth was confident in his security, fearing no attack from the Knights of Dur, or any other force that might roam these northland forests.

Slowly, anticlimactically, observed by none but half a dozen uninterested goblins, the eight travellers crept from the Riever camp at Ahockûl Crest, and into the shelter of the dark forest. Leighor breathed again as the forest closed in around them. Apart from the distant noises of the goblin camp, there came no sound at all from behind. There were no alarms, no angry cries, nothing at all to indicate pursuit. He would not have believed it possible, but the mercenary had been right. The eight of them had indeed been able to walk right through the heart of the Riever camp undetected. For the first time since catching sight of what lay beneath the Shattered Mountain, Leighor began to feel that they had a real chance of escape.

Chapter Eighteen
THE INN AT THE BRIDGE

Moving ever onward with no thought of halt or rest, the travellers journeyed north into the grey rising dawn. How many leagues they covered that night and the day following none of them could have guessed. Much of the journey passed for Leighor in a formless, numbing blur. Hills rose and fell all around them as the forest flowed endlessly on and on, an unbroken blanket across the face of the land. Nothing ever seemed to change, and for all the southron could tell they might have been walking in circles.

It was almost dark when they came to the river. A broad, majestic, king of rivers, that flowed slowly and regally down from the north-west. Indifferent to the puny concerns of those who trod its banks, it rolled quietly on into the south. Some distance upstream, a great stone bridge of a dozen turreted arches spanned the river. Still, grey, and immeasurably old, it had an air of unreal ghostliness in the evening half-light, as if lifted by some faerie magick to a time and place to which it no longer belonged.

'Now I know where we are!' Haflas broke the silence suddenly. 'This must be the Malûn River! That is the only great waterway that runs southward from the plains of Scûn towards the Rathul Sea. And there is but one bridge across that river that still stands; the bridge of Vhori.'

Keran sighted bare treeless hills rising out of the forest upon the farther shore, and her spirits rose. The forest was ending. A day's further travel and they would be beyond its dark embrace. Out in open country, where they would at least be able to see whatever dangers still lay ahead of them. There was a house ahead, she noticed abruptly, a run-down shambles of a building that clung to the western end of the great bridge as if it needed the support of the older, mightier structure to remain standing. It was a poor looking place, yet perhaps they might find some shelter there for this coming night. Their tents were lost, abandoned with their mule on the far side of Ahockûl Crest, and all else that they had possessed in the way of food and equipment lost with them. They had gone two days without sleep already. Without food and shelter they would soon be in a parlous state.

The bridge was farther away than it seemed, distances being distorted by the sheer size and scale of the landscape and of the great river that rolled along beside them. As they approached, the structure of the building began to take clearer shape. It, like the bridge, was larger than it had at first appeared, and seemed to have been built in stages by many different hands, new rooms being added as and when needed down the centuries. The stones were rough and irregular, of a hundred different shapes and sizes, and appeared to consist entirely of crumbled masonry that had fallen from the great bridge over the years. A line of small, irregular windows stared down at them from beneath an untidy roof of rotting straw. Iron grilles, bolted to the stone, guarded every window. The whole lay still, in eerie silence.

The travellers made their way slowly around to the front of the building, where it faced on to an overgrown roadway which must once have carried much traffic over the bridge. Keran was surprised to see a painted inn sign still swinging above the low, timber doorway. It bore the faded representation of a great king who held a silver sceptre in one hand and a flaming sword in the other. Below the picture was a short line of inscription written in the Durian rune-script of Xhendir, a stark, barbarian form of lettering long since displaced in most lands by the more elegant, spindly scripts of the south. And although she had been taught the rudiments of the new writing, Keran had no way to decipher these ancient letters, and was glad when Uhlendof supplied the translation without her having to ask.

'Most Royal Inn of King Vhori, Ruler of the Four Kingdoms of Scûn,' he read slowly, nodding quietly to himself. 'An ancient title, though not so ancient as the bridge itself. No Durian king could ever have raised such a bridge as this, although many would have liked to claim the credit.'

'Be that as it may,' Telsyan cut in quickly. 'Our business now is to discover whether or not it is still inhabited.' He advanced towards the door.

'I think I saw a movement!' Haflas warned quickly. 'Behind the shutters!'

Zindur's sword flashed noisily from its sheath, and others quickly followed. There came a sudden rattling from behind the small door, Telsyan backing hurriedly to one side as it swung open.

A large, square-faced man stepped out into the gloom, a smouldering oil lantern swinging from one brawny hand. He showed no apparent surprise at the drawn weapons all around him, nor did he seem to find the wary watchfulness of the eight strangers at all unusual.

'Good day to you, sirs,' he said, holding out his free hand. 'I am Thurin, the bridgemaster. Do you seek board and lodging this dark night at the King's Inn?'

The travellers stared at one another in amazement.

'Who set you here to guard this ancient bridge?' Telsyan asked, somewhat later, when they were all slumped in chairs about the low peat fire that smouldered dimly at one end of the inn's dark, low-ceilinged hall.

'I keep the bridge open for the Knights of Dur,' Thurin replied slowly, breathing a puff of smoke from his clay pipe into the already murky air. 'This inn is under their protection. I am but the warder. Such has been my family's duty for generations beyond number: to repair the bridge, to keep the roadway clear, and to keep an inn for travellers. We were bridgemasters to King Vhori and to the nameless kings who ruled before him. Ours is an ancient trust.'

'But what of the Rievers?' Yeon asked. 'And of their chieftain, Embor-Horeoth, who rules at Ahockûl Crest? Does he not trouble you?'

Thurin shrugged. 'We hear many strange tales here, my sons and I. Your Embor-Horeoth is not unknown to us, yet he has never cared to cause us any trouble, and we do not choose to trouble him. We keep to our appointed tasks and interfere with no one else.'

'Yet you are in great danger, both here and in Hith-Gibor,' Uhlendof warned. 'Can you not raise some warning? For Embor-Horeoth assembles goblins and Rievers in their thousands beneath his dark tower, and I fear that his purposes are evil.'

'Nay, good sirs.' The bridgemaster smiled and shook his head. 'There you are mistaken. I know for a fact that Embor-Horeoth is on good terms with the Knights, and with the folk at Hith-Gibor. He holds lands that others, less friendly, might occupy were he not there. He makes good the forest roads, and sends much gold and trade in the way of the Knights of Dur. I cannot think he now means to attack them.'

'Then you know not what we have seen!' the monk broke in abruptly. 'Embor-Horeoth is utterly corrupted by evil! He is far too dangerous and powerful to be trusted!' Swiftly Uhlendof recounted the story of their passage through the Riever camp at Ahockûl Crest, and of what they had witnessed there.

When he had finished, Thurin was silent for several moments. 'You bring grave news, my lords.' He shook his head. 'If this tale of yours be true, and the Lord of the Shattered Mountain has indeed turned to works of ill, then there are few in all these lands with power enough to stay him. It is my honest hope that you are mistaken. But I shall send word at once to the knights, and keep close guard upon my door until I have better news.'

A small door creaked suddenly open in the dark-stained panelling that lined the walls. Two large figures entered, bearing trays of ale.

'These are my sons,' Thurin announced proudly, rising to introduce them: 'or two of them, at least: Tvorek, the eldest, who works on the bridge, and his younger brother, Idurn. My third son, Vaerd, readies your meal.'

The two young men nodded dourly. Both were strongly built and square-faced like their father; their eyes keen, their hair close-cropped, and their faces overrun with dark stubble. Tvorek was the larger of the two, and wore close-fitting garments of dark leather, whilst Idurn seemed content with leather breeches and an old shirt of stained brown linen. Neither seemed particularly pleased to welcome the strangers, and neither spoke a single word of greeting.

The ale itself was dark and warm. It came in large wooden tankards, almost black with age, each artfully fashioned into the form of a giant's head: staring eyes set deep into furious, bearded faces that glowered unsettlingly into the eyes of the drinkers as they raised them to their lips. Everywhere Keran looked she saw rich carvings; on walls, mantel, ceiling beams, even the chairs themselves. There was not an inch of free wood that was not carved into some fantastic shape. Trees, giants, trolls, gryphons and dragons without number wound, coiled and stared back at them from every corner of the dark chamber.

'Do you find the skills of the ancient stonemasons difficult to master?' Uhlendof was asking. 'It is rare to see anyone in these days attempting to maintain the ancient works.'

Tvorek shrugged. 'When a stone falls we find another to fit. If we cannot, it must be left. So long as the roadway is firm, the rest matters little.'

'But the arches,' Uhlendof insisted. 'How do you repair them?'

'We cannot,' Tvorek grunted darkly, as if already bored with the conversation. 'If an arch falls, it falls.'

'One has already fallen near the centre of the bridge,' Thurin added. 'We have not the skill, nor the numbers, to build it up again; but the gap is small and safely spanned with timber.' He shook his head sadly. 'That is all we are able to do. Perhaps some day the knights will spare us some masons and some new stone, but until then . . .' He lapsed into silence.

Shortly thereafter Thurin and his sons departed, leaving the travellers on their own, with only the dim light of a single lantern to drive the shadows away. The low, flickering light seemed to make the carvings all around them come alive, with eyes that moved and hard-clawed bodies that writhed and twisted to the silent music of the flame. A wind was rising in the south, rattling unseen shutters and window panes in the dark corridors beyond; the whole building seeming to creak and shudder with each new onslaught.

It was clear that the travellers had much to discuss concerning their flight and their plans for the immediate future. But they were far too weary to decide anything of import that evening, and had fallen into an exhausted silence when two goblins in tattered linens brought in their meal. The sight of the goblins came as something of a shock. But Thurin, following on behind, quickly reassured them that these were his trusted servants. The travellers nodded, and after eating the welcomingly thick broth Vaerd had prepared for them, announced themselves ready to retire.

Thurin himself led them to their chambers on the upper floor: two adjoining rooms with four narrow beds crammed into each. They were cramped and shabby, but the travellers did not complain, thankful only to fall into real beds once more.

'I have but this one lantern,' Thurin told them as he prepared to leave. 'But if you desire light, you will find wax candles in the window.'

He pointed past Keran. And sure enough, she turned and found the candles; two, of dark brown wax, held in candleholders of shiny, tinned copper. The design of these was as curious as that of all else in this inn, each being in the form of an upturned goblin face, the mouth wide agape to hold its candle upright, clenched tightly between bright metal teeth. Her eyes were held by the strange design, even as the candles were lit. They guttered, sparking and smouldering, but producing little light for all their efforts, barely brightening the still, dusty air of the linked chambers.

Thurin departed, and the travellers prepared for sleep. The beds were old, hard and covered in dust; as if they had not been disturbed for many months. Keran brushed a skein of cobwebs from the carved headboard above hers, and then sat to let Tavolir pull off her damp boots. She felt more tired than she had for years – since the long journey she had once made to Vliza, as a child with her trader father, along the great rivers of the north. The days had been long that summer, and the oarsmen had rowed deep into the night, until at last it had come time to halt and make camp. She fancied that she could still smell the woodsmoke, sharp and fragrant on the evening air. Without noticing, she drifted into a deep sleep, lacking even the energy to crawl beneath the bedclothes.

But now someone was pulling at her, shaking her awake. Surely it could not be morning already? She had only just closed her eyes. She forced them open.

They felt as if they were lined with sand . . . No, it could not be morning. It was still dark. The candle still burned on the mantelshelf. She tried to close her eyes again . . . it was too early. She must sleep.

'Rouse yourself, lass!' the whisper came harsh and fierce in her ear. It was Inanys. Inanys here? Her brain was fogged by sleep, and it took several moments for the wrongness to work its way through to her conscious mind. Something was wrong. Inanys should not be here. He had abandoned them at the crest . . . She forced her eyes painfully open once more. The familiar face stared sidelong into hers.

'Hurry!' it hissed. 'Or we shall be too late!'

Fully awake now, Keran sprang to her feet. 'Grey One!' she breathed. 'What do you here?' Then she saw the bodies of her companions, all slumped across their beds, just as she had lain, uncovered and half dressed, in the deep embrace of sleep. 'How . . . ?'

'There will be time enough for that,' Inanys smiled smoothly, his face dark-shadowed in the candlelight. 'Time enough, once we are gone.'

'Gone?' Keran repeated dumbly, wondering whether her mind was not still clouded by sleep. 'Where . . . ? Why . . . ?'

'We must make haste, girl,' Inanys whispered. 'Lest your life be forfeit. And would not that be a wicked thing – to waste such talent as thine? Fool was I not to realise what I had chanced upon at Silentwater . . . I nearly lost you then. But Inanys does not make such errors twice . . . Oh, no . . .' He shook his head, chuckling grimly to himself.

Keran's mind spun. This was all too much to take in. And despite the shock of the crookback's reappearance, she still felt dark sleep battling to overcome her. She must not let it. She must do something – anything – to regain at least partial control over her own destiny. She began to inch sluggishly away from the bed.

'I shall wake the others,' she said as firmly as she could, forcing herself to pronounce each word clearly.

'Oh no,' Inanys hissed, shaking his head briskly as he rushed forward. 'That won't do at all! It must be just you and I. You and I alone. No more. Come!' One finger curled, beckoning her to follow him.

'No!' Keran pulled away sharply. 'I shall not!' She turned and called out to the sleeping figures behind her, 'Zindur! Master Telsyan! Haflas!' Her voice echoed alarmingly about the darkened chamber, but no one stirred. Not one of them seemed to have heard her voice – or was able to respond to it if he had. She made to shout again. But at once Inanys spun her about to face him, his grey-green eyes catching hers, and holding them.

'Oh no, my lass,' he shook his head gently, the rat tails of hair swinging hypnotically from his balding pate. 'No noise! we cannot do with that now, can we?' He smiled again, raising one thin, bony finger to trace a figure in the air between them. And where his finger moved, the air seemed suddenly to thicken, congealing into phantom lines of deep emerald green that glowed through the darkness. A shimmering symbol slowly took shape before her. It floated in the air before her eyes. It was a rune. A rune of power. Deep down within her Keran knew this, recognised it instinctively for what it was. An ensorcelment. A trap! Yet she could do nothing whatsoever to extricate herself. The flickering shape seemed to move with her eyes, maintaining its position, just out of reach, in the centre of her field of vision, no matter where she tried to turn. Slowly it bound her, sapped her strength; the writhing green rune burning itself into her consciousness, embedding itself there, so that nothing she could do could drive it from her mind. She tried to shut her eyes, to blot it out, but she found that she could not. Somehow the rune prevented her, negating even so minor an exercise of her will. She could not speak. She seemed no longer to have the will even to move her own lips, her own body. She could but stand motionless, her eyes entrapped in the glowing coils of the shining spell. Utterly helpless, as though imprisoned in a dream.

Behind the rune she hardly saw the crookback moving towards her, yet she felt him approach. She felt his bony arms encircle her, felt herself lifted bodily from the ground, her weight taken easily across one scrawny shoulder. Dimly, at the back of her mind, she registered surprise at the small one's strength. He lifted her like a child, and now bore her to the doorway seemingly without effort. Still she seemed unable to force her mind to think clearly, to concentrate. Even now sleep threatened once more to overwhelm her. She must resist! Where was the crookback taking her? What did he want? She could not begin to guess, yet she knew that she must try to prevent it, whatever it was. Why was he so anxious to be away, to abandon the others? What did he fear? Had he not earlier mentioned a threat? She tried to remember . . . A threat of death . . .

A cold shock of realisation flooded through her. The way she had slept – the way the others still slept – it was unnatural! It came to her suddenly that none of them were ever meant to waken. Yes. The stench of death hung over this whole chamber. She could smell it now, bitter as aloes and sharp as a knife. All who remained here in this room would soon be dead. That was fact, visceral, undeniable. They lay in wait upon some terrible doom – one that she could do nothing to prevent. She felt an icy shaft of fear. She must stop this somehow: warn the others! Yet the fiery rune still pulsed before her eyes, and before it she was helpless.

No! She could not let this be! With all of her will she strove against the spell; straining to move an arm, a hand, the smallest of her fingers; straining to call out, to do anything at all that might have some effect upon her destiny and that of her companions. The crookback paused to fumble with the doorlatch. In a moment they would be out of the chamber, and it would be too late. She must free herself now! But the rune held firm, and she relapsed into bitter defeat, inwardly sobbing at her own pitiful weakness.

A bolt flew back, and the door began slowly to creak open. A draught of cold air gusted into the room, making the candle gutter, almost dousing its flame. In moments she would be beyond all aid. With a lurch, Inanys straightened beneath her. The movement loosed the small gold medallion from its place beneath her leather jerkin, to set it swinging free from her neck, its chain brushing gently against her face. Out of the corner of her eye she could just see the tiny Ginara Stone fused to its surface. It glowed dimly at her through the darkness, and a new hope rose within her. There was power in it, of a kind. Perhaps somehow it could help her. If she could but lift her head the few inches necessary to see it clearly, she might then, perhaps, be able to use it . . . Be able to focus what was left of her will upon it . . . To break the spell . . .

Slowly, concentrating all of her remaining energy upon this one task, she tried to raise her head, letting it swing backward with the lurching movements of her captor until she could at last focus upon the tiny stone. Straining every fibre of her being, she froze in that position. At the outermost edges of her consciousness she noted that they were now passing out through the doorway, that it would soon close behind them, and her struggle would be lost before it had begun. She must act quickly!

The rune now seemed to hover between her and the Ginara Stone – only inches away – party obscuring it. Yet she could still just discern the pink glow of the Ginara Stone, even through the writhing green wall of Inanys's spell-rune. She must try to break through. Focus her will, all of her fear, all of her loathing of the vile crookback who now bore her who-knew-where, focus it down into the jewel.

Almost imperceptibly at first, the pink glow brightened. Brightened and then grew stronger. Yet for long moments the rune held, resisting her silent onslaught. She despaired. And then at last it began to alter: trembling, shivering, straining against itself; its shape distorting, twisting, breaking! With one final shudder, it flew apart, shattering abruptly into a thousand gleaming fragments, like a crystal goblet falling from a great height on to a bare stone floor . . . The fragments blazed for an instant, and then died. She was free! She felt something released inside her in the instant of her victory. And in that same instant, the crookback staggered beneath her, as if he had been in some way physically wounded by the sudden breach of his ensorcelment, lurching crazily as he struggled to keep his footing.

Now Keran fought like a wild thing. Her fingers tearing desperately at the jamb of the fast-closing chamber door, her knees hammering ruthlessly into her captor's chest, she screamed for her companions to awaken. Inanys reeled beneath the sudden onslaught. Keran was a deal heavier than he, and the loss of his rune-spell seemed indeed to have weakened him. He cursed fluently in some unknown tongue, slamming the chamber door hard upon her hand. Now it was Keran's turn to cry out in pain, releasing the door jamb in an agony of cut and burning fingers. Yet the pain only increased her desperation and the intensity of her fury. And despite the crookback's still remarkable strength, he was now unable to bear her any farther along the passage. She cried out again and again: to Telsyan, to Zindur, to Leighor, to Uhlendof, to any who would hear her, praying for some response. But those within the bedchamber might have been dead already for all the answer they made. She lashed out hard with her stockinged feet, hurling them against the darkwood panelling that lined the corridor. Yet still there came no response. None at least from where she sought response: but somewhere below harsh voices rose suddenly in surprise and anger, and the sound of heavy-shod feet began to pound along wooden corridors not far beneath them.

Abruptly Inanys released her, letting her slip unceremoniously to the floor in front of him. 'Well, lass,' he hissed. 'You have won. For all the good it will do you! Now we are all lost! Quick!' He turned sharply back for the chamber door, grasping her hand in a claw-like grip to drag her after him. 'We must go back!'

Utterly disorientated by this latest turn of events, Keran allowed herself to be dragged, unprotesting, back into the small chamber, watching dumbstruck as Inanys slammed the heavy door behind them and crashed the double bolts firmly home.

'Wake the others, fool!' the crookback shouted across at her. 'Or do you truly wish to die?' Without waiting to see whether or not she obeyed him, Inanys seized up the smouldering candle and skittered off with it into the adjoining room. There Keran watched him quickly snuff out the other and then hurl both of his prizes out through the small glass window to clatter on to the windblown roadway below.

There came a sudden thunderous pounding on the bolted door. Someone hammered loudly against it from without, and a harsh voice called on them to open. Yet despite even this great commotion, Keran's seven sleeping companions seemed to be coming to only sluggishly.

'Have you not roused them yet?' Inanys spat from the connecting doorway. 'Open the windows! Speed out the fumes. Then let us begone! Before the others come!'

'Others? . . .' Keran stumbled towards the window, thankful for a dim moon that supplied just enough light for her to see where she trod. Once there, she tugged the small casement briskly open, surprised at the sharp, invigorating freshness of the air beyond. It felt almost as if a dark cloud had been suddenly lifted from her mind, and for the first time since entering the inn she felt fully awake.

'The candles!' she realised sharply.

'Aye, the candles!' Inanys sneered. 'Dark candles of intoxication, lit by fools, to make them sleep for ever!'

'Wh-What?' Someone was coming to on a bed nearby.

'Hurry, fools!' Inanys voice screamed. 'The Rievers will soon be upon us!'

Before the words were out, there came another reverberating crash against the bolted door. Someone was trying to break it down. Freed of the clammy hold of the black candles, the other travellers flew to their feet. Yet it took many long minutes for Keran and the crookback to drill any sense at all into their muddled heads.

'Thurin has betrayed you,' Inanys said quickly. 'Even now he fetches Rievers from the Shattered Mountain to carry you back to face the lord of that place!'

'Back?' Uhlendof repeated sleepily.

'Aye, back!' Inanys sneered once more. 'Alive, or dead!'

But the urgency of their predicament quickly made itself clear. And in moments the chamber was a confusion of arms, legs and elbows, as boots were dragged on, clothing hastily donned, and weapons readied.

'How do we escape?' someone asked.

'Through the window!' the crookback hissed. 'Down, and then across the bridge. Hurry!'

'But the windows are all barred!' Telsyan's rings rattled against the iron gratings.

'They may be prised free,' Haflas said quickly. 'The iron is three quarters rotten already.'

Yet even as he and Zindur applied hammer and axehead to the task, the door to the chamber burst inward in a shower of screaming wood. Two men entered the room, armed with primed crossbows: Idurn and Tvorek. Another lurked behind in the shadows.

'Hold!' the larger shouted. 'Hold, or I fire!' His finger pressed gently against the cocked trigger. Haflas and the mercenary turned from their task, but Inanys did not, continuing to claw at the windowframe with one of his sharp knives.

'Hold, I say!' Tvorek's finger pressed a little harder, preparing to fire.

'No!' Tavolir flung himself upon the larger man, knocking the crossbow sideways to send its murderous shaft screaming askew into a carved wall-beam.

Instinctively, Idurn too fired, but his panicked shot was not true, and though the crossbow bolt struck deep it was only into the musician's leg. Tavolir gave a sharp cry of pain and slumped to the floor. Yeon sprang forward in fury, leaping one of the low beds to hurl himself upon the firer of the shot. Both fell in a mass of flailing arms and legs. Uhlendof advanced slowly upon the other, sturdy quarterstaff gripped tightly in both hands.

'Hurry!' Telsyan shouted urgently from the window. 'I see lights in the forest. Moving lights!'

'Where?' Keran leaned forward fearfully, pressing her head to the iron window bars to see farther into the darkness. At first she saw nothing. And then, suddenly, they appeared from behind some invisible obstacle. Flickering dots of orange flame, far off in the darkness of the west. Torches! Ten, twenty, thirty of them! Moving steadily down out of the hills towards the inn! And from the way that they bobbed up and down as they drew nearer, whoever bore them must be running. Running at some speed. 'Rievers!' she gasped.

At once there was a flurry of movement across the room behind her. A short brutish man stepped into the chamber, crossbow in hand. Keran had not seen him before but guessed that this must be the third brother, Vaerd. He was flanked by three grinning goblins, all bearing razor-sharp kitchen knives. A bolt from the newcomer's crossbow whistled across the room to catch Haflas in the shoulder. The miner gave a sharp cry, more of surprise than pain, and fell to his knees clutching at the afflicted shoulderblade. With a roar, Zindur spun upon their attacker, hurling the axe he had been using seconds before to attack the iron window-grille.

Vaerd managed to duck out of its path, but one of the goblins was not so lucky, screaming in pain as its arm was shorn away at the shoulder. Drawing his great broadsword, the mercenary followed after, leaping hotly into the thick of the fray.

Yeon, meanwhile, had made short work of Idurn on the floor, and now dragged himself back to his feet to help Leighor and Uhlendof with the eldest brother and two knife-wielding goblins. Falling on Tvorek from behind, his long arm dealt a shattering blow to the side of the bridger's face, leaving the jaw jutting unnaturally forward. Two more blows doubled the larger man up to send him crashing into a side wall. Keran caught a brief glimpse of Leighor, engaged in a scratching tearing struggle with the two goblins, even as a hard sharp blow from Uhlendof's staff sent Tvorek headlong into the body of his semi-conscious brother.

Zindur now made for the disarmed Vaerd – who turned at once to flee towards the doorway. But before he had taken two steps, the warrior's sword clove deep into his side. The shorter figure crashed heavily to the floor, his leather tunic leaking blood.

Yet the warrior's triumph was shortlived; for in seconds he too was crying out in pain as a goblin knife bit deep into his thigh. Zindur spun instantly, about to run the goblin through, but at once another was upon him; sharp, serrated knife in hand, lunging for the mercenary's throat. Leighor threw himself forward, trying to drag the biting, snarling creature from the warrior's back . . .

To Keran, at the window, all was confusion. Blades glinted and knives flashed through the darkness. Weapons clashed, screams rose and bodies fell. She could not tell which way the skirmish went. Yet that was not her task. She was of more use here, labouring feveredly with Telsyan and the crookback to tear free the rusting supports of the window-grille. But even now they seemed no closer to dislodging it. It clung tenaciously to its stone mounting, despising their efforts. And all the while, the bobbing lights crept closer.

'Leave that!' Zindur's voice now rose triumphantly from the doorway. 'We have done with the house scum. The way through the inn is clear!'

Keran turned from her work to see that the warrior indeed spoke true. All three goblins now lay either dead or wounded on the floor, and the three sons of Thurin had fared little better. Vaerd lay in a pool of blood near the doorway where Zindur's sword had cut him down. And Tvorek's form lay slumped on the floor, next to where Yeon and Leighor were even now engaged in binding the half-conscious Idurn, who had been the first of the attackers to fall, and was consequently the least injured.

It took but a few seconds more for the members of the company to retrieve their lost clothes and fallen weapons. It took far longer, however, for them to drag themselves from the darkened inn and down on to the open road with their hurt and wounded. Leighor, Zindur and Uhlendof, despite various cuts and bruises, did not seem to be too badly hurt. Neither were she, Telsyan and the crookback. It was Haflas and Tavolir who had taken the worst of the injuries: Tavolir could not walk at all and had to be carried between Yeon and the mercenary; Haflas was able to walk, but the short quarrel still remained in him, driven deep into the shoulder-bone by the force of the crossbow, and he was in considerable pain.

It took an agony of dark passages and twisting stairways before they at last found their way to the inn's low front door. The doorway itself was neither locked nor barred, swinging open easily at Telsyan's touch to admit a draught of ice-cold air and a thin shaft of moonlight.

'Wait here,' Zindur ordered quickly, going through before them. 'I shall see if the way is clear.'

The rest of the travellers awaited his return in tense silence. At last he reappeared, a dark shadow-form clinging to the inn wall.

'The lights are closer,' he whispered harshly. 'Very close. We don't have much time. Stay in the shadows until we are on the bridge, and then we must be across quickly!'

'And what if the Rievers follow us across?' Leighor demanded.

'If we are over before them, we can lose ourselves in the hills beyond. If they catch up with us on the bridge . . .' The mercenary shrugged. 'We shall just have to make a stand. Either way we cannot remain here. The bridge is our only chance. Now let us go!'

The great dark sweep of the bridge rose up starkly before them as they stumbled out on to the roadway, climbing gently towards its own enormous central arch, which lay a good sixth of a league distant, high above the swirling waters of the Malûn River. The nine crept furtively from beneath the protective shadow of the inn, to climb up on to the ancient bridge itself. The moon now seemed alarmingly bright as it glinted across the surface of the great river, throwing their shadows into sharp relief against the old grey stonework.

From nowhere, a crossbow quarrel suddenly clattered into the high stone balustrade to Keran's left. Zindur swung sharply around to see a pale face momentarily peering down from behind the grille of one of the upper windows. He cursed.

'You were fools not to finish them when you had the chance!' Inanys hissed with finely-wrought contempt.

'Never mind that!' Uhlendof ordered. 'Run! Run now! Before the man reloads.'

But in their present state, few of the travellers were capable of much more than a slow jog. This proved enough, however, to get them out of immediate firing range of the inn before their attacker could loose another shot. And again they halted to catch their breath. They were still barely a fifth of the way across, but already the rise of the bridge had carried them above the level of the inn roof. And somewhere in the shadows beneath, Keran thought she saw two figures move.

'There!' she pointed. 'More goblins. I think they follow us!'

'They will do us no harm,' Zindur grunted darkly, pointing past the inn roof to a point where the trackway from the bridge ran into the deeper forest. 'It is those we must worry about.'

Keran followed his pointing finger to see the first group of torch-bearing warriors emerge from the shadow of the trees no more than half a mile away. She could not make out the individual shapes of the running men in the darkness, nor their number, but that seemed only to make the prospect all the more fearful. She had to imagine the dread figures that ran beneath those crimson torches, the soulless faces that stared out from beneath those dancing plumes of fire.

'Run!' Telsyan screamed. 'Or they will be upon us before we are half way across!'

With fearful urgency the company broke into a run once more, Zindur still helping Yeon to bear the burden of the wounded Tavolir. Even so, Haflas was unable to keep up. The back of his leather tunic was now slick with blood, and he staggered on with only his courage to keep him upright. Keran and Leighor offered him what assistance they could, but even with their help he was unable to increase his pace by more than a fraction.

The travellers struggled despairingly onward; yet still their pace seemed immeasurably slow, the great bridge endless. They could hear the Rievers behind them now: snatches of some wild war-chant blown on the wind; the sound of javelins crashing against leathern shields. Keran chanced a look back over her shoulder to see the first of the torchbearers emerging from the shadows of the low inn wall.

They halted for but a moment, to exchange sharp words with someone who waited beneath, and then with a mighty roar began to run for the bridge. A racing column of dark-helmed figures raged towards them, fearsome and full of running – like a stream of angry ants, at this distance, beneath their fluttering torches. Their appearance gave wings to the travellers' feet, bringing new life to their drained, exhausted bodies. Keran ran as she had never run before, trying to drag Haflas along with her, trying not to stumble upon the uneven stones. But still the Rievers drew closer behind them, seeming to gain upon the wounded party with every stride. It was hopeless! They could not now be more than a few hundred paces behind! Javelins and other missiles began to clatter on to the roadway only a few yards behind them.

And then, without warning, a great chasm opened up in the bridge ahead. Through it Keran could see right down into the oily waters of the Malûn far below. They were at the high point of the bridge, and this was the arch that had collapsed! They could run no farther. They were trapped!

'There is a crossing here!' Telsyan shouted to her relief, somewhere away to the right. 'The wooden section raised by Thurin.'

And there it was! So dark and slender she had failed to see it, just wide enough for a horse and rider to cross, barely a sixth of the width of the old way itself. It was built from the southern parapet of the ancient bridge, stretching across the broad gap to where the crumbling masonry took up again upon the other side. They could cross! Perhaps even defend this narrow passage until it could be thrown down, or some other means of escape worked out.

As if he had read her mind, Zindur turned back to her, a fierce grin creasing his face. 'This is where we make our stand,' he declared, almost as if he relished the coming battle.

Arrows and javelins clattered down all about them as they stumbled across the wooden bridgeway, but all managed to make the crossing in safety. The two wounded were set at once in the shelter of a high parapet – one of many that supported the several empty stone arches that towered high above the roadway, and seemed to serve no useful purpose. Yet now these piers at least provided some shelter from the Riever missiles: even as the advance guard of that fearsome host drew near to the western edge of the chasm. Here they hesitated at the foot of the bridgeway. The shapes of goblins, tribesmen and grey-swathed *tarintari* could all now be discerned beneath their flickering lights.

'Cover us with your bows!' Zindur ordered, moving forward with Uhlendof. 'We two shall try to dislodge the bridgeway!'

But the cover provided by the four others was neither strong nor accurate enough to long hold the Rievers back from the chasm. And Zindur and Uhlendof were quickly driven back from the timber bridgeway by a far more threatening shower of Tarintar missiles from across the gap.

'There is nothing we can do!' Zindur gasped, after a hurried dash back to the shelter of the high stone pier. 'If we stand out there in the open for more than a minute, we shall be cut to pieces!'

'How else can we destroy the bridgeway?' Yeon demanded.

Zindur shook his head. 'I do not know. But we can at least prevent them from crossing as long as we have arrows left to fire.'

'And how long will that be?' Inanys asked scornfully. 'Must we wait here until dawn before we die, or will it take us but an hour?'

'What would you have us do then, little man?' Zindur growled angrily.

But before the crookback could reply, another voice rose up, hard and familiar, across the gap. The voice of Thurin, their betrayer.

'Come, strangers,' he called. 'Surrender yourselves to these men now, and no harm shall come to you. You shall be the honoured guests of Embor-Horeoth the mighty: Embor-Horeoth, Governor of the Eastern Marches.'

'Governor of what?' Zindur bellowed back. 'Of what muck-laden dunghill does your Embor-Horeoth claim to be the governor?'

Thurin affected to ignore the insult. 'Embor-Horeoth rules all the lands of the Malûn River: by order of the Knights, and of the Master. Here he is lord of all, and all must make obeisance to him. Come strangers, our lord desires only to know what pressing business you have, to make you scurry so discourteously through his encampment, unannounced – like thieves in the night.'

'Aye,' Zindur responded with scorn. 'Is that why he sends a hundred armed men with his invitations? And less than men, and goblin scum. Is that why you drug us in our beds and send your goblin-bred sons to slay us? You lie! Your mouth is a midden of lies! Your lips run with deceit! The very worms of the earth would choke upon your lying tongue!'

'Is all this really necessary?' Uhlendof hissed beside him. 'Surely we have no need to anger these men further!'

'What matter how we anger them?' Zindur shrugged. 'The end is the same.'

'Enough!' A taller man stepped forward beneath a raised torch, pushing the stolid figure of the bridgemaster aside. This was no barbarian, for his features were noble, and he was dressed in long robes of pure silk that shimmered in the light of the flames. 'Enough of this time-wasting!' he continued sharply. 'Realise, strangers, that all things in these lands belong to my master: this bridge, the inn, even this doltish innkeeper – whose task it is to report all unescorted travellers who might be of interest to my lord. All others he may do with as he wills.' His eyes narrowed. 'You will now come with me. No choice is offered you. You have injured or slain several of my master's servants. You pass through his realms without leave, and we would know your purpose. You have but one decision to make, and that is to surrender or be slain where you stand. What is your answer?'

There was silence for several moments, the only sound the wind tearing noisily through the flames of the Riever torches. No one moved, no one dared to speak. Then suddenly, before anyone could stop him, Yeon raised his bow and fired.

The arrow missed its target, clattering into the rough paving stones at the tall man's feet. But it struck close enough to make the robed figure stumble several undignified steps backward before falling clumsily into the arms of his followers. Furiously brushing all restraining hands aside, he staggered back to his feet.

'It shall go the worse with you when you are taken!' he hissed, turning to face the watchful ranks of warriors behind him. 'Slay them all! All but the one who fired the arrow.' He pointed towards Yeon. 'Him I want alive!'

The first storm across the planks was a reluctant one, and met with a hail of arrows that drove most of the warriors rapidly back to the western arch once more. Only one of their number, a great warrior bearing a spiked flail and a flaming torch, still came on; almost reaching the end of the narrow walkway before a bolt from Telsyan's crossbow finally struck him down. He fell lifeless to the hard boardwalk, his torch still burning in his hand.

'The torch!' Telsyan hissed. 'Mayhap it will fire the bridge! Let no one approach it!'

And, for the moment it seemed that none upon the farther side were over anxious to attempt another crossing.

'Forward, you dogs!' their commander roared. 'There are but seven of them and a girl, and half of those wounded! Take them! A gold throne-piece to the first man across!'

Another small group of warriors charged forward, only to be repulsed with equal swiftness. And still the fallen torch smouldered on the timbers. But the flame did not seem to be catching, nor spreading with sufficient speed to do any damage to the structure. The travellers watched in silence, waiting whilst the grim warriors across the gap slowly re-ordered themselves.

'The flame will never catch!' Telsyan whispered sullenly. 'Is there no way we can aid it?'

There was no answer, the entire company silently willing the pitifully small flame to spread, to fire the bridge, and so save their lives. But the tender flame only lapped and flickered in the rising wind, half threatening to go out altogether.

There was renewed movement on the far side of the gap as another close-packed group of Tarintar warriors approached. This time they came slowly, with no shouts or war cries, large wood and leather shields held up before them to dash away missiles. There were thirty of them at least, and the narrow wooden walkway groaned as it took their weight.

'Fire now!' Zindur ordered sharply. 'And keep firing. They must not cross!'

A hail of arrows flew from the defenders' bows, but most of these were deflected upon the great oval shields, or else plunged uselessly into the river. Only one or two of the attackers fell, from arrows either to arm or leg; the rest came on remorselessly.

Keran squinted hopelessly down her bowsight. Her store of arrows was nearly spent, and it seemed no matter how many she was able to disable, others always came forward to take their place. They were almost halfway across, nearly at the spot where the fallen torch still fed its small circle of flame. She was down to her last arrow now, and this she decided to hold. It would make little difference now, but might make much later.

Alongside her, Leighor, Telsyan and Yeon were rapidly running out of missiles too, even after using up Tavolir's small supply. Their brief defiance was all but over. His arrows spent, Zindur threw down Tavolir's borrowed bow to take up his own great double-headed axe once more. Telsyan, Yeon and Leighor drew their swords to stand at his side, and a little behind these, Uhlendof stood ready with his staff. Slowly, Inanys started to back away into the darkness.

'Oh no!' Telsyan swung round with surprising speed to catch the stunted figure by sleeve and collar. 'You are far too nimble on your feet when there is trouble stirring. This time, my friend, you shall remain here with us!'

Inanys hissed like a snake, struggling fiercely to break free. But the merchant's grip was firm.

'Aye,' Zindur smiled grimly. 'Come, good brother in arms. Will you not rally to the defence of your comrades?'

'Fools!' the crookback snarled, finally managing to twist himself free of the merchant's grasp. 'Not content to await your own deaths here, you would have me accompany you!' Half in frenzy, he tore open his long, grease-stained coat, to hurl a large earthenware vessel concealed beneath into the warrior's hands.

So surprised was Zindur that he almost dropped his weapon in order to catch it. 'What is this?'

'Lamp oil, from the inn.' Inanys' lip curled contemptuously. 'It seems that I alone have brain enough to plan ahead. Use it, dolt! Use it quickly – before we all die!'

There came a roar of triumph from the bridge. The Tarintar warriors, at last realising that the travellers had used up all their missiles, began a concerted charge across the bridgeway.

Zindur removed the plug from the jar.

'Throw it, you fool!' the crookback screamed.

The mercenary glowered, but turned instantly on his heel to hurl the heavy earthenware vessel into the wooden walkway. It landed just where the fallen torch still smouldered – not half a dozen yards in front of the advancing host. The jar shattered at once, sending a sheet of scarlet flame flooding across the bridgeway, setting light to all it touched.

Suddenly all was confusion. Panicked screams rose from the bridge. The flames seemed to spread everywhere at once, licking hungrily at dry timbers that now burned bright enough even for Telsyan. Shrieking warriors crashed wildly into one another in their desperation to escape the flames, those at the front being hurled forward by the momentum of those behind. Ragged, burning shapes hurled themselves into the river below, screaming as they were swept away by the current. All but a few of the rest managed a chaotic retreat to the stone safety of the western arch, beating out scattered flames as they fled.

Four warriors, however, were unable to get back to the western arch. These managed somehow to battle their way through the fires, to stumble, gasping and choking, on to the eastern span. Seeing themselves trapped with the fugitives on the Xhendir side of the bridge, they drew their swords, the sharp, curved blades glinting in the light of the flames. At once Zindur leapt forward: Yeon, Telsyan and Leighor close behind.

There was a sharp confusion of swift, silhouetted shadows and drawn blades. Keran could make out next to nothing of what passed in the smoke-filled darkness. And with a sharp order to her to remain where she was, Uhlendof too rushed forward to assist the others.

Only then did she see it: a furtive movement opposite, in the murky shadows of the northern parapet! Her heart chilled, recognising the shape at once. Somehow one of the Rievers had managed to evade the others, and was making straight for her! He came quickly now, low and silent. She cried out for help – but her companions were still embattled, and Inanys was nowhere to be seen. She was alone!

It was too late now to use her bow. She drew her sword. It felt unexpectedly cold and heavy in her hand. And before she had time to wonder whether she would truly be able to use it, he was upon her: tall, grey and demon-eyed, a deadly grin upon his hooded face. He thought this battle already won. Perhaps he was right.

Keran stood rooted to the spot as he towered up before her, almost as if hypnotised by the dreadful, swaying form. And so she remained, even as he slowly raised his great hooked scimitar to strike her down. Yet surely he would never strike the blow . . . She could never die . . .

Only a sharp scream from somewhere behind her snapped her out of her trance in time to lift her sword; to place it between herself and the descending blow, and so save her life. The impact was bone-wrenching, nearly tearing the weapon from her grasp. She staggered backward, feeling that her arms must surely have been ripped from their sockets. But she was still alive. Still relatively unhurt. And she still held her sword.

Again the Tarintar warrior came forward. But this time she was ready, and parried the blow as Zindur had taught her. Yet she could do no more. She was not as strong as he, nor as practised. She could not hope to attack, only defend, and she knew that sooner or later she would make an error and he would break through. Again he struck out, and again. Each time, she somehow managed to find the strength and skill to parry the blow. But each time she stumbled several steps farther backward, and each blow seemed to weaken her a little more. Her back struck suddenly against the cold stone of the parapet. Now there was no further retreat. The shadow loomed before her, eyes like burning embers blazing into hers. She tried not to see them, tried to drive all out of her mind but the gleaming sword. But she could not. She knew she could not win this battle – and that knowledge betrayed her . . .

Once more the scimitar descended. And this time the sword was torn from her grasp. She watched it fly to the ground a dozen feet away, far beyond her reach. She looked up again, and screamed, seeing the Tarintar's sword poised high above her. Its next descent would bring only death . . . She held up her arm in instinctive but ineffectual defence against that dark, final blow she knew must come . . . And than it ended.

The warrior seemed to pause in mid-swing, the great sword held motionless in his linked hands. And then, like a plaster statue, he fell slowly forward, to crash into the stone roadway in front of her, Zindur's war-axe embedded deep in his back. For long seconds Keran just stood there, still and unbelieving, as the others gathered round her.

'It's all over, lass,' Zindur said, bending to retrieve his weapon. 'The three others are dealt with. You did well. Better than I had hoped.' He smiled, clapping a heavy arm about her shoulders.

She looked down at the sprawled body of her foe, yellow ichor oozing from his death-wound, and then back up to the rest of her companions. They all bore new cuts and scratches, but none looked to be too badly hurt. None but Leighor, whose right arm now hung limp and awkward at his side, blood streaming from a wound half way between elbow and shoulder.

'What has happened . . .' she began, shocked.

'It is a bad wound,' Uhlendof shook his head as he applied a rough tourniquet to staunch the bleeding. 'But we must deal with that, and much else, later. Let us go now, whilst we can.'

The others nodded. The wooden bridgeway was now a raging inferno, a pall of dark smoke rising high into the star-flecked heavens as the fires burned and spread, whipped up by the brisk south wind. In their harsh light Keran saw the bridgemaster walk to the edge of the stone chasm, his face stricken with grief and despair, until it seemed that he sorrowed more for his precious bridge than for his three injured sons. And even as he watched, there came a sudden great groan from its tortured timbers; the whole structure slowly collapsing, still flaming, into the dark, oily waters of the Malûn River. With a surprisingly gentle hiss the fires were quenched, and the two banks were sundered once more.

The rest of the company had already begun to turn away, limping painfully from the scene of the conflagration. Uhlendof supported the shaken southron while Telsyan helped the half-conscious Haflas back to his feet. Tavolir still could not walk at all, and with Zindur needed to guard their backs, it fell to

Yeon to bear the burden alone, scooping the injured musician up into long, limber arms.

Keran picked up her fallen sword and ran to follow, hearing behind her the frustrated shrieks and howls of the Riever band. A few arrows struck into the broken stonework behind them, but none had the range to do the fleeing travellers any harm, and gradually, as they passed eastward along the great stone bridge, even these sounds faded behind them.

Another great vacant archway loomed above them. And beyond that, another: the final arch before the end of the bridge at last came in sight, the dark hills of Northern Xhendir rising up behind. All was quiet. Then suddenly, there came a heavy fluttering sound overhead – like that of wind gusting through great canvas sails. There was a downrush of chill air. Keran looked up to see dark, leathern wings beating through the sky above her, and cried out in horror.

They seemed at first like bats: dark, man-sized bat-things. Two of them, wholly hidden in the darkness, until – occasionally and briefly – one was silhouetted against the moon or a cluster of stars. As she watched, a third detached itself from atop the nearest of the high stone archways.

'Haroodin!' Zindur hissed sharply. 'They fly with the Rievers! Tracking and following by night. We must hide!'

'Aye, run for the trees!' Telsyan ordered. 'We may lose them there!'

As if they too had heard the order and understood, the flying things began to attack: swooping down to rake the fleeing travellers from behind with teeth and razor-sharp talons before retreating once more into the dark safety of the skies. They were too weak and light to do much damage, but each time the travellers had to halt and turn to beat them off with swords and staves.

Close to, the creatures resembled nothing so much as winged goblins: scrawny goblin bodies covered in short greasy fur, wide goblin eyes gleaming beneath hooded eyelids, hands and arms stretched and twisted beyond all recognition to form ribbed leathern wings that bore vestigial claws upon their fringes. Sharp-taloned feet swung beneath cadaverous bodies.

There was a sudden sharp flurry of wings behind them, and Yeon's bow was gone. A screeching goblin voice rose in triumph as one of the creatures sped skyward with its prize. A scarlet weal scored the back of Yeon's neck.

He whirled, his sword still in his hand despite the burden he carried. But he was far too late to salvage his lost weapon.

'You still have one arrow left!' he beset Keran angrily. 'Use it: or give it to someone who will!'

Stung, Keran released her hold on Haflas and turned to wield her bow. The three winged things still circled above them, yet she hesitated. This was a different matter indeed from firing blindly into an advancing throng, not knowing who she hit. Were these sentient beings?

One of the creatures swooped, shrieking, towards her. And instinctively she acted: drawing her bow, taking aim, and loosing the bow-string, all in the space of a heartbeat. Before the creature had travelled ten more yards her arrow pierced its wing. Screaming horrifically, it plummeted past the parapet of the great bridge into the river beneath.

'Good shot!' Zindur growled. Yeon said nothing.

Keran breathed deep. She had no more arrows left, no other weapon but her sword. Nothing now upon which she could truly rely to defend herself. But at least the remaining Haroodin did not now attack, staying well out of bowshot as they circled high above the travellers, content just to watch them as they ran for the eastern shore. Almost carrying Leighor and Haflas along between them, the company descended at last from the ancient bridge. And still they ran, gasping with pain, exhaustion, and the sheer effort of drawing breath. They ran until they could run no more, and when they could no longer run, they walked; shaking, stumbling and gasping for breath as they made for the dark shelter of the trees.

Chapter Nineteen
SILITH RACE

Only once huddled beneath the tall firs of the Xhendir bank did they dare halt to take a last look back at the inn and bridge of Vhori. Fires still burned along the western arch of the great bridge, unseen figures bearing torches that moved back and forth in milling confusion between the vanished central span, the inn, and the forest beyond. But for the moment an untraversable gap separated the Rievers from the eastern shore and the prey they hunted.

'Come,' Telsyan said after a time. 'We cannot remain here.'

'Why not?' Haflas groaned. 'The bridge is down. The Rievers cannot cross. And I can go no farther.'

'We cannot stay!' the merchant shook his head quickly. 'Who knows what other means they have, or may yet obtain, to cross the river? If we remain here too long we will most surely regret it.'

'Then leave me,' Haflas insisted. 'I know these lands. I shall find somewhere to hide. But I can do no more running. I will only slow you, and the pain is too great.'

For a moment the travellers stared at one another in despair. Then Telsyan spoke again, turning to Leighor who sat slumped at the base of one of the thick-boled firs. 'Is there nothing you can give him?' he asked. 'Nothing that will kill the pain?'

'If you will remove my satchel,' the southron breathed painfully, 'I can look. But I have little left of much potency.' With some difficulty the satchel was removed from beneath his outer robes. With his one good arm, he searched through it, finally producing a small, precious phial. 'Apply this to Haflas's wound, and to Master Tavolir's. It is a smokesalve of Miriume. It will help ease the pain for a time.'

Wordlessly this was done, and although neither of the crossbow quarrels could be removed, the rest of the company's wounds were cleansed and bandaged. Leighor's arm appeared to be badly broken, and could only be crudely set with makeshift splints.

Alone among the company, Inanys bore not the slightest cut or mark from the night's adventure. And when the travellers strove to press him about his sudden disappearance and opportune arrival at the inn, they could at first get nothing more from him than a weak tale of his following a league or so behind them to guard their backs.

'That will not do!' Zindur turned on the crookback angrily. 'Where did you go when you abandoned us upon the ridge, foul one? Tell me that! Did you go perhaps to call upon your friend Embor-Horeoth and inform him of our path? How else did you get through his camp unharmed? You came not with us!'

'You dare accuse me of treachery!' Inanys spat. 'I, who have just saved all of your worthless lives! What gratitude! What noble reward for my endeavour! Without me, you would all still be lying drugged at the inn to which your own stupid folly led you. Aye, and in the hands of Embor-Horeoth besides! But it is ever the way of fools and the ignorant to turn upon their benefactors!'

'Worm!' the mercenary spluttered, reaching for his sword. 'You shall not call me "ignorant fool" so lightly!'

'Nay. Nay!' Telsyan interposed himself hurriedly between them. 'Let us not turn upon one another now!' He drew a breath. 'Even so, the crookback must answer, and answer well, if he wishes to remain with us.' He turned upon Inanys. 'Why, my friend, did you abandon us at Ahockûl Crest, and what had that to do with Embor-Horeoth's pursuit of us?'

'Nothing, my lord,' Inanys replied, now edging backwards. 'I was fearful. That was why I fell behind. I dared not pass through the sorcerer's lair, and so went back, trying to find a way to encircle the Riever camp through the mountains. And it took long indeed for even poor Inanys to find such a way. I must needs scramble many deep clefts and perilous scarps. When finally I gained my end, I was far behind you, and knew not which way you had gone. Only when I saw the Riever column, led by the accursed bridger, marching east, did I guess where you were, and race to your rescue.'

Telsyan snorted. 'There are still many things that I do not like about this tale of yours, crooked one. Yet your intervention was timely, I admit. And without proof of your treachery, I am loath to break an oath, whether given freely or no. You may remain with us if you will – but be careful, be very careful, for I and many others will be watching you.'

Inanys gave a bow. 'You are most generous, my lord.'

Keran was uneasy. The crookback lied: of that she was certain. Yet she knew not why. She tried once again to recall the exact order of events surrounding Inanys's reappearance at the inn that night, but the memories just would not come. She could quite clearly remember the fight with Thurin's sons, and the company's subsequent flight across the bridge. But of all that had passed before that, from the moment she had fallen asleep on top of her bed to the attack by Tvorek and his brothers, there was just a grey impenetrable haze. It was as if the memories had been stolen, locked away somewhere deep in her mind, with a key she no longer possessed. There was something very important she ought to remember, something that concerned the crookback, something that proved that he lied. Yet hard as she tried, she could not remember, and she could not tell why.

The brief rest was soon over. Telsyan rose, and wearily the others followed. Crude stretchers were made for Haflas and Tavolir from their own grey cloaks and stout poles cut from the forest. These were borne by Telsyan, Uhlendof, Zindur and Yeon. Keran helped where she could. Mainly this meant assisting Leighor, who kept watch at the rear of the column. Inanys walked in front, where Telsyan could keep a watchful eye upon him, and he in turn could serve as look-out ahead. And so the depleted company began the long slow march away from the river, and up into the Xhendir hills.

The travellers kept away from the remains of the old road, which headed straight as a die east and south towards the ancient heart of Xhendir. Instead they journeyed north, keeping to the shelter of the trees and the trackless forest. Just about daybreak they reached the crest of the first line of hills that overlooked the Malûn River. Here they slumped to the ground beneath the stunted trees, heeding Zindur's grunted warning to stay hidden in their shadow until the sun rose.

'The Haroodin can see in darkest night,' he told them. 'But the sun will rid us of them. It blinds their eyes and they cannot fly.'

Keran nodded, looking down at the Malûn River as it curved slowly around the base of the hills far beneath. She could just make out the shape of the great bridge in the pre-dawn light, and fancied for a time that she could still see a thin column of smoke rising from its central span. But of the Rievers, and of the fell creatures that flew with them, she could see no sign. There did not yet seem to be any serious attempt in hand to repair the bridge or to put boats on to the river. But that could still happen, and all too quickly for their liking.

Turning back to the company, her spirits fell once more. They looked so tired and beaten. For the first time, she began to wonder whether their quest might not fall apart before this day was over. Haflas and Tavolir looked no worse, if indeed they looked no better. But she knew that only the pain and the awkward bumpy discomfort of their travel kept them even half-aware. Leighor too was clearly in considerable pain, and threatened constantly to drift into semi-consciousness. Telsyan looked wearier and closer to breaking point that she had ever seen him. Even Zindur, in his unguarded moments, was beginning to show signs of debility from the several minor wounds he had received on the bridge. Only herself, Yeon, Telsyan and Uhlendof seemed in any fit state to travel – and of course the ever-unscathed crookback, who led a charmed life. She shuddered involuntarily. *The Dark One protects his own*: the old saying was well spoken.

Telsyan too had been looking down at the river. Now he sighed and turned away to kneel down beside the wounded miner. 'Master Haflas,' he said slowly, trying to make him hear. 'We need your help. You know this country better than any of us. Is there anywhere nearby we might find friendly folk to grant us aid and shelter?'

For a moment Haflas did not answer, and Keran began to wonder whether he had heard, but then the miner slowly shook his head. 'There are few who dwell in these lands, my lord. Even the writ of the Durian Knights does not run beyond the banks of the Malûn River. There are some scattered folk in the Bare Hills: goatherds, hermit folk who scratch a living, miners searching for gold, but little else. I have not journeyed here . . .' He lapsed once more into silence.

The merchant rose slowly to his feet. 'The Bare Hills it is then,' he announced with a sigh, turning to chide the weary travellers into motion once more.

Keran hung back to walk beside the injured Leighor at the rear of the train. 'Are you all right, southlander?' she asked.

There was a vague grunt of acknowledgement.

She looked across at him sharply. He seemed to be falling into a state akin to sleepwalking. 'What land are you from, physician?' she asked at once, hoping that conversation might help to keep him alert.

'Syrne,' he replied, his voice a little clearer. 'It lies far to the south. You would not know of it. A harsh land of sun and heat, yet fair.'

'And have you such evils there as we face in these lands?'

'There are no Rievers,' Leighor considered. 'Although there are some raiders in the wastes, and many evils of a subtler sort . . .'

'No Rievers,' she said in wonder. 'Then why did you ever choose to leave such lands to venture here?'

'I had little choice . . .' he began, but broke off as they began a long steep climb which seemed to require all his concentration, forcing him to withdraw into himself once more. At length, Keran gave up hope of receiving any reply, and struggled on in silence.

The sun was risen now, and the day looked bright and fair, with a cool eastern breeze; ideal for travel under better circumstances. And so the day remained: the bright cheerfulness of the elements in stark contrast with the broken weariness of the travellers who toiled through them, with their double burden of exhaustion and injury. The time passed slowly, with many halts for rest. They drank often from the many fast-flowing streams which coursed through this upland country, trying vainly to wash the numbing tiredness from their faces in the cool waters. Evening found them stumbling slowly down into one of the many steep wooded vales that dissected these hills.

'We can go no farther this day,' Zindur said, stooping to wash his face with water from the broad stream that hurtled down the vale. 'Let us camp here, and then we may scour for food.'

'Camp?' Uhlendof muttered irritably. 'How do we camp? We have no tents, no groundsheets, not even the barest makings of a fire!'

'We could not risk a fire, even if we had the means,' Telsyan warned. 'We can chance nothing that might give our position away.'

'You do not think they still follow?' Keran asked anxiously, her eyes rising to scour the hilltops behind.

'We cannot stake our lives that they do not,' Telsyan shrugged. 'And in our present state we would be hard put to drive off a pair of goblins, let alone a Riever war party.'

Zindur had been staring into the fast-flowing stream, deep in thought. Now he turned back to the others, who mostly lay slumped, exhausted, on the ground around him.

'Into which river will this stream flow?' he asked.

'Into the Malûn I suppose,' Uhlendof answered wearily.

'But the Malûn lies to south and west of us, does it not?'

The monk nodded.

'Then why does this stream flow north and not south?'

The monk quickly checked to see that this was true, and shrugged. 'I suppose it must run back on itself.'

'I do not think so.' Telsyan rose, staring thoughtfully towards the south. 'There is no way that these long valleys could turn back on themselves. No. If this stream runs into the Malûn, it must meet it farther north. The river must make a great westward curve around these hills as it flows south.'

'So?'

'Do you not see?' Telsyan asked impatiently. 'All the while we have thought we have been walking away from the Malûn, we have actually been cutting straight back towards it again!'

There was a long silence.

'You mean we may not be a day ahead of the Rievers?'

Zindur nodded. 'If they even suspect which way we travel, they could easily send forces north to cut us off. They will have been able to travel far faster than we along the open ground by the river.'

'Then we cannot remain here!' Uhlendof hissed.

As if in answer, there came a sudden harsh scream from somewhere to the north. Telsyan swung sharply round to see, high above the trees, two dark bat shapes circling in the embers of the passing daylight.

'Haroodin!' Zindur spat. 'They have seen us! We must fly – before they can warn their masters!'

'We cannot run far,' Uhlendof said quickly. 'We must find somewhere to hide.'

Plunging through the onrushing waters, the travellers raced for the dark eastern wall of the valley: now scrambling through tangled woods, now through thorny undergrowth, the clumsy litters of Haflas and Tavolir slowing them as they ran. Bursting through a last thin line of trees, they found a sheer cliff-wall rising up before them. The way forward was blocked.

Brambles and coiling tangled briars grew in thick, knotted clumps between cliff and forest, barring the way north. Gnarled hawthorns clung to the cliffside, their branches heavy with scarlet berries and long thorns that tore into the travellers' unprotected flesh as they tried to force a path southward. But their progress was unbearably slow, and they were still toiling desperately on as night fell.

The distant clashing of Riever spears upon shields and the high-pitched, haunting cries of the *tarintari* now carried south to them upon the wind. Somehow, the Rievers had indeed crossed the river! For some reason – perhaps only revenge for the humiliation of the previous night – the Riever army still pursued them. The sounds brought despair to the travellers' hearts: a dark hopelessness that only deepened as the sounds of pursuit drew steadily closer behind them and no sign of shelter appeared ahead. The dark, croaking cries of Haroodin now filled the valley.

There was a sudden movement somewhere to the right, within the dark mantle of the forest. The party froze, the men hurriedly lowering their burdens to draw wavering, unsteady blades that glinted in the moonlight.

Zindur fell into a low crouch. 'Who moves there?'

'Are you the ones they hunt?' A low voice, but unmistakably human, and female.

'Approach woman. Who are you?' The warrior stepped a wary pace towards the voice. 'We shall not harm you – if you mean us no ill.'

Slowly, a small shape pushed its way through the undergrowth to emerge beneath the cliff a little way ahead of them. She was of middle years, yet seemed sturdy and strong of build. Dressed entirely in dull browns and greys, she bore a large, roped bundle of wood upon her back, presumably for a fire.

'Who are you?' Zindur demanded once more.

'Guddrun, my lords,' she nodded. 'Guddrun Stoutback they call me. I dwell here alone in this vale. And who may you be, good sirs, to bring ten score of the Curséd Ones a-hunting after you?'

'We are travellers who seek shelter and safety,' Telsyan cut in quickly. 'Do you know of anywhere we may hide? For as you can see, our need is urgent.'

The wry flicker of a smile lit the woman's dour features. 'I see indeed! But you must not hurry an old woman. How do I know that I may trust you?'

'And how are we to trust you?' Yeon broke in angrily.

'That is your concern.' The woman rocked back and forward on her heels. 'Yet I need not have approached you when I saw you flying across the vale just then. If indeed I meant the Curséd Ones to have you, I could have left you – for left alone they would have you soon enough!'

'Then why do you approach us, if not to help?' Uhlendof demanded.

'I am no friend of the Curséd Ones! If you are their enemy, perhaps I shall help you.'

'We are their enemy, right enough,' Zindur said darkly. 'For they have slain all who dwelt at my lord's keep upon Silentwater; all but we few you see before you. And we who escaped have been harried near-on all the distance between there and here.'

'How many then were slain?' The women's eyes widened.

Zindur grunted softly. 'At least two score, perhaps closer to three: men and women.'

The woman shook her head, clucking anxiously to herself for a moment; and then, having apparently made up her mind, she grasped Zindur firmly by the arm, making to lead him back the way they had just come.

'Hold!' The mercenary shook himself free of her grip. 'We have seen no shelter that way.'

'It is a poor hiding place that is visible to every lumbering dolt who passes!' the woman said sharply. 'Now do you come or no?'

Zindur looked quickly back to Telsyan, who nodded wearily. 'We come,' he said.

Perhaps a quarter of an hour passed as the travellers made their way slowly back through the darkness. The screams and wild howls of the Tarintar horde grew steadily closer. Within minutes they seemed to be on top of them, rising up from every corner of the narrow valley. A crash of shields came suddenly from somewhere to their left. Again the company froze. But, thankfully, the Rievers passed on by.

'Where is this hiding place, woman?' Telsyan hissed.

'Almost there now,' Guddrun nodded encouragingly. 'Come!'

Keran began to wonder whether this woman did not, like Korzhlin, intend to lead them all into some trap. They seemed to be moving deeper and deeper towards the heart of the pursuing band. She wondered how many Rievers there must be. What had the woman said . . . ten score? Two hundred! She shuddered. If this woman did indeed intend to betray them, they had little hope of escape.

Guddrun halted abruptly and pointed upwards. Keran could see nothing but a large mass of bramble and trailing briar that hung down from a narrow ledge some twenty feet above them. A skein of thorny branches trailed down across the cliff face to merge with a solid tangle of gorse and hawthorn that rose up to meet it.

'What are we supposed to look at?' Telsyan asked irritably, and somewhat louder than he had intended. 'There is nothing here!'

In answer the dark-haired woman worked her way quickly in towards the foot of the cliff, where she began to tug at a tangled mass of hawthorn. To Keran's surprise, a large section of the thicket pulled easily away in her hands to reveal a narrow pathway through its centre. Less of a surprise, once this was revealed, was the set of earthen steps that led down from its heart into a low cave beneath the cliff. The travellers followed their guide warily down. The cave roof was only a foot or two above ground level, but the floor had been dug down some five feet below the surface, so there was height enough to accommodate the tallest of them.

Once the wounded had been negotiated into the confined space, Guddrun ran back to eradicate their tracks and draw the hedge-wall shut behind. Wearily the travellers seated themselves around the rough cave walls, only their laboured breathing echoing through the darkness. Untying her wooden bundle, Guddrun began to pile dry branches on to the embers of a dull fire that smouldered at the back of the cave.

'Will not someone see the light?' Telsyan warned quickly. 'Or the smoke at least?'

Guddrun shook her head. 'No, my lords. The smoke rises through clefts and cracks in the rock, and the flame cannot be seen from without.' Humming tunelessly to herself, she raised a battered bronze pot on to a support above the fire and began slowly to stir the contents. The travellers watched in silence – most of them half, if not fully, asleep.

Keran felt somehow safe and protected in this small cave: the sounds of the pursuit outside receding into the far distance. She felt, for the first time in many days, that it was safe to close her eyes.

Guddrun's low voice woke her. 'Take this, girl.' A bowl of thin vegetable broth was proffered her. 'I have not bowls nor spoons to feed you all. You will have to share between you.'

Keran nodded weakly.

'You will have had a long journey.' Guddrun spoke to no one in particular. 'A hard journey.'

'Aye,' Leighor nodded, seeming somewhat recovered after his rest. 'Many of us are wounded, Masters Haflas and Tavolir quite seriously. There are arrows imbedded and bones broken. I myself have an arm badly broken. It hurts far more than it should, and I fear there may be poison in the wound. Can you do anything to help us?'

The woman stepped forward to examine the injuries of the three worst afflicted of the party. She sniffed shortly and turned away. 'No.' She shook her head briskly. 'No. Leave them. There is nothing I can do for wounds such as those. Nothing in this dark. Little more when light comes. But there are some who may help upon the morrow. If we survive this night.'

'Who?' Telsyan asked. 'Where?'

'Over the hills.' Guddrun gestured vaguely towards the north-east. 'There dwell men of your ilk who may help you.'

'Then there is a way over this cliff?' Uhlendof asked quickly.

'Aye,' Guddrun nodded again. 'But it is not safe at night. At daybreak I shall show you.' She sat down beside her cookpot once more, taking occasional sips of the hot liquid.

'And this place where we lie,' the monk asked at length. 'What is it called, and how came you to bide here?'

'This country has no name,' Guddrun began quietly. 'Or if it had, it is long forgotten, for no one dwells here now: none but I. And I shall not see many more winters.'

'But you spoke of others . . .' Uhlendof broke in.

'Not here,' she shook her head. 'Over the hills. High above the Trimsil Gorge, there do they dwell. They are good enough men no doubt: but I prefer my own company.'

'Have you always dwelt alone?' Keran found herself asking.

Guddrun nodded. 'Here have I lived these thirty years alone, and here I shall remain. This is my vale. Mine alone since the elders left, and went away into the east. Only I would not go. Only I chose to remain in the vale of my birth, by the cold waters of Silith Race.'

'And was it Rievers who drove your folk away?' Uhlendof pressed.

'Aye, each winter they fell upon us in greater number, until our folk could bear no more, and the elders at last chose to leave – to fly eastward to less endangered lands. But all my kin were already slain, and I would not leave them to lie untended in this place. The elders would have made me go; but I hid here, in this cave, until they tired of their searching, and departed – whither I know not.'

'And what . . .' Keran began.

'Hush!' Zindur held up his hand, commanding silence. 'I thought I heard something!' Rocking to his feet, he crept silently towards the cave mouth.

Now Keran could hear the sounds also: cautious footsteps through the dry undergrowth outside. At once Guddrun sprinkled earth upon the fire to quench the flames.

'What is it?' Yeon and Telsyan were standing now.

There came a loud snuffling sound from somewhere close by, beyond the briars. And then a voice: deep, yet grating, in coarse, halting Durian. 'They are near. I smell the blood. They are close. Close!'

'There is nothing here,' another voice came, harsh and impatient: a westron warrior out of Khiorim. 'Naught but rock and stone and scratching briars! Let us go, before we are missed!'

'No!' the first hissed. 'They are here. They are here somewhere. I know! The blood is still warm!'

The sound of sniffing drew closer. Zindur readied his axe.

'I see nothing!' the westron repeated suddenly, almost on top of them. 'No tracks, no caves: nothing! Your crooked nose betrays you. The southerlings are far gone from this place. Let us go!'

Keran was surprised how loud and close the voices were, almost as if they were here in the cave with them.

'What can you see with your feeble eyes?' the other hissed with contempt. 'Your kind are of less use than a night toad without the flame of the sun to guide you. You see nothing, smell nothing, know nothing!'

'I smell you, sure enough, Tarintar scum! Stay if you will. I have poked through these briars long enough. I am back to report to Urnûk. If you're missing, that's your worry!' Feet crashed heavily away through the undergrowth.

For a few minutes there was no sound, and Keran began to hope that both hunters had left. Then suddenly the sniffing started again, this time even closer to the cavemouth. There was a dull scraping of briars and then silence. The travellers remained entirely still, fearing even to draw breath.

And then a spear stabbed abruptly into the cave, sweeping the thin veil of brambles aside. Keran gave out an involuntary squeal.

'So!' a voice hissed triumphantly. 'Here you are. Thinking to escape us in your little hole! You may escape the Khiorim fools. But none escapes Serghasz the hunter. Come! Come quickly. The captain awaits!' A bony hand waved them upward.

'Aye,' Zindur growled. 'Do not harm us. We surrender.'

'Surrender?' Yeon gasped. 'But there's only one . . .' His voice was stifled as Zindur's hand clamped tight across his mouth.

'We surrender,' he repeated swiftly.

Yeon wriggled fiercely free of the mercenary's grip. 'But why . . . ?'

Zindur was already on the stair.

'Throw out your weapons first!' The other commanded.

'There are wounded,' Zindur said. 'They will have to be carried up.'

'First your weapons!'

Wordlessly the warrior complied, removing sword, axe and mace to throw them to the ground at the feet of their captor. 'You too,' he nodded, turning back. 'Hold back nothing.'

'I shall not!' Yeon insisted. 'You saw what happened at the camp . . .'

'Do as you're told, lad!' Telsyan dug him sharply in the ribs. 'Quickly, and don't argue!' He in turn stepped forward to hurl his sword and crossbow out on to the open ground then, following Zindur, he climbed out into the dark clearing beyond. Knowing not why she did so, Keran followed his example.

The glade shimmered with moonlight. Their captor faced them, crossbow in hand, tall and silent across the confined space. Hooded face mostly hidden in swathes of tattered bandaging, only red glinting eyes and a thin cruel mouth were visible.

'Come on! Hurry!' Zindur hissed.

Quickly the others – all those still able to do so – followed Keran up into the moonlight. Only then did the Tarintar realise his mistake. There was very little open space between the cave and mouth and the surrounding ring of thorn, and captor and captives were pushed into closer and closer proximity.

'Stand back!' he croaked urgently, waving the crossbow from side to side to keep them all covered. 'Back in the cave. All of you! Go back!' Falling unto sudden panic, he turned anxiously to call for assistance.

In that instant Zindur struck, his left arm knocking the crossbow upward to send its steel bolt flying harmlessly off into the night, his right arm coiling about the Riever's neck and squeezing tight. Their captor's cry died in his throat. There was a sudden wrench from Zindur's arm, a dull crack, and the cowled figure slumped limply to the ground.

'It is finished,' the mercenary smiled grimly; 'and he had no chance to cry out. That was the whole purpose of our little exercise.'

'We need not have so dishonoured ourselves,' Yeon protested. 'It could have been done without deception!'

Zindur showed little patience with this argument. 'We are alive, boy. That is the point. Better a live liar than a dead fool!'

For what seemed like hours the travellers waited in the still darkness of the cave. But no one came looking for their Riever assailant, and eventually most of the company slept.

Guddrun awakened them at first light, moving from bundle to close-wrapped bundle, shaking the huddled fugitives back into the realm of pain and hunger and consciousness. Keran felt her way to the narrow cavemouth to look outside.

No sounds of pursuit now echoed through the long vale. No dark things flew overhead. Nothing at all seemed to move through the early morning stillness. For all she could tell, the valley might be clean of Rievers once more. But a nagging feeling deep within told her it was not.

'We must hurry!' Guddrun's voice rasped as she pottered with her cookpot once more. 'Soon they will search for the missing one. By then we must be gone, for the other will surely lead them here.'

Only then did Keran notice that the Riever's body no longer lay where it had fallen, in the thicket beyond the cave. She spun about in alarm.

'I hid it while you slept, girl,' Guddrun said swiftly. 'I want no Riever scouts smelling it out!' She turned away. 'Most of them are gone, I think – farther south. But some still keep watch at the head of the vale and others camp by the water.'

'Then how do we get away from here?' Telsyan asked.

'You shall see,' Guddrun promised.

Many sounds filtered through the ranks of forest trees as they made their way northward once more: sudden unidentifiable crashings through the undergrowth, that might have been forest animals – and might not. The sharp cries of birds rang from the treetops as the travellers passed beneath, and occasional distant shouts could be heard from somewhere unseen across the valley. The whole company walked a tightrope of tension, ready to freeze and draw their weapons at the snapping of a twig. As the morning wore on, the blanket of silence grew ever more oppressive, until it seemed that their every footfall could be heard on the mountaintops. Last night they had at least known roughly where their pursuers were. Now they knew nothing, and must be ready for an ambush at any moment.

Suddenly the column halted. Keran, at the rear, could not see why, for there seemed to be no obstruction ahead. But after a few moments Telsyan came back.

'There is a narrow passage here,' he told them. 'A tunnel through the cliff. It is the only way out of this vale, it seems, so we must take it. But the old woman says that it will not be long.'

'What of the stretchers?' Uhlendof asked. 'We cannot bear them through narrow twisting passages.'

'She says it is wide enough,' Telsyan shrugged. 'Besides, we have little choice.' He nodded back towards the vale. 'Consider the alternative.'

The tunnel was a natural one, formed at the base of a long narrow fissure in the cliff face; its entrance a vine-draped cleft that ran deep into the rock. In many ways it reminded Keran of the entrance to the hidden temple in the forests above Irnpool, where she had found her Ginara Stone, and that seemed to her a good omen. Yet Yeon and Zindur ahead of her, bearing one of the two stretchers, cursed and grumbled continually as they stumbled upward on the uneven footing, constantly grazing elbows and knuckles against the rough passage walls. The way itself, however, remained remarkably straight, twisting neither to left nor to right as it rose steadily through the solid rock. The passage was never in total darkness, for a dim grey light always managed to filter its way down through fissures in the arching roof from somewhere high above them. Yet this was little enough to see more than dim shadows on the path, which ran with water like the bed of a small stream. How much water ran through this passage when it rained heavily, Keran did not like to imagine.

The light from above grew steadily brighter as they rose, and Keran occasionally caught glimpses of a cloud-scattered blue sky through breaks in the arching rock. The travellers' spirits rose as they climbed. And in minutes the rock roof had fallen away entirely, transforming their narrow passage into a deep, vertically-walled ravine, open to sun and sky. The gully rose steeply for perhaps a thousand paces more. Where it eventually broke surface, the travellers could still not guess, but they toiled on, steadily and with few pauses for rest, encouraged by the prospect of a safe haven ahead.

They were all sweating profusely when they finally emerged from the ravine, and the breath of fresh air which hit them as they clambered the last few rocky feet to the surface came as a welcome deliverance. Keran gasped at the view she now saw before her. They were high up; on the flanks of a steep, rocky hillside, looking down upon the green vale of Silith Race far below. Beneath her, she could see the dense walls of forest that lined the vale, and the long ridges of forested hills rising up behind to south and west. She even fancied that she caught a glimpse of the sun reflecting off the gleaming surface of the Malûn River, far away between the hills.

Small brown dots moved upon the sparse patches of open ground along the banks of Silith Race. Rievers. There was a rough encampment downstream, and from it small groups of dark specks – hunting parties – were spreading out in all directions across the vale.

'Do you think they can see us?' she whispered to Uhlendof, feeling painfully exposed upon this open hillside.

'Small chance of that,' Guddrun responded briskly, her voice seeming alarmingly loud – as if it might somehow carry all the way down to the questing Rievers below. 'The eyes of the Curséd Ones see not well in the sunlight, and the greys that we wear lie well against the mountainside. Aye, and even if they do see us, they know not how to follow. Come!' She waved them onward and upward. 'We have far to go before we rest again.'

The hill rose another six or seven hundred feet before reaching its summit, a narrow pass between two bald humps of rock. They continued to follow the stony path of the rivulet as they climbed, for here the way was easier than elsewhere, if still a little loose and unstable. Keran, Guddrun and even Inanys were now required to assist the others as they struggled uphill with the heavy litters. Halfway up Haflas offered to try and walk, but he could manage only a few short steps before he grew too dizzy to struggle further, and had to be carried once more.

Yet once at the summit, a vista of towering majesty, magnificent and unforgettable, opened up. As far as the eye could see, range upon range of bare, stony mountains towered up before them. The nearer ones were low and rounded like their own; those farthest away, into the purple distances of the north, towering and high-pinnacled, soft caps of piercing white snow already crowning their peaks, sparkling like silver fire against the deep blue of the sky.

'It is beautiful!' Uhlendof sighed, shaking his head.

Yet in all of the vast, wild expanse that lay before them, Keran could detect no sign of human life, nor any single form of human husbandry or habitation.

'What have you brought us to?' Telsyan gasped. 'Where can we hope to find aid or shelter in such a wilderness as this? Where do you lead us?'

'You shall see,' Guddrun chuckled softly. 'Little safety would there be, should it lie for all to see! But come! You must go quick, if you would be there by nightfall.'

Wearily the travellers set off again, this time upon a long downward traverse, stumbling down boulder-strewn slopes of dizzying steepness towards a barren vale some half a thousand feet beneath them. Their knees straining with each uncertain step, the muscles of their legs screamed their protestations at the effort.

The vale itself was high and cold. Yet once in its bleak embrace, there were at least a few scattered patches of hardy, close-cropped mountain grass to walk on, and a small burn to mark their way as it tumbled gently down towards the north-east. The going was easier now, and the best of the day still lay before them as the sun began slowly to warm the high, upland pastures. Scattered animal droppings bore witness that this place was not entirely lifeless, and occasionally one or other of the travellers might catch sight of a shaggy, mountain goat or perhaps a lone stag, watching them curiously from some precipitous granite crag.

'If I had but a single arrow,' Zindur promised, 'our fasting would end this moment!' But without the wherewithal to test this claim, his boasting came to naught.

Early in the afternoon the travellers came down into a deep gorge, broad and high-walled, through which a mighty torrent raced. River and gorge ran a sharply twisting path into the north-west. The trapped river was no more than a dozen yards across, yet swift and powerful, its waters scouring deep into the mountainside as they fled into the west.

'This is the River Trimsil,' Guddrun told them. 'We shall follow its path for a while.' Offering no further explanation, she turned sharply upstream, where a rocky pathway ran beneath the eastern wall of the gorge, only feet above the raging waters.

Knowing better than to argue, the travellers followed her along the twisting path. The river ran a narrowing course between the mountains. The canyon walls rose higher and higher above them as they climbed, closing in ever tighter until the company began to feel that they walked into a giant's maw: the great rocky teeth all about them, the endless river raging through its dark gullet. Keran found herself shivering. The gorge walls had long since cut off direct sunlight, and with it they had stolen all the warmth of the dying day. A freezing wind swept down the canyon towards them, bearing clouds of ice-cold spray from falls and rapids as yet unseen. She was tired now, and hungry. It was well into the afternoon, and the tiny drop of thin soup she had swallowed at dawn had done little to sustain her. Yet she dared not complain, and laboured on in silence.

All but Leighor had now to take their turn with one or other of the stretchers, so that each might have some relief from the back-breaking labour. Only Zindur always refused to be replaced when his turn came – as if he were trying to prove something to them all, or to himself, of his continued fitness. The day was fading now, and already night was beginning to fall, cold and grey, all about them. Keran glanced nervously into the darkening sky, dreading to see the familiar black-winged shapes of the Haroodin circling above them: a sight that must mean that the Rievers still followed close behind. But to her relief she saw nothing but a lone, mountain hawk circling against the vault of the sky.

And then, unexpectedly, around a sharp bend in the gorge, the end of their long agony came finally in sight.

A slight stone footbridge, just broad enough for one man and a pack-mule to cross, carried their path over to the far bank, where it began a sharp climb away from the torrent. The water racing beneath was turbulent and filled with power. Halfway across, Keran halted to look upstream. Cold spray soaked her through. But through all the noise and mist something caught her eye. She was sure that she could see a meeting of rivers some half a league ahead of them, two high gorges merging to form the single great channel through which they walked. And there, high upon a tall pinnacle of rock between the two rivers, stood a great building, or perhaps a cluster of lesser buildings.

'Look!' she shouted, pointing up into the mists.

Startled, the travellers turned to follow her gaze. And in that instant clouds parted somewhere high above them to bathe the distant buildings in the last crimson glow of the setting sun, picking out red roofs, high-domed towers and long, rose-pink halls.

'Aye,' Guddrun nodded with satisfaction. 'That is where we shall take our rest. The place that those who dwell within name Valmaalina.'

Chapter Twenty
VALMAALINA

Leighor screamed. Pain, sharp, mind-jarring pain, coursed through his body like fire, threatening to tear his being asunder. It endured for one long, endless moment; and then, suddenly, was past. Not gone entirely, but subsided into a low, nagging ache that centred itself somewhere in the middle of his upper arm.

'There!' a satisfied voice came from somewhere to his right. 'It is done. The worst is over.'

Leighor felt his arm being bound tightly with splints and bandages, each successive layer painstakingly pinned and knotted into place.

'It is as I said,' the voice continued. 'The arm was badly set, and needed to be altered. A little longer as it was and you could have been crippled for life. But now, with a lot of rest and a little good fortune you should be as right as rain again in a few weeks.'

'Weeks!' Leighor groaned. 'But the journey ... We have to get to Darien ...'

'I would not advise further travel in your present condition,' the other said firmly.

Leighor twisted on his pallet, irritated at being unable to see the man who spoke to him. But his face was turned in towards the whitewashed wall, and for some reason he seemed unable to move.

'Stay still!' the voice said sharply. 'They say you are a physician. Then you should know better than that! You are strapped down for your own safety. Whatever caused your injury left some poison in the wound, and it would not heal until we used a little agent of our own.'

'What was in it?' Leighor asked, professional curiosity overcoming the pain and the giddy spinning in his head.

'Now is not the time,' the other said. 'Perhaps when you are a little better we shall have occasion to talk of such things.'

Two pairs of hands unbound Leighor and gently raised him into a more comfortable position. For the first time the southron had the opportunity to see his torturer/benefactors. There were two men, both in priestly robes of brown and black. Their faces, though lined and weatherworn, seemed serene and at peace with the world.

'Where are we?' he demanded, although he already knew the answer in general, if not precisely.

'Valmaalina,' the taller of the two replied. 'High cloister of the servants of the One. You and all your friends are safe here for as long as you choose to remain with us.'

'Monks . . .' Leighor repeated dreamily; '. . . serving the One. Are you then Mallenians, like our good comrade Uhlendof?'

The other smiled. 'Not Mallenians, they are a worldly order indeed; although perhaps in some ways we serve the same goal. But ours is a separate path.'

'I see,' Leighor nodded, not exactly sure whether he did or not. 'Yet you are friends to the woman who brought us here.'

'We know her,' the younger man spoke. 'In many ways she is much like ourselves, desiring only separation from the evils of the world. She has already departed to return to her valley.'

'And we too must depart,' the other added quickly. 'Now that you are awake you must eat, and then later perhaps you may speak to your friends.'

With a whisper of sandalled feet on the polished floor they were gone, leaving Leighor alone in the airy whitewashed chamber. For a moment he studied his newly splinted arm, but there was little he could complain of in the manner of his treatment, and he turned his attention to the chamber of his incarceration and its square, white-painted windows. He wished he were able just to stand up and look out, to see exactly where he was. He could remember little of the past days: little but the fear, and the need constantly to fly from their remorseless pursuers. And what had happened to those pursuers? The Haroodin, the Rievers, the dread Tarintarmen? Had they indeed eluded them? Or did the raiders still hunt them, somewhere out there beyond those windows?

His train of thought was broken by the arrival of his meal, a vegetable broth remarkably similar to that which the hermit woman had given them in her cave. He ate it with surprising relish, finding himself disappointed when, all too quickly, it was gone. The door to his sick-chamber opened again, and there were Telsyan, Zindur and Uhlendof. They crowded, smiling, about his bed; and although they tried to hide it, the concern upon their faces was obvious.

'How do you feel?' Uhlendof asked.

'Well enough.' Leighor tried to smile. 'The brothers have treated my wounds and re-set my arm, although they spoke of poison in the wound.'

'That should not trouble you greatly, southron,' Zindur laughed. 'I too was cut by the Tarintar swords, remember? – and I am not ill.' He lifted a bandaged arm. 'No, if there was any bad poison in your wound it should have killed you long before this.'

'I do not know if that is precisely the kind of reassurance he needs at this moment,' Telsyan smiled.

'How are Tavolir and Haflas?' Leighor asked. 'How do they fare?'

'Quite well,' Uhlendof nodded. 'Very well, considering their injuries. Both awoke before you did. They are in separate rooms along the hall. Both arrows are out, but bones are shattered, much blood has been lost, and that will take time to heal. Neither will be able to travel for many weeks.'

'So what of our quest?'

'We must go on, of course,' Telsyan said shortly. 'We can tarry here but a day or two, at the most. And then those who are able must journey onward.'

'And I?'

There was silence.

'We shall see how you progress,' Uhlendof said quickly.

'Tomorrow we meet with the High Brother,' Telsyan added. 'And he will tell us how far we must travel and what aid he can give us. Perhaps if you are well enough, you will be able to join us then.'

'But for now you must rest,' Uhlendof insisted. 'We are only allowed to see you for a few minutes, and we must go.'

'What of our pursuers?' Leighor asked hurriedly, determined not to let them go before he had an answer to this, his most urgent question. 'Have they managed to follow us here? Is this place safe?'

'Safe enough,' Zindur assured him. 'These brothers may speak of peace, but their abbey could be defended by five good men against an army. Any approach can be seen a league off along the great ravine, and there is but one narrow stairway that leads upward. If Silentwater had had such defences we would have held it yet!'

'And besides,' Uhlendof added, 'we have seen no sign of Rievers or Haroodin since we left Silith Vale. I think we have lost them.'

Thus reassured, and perhaps drugged by something the brothers had put in his broth, Leighor slept.

The next morning Leighor waited impatiently for one of the brothers to come and assist him. So much depended on his being able to walk; to walk well enough to convince the others that he was fit to accompany them. All that, in a day or two at most. He must make those first few steps today.

Before he had chanced to fall into the web of Lord Darvir's intrigues and so been precipitated into this desperate adventure, he had been almost content with his life as a purposeless itinerant. But now, he discovered, somewhat to his surprise, that had changed. He himself had changed. He knew now that he could not simply fall back into his old way of life. Nor could he lie still in his bed while others fought, whilst others decided his destiny and that of all who dwelt in these lands. That would be torture beyond bearing. To lie helpless here, wondering whether his companions lived or died, went on to triumph or disaster: and not to know . . .

'Do not chafe against bonds you can do nothing to break,' a young brother smiled, suddenly beside him. 'If you can walk, it is the will of the deity. If not, it is his will also, and you must accept it. Whichever it be, the eternal will is preserved, and all shall be to the good. Now let me help you.'

Once he was on his feet, Leighor found to his surprise that his legs felt quite firm beneath him; and only a sense of almost overwhelming dizziness made him seek the continuing support of the young brother as they walked slowly across the room. The dizziness seemed to centre in his injured arm and flow up from there – a dark, churning cloud, ever threatening to roll forward and overwhelm him entirely.

'You do very well,' his supporter said. 'Can you go on?'

'Yes,' Leighor nodded. 'I would like to see my companions.'

'Are you sure you can walk so far?'

'Aye,' Leighor insisted. 'I must learn. My legs are undamaged. They will bear me.'

Slowly, painfully, Leighor and his young helper worked their way out of the chamber, along several whitewashed corridors, and down a flight of broad stone steps. They rested often, pausing to let Leighor regain his breath every few dozen paces. And eventually he had his reward: a low wooden door opening before him to reveal a sparsely furnished chamber with a peat fire smouldering in one corner. There, looking up, surprised to see him, were all six of his uninjured companions.

'My friend, you are unwell . . .' Uhlendof rose hurriedly from the cushioned bench he occupied by the fire. 'How did you get here?'

'I walked,' Leighor answered hazily.

'Then you should not have done so,' Telsyan said reprovingly. 'By such foolishness you only delay your own recovery.'

'He is not ill,' Zindur cut in, 'only injured – as I have been many times. And what is best for a man at such times is good food and strong ale, not mollycoddling and cold broth. Let him remain if he wishes.'

'He desired to be with you,' the young brother added, 'and he will heal as well here as in his bed. When he wishes to return to his chamber you may send for me.' Silently he withdrew.

Leighor sat down next to the hearth, and soon began to feel somewhat more alert. The rest and the warmth of the fire began to drive away the black cloud of darkness and confusion that still lurked on the edges of his mind, pushing it back to its own dark corner where he hoped it might be contained, or at least lie dormant for a while.

'You have missed much that is good, Master Leighor,' Keran offered him a sweetmeat, which he refused. 'This is a beautiful place, one such as I never dreamed existed in these lands.'

'Aye,' Uhlendof agreed. 'We are surrounded here by mountains, and set high above the fairest of lakes. When you feel a little stronger we shall help you to the window and show you all there is to see.'

'I am strong enough now,' Leighor insisted stubbornly. 'I would much like to see what country surrounds us, and how we lie.' He made to rise, and reluctantly Uhlendof helped him to his feet, guiding him to the high window.

'This chamber is set in the outer wall of the main building,' Uhlendof told him. 'From here we can look right down across the lake, and to the mountains beyond.'

Indeed the view fell away with such alarming suddenness that it brought Leighor's vertigo racing back. He clung grimly to the wooden windowsill, fearing irrationally that he might somehow plummet into the gaping void in front of him. He tried to concentrate upon the topography.

Far beneath him lay a lake, small in comparison with the tree-girt monsters of Hathanwild, but still more than half a league across. In shape it was a rough oval, with several small fingers that probed outwards from its rim to nestle between the feet of the mountains. Girded by steep meadows, and surrounded by snowcapped peaks; the late morning sun glinted across its surface, burnishing it with silver.

'That is Shiningwater,' a soft voice came suddenly from behind them. 'The lake of Valmaalina.' The travellers spun sharply around to face the new arrival, who had entered the room so silently that none had noticed his coming.

He was a tall man, gaunt and ascetic of aspect, yet with an amiable face that spoke of a deep sense of humour and a basic satisfaction with the world. His age Leighor could not guess, for it could have lain anywhere between fifty and eighty. His hair, from what could be seen beneath the cowl of his dark robe, was of a hard, steely grey.

'Do not let me distract you,' he smiled quickly. 'For you admire a noble vista which is both our pride and our joy. In fact let me be your teacher, and name for you all that you see. You are fortunate indeed that the weather is so fair,' he nodded, approaching the window. 'For you would see but little if we had the rains and mists that are more normal at this season. But today all the kings of the eastern ranges are here, attired in their finest raiment, for you to look upon.' He raised a finger to the glass, pointing out each feature in turn. 'Below, as we look toward the north and east, you can see Shiningwater. The river that flows from its south-western corner is the Trimsil, whose course you followed to come to this place. We stand now upon a high pinnacle, between the gorge of the Trimsil to the east, and that of the River Thurgond which feeds into it from the west, and guards our nether flank.

'The three low peaks that face us beyond the lake are the three sisters, Desan, Deresen and Desuna. Legend has it that these were three witches who once dwelt at the far end of the lake and were turned to stone by the goddess Celatha Ghemirieth for their impudence. Behind them you may see Fara with her double peak, and grey-walled Malthren with his head in the clouds. Farther south, the tall, sharp peaks with snow on their summits are Fangthrim, the many turretted, and Edothrim the mighty; and there, closest to the lake, is their brother, the slumberer, Enthrim. But the highest mountains lie to the north: Lollfin, whose flanks run down into the lake waters; and behind him, Sullagorn, the white mountain . . .'

'All the mountains to the north are snowcapped,' Yeon broke in suddenly, 'but few to the south. Is it because the northern mountains are higher?'

'Yes,' the other nodded. 'The northern mountains are much the greater. They draw the snow and the cold winds down upon them. It is a cruel country for travel . . . But that, it seems, is where you still intend to venture . . .'

'Aye,' Telsyan admitted. 'That is so. We have an urgent errand that calls us north, and we must be in Darien before the snows.'

'Brother Hindar has told me of your quest,' the other replied quickly. 'And of your search for the testament of Eridar. Yet I feel it my duty to advise you not to attempt such a journey. There will be few more days as fair as this one before winter is upon us, and when winter falls in these climes, she falls quickly. Besides, it is said that there is little welcome in Darien these days for uninvited travellers.'

'Perhaps,' Telsyan grunted. 'But much as we might prefer it otherwise, we cannot linger here. Our errand is of prime urgency and will brook no further delays. Surely you have knowledge of the evils now astir in these northlands and in the Varroain lands beyond? You have seen the Riever hordes that pour through these dark forests. You have heard of the Mage Metal, *harrunor*, whose purposes seem ever turned to those of evil . . .'

'I have heard of all these things,' the elder nodded slowly. 'And I have been told your story by those who first met you at the gates and upon the stair. Indeed I know much of these matters, and many others, that might surprise you . . .'

'Then you will understand the importance of our quest,' Telsyan insisted.

'I understand the importance of these events, yes,' the other sighed. 'But whether your quest is as important as you believe, I do not know. You may in some small way be able to delay or alter what is to come. You may not. Yet you will gain nothing by undue haste.'

'But you do not understand!' Yeon broke in. 'If the proxy vote of the Sielders is not in High Tershelline by the spring, then the wrong man may become High Lord of the Varroain, and all will be lost!'

'Much, perhaps,' the elder said softly, 'but not all. Arminor and Misan may be but two sides to the same coin. One may bring things to a head a little sooner, perhaps, but in the long view it may matter little which is chosen. Come,' he waved them back to the benches beside the fire, seating himself upon a high stool between. 'There is much that you must learn of the ways of our little world.

'I am the elder, the High Brother of Valmaalina,' their host continued. 'We are a small brotherhood and have dwelt in this place for but a few hundred years. Yet our order is an ancient one, and these mountains more ancient still. How long have these mountains stood? How long indeed have men walked the face of the earth? We know not. But we know that all these things were created, and may only be destroyed, as it pleases the eternal will. Perhaps all of these lands are meant to fall beneath the dominion of evil for a time. But even if all must fall, the rule of evil cannot endure for longer than the deity will permit.'

'But surely you cannot suggest that we just sit back and wait to be overwhelmed?' Telsyan's voice rose impatiently.

'We do not sit back,' the elder said firmly. 'Ours is a lifelong duty of prayer. A burden that bears with it great responsibility. This whole monastery is a vast engine of prayer to the One. Prayer which sustains much in this world, and which fuels many struggles of which you know but little.'

'But it is said that the One has little interest in the affairs of men,' Zindur broke in. 'That prayer is better directed to other gods?'

'Not at all,' their host smiled. 'The other gods, as you call them, are but wayward children of the One. The gods of the first creation: Arul, Helior, Ethimathé and Ginara, were banished forever from the earth. Only the blasphemous Heliards would deny this. The gods of the second creation are far weaker than these. They have many differing names in many lands, although you might know some of them as Thall, Eldalis, Nohul or Skereor. None has the power or the wisdom of the One, although their cultists might betimes imagine so. Many are but pawns of the Evil One. Their worship is false.'

'This is all very well,' Telsyan broke in abruptly. 'But it gets us precisely nowhere! What we wish to know is whether you will help us in our errand, or no!'

The High Brother shook his head. 'You trust too much to your own emotions, my child; to your own simple view of things. The world works in other ways than those of human will, and for other reasons. Yet I will not try to halt you in your endeavour, for that too would be to interfere. Mayhap you have indeed been chosen for some great work, greater even than you may imagine. Therefore I only advise: do not be overhasty, do not be foolhardy, do not tempt the forces that watch over you.'

He rose, turning suddenly to stare at Uhlendof. 'Frankly I am surprised to see a monk, even of your sort, engaged in such worldly business!'

'As you say, the One may be served in many ways,' Uhlendof answered. 'Your path is your own, and who am I to gainsay it? Truly there are far too few places as fair as this upon the earth. But we have the gift of free will, or if you will, the curse; and we must determine our actions as the need arises.

For sometimes to do nothing is as positive an act as any other.'

'To pray and to contemplate the unity of the One is not to do nothing!' the elder frowned. 'Yet I take your point. We shall do all in our power to assist you, once your choice is made. You may stay here for as long as you wish; and that is what I hope you will finally decide to do – at least until the spring, when it is safe to journey abroad once more. But if your destiny is indeed to venture north through the mountains upon your quest, then I shall pray that the One may smooth your path, and go with you through the dangers.'

'For that we give you thanks indeed.' Uhlendof rose.

The elder nodded. 'Perhaps on the morrow I shall have time to speak with you again. But until then I must bid you farewell.' He made a brief bow and was gone, the door clicking shut behind him.

'Well?' Uhlendof asked, as soon as they were alone once more. 'What shall we do? Take his advice and remain here for the winter, or move on as soon as we may?'

'We go on, of course,' Telsyan said brusquely. 'We have no reason to remain, other than our imagined safety – and that may prove to be nine parts illusion. The whole of our task lies still before us, unaccomplished.'

'Then when do we leave?' Yeon asked.

'As soon as possible,' the merchant went on. 'If we are to leave, it must be before the weather fails. This is a pleasant place, but it is folly to remain here. I am afraid that these lost brothers know little of the true ways of the world. We are rested; anyway, as rested as we shall be. I would leave tomorrow; but that would be too abrupt, and there are provisions to organise. But it must be the day after.'

'And what of the wounded?'

'I have already spoken with Haflas and Tavolir,' the merchant turned to stare into the fire; 'and they have both agreed to remain. Haflas might be well enough to come with us in a week or so, but we cannot delay that long. And anyway, the musician will not be able to walk for many weeks. So Haflas has agreed to remain here with him, and they will journey south in the spring to meet us in High Tershelline.'

'You seem to have this all organised,' Uhlendof sniffed.

'I have not been idle,' Telsyan nodded. 'And it is well so. We have been spared thus far through good fortune, and perhaps yon High Brother is right when he says we have been spared for a purpose. So then, let us be about it, and see that this providence goes unwasted.'

The monk nodded. 'But what of you, friend Leighor?' He turned to look down at the injured herbalist in his seat. 'Are you yet well enough to continue with us; or would it be better for you to remain here with Tavolir and Haflas?'

'I would come with you,' Leighor answered firmly. 'If that can be at all possible. I feel that I have a part in this quest which is not yet done. I would see it to its end.'

'Aye, well enough said,' the merchant admitted. 'But you are weak, although it is but one arm that is damaged. We shall have to see how well you are upon the day. You have made much progress, but if you are then no better than you are now, I should have to say that you were unfit for travel and must remain behind.'

Glumly Leighor nodded.

Next day, however, he felt a good deal better. The pain in his arm had greatly decreased, and the lesser wounds to his side seemed also to be healing well, when the brothers re-bandaged them that morning. For the first time in many weeks he attempted a reading of the *Rudäis*, to determine his future; but the pieces fell irregularly, and the prediction gave him scant encouragement, only hinting at vague dangers and hidden obstacles ahead. He descended unaided to eat a light breakfast with his companions, feeling sure enough on his feet to agree to accompany them on a brief tour of the abbey and its outbuildings. He carried Erchoron's staff with him for support, but used it as sparingly as possible – at least in the sight of the others.

Once again the High Brother was their guide, conducting the travellers through dark-walled cloisters and high, candlelit chapels that echoed to the chill sound of plainsong. Once they passed through a great library where brothers worked upon vellum manuscripts in ordered rows beneath the shadow of the mountains. Here Uhlendof would have stopped awhile, to peruse some of the histories and the older volumes, but the elder seemed in a hurry to move on, and they saw no more of these things.

Halfway through the lengthy tour Leighor began to flag. His earlier dizziness was returning and he found himself rapidly losing interest in anything but finding a safe place to sit and rest.

They had come out suddenly on to one of the high outer walls that surrounded the interconnected maze of chapels, dwellings and workshops that was the abbey of Valmaalina. It appeared that they would have to walk along it to reach the nearest of the high abbey towers. He could not have found a worse place to suffer an attack of giddiness! On one side they overlooked one of the large inner courtyards, on the other only a low parapet separated them from a dizzying drop into the stony gorge of the Thurgond far below.

He stumbled, clinging desperately to the crumbling masonry. A small piece broke away from the top of the parapet to tumble slowly towards the hurtling waters far below. He watched in grim fascination as it bounced off the ravine walls, shattering into a dozen fragments before finally being swallowed by the Thurgond.

Telsyan and Uhlendof rushed back to help him.

'I am all right,' Leighor insisted, trying to sound better than he was. 'A little dizziness, that's all. It will pass.'

'Do you wish to be taken back down?'

'No.' He shook his head. 'I shall rest when we are at the top, if you will help me.'

Uhlendof and the merchant exchanged glances, but they did as he requested, helping him the rest of the way along the wall and then up the precipitous open stairway that led to the tower. Here, beneath its gilded onion dome, an open platform overlooked the surrounding country. Hard wooden benches lined the walls. Leighor slumped thankfully on to the nearest of these, struggling to regain his breath and sense of balance. Yet this was no mean task.

A sharp breeze swept through the small enclosure, with the smell of snow upon it. The altitude was dizzying. High mountains hemmed them in on all sides, towering so impossibly high that it seemed that one must surely topple forward to crush them all. They induced a special kind of vertigo all their own, so that he dared not look far beyond the sturdy wooden framework of the tower.

The others still clustered around him. He waved them irritably away, saying that he would recover far better if left on his own for a while. He despised himself for being so weak. His body mocked him, ridiculed his efforts to prove himself fit enough for the onward journey. He could no longer walk the long, hard distances that would be required in order to reach Darien in time. All too soon he would have to admit that fact: admit that he would most probably have to remain here until the spring . . .

He looked up, trying to take more of an interest in what was happening around him. The High Brother seemed to be explaining something. He held a bird in his hands; and for the first time Leighor realised that there were other birds flying above them, within the high dome; grey and white doves that filled the air with the fluttering of wings and with their soft, reproachful calls. The bird in the High Brother's hands struggled gently as he removed a scrap of parchment that had been attached, by means of a small metal band, to one of its legs.

'The birds are from various houses of our brotherhood set about the eastern lands. Each will return to its home once released, and they bear with them news and messages of import.' He pointed upwards. 'When a bird enters the loft it rings a bell below, and the nearest brother comes up here to release it from the trap and remove the message. It is a system that works well.'

Telsyan looked on with interest. 'How long would it take one of those birds to reach Darien or Tershelline?'

'A day to Darien, two or three to Tershelline, at the most.'

'Who else knows of this?'

The elder smiled. 'The principle is well known, but it takes great patience to train the birds, and then to transport them to places where they will be of use; and that is a rare thing in these days.'

'And does this bird bear any message?' Yeon asked.

'Indeed it does,' the elder nodded, unwrapping the thin scrap of parchment as he released the dove into the dark space of the loft. 'It is from three of our order who live by the shores of the Eastern Sea, a hundred leagues and more beyond the mountains. They have little news: one of them has had the fever, the seas have been high and the frosts are early. They think it will be a bad winter.' He looked further down the tiny page, his eyes squinting as he struggled to read the minute writing. He nodded slowly. 'They have been much troubled by goblins who dwell in caves beneath the sea cliffs. The sand dwellers have increased greatly in number, and grow daily in viciousness . . .' He sighed. 'It is as I feared. The brothers fear for their lives, and debate whether or not to try to return before the snows.'

'It seems that the forces of the dark now hold sway even to the edges of the eastern shore.' Uhlendof noted grimly.

'I have told you that the task you face is a stern one,' the High Brother responded. 'You fight an enemy whose reach is long, and whose power is great. Take care.' He turned away to climb the narrow ladder into the loft. When he descended again a small, blue-grey dove was cupped between his hands.

'Have you made your decision?' he asked, looking hard at Telsyan and Uhlendof, who stood before the assembled company.

'We have,' the merchant answered firmly.

'And it is to leave?'

Telsyan nodded.

'I did not doubt it.' The High Brother seemed at that moment very old and frail. 'It is not the choice that I had hoped you would make, for you face a hard journey of many dangers. However we shall keep our promise, and give you what aid we may. You shall have whatever provisions and equipment we can spare, and all other help we may provide for you. This we give freely, in the hope that a little good may be added to the balance thereby.'

'For this we are deeply grateful . . .' Telsyan began. But the elder would hear no more.

'No. No. It is but our duty. There are other matters more important.' He motioned Telsyan and Uhlendof to one side, out of the others' hearing. 'It is of the crookback I speak,' he whispered. 'The one you term Inanys. I see something within him dark and evil. I am sure that he schemes in some manner to betray you. If you would ensure your safety I would beg you to leave him behind; here with us. If you wish we shall detain him here until you are safe away.'

'That we would gladly do,' Uhlendof replied quickly. 'But we have pledged him our oath that he may remain with us as long as he wishes.'

'You have sworn?'

Monk and merchant both nodded.

'That was foolish. Most foolish. Yet if you have made an oath, you must not break it. That would bring naught but greatest ill-fortune upon you, perhaps even the anger of the One himself. No, only if you can trick him into parting with you of his own free will must you send him away. But beware. Guard yourselves!'

He turned back abruptly to the others. 'As I have been telling your companions,' he raised the dove aloft in both hands, 'this bird is destined for the agent of our order in Tershelline. I have asked him to give whatever help he can to those who come bearing this.' He handed a small bronze seal-ring to Uhlendof. 'The ring is to be given to the agent of our order, should you come safely to Tershelline in the spring as you plan. I have said nothing else in my message to identify you, and have written nothing of your errand. Is there anything you wish me to add?'

'No,' Telsyan said firmly. 'The less that is known in advance of our coming, the better. Leave it as it is.'

The older figure nodded and secured the message. When he was ready, he turned to the south-west, holding the dove in both hands before him. Saying a short blessing over it, he spread his hands, releasing it to the care of the four winds.

The bird seemed joyous to be free at last, taking to the air in a rush of wings. It soared high above the straggling buildings of Valmaalina, circling them and the shining lake several times before flying finally beyond the travellers' vision, southward into the sun.

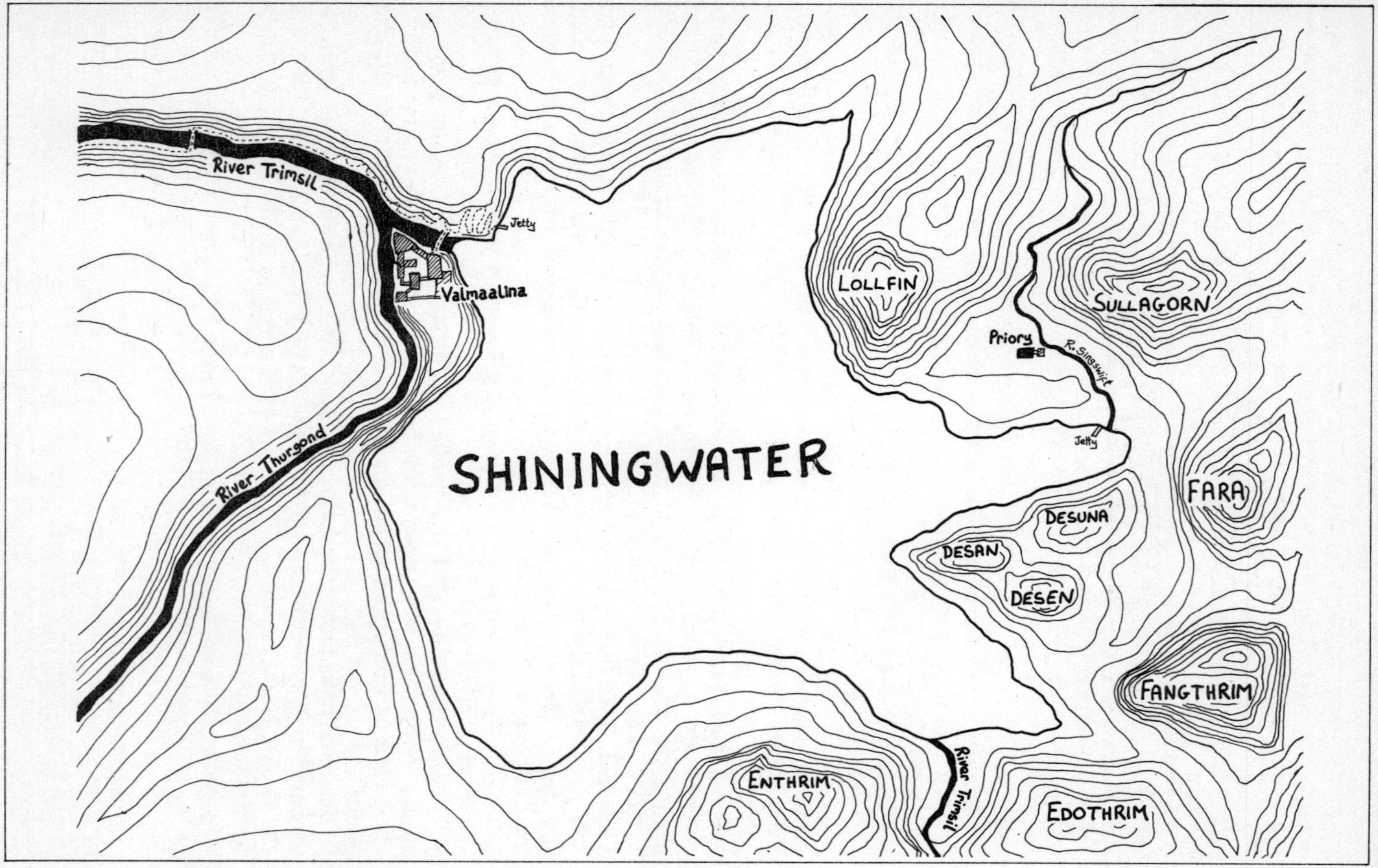
SHININGWATER
River Trimsil
Jetty
Valmaalina
River Thurgond
LOLLFIN
SULLAGORN
Priory
R. Singswift
Jetty
FARA
DESUNA
DESAN
DESEN
FANGTHRIM
ENTHRIM
River Trimsil
EDOTHRIM

Part Four
CITADEL

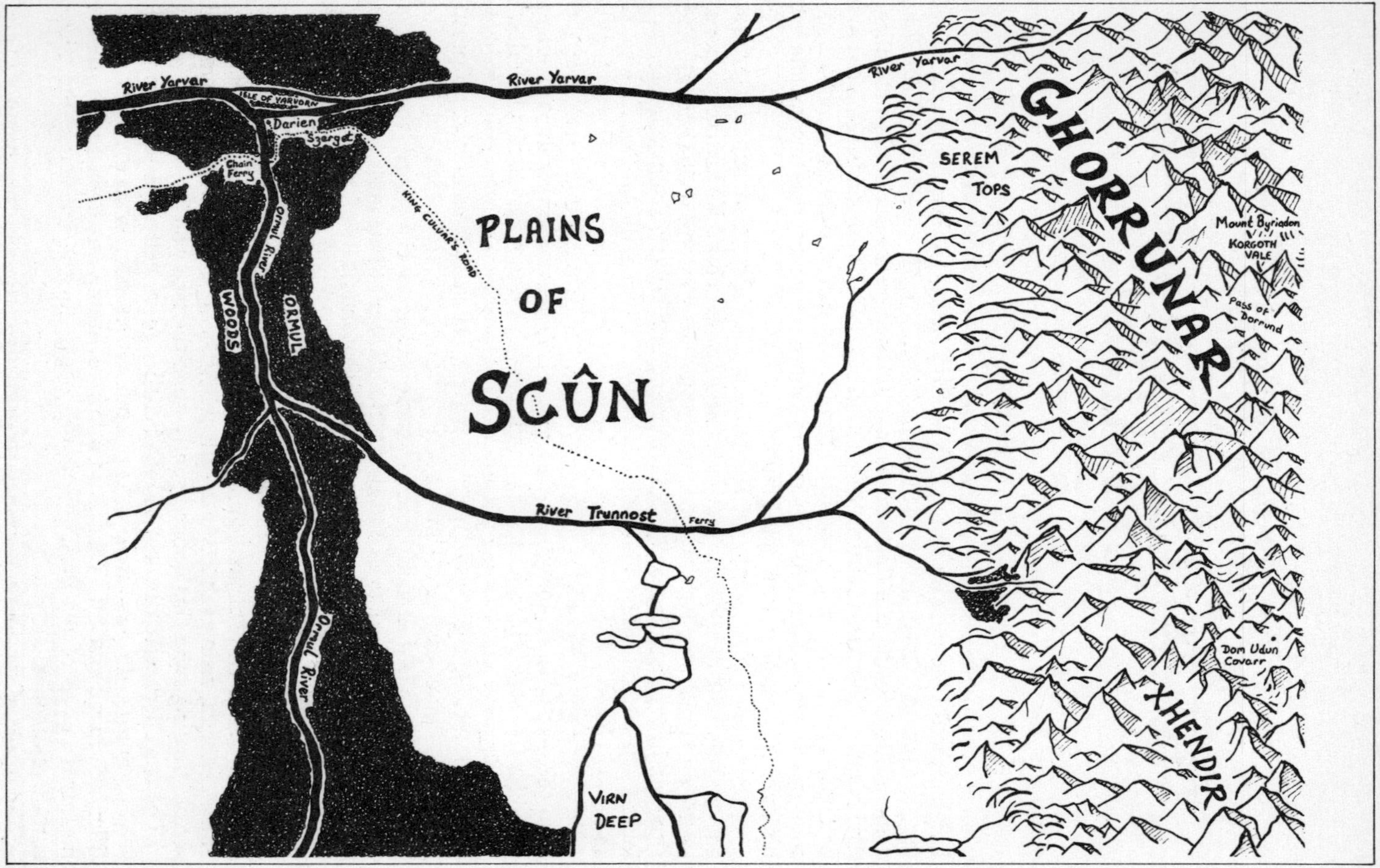
River Yarvar
Isle of Yarvorn
Darien
Szargat
Chain Ferry
Ormul River
Woods
Ormul
King Culvar's Road
Plains of Scûn
River Yarvar
River Yarvar
Serem Tops
Ghorrunar
Mount Byriadon
Korgoth Vale
Pass of Dorrund
River Trunnost
Ferry
Ormul River
Virn Deep
Dom Udun Covarr
Xhendir

Chapter Twenty One
THE WALL WITH NO WAY

Leighor awoke the next morning with a heavy heart. He knew at once that he felt, if anything, even worse than he had done the day before. The lurking demons of confusion still lingered just out of reach on the edges of his memory. And much as he strove to drive them out, the dark clouds of giddiness could not be held at bay. He knew now that a long day's march through mountainous country was beyond him. And so, steeling himself for what was to come, he left his chamber to seek out his companions.

To his surprise the others were not waiting for him in the guest refectory, and he was taken instead to the outer courtyard, where all his companions, including Haflas and Tavolir, stood assembled. Haflas looked well enough, and although heavily bandaged, was able to stand and walk. Tavolir however, still looked pale and bloodless, and had to be borne by two of the brothers in a wood and canvas litter.

Before Leighor could do or say anything, the High Brother had emerged from the main chapel, followed by a dozen of the lesser monks, all cowled and robed for travel. With a silent nod he indicated that the travellers should follow. The broad outer gates swung silently open before them as they left the abbey courtyard, making their way across the narrow bridge that spanned the Trimsil gorge, and thence eastward, down a steeply winding path towards the lake.

It took them a full half hour to come down to the placid shores of a Shiningwater still shrouded in its overnight blanket of pale mist. A newly risen sun peeped timidly down from between the dark shoulders of the mountains, its rays as yet too feeble to dispel the swirling mists. The path ended at a small jetty which ran out into the lake. And moored at its far end, half-shrouded in mist, lay a slender barge of sun-whitened pine. It was a curious vessel, with many long oars set in twin banks behind a high, curved prow; a single great tiller, almost as high, rising at the stern – the whole being constructed to resemble a serene, floating swan that bobbed gently upon the lake waters.

The travellers were directed to take benches in its belly, the brothers themselves manning the twin rows of oars upon either side. With the elder at the tiller, the barge cast off. Taking up a low plainsong chant, in time with the measured sweep of the oars, the monks began to row out across the silent surface of the lake.

The whole of the journey seemed to pass as in a dream: the chanting of the brothers stirring and melting into the floating mists, rising gently up with them to gird the far-flung mountains, snowcaps pink in the morning sun. Far above them on its high ridge, Leighor could still see the sun glinting off the bright walls and rooftops of Valmaalina. He could just make out the path they had descended – pale white against the grey stone of the mountain wall – and the shape of darker mountains and deeper valleys beyond.

Slowly the far shore emerged from the mists. A small wooden jetty awaited them, at its side a narrow path that wound up through open meadow into the trees. To their right, the three sisters, Desan, Deresen and Desuna rose up sharply out of the lake; and the high crags of Lollfin towered above them on their left. The white barge moored in total silence, leaving scarce a ripple in the cold lake waters to tell of its passing.

Once ashore, the small procession quickly reformed, passing up through the thin line of pines to emerge before a broad, high-domed timber building that none of the travellers, until that moment, had suspected existed. It stood in the middle of a broad meadow, between the feet of the mountains, fully hidden by its protective wall of trees, both from the lake and from the high monastery upon the farther shore. The building itself was tall and many-chambered, with pillared porticoes and flowered balconies, its every timber brilliantly white-washed so that it shone with light.

A half dozen grey-robed figures emerged from the building: women.

'Aye, there are sisters of our order also,' the High Brother noted, seeing their surprise. 'This is their house which stands beneath the mountains. Here we shall be made welcome.'

A tall woman, not young, yet swift and graceful in her movements, stepped forward to welcome them; dark hair tight-constricted beneath a long grey shawl. 'We have food and drink prepared for you,' she smiled austerely, 'and full provisions for your onward journey. Yet you are still welcome here if you have changed your mind, to rest and to dwell for as long as you wish.'

Telsyan bowed. 'For your generosity we thank you, ma'am; but we are set upon an urgent errand and cannot remain.'

The abbess nodded. 'So be it. All is readied for your going once you have eaten. Come.' She turned away to lead them up into the main hall.

Here a great table had been set out with pies and meats and other good things. Yet of these the monks and the sisters partook but little, seeming content to watch the hungry travellers as they ate.

The late breakfast was quickly done, and the guests were ushered out into an open courtyard behind the building. Here a broad stream tumbled down from a high vale between the mountains to pass beneath the priory wall; a stony trail followed its course upward, into the north-west. Leighor swallowed hard.

Haflas seemed to have read his thoughts. 'I fear that this is where our company must part,' he said morosely.

'Yes,' the abbess nodded. 'Some must go and some must remain; that is the price of the choice you have made.'

'And I fear that I am one of those who must pay that price,' Leighor admitted out loud for the first time. 'Much as I would like to go with you, I fear I am not yet strong enough to hike such long distances through the mountains.'

Telsyan nodded. 'This is not your hour, southron. You will be better off here, well cared for by these good folk. And you shall have Haflas and Tavolir for company. Wait until you are fully recovered, and hope that we shall all meet again in the spring, in Tershelline.'

'Mayhap you need not take your parting yet.' The abbess intervened unexpectedly. 'Not if you do not wish it. For if walking is your only problem, then provision is already made.' Swiftly she clapped her hands; and from an outbuilding to their right emerged a sight that made Leighor break into a broad smile. Seven black horses were led from the stables, each saddled and harnessed, and equipped with bulging packs that must contain food and equipment enough for a journey of several weeks.

'As you see, all has been made ready for you to ride,' the sister smiled. 'You would never get through the mountains of Ghorrunar on foot at this season. Upon these you may; for the vale horses are stout and strong.'

Indeed the horses were sound, firm muscled and lean built, fit certainly to bear the scions of kings.

'We cannot accept . . .' Uhlendof began. 'You give us too much . . .'

'It is no more than our duty to give help to travellers in need of assistance,' the abbess held up her hand up firmly. 'And I can think of few in greater need of assistance, or upon a better cause. Besides, what we give you is a loan, no more. These horses are no more ours than they are yours. This vale is their home, and to it they shall return, wherever you may release them in these northlands. And thus they are neither to be sold nor to be bartered, nor are they to be taken into the lands of the south.' She paused. 'Do you promise this?'

Telsyan nodded. 'This we do with pleasure, good lady. We will not misuse this noble gift.'

He turned once more to Leighor. 'But are you sure, physician, that you can manage the long journey that still lies ahead of us?'

'I can manage,' Leighor insisted, his face set. 'My only fear was for my legs. I can ride as long as I wish.'

'Indeed,' the abbess nodded gently. 'I have the feeling that your destiny lies not here with us but in the harsh lands beyond. Your road shall be long and hard, southron healer, there will be times when you shall wish that this was not the way that you had chosen, but you must go.' She turned abruptly away, leaving Leighor somewhat shaken and perplexed.

Telsyan looked at him curiously for a moment and nodded. 'We shall see . . . we shall see. Let us see how you do upon this first day's journey. The lady would have you come with us, it seems; yet I trust not this talk of feelings and destiny. We shall rely upon more solid proofs. Ride with us today; but if you are unable to keep up, then tomorrow you must return, and we must proceed without you. Is that agreed?'

Leighor nodded. He was on trial, but at least this way he still had some chance of remaining with the company, and for now that was enough.

Haflas and Tavolir tried to look pleased to see the rest of the travellers on their way at last, but it was clear that they were both deeply saddened not to be going with them. There were many words of farewell for both the brothers, and the sisters who had done so much to set them on their way once more. But it was quickly over. A few parting words with the High Brother, a last leavetaking of Haflas and Tavolir, and it was time to mount and be gone.

Zindur and Telsyan helped Leighor on to his mount; but once firmly ensconced in the saddle it took him only a short while to grow used to controlling the horse with his one good hand. He only hoped, as he watched the others mount, that he would be able to maintain this level of concentration throughout the coming journey.

Leighor found himself third from last in the brief column, as the seven horses and riders moved slowly away from the wooden priory to follow the course of the hill stream upward into the mountains. Only Zindur and Inanys rode behind him; ahead were Keran, Uhlendof, Yeon, and, of course, Telsyan – in the lead as usual. For a moment Leighor considered the hunched figure of Inanys, seated unsteadily astride his jet black horse as it trotted along behind them. He wondered why this spite-filled stranger, who could have no possible interest in the outcome of their quest, should stick with them so through every danger? The question concerned him, but his mind was still not clear enough to think things through, still less to concentrate upon two tasks at once. Best now to concern himself solely with the difficulties of the ride.

They were now a good distance above the rambling convent, and the group of indistinguishable figures gathered before the building had already begun to disperse. Leighor supposed that the seven horses and their riders must now seem little more than so many dark dots against the giant backcloth of grey mountains that swept down upon them from east and west.

The steepness of the slope left barely an inch or two of level footing beside the stream. Yet still the horses managed to find their way slowly onwards and upwards, towards the higher mountains. They ventured now into unknown, unmapped territory. Even the sisters had had only the vaguest idea of what lay beyond these barren peaks. All the travellers knew was that there was a route, roughly north and west through these mountains, that would eventually bring them down into the plains of Scûn. Exactly how the land lay they knew not. They would just have to find their way as best they could.

The stream waters tumbled violently down towards them now, as if desperate to be free of the embrace of these snowcapped northern mountains, and to merge with the gentler waters of the lake below. Strangely, Leighor found himself envying them. He took a last look back at Valmaalina just as the lake and its twin abbeys passed out of sight behind the towering bulk of grey-flanked Lollfin to the south. To the east, cold Fara and snowcapped Sullagorn glared haughtily down at the few puny travellers who dared to disturb their deep stillnesses. And ahead lay naught but row upon row of strange, nameless mountains, higher and loftier still; all seeming utterly disdainful of the presumptuous band of humans who rode in their dark shadow. Despite his six companions, Leighor felt suddenly very alone.

The rest of the day passed slowly. For although the horses were still fresh and strong, and could have been pressed harder if the travellers had wished, Telsyan thought it wiser to keep to a slower pace so as not to exhaust their mounts too early – especially when they knew not what need they might have of their horses' strength in the days to come. And as they climbed, the air about them seemed to grow thinner and the sparse vegetation dwindled, until by noon the travellers were riding through a barren wasteland of shattered boulders and crumbled rock.

A low pass led them into a dry vale between the mountains. Here they halted for a brief meal of bread, cheese and some of the sweet, yellow cloudberry jam the sisters had given them. For several hours more they continued along this stony vale, until the welcome sight of a fresh stream going north set them on a downhill course once again. Yet the vale had not ended, or lost a great deal in height, before darkness finally caught up with them, and they must halt.

'The cold comes on as soon as the sun sets at these altitudes,' Telsyan warned them as he dismounted. 'We must make a fire, quickly!'

The weather was as good as his word, and the mildness of the day was fast replaced by a bitter cold, borne on the north wind, that cut right through to the bone. The rough canvas shelters which the sisters had provided were no substitute for the solid leather tents they had left behind at Ahockûl Crest. The icy wind cut through the thin fabric like a knife, to drive every remnant of warmth from their cramped interiors. The travellers had been able to find only a few poor twigs and branches nearby, and the resultant fire provided scarce warmth enough to heat a single small pot. And even at this rate it looked like consuming their meagre store of fuel long before the night was ended.

In spite of all these hardships, however, Leighor still felt more satisfied than he had done for a long while. He had survived the day's journey, he had kept his weakness and giddiness at bay. He would not have to return to Valmaalina in the morning: he could go on. He was one of the company once more.

A sharp frost fell during the night, the first of winter; decking grass, stone and moorland sedge in a silver mantle that glinted like a thousand diamonds in the morning sun. Yet despite its great beauty, the travellers looked out upon the scene with foreboding. It was the first day of *Vilvereem*, a winter month this far north; and this was the first herald of that overmighty season, a grim reminder of her greater legions soon to come. And although the frost began to melt away with the first kiss of the strengthening sun, it lent the travellers new urgency as they broke camp and prepared for the long day's journey ahead.

'What is our route today?' Zindur asked, clasping his hands for warmth as he untethered the last of the horses and checked the packs for the final time.

'Still north,' Telsyan answered, already mounted and waiting for the others. 'North and west until we come out on to the plains, and then hopefully, fair weather for Darien.'

'I hope that we descend soon,' Yeon grunted. 'I like not these icy mountains, and I fancy these fine horses like them less than I.'

'If it is to be a choice between cold and Rievers,' Uhlendof noted, 'then give me the cold. I would not be in too great a hurry to get back down on to the plains, my lad. Be thankful for such small mercies as we have.'

Most of this second day passed as had the first: a slow steady trek through lonely mountain valleys, with only the sun and the circling kestrels for company. On occasion they saw the odd mountain here, already half white in anticipation of the coming snows; or perhaps a small, timid rodent, that started from its hide to run in panic across the path of the advancing horses. Only once did the party stop, when Leighor sighted a strange bush growing high upon a rocky slope above them.

'What is it?' Telsyan demanded as the southron urged his horse gingerly towards it, halting the column.

'A frost rose!' Leighor shouted back, dismounting with some difficulty as the others began slowly to follow him.

'I know of it,' Uhlendof added, clambering up beside him. 'A rare find!'

The bush was short, straggly and covered with sharp thorns, its roots clinging tightly to the splintered rock around it, as if it dreaded to be torn free. Its branches bore several plump, bulbous rose-hips of deep royal blue. The flowers – of which only two still remained – were silver grey, the insides of the petals a pure brushed silver that seemed to glisten in the sharp sunlight.

'There are but two blooms left,' the monk murmured; 'and they shall last but a few days more. We are lucky to find even these.'

'What use are they?' Telsyan asked impatiently. 'Must we stop now for every bramble and rose-bush that we pass?'

'It is very rare,' Leighor whispered. 'The flowers might fetch a king's ransom in the right market, for their scent and beauty alone. But the hips are more useful for our purposes. They have great medicinal value; such as we may soon have cause to be very thankful for.'

'Well hurry!' Telsyan turned away. 'We may have less cause to be thankful if we are not through these mountains before the snows.'

The halt did not last long; and Leighor's pockets full, the travellers were soon remounted and on their way once more, the high peaks rising ahead of them. Yet Leighor still felt uneasy in the shadow of these dark mountains. Looming above them, still, grey and oppressive, they seemed to despise the very foot of man. He felt a hundred unseen eyes watching them from behind every sharp-toothed crag and fallen boulder. Their small company was weaker now by two; and weaker yet for the ill condition and lack of weapons of those who remained. Yeon's bow was lost at Vhori Bridge, and the rest of them had only a handful of arrows for what few bows remained – all that the brothers had been able to provide. If they were waylaid now by bandits or Rievers, they would be easy prey.

A loud oath from Telsyan, at the head of the column, shattered his train of thought. He looked up to see the merchant pointing forward and cursing fluently. They had been travelling steadily upwards for over an hour, yet only now could they at last see what lay ahead of them at the end of their narrow valley. The sight was not encouraging. The mountains closed tight in about the head of the valley, forming a high wall of sheer, precipitous peaks, with no sign of even the slightest gap between them. The way forward was blocked – as surely as if an iron gateway had slammed shut in their faces.

'Damnation!' Telsyan cursed once more. 'We have missed our way! We shall have to go back!' The travellers drew to a halt around him.

'Where have we gone wrong?' Yeon asked.

'One valley is much like another in these mountains,' the merchant shrugged. 'It is easy to lose one's way.'

'Easy indeed for you!' Inanys said sharply. 'It is a miracle you have managed to live so long, with such small journeycraft!'

'It is a miracle you have managed to live so long with your brutish impudence!' Telsyan spluttered angrily. But Uhlendof restrained him.

'There is no time . . .' he said quickly, pointing ahead. 'There are other matters – look!'

The travellers followed his pointing finger, to stare up into the grey flanks of the mountains ahead, noticing for the first time the ruined walls and watchtowers that glowered broodingly down from the shelter of their stony heights. Grim fortifications that had been raised up in some age long past from the self-same stone as the mountain itself, so that they blended almost perfectly into the crumbling stone ridges: so well that it took a sharp eye to determine their full extent in the fading half-light. Beneath these, a long stone wall ran right across the far end of the vale, cutting it off entirely from the south.

'A ruined fortress,' Telsyan shrugged. 'Long abandoned by whoever once raised it. What is that to us?'

'It seems a curious place,' the monk observed slowly. 'One that might bear investigation. It grows dark, and we might perhaps find some shelter there for the night.'

Telsyan considered the idea for only a moment before rejecting it. 'No,' he shook his head. 'What would that bring us, bar more trouble? We have tents, let us camp in the open somewhere farther down the valley.'

'Do you not find it at all curious,' Uhlendof asked; 'that yon stone wall passes from one side of this valley to the other without a single break or gateway? Surely there must be some means of egress? And if that is hidden, mayhap much else is hidden also?'

'I do not follow your reasoning,' Telsyan said irritably. 'And I find it increasingly profitless to try to do so. We have lost far too much time already. Let us go.' He prepared to turn back.

'Nay,' Zindur warned. 'It grows already too dark to travel. We shall have to make camp somewhere. Why not here? In the full light tomorrow we may even find a way over the mountain and save a day's wasted travel.'

'No, let us go!' Keran hissed suddenly. 'I do not like this place. There is something hidden here. Let us go back!'

Unexpectedly Telsyan shook his head. 'No. This time I think Master Zindur is right. We cannot throw away the chance of finding a path through these mountains. We must stay.'

Keran frowned, but she said nothing.

The wall seemed to grow taller and broader as they approached; and once they were at its base it towered a good dozen feet above them. It was old. Old beyond reckoning, and set as firm in the ground as if it had grown there: a bastard child of the mountains themselves. And although its great unmortared stones crumbled at their edges and were decked in a heavy blanket of moss and lichen, not a single one was fallen or out of place. The wall was as complete and as effective a barrier as it had been on the day it was first raised.

'Whoever built this knew well his trade,' Uhlendof declared, dismounting to study the construction closer to.

'I suppose so,' Telsyan yawned, coming up to stand beside him. 'Since it successfully bars our way forward, and seems to have been made for no other purpose.' He removed his hat and held it out to test the wind. 'Well, at least we may use it for shelter.' He sighed, turning back to face the others. 'We shall set up camp here, where we stand.'

Wearily the rest of the company obeyed, dismounting to set about the familiar task of making camp. Yet Uhlendof did not join them, seeming totally absorbed in his examination of the wall.

'Surely its purpose is no mystery,' Leighor said, appearing beside the priest some moments later. 'It is to protect the old fortress above from attack from the south. There is nothing curious about that.'

'But there is no way through it or around it,' Uhlendof insisted stubbornly.

'No one builds a wall that they cannot themselves pass through – especially when the best land in the vale lies beyond it.'

'Then perhaps there is a secret way or a tunnel,' Leighor suggested, showing a little more interest; 'an entrance less obvious and easier defended than a gate.'

The monk nodded, rapping the damp grey stones irritably with his staff. 'Aye, that is what we must look for.'

Leighor turned to stare along the length of the wall. 'If there is a tunnel,' he shrugged, 'it could be anywhere. Perhaps we have even passed it by, somewhere back down the mountainside. Anyway, we shan't find it tonight, that's certain. This old wall will hold its secret for one more night at least.' He gave the wall a parting tap with his staff, and turned away.

Yet the moment his staff touched the stones, Leighor felt its power drive through him. A cold, tingling rush coursed through every nerve of his body in a single instant, and then was gone. The staff flew from his fingers, leaving him utterly drained, to slump spent and exhausted to the ground. There was a gasp from his fellows, and cries of alarm. Something very strange was happening behind him. Yet from where he now lay, he could see nothing. His head whirled, and his brains screamed and jangled as if they had been stirred with a stick.

He realised suddenly that he seemed to be bathed in a faint blue light that had its source somewhere behind him. How could that be? All that lay behind him was the wall. Suddenly, deep down inside, he felt fear. He must turn; turn and see what was happening! With a major effort of will he rolled himself painfully over on to his injured side, eventually managing to right himself so that he lay flat out on his back, facing the wall.

But the wall had changed.

The whole of the great barrier now glowed eerily in the gathering darkness, a dim aura of irridescent blue clinging to the surface of the ancient stones. To left and right of him, as far as he could see, a wall of shimmering blue stretched out across the valley. His jaw dropped open; aghast at what he had somehow accomplished. Yet even as he stared, the glow began to fade, shrinking and diminishing as it concentrated itself upon a small area of wall some half a hundred paces to the west. Here the light intensified even as the rest of the wall darkened; taking upon itself the form of a shimmering blue archway that floated above the dark surface of the stones. Fiery letters clawed themselves out of the haze to dance and flicker across the lintels of the phantom arch. Letters in some forgotten runic script, that burned brighter and yet brighter as Leighor watched; flaring suddenly into an intense white sunburst of power that seemed to illumine the whole valley for one brief, intolerable instant – and then was gone.

The wall was restored to darkness once more; but Leighor's eyes were still filled with enchantment, and for a moment he could not see. The startled voices of his companions rose up all around him. Desperately he tried to clear his eyes, to see where they were pointing.

The vision seemed to return all at once – and for an instant he thought that he still dreamed. For there, where the phantom arch had so recently shimmered in its faery fire, there now stood a real archway of firm grey stone, piercing the long wall. Solid and dark-shadowed in the halflight, it looked as though it had stood there for half a thousand years – and the stunned and bewildered wayfarers had only their all too fallible senses to tell them it had not.

For long minutes no one moved or spoke, all of them trying to take in what had happened. Only Leighor, struggling to rise, eventually set the stunned figures back into motion, Zindur and Uhlendof rushing quickly forward to help him to his feet.

'What has happened?' Leighor gasped. 'What did I do?'

There was no answer, and silence fell once more, the travellers staring in wonder at the dark, beckoning archway.

Only Leighor glanced down at the innocuous looking ashwood staff that still lay upon the tussocky grass behind him.

'Well, bold adventurers . . .' Inanys's sharp voice cut through the silence like a razor. 'Will you stand here all night, gawping like dimwits on market day – or do we move?'

'Be silent!' Uhlendof hissed. 'Only fools venture into places such as these without thought.'

'It will do no harm to take a closer look,' Yeon ventured, stepping forward before anyone could stop him. Reluctantly the others followed.

Yet at first glance there appeared to be nothing out of the ordinary about the opening: a plain rounded arch some ten feet high, that passed right through the thickness of the long wall. The writings they had seen upon the glowing faery arch were now gone – if they had ever actually existed at all. The arch seemed as dull and ordinary as any of half a hundred others in the northern kingdoms.

It was nearly full dark now, and little could be seen through the archway but a stretch of rough tussocky grassland and the dark shapes of the mountains beyond. If any of them had imagined that some enchanted vale might lie upon the other side of the gateway, they were quickly disabused. Gingerly Telsyan stretched out a hand to touch the stone, prepared to snatch it away in an instant if anything untoward occurred. But the grey stone of the archway seemed as plain and as solid as any other. He slapped the rock disbelievingly. 'How is this here?'

'Mayhap this arch has always been here,' Uhlendof said softly. 'Only hidden behind a veil of illusion which Leighor has somehow broken.'

'Perhaps.' The merchant nodded, seeming somehow reassured by the suggestion. And, thus emboldened, he made to step through the arch itself.

'Beware!' Zindur warned sharply. 'You know not into what you pass!'

But he was too late. Telsyan had already stepped through the arch, and seemed to show no adverse effects from the passage. Slowly the others followed him, to find themselves in a rough valley bowl beneath the mountains. Somewhere to their left a stream trickled gently, half hidden by a tussocky dyke that ran away in a straight line towards the feet of the mountains.

'There is nothing here.' Yeon's voice sounded disappointed.

'Aye,' Telsyan nodded. 'Let us go back and make camp. We can do all our exploring in the morning.'

But Zindur was not listening. 'Hold!' he hissed, raising his hand abruptly to silence them. 'I thought I saw something move!'

The travellers followed his darting eyes as they scoured the thickening darkness beyond the hillocks.

'Where?' Keran whispered fearfully. 'I see nothing.'

The warrior hissed her silent, hurriedly unhooking the giant war axe from where it hung across his back. Fearful now, although none of them had yet seen anything to fear, the others began cautiously to draw their own weapons. At once a bloodcurdling war-howl tore through the air; and all around them the ground seemed suddenly to spring into life: dozens of small dark figures swarming over the low dyke towards them, bearing swords, pikes and glinting axes. A great purple banner shimmered through the darkness, emblazoned with silver runes.

'Form a circle!' Zindur roared above the mayhem. 'Defend yourselves!'

Fearfully the travellers rushed to obey, raising a serried rank of swords and bows against their unknown attackers. Even Leighor held a sword uncomfortably in his good hand as he waited for the horde to reach them.

The attackers were almost within striking distance, when suddenly they halted; keeping a good sword's length away from the huddled travellers as they spread out to encircle them, cutting them off from the wall and their only way of escape. The figures were short and stocky, clad in leathers and woven yarns; many of them also wearing dark coats of chain-mail, or carrying iron-studded shields.

'*Maezgrull!*' Zindur hissed. 'The Dark Hillfolk!'

For a moment the two groups faced each other in tense silence, weapons drawn and barely two swordpoints apart. No one moved or spoke.

'I think we had better parley,' Telsyan muttered quickly.

'A wise decision,' Inanys sneered.

'Ho!' Zindur called out aloud. 'We come in peace. We seek no quarrel with you or your folk. We are but honest wayfarers venturing north. Let us pass on in peace and we shall cause you no trouble.'

'Aye, mighty sons of men,' an answering voice called back, in a Durian even more harsh and sharply accented than Korzhlin's had been. 'You shall indeed cause us no trouble if we slay you – now where you stand – and bury your bones beneath these mounds. Aye! Then manlings, shall we have true peace!' There was a dark rumble of assent from the ranks of the Hillfolk.

'We shall sell our lives dear!' Zindur warned. 'Many of you will perish before we fall. Why waste our blood upon such foolishness, when we have no quarrel?'

'We have quarrel with all who trespass on our lands.' The other spoke again, stepping forward to reveal himself for the first time. A broad, powerfully built figure in fine-wrought armour; not yet old, with a full black beard and an accompanying shock of long dark hair, half hidden beneath an iron helm. 'Aye,' he repeated. 'Especially when they be ill-spawned, thieving sons of men!' There was a louder roar of approval from the warriors behind him.

'Let us not re-open old quarrels,' Uhlendof stepped forward quickly. 'Rather let there be peace between us, for together we may have to face evils greater than you dream of.'

'When you are few in number you talk of peace,' the Hillman leader spat. 'And when your numbers grow great we see the truth behind your words! What do you seek this day, sons of men: our gold or our lands? Whichever, it will take more than fair phrases to take them from us.'

'We seek nothing from you!' Uhlendof insisted angrily. 'Nothing bar shelter this night, and guidance on our way tomorrow. Our enemies are the Tarintarmen, and the foul ones who run with them. And to harm these, we must be in Darien before the snows.'

'Darien?' another of the Hillmen repeated with scorn. He was slightly shorter than the first, and wore no fine armour, only a dull coat of grey mail. 'What business could those who fight Tarintarmen have in Darien? Only the Knights of Dur dwell in that foul sump, and they are as much in league with the *tarintari* as any goblin hellspawn!'

Hillmen weapons began to rattle impatiently, and angry voices rose in the *mazgroll* tongue. And although Leighor could not understand the words, their meaning was clear enough.

'If words cannot persuade you,' Uhlendof roared above the rising hubbub, 'then deeds must. We will lay down our arms before you, and then you may slay us or not as you will.'

'What?' Yeon hissed, outraged.

'It is the only way,' the monk nodded gently. 'Any other and we are lost.'

Reluctantly the travellers followed Uhlendof's lead, and let their weapons fall to the ground in front of them. The ranks of Hillmen stood perplexed.

'Now slay them all!' a voice cried: but the grunts of approval were fewer. The mailed warrior who had spoken earlier shouted some harsh words in his own tongue. But the leader shook his head, and an incomprehensible argument developed in which many took part. Leighor tried to make sense of the dark, convoluted words of the Hillman speech; the long, sonorous earth-grinding vowels that ran into one another like the coils of some great serpent that burrowed away secretly beneath the mountains: the half-forgotten language of a vanishing barbaric race. Then, abruptly, the debate was over, and the leader turned to face them.

'Your act of foolishness has intrigued us; and for the moment you are to be spared. Yet beware: many of our number are unconvinced by your tales, so do nothing to feed their suspicions. Now come!' He turned away, and the ranks of the Hillmen parted before him, forming a well-armed corridor through which they all must pass.

A score of armed warriors marching along beside them, they followed the *mazgroll* chieftain across the vale, and thence up towards the dark ruins that stood lonely guard upon the mountainside. The upward way was hard and stony, and many times the travellers stumbled and fell in the thickening darkness before finally they reached their goal. Each time, nervous Hillman guards would rush forward with swords drawn, ever suspicious of some sudden treachery.

The travellers were loath to leave all their supplies and possessions in the hands of the Hillmen below, but they had little choice; wondering, as they stumbled upward, just what they would meet in the dark ruins above them. Their path ran for much of its distance beneath a line of ruined ramparts, whose towers rose like dragon's teeth from the rim of the mountains.

As they drew closer, Leighor scanned the crumbling heights of the great octagonal towers. Yet even at this range he could detect no sign that any living creature dwelt within, or had done so for centuries. The towers, and all their neighbouring walls and fortifications, seemed utterly abandoned and forsaken. It was as effective a hiding place as any he could imagine for a tribe of Hillman warriors – for who, besides themselves, would trouble to investigate these dismal ruins? Ruins identical to so many score that dotted the northlands. And if any did approach, then these broken walls and towers were not so broken – when one bothered to examine them closely – that they could not still make up a formidable set of defences, with a few dozen seasoned warriors to man them.

They were taken to the base of the nearest tower, coming at last to a small doorway, half hidden against the mountainside. There were no sentries to guard the open door, nor any visible in the tower above, yet Leighor felt certain that they were all well marked by many hidden eyes as they passed inward.

A moment later they were feeling their way down a flight of steep, twisting steps, in a darkness so total that Leighor could barely make out the shape of his own hand before his face. For long minutes the travellers could only feel their way downwards through the dark. And then at last a dim glow appeared far beneath them, growing slowly brighter until it seemed that they journeyed down a steep well towards a distant pool of light. Here the stair ended: in a small, bare cave lit by a single guttering torch. Only here, Leighor realised with a start, could even a solitary flame be allowed – here, where not a single flicker of light could possibly escape to the surface to betray the presence of a tribe of Hillmen dwelling deep beneath the mountains.

From this bare entrance chamber they passed along another passage to enter a far greater cavern, lined with scores of dark stone seats carved from the living rock. A low fire was banked up in a stone trough that ran the length of the room, and by its light Leighor could see the many stone friezes that had been carved into the walls. The carvings held his eyes despite himself. They enthralled him, drawing him deep into their intricate, finely-worked fastnesses. They were in a style that he had never seen before: a sharp, coiling, detailed style that seemed to make the pictures come to life in the shifting firelight. Here were scenes of long-forgotten battles, high-towered fortresses, and great hunts on horseback through wild, virgin forests.

Leighor's eyes made out many creatures prowling and skulking through that stone forest; from birds and forest rodents to grizzled bears, stags and flame-breathing dragons. Two-legged creatures were here too in abundance: both true men and the stunted Hill Folk, as well as goblins, Tarintarmen, and other races he failed to recognise. Over all was depicted a gigantic carved throne upon which sat a great king of the *maezgrull*, crowned and garbed in his majesty, and surrounded by rich treasures. Men of all kingdoms knelt before him, bearing gifts of jewels, spices and precious metals.

'That is Zarun-Dur.' The Hillman chief followed their gaze upwards. 'The greatest king of our race, whose kingdom was the mightiest and most magnificent these lands have ever known. Ancient *Qhirrürron-ár*; that extended from the Seas of White Crystal south to the great rivers, from the shores of the Eastern Ocean to the far limits of the western wastes. All lands once ours. All now gone.' He swung around quickly to face the waiting travellers, his eyes hard. 'Stolen from us by the sons of men!'

'You speak of times long past . . .' Uhlendof began.

'Past? How long past?' the chieftain cut angrily through his words. 'Are our folk not still harried and persecuted by your own? Do you not still ally yourselves with Rievers, goblins and all who will fly to your banner against us? How many years have passed since the last of our kind were driven with fire and sword from their ancient places in the grey mountains of Felldur and the dales of Elerian? None of these things are past. And now you come even here, to these dark mountains where we must dwell amid the ruins of our former glory, and dare to tell us that all is past? Aye,' he nodded. 'With your kind all is ever past, until it is time to come again in force to steal what little we still have left! Do you truly think us such fools?'

'Nay, my lord,' Uhlendof apologised hastily. 'We do not think you fools. And in truth there has been much bitterness in centuries past between the children of *Mûrond* and the sons of *Mirvandär*. No doubt there have been many dark deeds done upon both sides. Yet surely the time has come when these ancient hatreds can no longer be borne? When Rievers swarm without number through the great forests; and the Mage Metal, *harrunor*, has once more reappeared in the hands of evil.'

'*Harrunor*?' the chieftain questioned sharply. The word seemed once again to have had its magical effect. 'What know ye of that?'

Briefly Uhlendof told him: and during the telling many others of the Hillfolk came into the great chamber to listen. Leighor watched them silently, noticing for the first time that there seemed to be no women at all among their number. Mayhap the women were hidden away somewhere deeper in these workings; or perhaps the old tales were true, and the dark folk of the hills had no womenfolk, being birthed from eggs hatched in their deep furnaces. But he had seen little yet of their habitation here, and he was not sure how much more they would be allowed to see. Most of the men gathered around them still looked very hostile: their hands staying close to their weapons, their hard eyes watchful and full of suspicion. Yet Uhlendof's tale of their travels and of their flight from Ahockûl Crest seemed to have impressed many of the warriors, including their leader; as soon as the monk had finished speaking, he retired thoughtfully to one of the carved stone chairs and seated himself.

'You speak well, holy man,' he said after a while. 'And you have given us much to think upon. But ask me to make no decisions now. I must first take counsel of the elders. Yet I may tell you that the waxing power of the *tarintari* and of the men of Khiorim is of great concern to us. Even this great fortress of Dom Udun Covarr could not hold for long against a legion such as you describe at Ahockûl Crest or at Uberezeg Ingur. And with the power of the *Gath-Harrunnor* added to their number, the forces of the Curséd Ones would surely be invincible, so that none might dwell in these lands unless at their pleasure.'

'My lord,' Uhlendof broke in quickly. 'You speak of the *harrunor* as one who knows of its properties and origins. Is there aught that you can tell us that may help us to counter its power?'

'Little.' The chieftain shook his head. 'Once there was naught in this world that could lie hidden from the metal-masters of the *maezgrull*. But in these days the greater part of our ancient lore is lost, scattered amongst the tribes of the *U-Zumur*. Nearly all of our knowledge, beyond the simple ironcraft, is gone – perhaps forever . . .'

'Why do you demean us so before these strangers?' one of the older warriors broke in angrily, striding forward to stand between the chieftain and the travellers. 'What use can it be to parade our weaknesses before them?'

'I speak only the truth,' the other said wearily. 'These folk offer us little threat, and I grow too tired to play to your dreams of ancient grandeur. Is it not time we ceased to deceive ourselves? For surely we deceive no others. The world grows old. Our race diminishes. We can no longer stand alone.'

'We stand alone or we perish!' the elder barked angrily. 'Nothing good can come of consorting with outsiders! Only evil has ever come to our race from the *U-Zumir*, and you are fool to believe otherwise!' He turned abruptly on his heel to stride out of the great chamber, followed by several of his supporters.

'Ours is a stubborn and quarrelsome race,' the chieftain observed sadly. 'Quick to anger and slow to forget. Whichever way our council shall go, the presence here of such a number of strangers will not be tolerable for long. Your stay with us, travellers, must be brief.' He rose. 'But this night at least you shall be royally entertained after the ancient manner, and you shall see a little of the true face of the *Zumur-on-dazar*.'

'And may we know to whom we speak?' Telsyan asked.

The other nodded. 'It can do but little harm for you to know my out-name. It is Kazmir of the Iron Helm who stands before you. Chieftain of the *maezgrull* race, and governor of this great fortress of the Hill King, which is Dom Udun Covarr, and of all the lands around.'

'The Hill King,' Uhlendof repeated softly, as if slowly recalling some half-forgotten tale. 'Does such still exist in these eastern lands?'

'None of the ancient line,' Kazmir admitted slowly. 'Urflasz, the last of the true line, perished at Virn Deep in battle against Rievers in the year 596 as the men of the Varroain count; 3140 in the years of Samar. Either way, a good two hundred winters past. Since those days few of our folk have dwelt west of the Malûn River.'

'And this Hill King, where does he dwell?' Telsyan asked.

The Hillman chief smiled briefly, shaking his head. 'Now you ask too many of our secrets, stranger. The king dwells in the hills, moving where he will. Let that be an answer.' He turned away.

Dom Udun Covarr was a place of many halls, the travellers soon discovered. Dark, gloomy tunnels ran off in all directions from the Hall of the King, each leading to some other spacious chamber that had been hollowed out of the living rock of the mountain. The small party, now unaccompanied by any armed escort, were led from the hall by a single dark-haired tribesman. Their guide had few words of Durian, other than those three or four necessary to give the briefest and curtest of instructions; and none of any other language of men. And so the travellers passed in almost total silence through a maze of dark passageways and cold, ill-lit chambers; some piled high with stores, some empty, some with small groups of Hillmen working in them, others that looked as though nobody had set foot in them for centuries.

Leighor wondered at this surly race of Hillmen, the tallest of whom came barely to his shoulder. In all respects, apart from their stunted build and their somewhat coarsened features, they seemed entirely alike to other men. Yet there was something indefinable about them that was strange and alien. Something in the way they moved, fluid yet deliberate – as if each motion had been somehow sundered into a hundred separate segments and then patched together again so that there was no noticeable pause, but leaving the tantalising hint that there had really been no movement at all. They also seemed particularly adroit in suddenly ceasing all motion to become as still and silent as the stone carvings that lined the walls; remaining that way for minutes on end, until, disconcertingly, they broke into movement once more. Speaking to each other only in hushed, whispered voices, the Hillfolk turned silently to watch the unknown strangers; staring at them with suspicion and open hostility as they passed.

In one of the deeper caverns, an underground stream had been dammed several times to form a series of deep, clear pools whose waters trickled gently through the cave, passing from one to another in the cool darkness. Farther along, they were led through a low armoury, piled high with swords, pikes, axes and crossbows, along with many other weapons of ancient and more curious design. This led into a much wider cavern, filled with the noise and heat of a dozen furnaces. Here the *mazgroll* smiths worked, bending cold grey iron and earth-red bronze to their will with fire and water, hammer and anvil and tongs. The metal hissed and screamed in impotent fury beneath the unrelenting torture. Smoke from glowing braziers and shimmering furnaces rose in thick clouds towards the dark, unseen reaches of the roof, leaving thick grey coils to swirl about the vast chamber. Despite the smoke, the black earth-coals which the Hillmen used burned hot and strong, filling the cave with heat; and for the first time since leaving Valmaalina the travellers felt warm. The walls of this cavern, too, were covered in finely carved friezes, depicting the forging of great treasures in gold and silver by the great metalcrafters of the past. Swords, rings and jewelled crowns long gone from the world looked down upon them from the dark stone walls; treasures that drew the eye to them like lodestones, so that the travellers were loath to pass on.

To their left, narrow tunnels sloped down towards mines that lay even deeper within the heart of the mountain. But these the travellers passed by, following their taciturn guardian along more level passages, to come finally into a large chamber of assembly.

Nearly circular, and close to thirty paces across, this cavern was fully bordered by two long, semicircular tables of carved stone. The seats all faced inward to form a spacious arena, at the centre of which burned a great iron brazier piled high with black earth-coal. The tables were already partly filled. And as the travellers entered, Kazmir emerged from the far side of the chamber. He took his seat at the centre of the inner wall, motioning the strangers to occupy seats nearby.

Leighor suspected that they had been led to this chamber by a circuitous route: whether to impress them with the size and grandeur of the underground fortress, or to confuse them about their true whereabouts, he did not know. But Kazmir's sudden reappearance only tended to confirm the suspicion in his mind that all was not quite as the *mazgroll* chieftain wanted it to seem.

'This is the hall of Nuraz-tûr,' their host rose to greet them; 'which is more used by us in these days than the Hall of the King, for that is overgreat and cold for our present number. Be seated, strangers, and take your ease.'

The entertainments of the *maezgrull* proved plain enough. The company were served with large platters of roast meats accompanied by rounds of flat barley bread hot from the oven. With a flagon of strong ale to wash the meal down, this was the sum of the repast. After the meal there were songs. Long songs of war, and quests for treasure, sung unaccompanied in deep solo voices; and rousing choruses of battle and the hunt, in which all around the table, including Kazmir, took part. Yet even the singing did not last for long, the Hillmen seeming quickly to tire of it, and grow melancholy. And there came a brief lull in the proceedings.

'All of your men do not seem to be with us this night, my lord,' Telsyan observed, indicating the empty spaces about the table.

'Aye,' Kazmir nodded absently. 'A strong watch must be kept in the vale this night, for it will take our enchanters many hours to remake the spell of warding which you shattered upon the outer wall.'

'Then there are users of magick here,' Uhlendof frowned.

'Only a few illusionists,' Kazmir shrugged. 'None who could be of any use to you. Our magicks are of a simple sort: a spell of warding, a charm for good fortune, no more. Nothing that will avail against the power of *harrunor*.'

'Surely the enchantment upon the vale wall is a thing of greater power than any common charm?' Leighor insisted.

The chieftain shook his head. 'That is an old ensorcelment, beyond our present powers to create anew. Our greatest power now lies in tending the eldrin fires that burn within the mountians. These are the fires of life; without them these mountains would lie dead indeed.' He fell into a morose silence for a moment, as if lost in thought. But then suddenly he rose and clapped his hands. 'Come!' he said loudly. 'The night grows too sad and sombre for my taste. It is not yet time for sleep. Let us see some combats!'

A ragged cheer rose up from around the tables as *maezgrull* stepped forward to engage in bouts of axe and swordplay within their circle. The fights were brief, and fought only to first blood, yet all aroused fierce excitement. Much silver changed hands upon the outcomes, the various combatants either being cheered for their valour or jeered for their cowardice. The fighting brought the hall again to life, and many, even the servitors who had waited upon the tables, now crowded the doorways to watch. There followed wrestling in a peculiar Hillman style, the combatants stripped to the waist and greased to make the holds more difficult. But Leighor remembered little of this, nor how the evening finally ended and they came at last to their beds.

Chapter Twenty Two
THE HALL OF THE STORMGIANT KING

'We have argued long and hard while you slept,' Kazmir began briskly, when the seven groggy travellers were brought back into the presence of the Hillman elders the next morning. 'And we have come to a decision...'

There was a pause.

'Well?' Telsyan demanded. 'What have you decided to do with us?'

'You may go free,' Kazmir answered. 'But on one condition.'

'And that is?'

'That you swear upon your holiest oath to reveal to no one what you have seen here at Dom Udun Covarr; and that you shall tell none of the whereabouts of this place.'

'That we shall swear,' Telsyan nodded quickly. 'In fact I do not think we could find our way here again even if we wished it.'

'You would be wise to ensure that that remains so,' the other replied without humour. 'It is a great risk we take in releasing you, now that you know so many of our secrets – a risk many of us would prefer not to take. Make sure that you do not give us cause to regret our decision.'

'And our horses and possessions: our weapons?' Uhlendof asked. 'Shall they be returned to us?'

'We are not thieves!' The chieftain's words grated. 'All that is rightfully yours shall be returned to you. Yet before you depart, I would ask whether you truly wish to learn more of the Mage Metal, *harrunor*, and of those who rule its secrets?'

'Aye,' the monk said cautiously.

'Then if you truly seek that knowledge, perhaps I can tell you where you may find it. A place quite close by, yet where no man of your race has ventured for half a hundred years.'

'What place?' Telsyan asked at once. 'Where and how far?'

'It will not be far out of your way: two days, three at the most, on horseback – and one of my own men will guide you.'

'But where?' Uhlendof asked again. 'And what shall we hope to find there?'

'The where is *Byriadon*, the cloud bringer, king of High Ghorrunar. A tall mountain and cold, yet you will find the climbing easy enough. Easier by far than those you will meet there. The what, is knowledge: the wisdom of he who dwells there; Karadas-Ulgar, the Storm King.'

'Is this a king of your people?' Leighor asked.

For the first time Kazmir smiled. 'I am sorry,' he apologised quickly. 'But your error is indeed great. Karadas-Ulgar is no king of my race, nor of yours – nor yet of any line of men. Have you not heard tell of the Stormgiants of High Ghorrunar? For it is they you must seek out if you would gain true knowledge of the *Gath-Harrunnor*.'

'Stormgiants?' Yeon's jaw dropped.

'Aye,' the chieftain nodded grimly. 'The first children of the old gods. Wise and mighty, proud and terrible. Do you have courage enough to venture upon their domain, manlings? Or is your desire for knowledge not now so great?'

'I think I would like to meet a Stormgiant,' Uhlendof announced suddenly. 'Or to see one at close hand at least. I have often wondered at the tales travellers bring of such creatures, to warm lands and credulous folk. Let us take this chance, and see if the old legends truly live.'

'They live,' Kazmir told him darkly. 'And you may find it little to your liking that they do. For they can be capricious and unpredictable, their humours good or ill as the weather turns. Beware!'

'Your warning is well spoken,' Telsyan nodded. 'And these giants may have no knowledge of the *harrunor* worth the telling. Our main task remains to reach Darien before the snows, and we have few enough days of good weather left for that.'

'But we cannot let such an opportunity pass us by,' Uhlendof insisted. 'This Storm King may hold knowledge that we would curse ourselves later for not learning. We have until the spring to reach Tershelline: what difference will two days more make?'

'Perhaps more than we know,' Telsyan grunted. 'Yet I suppose we had better do as you suggest – even if the journey proves as fruitless as I fear.' He nodded to the waiting *maezgrull* elders. 'We shall accept your offer.'

It took three days of hard riding to reach the foot of Mount Byriadon. Emerging from one of the lesser tunnels on to a bare, north-facing mountainside, they rode north behind their solitary Hillman guide. This was one Harstond, who spoke little as he urged his small, fleet-footed pony along stony vales beneath dark-towered mountains. A cruel wind whipped down constantly from the north-west, unremitting for the duration of their journey; and although a pale sun shone, its rays seemed not to have the power to dispel the cold.

On the morning of the third day, the travellers awoke to find the skies no longer blue. A thin blanket of watery cloud had crept up under cover of darkness to drape the skies in grey.

'Do you think we shall have snow?' Leighor asked apprehensively as they made ready to depart.

'Not today,' Harstond declared firmly, lifting his head to sniff the north wind. 'Tomorrow perhaps: the day after for certain.' He turned away to see to his mount's harness, leaving the travellers to stare at one another in dismay.

'And shall we be at Mount Byriadon before then?' Telsyan asked quickly.

'Mount Byriadon?' Their guide's voice bore traces of surprise. 'That *is* Mount Byriadon. You see him now before you!' He nodded absently towards a bare, twin-pinnacled peak that jutted high above the lesser mountains all around it.

'Why did you not tell us before?' Uhlendof asked irritably. 'We have been staring at that peak since noon yesterday!'

Harstond shrugged. 'We shall be at its foot this morning. Then you shall see it even better.'

They still had some way to go, however, and many twisting mountain valleys to traverse before they got there.

'How much farther?' Telsyan asked after an hour of riding.

'Three leagues, no more,' the Hillman answered. 'We ride now through the Pass of Dorrund.' He nodded towards sheer cliffs that closed in rapidly on either side: cliffs that had already cut off all sight of the gaunt mountain that was their goal. 'Soon now you shall see the first of the giants' workings: the gates of Korgoth Vale.'

Harstond proved as good as his word, for around the next bend a truly awesome sight met the travellers' eyes. At the head of the pass the granite cliffs nearly met, their bases only some twenty yards apart. And here the shattered remnants of a single enormous stone gate lay strewn across the pass, the fragments so vast that the smallest of them must easily outweigh any two of their mounts. Leighor drew a sharp breath of wonder. In its original state the monstrous wheel of rock must have stood at least fifty feet high, its weight incalculable. What power on earth could have created, or even moved, so monstrous an artefact? And what other power, still greater, could have so utterly destroyed it?

There was a sickening feeling deep in the pit of Leighor's stomach that he knew the answer to that question only too well.

Urging their horses onward, the travellers traversed a sunken ditch to make their way on down the pass. The giant workings grew even more numerous as they proceeded. Here and there huge caverns had been cut into the living rock: some set behind great archways of carved and graven stone, others behind pillared porticoes approached by steps a yard high. Perhaps in some past age these had once been guardhouses or dwelling places. Now all lay long abandoned, inhabited only by a handful of timid rodents and dark-seeking bats.

The travellers rode on past fallen pillars and humbled statues, their features long since scoured away by wind and weather. Most still lay where they had fallen long ages before, yet a few seemed to have been moved in more recent times to clear the way. Smothered beneath rough coats of moss and lichen, all of these massive artefacts were being slowly strangled by twining tendrils and tough, tenacious roots.

The Pass of Dorrund had suddenly become a cheerless and oppressive place.

It took nearly an hour for the mounted travellers to complete the passage of the pass. Emerging suddenly into the deep vale beneath Mount Byriadon, they saw the peak at close quarters for the first time.

It was indeed a noble mountain, the true king of High Ghorrunar. Soaring high above them into the clouds, it dominated all else around it, its cold grey flanks savage and magnificent beneath a white mantle of snow. A sparkling blue glacier ran down from its westernmost col, to break and tumble down a vertical cliff-face a thousand feet in height. The wind whipped clouds of snow from its flanks to send them cascading into distant valleys far beneath.

'How on earth are we to climb that?' Telsyan gasped.

'There is a way,' their guide replied softly, urging his pony on towards the splayed feet of the mountain.

Having no other option, the others reluctantly followed.

It was noon when they crossed the last small valley stream to begin the ascent. The travellers approached with trepidation, not daring even to guess how they might scale such a terrible peak. They had seen no more of the giants' workings since leaving the Pass of Dorrund, and there was nothing now to indicate that intelligent creatures had ever dwelt here.

Harstond, however, pressed on undaunted, leading the travellers along a gently rising trail that coiled up the lower flanks of the mountain. Leighor hardly dared glance upward as they rode – the sight of the wind whipping through the high snows above, was enough to chill him to the marrow before ever he felt its touch. He pulled down the hood of his heavy robe and rode on.

The trail wound steadily upward for an hour or more, passing gently from green meadow to steep, boulder-strewn scree. Looking back, Leighor was surprised to see how high they had already come. The narrow entrance to the Pass of Dorrund now lay far beneath them, and great new vistas had opened up before and behind. With a start he realised that it would take but one misplaced footfall to send both him and his mount tumbling thousands of feet to their deaths. He rode with more care thereafter, impatient now for the moment when they must all dismount and continue on foot.

Yet to his surprise, when the signal finally came to dismount, it was only in order to lead the horses up from their rough trail on to what looked to be a broad stone platform some twenty feet above them. He wondered what possible purpose such a platform could serve halfway up the mountain. And then, with an icy chill of disbelief, realisation struck. Truly it was no mere platform that he stared at . . . It was nothing less than the beginning of a great stone roadway up the mountain! For a moment Leighor feared he must be dreaming, refusing to believe the evidence of his own eyes. But the startled exclamations of his companions, and the fact that the road refused either to melt away or to dissolve into the mists, forced him to accept it.

More tangible proof came when the travellers finally struggled up on to its broad stone surface. Six yards wide, and raised of stone blocks two yards square, it clung limpet-like to the side of the mountain. In fact the enormous roadway seemed fused by some impossible magic to the sheer cliff face, snaking its way up in series upon series of precipitate hairpin bends, finally to lose itself in the clouds. In places it overhung sheer drops of thousands of feet; in others it followed a gentler path. Yet always it maintained the same smooth gradient, and nowhere did it seem to narrow or fall away. Leighor could not even begin to guess at its antiquity, but he marvelled at its construction, at its enormity, and at how it had so withstood the ravages of time and weather.

Moss and lichen carpeted the stones, making them unnervingly slippery beneath their feet. Yet without this road the near-vertical walls of Byriadon would have been impossible to climb, and the travellers mounted once more in awed silence.

The temperature fell as the long hours of the climb went by: slowly at first, and then more rapidly as the winds strengthened. A constant hail of snow and ice rained down on them from above, cutting into hands, faces, and all exposed areas of skin. Small patches of snow began to appear wherever the wind permitted it to gather, in the deeper cracks and crevices of the rock. And there was ice too: where snow had melted in the sun, or a small summer rivulet had once spilled across the roadway.

A magnificent vista now opened out to the east, where great Korgoth Vale cut through snowcapped mountains towards an unseen horizon. It was a truly majestic sight. The travellers could watch the fleeting patches of sunlight racing across the meadows thousands of feet below. The sheer scale of the landscape was awesome. Surely this was a country fit for giants.

They had begun to ascend into high cloud. Lank, smoky tendrils swirled down to meet them, gathering the mountain in a veil of white. Even the ghostly figure of Master Telsyan, two horses up the line, was barely visible now as it retreated into the mists. Time passed slowly; the sky growing steadily darker overhead; the hovering curtain of cloud billowing gently all around them. And still the travellers climbed, mist-sodden and silent, through the aching cold.

Just as Leighor was growing resigned to their journey lasting well into the night, the fog began to thin around them. In moments they were above the cloud, and riding into the last cold shadows of the setting sun. Now they could see the way ahead once more, and there was far less cold grey mountain above them than there had been. They were approaching the summit.

The stone roadway twisted twice more, bringing them within a dozen feet of the final rise. The wind was bitingly cold now, and the travellers were glad indeed that it blew only at their backs. Even so, the gusts held frightening power.

Expectantly they rounded the last loop in the road to crest the ridge. Leighor was disappointed to discover that this was not yet the summit, for the road still climbed – upon a gentler incline – towards the true peak, a good quarter of a league distant, and some five hundred feet above them. Ahead rose a wide, snowswept waste which climbed in a series of broad sweeps towards the central peak. A steeper rise towards one of the lesser spurs on their left now protected them from the full force of the wind.

And then Leighor saw them: two men – or so they seemed at first – sitting beneath an overhang of rock not fifty feet away. Thickset and bearded, they were dressed in shaggy tunics of goatskin and fur, with heavy leather breeches and thick cloth leggings against the cold. Yet it quickly became clear that these were no ordinary men. For each must stand at least twice the height of any of the travellers, and weigh many times more.

'Giants!' Leighor hissed.

'Aye, stranger,' one of the two nodded grimly, giving the travellers only a brief sidelong glance to acknowledge their existence. Yet he spoke in perfect Durian, his voice deep and resonant, as though it might shake the very bedrock of the mountain if he willed it to. 'Who else might one expect to find atop stark Byriadon? Yet why come you here, to trespass upon our sacred mountain?'

Neither of the two attempted to rise or approach, both seeming totally engrossed in a game of dice which they played on the open ground between them. Seeing that their Hillman guide had no intention of answering for them, Telsyan urged his horse forward.

'Sirs,' he began, in as loud a voice as he could muster. 'We seek audience of your king, the noble Karadas-Ulgar. We are eight travellers, come from far and distant lands to seek his most wise counsel!'

There was silence for several minutes as one of the giants threw six stone dice as big as goose eggs to the ground in front of him, bending to study the result before speaking again. 'The king has no business with strangers,' he growled darkly. 'From wherever they come! You were not summoned here. No invitation has been sent. So go! Back to whatever dark fleapit spawned you!' He turned curtly back to his game.

Telsyan's jaw dropped open. 'Sirs, you cannot treat us so!' His voice was almost inaudible, torn apart by the sheer force of the wind. 'You know not the business on which we are come to this place. Do you not know that there are forces at work in these lands that threaten all things living? Forces that may threaten even you in time, if you do not now aid those who struggle against them. If you, in turn, do not accept our aid . . .'

'We have need of no aid that you few puny wretches have to offer,' the second giant snorted. 'Now depart, and trouble us no more!'

'How can we depart?' Telsyan rallied angrily. 'Can you not see that darkness now falls? That none of us could survive a single night unprotected on this mountain? Is there not one speck of honour or hospitality amongst you?'

'Speak not to us of hospitality!' the other giant turned on them in fury. 'Who has invited you here to this our dwelling place? Did any of our number? Nay. What befalls you then, lies upon your own head. Part! You are no guests of ours!' Picking up a small boulder that lay nearby, he weighed it idly in his hand, and then suddenly hurled it towards the travellers. Leighor watched it come with a disturbing sense of detachment, hardly flinching as it flew over his head to miss the rear of Zindur's horse by inches, shattering into a hundred pieces against the harder rocks below.

'Dog!' Zindur roared, striving to control his startled mount. 'Coward! Brazen whelp of a she-cur! Come forth and fight like men: and I shall slay the both of you! One by one, or both together – as you will!' Before Telsyan could do anything to stop him, the warrior, managing at last to rein in his horse, had unhooked his great war-axe and hurled it directly at the astonished giant.

Not expecting such a vigorous response, the giants stumbled, startled, to their feet. Zindur rode straight towards them in white-hot fury. On horseback he came almost to the shoulders of the standing giants. He struck out with his sword, sending the nearest of them stumbling several stunned steps backward.

'Hold! This is madness!' Telsyan roared, reaching forward to grasp the bridle of Zindur's mount – even as the second giant produced a heavy stone club as large as a man.

'Nay!' Zindur broke angrily from the merchant's hold. 'I will not die like a cur on this open mountainside! If we are to die, let us at least take some of these beggarly dogs with us!'

The others drew reluctantly closer, circling the two giants at what they hoped was a safe distance, weapons drawn and ready. Yet in truth they knew not what they might hope to achieve against a pair of such awesome foes. The bones of horse and rider both might easily be shattered by but one blow from a giant's club.

Yet to Leighor's surprise it was the sound of deep, guffawing laughter that next assailed his ears. He looked across in astonishment to see that it came from the stouter of the two giants – who stood watching from behind as the other fended off Zindur's mount with his great club, holding both it and its furious rider securely at arm's length. In fact Zindur did indeed look a vaguely comical figure as he struck out impotently against an opponent permanently beyond his reach.

'Hold! Hold!' the first laughed, wiping the tears from his eyes. 'I have not had such merriment for many a long day. It would be a sad shame to slay such eager foes as these! Put away your swords, fine fellows. We only sought to test your mettle, and to have a small jest with you. It is enough!'

Somewhat sheepishly the travellers lowered their weapons.

'There, good fellows,' the first repeated, bending to retrieve Zindur's fallen axe, and handing it back to him. 'You are bonny fighters for all your size, and we are well met. Follow, and we shall take you into the presence of the Great King directly.' He swung sharply about, to lead the eight mounted travellers on across the snowy plateau; glancing back over his massive shoulders every few yards or so to chortle deeply into his great woolly beard.

Leighor began to notice a number of vast constructions built into the iron-grey mountainside on their left; long, stone-built galleries, whose dark, vaulting arches ran parallel with the rising roadway for several furlongs. Yet all now lay roofless, snowswept and utterly abandoned. What purpose these massive structures had once served, he could not guess; but they seemed one more indication of the diminishing power and numbers of even this great race of giants. Slowly, as the road coiled up towards the dark peak, more ruins revealed themselves: great ageless halls and bastions, of tumbled stone and crumbling mortar, constructed on a scale to astonish the eye. Unbelievable, were it not for the still grander scale of the savage peak that towered above them.

Then, at last, their goal came in sight: a mighty stronghold indeed, raised of the same dark stone as the mountain into which it was built. A broad stair of shining stone coiled upwards from its high ramparts to reach a single tower, growing like a thin, pointing finger from the very summit of the mountain. Tall, grim and high-turreted, the walls of this gaunt fortress glowered disdainfully down upon all that lay beneath.

Leighor shuddered as they passed beneath an open gateway that arched a full hundred feet above them. Gargantuan blocks of ice-clad stone, a dozen feet thick, hung poised above their heads. Alien designs and unknowable scripts were etched into the walls, and a fearsome wind still blew. Surely they had come to the ends of the earth.

Apart from their two giant guides, there seemed to be no one living in all of this colossal fortress. A hundred windows stared, open and unglazed, into the night. And in all this dark immensity no light shone. The giants led them straight up into the main citadel, only halting for the riders to dismount once they were within the actual building. Here the ceilings rose seventy or eighty feet into the darkness, and even the small chamber where they unburdened and tethered their horses seemed at least a hundred paces across. They followed on foot now, through great darkened hallways and up several flights of monstrous stone steps whose treads were so high that they had to clamber rather than walk up them, passing along several more broad passages to come at last before a pair of immense wooden doors.

'Prepare yourselves, strangers,' the first giant instructed sternly. 'You are about to enter the presence of Karadas-Ulgar the mighty, true son of the Elder Gods, King of Storms and Lord of the High Reaches.'

The great doors swung open before them. And trepidly the travellers advanced into the darkened chamber beyond, wondering what greater wonders they must yet face.

The room was dark and cold. An icy wind blasted through it, almost as stern as that which scoured the barren mountainside beyond. For an unnerving minute Leighor could see nothing, not even the vast ceiling that soared above them into the darkness, supported by a forest of stone pillars, each broader than any four of the greatest trees of Hathanwild. He felt for a moment like some lowly insect that had had the temerity to crawl into a tourney hall. An insignificant nothing, surrounded by such greatness.

A dull flame flickered in a far-off corner of the hall, and it was towards this that the travellers were led, slowly discerning the great stone-carved, ice-encrusted throne that rose out of the gloom before them. Behind it, six high-vaulted windows stared sightlessly out across the open mountainside, granite sills half-buried in piles of drifted snow. In front of the throne, in a round stone hollow, a roaring pyre burned, the thin veils of smoke partially obscuring he who sat behind.

It was only slowly that Leighor managed to make out the massive figure bathed in its crimson light. A daunting titan in long robes of bearskin and ermine, seated upon a throne that dwarfed even him: the Storm King. Their two guides fell to their knees before him, and the travellers felt it wisest to do likewise.

'Greetings, wayfarers.' As the king rose from his seat to welcome them, Leighor noticed for the first time the open crown of beaten gold that rested upon his brow. In sheer weight of metal it must be worth a king's ransom – should anyone ever have the temerity to steal it. The king nodded to them graciously. 'You have been long expected.'

'Long expected?' Uhlendof queried, rising to his feet. 'How so, my lord?'

Karadas-Ulgar smiled, the action emphasising the lines of age that creased his face, and the great beard that was now three-quarters grey, where once it must have been as black as the earth-coals of the *maezgrull*.

'Aye,' he nodded once more. 'It is not for naught that we dwell atop this high mountain, for here we may see all strangers coming from afar. You were first sighted by our watchers a full two days before you ventured into the Pass of Dorrund.'

'Two days?' Telsyan sniffed disbelievingly.

'Indeed, stranger.' Their host drew back the mottled skin from one bewrinkled eye. 'The eyes of a giant are passing strong, for we must needs see far beyond the vision of other men. Indeed, that is why I sent forth my servants, Evok and Tharlas-din, to the lip of the mountain to welcome you.'

'And fine welcome we received!' Yeon muttered as the king returned to his seat.

Leighor found himself hoping that a giant's hearing was not as good as his eyesight. But the Storm King seemed not to have heard the youth's remark, sprawling back into his stone-carved throne with a cavernous grunt. He clapped his hands sharply together, producing a fierce sound that echoed and re-echoed around the vast stone chamber.

For a moment there seemed no response, the echoes dying slowly away into the whistle of the dark wind. But then Leighor detected a movement, small and indeterminate, in the gloomy distances of a lefthand gallery. A figure approached, and as it drew closer he was startled to realise that it was female.

A female giant! Somehow he had not imagined such a creature. She seemed only slightly smaller than her male companions, with a round, lumpy face tightly confined within the folds of a red woollen headscarf the size of a bedcloth. The rest of her clothes were of more sombre hue, being for the most part of dappled brown homespun: a close fitting bodice that emphasised her heavy build, and a long, shapeless skirt that billowed softly around her leather-shod feet. She approached the fire and waited silently for the king to speak.

'Fair Hemmega,' he smiled. 'Fetch food and wine for our guests, and soft pillows for their rest, for they will be both tired and hungry from their journey.'

'Aye, my lord.' Her voice was softer than the king's, but it seemed just as sonorous. She inclined her head briefly in acknowledgement, and was gone.

A cold silence fell once she had departed, and to break it Telsyan ventured a compliment. 'You have a very good command of the Durian speech, my lord. In fact it is the fairest I have ever heard that tongue pronounced by one not born to it.'

'Indeed?' the king nodded, giving the appearance of pleasure. 'I have learned to speak many of the tongues of men in my time: the Durian, the Giellin, the Varroain, the dark speech of Khiorim and even the Qhilmun tongue of old.' He marked them off on his fingers as he named them. 'Besides which, I have a fair knowledge of the *mazgroll* speech and those of the other races of lesser men.'

'An impressive feat, sire.' Telsyan bowed his head. 'For in all my years of travel I have been able to master no more than the barest rudiments of three languages beside my own.'

'In all your years?' Karadas-Ulgar snorted. 'How many years have you, fleabite? Two score? Two and a half? Three score, no more! And do you know how long I have sat here upon this granite throne? Guess,' he commanded suddenly.

'Ninety years?' Yeon ventured.

The Storm King laughed out loud. 'Ninety years! Nay, even Durugahr, whom we term our youngstrel, has seven more than that; and we think him only fit to tend the goats! Yet he had reached his manhood before your grandfather was born. No, stranger, next midsummer day I shall be in my four hundred and eightieth year; and that is old even for one of our race.'

'Four hundred and eighty years!' Keran gasped.

'Aye, girl.' The king's tone grew more sombre. 'We are a long-lived race by the standard of your folk. Aye, and of most folk who yet dwell upon this earth. We are few in number, and in recompense we have been granted wisdom and length of days. But it was a hard bargain, for there have ever been more men than women amongst us, and now fair Hemmega is the only woman who remains of all our race.' He paused a moment before speaking again. 'Her last child was Durugahr.'

'And if there are no more girl children?' Keran began.

The king shook his head. 'Then there will be an end to the race of Stormgiants; and in the long centuries to come our memory shall become no more than legend – a half-remembered tale that your decendants yet unborn shall tell to their grandchildren over the winter fires.'

There was silence for many minutes, before the king spoke again. 'Now, wayfarers.' He sat back. 'Tell me the story of your travels, and why you seek audience of me.'

Again the travellers' story took long to tell, for Uhlendof left out very little of importance, describing their quest, and all that had occurred since its outset, in detail. Throughout, the king sat with eyes closed, making no comment and asking no question, only nodding or giving the odd grunt of acknowledgement to show that he was still listening. Even when the monk had finished his tale there came no immediate reply, and for long minutes only the laboured breathing of the Storm King broke the stillness. The travellers glanced at one another dubiously.

Telsyan stepped forward. 'We have come to seek your counsel, sire!'

'Hmmn?' Karadas-Ulgar shifted suddenly in his seat as though startled from some half slumber.

'For your counsel, my lord,' Uhlendof repeated. 'We have come to seek knowledge of the *harrunor*. Knowledge that may help us to withstand the onslaught of the dark enemy whose forces now fill these northlands.'

'Counsel?' The king sounded surprised to receive such a request, sitting back in his throne to comb thoughtfully through his great beard with the fingers of one hand. 'What form of counsel do you seek of me?'

'Knowledge, sire,' Uhlendof repeated. 'Of the *harrunor* and of the amulets: of who constructs them, and what gives them their power; of who controls them, and how they may be countered.'

'You ask much,' Karadas-Ulgar smiled. 'What makes you think that we have such knowledge?'

'It has long been held amongst our folk that the giants possess great knowledge and wisdom; and this we have also been told by the *maezgrull* of Dom Udun Covarr, who led us to this place. If anyone in all these northlands has such knowledge we are sure it will be you.'

The king nodded. 'Perhaps, Master priest, perhaps. Mayhap there are indeed some things I could tell you that would be of use to your cause. But what payment could you make for such knowledge?'

'Payment?' the monk was taken aback. 'Payment . . . ? We have but little gold . . .'

'I do not speak of gold!' Anger flashed in Karadas-Ulgar's eyes for the first time. 'Do you think that we, who have warded the treasures of High Ghorrunar for a score of centuries, hunger for your few paltry coins? I speak of payment of more fitting kind. Payment more in accord with what you ask. What have you to offer that is of real worth?'

'We offer friendship,' Telsyan said quickly. 'Allies willing to join with you against a common foe; willing to face that foe before it falls upon you. There are many in the lands below who would fight if they could only be warned of the danger, given some means to resist – some means by which they might hope to defeat the power of those who wield the *harrunor*.'

The king did not reply immediately, but waited as Hemmega returned, a pile of heavy cushions in her arms. Seeming to consider the merchant's words at length, he watched as she laid them in a neat row before the firepit. Impatiently he motioned the travellers to sit, and only when they had done so did he finally speak.

'Well is it said that a manling's promises are like the snows of springtime – ever present in abundance until summer comes and one has need of them. No.' He shook his head. 'Your promises are no payment. And even if they were worth all the gold in Azaranth we would still have need of no allies. For none would be so foolish as to attack us here upon our sacred mountain.'

'Then who has shattered your gatestone?' Inanys queried archly. 'Or did it fall by mischance into a thousand fragments in the Pass of Dorrund?'

Karadas-Ulgar's face darkened visibly, Leighor shuddering at the speed with which the crookback's smallest intervention could provoke its habitual response. 'We are secure enough without your aid! Let that suffice. And as for that which shattered the stone; that, and much else best forgotten, is long departed from this world.'

'Then what is your price?' Leighor begged in exasperation. 'Name it, and if it is ours to give, you shall have it. Do you perhaps desire some magical artefact or thing of power? If so, this staff that I hold is all that we bear. Yet it works strange magicks which I myself do not fully comprehend; and if you wish it, it is gladly yours.'

The giant leaned forward to pluck the staff from Leighor's fingers, holding it daintily between thumb and forefinger as he perused it, studying it with some interest before smiling softly to himself, as if at some secret joke, and handing it back to its owner. 'You had best keep it,' he told the southron gravely. 'You will have more need of it among your folk than I amongst mine. Again that is not the payment I desire. No, strangers,' he smiled, sitting firmly back in his great seat once more. 'All I desire of you is what you are most free to give; some small amusement to lighten our dark night hours. There are but five of us who still dwell on this mountain; and four more who live beyond: Kharst and Fornstall, who farm the lower lands of Korgoth Vale,' he pointed vaguely away into the darkness, 'and Athors and Durugahr who herd sheep and goats on the slopes of the far mountains. Such is poor company at best, and grows the more jaded with the passing years, even as the visitors we receive grow fewer. On winter nights these halls throng with the ghosts of the departed, so that naught may dispel them.'

'Then would you hear tales of distant lands?' Telsyan asked, rising to stand alongside Leighor. 'For there are few places in all the eastern realms which one or other of us has not visited, and there are few fair tales I could not tell you; and much news besides.'

'Nay,' the giant shook his head once more. 'Of these things I know enough; and I trow I could tell more tales than ye, had I the mind to recall them all. We care but little for the affairs of humans; to us their lands and squabbles seem small and petty and very much alike. As for these other places: could any compare with what I have already seen? The green ice floes of the Sea of Crystal, which sunder the continent of men from the land where all ice and snow have their birth, where lies the cave of the North Wind, and where the ruler of the Nine Winds himself has his resting place? Have you seen such wonders as lie there, merchant? The bellows of the North Wind that makes the Zephyrs dance, and can tear the masts from the golden galleons that ply the seas a thousand leagues to the south? No, I need no travellers' tales.'

'Then what?' Telsyan asked, defeated.

'A contest!' the king grinned good-humouredly. 'And upon the result shall hang your answer. Here. Good Hemmega comes once more, with your food and drink; and whilst you eat, we shall prepare. Evok!' He beckoned to one of his escort. 'Fetch us good Master Mhindoran with his cage, and then set out the table!'

Chapter Twenty Three
THE STRATAGEMS OF KARADAS-ULGAR

The travellers were given little time to dwell upon what lay ahead of them, Hemmega quickly dispensing vast wooden bowls of thick soup, which they ate hungrily as Tharlash-Din set up a great chess table before them. Carved from a single piece of cream-coloured ivory, and inlaid with polished teak, it stood at least five feet high and a good half a dozen square. Carefully, the retainer set up the twin rows of jade and ivory pieces. Leighor stole a quick sidelong glance at the merchant as he did so, to see that his eyes too were firmly fixed upon the tall, elegantly carved figures. The southron could not even guess at their value, but he had a fair idea that Telsyan was even now estimating, to the nearest silver mark, just what they would fetch in the Gold Market at Selethir. He turned back to his bowl, wondering uneasily whether the bargain was as simple as it seemed.

The rest of the company had not long drained their bowls when Evok returned, accompanied by another, still broader, giant – who must be the summoned Mhindoran. The newcomer was clad entirely in stained, loose-fitting leathers; his arms bare but for the thick brazen bands that girded each. Yet broad as these bands were, even they looked as if they might snap like dry twigs at the slightest exertion of the immense muscles that played beneath. He alone of all the male giants wore no beard, and his face was square and heavy-boned, bearing a single white scar from cheek to chin. A heavy iron cage some four feet square swung from his left hand, its contents silent and invisible beneath a cover of coarse brown cloth. Somehow this troubled the southron more than anything else that lay prepared for them, and he could not tear his eyes from it. Nervously he watched as the giant dropped the cage to the floor in front of the throne and sat down upon it. Within, something stirred.

'Have you had your fill?' Karadas-Ulgar asked, studying the travellers expectantly from beneath hooded eyes; much as Leighor had seen the charmers' snakes in distant Syrne study the small rodents that were to supply their next meal.

The travellers nodded.

'Good!' The king sat forward. 'Before us lies a game which all men of affairs should play well. Let us see what you are capable of . . .' he laughed softly, '. . . you who would save the world from the Dark One. We shall play three games. If you win but one of three, your debt shall be honoured in full.'

'And which of us would you play against, sire?' Telsyan asked.

'Your best,' the giant smiled. 'Yet I consider myself a player of fair merit; and to make the game fairer, you may confer together if you wish. But you must elect a headman to play your move for you.'

Like all who dwelt in the southern lands Leighor had a passing knowledge of such games, yet not the skill of a master. And of the others, only Uhlendof, Telsyan and Harstond would admit to any greater experience. And so it was these four who stood to face Karadas-Ulgar, with Telsyan as their arbiter and spokesman.

The other giants drew up low stools around the table as the game began, that they might have a better view of all that passed, Evok being assigned the task of moving those pieces which Telsyan himself could not reach. Yet despite these early distractions, the run of the game seemed at first to go well enough, the initial tentative moves being swiftly made on both sides. But as the game progressed, and the position upon the board grew more complex, the king's decisions continued to be made with the same discouraging speed. So fast, in fact that the travellers had barely time to draw breath after making their own move before it was their turn again, Karadas-Ulgar tutting and drumming his fingers impatiently against the arm of his chair all the while. Placed under such pressure, the travellers' moves grew hurried and slapdash. And Leighor was not truly surprised when, early on in their deliberations, Karadas-Ulgar's ivory Thaumaturge swept forward into the heart of their jade-green ranks to secure an easy victory.

'That was a fair game . . .' the king sat back in his chair, a broad grin forcing its way across his face, '. . . yet short. You had best play a little longer next time, manlings, or you may soon lose all.'

Inanys chuckled quietly to himself on the cushions behind them, as Evok re-set the board.

'This time we must not allow ourselves to be hurried!' Telsyan whispered sharply. 'We cannot afford to give him another game so easy!'

And indeed, the next game went a deal better. For no matter how much the king might drum his fingers or roll his eyes heavenwards whilst he waited for them, the travellers took their time. And slowly the four companions built up a strong defensive position; the all-important Warlord and his Vizier protected by firm wedges of unswerving Peons, while the twin Thaumaturges and their attendant Knights spearheaded an attack on the right flank. Leighor's hopes began to rise still further when one of the giant's own Knights fell. The whole of Karadas-Ulgar's left flank seemed suddenly weak and exposed. It would take but the removal of a single Castle to bring about a total collapse . . . A slow grin forming on his face, Telsyan gave the instruction.

It was only when Leighor looked upward and saw the triumphant smile upon their opponent's face that he realised that all was not quite right. His eyes fell hurriedly to the board; and then he saw it. The removal of the Castle had opened a path for the King's Vizier across the board, so that every move now open to them seemed to lead only to disaster . . . A carefully prepared trap had slammed shut around them. Their whole well-ordered plan of attack had been foreseen, and turned against them! The travellers looked on aghast as their Warlord was toppled in just three more devastating moves.

'You have done well indeed, wayfarers.' Karadas-Ulgar's eyes twinkled wickedly. 'You have lasted close on a full hour! You improve! Perhaps, with a little good fortune, you may yet win the last.' He turned to whisper something to Mhindoran on his left.

The travellers could only stand in silence, to await the re-setting of the board. The other giants watched grimly and without comment.

'How are we to do better?' Uhlendof whispered. 'He defeats us as easily as if we were children. Is there not some trick, some new stratagem, that he may not know of?'

'Nothing that is certain.' Telsyan shook his head. 'I have already used most of my best plays.'

'So it seems.' Inanys's voice curled up mockingly from where he sat, a yard or so behind them. 'Have all your noble minds together not the wit to defeat one aged giant?'

'And yours has?' Telsyan swung round on him angrily.

The crookback shrugged. 'I could not of course aspire to such noble heights as yourselves . . .'

'Enough of that!' Telsyan snapped sharply. 'Can you play or no?'

'A little, my lords,' the hunched figure lowered his head in mock humility. 'I have had a game or two – of sorts.'

'Then drag yourself up off the floor and assist us!' the merchant growled. 'We need all the help we can get – even yours!'

Inanys smiled softly and obeyed.

The final game began slowly, and from the beginning it did not augur well, the travellers' disagreements growing ever more numerous as the game proceeded. For whatever the others thought the wisest or more prudent course, Inanys immediately rejected out of hand, always suggesting a move that seemed either completely irrelevant or openly foolish. Yet each time the travellers rejected his advice, their overall position only worsened; Karadas-Ulgar seeming ever able to foresee and confute their most carefully planned attacks. Gradually the travellers' play grew more and more defensive and demoralised, while Inanys's comments grew ever more derisive and filled with scorn. And so at last Telsyan decided to give him his head.

Once the decisions were his own to make, the game seemed to hold a fatal fascination for Inanys; and from that moment on he never took his eyes from the board for a single moment. He moved rarely, and then for only an instant, to see the disposition of the pieces from a different angle. Otherwise he stood almost motionless, his face a mask of single-minded concentration, which broke occasionally into a thin smile of pleasure when he found some stratagem that pleased him.

He played like a demon, Leighor thought, engrossed for the moment in this game alone; almost as if it were the only thing that still mattered in the whole of the world, as if his very life depended on it. He played after a fashion that none of the travellers had ever seen before, a style that ignored all the basic rules of defence and strategy. His moves seemed those of a madman; or of a child going through the motions of a game he did not fully understand. Yet somehow, although disaster always seemed to threaten, it never came. A hundred times it seemed the crookback played right into the giant's hands, a hundred times the travellers almost cried out in despair as a clumsily foolish move seemed set to throw away all that had been gained. But each time the trap failed to close.

Some counter, some threatened response, unseen by any but the two players, prevented the jaws of death from closing; and for a moment the travellers breathed again. For the first time Karadas-Ulgar began to look concerned – now playing intently and with full concentration. He and all the other giants were so engrossed now in the game that Leighor would have wagered that the rest of the company could all have risen and left the chamber, and none would have noted their parting.

It seemed to endure for hours, the time between each move stretching out as the game went on. Slowly the number of pieces on the board grew fewer, yet the basic balance remained unchanged. There was no sound now, throughout the great chamber, bar the soft howling of the north wind, the whispered instructions of Inanys to Evok, who moved his pieces, and the occasional indrawn breath from one or another of the giants in response to some unexpected move. Leighor shivered. Even as close to the fire pit as they were, the cold was shattering. No fire could warm such vast, empty halls as these, their windows open to wind and weather; and surely no heat on earth could counter the cutting wind that swept in unfettered from the mountainside beyond. This race of giants must be hardy beyond measure to endure these conditions for so long. Leighor tried to warm his cold-burned hands at the fire, praying for the game to end.

But the game went on seemingly endlessly, the moves only growing fewer and longer between, until king and crookback were left with but three men apiece – their Warlords and two others. And it seemed that neither could gain the advantage. A look passed between the players; and Inanys stood back from the board, turning to face his companions.

'Well?' Telsyan demanded.

'A draw,' the crookback shrugged. 'It was always the best I could achieve – given the position you left me. If you had but taken my suggestions earlier . . .' He smiled. 'Who knows?'

'You are a fair player, crooked one.' The king sank back expansively into his seat. 'You have given us much pleasure. Perhaps the best game we have had since the passing of old Morgreant Blackstaff. Your visit has been an opportune one, wayfarer.'

Inanys gave a gracious bow.

'And what of the answers we seek?' Uhlendof stepped forward. 'Will you now tell us that which we must know?'

'But you have not fulfilled the bargain, my friends.' The king shook his head. 'You have won no game. Not one of three. How then can I break my word? How may I tell you what you wish to know?'

'But we have drawn a game,' Telsyan protested. 'Surely you knew that we could not hope to win against such a noble player as yourself? A draw must be enough to satisfy honour.'

'Perhaps.' The flicker of a smile passed across Karadas-Ulgar's lips. 'Not enough to settle your debt perhaps, but enough to give you a further chance . . .'

'You mean another game?' Leighor asked, his conscience pricking him at how relieved he felt when the giant shook his head.

'No. That is past.' He waved absently for the board to be removed. 'There is another test I have in mind. One I have set by for just such a circumstance as this. A combat – with our champion.' He nodded sharply to Mhindoran, who at once rose to pick up the cage he had been seated upon, raising it high in one massive hand.

'Behold!'

Leighor looked up through the gloom to see a small, startled goblin creature peering out sleepily from behind the bars.

'That!' Yeon pointed scornfully. 'You wish us to fight that?'

The king nodded.

'Which one of us?'

'Any who so wishes. None, if it displeases you. But if there is no contest . . .' He shrugged.

'We will fight,' Zindur said at once. 'Release the creature and I shall take it on. I trust you wish it no great harm done?'

Karadas-Ulgar nodded gravely. 'Be not too unmerciful. Uthri has been with us many years, and we would be loath to lose his company.'

Mhindoran lowered the cage to the ground, unclasping the latch to let the creature crawl stiffly out. To Leighor it no longer seemed quite so much like the goblins he had seen earlier. Its skin was pitch black, without a single mark or blemish, and its limbs were long and angular. Its eyes, too, seemed somehow quicker and more fiery, almost as though they were formed of living amber; totally belying the slowness and stiffness the creature now displayed. Even so, it was in no way large or overthreatening. Its webbed feet splaying out beneath, it stretched itself slowly to its full height – and even then, its ragged ears only just came level with Zindur's hip.

Snorting dismissively, the warrior advanced upon the goblin-thing, arms outstretched. The creature paused, leaning back on its haunches and swaying slowly from side to side as if to study its adversary. Then suddenly, unexpectedly, it darted forward, evading Zindur's grasp like a greased pig to seize the startled mercenary about the legs; lifting him off the ground as though he were a straw-filled doll.

Then, just as casually, it tossed him aside, to skitter along the floor on his back until he was brought to a stunned halt at the foot of Karadas-Ulgar's throne, black burn marks smouldering wherever the goblin's fingers had come into contact with his clothing.

Yeon leapt forward at once, to receive roughly the same treatment; the creature's thin, spindly arms hurling the struggling youth half across the chamber, as it turned triumphantly to face the remaining travellers. Telsyan's sword flew from its scabbard; but it proved of no more use to him than had the warrior's strength. The creature, moving almost too fast for the eye to follow, dipped swiftly beneath his guard; seizing him by arm and shoulder to send him spinning across the cold stone floor. The merchant cried out as his doublet caught afire; rolling frantically over to try and smother the orange tongues of flame that had arisen wherever the goblin's hands had touched.

The creature turned again, stepping forward menacingly, arms outstretched.

'Enough!' Karadas-Ulgar's voice boomed out through the dark. 'These others, I think, have no wish to continue the contest.'

The dark goblin halted at once, slinking obediently back towards its cage at the king's command. The three chastened travellers struggled back to their feet amid gales of giant laughter.

'What . . . what is that thing?' Zindur gasped breathlessly.

'It is no goblin!' Yeon spat, dusting himself down and eyeing the retreating figure with malice.

'No,' Uhlendof stared directly up into the king's eyes. 'I think not.'

'You are correct in that, at least,' Karadas-Ulgar nodded. 'Uthri is no mere goblin, manling. Can it be that you have never before seen a Fire Imp? It is clear that you have not had cause to pick a quarrel with one before this, or you would not have been so incautious!' He chuckled softly.

Telsyan strove visibly to restrain his anger. 'You may consider this a great entertainment, my lord,' he said between gritted teeth. 'But we are come here on matters of great import; of deadly earnest for all who dwell in these lands. And all you have done thus far is to mock and make sport of us for your amusement! Setting us hopeless tasks which you knew we could never accomplish. Is this your way? To turn all of importance into foolish riddles and games for children?'

'Nay,' the King's face grew serious once more. 'We make no mock of you, manlings. But the knowledge that you seek is great, and the tasks you must perform to earn it cannot perforce be light. The tests we have set you have not been impossible; for that would indeed be to deceive and make sport of you – and that is not our way. The tasks can be performed, with skill and knowledge enow – but these you have failed to display.' He shook his head almost sadly. 'How shall you fight the great evils of which you speak, if you have not the skill to win a simple game of chess, nor the prowess to overcome a common Fire Imp? Nay, wayfarers; such knowledge as you seek holds many dangers, and cannot idly be given to those unworthy of its trust, lest in that manner still greater disasters befall.'

There was a silence.

'Indeed, my lord, I see your meaning,' Uhlendof said quietly at last. 'Yet I fear that in their main purpose your tests are mistaken. They may establish strength and craft and cunning, aye; but they cannot reveal truth, or courage, or resolution – and it is these which are the more important qualities for an endeavour such as ours. And that is why we shall proceed with our quest, until we meet with success; whether you choose to help us, or no.'

'Your courage is great,' the king admitted. 'Were it not so, you would not have dared to venture even so far. Perhaps, as you say, that is enough. Yet my word as king must stand; and you have not passed the tests. Therefore I may not grant your boon.'

'Have you no other test?' Yeon asked. 'No other riddle?'

Karadas-Ulgar shook his head. 'The imp was your test, fail with him and there can be no other.'

In that instant Yeon's chance word struck home; and Leighor suddenly realised . . . A riddle! Of course! The imp . . . This second test . . . It too was no more than a riddle! One such as filled any of a score of the sagas spun daily by the taleweavers of the Syrne markets. 'I have the answer!' he cried out suddenly. 'Let me take on your imp champion!'

'What!'

'Are you mad?'

The rest of his companions turned to stare at him in amazement.

'What nonsense is this?' Uhlendof demanded. 'How can you hope to fight such a creature, with one arm strapped and broken?'

'I have a way,' Leighor said firmly, pushing past him to stand alone before the throne. He looked across at the king. 'Will you accept my challenge, Sire?'

The king nodded, giving Mhindoran the signal to release the imp once more.

But Leighor did not wait for the creature to emerge from its cage. He knew now how deceptively fast and powerful it was; knew its hands would burn like coals, if ever they came into contact with his unprotected flesh. He had but a single chance, and that he must take at once!

Before the cage gate had swung fully open, he had turned on his heel and was racing, as fast as his aching body would carry him, towards the nearest of the great open windows that flanked Karadas-Ulgar's throne. Ignoring the cries of surprise and alarm behind him, he ran on; only hoping that he would have time to reach it before the imp caught up with him.

He was but a half-dozen paces from his goal when a bony hand pinioned his trailing ankle, dragging him to a halt. He cried out in pain as the foot of his robe dissolved in a curtain of black smoke; the imp's fingers burning like red-hot pincers as their grip tightened. He sought despairingly ahead. The great window was still a good four yards away – out of reach. Yet directly above him, to his right, rose the great stone frieze that towered up behind Karadas-Ulgar's throne; its grey stones encrusted with ice, a frozen cascade of glinting icicles clinging to its upper reaches.

Abruptly Leighor's leg was torn out from under him, and he was unable to keep his balance. Yet using the last iota of his remaining strength, he was at least able to direct his fall, hurling himself solidly into the base of the great frieze. An intense shock of pain knifed up through his injured arm. Pain enough to make him fear that he must surely have shattered it anew. But the giant base-stone trembled, sending a hail of icicles and brittle ice crystals showering down upon both him and his assailant.

The imp gave a sudden howl of pain, and released him to stagger drunkenly backward, the few ice particles that had chanced to alight upon its skin hissing and spattering away in a cloud of exploding steam. With a gasp of relief, Leighor forced himself back to his feet, ignoring his still-smouldering robes as he stumbled on towards the open window. Hastily scooping up a great armful of the snow that lay piled beneath its vaulting arch, he turned to face the imp once more.

'Hold!' Karadas-Ulgar commanded, as the dark creature began to back warily away, pale yellow welts forming on its skin wherever the ice had touched. 'You have proved your point, southling. Poor Uthri cannot bear the touch of water, in any of its forms. The answer to our little riddle was as simple as that. It is a pity indeed that you were unable to discover the solution entirely on your own . . .'

'What!' Leighor demanded, outraged. His injured arm did not seem to be as damaged as he had feared, but the pain was still intense enough to fuel his anger. 'We have done all that you have asked of us!'

But the king shook his head. 'I do not think that yours can be truly counted a fair victory. Once you had been told that Uthri was a Fire Imp, the solution was simple!' He drew a breath. 'Yet I shall not be too harsh. You have perhaps done enough to earn a final task.'

'And what is that to be?' Zindur asked sourly.

'I think a song,' Karadas-Ulgar said, watching the surprise upon the travellers faces with unconcealed amusement. 'That will not be too hard, will it, my friends? Yes,' he settled back into his seat with a sigh. 'It has been many long years since a visitor last brought us a new song; and the old are now become but poor amusement. Sing me one song that I have not heard before; if I know it not and cannot finish it for you, then you shall have won your prize. Which of you shall begin?'

In the end it was Telsyan who went first, stepping forward to sing a sailor's song from the taverns of Selethir. It was melodious and sad, and told of far-off lands where the sun shone, dark maidens sang, and life had few cares. But he had barely got through one verse when Karadas-Ulgar stopped him, reeling off the next few lines word-perfectly, before nodding briskly towards Leighor. 'That is a dry old song, well enough known since my father's time! Let us hope that you have a better.'

'Try something newer,' Uhlendof whispered quickly in his ear. 'Something that will not yet have reached this place.'

Leighor's mind raced, rejecting an obscure childhood song that he had already half decided upon in favour of a topical ballad he had heard only recently in a Felldur tavern. Yet to his surprise this fared no better than Telsyan's, and the giant broke in to finish it off in a trice, leaving him sorry that he had forsaken his earlier choice.

The others followed in quick succession: Harstond singing a low *mazgroll* song; Yeon; Zindur; and then Inanys, with a sibilant, mellifluous chant in some unfathomable tongue which Leighor could not identify. Yet Karadas-Ulgar knew even these, naming each and continuing the melody with evident pleasure. Now only Keran and Uhlendof were left, the monk seeming so engrossed in his own thoughts that Keran must needs go first. She chose a long ballad which Tavolir had once sung, called *Celandamir the Fair*, which told of a king's daughter promised to the sorceror, Megron; but who instead fled into the northlands with a young esquire, and so brought down great tragedy upon all her kinfolk, finally hurling herself from the sorceror's high mountain tower.

Karadas-Ulgar heard this through in its entirety before quietly applauding. 'Well sung, my girl.' He nodded his head. 'Yet your song is old, old even beyond your imagining. Your version sounds well enough, but the original has more truth, for it dates from the years of the Lost Kings and is better known to us in its original tongue; the High Qhilmun. Though it is many years since last I heard it sung so.' He began to hum the deep melody quietly to himself, gently lapsing into song in a tongue that sounded vaguely similar to that which Inanys had just used.

> *Qua-lun-damar qual demizir,*
> *Koth ulda-ron, koth ulgazir,*
> *Qua-lun-damar fol membrizeer,*
> *Qua-lun-damar Qua-rûn.*

His voice trailed off into silence, as though the song had uncovered some distant, half-forgotten memory, and again he shook his head, turning at last to look at Uhlendof.

'You are the last, priest. I hope that you have something new to sing to me, or our time together shall indeed be ended.'

'I do not think you will have heard this before, Sire.' Uhlendof stepped forward. 'Although this is a song from some time past, when I was but a young apprentice.'

'Then proceed,' Karadas-Ulgar nodded indifferently, 'but be sure that it is chosen well.'

Uhlendof nodded in return, then quickly drew breath and began to sing, the tune unexpectedly light and frivolous:

> *I want to go back to bed,*
> *I want to go back to bed,*
> *I've only just got up, I know,*
> *But I want to go back to bed.*
>
> *My eyes are like sand,*
> *And my brain is on fire,*
> *My head it doth ache,*
> *Like a bellowing choir,*
> *My bones are all throbbing,*
> *And not with desire,*
> *And I want to go back to bed!*
>
> *I've got to get up,*
> *There are things I must do,*
> *There is scouring and scrubbing,*
> *And woodcutting too,*
> *There's my master to see,*
> *And there's money that's due . . .*
> *Oh! I want to go back to bed!*

The song ended, Uhlendof stared the Stormgiant King boldly in the eye, folding his arms before him. 'Well?' he demanded.

'Is that then your song?' Karadas-Ulgar asked, his face expressionless.

Uhlendof nodded, and for a moment there was stiff silence between them.

'Well done!' the Storm King boomed at length. 'Yours is a fine song, and I am glad indeed to have heard it! You have won, priest. You have passed the test. Yet how is it that we have never heard this fine song before?'

'Because it is my own invention,' Uhlendof said simply. 'Which, for the greater part of its existence, has been no more than a forgotten scrawl upon an old fly-leaf.'

'Then you have solved the third riddle also,' the king growled good-humouredly. 'For we have been granted a knowledge of many things, and I would take a fair guess that there is not one known song in all the Great Continent that we could not divine if we chose. And therefore perhaps the only way you could have won the contest was with a song of your own devising.'

'Yet how so?' Leighor asked. 'How can you know of even the newest and most recent of songs, here in this isolated place?'

'There are other magicks beyond those of *harrunor*,' Karadas-Ulgar smiled softly, raising his right hand slowly into the darkness. 'See!'

A sudden cold wind gusted through the great chamber. Its path marked by the cloud of dust and debris that it threw up before it as it raced towards them, it roared through the hot flames of the fire-pit before vanishing into the dark galleries beyond. Yet an instant later it returned; whipping the tattered tapestries above the throne into a wild dervish-dance of despair as it whistled past. Now it began to circle the stunned group, drawing in ever closer to the king's upraised hand, until the travellers were forced to shield their eyes from the storm of dust, sand, and stinging ice-crystals that it whipped into their faces.

As quickly as it had arisen, the storm abated; the miniature whirlwind drawing slowly in upon itself, seeming to gather up more dust and light as it shrank. Slowly it descended towards the giant's upraised hand, hovering just above his broad fingers as the matter within began to swirl and condense; the whirling particles of dust and smoke coalescing to take on a wispy, insubstantial, human form.

The travellers blinked and rubbed their eyes, but the apparition still remained: unmistakably human, true in every detail, yet in perfect miniature – a phantom child that glanced out of the vortex of swirling wind with supreme uninterest. It chose to smile for an instant; perhaps at the astonishment on their faces, perhaps at some secret merriment. Yet that smile was not soft and childlike; but hard and knowing – as if it had seen much in its life of both good and ill, and cared little for either. Its eyes too were hard, hard and quick, constantly darting this way and that, sharp and unforgettable.

The vision remained but an instant, before dissolving back into the grey formlessness from which it had arisen. And with a sudden high-pitched shriek it was gone, tearing up the dust and debris into a blinding cloud behind it as it roared out through the ice-draped windows.

'What was that?' Yeon gasped, his voice echoing thinly in the sudden silence it had left behind.

'A Zephyr!' Karadas-Ulgar smiled. 'Nothing less! Berizel, one of the smaller and more harmless of the several that I have bonded to my service. I could call upon several greater if I chose – some that might tear even this great fortress to the bare stone if so commanded. Berizel though, is an errand-runner, and he brings me much that is new.'

'And this is how you gain your knowledge!' Keran exclaimed. 'Zephyrs who run your errands!'

'In part,' the king nodded. 'But we have other ways also.'

'And will you now tell us what we wish to know?' Telsyan demanded, stepping forward.

'I suppose I must,' the king nodded again. 'You have earned the knowledge. Good Mhindoran, our master of metals, shall answer your questions, as far as he is able.'

'As far as he is able?' Yeon repeated with open suspicion. 'I thought that you knew all?'

'Even our knowledge is not total,' Mhindoran chided softly. 'We too are but mortal, and our wisdom is not without limit. Yet our memories are long and our histories longer still – longer by far than any that yet linger in these eastern lands. So I shall answer your questions as fully as I can – to the limits of my knowledge.'

'Well then,' Telsyan sighed. 'Let us proceed until we reach those limits. I have but three questions to ask: What is *harrunor*? How is it used? And how may it be countered?'

'You will forgive me ...' Mhindoran drew his makeshift seat further forward, 'if I do not at first answer your questions directly. But what I have to say has direct bearing upon the knowledge you seek.' He leaned forward. 'You have all heard tell of ancient Qhilmun, have you not?'

The travellers nodded their heads, some a little more hesitantly than others.

'Then you shall know,' the ironmaster went on, 'that in the elder days of the world, and for close upon a thousand years, there was but one great kingdom in all the lands of men, and it was Qhilmun. Great was Qhilmun and mighty in her raiment of splendour. Qhilmun it was that built the ancient ways which still cross the scattered lands; Qhilmun that raised the great bridges that span the deep rivers – works such as none amongst all the races of man can now build anew. And even these are as nothing compared to the myriad other wonders that have passed away since fair Qhilmun fell ...'

'You say "fair," ' Leighor objected. 'But all the histories speak naught but ill of Qhilmun and her Spellbinder Kings.'

'So they do,' Karadas-Ulgar agreed. 'But in this they tell only a part of the truth – although understandably so. For at its height Qhilmun was truly the bright realm, the fairest kingdom of men that ever did exist upon this earth, or ever shall again. And her kings were as the sons of the dawn in their power and their splendour. And truly were they named the Spellbinder Kings, for they had powers to cure many ills. Powers granted them by the High One in repentance for the Ages of Mortification that had gone before. Power for healing and for easing pain; power to make sour lands blossom and the poisoned waters clean, to call forth fair fruits and harvests in abundance where once had grown only thistle and briar. Power to build the great ways and raise high cities. Power to maintain peace in lands torn asunder by war.

'Yet as the years passed and the Mage Lords of Qhilmun grew in number, so too did their powers slowly wane. And more and more they began to seek out the forbidden secrets of the darker lore in the hope of regaining their former strength. Yet all who took this path fell only into greater evil; for to touch such forbidden power, even briefly, is to darken the soul, to stain it with a blackness that may never be removed, but will only lurk and fester and grow. For he who has the touch of the dark cannot rest, but must delve still deeper, craving ever more knowledge, ever more power, ever more dominion over the minds and souls of others, until his own be truly lost. And so did the Sorceror Kings of old grow corrupted, forgetting the healing arts and the ways of peace; forgetting all but their desire for power and riches and to increase the span of their years. Seeking now only to oppress and enslave those over whom they ruled; to make war one upon the other, and to inflict anguish and terror upon all who dared deny them.

'And when the peoples could bear their oppressions no longer, they rose up in their scattered nations: the men of Dur and of the Varroain, the men of Samar and the Giellin – although many did not yet bear the names by which we now know them, or dwell in the same lands. The wars were long, cruel and unrelenting, but finally were dark Qhilmun and her cruel Mage Lords overthrown, and driven into the uttermost west. Those who survived fled across the great wastes to their own dark redoubts behind the Lost Mountains. So were the glories of Qhilmun lost, her lands despoiled and her peoples scattered. And thus fell a great dark age upon the lands of men, an age that in part lingers still. And little was remembered of the Spellbinder Kings and of the builders of the great ways; little but a fear of great magicks, and a formless yearning for a more noble past that is forever lost.'

'But what has this to do with the *harrunor*?' Telsyan asked.

'Much,' Mhindoran grunted. 'For this is where the story of the Mage Metal truly begins. For it was at some time in the year 2034, as it is reckoned in the calendar of Samar, at the time when the last of the Mage Lords were fleeing into the west, that the importance of the purple metal, *harrunor*, was first discovered by men. Some say it was a minor mage called Berazh-goram who first divined its secrets, and became great and powerful thereby. But whatever the truth of the tale, the secret seems soon to have become the closely-guarded property of a small inner circle of the exiled Mage Lords of the west . . .'

'2034?' Uhlendof broke in quickly. 'But this year is 3328 in the Samarite reckoning, 784 in that of the Varroain. All this took place thirteen hundred years ago! How is it that *harrunor* has not been used until now?'

'It has been used,' Mhindoran grunted darkly. 'But for most of this time only in the deepest redoubts of the far west. For although *harrunor* is a wondrous metal and capable of great power, its secrets are deep and hard indeed for even the greatest of sorcerors to divine. And this was the toil and the vexation of the Mage Lords. It took many years of experiment and dark invention for them to uncover the simplest of its secrets. Many long centuries, before even the first of the Dark Amulets was made.' The ironmaster leaned forward, as if to confine his words only to those who sat in the sharp light of the fire. 'For in truth the *harrunor* has little power of itself. It is but an empty vessel into which power must be infused by one who knows its secrets and has that power at his command. Only then does it become an amulet of worth. And therefore the first of the amulets held but little power, and that was raw and unchannelled, and could be used but once before the amulet must be re-made. Such an amulet might produce a single burst of Magefire, no more; perhaps enough to slay a man; and then it was finished. As long as the amulets remained thus, they could be little more than dangerous playthings, offering but small threat to the enemies of those who had created them.

'Yet still the Mage Lords persisted; for their exile was harsh to them, and bitter as gall, and they craved the return of their former power. And growing at last impatient with the clumsiness of their individual efforts, they set apart five of their number, whom they termed the Wrights of Elnar. And these were sent away in secret with no other task but to perfect the use of *harrunor* as a weapon for the enslavement of men. And so, all the while that the younger kingdoms of men have arisen and grown strong in the east, these great lords have been secretly honing and perfecting the powers of *harrunor* and creating new and greater amulets. One thing alone has prevented their total triumph: that *harrunor* has ever been the rarest and most precious of metals, existing for the most part in quantities too small to be of great use . . .'

'That has changed, I fear,' Uhlendof broke in quickly. 'From what we have witnessed since leaving Sonsterness, it seems clear that *harrunor* has grown far more common of late.'

'That is indeed so,' Mhindoran nodded. 'We have recently learnt that rich veins of the Mage Metal were discovered a little over two centuries ago in the deep bowels of the Westron Isznells. All the amulets made so far have come from this single source. The mountains were quickly scoured clean, and the metal carried back into the uttermost west where it could be prepared for use – by what means we know not, for the five have guarded their secrets well. Only they know how the amulets are made and bound to their will. Only they know the dark spells and hidden rituals that bind the living power within the cold metal. And only they know whence comes the dread power to fill each amulet with living fire, so that the greatest of these may make a common man a sorceror, and a sorceror a king.'

'Yet if they have found such power,' Leighor asked softly in the silence which followed, 'why do they not keep it for themselves? Why do they hand it to men such as Darvir and Claighar, Korgul Slainhand and Embor-Horeoth?'

'As I have said,' Mhindoran's words came slowly, 'this is but a part of their greater strategy; the reconquest and subjugation of all the kingdoms of the east.'

'Nay,' Telsyan shook his head firmly. 'I have followed your tale thus far, but this I cannot believe. The northlands, perhaps, may fall to these mages and their Riever allies; but the rest, never! No power on earth could conquer all the kingdoms of the east . . .' Quickly he began to number them, 'Eleven kingdoms of the Varroain; and then Scûn, Oleiyor, Azila, the twenty kingdoms of Samar, and dozens more farther south . . . Even if Khiorim is already half theirs, none could break all these!'

Karadas-Ulgar frowned. 'The lords of power are not so foolish as to strike now, openly, when all men would indeed stand against them. No, their conquest shall be ensured by means more subtle and more suited to their ways. Means that play upon the desire for wealth and power that lies within the hearts of all men. It is for this that the amulets were fashioned. That they might be given to Riever Chieftains, to ambitious and disaffected noblemen, to petty mages and would-be sorcerors; aye, and even to kings. All whose greed makes them easy prey. For there are many forms of amulet, suited to the needs and capacities of many kinds of men. The greatest may give a man the power to strike down a whole company in flame and thunder, or bind the souls of many men to his own. Even the lesser may give a man strength and agility beyond his mortal means, or the power to convince others of his worth, to perform minor magicks and sleights of hand. And there are men enough willing to sell their souls for such fruits as these – poisoned though they be.

'By what means the amulets are spread we know not, but they appear now everywhere in the eastern kingdoms, and ever in the hands of the vilest and most evil of men . . .'

'But what end is achieved thereby?' Telsyan asked. 'From such madness all that can come is anarchy and darkness!'

'What better way to win a world?' Karadas-Ulgar asked, spreading out his hands before him to form a globe and then suddenly breaking it asunder. 'Anarchy will shatter kingdoms that armies alone cannot. Men dream only of treasures and of making war upon one another. The *harrunor* assists them and gives them cause. In a way you are correct, Master merchant; the *harrunor* may not of itself have the power to destroy great armies, but used with cunning and artifice it may yet corrupt them, and build greater legions of its own. Those who are given the amulets are chosen well; for their ambition, for their greed, for their hunger for power. Slaves they are already to these things, willing to sacrifice all for them, and so shall they all the more readily become the willing slaves of a new master.

'These, then, are the ones that the power of the *harrunor* shall place in power over all the armies and nations of the east. Yes,' he nodded, seeing the travellers' disbelieving faces. 'For if Rievers attack from the north, if civil strife rages in the south, what better reason for new men to rise? Each committing new crimes, new atrocities, to avenge those already committed by others of their kind. And out of murder and anarchy, out of fear and greed, out of slaughter and kin-strife shall come the final rule of the Lords of Evil.'

A bleak silence fell across the hall as the wayfarers took in the full import of the king's words. And in the end it was only Telsyan who found the voice to break the silence.

'But surely even then your Mage Lords will not rule?' he objected. 'For they will only have created new, more powerful masters to reign in their stead.'

'Not so, manling,' Mhindoran stated flatly. 'Once they have accepted the amulets, all men who receive them – knowing or unknowing of their true provenance – can be naught else but the vassals of their true creators. For when a man makes use of any of the amulets, his whole mind is laid bare to he who made it. Any who begin to suspect, any who begin to plot rebellion, may so be swiftly dealt with. Nor do the Mage Lords fear that their own amulets may be used against them, for the power is entirely theirs, its true source secret and close-guarded. And thus all who rebel may quickly be reduced to their former powerless state, and many to a condition far worse.'

'How so?' Leighor asked.

'Some of this we only guess,' Mhindoran admitted. 'Yet we ourselves have had cause to deal with *harrunor* in past times, and we know that it can be made to draw some of its strength from the living body of he who wields it. In this wise, for as long as the amulet is worn, the wearer will feel stronger – and he shall truly be stronger, for the power of the amulet supports and nurtures that which it devours. Only when the amulet is removed, or its power fades, will the bearer at last feel the full lack of what has been taken. The life-force that has been slowly drained; the imagined vigour that is suddenly departed; that and much more. After too long in its thrall a man may not even be able to survive the loss unaided: he will have become truly its prisoner.'

'And do none of them suspect this?' Uhlendof asked.

'Some may suspect after a time; but few will have the strength willingly to part with such power.'

'And how come you to learn all this?' Yeon demanded suddenly; a sharp note of suspicion in his voice that brought an answering chill to Leighor's spine.

Mhindoran and Karadas-Ulgar swung about as one, their eyes suddenly hard and fierce, as if about to kindle into fiery anger. Yet to Leighor's relief no explosion came, and unexpectedly the king smiled.

'Do not fear, manling. We have no part in these conspiracies. The affairs of men now concern us but little. Although it was different once, long ago. In these days we do but gather knowledge of things that might at some time come to threaten us . . .'

'Then you will know of Enalkur,' Yeon broke in abruptly. 'Styled "Master of the North." Who is he?'

'Oh! Young one!' the king laughed out loud. 'You bandy names of power about like turnips in the marketplace! Enalkur indeed!' He snorted with derision. 'How is any to know who this Enalkur may be? For none has ever seen him; nor lived to tell of it if he has. His name fills these northlands like the leaves of Faestan month, yet nowhere does he care to show himself. Perchance he is a great Mage Lord from out of the west, well able to hide himself from our poor eyes and ears; or yet again a humbler sort who bides his time in some dark secret place. Perhaps he is truly the Goblin King of legend, arisen like a storm to banish hated man from the north; or else a great lord of Rievers who plays his part all unknowing of its true purpose. Mayhap he has no real existence at all, and is naught but a name of power, used by those who plot in secret, to unite the sundered Riever clans. Who knows, manling?' He shook his head. 'Who knows?'

'There is one other thing we have not so far revealed, sire,' Telsyan stepped forward. 'We have discovered that *harrunor* was being mined at Silentwater. We believe that is why the Rievers laid it waste. The metal was being sent south to a sorceror in Helietrim; a man named Ariscel.'

'Aye,' Zindur spat. 'And I trust him not – though he claims to be a servant of our king. From what you have told us, he is most likely an Amulet Bearer, a tool of the Mage Lords!'

Many of the company nodded their agreement.

There was a brief silence before Karadas-Ulgar spoke. 'I know well your minings at Silentwater,' he nodded gravely. 'We have long suspected that a little *harrunor* might be found in those old hills, but it was ever our hope that none would delve deep enough to discover it. It is ill-news indeed that they have done so. As to this Ariscel, I cannot say. I know of him. He dwells in Norndale of Helietrim. But until this day he has given us no cause to inquire too deeply into his works.'

'Do you think he can be trusted?' Leighor asked.

'Trust no Amulet Wielder!' The giant's eyes flashed. 'If Ariscel wields an amulet of the Mage Lords' devising, he is your enemy. Yet this may not be so. Perhaps he investigates the metal on his own account. I cannot see why else an attack would be made upon the mines. Why would the Mage Lords wish to destroy what is already theirs? But in any event, be wary.' He began to rise.

'One further question,' Uhlendof asked quickly, before the audience was ended. 'How may we recognise and counter these amulets?'

Mhindoran drew a sharp breath. 'That is a hard question indeed, my friend. For the amulets may be worked into any shape their maker desires, and so may be hidden anywhere upon the person of the bearer. Most commonly the amulets are circlets or bracelets, or else medallions that hang from chains about the neck. But they may take many other forms and be disguised in silver, gold or enamels. Thus veiled, they may be fashioned perhaps into a brooch or a ring, a staff, a buckle, or a comb in the hair – even the haft of a knife. There is but one saving grace; and that is that the greater the power of an amulet the more pure *harrunor* it must contain, and so it becomes the less easy to conceal.

'As for the second part of your question.' He paused. 'We know of no way to counter the power of *harrunor*; except with stronger magicks of your own. And such powers are rarely to be found in the world of men in these days. Neither do we have any great magicks that might help you in your cause. I can offer you little hope to avert the evils that are to come. None at all, unless you are able somehow to discover the means to weaken the hold of the Mage Metal upon the souls of men.'

Abruptly the king rose. 'It is late. Sleep now, strangers. And at first light you shall see something more of the power of *harrunor*!'

Chapter Twenty Four
FAIR WEATHER NORTH

The travellers passed the night comfortably enough, sharing the shelter of a great four-poster bed that stood alone in one of the dark ante-chambers of the king's hall. Morning, coming all too soon, brought with it a brisk awakening from Hemmega, who tumbled them rudely from their warm nest among the damasks and velvets.

'The sun is up,' she scolded, 'and the king is long abroad. What manner of wayfarers are you, to spend the best of the day abed?'

A befuddled Keran tried hard to keep her eyes open. She wondered idly just what reason giants had to rise so early. It seemed weeks since she had had a good night's sleep, and her weariness was overwhelming. Sharp lances of light from the great windows burned into her eyes. She realised suddenly that it was snowing outside. Snowing quite hard.

'You do not think these snows will block the valleys below?' Telsyan asked anxiously.

Hemmega shook her head. 'Not so early in the winter. And this blows in from the west, not north. Below it will be but rain.'

'That will be quite bad enough!' Uhlendof grumbled, shuddering as he set stockinged foot to cold stone floor. 'I have no relish for ten days' ride through freezing rain either!'

Even the brilliant daylight seemed unable completely to penetrate the gargantuan fortress through which the travellers now passed once more, stumbling like a straggled column of unwary insects towards the great audience chamber. Black pools of darkness lurked like thieves in distant corners, despite the colonnaded rows of windows that stared out over the bare mountainside. High, vaulted ceilings reared cumbersomely above them, their massive arches meeting in keystones eighty feet above their heads. Unnervingly lifelike, the graven heads of giants stared down at them from every wall and ceiling, so that there was not a single pillar not topped by some grotesque, bearded head, nor a bare patch of stone not formed by laborious artifice into the shape of some dragon or gryphon, wyvern or cockatrice.

Most of the rooms were bare, as though they had been left uninhabited for many years. But one or two still held a few spartan furnishings. A table perhaps, with a chair or two; an iron-bound chest, rusting and coated with ice; a stone shelf which might hold a battered shield or a cracked stone pitcher. Once Keran saw some books, piled high upon a stone ledge sheltered from the worst of the wind; great leatherbound tomes, which she seriously doubted she would even be able to lift, had she the need to do so.

Suddenly she saw a large spider, skittering into a crevice between the books. And then, looking around her, she began to notice dozens more: in crevices and corners, archways and recesses, taking shelter where they could from the constant winds. Keran shivered, suddenly glad that she had not seen them before this; or she would have had no sleep at all. Fat and grey, spinning their ragged webs in the dark, dusty heights, they stared down at the passing wayfarers with cold intelligence in their gleaming red eyes. Again Keran shivered, and this time not from cold.

Karadas-Ulgar awaited them all in the great audience hall. He said no word of greeting, sitting in silence while they ate their breakfasts of hot meal porage, seeming for the moment entirely absorbed in his own bleak thoughts. But the instant they had all finished, he rose abruptly, indicating that they should follow as he led them through the empty halls.

Shortly, they emerged on to an upward-sloping passage, whose unglazed windows stared out on to the west. Through these, snow had blown, to pile in the covered passageway – as thick and as deep as if it lay out of doors. The passageway steepened, transforming itself into a long, covered stair that rose into the grey murk of morning.

Within minutes the little remaining shelter fell away, and they found themselves suddenly on the high, exposed stair they had all seen from the courtyard the previous evening. Bright and snowswept, it coiled precipitously up before them, towards the mountain peak.

Fully a dozen yards broad, the stair reared twice as high again out of the tumbled rock of the mountainside. Great crenellated balustrades soared up on either side, but even these could do little to protect the travellers from the bitter winds that now assailed them. Winds that tore through thick layers of clothing as if they did not exist, whipping up sharp flails of hail and ice to hurl them into unprotected faces, plastering shivering bodies from head to heels in wet, congealing snow.

A solid stone tower, grey, circular and massive, crowned the summit of the mountain; and it was to the top of this that the stair led. The tower had no doors, no windows, no means of inward access, just a flat stone roof with a low parapet, open to all the elements. And for this reason Keran was loath to step on to it, fearing that here the winds would be at their strongest. Yet, to her astonishment, the instant her foot touched the stone tower the winds miraculously fell away. The forty yard circumference seemed an unnatural vortex of calm, about which the shrill winds still screamed in all their fury. Keran caught her breath, only after some minutes daring to look about her.

Beneath them, to the south and east, lay the vast sprawling hulk of the giants' fortress, with the abandoned galleries that ran down from it. The more distant view was lost in a white wall of falling snow. To the north, however, the mountain fell away less sharply to form a vast, almost circular bowl, perhaps a quarter of a league across, of which this peak formed only the highest point of its sharp, many-pinnacled lip.

'We stand now upon the true peak of *Byriadon*,' Karadas-Ulgar announced suddenly. 'King of High Ghorrunar, and oldest of mountains.' He pointed down into the vast bowl of shattered rock that yawned beneath them. 'Here in ancient times did grow the roots of the great Earth-tree, *Pharlondor*; north-easternmost of the four True Trees planted by the Elder Gods to support the mighty vault of the sky.'

'Indeed?' Inanys sniffed, looking thoughtfully up into the grey, stormy void above them. 'Then what supports it now?'

'The universe grows,' Karadas-Ulgar answered absently, 'and her needs alter. The sky is no longer as it was in the first days of the world, when creation was young and only part-formed. It has grown since, to spawn new worlds, new stars to light the winter dark. Even now it expands beyond knowing in the far reaches of the void, growing eternally in the unimaginable mind of the creator. All things change; yet men know only what is, and imagine that that is what has always been.' He turned away, striding towards the centre of the tower.

Here, where the concentric rings of flagstones that paved the tower roof converged, was a single dark hole, less than a handspan broad. The king stooped, falling down upon one knee and stretching out his hand, as if to grasp something unseen that stood embedded there. The travellers watched in nervous silence, wondering if the king's mind wandered. Yet even as his hand closed about the invisible object, there was a sudden shimmer of dazzling white light.

Instinctively Keran flinched away, shielding her eyes from the unexpected brilliance. Lowering her hands only as the flare died, to see a great staff of white stone shining before her in the king's hand.

Slowly Karadas-Ulgar rose to his feet, raising the staff up in his hand until it speared into the heavens above him. Keran drew breath in wonder. Although she had never seen its like before, she had no doubt that this was an artefact of great power. Taller than any living man, it was fashioned from a single piece of pure white marble. No . . . not entirely pure. For thin, intertwining veins of gold and *harrunor* streamed along its entire length, glinting amber and purple in the snowlight. Smooth and slender as a willow bough, it broadened slightly towards its crystalline tip; where it must at some time have been sheared from the parent rock. Yet that breach had been carefully camouflaged; carved and worked with most delicate art into the semblance of a crown of living white flame that glittered and sparkled with diadems of gold and *harrunor*.

Now that he held the staff aloft, the Storm King seemed somehow stronger, greater, more awesome in his power. His dark eyes burned with a fire otherwise long departed, and even the dull greys that braided his hair seemed somehow to darken and diminish before their eyes, revealing him in the full vigour of his youth.

'Behold the Stormstaff of Lor-Karaiéth!' he roared, his voice as dark as thunder and as deep as the roots of the mountains. 'Behold the power of the Kings of High Ghorrunar!'

In that instant there came a sudden, terrible flash of lightning, accompanied by a crash of thunder to make the mountain shiver. Intensely loud, unbearably bright, the bolt passed between blazing staff and roiling clouds above; whether from clouds to staff, or staff to clouds, none could tell. Yet all present were struck dumb with awe and terror; cowering away from the force of the thunderbolt to seek refuge against the parapet, almost as if they hoped it might swallow them up in its cold embrace.

But Karadas-Ulgar seemed now not to notice any of them, staring intently upward into the crown of the great Stormstaff, entirely absorbed in its magic. Streaks of white lightning screamed upward from the Stormstaff to strike into the rolling clouds above; and answering bolts began to sear down all around them. Beyond the tower the swirling snows redoubled in fury, and the storm winds turned and strengthened until they shrieked in from all sides across the wild mountainside, driving snow and hail before them like fiery missiles. Yet within the circle of stone no snow fell, and the wind was stilled – almost as if an invisible wall somehow shielded them all from the raging elements beyond.

Overhead the storm clouds churned like a tempest sea, transposed by some fell sorcery to hang above their heads; circling in now tighter and tighter, darker and darker, about the peak of Mount Byriadon, as though summoned and strengthened by the Stormstaff itself. The sight of such terrible power both frightened Keran and in some dark way thrilled her; and unlike Harstond, who cowered in terror beneath his dark mantle, she could not draw her eyes from the stirring winds that raged overhead and the furious lightning bolts that powered down like blazing rain all around her, rending and shattering the ancient rock of the mountainside as they struck home.

And still the storm deepened. The snow, turning to iron-hard balls of hail as big as a man's fist, crashed into the stone buttresses of the tower with such force and wrath that Keran knew none of them would survive more than a moment or two, were their miraculous protection suddenly removed. The sky grew dark as night, with only the fearsome thunderbolts to light the scene; the wind tore great boulders from the mountainside to send them crashing into the dark abyss below. If the storm grew any stronger Keran feared that the whole mountain must surely crumble before it.

And only when the Stormtower began physically to shudder with the sheer force of the elements raging against it did the Storm King at last lower his staff, pointing it past Telsyan's shell-shocked form, into the far south. And slowly, incredibly, the storm followed. Its raging heart drifted gradually southward, as gently as might a summer shower, until it was no longer directly above them, and the winds tore in from one direction only.

The travellers watched in awestruck silence as the storm moved slowly away across the mountaintops; the elements gradually calming all about them, the clouds thinning and the fierce north winds at last abating. Slowly the harsh explosions of thunder dwindled away into the south, the bright lightning flashes sundering the skies above distant mountaintops.

Wearily Karadas-Ulgar lowered the Stormstaff, bending with an aching sigh to return it once more to its dark niche at the centre of the paved circle.

'I have thrown the storm into the faces of your enemies,' he announced grimly, standing erect once more. 'You shall have clear skies and fair weather to Darien.'

The staff relinquished, he looked as old and as time-ravaged as he had ever been: in fact, to Keran's eyes, far more so, as if the use of the Stormstaff had taken much out of him.

'Aye,' he nodded, seeing their startled faces. 'The *harrunor* in the staff doth truly sap the life-essence. So was it made by Lor-Karaiéth at the dawning of the world, and such is ever the payment for its use.' He stared southwards after the storm – whose black heart was fast vanishing behind the peaks of the far mountains – and sighed. 'That was a storm as has been but rarely raised in these latter days. If the minions of Embor-Horeoth, or any other, still pursue you, then they shall meet with something they shall not much enjoy!' He chuckled darkly to himself and turned for the stair. 'Come! We have already lingered in this place too long!'

Looking back, Keran noted that the staff had once again disappeared, although she imagined that she could just detect a faint shimmer of power hovering in the air where it should have been. It was as if it had been silently swallowed up in the surrounding stone, or else hung under some spell of illusion that shielded it even from eyes that knew its true shape and location. Surely it must be this which protected the tower from the awesome forces of the elements, and which was the fount of the Stormgiants' power. Yet none of the travellers dared to approach, and even Inanys stayed well clear, following the rest of them meekly back down the stair towards the main fortress.

The sky brightened slowly, clearing from the north as they descended. The late morning sun emerged suddenly from behind a last fleeting wisp of cloud to shine weakly down on them, like a small gold coin from out of a cold winter sky.

It was past midday when they finally departed the halls of the Stormgiant King. Their horses had been fed and watered overnight, so there was little for the wayfarers to do but mount and ride out through the bleak inner courtyard on to the ancient way. Evok and Karadas-Ulgar strode with them as far as the great ridge, where the upland plateau tumbled sharply down into the depths beneath. Despite the previous day's climb, the travellers were quite unprepared for the dizzying nature of the drop that now opened before them, staring grimly down at the precipitate, twisting path they would have to follow. There were no clouds now to screen the awful fall beneath, and every foot of the way, right down to the green valley floor thousands of feet below, was all too clearly visible.

'Fear not, manlings!' Karadas-Ulgar boomed in encouragement. 'The road has stood here near as long as the mountain itself. It will bear you down in safety if your courage fails you not, and you do nothing that is foolish.'

'Farewell, then!' he shouted after them, once they had all passed beneath him, and were well into the twisting descent. 'Farewell, manlings! May the All Highest watch over you on your journeys!'

Keran turned back in the saddle to give a rather nervous backward wave to the two watching giants. And the last she ever saw of them was as they turned slowly away to stride back across the cold, snowy plateau towards their bleak dwelling place.

'Waving goodbye to a giant!' she laughed suddenly. 'Who in all of Darien could ever have imagined such a thing?'

'Keep your eyes on the road!' Telsyan warned sharply, behind her. 'Or you won't live long enough to tell of it!'

The descent was slow, and it was nearly dark when they finally came down into the narrow green vale between the mountains which they had last passed through nearly two days before. Here they made camp, beside a tumbling brook that flowed strong and cold between open meadows, passing the night within clear view of the towering summit of proud Byriadon.

At morning the party divided: Harstond to journey south alone through the Pass of Dorrund, and thence back to bear what tidings he had to Dom Udun

Covarr; the rest of the company to travel north and west through the mountain passes towards the plains of Scûn and Darien.

'Do not descend into the plains before you must,' Harstond warned them before he departed. 'Keep to the heights as far north as you can, for the hills will give you cover that you will surely lack upon the open plains. Even on horseback it is hard to long outdistance a band of Rievers once they have smell of you.'

The travellers bore his advice well in mind as they rode out through the long vale, leaving Mount Byriadon gleaming crystal pink and white behind them in the early morning sun. Keeping to a steady pace, they passed northward between the glowering mountain Harstond had named Khorambar – burial place of half a hundred generations of giant kings – and a dumpier, nameless peak that rose up steeply to the west. New lines of peaks opened out before them as they rose.

For four days more they journeyed north and west through the high peaks and lonely vales of Ghorrunar, all the time meeting with nothing more fearsome than the occasional snow-white hare or undernourished mountain cat. Once Keran fancied that she glimpsed the fur-clad figure of a giant – perhaps one of the three goatherds – moving somewhere far away on the high slopes of one of the distant mountains. But the movement was too briefly noticed and too far distant for her to be sure. The rough clothing of greys and browns that the giants wore blended in all too well with the surrounding landscape. Keran sighed and looked away. It would take a better pair of eyes than hers to pick one of them out on the bare mountain slopes if he truly wished to remain hidden.

Yet the travellers had reason enough to be thankful to the giants, whether they watched over them or no. For the fair weather that had persisted throughout their sojourn in these mountains still showed no sign of breaking. Each day dawned as bright and sunny as the last, and each night was cold and clear, with a good hard frost to firm the ground each morning. There were no harsh winds, and none of the deep snows that might have trapped them in these bleak passes all winter, or until they all perished from cold and hunger. Indeed, as Uhlendof told any who dared complain, they had much to be thankful for.

On the fifth day they came down out of the high mountains and into a bare, rolling country of bleak hills and barren vales, which reminded Leighor somewhat of the Grey Fells above Cleafedale where he had had his encounter with the baleful *Roegannaith*. Yet these hills seemed in some manner cleaner and less troubled by ancient evils than those other hills so many leagues to the south; perhaps because they had in their long ages seen far fewer of the works of men.

'These hills are known as Serem Tops,' Telsyan told them at their midday halt, pausing from his journeybread to examine the brief sketch-map that Harstond had made for him. 'We must travel due west from now on: and if I am right, tomorrow we should come out on to the plains.'

In the late afternoon the company came across a lonely, ruined inn, roofless and deserted, at the foot of its own stony valley. But this smelled dank and unwholesome, and they gave it a wide berth. Instead they rode on for another hour or so, before finally halting to make camp in a deserted glen, watered by a single brackish stream.

The travellers' first sight of the plains of Scûn came abruptly, when they had barely begun the next morning's ride. Coming suddenly over the brow of a low hill, they saw the vast treeless emptiness at last spread out beneath them. From this distance the plains seemed a uniform dull yellow-green, rolling onward and outward for league upon league into the hazy distance. For as far as they could see, there was nothing to attract the eye: no forests, no roads, no settlements; no single feature by which they might measure the awesome scale of the landscape. Even the hundreds of lakes that speckled the green seemed no more than the tiniest of puddles, and could truly have been of any size – as broad as Silentwater or as small as a village newt-pond.

'How far does this extend?' Leighor asked at last.

'I am not quite sure,' Telsyan admitted after a short pause during which he again consulted his rough map. 'More than a hundred leagues in any event, probably half as much again. Aye, a hundred leagues at least, until one comes to the thick woodlands along the Ormul River; and then it is twenty more to Darien.' He turned and pointed north, towards a thin clear line of sparkling water that coiled far away into the west. 'That must be the River Yarvar, which flows straight across the plains to meet with the Ormul at Darien. If we keep the river always in view as we ride, we shall have little chance of getting lost.'

Leighor studied the distant river. He had heard that the Yarvar was great and broad: at least as great as the Thurond or the Caethalon, probably as broad as the Malûn itself. Yet against the backdrop of the plains it looked as small and inoffensive as any of the sleepy streams of Low Sielder.

Once down upon the soft spongy ground of the plain, the travellers could see little. There was not as much as a six foot rise anywhere ahead of them. A few dark birds flew on the western horizon. Some vicious looking black flies buzzed angrily above the marshy puddles. Otherwise nothing broke the silence but themselves. There was little chance of anyone creeping up on them here – in daylight at least. But by night they would have to keep their campfires small and well concealed.

Over the next few days Leighor discovered that there was much else, besides themselves, that moved on these open plains. Great herds of slow-moving elk and reindeer grazed idly upon the open steppe, their paths shadowed by slinking groups of slim grey wolves. Sharp-eyed snow-rabbits and countless small northland rodents emerged only briefly into the sunlight before fleeing back to their dark burrows once more. Hosts of geese and mute northern swans floated on ice-girt lakes and pools, enjoying the last warm days before the winter. Overhead the great carrion-eaters and birds of prey circled tirelessly, ever on the watch for the fallen and the dying. Only once did the wayfarers pass close to a tribe of mastodons.

These were unavoidable, grazing right in their path, and the travellers had to circle several leagues out of their way to pass them by. Even so, at one point they came within a mile of some of the stragglers, their great-tusked leader raising his head to trumpet in alarm as he caught their scent on the breeze.

But the moment of danger quickly passed. The gargantuan beasts, seeming to have decided that these few interlopers posed them no real threat, returned quietly to their grazing, leaving the riders to spur their horses hurriedly onward.

It was about mid-afternoon on the eighth day out from Mount Byriadon when the travellers at last caught sight of the thin dark line of the Ormul woodlands on the western horizon.

Far away to their right, the River Yarvar curved gently away into the dark forests of the north, and out of sight of the seven riders. But ahead of them, unmistakable in its crumbled grandeur as it ran north-west across the open plain, was King Culvar's Road. The old way seemed as lonely and devoid of traffic as ever, and it was with some trepidation that the travellers approached it once more; climbing watchfully up on to its broken surface to follow its path north and west across the plain until they were finally swallowed up by the dark forest.

Almost immediately they came upon signs of human habitation. The scattered stumps of trees stood stark and exposed close by the road's edge; and here and there, piles of logs and smaller stacks of bundled firewood lay as though awaiting collection. Small clearings soon appeared in the forest to either side of them, with the stubble of a sparse grain crop not yet ploughed back into the thin, grey soil. But nowhere was there a sign of even the humblest shelter or dwelling. Whoever worked these fields must live elsewhere.

The road bent again, back down into the west, and here they came of a sudden upon a small settlement of log huts and wooden shanties, part veiled in a blue haze of woodsmoke. Keran recognised it at once as Szerget, a small out-village of Darien, from which a winding cart track ran due north to the only ferry crossing of the Yarvar, half a dozen leagues away.

'We had best spend the night here,' she told her companions quickly. 'There is a small tavern for travellers – and we shall not now get to Darien before curfew.'

The tavern was a poor enough place; little more than a common log cabin that rose up next to a smouldering charcoal-burners' mound, with only lumpy straw pallets for the travellers to lie upon. Yet even so, they felt like the height of luxury after the long privations of the ride; and the travellers slept well, rising late the next morning to resume their journey.

Keran found herself approaching Darien with mixed feelings. For her this was to be the end of the journey, the end of her involvement in the greater events that so troubled the world beyond. Events that she had never dreamed to play a part in, and which in the past she had comprehended only vaguely, if at all. For the others, for the rest of her ill-sorted companions, Darien would be but a brief halt upon the way; a place to rest, to collect the few items and messages they sought; and then to depart, returning southward once more, to unknown lands and kingdoms that to her would never be more than distant, half-formed imaginings. Half of her longed to go on with them, but more still held her here.

The longing to see her father, the rest of her family again, now grew in her with every mile they trod – and was this not the sole reason she was on this expedition at all? Yet now, as their arrival in Darien drew ever closer, she found herself increasingly unsure of the sort of welcome she would meet; unsure of the sort of life she would soon have to lead in the close-timbered traders' backwater that was Darien. Unsure of how she would take her final parting with her companions of the road, and saddened that this would be her last full day in their company. Deep within her she knew it most likely that once she took their leave she would never meet any of them again; never know what became of their great quest. Until, perhaps, the Dark Lords did indeed come out of the west, as rulers of the Riever hordes, to claim dominion over all. The thought chilled her to the bone – as did much else of which the giants had warned them. She had thought once that no Riever horde could ever take Darien; but here, amongst these dark northern forests, she was not so sure.

Thus occupied in her own thoughts, the ten leagues or so to Darien passed quickly, and it seemed no time at all before they must turn from King Culvar's Road, leaving the ancient way to run its lonely course westward to the chain-ferry across the Ormul, and thence on half a thousand leagues to Vliza. Instead they turned north on to the broad way of split logs that would carry them the last three and a half leagues to Darien. Every tree, every twist of the road, every low hillock, now brought familiar memories flooding back into Keran's mind: of her childhood; of summer picnics on the banks of the Great River; of journeys with her father to farmsteads and out-settlements to gather furs and timber, horn and amber, for the southern trade. Everything seemed just as it had always been, as if nothing had changed, as if she were journeying slowly backward in time . . .

Despite her misgivings, Keran was now desperately anxious to see again the city of her birth, and to discover what had happened to all those she had known within, during her years of exile. There was but one low rise left before the city. Unconsciously, she spurred her horse onward.

Chapter Twenty Five
DARIEN

The rest of the travellers were no less anxious to see the city that had been their goal for so long, and which at times they had doubted they would ever reach. Yet here they were, within a league of Darien, and riding fast towards it through the bright cold sunlight of a winter's morning. The damp logway clattered beneath their horses' hooves as they rode up a final muddy incline to see the town at last spread out before them.

Leighor gasped: it was not at all as he had imagined it. He had envisioned a civilised town; somewhat like Irgil, or perhaps Sonsterness, with walls of stone, well-made buildings, and a central keep. Instead what lay before him was a sprawling collection of log houses and timber shanties that seemed little better than the wretched dwellings of Szerget and Furthka – only here they were in greater number, and contained within a high wooden palisade.

To the north, the settlement bordered upon the River Yarvar. On his left, the River Ormul swept northward to join the greater river, before turning with it into the west. Judging one river against the other, there was little to argue between them: both being at least half a league in width, both dwarfing the tiny township that presumed to occupy the triangular spit of land between them. A deep, water-filled ditch connected the two rivers, separating the town itself from the level fields to south and east. A high stockade of sharpened logs completely encircled the town, fencing it in even from the rivers.

There was but one visible break in the stockade. It ran beneath the twin wooden guard-towers of the landward gate. Another, far smaller, must permit some egress to the west – on to the Ormul river – where several small jetties ran out into the water.

Before the main gates, however, there lay a large sea of tents and rough-built shanties, unprotected by the stockade-walls, and crowding in upon the main road. Small, wretched figures moved between the makeshift dwellings, or sat idly about smouldering fires, their shapes sinuous and unmistakable . . .

'Goblins!' Yeon hissed. 'There must be a thousand of them! . . . Camped all about the city!' He glared at Keran accusingly. 'Is this normal?'

She shook her head. 'There have ever been one or two of them, who scavenged the fields and the waste-pits about the town, but never so many . . .' She stared out across the town aghast. 'I do not know if it is only after my time in the south, but the city seems much changed: poorer, less cared for than I remember it. Never before would it have been allowed to become so wretched. What has happened?'

They rode down towards the gates in silence, passing through the sprawling goblin encampment to come at last beneath the twin guard-towers. Looming high above them, each was crowned with the gold and crimson flags of the Knights of Dur, leaving no doubt whose city this was. The blue and white banners of the Kings of Scûn lay nowhere to be seen.

No guards seemed to man the high watchtowers, and only two surly men in shabby red surcoats stood guard upon the gate. These studied the seven travellers idly, with little interest, as they passed across the moat into the town.

Within the stockade, conditions appeared little better than they were without. The poorest quarter lay nearest to the gate; and here there were scores of low wooden shanties, inhabited by some of the most surly, sullen and beaten-looking people Leighor had yet seen. Poor, and oppressed beyond caring, they seemed totally without hope. These were the lowest orders of the city: serfs, vassals and bondsmen, the chattels of the Knights and of the greater merchants who ruled here.

The poor quarter ran on for another fifth of a league, the lines of shanties broken only by a few long barrack buildings that housed more surly mercenaries. Farther along, a wooden bridge led across a second ditch to the richer, northern half of the city.

The citadel of the Knights of Dur was a straggling brick and timber building in the heart of this section of the township. Yet when told of their desire to see the Knight Commander, the grey-robed functionary who ruled here seemed singularly unimpressed.

'The Master of the Knights and all the High Nobles of Darien shall meet in High Council upon the morrow,' he told them briskly. 'You may place any entreaties before them there, and they will be heard.'

'But ours is a private business,' Telsyan insisted. 'Not for the ears of all who may care to listen at public assembly! Can we not see the Master in private and at once?'

The official shook his head, not deigning to look up from the sheaf of papers that lay before him. 'His Excellency has important business, and may not be disturbed today. You may present your appeals at the proper place tomorrow.' He nodded briefly towards the far door in dismissal.

Yeon's face darkened, and he seemed on the point of doing something forceful to draw himself to the other's attention, when Uhlendof intervened.

'We have waited two months,' he whispered quickly. 'We can restrain ourselves in patience one day further. Besides, we must do nothing to make enemies of these people. Here they are the law.'

'Aye,' Keran added quickly. 'My father, perhaps, will be better able to aid us in this. He himself may no longer have influence with the knights, yet he will know those who do, and the ways to gain an audience.'

Reluctantly the travellers nodded, following her out of the citadel and westward, along narrow alleyways, towards the Ormul River. Here the spacious properties of the Knights and High Merchants bordered one another, separated by their own palisaded compounds.

She halted before a pair of tall wooden gates, rapping hard with her bare knuckles.

It was a short, nervous wait before the summons was answered. One of the gates creaked slowly open to reveal a small threadbare figure who looked without recognition at the new arrivals.

'Yes?' he asked nervously, his voice cracking with age and infirmity. 'What do you want here?'

'Oh, Kaedban!' Keran threw back the hood of her cloak to reveal her face. 'Do you not know me? It is I, returned to see my father.'

'What? . . . Can it be? . . . It is never Keran!' A warm smile spilled across the old man's face, only to depart with equal swiftness when he took in the rest of Keran's words.

'Ah, Mistress Keran,' he looked behind him nervously. 'Would that you had returned in happier times . . .'

'Happier times?' Keran's smile too began to fade, and apprehension crept into her voice for the first time. 'How so? What is wrong?'

Kaedban's eyes fell to his feet, and slowly he shook his head. 'Things have changed much here, mistress, since you left us; and most of them not for the good . . .' He fell silent, still standing in the half-open crack of the gateway, as if fearful that someone within might see with whom he spoke. 'I know not if I am the rightful one to tell you of these things, mistress, but—'

He got no further, for there came a sudden harsh shout from within the gates. 'Who is that, Kaedban? To whom do you mutter so long? Have I not warned you often enough never to mumble in secret at my gate?' The voice drew nearer. 'If it is Jorkath, admit him. If it be any others, seeking favours, send them away!'

A large hand gripped the gate and flung it open. And suddenly the travellers found themselves face to face with a tall, fair-haired man just on the borders of middle age. He was attired in rich damasks and furs, yet despite his height he was thin and bony, his eyes dark and deep-set in a narrow, mean face.

'Well, man: who are these people?'

Kaedban cowered away from this new apparition as if he feared to be struck. 'It is Keran, my lord,' he stammered. 'Keran, my lady's young sister.'

'Oh,' the thin mouth dropped open in surprise, its owner staring direct into Keran's green eyes, which were just about on a level with his own. Slowly recognition dawned. 'Keran . . . Keran? . . . What are you doing here? We thought you well settled as lady to the wife of some southland lord?'

Keran nodded blankly, and then quickly shook her head in negation. 'No . . . no more. Much has happened since . . . But you? Are you not Hoethan, one of the knights?'

'Aye,' the other nodded grimly. 'I was. Although that, and much else, has altered since you were last here. Much, it seems, that you have not yet learnt of: for I am now Vice Commander of the Knights in Darien and of the Wardship of Eastern Scûn; and you should address me as such. Besides which, I am also husband to your good sister, Kerel, and master of this house—'

'Master of this house?' Keran broke in abruptly, her jaw rapidly slackening. 'But what of my father?'

'He is passed away these two years since,' Hoethan answered quickly. 'Aye, two years last autumn, of the grey fever. I have been master here since then.'

'Dead?' Keran's voice crumbled in disbelief. 'Dead . . . And you never sent word . . . You never sent me word?'

'We tried, but we knew not where you were, lass. How could we let you know?' He placed a consoling hand upon her shoulder, but she shook it angrily away.

'Where is my sister?' she demanded. 'I must see her! I must speak with her – alone!'

A sharp look crossed Hoethan's face like a stormcloud. But the irritation was gone in an instant, entombed beneath a sympathetic smile. 'Of course, you shall see her at once. She will be surprised and delighted to receive you. And even though your arrival is a trifle unexpected, you know that you are ever welcome here.' He placed an arm about her shoulders once more, and this time she did not resist.

'My lord,' Telsyan stepped forward before the Vice Commander could turn away. 'It is perhaps propitious that we find you here. We have journeyed all the way from the Sielders in search of vital papers held here in trust by the Knights. The papers concern . . .'

'Now is not the time for such matters, my friends.' Hoethan shook his head. 'But be assured, they will be dealt with in due course. Where do you all stay?'

'At the Strangers' Inn,' Telsyan said quickly.

'Good,' Hoethan nodded, as though satisfied. 'It is a fine establishment. Perhaps we shall have the opportunity to speak again tomorrow, or at some later time if you prefer. But now, as you will understand, there are griefs to be borne, and many other things that must pass between us in private.' He gave a brief nod to Kaedban to open the gate just wide enough for himself and Keran to enter. 'You will forgive us . . .'

Leighor looked uncertainly towards Telsyan and Uhlendof. He had not expected to be separated from Keran so abruptly. She herself seemed half on the point of protesting. He had just opened his mouth to object, when both men nodded, and the moment of decision was past.

'Aye,' Telsyan acquiesced. 'Perhaps after such ill news our business is best postponed. We shall return at a better time, lass. And worry not, we shall surely see you again before we leave.'

Hoethan smiled. 'As I have said, you are welcome here at any time.' He turned away and was gone. The gate swung firmly shut behind, leaving the six remaining companions suddenly alone on the cold and darkening roadway.

'I do not think that was well done,' Leighor said at last. 'We should not have left her on her own.'

'It is not our place to interfere between the girl and her family,' Telsyan said firmly. 'It is by her own choice that she comes here. Her future lies with her own folk, and she must face it alone.'

Uhlendof nodded, turning to walk away.

He had taken only a few steps when he halted suddenly to swing round upon Inanys. 'Surely it is time for our ways to part also, grey one?' he demanded. 'You said when you joined us that you were journeying north. Well here we are, as far north as we intend to go. Our bargain is at an end.'

Inanys shook his head. 'Nay, my lord. You grow forgetful. Our bargain concerned no direction of travel. It was simply that I might remain with you for as long as I wished—'

'Oh no!' Telsyan broke in angrily. 'You have journeyed with us so far on pretext of travelling north – or was that but another of your foul lies? Where are you truly bound, crooked one, and what is your real reason for following us to this place?'

'I did not lie to you, my lords,' Inanys said quickly, stepping back, his feet skating on the ice in a frozen rut. 'I have business of my own here in Darien. Business I must quickly attend to. Yet our bargain still stands, my lords. A word given may not be broken.' He paused to draw breath, his lips twisting once more into their usual mocking smile. 'But fear not, it is likely I will have to remain here far longer than yourselves. Until you must leave, however, there is no reason we should not stay together.'

'Aye,' the merchant nodded grudgingly. 'Until we leave.'

Yet even the prospect of finally ridding themselves of Inanys could not lift the travellers' low spirits as they made their way back to the inn. Keran's disappointments, along with the off-hand way in which they had been treated since their arrival in Darien, seemed to bode ill for the success of their errand.

Leighor had somehow imagined that all their troubles would be at an end once they reached Darien – but instead they seemed only to be beginning . . . Their journey money was now all but spent, they had very little prospect of obtaining more, and they still had a long and dangerous journey south ahead of them – if they ever actually obtained the testament of Eridar they sought.

What if, for some reason, it was not here? If it had been moved elsewhere, or had already been collected by agents of Misan during the long months they had lost in these northern wastes? What if the Knights still held Lord Eridar's legacy, yet for their own purposes denied all knowledge of it – or refused to release so valuable an item to such a ragtag group of strangers? Thoughts like these passed through the minds of all the travellers during the long evening and the fitful night of sleep that followed. And breakfast found them increasingly worried and irritable.

The others at table were either fur-traders, hunters or miners, settled in for a long lazy winter in Darien after three seasons of toil in the out-country. All were appalled at the travellers' plans to leave for the south as soon as their business was completed.

'You are mad to think of travelling at this season!' said one. 'In a normal year the snows would already be many feet deep, and all journeying over until the spring. You know not how the weather turns in these northlands. We have blizzards here to freeze the very blood in your veins as you walk! Your first such storm would be your last, my friends: so, whatever your business, it can wait.'

'There have already been bad snows farther south,' said another. 'I have heard that the road is covered to the depth of a dozen feet, not half a hundred leagues from here, and that there have been hailstones the size of dragon's eggs . . .'

'Then you have had recent news from the south?' Uhlendof broke in quickly.

The other shook his head. 'Little but rumours and trappers' tales. No knights or traders have come north up the Great Way for many weeks.'

'Have you seen no party of Varroain traders bound for Vliza?' Yeon asked. 'A large party: twenty men and a dozen mules?'

The other breakfasters exchanged blank glances and shook their heads. 'No, there has been no party of that size through here since *Gurnithun* month.'

'Then what has happened to them?' Yeon asked again. 'For we parted with such a company upon the road, but four weeks since.'

'Perhaps they did not choose to halt at Darien,' the first trader answered. 'If I were they, I would lose no time in getting to Vliza at this season. Perhaps they have passed on by.'

'Aye, perhaps.' Zindur grunted.

The twelve men of the High Council of Darien passed through the crushed multitude like princes in their gleaming silks and furs. Preceded into the Guild House by four trumpeters and two score halberdiers, they created a hush of excitement and suffused expectation as they passed. There were seven knights; all dressed alike in rich robes of crimson and gold, overlaid with gleaming tabards in the same two colours. Behind these came five others in the rich robes of merchants, of varying hues and fabrics from velvet green to deepest purple satin. All seated themselves upon a raised dais facing the crowd; the close-bearded Master of the Knights taking the central, high seat. To his right sat Hoethan, barely recognisable now in his knightly robes; of Keran there was no sign.

Silence fell upon the hall as the High Council began. First came the announcements of new rules and regulations controlling trade and order within the townships and its vast hinterlands, all read out from beneath the dais by a grey-robed functionary.

Then came the justice-giving, during which a long succession of insubordinates, drunkards and petty criminals were dragged before the assembled lords to receive sentences ranging from a light flogging to brandings, mutilations, and months – or even years – of bonded labour.

Leighor swallowed hard. He had seen such justice-givings often before, in many different places – but seldom after such a manner. No one, once charged, seemed ever to be released. None seemed to receive even the pretence of a fair hearing, the judges cutting off the defendants in mid-sentence, to pass on in haste to their usually stern judgement. Two men objected that the guards who accused them lied, and were in the pay of their enemies. These only received harsher sentences than the rest, who had gone more meekly to their ordained punishment. It was as if the judges cared nothing for the rights and wrongs of particular cases; concerned only with the maintenance of a quiescent order through fear and harsh example. Leighor shuddered at the prospect of ever himself facing such a tribunal.

Finally the judgements ended, and it was time at last for the presentation of petitions. At the call, a great multitude surged forward all around the crushed wayfarers, waving tally-wands, papers, and scraps of parchment to attract the attention of one or another of the lords upon the raised dais. And the various lords of council, as it took their fancy, would nod in the direction of a particular supplicant, whom the guards would then allow through to the fore to present his plea.

Most of the petitions concerned minor disputes between townsfolk about property, payment or passage rights; or else were pleas for pardons, preferences, trading licences or permissions – perhaps to graze goats in the town fields or to cut timber in the surrounding forests. All of these were either refused or granted on the spot, often in what seemed a highly arbitrary fashion, and occasionally against the clear run of the evidence.

As the press of petitioners slowly began to thin around them, the travellers grew increasingly anxious. They had still not been called. None of the Lords of High Council appeared able to see them, and even Hoethan studiously ignored their several vain attempts to catch his eye. Perhaps it was the rule that those previously known to the members of High Council were summoned first, and strangers left until last? If so, then they had a long wait ahead of them. And since none were permitted to approach the dais until they had been called forth to do so, they must possess themselves in patience.

But then, suddenly, it was all over. Without warning, the Master of the Knights rose from his high seat, and the audience-giving was at an end.

Before the travellers fully realised what was happening, they were thrust roughly backward by a wedge of cursing mercenaries who cleared a path for the members of High Council to leave the hall. Telsyan was the first to regain his composure, forcing his way forward to try to call out to the departing Councillors. But they either did not hear, or else chose not to, and the merchant received only a vicious elbow in the stomach from one of the guardsmen for his pains.

Within seconds the High Council of Darien was gone, and the great assembly had fragmented into a pushing, shoving multitude, clogging the narrow doorways in the rush to gain the best places to witness the punishments in the square beyond.

'What shall we do now?' Leighor asked as the small group reassembled. 'The lords will be long gone by the time we get out into the square.'

'And even if they aren't,' Zindur grunted, 'I doubt that their cursed guards will let us near them!'

'Then what shall we do?' Yeon demanded irritably. 'We cannot wait a month till next council!'

'We shall just have to return to the citadel,' Telsyan said, 'and demand to see the Master in private.'

'I do not know how far we can *demand* anything in this place,' Uhlendof said quietly. 'Perhaps it would be better if we tried to speak with Keran's brother-in-law again – he may be able to help us.'

'Oh dear! What shall we do?' Inanys mimicked gleefully, forcing his face into a vacant, village-idiot expression. 'We are lost! We shall have to wait for the next council! Truly you are the dullest group of witless dolts ever to wander into the northlands! You see nothing – understand nothing! Even when it is as plain as the nose upon your face. And in your case, Master Merchant, that is plain indeed!' He shook his head, cackling merrily to himself.

'If you have anything of value to say, then say it,' Uhlendof snapped. 'Otherwise be silent!'

'You wish my counsel?' the crookback asked, as if surprised.

'If you have something useful to tell us,' Telsyan replied stonily.

'Then still you do not see?' Inanys smiled, taking his time. 'You seek everywhere for a noble lord to give you audience. Yet you cannot see that there is but one ruler in this place, but one king – though he be strong and mighty withal, so that through him all may be achieved and all desires made flesh . . .' He paused expectantly, as if waiting for them to take his meaning. When certain that they did not, he smiled again; and suddenly a small gold coin was in his hand, with the king's head upon it.

'There!' He cast it casually across the wooden floor; watching as it rolled into the midst of the straggling throng at the doorway.

At once the well-ordered crowd fell into a kicking, struggling rabble, each striving with his neighbour to claim it for himself.

'There!' Inanys croaked with scorn. 'There is the true king in Darien: gold!'

'Strike me for a fool!' Telsyan smote his forehead in disgust. 'Of course! What has befuddled my brain? It was so obvious. Only I had not expected it of the knights – even in such a place as this. That is the reason for the curious decisions of the judges, and all else in this town! To get anything done here one must first cross the hand of the right person with gold!'

'But we have no gold,' Uhlendof protested. 'Barely enough to buy us even the few sacks of meal we need for the journey south . . .'

'Ah! Then we must thank our good friend for reminding us,' the merchant clapped a friendly arm about the crookback's shoulder. 'For reminding us of the gold he . . . obtained . . . in Biren; and with which he ever promised to pay his way in our company. And now is as good a time as any for him to honour his bargain!'

Inanys freed himself of the merchant's arm to produce a familiar leather pouch from deep within his coat. 'Ah yes, the gold,' he smiled, the dappled daylight from the windows seeming to strike oddly upon his yellow teeth. 'The seal upon our bargain! If you now desire it, it is gladly yours.' He opened the bag to pour a gleaming cascade of silver and gold coins into his left hand. 'You see . . . Inanys keeps his promise.'

'Beware!' Uhlendof said suddenly. 'He seeks somehow to entrap us! The money is tainted, stolen! We cannot take it!'

'We have no choice,' Telsyan said, stepping hurriedly forward to shield the coins from curious eyes, before sweeping them quickly into his pouch. 'You know how little we have left. And it is high time that our friend paid something towards his keep. Besides, we cannot be certain that the money was stolen. Let your conscience rest!'

He turned for the gateway with new determination. 'We have already wasted two days here in foolishness. Let us go at once to the Citadel, and find out just how much it costs to speak with the Master of the Durian Knights!'

'Greetings, strangers.' Vairdos, Commander of the Knights in Darien and the Wardship of Eastern Scûn, rose to welcome them. He made an absent motion with one gloved hand to indicate that they should seat themselves on the twin horsehair sofas that faced his desk. 'I am led to understand that you have urgent business with me?'

'Yes, my lord,' Telsyan made a perfunctory bow, giving the Knight Commander an abridged version of the death of Lord Eridar and of their mission north; first to Irgil, and now here, to collect his Testament. Finally he produced the sealed forms of authority which Careil had given them two months before in Ravenshald.

Vairdos examined these for several moments in silence, nodding once or twice as he did so. 'Yes,' he acknowledged finally. 'Your papers seem to be in order. And the documents to which they refer are indeed here in our safekeeping. They came to us a little over two months ago, having come north, along with much else pertaining to our southern affairs, in the last great caravan from Irgil. Wait, and I shall have them brought for you.'

A dark-robed assistant swirled silently into the room at his summons, bearing a small, decorated silver casket. Light, and worked with intricate skill, it was secured by three small padlocks, each sealed with the stamp of Archbaron Eridar. Vairdos received it into his own hands before presenting it formally to Telsyan for his inspection.

'You will note that the seals are unbroken.'

Telsyan nodded.

'Then you will have no objection . . .' Vairdos produced a sheaf of parchment, 'to signing a document to that effect? It is a minor formality, but necessary, as a safeguard for us all.'

The merchant forced a smile. 'Of course.'

'Then our obligations shall have been discharged in full. It has been a great honour to have performed even so minor a service for the noble Lord Eridar.'

Telsyan responded with a brief nod. 'The honour, my lord, is entirely ours.'

Even as Telsyan and Uhlendof signed Vairdos' paper, Leighor held his breath, finding that he could not draw his eyes from the tiny silver casket. It was for this that they had journeyed so far and risked so much. And now it was finally in their hands, and seemingly untouched. Things seemed to be going surprisingly well.

'And your new ruler,' Vairdos asked suddenly. 'Who is he?' I notice that his name appears nowhere upon your papers.'

'That matter was not quite settled when we left Ravenshald,' Telsyan said quickly. 'It was not, therefore, deemed fitting for any but the High Counsellor's name to appear. But it was considered fairly certain, even then, that my lord Darvir would succeed.'

'Ah, Darvir,' the Knight Commander scratched his dark beard thoughtfully. 'He is of the party of King Misan, is he not?'

'You are most knowledgeable, my lord,' Telsyan smiled, 'with regard to affairs in lands so far distant.'

'All such things must concern us. For there will be great turmoil in the southern lands if the succession to Galdan is not quickly settled. It is a wise precaution to gain as much knowledge of these matters as we may.' Vairdos turned sharply to look him straight in the eye. 'There are many who might suppose that the contents of this very casket may have bearing upon the final outcome . . .'

'I hardly think so,' Telsyan said quickly. 'We have been told little of what lies within, but I cannot think it as important as you suggest. To my knowledge it holds nothing more than some personal legacies that must be settled soon, so that the new Archbaron may know what is his and what is not. The disposition of lands, various small manors within the Sielders: only so much.'

'Then all is well,' Vairdos said, rising to indicate that the audience was over. 'Thall praise that I have been of help to you. You will, of course, remember me to your lord . . . Darvir?'

'Of course.' Telsyan rose with his companions to leave the chamber. 'We shall do so as soon as we meet.'

'Good, good,' the Knight Commander returned to his desk and pulled gently upon the summoning cord that hung there. 'Lord Hoethan, my deputy, shall see you to the gate. I bid you farewell.'

'How is our friend Keran?' Leighor asked as soon as they met with Hoethan outside Vairdos' chamber. 'When may we hope to see her?'

'To take your farewells?' Hoethan asked. 'For I hear that you plan to leave upon the morrow.'

'Aye,' Telsyan answered. 'We must leave as soon as we can, to escape the snows. So if we are to see Keran at all, it must be this evening or early tomorrow.'

Hoethan shook his head. 'I am afraid that will be impossible. For you see, Keran left this morning for Zaidar, one of the outer settlements, where most of her remaining family now dwell. She will return, I think, in three days or four, but unfortunately by then you will be gone.'

'She has left Darien?' Leighor repeated in astonishment. 'Without telling us? Without bidding us farewell?'

'She left you a message,' Hoethan corrected. 'Which I now deliver.' He delved deep into an interior pocket and produced a small folded letter. 'Here it is. It is addressed to all of you.'

There being neither the time nor the light to read the letter there and then, the travellers permitted themselves to be escorted from the Citadel in silence; Telsyan bearing the precious casket, and Leighor, Keran's letter. Taking their leave of Hoethan, they made their way back through darkened streets to their cramped chamber at the inn.

Leighor broke open the seal of Keran's letter at once, holding it up to the thin light of their single oil-lamp.

'It is very short,' he said at last. 'A few words to thank us for our companionship upon the road, and ending by wishing us a safe journey south. It is very strange . . .'

'How is it strange?' Telsyan demanded, plucking the letter from his hand to study it himself. 'It seems quite plain and straightforward enough to me. She has gone to see her relatives and wishes us God Speed. What more do you expect?'

'A little more than that, after so long together on the road. Do you not think it strange that she could not wait a single day to say farewell to us in person? There is nothing in this letter that a perfect stranger could not have written. Do we even know that it is in her hand?'

'Who knows her hand?' Uhlendof shrugged. 'None of us has ever seen her write. She may not have the art. It could be anyone's hand.'

'You have dwelt with her the longest,' Leighor turned to the mercenary, who stood beside him. 'Does this cool parting seem likely?'

Zindur shrugged. 'I barely spoke with her at Silentwater; she kept herself apart, with the women. Perhaps now she is back with that kind again – yet on the road she seemed a warm-hearted enough a lass . . . As to letters, I have naught to do with them; I cannot tell whether the hand be hers or not.'

'We have no good reason to believe that it isn't perfectly genuine,' Telsyan said firmly. 'So any further debate on the subject is a waste of time! What concerns me more is this casket we have been given. Is that genuine? It seems to me we have had it from the Knights far too easily.'

'Why not open it?' Yeon asked. 'And see what lies inside?'

'We cannot break Lord Eridar's seals!' Uhlendof's head shook with outrage. 'If the box is seen to have been tampered with in any way, then all its contents become suspect. Worthless! And my lord Vairdos made certain that we signed to show the seals unbroken when we received it.'

'That is true enough,' Telsyan agreed. 'Only Arminor, Darvir, or Misan himself, now have the authority to break those seals. Yet it irks me not to know what lies inside this little casket; and whether it be of importance or no. Whether it is even worth carrying all the way down into Helietrim to present to King Arminor.'

'Whatever lies within, the king is the best person to receive it,' Uhlendof studied the casket seals once more. 'If it contains the proxy vote of the Sielders, well enough. But even if all it holds is a few words that will prove Eridar's fears of Darvir and Misan, then Arminor is in the best position to use these things to advantage.'

'Aye,' the merchant nodded. 'I suppose you are right. But . . .' the idea seemed to have been troubling him for some time, '. . . the casket could not already have been tampered with in some way, could it?'

Uhlendof shook his head at once. 'I cannot see how. The locks are unbroken, the seals are full and undamaged, and they are undoubtedly genuine. I know Eridar's seals, and all their flaws and imperfections. This box was last opened by Lord Eridar himself, I would swear to it.'

A thin mantle of snow fell during the night. Only an inch or so, but it transformed Darien from a city of dirty greys and muddy browns into a place that looked quite clean and beautiful for the first time.

Yet the sight brought no joy to the travellers, and only confirmed Telsyan in his desire to be out of the city at once. It took them less than an hour to make ready for their departure. And, leaving a surprisingly silent Inanys behind them, they rode away from Strangers' Inn for the last time; reaching the city gates just as the sun began to rise, bloated and fiery red, above the dark forests of the east.

The guards let them pass out of the city without a word. And with barely a glance back at the snow-covered township of the Knights of Dur, the five travellers began the long ride south.

Chapter Twenty Six
HOETHAN

The fading embers of the fire still glowed a deep warming red, but there was little heat left in them. Keran huddled closer to the flames, feeling desperately alone. Despite the familiar surroundings, her father's house had begun to seem more like a prison to her than a place of refuge, and a mounting sense of impotence and frustration grew in her.

Darien had changed much in the two years she had been away. It had always been a ramshackle, corrupt place, but even under the harshest of Knight Commanders it had never been like this. The poverty, the cruelty, the sullen anger in the streets: all had made the city of her birth seem grim and oppressive.

Hoethan himself seemed never to be at home, spending most of the day at the Knights' Citadel, or elsewhere in the sprawling township that was Darien. But when Keran had asked to accompany him or to leave the high-walled compound to meet her friends, he had quickly found a dozen good reasons why she should not. Women were no longer welcomed in the inner councils of Darien. Neither was it safe for her to walk the streets on her own, and for the time being he could spare her no guard. All this she had accepted with good grace, yet when Hoethan also refused to allow her to attend the High Council, her temper had momentarily forsaken her.

'Why not?' she had demanded fiercely. 'It is my right to attend. It is the right of every citizen!'

'You should know by now the procedures of High Council, sister,' Hoethan chided. 'They are long and tedious, and the crowd will be an unseemly rabble. It is no place for a lady, and no place in which to meet your friends. I shall do the best I can for your companions, and I will try to arrange a meeting for you at a better time and place.'

Beyond this he would not be moved, and finally Keran had given in. But now she regretted her reasonableness, for this meeting had never materialised. And although she had been given the news that her companions now had what they sought, it seemed that they could not visit her that night. Perhaps tomorrow.

But tomorrow had come, and with it a thin covering of snow, yet still there had been no sign of her companions. She wondered at their lack of thought for her. She had half expected such behaviour of Telsyan; after all, by his reckoning, their bargain was now concluded. She had been delivered safely into the hands of her family, and his commitment to her was over. But she had expected more of the others: of Zindur, Leighor, even Uhlendof. Yet all had disappointed her, and she felt foolishly rejected and alone.

Her sister, Kerel, had provided but little warmth or company. Seeming always strangely aloof and distant, she spent much of the day alone in her chambers, nor did she ever seem to leave the house or have visitors, speaking normally only to Hoethan and her servants. This seemed so unlike the joyful, confident sister she had known. In fact, this Kerel was almost a stranger: embarrassed and strangely lost for words in her presence, seeming to find every moment spent with her younger sister an ordeal from which she retired gratefully at the earliest opportunity. The only person she would ever talk about with any enthusiasm was Hoethan, and when she spoke of him, her words were all of praise: for his wisdom and astuteness, his energy and determination, his rising power within the Durian order, and his ambitions for the future. It was as if Hoethan were the whole of her life, dominating every waking thought.

'And all that remained of our father's money and goods?' Keran had asked her. 'What of these? Have they too all passed to Hoethan?'

Kerel nodded. 'Of course, dear sister. That was only his right upon our marriage. And besides, the High Council do not long allow a woman to hold estates and money for her own in these days. And I suppose they are right, it is truly a man's task.'

'And to me: did our father leave nothing? Nothing personal?'

Kerel shook her head, giving her sister a small smile of consolation. 'He thought you well enough settled. And a great shame it is that he was so wrong. That such fearful things can happen as you have told us of . . . Still I know that Hoethan will do his best to find you some good settled station of your own.'

It was this prospect that was beginning increasingly to worry Keran, for it was obvious that there was no permanent place for her here. All the brightness and laughter seemed to have gone out of this house with the passing of her father, and it had become dark and watchful, suspicious and silent: a place of strangers.

There came a creaking from the gates beneath her window, and the sound of a horse entering the courtyard. Hoethan was back. It was late, it had been dark for several hours, but she would have to speak with him. Find out what news he bore, insist upon seeing her friends. Pausing only long enough to allow him to enter the house, she ran down to the large study where he was normally to be found.

Hoethan looked up in surprise as she entered. He stood at her father's great oaken desk, going through some papers. Unreasonably Keran bridled to see him there, where her father had so often stood: the new master in a house she still regarded as hers. He was dressed now in robes less formal than those he had worn for Council the day before, but he was still richly attired in silks and velvets of black and mauve, overlaid by a fur-trimmed mantle and thick chains of gold.

At first he seemed irritated by her presence here, uninvited, but then abruptly his mood altered.

'Ah, Keran,' he motioned her towards him almost cordially. 'I have been meaning to speak with you, either this day or tomorrow. This shall be our opportunity.'

'I too have been wanting to speak with you . . . brother' The term was unfamiliar, and Keran had almost to force the word out through a throat unwilling to suffer it. But Hoethan waved her into silence.

'Later. What I have to tell you is of greater importance.' He signalled her to sit, although himself pacing the floor in front of her. 'It is time that we discussed your future, Keran. Time we discussed it seriously. You must understand that many things have altered since you were a child here, and that, for many reasons, you cannot remain here indefinitely – not as you are . . .'

Keran opened her mouth to speak, but Hoethan pre-empted her. 'The position of a younger daughter without lands or dowry in these days is not a happy one. But I am willing to use my best endeavours on your behalf.' Abruptly he sat down on the sofa, facing her. 'You have tried the life of service with a noble lady, and you would not like that again?'

Keran shook her head, still not quite sure where all this was leading.

'Well then, there is but one thing left: marriage.'

'Marriage?' Keran repeated numbly, now quite sure that things were moving far too swiftly for her liking.

'Aye,' Hoethan nodded. 'You are certainly old enough. In fact most would say that it is well past time.'

'But how? To whom?' Keran objected weakly.

'In that you must accept my guidance, dear sister. As I have said, since you have no wealth and no dowry, you cannot be too choosy. But I think I can arrange a marriage with one of my followers who needs a wife, and would be grateful of the connection with my family. One Idthur, who is landreeve of the settlement of Garim, some forty leagues to the north-west.'

'Idthur?' Keran questioned, stunned. 'I have met no Idthur. Who is he? What is he?'

Hoethan smiled. 'He is my age, a good man: you will like him. But you will meet him tomorrow and see for yourself. And though your circumstances may at first be somewhat reduced, Idthur is an ambitious man. Your standard of life will soon improve . . .'

'And what if I do not like this Idthur?' she broke in, a sharp note of outrage beginning to colour her voice.

'Do not misunderstand me, sister.' Hoethan's smile hardened. 'I do not offer you a choice. Idthur shall be your husband, like it or not. Best do it with a good grace and save us all much trouble.'

Appalled by this sudden ultimatum, for long moments Keran could do nothing more than stare blankly across the room, too stunned to speak. She knew enough of Hoethan already to realise that he meant exactly what he said. She knew, too, that it would be little use appealing to her sister. Kerel was totally in Hoethan's thrall, and would do and say exactly what he wanted – and now, it seemed, she must do the same! The very thought made her seethe with anger: that this total stranger, this trumped-up mercenary horse-soldier should usurp her father's place, usurp his lands and title, and now presume to rule her; to control her life! It was beyond bearing!

'You cannot do this!' she said at last. 'Not if I do not wish it! I shall not consent!'

'Take care!' Hoethan's eyes were like cold crystals of ice. 'I truly care not what becomes of you, girl. I only do so much for you for the sake of your sister.'

'Then spare me your charity!' Keran seized upon his words with scorn. 'I may still leave your protection, and journey south with my friends. At least then I shall not have to live as your creature!'

A shock of fury passed across Hoethan's features, and she could see that he controlled his temper only with great effort. 'No.' He rose and shook his head firmly. 'Understand that this marriage is of great value to me. Idthur is a rising man. You will be my eyes and ears in his house, helping to ensure his continued loyalty. Besides which,' he added before she could speak, 'your companions are gone. They left Darien at first light this morning, and will be ten or fifteen leagues south by now. You may have cause to be thankful, in time to come, that you were not with them.'

'What?' Keran's mouth dropped open, aghast.

'Aye,' Hoethan nodded with evident pleasure. 'They are gone without a word. The guards at the gate so informed me this morning. That is how little your "friends" care for you. You would do best to forget them, and their foolish meddling.'

At first Keran could not believe it; but one look into Hoethan's eyes and she knew beyond doubting that it was true. 'You made it so!' she spat suddenly, determined in her anguish to place the blame on him, even if it were not so. 'You have done it! You have told them some lie, to make them leave without first seeing me – some foul lie!'

'No one made them leave, girl. It was their own choice. In truth they were probably as glad to be rid of you as I shall be!' He stretched forward to haul her to her feet. And for the first time Keran noticed the slim band of purple metal about his wrist.

'*Harrunor!*' she gasped in horror.

Hoethan froze – as if a knife had suddenly been driven between his ribs. And Keran knew at once that she had made a dreadful mistake.

'What do you know of *harrunor*?' he demanded, his voice sounding for the first time truly dangerous. 'Tell me, girl. Tell me quickly: what do you know of this?'

'N . . . nothing.' Keran faltered, her wits for the moment deserting her. 'Nothing at all!'

A violent slap wrenched her head backwards, startling as much as it hurt.

'Do not play fools games with me!' Hoethan's other hand tightened its grip on her arm. 'Answer!'

'I know little,' Keran pleaded, the pain of the slap stinging some of her former resolve back into her. She must reveal something: but what? How much would suffice to satisfy Hoethan in his present state? 'It is the strange metal we mined at Silentwater,' she stumbled at last, 'and which we sent in secret to Helietrim. We knew not why, nor for what purpose . . .'

'Ah . . .' Hoethan sighed, seeming relieved at this explanation, and the grip on her arm loosened a little. 'Yes, of course. Arminor's old workings at Silentwater. Why else would he delve so deep in that forsaken place? He has found something then, the old crow . . . Still, that is finished now.' These last words were spoken more to himself than to Keran. But now he turned his full attention back to her once more, pale eyes blazing directly into hers. 'Is that all you know?'

Keran freed herself from his grip and nodded, taking a surreptitious step backward.

'Good.' Hoethan seemed satisfied, and turned away. 'If you are wise you will forget, now and forever, all that you knew of these things, and never speak of them again. The consequences otherwise might be more serious than you imagine.'

Keran shivered and took another backward step. Hoethan had somehow gained possession of one of the dread Dark Amulets . . . The shock of the discovery overwhelmed her. Yet suddenly it all fell together . . . her sister . . . the servants . . . the harshness and corruption . . . the many dour unpleasant changes to Darien itself. *Harrunor* was at their heart: the alluring, soul-tainting poison of the Mage Metal! Had not the giants told them that the power of the amulets, whatever its form, was only for evil – either to hurt or to defile? And what power did Hoethan's amulet bear?

If it held anything like the power of the other two she had seen, then Hoethan was far too dangerous to be trifled with. She must take care. Pretend to agree with all he proposed, until she could find some opportunity to escape this place.

But Hoethan gave her no time for further reflection, turning sharply from his desk to face her again. 'Well, my sister.' He spoke softly once more. 'I now wish your answer to my proposal. Will you consent to this willingly, as I ask – or no?'

Hesitantly Keran nodded. 'If it is truly your wish.'

'Yes, it is my wish, dear sister.' Hoethan looked at her darkly, holding her eyes now with his own and staring deep into them with a cold, penetrating directness that seemed to see right into the depths of her soul. 'Yet I am no fool, as you shall soon discover; and I have my own ways of curing insincerity and deceit . . .' He raised one hand towards her – the hand which bore upon it the *harrunor* amulet.

Shaking her head, Keran backed away.

'Stay, sweet sister,' Hoethan smiled. 'You shall come to no harm, if you do as I say.'

Keran tried to retreat, but Hoethan's words seemed to place some strange compulsion upon her, and she could not. In some manner her will was already held in thrall to Hoethan's gently shimmering amulet. Her eyes fastened unwillingly upon it.

It gave out an almost visible aura of power, which seeped forth like a dank miasma to penetrate and fill every corner of the chamber, entangling her in its dense, smouldering coils. She felt dizzy, helpless, without bearings. The whole world seemed to be closing in on her, foreshortening, until only she and Hoethan were left.

'Now, sweet sister,' Hoethan spoke at last. 'Now you shall truly obey. Tell me, Keran, tell me true: what is the real errand of your traveller friends? What is their knowledge of the *harrunor* and its provenance? Whom do they serve? Tell me all, hold nothing back – and I shall be most gratified.'

Keran felt an overwhelming compulsion to speak, to tell Hoethan without reserve, all that she knew of their quest, her deepest secrets, anything he willed.

Deep within, she knew that she must try to resist. But she could not find the will. She bit her tongue, somehow knowing that should she allow even a single syllable to escape her, the floodgates would burst, and all her knowledge would pour out of her like a river. She felt utterly helpless.

But where else had one tried to entrap her so? It hovered just out of reach on the hazy edges of her memory . . . An inn? The inn at the bridge . . . Vhori bridge . . . and had it not been with Inanys? Or was that a dream? No, it had been no dream – she must believe so at any rate, for that was her hope.

What had she done then? The jewel . . . the Ginara Stone . . . it hung still at her neck. She must reach for it . . . use it.

Even to move one hand against the silken constraint of the amulet was an effort akin to scaling Byriadon. Yet slowly, imperceptibly, by sheer force of will, she did so.

And, as her questing hand found the gem, touched it, Hoethan's spell was broken. Shattered, as if it had never been: and instantly her mind cleared. She felt in full control of her own movements – her own being – once more. Hoethan too noticed the change, felt the breach of his carefully – woven enchantment, saw what had caused it.

'What is that thing?' he demanded, his voice quivering with fury. 'Give it to me!'

'No!' Keran shook her head firmly, still holding the jewel up before her like a talisman on its golden chain. 'It is mine; you shall not have it. And you shall not have me for your creature either! Allow me to leave. Give me but a single horse that I may follow after my friends, and I shall burden you no longer!'

There was an instant of electric silence as their eyes met and fought. And then, without warning, Hoethan lunged forward, seizing both her wrists in one large hand, holding her precious jewel suddenly hostage. Even in the midst of her fear and startlement, Keran wondered at Hoethan's speed and strength. His fingers bit into her bare wrists like an iron vice, shaking her from side to side like a rag doll. And much as she strove to free herself, she was unable to.

'Speak not to me of your precious friends again, girl!' he spat, wrenching the jewel and its chain from her neck with such force that she gave a startled gasp of pain. 'Do you truly wish to know what has happened to them? Do you, girl? They are dead! Done with! Or soon shall be . . .' Holding the jewelled medallion firm now in his right hand, he sent her sprawling to the floor with the other.

'Aye,' he glared scornfully down at her. 'The Council feared that they might grow lonely on the long road south, and so have sent word for some to meet them on the way. I fear that your friends have no chance of reaching either Helietrim or King Arminor alive. So be thankful that I did not indeed send you south with them to share their fate!'

'But why?' Keran gasped, although in part she already knew the answer. 'Why would you wish to harm them?'

'Because the Council, the Knights, and all with any sense in these northlands support the accession of King Misan to the Iron Throne. And whatever it is that lies within Eridar's casket, it will be of help only to Arminor. It is Misan who will rule – your friends are fools if they think they can alter that – and Misan will reward well those who bring about the destruction of his enemies.'

'And for this they will die?'

'Yes, sweet sister,' Hoethan nodded. 'What better way to be rid of casket and meddlers both? They shall all lie dead, with cold Riever steel in their bellies, before ever they reach the southlands. Aye, before even they cross the Ormul, if Foln is as swift as he is wont.' He turned away to examine her jewel more fully beneath the light.

It took a few minutes for full realisation of the scale of the Knights' betrayal to strike home. But when it did a wave of wild, animal fury swept through Keran and she sprang to her feet, borne upon a tide of loathing, to hurl herself at Hoethan's unprotected back. Wildly her fingers clawed for his face and neck, with desperate intent to do him harm.

But despite their near equal height, Hoethan's strength was so much the greater that he was able to restrain her with ease, twisting around to face her as he pinned her arms tight in his own. Yet as he did so, the Ginara Stone slipped gently from his palm to dangle down his wrist on its golden chain, seeming almost drawn to the coiled *harrunor* bracelet that hung there. Hoethan raised his arm as if to strike her once more – and at once the trailing gem slipped the last half-inch down his wrist to come into brief, momentary contact with the *harrunor*.

The result was utterly unexpected. There was a sudden brief ripple of painfully intense white light: and then, with a small crack, Keran's precious Ginara Stone burst asunder.

Hoethan let out a startled howl of pain and tore the amulet from his wrist as if it had stung him. Almost without thinking, Keran seized it as it fell, to hurl it hard across the room.

For an instant both combatants were too stunned and astonished to move, Keran staring in disbelief at the large scarlet burn that had appeared on Hoethan's wrist where stone and amulet had met. What had caused it? Whatever it was, it was none of her doing. Somehow her stone and the *harrunor* amulet had reacted against each other, in a conflict that had destroyed her stone utterly. Hoethan, too, seemed suddenly weaker than before. Not pausing to wonder at the reason, Keran took full advantage of it, tearing herself finally free of his grasp.

Ignoring her, Hoethan lunged after the fallen amulet.

At once Keran knew she must stop him. Once in possession of the amulet, he was back in control, and all hope would be lost.

Desperately she hurled herself into his path, striking him with just enough force to make his outstretched right arm miss the amulet by inches. She still had no idea what to do with the amulet should she chance to secure it; but she knew that she must have it, if only to deny it to Hoethan, and she fought for it like a creature possessed.

Hoethan was a good deal weaker now, and he was not able to overcome her as easily as before. But still he had the greater strength – if only by a fraction – and with a sudden sharp elbow in her ribs, he at last managed to tear himself free and reach out for the amulet.

Keran gasped at the pain, but she could not give up now. In desperation she threw herself on top of him, seizing his arm in the selfsame instant that it again caught hold of the amulet.

At once she felt the shock of the power as it surged back into him from the *harrunor*, filling him with strength. Somehow she must stop it, halt it. Before it was too late. He was still at a slight disadvantage, sprawled across the floor beneath her, his right arm splayed towards the amulet, her right hand clamped tight over his.

Yet he was growing stronger with each passing moment. Even now he tried to rise. In seconds, he would have the advantage once more.

She must act now . . . or never.

Bracing her left hand against his shoulder, and summoning every last iota of her remaining strength, she wrenched his outstretched arm savagely back against the joint. Unable to resist, the arm hurtled backward to come to a sudden shuddering halt against the solid bone of her knee. But the momentum was too great to be so halted; and with a single dry crack, the elbow gave way, his arm snapping like a rotten branch to hang awkwardly in her grip.

With a dull clank, the amulet fell from his suddenly lifeless fingers to roll away into the darkness.

Yet Hoethan gave out no loud cry: too shocked to emit more than a single, barely-audible gasp. Shocked herself by what she had done, Keran pulled away from him, looking on with something akin to horror as Hoethan tried vainly to come to terms with his sudden, calamitous disablement. Only now did he begin to feel the full agonising pain of his injury, emitting a low moan of pain as he tried to rise.

Sheer animal fury enable him somehow to stagger to his feet and take several lurching steps towards her, his eyes ablaze. A row of heavy carvings stood not a dozen feet away, on the mantelshelf. Keran made a desperate lunge for them, evading Hoethan's last blundering grasp to clutch one in her hand and bring it crashing down into the side of his head.

Seeing Hoethan lying at last slumped and unconscious at her feet, she allowed herself a deep sigh of relief. The immediate danger was past. But she must make good her escape quickly, before Hoethan recovered or anyone else chanced upon the scene. But then, with the chamber door half open, she thought better of it. Hoethan would soon come to, and she would not get very far once he raised the alarm.

Silently she pulled the door to once more, bolting it fast to prevent Kerel or one of the servants coming upon her unexpectedly. Then she bound Hoethan tightly, with stout cord torn from the curtains, choosing to err on the side of overcaution rather than haste.

She could not leave him where he was, however. He must be hidden. But where? Her eyes sought despairingly about the room. Then she remembered. Her father had had a deep store-cellar where many of his more important valuables had lain in safekeeping through the long winter months. There was an entry from this very chamber; a trapdoor in the middle of the room, approximately where a thin, knotted carpet now lay, between the two sofas. Eagerly pulling the carpet aside, she found it. A large iron ring, embedded flush with the floorboards, lay ready for her to drag it open.

Even with the ring, it took a deal of effort to lift the heavy trapdoor. But once done, she was rewarded by the sight of the narrow wooden stairway down into the darkness beneath. As she descended, the trembling light of her lamp caught an array of gleaming treasures. Treasures such as even her father – who had been no modest merchant on his own account – had never dreamt to possess.

Row upon row of rich furs: some bundled raw, others fashioned into shimmering capes and gowns of finest workmanship; all hung heavy from long racks, alongside countless other fine robes of silk, velvet and leathers. Here too were great piles of horns and ivories; chests brimming with delicate artefacts of silver, bronze and porcelain; numberless barrels of fine wines and stronger liquors from the south. Here was china so fine that she could see the colour of her fingers through it, and glassware that sparkled in the lamplight as if it were distilled from liquid fire. She had never seen so many fine things together in one place before, not even in the possession of Lord Fralcel and his lady. Yet here they all sat, piled high like common market-pots, in the cellar of her father's house in Darien!

Several small wooden chests stood alone to one side of the stair, and these she could not resist opening. Two were crammed to the brim with every kind of silver plate imaginable, a third was half-filled with precious amber jewellery, and the fourth contained gold. It was less than a quarter full, but there was enough there in plate and coin to buy up most of the poor farmland around Darien many times over. Hoethan had indeed done well for himself in two short years.

Keran had not dreamed to find anything like this; but now she took full advantage of it, quickly slipping out of her cumbersome linen skirts to find herself some stouter clothing for her travels: soft boots and breeches of dark leather, along with a warm, hardy-looking jerkin of the same material. To top these she selected a warm cloak of dull, forest green, trimmed with brown fox-fur. Hurriedly filling her pockets with handfuls of the bright gold coins – the least that Hoethan owed her for the loss of her rightful inheritance – and taking a long, regretful look at the brilliant amber necklaces she must leave behind, she made her way upward once more.

Hoethan was fully conscious now and his eyes were wide open, watching her with cold, impotent fury as she approached. There was such malice and blazing hatred in them that for a moment Keran lost all her resolve and would have retreated. But grim necessity made her go on, and she steeled herself to face him.

'I have found your little treasure-trove, brother,' she smiled at him sweetly, taking him securely beneath the arms and dragging him back to the waiting opening. 'And now I think it fitting that you spend a longer while with your treasures.'

Suddenly realising what was about to come, Hoethan began to struggle like a wild thing. But Keran had done her work well, and he was securely bound. His struggles served only to increase her nervousness, so that she did not treat him as tenderly as she might have, dragging his writhing form down the steep wooden steps. She let him slide the last dozen feet or so to the bottom on his own, climbing back up to close the heavy trapdoor on him.

She had only to ensure that the trapdoor was again hidden, and the rest of the room returned to some semblance of normality, and she could leave.

It was as she completed this final task that she found the amulet – where it had lain, forgotten, beneath one of the twin sofas. For a long moment she looked at it in silence. It seemed so harmless and commonplace there: dull iron-grey on the bare wooden floor. But now she knew the dark power that lurked beneath that outer shell, and she shuddered.

What should she do with it? She could not leave it for Hoethan to find and use again. Nor dared she try to use it herself. No, she would just have to take it with her, and hope she might find some safe means to dispose of it later. Gingerly she picked it up, hardly daring even to touch it with her bare fingers, but using instead the hem of her cloak to place it in her jerkin pocket.

Now she must go. She had already wasted far too much time. Pausing only to retrieve the blistered remnants of the gold medallion that had borne her lost

Ginara Stone, she unbolted the door and fled the chamber. It was late now, and the few lights left burning in the narrow hallway glimmered low. Yet even their scant illumination was enough to show her that the main door to the outer courtyard lay locked and barred. There would be no escape that way, not without the complicity of Hoethan's nightwatchmen.

She considered trying to make her way out through the kitchens, but that way too was bound to be guarded, and there would be many servants either working or asleep there. Besides, she would still have to get over the high timber palisade that surrounded the compound without being seen or heard. No, whatever the risk, she would have to try to enlist her sister's aid.

Yet Kerel had been acting almost like a stranger since their strained reunion two days before. Most likely she too had been under the baleful influence of Hoethan and his amulet. Perhaps that influence was now broken, and once away from this place her sister would swiftly return to her old self. It was a thin straw, but one on which Keran had no choice but to rely. She could not leave her sister here, and only with Kerel's authority behind her, had she any chance of being allowed out of this house and its well-guarded compound . . . Once out, she might realise the plan, already beginning to form in her mind, for escape from the city itself.

Kerel lay already robed for sleep in the folds of her vast, canopied bed. She looked up in startled surprise as Keran burst into the long bed-chamber she occupied on the upper floor. 'What do you want at this hour, Keran?' she asked nervously, pulling herself upright against the heavy bolsters. 'Why are you dressed so? And where is Hoethan?'

'I must leave this place!' Keran pointedly ignored her sister's other questions. 'And you must help me. At least help me to get out of this house so that I may warn my friends of the danger that awaits them.'

'But your friends are gone.'

'I know. Hoethan has told me. I must stop them!'

Kerel heaved a heavy sigh and rose from her bed. 'Do not be so silly, sister. Do you not know what hour it is? Have you never heard of curfew? Let me call Hoethan. Perhaps he may be able to talk some sense into you . . .' She began to make her way towards the door.

'I have already spoken with Hoethan,' Keran said quickly, moving to intercept her. 'There is no more time! We must go now!'

Kerel shook her head. 'We cannot go out at such an hour, and certainly not without my lord's permission! You should not even think to ask me such a thing! I like not this underhandedness, Keran. I think we had best have him sort out this whole business directly! Where is he?'

She made to push past, towards the door. But Keran was there faster. Making good use of her superior size and strength to pin her sister's arms tight about her waist, she forced one hand across her mouth to still her cries.

Yet still Kerel squirmed and fought like a creature possessed, clawing at Keran's bare arms and forearms with long, raking fingernails as if her whole life hung upon the outcome. But having overcome Hoethan at such great cost, Keran was not now prepared to let Kerel get the better of her. She had one hand already clamped tight across her sister's mouth, and it was little additional effort to pinch her nose shut as well, cutting off Kerel's breathing entirely, holding her grip firm until at length her sister's struggles ceased, and she slumped into semi-consciousness.

Gathering Kerel gently into her arms, Keran found herself surprised at how light a burden her sister had now become. She hardly felt the weight as she bore her back across to the bed and laid her down there. Kerel seemed so thin and frail, the merest shadow of her former self. What in the world could have happened to her?

Almost immediately Kerel began to come to. But even when fully recovered she could not be made to listen to any word spoken against Hoethan; refusing to consider that he might be capable of acting against Keran's companions' interests, let alone encompassing their deaths. And as the minutes passed, Keran began to grow more and more desperate. She had always imagined that if she could only get her sister on her own for long enough, she would be able to talk her around. But Kerel was like a stone wall. There was no getting through to her, and she had constantly to be restrained from attempting to escape or call for help. Hoethan's hold on her was strong indeed.

His hold – or that of the *harrunor*?

The thought came to her that she still held Hoethan's amulet in her pocket. Could she risk using it? Perhaps by doing so she might break Hoethan's control over her sister: free her entirely. The idea intrigued her. The dangers were great, but then so were those of any other course . . . She would do it. She would only put the amulet on for a minute . . . To see if it had any effect. That would do no harm. Surely?

She reached cautiously into her jerkin pocket, her fingers making brief contact with the cold metal. It seemed to leap to her touch. With trepidation she withdrew the purple-grey bracelet and placed it on her wrist.

At once the shock of raw power ran through her, streaming up her forearm and coursing through her veins like some dark poison. For an instant she wanted nothing other than to throw off the cursed amulet and hurl it from her. But before she could act, the feeling left her.

All too quickly she felt herself becoming reconciled to the amulet. It was warm and comforting now, her friend. And she felt at once stronger and more confident, as if nothing could defeat her; all the dark shadows seeming to retreat and dwindle before her eyes. She could hear more now, she was certain: every creak and grumble of this dark old house; the stamping of Hoethan's two guards in the courtyard beyond; even the squealings of the night-bats in the high, still rafters. She seemed suddenly open to new feelings, new sensations: a score of moods and undercurrents previously hidden from her own dull senses. Even her skin seemed to burn with a new inner fire . . . So this was the power of the amulets! No wonder they were so desired, and their loss so keenly felt.

Kerel now lay quiet and still beneath her, her eyes agape. 'The amulet . . . Hoethan's amulet!'

'Yes,' Keran smiled down at her. 'He has lent it to me for a while, and with it I think I may command you, if you will not help me willingly.'

Kerel said nothing, merely staring up at her younger sister in total astonishment.

'Now, sister,' Keran held her eyes fast with her own: deep green reflecting into amber. 'Rise and dress yourself, for we two are leaving this place. If anyone attempts to challenge or prevent us, you shall say that what we do is at Hoethan's command. Otherwise you shall say no word until I give you leave.

Do you understand?' She held Kerel's eyes until her sister nodded, and then released her, watching as Kerel rose silently and began to do as she was bid.

Keran marvelled at the amulet's power. Her power. For it seemed in no way evil. In no way did it attempt to control her will as she had feared, nor had it felt in any way uncomfortable or unnatural. It seemed entirely neutral, a tool which could be used either for good or ill as its bearer chose. Mayhap the giants were wrong; and there was no evil in the amulets themselves . . .

Kerel was now ready to depart, and waited silently at the door for Keran's further instruction. Hesitantly Keran nodded, giving her sister consent to draw back the bolt and pull the door quietly open. Kerel's obedience to the command of the amulet seemed entire, if unwilling. How to gain her willing consent, however, Keran could not guess. She dared not try to experiment with the amulet here. Best to wait until later, until they were safely out of this house. Then she would try.

They passed silently through darkened hallways to gain the barred outer door. Here Kerel again halted to seek direction. Keran held a finger to her lips. She was about to move forward to unbar the door herself when a dark figure stirred suddenly in the shadows, rising from a startled slumber to confront them.

'What would you here at this hour . . . mistress?' This was not Kaedban, as Keran had hoped, but a dour, heavy-built member of Hoethan's personal guard. One who was clearly disconcerted to find himself face to face with his master's lady in the middle of the night, attired for travel. 'It is long after curfew.'

'This is a matter of great need,' Keran said quickly. 'We must go at once to the Citadel upon an urgent errand for my lord Hoethan. Is this not so, sister?' She turned to give Kerel a quick hard stare, hoping that the amulet still held enough force to compel her sister's obedience.

There was a tense silence, Kerel seeming to engage in a long, internal struggle before she gave an answer. But at last she nodded. 'Yes, Birstan, that is so.'

Although only partly visible in the dull quarter-light, Birstan's face looked puzzled. 'But I have had orders that no one—'

'You have new orders!' Keran broke in sharply, trying hard to browbeat him into compliance.

The guardsman looked at her with growing suspicion, yet she could see that he feared to disobey openly.

'I shall accompany you,' he grunted at last. 'It is too late for any to walk the streets alone.'

'There is no need,' Keran insisted, wishing that she could somehow force her sister to speak again. But Kerel remained obstinately silent.

'There is need,' Bristan growled darkly, daring to speak to Keran as he never would to his mistress. 'It is Lord Hoethan's order. No one must journey beyond the gates without guard!'

'All right,' Keran nodded quickly. 'Perhaps you had best accompany us.'

Birstan nodded, seeming partially satisfied, and stepped forward to unbar the door. Taking up a blazing torch from the doorway, he led them through the snowswept courtyard and thence out into the pitch dark streets of Darien.

Keran felt an intense surge of relief as the gates finally closed behind them.

The house of Hoethan and Kerel had become a grim prison for her; and despite the many difficulties and dangers that lay ahead, she was – for the moment at least – free once more.

For long minutes they walked in silence through the deserted streets: Kerel treading soft and strangely subdued beside her, like some wraith only partly present with them. Ahead strode Birstan, all too solid and corporeal, his torch held high to light the way. Time was passing too quickly. She had told him that they were going to the Citadel, yet none of them must reach it – lest her deception be uncovered and the alarm raised. Again she must act swiftly is she were not to become ensnared.

Seizing her courage in both hands, she stopped, pulling Kerel to a sharp halt alongside her. 'Stay still and say nothing!' she hissed, hoping that her word would still be enough to make the order stick.

For the moment it seemed to be doing so, and Kerel remained silent and motionless at her side.

At once Birstan turned to investigate.

'Why do you delay?' Deep suspicion rose anew in his voice as he approached.

'We have told you a small untruth, Birstan,' Keran declared softly. 'Our plans are changed. We go not now to the Citadel. And from here on we must proceed alone. Return to your post and await us there.'

'No, my lady.' Birstan shook his head firmly. 'I may not. This whole midnight jaunt is not to my liking. I think it time we all returned – and discovered upon whose errand you truly journey!' He took a further step forward.

'Hold!' Keran cried, holding out her right arm before her. She tried to wield the amulet just as she had seen Hoethan do, to direct all its power into the subjugation of Birstan's will – yet to no apparent avail. He still advanced inexorably upon her.

Perhaps his will was harder to subdue than Kerel's. Perhaps, unlike her sister, he had never been subject to the amulet's thrall. Perhaps it was she: not skilled enough in its use. Whatever the reason, the force or her will seemed to dissipate ineffectually; she could find no way to concentrate her power and give it effect.

'What do you play at, lass?' He was nearly upon her. 'Do you try to bewitch me?'

Keran shook her head, taking several hurried steps backward, her feet crunching through the frost-sharp snow. It was not working! A moment more and she would have to flee: with or without her sister.

She wavered. And in that instant Birstan sprang for her.

Hardly realising what she did, Keran reacted without conscious thought. Instinctively marshalling all the force, the fear, the panic within her, she hurled it wildly against him.

And all at once the amulet blazed into life.

There was a sudden brief hiss of power. A sunburst of intense purple light, that for a single moment lit up the alley like day, throwing the walls of the dark timber buildings into sharp relief. Then, equally suddenly, there was darkness once more. A howl of agony rose from somewhere in front of her as Birstan's form vanished into a living ball of flame; which writhed, bright golden orange, in the snow. And in that instant Keran felt the amulet on her wrist become suddenly aware.

It was aware of her! Something far away, yet buried deep, had awoken to her presence . . . had realised, with that last terrible burst of power, that she who used the amulet was not its true bearer. She felt the shock of that distant realisation flood through her, felt something old and incredibly evil trying to recognise her, to probe her, to reach right into her . . .

Blind and deaf to all else now, she fought her own private battle with whatever it was that now attempted to use the amulet to enter her. It was as if some great leech strove to inhabit the inner core of her being: to attach itself to the roots of her soul.

Deep down inside she knew that there was but one cure: to throw off the amulet. Yet this was now the most difficult task she had ever tried to accomplish. Even after so short a time, the amulet seemed almost a part of her: her ward and protection against all harm, her only hope of releasing her sister from Hoethan's thrall.

Yet her terror of what now tried to *touch* her was the greater. Whatever it was, however distant, it was more powerful than she could even begin to imagine, and the intensity of its purpose appalled her.

In a sudden wave of revulsion she hurled the amulet from her wrist; feeling its loss even as she did so. Yet at once that terrible other consciousness was cut off, leaving her with nothing but a yawning sensation of utter weakness. For an instant she had to steady herself against a nearby wall, drawing great choking breaths of horror and relief.

But in truth she had no time to rest or recover, for her situation was now more urgent than ever. Birstan had somehow managed to beat out most of his terrible flames in the snow, the howls of his agony still echoing through the streets. His clothing hung in tattered cinders about him, his skin was seared and scorched almost beyond recognition, yet still he tried to rise and come towards her, death in his cold grey eyes.

With the amulet she had also lost all remaining influence over her sister. And now Kerel backed away from her, ashen faced, gathering up courage to scream.

Everything was going wrong . . . ! The whole of the city would soon be awake and upon her. She had no choice now but to fly: to abandon her sister, abandon the amulet, and escape alone.

With a sorrowful glance towards Kerel, she turned and fled into the darkness. Birstan lunged after her, but he was too badly burned to take more than a few faltering steps before collapsing back into the snow. Keran turned back momentarily as she rounded a last dark corner, to see her sister still standing in the light of Birstan's fallen torch, ignoring all else as she clutched Hoethan's amulet to her chest.

Keran shuddered, and ran on.

The utter darkness did not trouble her. Now she was a fugitive, and darkness was her friend. She knew these narrow, twisting streets like the back of her hand. But even as she ran, she could hear the growing commotion behind her, the hue and cry of the awakening burghers. Half the town seemed already to have roused itself into life to pursue her. How was she ever to escape them?

There was but one land-gate out of the city, and that would surely be barred against her. And besides, fleeing that way would mean passing through the dangerous lower quarters of the city and the still more perilous goblin encampment beyond. She dared not walk through those alone. No, her plan had always been to leave by a less obvious route – and she had bare minutes to accomplish this before the guards on the walls were alerted.

She ran roughly north through the still-sleeping Merchants' Quarter, her only fear that she might run into some mercenary patrol before she reached her goal. Yet she found the westward-leading way she sought without incident, running down it until at last she saw ahead of her the high wooden palisade beyond which slank the turbid waters of the Ormul. Here the wall could be climbed with little difficulty – and there would be few guards on patrol on such a frosty night as this.

Thankful for the meagre illumination of a young crescent moon, she clambered up on to one of the low boundary walls that adjoined the main palisade, maintaining a fragile balance there before half-hauling, half-scrambling her way on to the high walkway above.

She paused to catch her breath. So far there had been no sign of close pursuit, nor of any guards upon the walkway. She hoped the affray near the Citadel would give her time enough to make good her escape. She peered out beyond the spiked parapet of sharpened logs to see the great river streaming slowly past to join with the Yarvar somewhere in the darkness of the north. The wall was perilously high . . .

But she could delay no further. It must be done now! Hauling himself up on to the very edge of the parapet, she leapt, hitting the smooth water twenty feet beneath with a gentle *ploosh*.

The shock of the near-freezing water cut like a knife, but she forced herself to ignore the agony, and swim. Swim the hundred yards or so upstream, against the flow of the river, to the one place she might hope to find some boats drawn up against the riverbank. She had learned to swim in the placid pools of the eastern forests, but that had been long ago, and in summer. The great river in its numbing cold and its winter flood was an altogether different prospect.

The river was close on a mile wide at this point, the currents so deep and strong that it took nearly all her effort merely to keep from being swept downstream. What could have been an easy swim swiftly became harrowing struggle that seemed without end.

Yet somehow, through sheer despairing persistence, she at last managed to reach the first of the timber jetties, crawling exhausted into one of the several unguarded boats that bobbed beneath the dark palisade wall.

Out of the water now, her clothes sodden, she felt the full, raking force of the cold. Fortunately there was no wind. She could only hope that the long, arduous row that lay ahead would keep her warm enough to survive. Trying to find some feeling in her frozen fingertips, she struggled to free the mooring-line. At last cutting through it with her knife, she took up the single oar to paddle, as quickly and silently as she could, out into the waiting river, and away from the glowering city of Darien.

Chapter Twenty Seven
THE RIDE FOR THE RIVER

'I like not the look of those clouds,' Telsyan muttered, the morning sun on his back as he stared westwards. 'I know clouds, and those spell bad weather if any do. I would wager on it.'

'Mayhap they will pass away into the north,' Leighor suggested, having just risen to stand beside the merchant, shivering between the tents. 'We had best hope so anyway, if we are ever to reach Helietrim – let alone get through the Alisterlings to Clanamel!'

Telsyan nodded grimly. 'That is a prospect I begin now to doubt myself. I only hope we shall be able to get far enough south to make a short journey of it come the spring. These great rivers trouble me, they will be impassable when the snows melt. We must get to the south of them if we can.'

'Aye, but how far do you really think we will get?' Uhlendof asked, having just returned with Yeon and Zindur from scouring the breakfast pans at the stream.

The merchant shrugged. 'We must reach Helietrim, that is vital. The hardest months of the northern winter still lie ahead of us, and these flimsy tents will not long protect us should we be halted by rising rivers or deep snows.'

'But are you sure we even have food enough to last the winter?' Yeon frowned.

'If we are careful,' Telsyan nodded. 'There are but five of us now, and we have the advantage of Keran's spare horse and the supplies it carries.'

'Aye, and we could have had far more,' Zindur growled, 'had the crookback not kept that seventh horse. It was rightfully ours. The brothers surely never meant so fine a mount for such as he!'

'Be still,' Uhlendof said quickly. 'The crookback has kept his word for once, and remains in Darien. For that boon, one horse is but small payment. Let us only hope that this time he is gone for good!'

'And what of the casket?' Zindur asked. 'Where is that? These lands are wild and filled with danger. Should we not take some precaution for its safe-keeping?'

'It is quite safe.' Uhlendof tapped the small satchel he wore beneath his cloak. 'I carry it with me always, and it is packed in my pillow while I sleep. No thieving hand shall have it while I live'

'Aye,' the warrior nodded. 'But let us be quickly gone from here. There is no birdsong in these woods, no sound of life. I do not like it.'

Once drawn to their attention, the deep silence of the forest unnerved the travellers greatly, and they broke camp hurriedly, anxious now to be away.

Their mounts, however, seemed more settled this day that the last. Then, the snow had been fresh, and the hauling of the winter logs into Darien had caused many long delays upon the road. But now, five and twenty leagues to the south, the way was clear, and they made good steady progress along the old straight road, cutting through the high, dense forests of Darien towards the crossing of the Ormul. Here lay the shortest route to the central Varroain realms and the far borders of Helietrim.

As they rode, the dark banks of cloud they had seen at daybreak rolled swiftly in from the west to blanket the entire sky. Smothering the sun in dark swirling greyness, they made the snow-mantled forest seem somehow brighter than the fretful skies above – as if the daylight no longer came from above, but had its true source hidden deep within the bright-frozen ground.

The clouds spat sharp flurries of snow down at the travellers. Yet despite their bluster, they chose to release little of their burden upon these low river-lands, and the snows remained but a few easy inches about the horses' heels.

Even so, the five had still not reached the river-crossing when night finally overtook them, and they must needs halt and make camp for a second night. The days were growing short indeed now, and the distances to be travelled long.

Leighor had to pause every minute or so, as he struggled with the intransigent tent ropes, in order to breathe life back into his frozen fingers; and the work went slowly. Beyond their tiny camp nothing moved, the whole forest robed in a cloak of dank, oppressive silence. The trees crowded in so close about them that even the fading light of the western skies could not penetrate their shrouding branches, and all beneath was blackness.

Leighor disliked to stare too long into that brooding dark, for fear of what his mind might conjure up there. There could be no real danger so close to Darien, surely? Yet here he could believe in all evils, all terrors; and this forest felt evil – as it always had to him. If there had ever been a time when these northern woods had run with plenty and light, that time was long past. Now they were the abode of dark things that hunted by night, and a place of fear.

A sudden high-pitched shriek rang through the forest – from somewhere high up but far away in the darkness of the east. And then silence: as black and as total as before.

Leighor froze. 'What was that?'

'I do not know.' Telsyan shook his head. 'Perhaps a bat or some other night creature; but it was far distant.'

'It was like no bat I ever heard,' Zindur grunted. 'I like not the feel of this place. We had best set a good watch tonight, and keep our fire low.'

The others nodded, disliking the idea of a small fire in this sharp cold, yet disliking the prospect of what their light might draw down on them even more. They were just about to settle to their tasks once more, when Yeon called out: 'Be still! I hear something!'

The travellers went silent, at first hearing nothing but the stirring of the trees in the wind. Then they all heard it: the faint sound of a horse – or a number of horses – galloping towards them along the old roadway from the south.

'What could it be at this hour?' Leighor hissed.

'Someone in the service of the Knights, most likely,' Uhlendof hazarded. 'Perhaps an urgent message for Darien—'

'A message from where?' Zindur snorted, drawing his sword. 'There is nothing to the south but wilderness for a hundred leagues! Near Darien or no, these lands are filled with danger. Hide the tents quickly, and let us get away from the road!'

'We have not the time!' Telsyan cried. 'They are fast upon us! Just hide yourselves, and hope the camp lies unseen.'

Weapons at the ready, the travellers scattered, taking up positions in the dark shadows of the trees on the far side of the roadway.

'Do not shoot or show yourselves unless you have to!' Uhlendof hissed. 'The chances are, whoever they be, they mean us no harm.'

'There is but one,' Telsyan corrected, his voice all but drowned beneath the fast-approaching hoofbeats. The horse was nearly upon them.

Leighor saw no more than a shadowy shape in the darkness as the rider sped past, crouched over a tall ungainly mount, dark cloak billowing behind. Yet it did not seem to him to be a knight – who then? Horse and rider were already beyond Leighor's field of vision, and he thought them safely past, when the pattern of hoofbeats changed, the horse whinnying as it was brought to a sudden halt. He could hear the animal's each laboured breath with ringing clarity as it turned to come slowly back towards them. The rider must have seen their camp!

Nearby he heard Telsyan's crossbow creak . . . And then a voice: thin, clear and instantly recognisable.

'Telsyan! Uhlendof! Leighor! Are you there? Is anyone there? Answer me!'

Keran.

'What in heaven's name do you think you're playing at, girl?' Telsyan's voice rang out furiously through the dark as he stepped out on to the roadway. 'Have you fled your family now, to follow us here?'

'And how came you on the road from the south?' Uhlendof demanded.

Still Keran did not attempt to dismount, clinging to the neck of her rangy mount in what looked to be utter exhaustion. Her clothes, although new, no longer looked it, being frayed, torn, and stained through and through with mud and dirt-water.

'We have no time!' she gasped at last, her breath so short one might have imagined she had run rather than ridden all this way; and she shook visibly with cold. 'No time for questions! You must come. Follow me. You are betrayed!'

'How is this, girl?' Telsyan tried to calm her. 'Has this to do with your fleeing your family? Do they pursue you?'

'No!' Keran almost spat. 'It is the Knights. They do not wish you to reach the south! They have sent Rievers and brigands to waylay you, to ambush and slay you upon the road! When I saw the empty camp I thought you already taken . . .' She broke off into sobbing.

'Nay lass, do not fret,' Uhlendof comforted clumsily. 'We are all still here as you can see. Come down, calm yourself, and tell us the whole story—'

'There is no time!' Keran shook herself free. 'Did you not hear me? You are to be ambushed by Rievers! You must break camp now; cross the river tonight!'

'I think we had better do as she says,' Leighor cut in quickly. 'If the Rievers truly seek us out, we stand little chance here.'

'Aye,' Telsyan nodded. 'But if this is just some foolish tale to force us into stealing this girl away from her people . . .' He looked up, staring directly into Keran's face. But she did not flinch.

'All right,' he said finally. 'We shall break camp tonight. But while we do so, you must tell us the whole of your story, leaving nothing out; do you understand?'

'Yes, but hurry!' Keran urged, resigned now to the delay, but almost falling from her horse with exhaustion as she dismounted. 'I am sure they intend to strike before you cross the river.'

Keran told her story in short bursts as the others tore down the camp around her, so that not all of them heard her tale in full, but they all managed to gather enough to underline the urgency. The horse she now rode, along with a bow, some arrows and a small bag of dry provisions, she had purchased in a small settlement on the far side of the river. Since then she had ridden all day without break: nearly twenty leagues south along the western bank of the Ormul, until she had at last reached the chain-ferry at dusk. When the ferryman then told her than no one answering her companions' description had passed that way, she had feared the worst. Yet still she had taken passage across the Ormul and ridden back north through the gathering dark until she had come upon their half-constructed camp.

The others were still not ready when Keran finally finished her tale, and she waited fretfully beside her horse whilst the last laborious tasks were completed, her dark glances into the forest unnerving and unsettling them all.

'The tale rings true enough,' Telsyan grunted. 'For as long as the Knights held Eridar's testament, they were honour bound to protect it. The only way they could dispose of it without blame falling upon themselves was to give it freely to any who came for it, and then have the bearers waylaid upon the road, when the testament was no longer their responsibility . . .'

'Then cease to congratulate them, merchant,' Yeon called out from horseback, 'and ride!'

Quickly Zindur and Uhlendof helped the exhausted Keran back into the saddle of her no less weary mount.

'I like not the state of that horse.' Zindur looked it dourly up and down. 'It will not stand another long gallop, I think. A pity we no longer have the crookback's mount . . .'

'There is no time to go back over that now,' Uhlendof said firmly. 'Let us ride!' He spurred his horse into motion, and the others followed; southward into the darkness with the cold wind slicing into their faces.

'How far is the ferry?' Telsyan drew his horse level with Keran's, roaring the question across to her.

'An hour's ride,' she shouted back.

The merchant nodded and rode on.

Leighor felt a deal safer once they were on the move again, despite the bitter cold. Yet for Keran's sake the travellers could not ride as fast as they desired, having to slacken their pace to match that of her exhausted mount, cantering in silence through the forest with only the high wailing of the wind to accompany them. The dark-boled trees edged in ever closer upon either side until at last their high branches met above the riders' heads. They rode blindly now, for the moon had not yet risen above the shrouded forest, and dark swirls of cloud still burdened the skies.

A high-pitched howl cut suddenly through the tangled forest behind them. It sounded much like the distant cry they had all heard earlier, only this time much louder and far nearer. The cry of an animal: a large beast of the hunt: long, shrill and clear, and wild enough to freeze the blood in their veins.

Telsyan drew to a startled halt as two answering cries rent the air farther east. 'What are those?'

'Sounds I dreaded ever to hear again,' Zindur replied grimly, taking a hurried glance backward. 'Those are the cries of the *Broghast*, the Bale Hounds of Khiorim: Demon Dogs, used by the Curséd Ones of the Westron wastes to hunt their prey. They can run like the wild wind itself, and smell out a man's trail a month old—'

'Dogs?' Telsyan cut sharply across his explanation. 'You mean tracking dogs, like bloodhounds?'

'No mere bloodhounds,' the warrior replied tersely. 'I have seen one alone take down a horse and rider in battle, and slay both. They are true hounds of hell! We must fly: and stop for nothing until we reach the river. I fear they have already found our campsite!'

Another cry decided them, and in moments they were once more galloping south towards the ferry. Yet as they rode, the sounds of pursuit from behind grew louder and clearer: the baying of the unseen Demon Dogs augmented by the shrill, excited calls of those who ran with them. Whoever pursued them knew now how close they were to their quarry. And somehow, despite the speed at which the travellers rode, their pursuers seemed still to be gaining on them . . . Were they on horseback too: or could the Riever men truly run faster than a galloping horse? Icy terror sped the company onward . . . Would the river never come?

But the road ahead of them showed no sign of ending, and soon the horses must either reduce their speed or collapse. Keran's mount was already beginning to falter, and reluctantly the travellers dropped back to a canter, hoping that this would be enough to revive the horses. Yet all the while the sounds of pursuit grew ever closer behind them.

'How far away do you think they are?' Yeon asked nervously.

'No more than a mile,' Zindur grunted. 'If we do not reach the river soon we are done for.'

'How do they come so fast?' Uhlendof asked. But there was no answer; only the baying of the Bale Hounds, and the sharp cries of their Riever masters behind them. And then, abruptly, silence. Sudden, complete and total.

The travellers turned anxiously to stare at one another, their fears unspoken yet evident upon their faces; the cavernous silence at once far more fearsome than had been the frenzied sounds of pursuit. For now they could no longer tell how close their hunters were; nor where, nor how many. They could hear nothing but the cold song of the wind, see nothing but snow and bitter darkness.

'Come!' Telsyan ordered suddenly. 'The time for prudence is past. Let us ride!'

Leighor spurred his horse onward for dear life, hearing only its laboured breathing and the muffled thud of its hooves through the thin snow. The trees crowded in on them now like stooping crones, low branches clutching at their unprotected faces as they passed; each seeming capable of harbouring a score of lurking Rievers in its dark shadows.

And then – there it was! The River Ormul, dark and wide, not a thousand paces ahead of them, framed between the darker edges of the forest. To Leighor it seemed suddenly the most beautiful sight in the world as it rolled majestically northwards beneath the newly risen moon. The horses, too, seemed to sense the end of their travails, gaining in strength and vigour for the last few furlongs of their journey. They bore their burdens down at last to the banks of the waiting river, where the old road petered out into a flat terrace of frozen mud.

'Where is the ferry?' Telsyan demanded urgently, seeing nothing upon either side of him but mud and water. He seized Keran by the shoulder to shake her from the half-slumber into which she had fallen.

She started abruptly awake at his touch to stare absently about her – almost as if she did not recognise this place. But then she raised one hand to point downriver.

'There,' she nodded. 'Where the crossing is the shortest: beneath the trees!'

Leighor followed her finger north along the tree-girt riverbank, not liking what he saw; for there the darkness was as complete as it had been on the road, and he could make out neither light nor edifice, nor any sign of human life. But Keran led the way forward now with new confidence, and the others must follow: north along the frost-rimed banks of the river, beneath the shadow of the trees; north towards those who still pursued them. But they had ridden only a hundred paces or so when Keran halted; pointing down towards a great iron chain which ran across the ground in front of her, from some unseen landward anchor, out into the river.

The travellers' eyes followed the chain out into the darkness until it sank beneath the surface. And a hundred yards farther out, barely visible against the dark spread of the river, a low oblong shadow floated on the eddying current: the ferry!

'The ferryman will be on board asleep,' Telsyan whispered. 'We must rouse him.'

'No!' Zindur said quickly, holding up a hand in warning. 'We must make no sound! He may not answer any call at this hour, and to cry out now will only draw our enemies down upon us. Someone must go out silently and bring the ferry in.'

Before anyone could stop him, Yeon threw off his weapons and outer clothing to slip into the icy water and haul himself out along the iron chain towards the boat. Leighor watched him vanish into the darkness of the river; the silence so dense and all-consuming that it was all too easy to imagine that those who hunted them had somehow lost their trail or passed on by. Yet deep within, he knew that to be a vain hope.

Hours seemed to pass as the crushing silence held. Where on earth was Yeon? Leighor half wished now that he had volunteered to swim out to the ferry himself – even that would have been preferable to this endless waiting.

There came the fleeting sound of a raised voice across the water – quickly silenced – and then of what could have been a brief scuffle aboard the waiting flatboat. Then stillness once more. Then with a deep dull clanking and a jerk upon the chain, the ferry shuddered into motion, inching its way slowly in towards them. Cautiously the travellers permitted their hopes to rise. The ferry came slowly, imperceptibly slowly; and each passing moment brought only new opportunities for their pursuers to fall upon them. Leighor's fingers kept close to the cold comfort of his sword hilt.

Yet still no attack came: and within minutes the ferry had drawn close enough to permit them to wade out with their horses to the sloping boarding-ramp.

Leighor hauled himself aboard just after Uhlendof and Keran, his trembling horse struggling up after him. He raced forward to drape a warm cloak about a cold-shocked Yeon, turning at once to see how Zindur fared behind him.

And then it came. The shrill battle-howl of half a hundred inhuman voices in ragged unison; a host of spectral, shadowed figures emerging suddenly from the dark edge of the forest behind them. Rievers!

'Pull away!' Telsyan screamed, scrambling up beside him; Zindur already at his side. And somewhere ahead the dull clanking took up again, as Yeon set to turning the great two-handled wheel that hauled the boat across the river on its iron chain. But the ferry was built for endurance rather than speed, and even at its swiftest it could travel at no more than a slow walking pace – not nearly fast enough to bear them safe away from their attackers.

Yet the wild Riever cries turned to howls of dismay the moment they saw the swirling river before them; and for several moments their hatred of fast-moving water held them back, hesitating at its edge.

All too soon, however, the first of them began to overcome their dislike, and started warily into the water.

'There are few enough of them,' Zindur muttered. 'If we but had the bows we started with, I am sure we could hold them until we were safe in deep water.'

'How many have we?' Leighor asked.

'Three . . .' The warrior turned quickly to relieve Keran of the longbow she bore. 'This, yours, and Master Telsyan's.'

But even as he took his place alongside the merchant on the open stern platform, two dark shapes burst out of the forest to hurl themselves into the river behind the pale Tarintarmen.

'The Demon Dogs!' Zindur screamed. 'Ignore the warriors! Fire at them!'

Telsyan obeyed, as Uhlendof ran back to help Yeon with the clattering cogwheel that impelled them onward. Yet the dogs seemed too fast for any arrow to touch; bounding through the oily water towards them, their solid blackness broken only by ochrous fangs and crimson eyes.

Already the first was almost upon them, its size unbelievable. Large as a fair-sized horse, easily the height of a man from foot to shoulder, its jaws dripped great flecks of foam. With a curse Zindur flung the useless bow aside, and hurled his heavy war-axe straight into the creature's face.

Spinning through the air like some terrible glinting star, it struck home in the middle of the Bale Hound's forehead. The creature screamed, and the fire in its eyes began to die. Yet still its momentum drove it forward, to crash, writhing, into the ferry's after-deck. Leighor watched in horror, unable to tear his eyes from the howling, maddened spectacle of the monstrous Demon Dog as it lashed out in its death agony.

One of the horses was caught by a flailing claw. It reared screaming, so panicking the rest that it took all of Keran's efforts to stay them. Leighor and Zindur too retreated, not daring to approach the fearsome monster close enough to finish it off.

And then, seemingly from out of nowhere, a ragged, grey-clad figure appeared beside them. Stumbling blindly forward as if his mind had left him, a thin trickle of blood ran down one cheek; and for an instant Leighor and Zindur stood stunned.

'Brigands! Thieves! Murdering dogs!'

Turning with a sudden wild scream, he flung himself upon Leighor, his fingers clawing for the southron's face, his face a mask of fear and wild unreason. Before the southron could react, the struggle had dragged them both out into the centre of the boat. And in that selfsame instant, the second Bale Hound came upon them. Screaming out of the darkness, it struck them with the force of a galloping charger, hurling both men to the deck beneath it.

Had it not been for his mysterious assailant, Leighor would certainly have perished there and then. The other took the brunt of the impact, pinned to the ground beneath the dog's terrible jaws while Leighor managed somehow to struggle free, forcing his body backward across the bare deck.

But now he was again in agony from his injured arm, the pain so great that it was all but impossible for him to take in anything else. Hardly registering the agonised screams that tore the darkness ahead, he felt only the slick pool of warm blood that spread slowly across the deck beneath him. Was it his own? He did not know. And for the moment, he did not care.

The boat jolted suddenly in the water, rolling him over just far enough to see Zindur and Telsyan hacking wildly at the back of the feasting creature. Of Keran, Yeon and Uhlendof, he could see nothing. And even as he thought of his companions, the giant Bale Hound broke suddenly free of its meal. Shaking the giant warrior from its back like some irksome insect, it leapt forward to tear into the flimsy wooden superstructure ahead.

Now Leighor could see nothing of what passed. But the sounds alone were fearsome enough: the roaring of the great hound, the cries of his companions, and the rending and splintering of wood and metal. It sounded as if the whole vessel were being physically torn apart! Where were the rest of the Rievers? If they were but to press their attack now, all of them were finished . . .

That thought alone somehow gave him the strength to stagger to his feet. But the sight that at once met his eyes appalled him. They were still barely a furlong from the riverbank, where the Rievers watched and waited in total silence – as if they dared not approach whilst the Demon Dogs did their work. Turning about, he saw the rest of his companions trapped with the horses at the prow of the boat, fending off the monster with swords, knives and makeshift wooden staves from the wreckage of the wheelhouse.

Yet still the Bale Hound advanced upon them, growling deep within its cavernous throat, preparing to spring. Not knowing quite what he intended, Leighor picked up one of the long, shattered spars that lay at his feet. It was a good sturdy weapon, but he had only the one good hand with which to wield it and despite the fact that he stood for the moment forgotten behind the creature, he hesitated.

And then some sixth, inner sense forewarned him. The creature knew that he was here behind it. He had but a split second before it turned! Instinctively he raised the sharpened spar, bracing the blunt end against his body as the monstrous hound swung snarling to launch itself against him.

There was a terrible scream as the stave pierced the monster's side. A fountain of dark blood gushed from the wound. The creature reared. Leighor felt himself lifted with it; borne dizzyingly higher and higher on the end of the spar – until at last he was shaken free, to fall back to the hard unevenness of the deck once more.

Now all about him was chaos and confusion. There were screams, both human and animal. A frenzied crashing. And then a single shuddering wrench that shook the whole vessel like a peapod, so that for a moment Leighor feared it had broken its back and was about to take them all to the bottom. Sprawled painfully on his side, he could see nothing but the black skies above him, hear nothing but the loud clattering of the chain beneath the boat. And then silence. Dark, seamless silence. The cries of the Demon Dogs were stilled. There was no movement anywhere about him.

What had happened? Was he the only one left alive? If so, they why did not the rest of the Rievers now attack?

There was a fearsome howl – like one of the great Demon Dogs, but far away in the distance, to his right; and many answering Riever cries. But why did they sound so distant? The ferry could not have pulled out so far on its slow chain.

There was a sudden movement somewhere behind him. He tried to move, to raise himself upon one arm to see behind: but he could not. Unable to sustain the action, he fell painfully back into the hard deck once more, and blackness overwhelmed him.

Part Five
THE GREY SWORD

Grimmerfen
White Pass
NORNDALE
Darkrigg
WASTARL DALE
Hythni's Pass
TRIM
ALISTERLINGS
HELIE
River Eld
EASTERDALE
River Irthing
River Torjal
NECK OF CLANAMEL
Clanamel
Irun's Teeth
LEE OF CLANAMEL

Chapter Twenty Eight
HELIETRIM

He awoke to the broad light of day. A pale, wispy-grey day, with thin, fleeting clouds speeding by above him. He rested on hard boards which no longer bobbed and swayed with the river current. Where was he? Captured and in some Riever encampment; or still with those of his companions who had survived this past night, somewhere to the west of the Ormul?

His answer came quickly enough as the bulky shadow of Zindur drew across him.

'So you have come to, bold one?' the warrior grinned down at him wryly. 'It seems then that we have all come through this night's ordeal far better than we had any right to . . .'

Leighor saw now that they were still aboard the ferry, or what remained of it. For it was thrown up, sideways-on, upon a gentle rise of the riverbank, its wheelhouse a shattered pile of wreckage, its deck strewn with broken timbers. A campfire burned beneath the trees. The horses grazed through the snow nearby. His eyes widened at their apparent carelessness.

'We are safe enough, southron,' Zindur smiled. 'Borne to the western bank when the chain broke.'

'The chain?'

'Aye,' Telsyan nodded. 'After you wounded the Bale Hound, it went mad; tearing the wheelhouse apart, and so shearing us free of the chain.'

'Then what of the Demon Dog?'

'Gone,' Zindur answered. 'Hopefully it perished in the river once we had forced it from the boat. Either way it shall not trouble us again. As for the rest: none of us are too badly injured. One of the horses will not bear a rider for a while. Only the poor mad ferryman was slain . . .'

'So it was he who saved me,' Leighor broke in. 'What happened to him?'

Zindur nodded out into the river. 'There he lies. It is the best place for him. The ground is hard frozen, and we had not the tools to give him a proper burial.'

For the first few days of their journey south the travellers could still hear the cries of a frustrated pursuit paralleling their course on the far side of the river. But nowhere was the Ormul less than a quarter league in breadth, and it remained an impassable barrier.

On the fourth day south from the chain ferry all sound of their pursuers ceased, and a disturbing silence fell upon the great forest.

'Do you think the Rievers still follow us?' Karen asked nervously.

'I cannot tell,' Telsyan shrugged. 'It is said that Tarintarmen hate water in all its forms. If they haven't found a way to get across the Ormul to us by now, they may well give up the hunt. They will have had many troublesome rivers to ford as they pursued us south. It would be far easier for them to return and tell the Knights that we were all slain at the ferry, and the casket lost in the river.'

'Aye,' Zindur nodded. 'Rievers will not persist on a profitless chase for long. Yet these may be more cunning than most. They may seek to trick us. We must remain on our guard.'

'Then let us ride fast for Helietrim!' the merchant said. 'I, for one, will not feel secure until we have had counsel of Arminor and Ariscel.'

'Ariscel!' Zindur snorted. 'I would have no dealings with such as he! I trust that fell sorceror even less than I do the Durians!'

'We have no choice,' Uhlendof said briefly. 'Our cause now depends entirely upon King Arminor. Ariscel is his servant. Even the giants have said as much – for if Ariscel were truly traitor or in league with King Misan, there would have been no need for the sack of Silentwater.'

'Still, I will not trust him,' Yeon said. 'I will not trust anyone involved with this *harrunor*!'

'Aye,' Telsyan nodded. 'In that you do well, lad. But whoever this Ariscel serves, he is but one man. If he is traitor to our king, then we must unmask him. If not, then he may well prove the staunchest ally we possess against the threat of the amulets. Either way, he is a man we cannot ignore.'

The others nodded slowly and prepared to move on.

Making their way roughly southward, they followed an overgrown and ancient trail that hugged the steeply sloping banks of the Ormul. There was little further snow now, but the weather remained bitterly cold. Each night the slow-moving pools and eddies along the banks of the great river would frost over, so that each morning the travellers must break through a thick layer of ice to obtain fresh water.

Yet thus far their journey had been peaceful enough, permitting them a brief but welcome respite, in which their strength slowly returned and their wounds began to heal. For nine days more they continued to follow the river south through dense, unchanging woodlands, their trail climbing briefly into a boggy upland country before sinking once more into the great inland sump of Grimmerfen, in which the great river had its source.

Grey, flat, and exposed to every blast of the unchecked northern wind, the deeper swamps of Grimmerfen never froze, not even in the hardest of winters. Vast expanses of bleak fen and reedswept bog clothed the land, numberless twisting rivulets interlinking and meandering to form a maze of still pools and low ridgeways. Yet the barely-marked trails that criss-crossed these wastes were frozen hard; providing firm footing for which the travellers had good cause to be thankful, despite the bitter cold and the frozen, comfortless nights.

It was now *Silstereem*, the second month of the northern winter – the first in more temperate latitudes – and the wind blew cold indeed.

The company saw the high peaks of the Alisterlings rising up out of the flat, silent swamplands ahead of them, when they were still a good two days' march away. Yet the sight did little to raise their spirits, for the mountains were clearly deep adrift with choking snows. Snows which robed all but the most precipitate slopes in a mantle of intense, eye-blinking white; giving the distant mountains the appearance of a high white rampart in their path – as if to ward some faerie kingdom of legend that lay hidden beneath the iron-grey sky. And the Varroain realms might indeed be as inaccessible as any faerie realm, if the travellers could not force a way through those distant high-cragged peaks.

It was on their sixteenth day south from the chain ferry that the company finally came to the southern edge of Grimmerfen. The vast swamp ended abruptly against the rising foothills of the Alisterlings, and their path now wound gently upward, along the vale of a frozen streamlet that fell down from out of the still distant mountains. A wide stone archway stood alone at the head of the vale, curving high above the narrow trail, as if this had once been a much greater way. And the travellers halted to read the weatherworn inscriptions graven into its snow-grimed surface.

'It is the North Gate to Helietrim,' Uhlendof declared, after studying it for some minutes. 'One of eighteen great arches set up by the Elder Kings to mark the bounds of their realms.' He sighed. 'This must indeed have been a busy trade-route in past ages.'

'Aye,' Telsyan nodded. 'So it is accounted in the old journey-books. The traverse we have just made across the great marsh was then termed Oloro's Way, or more lately, the Wetfoot Road; for like most things in these days it is fallen greatly into disrepair, so that few might guess that a more noble way once ran here.'

The travellers would have lingered longer at this spot, but the wind was bitter cold and the hills bare and lonely, offering little shelter. And they moved on in haste, passing back into the Varroain realms with little observable change in the landscape to show that they had at last left the northron wilderness. Yet each one of them now felt a little more hope in his heart in the knowledge that they were now, officially at least, in the lands of Arminor, King of Helietrim.

On the following day the climb up into the mountains began in earnest, the snows gradually deepening as their path wound its way upward. The horses were now more and more reluctant to go on, stumbling through the deepening snow, and bridling at any sudden pull upon the reins; until it seemed that they wilfully resisted every onward step that the travellers forced upon them, and the riders had to use all their efforts to make them go forward at all. It was only after many hours of this tortuous progress that the monk finally realised . . .

'We are out of the northlands: that is it!' Uhlendof declared suddenly. 'Our bargain is ended. We must give up the horses!'

'What?' Yeon turned sharply to stare at him, grey eyes glaring out in disbelief from beneath a snow-flecked hood.

'Aye. That is the truth,' Zindur nodded. 'Though we have come to think of them as ours, the horses were not given, only lent: and they pass unwillingly from the lands of their abiding. The bargain was always that we must release them when we left the northlands . . .'

'And that we should have done yesterday,' the monk broke in. 'As soon as we passed beneath the arch of the High Kingdom. We have already broken our oath!'

'Then perhaps it will do us no harm to break it a few days longer,' Yeon said quickly. 'Just until we are safe through these mountains. The task will be near impossible on foot.'

'Nay.' The monk shook his head firmly, and swung down from the saddle to land heavily in the snow. 'We must free them now; these five that remain to us. The horse Keran bought we may keep, and use that for our packs if we must. But as for the others, they must be allowed to return to their true owners at once.'

'But how will they get there?' Telsyan demanded. 'How will they find their way home through these snows; the mountains, the forests, all the way to Valmaalina: half a thousand leagues! It is madness!'

'How quickly you forget your own promise,' Uhlendof chided, his face weary and lined with stubble beneath its dark cowl. 'A promise once given must be honoured, for we know not the reason it was demanded. These horses have served us well, but now is the time to let them go!' He began to remove the packs and various pieces of burdensome tackle from his mount's back, and Zindur, after watching him for a moment or two, began to do the same.

'You are a superstitious pair . . .' Yeon began, but he had not time to finish the sentence before his mount bucked suddenly beneath him, throwing off several of its packs and almost unseating its rider.

The action could have been no more than a coincidence, but it seemed to confirm the issue in the minds of most of the travellers. The other horses too were now growing increasingly unsettled, and it was not long before even Yeon and Telsyan realised that they could take their unwilling mounts no farther, and reluctantly dismounted.

Yet once released of their packs and burdens, the five horses did not run off immediately, but remained nearby – whether out of habit, or in some strange, silent leave-taking, the wayfarers could not guess. And then they seemed suddenly to taste some distant scent upon the breeze; turning as one into the north to follow their own trail slowly back down towards the frozen marshes, picking up speed as the tug of freedom grew stronger within them and they gained in confidence; until at last they were galloping together through the deep snow. They were a strangely stirring sight, the five jet black horses, silhouetted strongly against the snows, running so purposefully together that it seemed they must still bear invisible riders who drove them onward. Yet now they ran as they had never run with the travellers upon their backs, entirely wild and free. The travellers watched them in silence for several minutes – until they were but small black dots set against the white flanks of the mountain far beneath – before turning reluctantly back to the more urgent task of re-ordering their scattered possessions.

All of them must journey now on foot, and their progress was slow; trudging in single file through knee high snows. Glad now of his ashen staff, which had hung unused across his saddle packs during the long weeks of their ride, Leighor pressed it to the mundane task of feeling a way through the deep drifts. There was little in the way of a clear trail left to follow, and only a vague flattening of the snowswept mountainside to show them where the road lay. Clearly no one had passed this way since the snows had first fallen – and who knew how long ago that had been?

The pass – so high above them that they could not yet even see it – might be long closed for all they knew. And if so, they could find themselves trapped here on this bare mountainside until they froze. Yet the prospect behind them was no better: winter was deepening everywhere, and there was no shelter for them to the north, not for many hundreds of danger-filled leagues. Ahead at least there was hope.

They paused often for rest now, the packs unaccustomedly heavy on their backs, the path rising steep before them, winding constantly back on itself in great circling loops to ease the gradient of the ascent. They halted at last where the trail levelled out into a high, bleak vale between the mountains, and here they spent the night. Yet with no fuel for a fire, there was no hot food and little comfort, the night as long and as cold as any they could remember.

The second day found them still amid the high, bitter snows of the Alisterlings, their only comfort that this day, at least, there was to be little more hard climbing and no new snow. By the third day, however, they were all beginning to weaken, and their progress slowed alarmingly. Telsyan's estimate was that yesterday they had gained no more than three or four leagues. Today they all knew that their rate of advance would be even slower.

A sharp climb had begun again, towards the high point of the pass, still several thousand feet above them. Their pauses for rest, and to rub life back into their blistered toes and fingers, grew ever longer and more frequent as the day wore on, until each onward step became a nightmare; a test of endurance, an awesome effort of will.

Towards evening it began to snow again: lightly at first, a few soft flakes floating down from the leaden skies above; but then harder and heavier, until the air was alive with cold white bees that swarmed silently about them, dancing on the freshening westron breeze.

Leighor could barely see the next person in line ahead of him as he followed the rest of the company, leading Keran's laden horse. Ahead, Zindur and Telsyan took turn and turn about forcing a rough pathway for them through deepening snows that rose at times to waist height and beyond.

The southron's hands and feet were completely numb with cold now, and he slipped and stumbled times without number as he struggled onward. Surely he had never been so cold? He longed to halt, to make camp and rest, but Telsyan would not allow it.

'We must keep on!' he bellowed back, across the rising wind. 'Keep on through the night if necessary, to reach the pass! If it snows up before we reach it, we are done for!'

Leighor nodded, yet the fear was growing in him that their task was hopeless. The air was so cold now that it became painful even to draw breath. Very soon it would be dark, and they would have to feel their way up the mountain. They had no light, nor any means of making any. He began to imagine how they might be found come the spring: frozen, white and still amid the melting snows, like the lost travellers of many a northron tale.

Their pace slowed again, those at the rear of the column having to stand waiting for long minutes whilst the two in front struggled to force a narrow path. It took almost an hour now to progress a few hundred paces, and it soon became clear to them all that they were never going to get across the pass like this. They gathered for a hurried consultation: but the way back was already fast closing in behind them. They had no choice but to keep going until they found somewhere to shelter.

Yet the path only steepened ahead of them, the snow-clad slopes sheering almost to vertical both above and below. Through the darkness they could hear the deep crump and boom of heavy snowslides and small avalanches crashing down the mountain all around them: sounds that filled Leighor with alarm and the fear of a sudden, meaningless death. The snows were too thick, far too thick for such steep slopes to bear. And still the ice-winds piled them ever higher upon the overladen mountainside.

A sudden pinprick of light flickered across the edge of Leighor's vision, somewhere in the snowy darkness high above them. For a moment he thought he had dreamed it, or perhaps had caught a glimpse of the moon through a break in the clouds. But then he saw it again; clearer than ever, the unmistakable glint of a naked flame.

'There, look!' he shouted, pointing wildly upwards. 'A torch!'

'Where?' Uhlendof demanded, following his pointing finger. But the light had vanished again, and for long minutes it did not reappear.

'Your eyes play tricks on you,' Telsyan snorted at last, turning impatiently back to the pathway. 'Who else but we would be fool enough to be out on the mountainside in this weather?'

'No, there it is!' Zindur suddenly seized the merchant's shoulder and pointed up into the dark. 'A light! A light indeed! There *is* someone else out on this mountain!'

And there it was: plain for all to see now, several hundred feet above them, its crimson-yellow aura glinting like a phantom circlet across the surrounding snows. It was an eerie sight, approaching silently yet remarkably swiftly down the mountainside.

As it drew closer, Leighor could see that it came not from one, but several individual torches, blurred together through the snowstorm. He could also now see the dark thickset figures who bore the torches; so deep in shadow against the snows that he could make out no clear detail of their outward appearance. Who were they?

For all he knew they might be a band of Rievers come down to spill their blood across the snows. But even that prospect now seemed somehow less appalling than the frozen hopelessness of their present journey.

'Ho there, strangers!' A deep voice called out suddenly from above, in a heavily accented form of North Varroain into which a good few Durian words seemed to be admixed. 'Who are you, and what is your business at this season in the lands of King Arminor?'

The men were bearded and strong-built, clad in the dark leathers and stout wools of the mountain farmers of Helietrim. A full dozen, they bore crossbows, yeoman shortswords and sharp-bladed halberds whose long shafts pierced the snows. The reason for their fleetness was now apparent, for all of them wore broad pine and wicker snowshoes which spread their weight across the snows.

They were at first highly suspicious of the unknown strangers who toiled up the mountain towards them, but their attitude quickly altered once the name of Ariscel was mentioned.

'You are in luck, strangers, if it is Ariscel you seek,' said one. 'For we are from the village of Darkrigg in Norndale where he now bides. If you are willing, we shall conduct you there.'

Leighor thought that the scouting party were probably determined to conduct them there whether they were willing or not. But he had certainly no objection to their guidance and protection, especially in the current circumstances.

The men had no spare snowshoes to offer the travellers, but endeavoured to help them as far as they could by beating a firmish path upward for them through the snow, hauling and manhandling them across the deeper snowdrifts.

'It was highest folly to attempt the pass at this season,' their leader, a grey-bearded man named Elfath, admonished as he strode along beside them. 'If we had not seen you from our watch-point upon White Pass, you would all most surely have perished here. Were it not for the unseasonable lateness of the snows this winter, you would never even have got so far. But a single day later, and even we would have been gone from our watch on the pass, and back down in the safety of Norndale.'

'Is that where lies Darkrigg?' Telsyan asked. 'And the sorceror?'

'Aye,' the other nodded. 'Though we of Norndale term him Ariscel the Seer, for that is his true business.'

Telsyan nodded silently, and struggled on.

The augmented company did not pause for rest at all that night, climbing steadily through the snows until at last they reached the frozen summit of White Pass an hour before the dawn. But even here they did not halt, for the wind blew now at its strongest, hurling the blizzard snows into their faces like a hundred thousand tiny splinters of glass.

Through such snowy dark Leighor could see virtually nothing, but he sensed that from this spot by day there must be a truly magnificent vista; the high mountain peaks towering all around them, and great valleys stretching away to north and south. The descent began at once – only a little less steep than had been their climb, their path winding a precipitate downward course between the flanks of the mountains.

Dawn came grey and bitter cold. And still the snow came down relentlessly – Leighor thought the heavens must surely have come close to bursting beneath the weight of it all.

All sense of time and place, all sense of existence itself, seemed somehow to have become blurred and smudged into an endless cold greyness, that only seemed to deepen as they toiled onward, dragging their way down the mountainside beneath leaden skies. Unable to see more than a dozen yards in front of them, they could hear nothing bar the howl of the wind and their own tortured breathing. And still they trudged onward through the snow.

Leighor had no idea what hour it was when they finally came down to some solid wooden structure. It might have been morning, midday, or even late afternoon. All he knew was that, whatever the hour, he desired only warmth and rest. It soon became apparent, however, that this was not Darkrigg, as he had hoped, but only an empty garrison hut, long abandoned by its military builders, and now used only by occasional patrols of the Norndale yeomen who had replaced the king's soldiers as guardians of the northern border. The accommodations within were bare, but comfortable enough once a fire had been lit; and the travellers fell quickly into a deep sleep from which they were aroused with difficulty the next morning.

'The snow has ceased,' Elfath said, as he prodded the rolled-up bundles into life with a fur-booted foot. 'Time to be up and on our way. It is but a few more leagues now to Darkrigg.'

The travellers rose bleary-eyed to find that the snowfall had indeed ended and that the skies were clear. Only a few fluffy white clouds still remained, scattered across a sea of blue, to remind them of the previous day's storm. A bright sun blazed down with such force that it seemed the snows must surely melt away before it. Yet somehow they resisted its fury, reflecting the light back up in a myriad eye-dazzling shades of pink and white and palest blue – so brilliantly that Leighor had to squint to see anything at all. But once his eyes had accustomed themselves to this wall of light, he found himself completely overawed by the sheer brazen beauty of the mountainous panorama all around him.

The mountains looked deceptively tranquil and harmless now; and White Pass, towering high above them, seemed only a pleasant afternoon's stroll away. Yet they all knew just how close they had come to an icy death no more than half a dozen miles from where they now stood; and none were tempted to stray from the path or the capable ward of their escort.

An hour later the whole of Norndale opened out abruptly before them. The twisting trail fell sharply away beneath their feet into a long, narrow valley that ran south for half a dozen leagues between high white mountains. A frozen river, the Norn, coiled southward along the valley floor, until it was forced sharply eastwards by a line of high-towered peaks that blocked off the far end of the vale. From here on, Norndale and its river passed out of their vision, into the clutch of the eastern mountains.

Halfway down the valley the river was bridged, and here it was bordered by a cluster of irregular dark specks: Darkrigg, upon the Norn.

The village itself was without wall or stockade, its angular houses of stone and dark timber standing apart from one another in their own small tillage-plots, so that only in the very centre of the settlement did they come close enough together to form a recognisable street. Few of the houses had more than two storeys, but all bore narrow balconies beneath steeply-sloping roofs. Friendly streams of grey woodsmoke poured from a score of chimneys.

A small square, open on to the river, marked the centre of the settlement, and here stood a small stone fountain, a single-arched bridge which crossed the Norn, and the town's only inn, the Good King Virostan, which towered over the rest of the village.

The house of Ariscel stood alone above the village, on the far side of the river. It looked down from a sloping ridge that clung to the steeply rising western side of the valley, where the feet of the mountains tumbled down in great stony sweeps to bathe their toes in the Norn. As seemed the fashion with the dwellings of all such eccentric folk, the house of the Seer was tall – fully four storeys high from stone foundation to timber-beamed roof. Its back slumped against the rising hillside, into which its lower storeys were built. A great elm tree towered over its north-easternmost corner, and this seemed over the years to have grown into the very fabric of the building: the girth of its trunk supported the overhanging upper walls, and its living branches braced many of the great crossbeams that held the structure together. In fact tree and house were so closely entwined that in places it was hard to tell where one ended and the other began. Leafless branches, trembling in the icy northern wind, coiled about leaded window; crooked twigs, like bare skeletal fingers, poked threateningly out through crumbling rooftiles; and grey, twisted roots embedded themselves grimly into the foundations.

The tree looked cold and lifeless, stripped bare by the onslaught of winter; yet deep within, it still seemed to Leighor somehow aware. As if some ancient consciousness plotted deep down inside, and took careful note of all that transpired around it . . . And remembered. Surely, the thought struck Leighor suddenly, it was aware of him even now, as he shivered at its feet?

He hesitated before the low oaken door. Its lintel, formed from one of the larger of the ancient branches, sagged across the doorway like the wrinkled elbow of a giant.

'Do not fear.' A soft voice came suddenly from their right, startling the travellers and the two remaining villagers who had been assigned to escort them thus far.

A tall figure stood watching them from the side of the building, where a ragged kitchen-garden tumbled down the hillside. He was willow-thin, and old; although his face bore evidence of a deep strength and a cutting swiftness of intellect. Forceful eyes burned with gentle humour from behind a small pair of round spectacles. His beard, like his windblown mop of thinning hair, must once have been jet black but was no longer.

He gave a sudden wry smile. 'The old fellow will not harm you, my friends. He has been here longer than any of us, and will be here still when we are all gone and forgotten.' He stepped forward, a loose-fitting robe of plain grey cloth trailing through snow at his feet. 'If we trouble him not, he will not trouble us. He is *Zynar*. This house was built here long ago to gain his protection. I am but a recent interloper in this place, yet his purposes seem to coincide with my own, and for that reason, if no other, he is our protection: for he will suffer no person of evil intent to bide here long.'

'You speak of the tree?' Telsyan asked, perplexed. The other smiled again. 'You think it strange that I speak of a tree so, merchant? Yet perhaps you have little feel for such things.' He shrugged. 'If it pleases you, ignore it. Little that we do or say troubles him. Nothing yet has confounded him, and nothing understands him fully. But we get on well enough together now, he and I, and he will tolerate us if we will him.'

'Enter,' he urged cordially. 'I am Ariscel, and you are welcome in my house. You have been long expected.'

'Long expected?' Leighor repeated once they were all assembled in Ariscel's long, upper library, whose two small windows looked out upon Darkrigg and the white mountains beyond. 'You mean you knew that we were coming?'

'We have known for some time,' the seer nodded. 'Ever since another party of travellers came through here in the autumn.'

'You mean my lady Gwildé and her company?' Keran started up eagerly.

'Yes,' Ariscel nodded again. 'She, a knight – whose name if I recall it aright was Uldain – and several others, came down White Pass on the seventh day of *Vilvereem* month. They gave me a description of some others who might follow them south across the mountains before the snows came. I had almost given up on you.'

'And they are gone on?' Yeon asked.

'Many weeks ago, to Clanamel and beyond.'

'And how soon may we follow them?' Telsyan said quickly. 'If my lady Gwildé told you anything at all, you will know that our errand is of the utmost urgency!'

'Indeed it may be,' Ariscel shook his head. 'But however great the importance of your errand, you shall get no farther now until the spring thaw.' He rose and turned to the window to point southward along the valley. 'Look there, and tell me what you see.'

'Naught,' Zindur answered. 'Naught but snow and mountains.'

'Aye,' Ariscel nodded. 'And that is all that lies between here and Clanamel. Perhaps a hundred leagues as deep in snow as White Pass: high, bare, and all but uninhabited. Do you see there, between those two high mountains; Snaecoll and Gryphonsfang?' He pointed out the spot with one bony finger. 'There runs Hythni's Pass and the road south. And there, upon the upper slopes of Snaecoll, when the snow is low enough to cross the pass in safety, you will see a long dark streak which is known as Hythni's Stone. Until you can see that clearly from the village, the way south is impassable.'

'And there is no other?'

'None.' Ariscel shook his head decisively. 'In fact I now find myself in the same position as yourselves: I too would be south at the turn of the year, to have audience of King Arminor. So mayhap I shall be able to travel with you when the pass clears. Until then you are all free to remain here as my guests.

'But perhaps now you will tell me a little of your story, and of your adventures since leaving Hallad's Keep.'

Again their tale took long to tell; the seer listening quietly, and grunting at intervals to show his continued interest. When they had finished, Ariscel asked to see the locked casket, examining it closely before he spoke.

'Yes,' he nodded at last. 'It seems to be untampered with. And the fact that the Knights acted quickly to try to prevent it reaching these lands, makes it all the more likely that it contains items of value to Arminor's cause. Yet even so, I fear that the information you bring south concerning the spread of the *harrunor* may prove in the end to be of greater concern to us all.'

He raised an eyebrow. 'You know of course that all of the *harrunor* that was mined at Silentwater came here to me?'

The travellers nodded.

'Well, the reason for that was simple enough: Arminor and his advisors have known for many years of the threat posed by the reappearance of *harrunor* in the eastern lands, and lately of these new and more terrible amulets. And so, when a few scraps of the purple metal appeared in a consignment of lead from a long-neglected mine in the North Felldur Marches, I was sent north to investigate. And in consequence the king ordered that all the metal there discovered should be mined in secret and transported south for me to experiment upon – in the hope that I would be able to fashion some useful artefact from it.'

'And have you?' Yeon broke in eagerly.

Ariscel shook his head. 'Things have not turned out as I had hoped. There have been many trials and difficulties. And at every turn I seem to have met with naught but frustration and failure. Perhaps I was wrong to imagine that we could ever make use of the *harrunor* as a force for good, or make of it a weapon that would serve us as it serves the enemy . . .'

His voice trailed off into silence.

'So you have discovered nothing,' Telsyan said.

'A little more than nothing,' the seer replied quickly. 'But yes, I admit, little of great practical worth. I have made one artefact, and am now at work upon another. Yet although there is much *harrunor* in their making – a deal more than can be found in most of the Dark Amulets – I have so far been able to imbue them with little true power. And even that holds many dangers; for the form of power that the metal will accept is a dangerous and corrupting one.' He drew a breath. 'I fear that these things will be more artefacts of flash and show than of any real worth. One is already in Arminor's hands. The other I still work upon and try to mould to more practical purposes; but the magics that are least corrupting are not those that are of greatest use in war . . .'

'And do you think there will be war in these southern lands?' Uhlendof asked.

Ariscel nodded. 'Even these things that you bring with you out of the north can do nothing but bring war closer to us. For if Misan fears that the vote in Tershelline will go against him, he will most certainly try to pre-empt the decision – force Arminor's hand before the election can be held, and provoke him into a confrontation that he cannot hope to win.'

'But surely he will not allow himself to be so provoked,' Leighor said, 'if it only serves Misan's interest?'

'You do not know King Arminor,' Ariscel shook his head. 'Nor I fear, the power of Misan. He and his allies will not easily release the reins of power they now hold in these lands; and they will use every available means to secure some pretext upon which to attack King Arminor and destroy him. It is my greatest fear that without good counsel Arminor will allow himself to be provoked into some rash act that may lose him all. I wish only that I knew what passes now in Clanamel, even as we speak—'

'Yet are you not a Seer?' Yeon broke in. 'So they have told us in the village . . .'

'I fear that you mock me, my lord,' Ariscel said gravely. 'I am a Seer of sorts, yes. But those things I am permitted to see do not come as I desire them. In my glass I glimpse only portents of what is to come, and these are more often worrisome than enlightening. Yet I see most often warnings of great danger from the south.'

'And none from the north?' Leighor frowned. 'Are you truly so secure in this place that you fear not the dark legions of the north?'

In answer Ariscel turned once again to the window and the broad vista of snow-capped mountains that lay beyond. 'These bright mountains of Helietrim, which the ancients termed the *Monath Jiastor*, the Shining Mountains, these have ever been our bulwark against all enemies to the north. The Alisterlings have been the northern rampart of the civilised realms for as long as any can remember . . .

'Yet in a way your perceptions are correct; the threat from the north grows ever stronger. Even these noble peaks slowly darken, growing daily more corrupted and foul. We hear many tales of fell creatures that creep anew into the deep bowels of the mountains, and lurk in the high, lonely places. Riever raids over the northern passes grow ever bolder and more common, and villages little smaller than Darkrigg have lain under siege. In the outer dales lonely farmsteads are destroyed each year, with much loss of life: and many honest folk have fled southward.

'To the east there are many small valleys no longer peopled; and to the west, even great Wastarl Dale now lies empty – the abode only of Rievers and Tarintarmen, who now make their camps openly in the heart of Helietrim!'

'These are indeed ill tidings.' Telsyan shook his head grimly. 'I had not heard of these losses.'

'It is not thought prudent to spread such news too widely,' Ariscel said; 'lest Arminor be thought weak. For it is all we can do now to hold on to what we have. This is now the most northerly inhabited dale, and we are surrounded by enemies to north and east and west. Our only protection lies in the road south, upon which soldiers may still be sent quickly from the garrisons at Clanamel should we have need of them. Otherwise we are entirely alone.'

Keran looked out at the deep snows, and shivered. 'So this feeling of safety and security here: it is all illusion . . .'

'Not wholly,' Ariscel smiled. 'Or we would indeed be fools to sit here gossiping like alewives in the midst of the enemy. The mountain walls are high and strong, near impregnable while winter holds. And even in summer we have so far experienced no more than a few small skirmishes on the high meadows. But we must never forget that beyond these white mountains lurks a legion of enemies who only grow in strength and number.'

'Then why does not Arminor garrison this valley?' Yeon demanded.

Ariscel shrugged. 'I have urged it upon him many times, but he can afford few paid troops, and those he has, he keeps close by him in Clanamel. The mountain passes are high, and he has little fear of successful invasion from the north. He sees the greater threat from the south, from Misan.'

The chamber fell to silence; during which Leighor caught sharp glimpses of his companions' faces as they stared pensively out at the high-towering mountains that held back such ill.

It was Ariscel himself who broke the spell, rising abruptly to announce that he must leave them. He bade them brief farewell and was gone, leaving the six travellers alone with their thoughts.

Chapter Twenty Nine
WHITE DEATH

'At least it is a fine day again!' Zindur peered out through diamond frosted windows to the white valley beyond. The homely smell of new-baked bread filled the darkness behind him.

'Fine, but still freezing cold!' Yeon complained, clapping his hands together for warmth, although he sat nearest of them all to the single pot-bellied stove that warmed the long kitchen. 'With so much sun, some of this snow must surely melt!'

'No snow will melt until the wind blows hard from the south,' Telsyan said briskly. 'And that is a rare occurrence in these mountains. Face the fact that we must remain here until the spring. It is as much as I had hoped to get this close to Clanamel before the snows stopped us. Be patient. When the thaw comes we shall not have far to travel.'

'But when the thaw comes it may be too late! Arminor may be long departed – or the election over! We should be seeking out some way over the mountains, instead of just sitting here . . .'

Keran rose quietly from her seat, leaving the others to argue. She had listened to this same debate many times over the past three weeks, and she was weary of it. There was nothing more to say. They could not leave Norndale now, even Telsyan had accepted that. They would just have to make the best of it. In a guilty, surreptitious way she was pleased that they were forced to remain here for a while. She liked this vale with its high soaring mountains and its grey, dark trees. She liked the peace and unhurried friendliness of this quiet place, and she had a concealed liking for Ariscel.

The travellers' suspicions of Ariscel had largely evaporated in the three weeks since their arrival, yet they had seen him little, and it began to seem almost that the Seer deliberately avoided them. Taking his meals separately from his guests, he came upon them only by accident: perhaps passing hurriedly in a narrow corridor, or strolling alone through the half-wild gardens beneath the house. At these times Ariscel would exchange a few brief pleasantries, or enquire politely after their health and comfort, before hurrying on. And so for the most part the travellers were forced to content themselves with the company of the various other members of Ariscel's household: Thera, his thin, taciturn wife, who spoke little and seemed never apart from her embroidery hoop; Pot Bethda, who ran the kitchen and served them their meals; and several fleeting acolytes who appeared also to dwell somewhere in Ariscel's house but who rarely lingered long enough to talk.

The village folk seemed friendly enough, most having little else to do during the long winter months but talk: about the crops, the weather, or their own petty gossips and rivalries. They were interested too in the travellers' tales of foreign lands, for few of them had ever been farther afield than Easterdale – a dozen leagues to the south across the mountains. A man who had been to Clanamel was considered a rare traveller, and few had ever ventured into Grimmerfen or the northlands beyond.

'That is bad country . . .' they would say, shaking their heads gravely; '. . . from which few return. Even the soil is poisoned, so that nothing grows well. If the Rievers want it they can keep it, so long as they stay there and don't come south to trouble decent folk.'

Keran smiled at that. After all, were hers not decent folk? And those – oh, so many – who had perished at Silentwater? To hear these Helietrim burghers talk one would suppose that the world ended at White Pass; and all who lived north of it were of little worth. No doubt these were good people, and if more refugees like themselves struggled south across the mountains they would do all they could to feed, clothe and shelter them. But they were lacking in some vital spark of imagination, and could not envisage that others, not of their community, might share similar fears and desires to their own.

Whilst thinking these thoughts Keran had been wandering the familiar passageways of the lower ground floor. Yet now she halted, surprised to find a new passageway in front of her, where previously she could remember none. A narrow passage, which sloped gently down into the darkness of the foundations, with no doors visible on either side.

Something within her warned that it might not be wise to investigate further; yet a compulsive curiosity pulled her on, and she began to venture down the corridor. After all, had not Ariscel himself given them permission to roam where they pleased? Not wholly convinced, even in her own mind, she walked on until she came to a low oaken doorway, half hidden in shadow, that crouched upon her left at the end of the passage. What now?

Feeling it a waste to have ventured so far without at least trying the door, she took hold of the iron door-ring and twisted, half hoping that it would be locked. To her surprise it was not, but swung open silently at her touch to reveal a small dusty antechamber, empty but for a festooning garlandry of cobwebs.

She was just about to shut the door again when she felt it – a strange, shimmering, yearning power that seemed to have its source somewhere on the far side of the blank stone wall that faced her. This was not the all-encompassing aura of the great tree, calm and protective. This was power of a different order, sharp and highly concentrated, a solitary pinpoint of power, yet disturbingly potent – somewhat akin to the cold-warmth of Hoethan's *harrunor* amulet. It made her shudder, and not entirely with fear. She recognised with sudden disquiet that this was the force that had called her here.

The invisible probing fingers of power seemed to delve deep into her soul and draw her nearer, so that it seemed that her heart must surely tear asunder should she turn away . . .

Someone caught hold of her suddenly from behind. Rough hands slammed her hard into the wall. She could not see who her assailant was, but he showed no gentleness in his handling of her.

With desperate urgency she dug her fingernails deep into his wrists, taking a sharp thrill of satisfaction from the gasp of pain this elicited. Using the momentary slackening of his grip to twist herself free, she turned sharply to look her assailant in the face – to discover that it was Kovir, one of Ariscel's dour young apprentices.

'How did you come into this chamber, outlander?' he hissed. 'What do you seek here? Spy!' This last word he spat out as he tried to take hold of her arms again.

But this time Keran was forewarned and evaded him, her right hand slipping from his grasp to strike out purposefully, hurtling its compact fist fiercely upward to make painful acquaintance with his left eye.

With a howl of outrage, Kovir stumbled backward, shocked as much by the unexpected vehemence of Keran's response as by the actual blow itself. Nursing a cut beneath a left eye already beginning to darken, he swore fluently.

Keran backed away. But Kovir seemed more wary of her now, and chose only to trace a small sign in the air before her.

At once a great wave of giddiness and confusion crashed down upon her. Her eyesight was blurred and unclear. The room pitched and swirled before her eyes. She heard nothing – other than a dull, reverberating echo that seemed to come at her from a great distance. And even her sense of balance seemed to have left her, so that it was all she could do to remain unsteadily upon her feet with her back propped against the wall. Yet even through the fog of her numbed senses she could still see Kovir's twisted face advancing towards her, grinning exultantly. He thought he had won . . . beaten her with his puny apprentice spell!

A tide of fury welled up within her. She would not allow herself to be so humbled by this snot-nosed apprentice boy! She would fight his ridiculous cantrip, and break it to smithereens – as she had broken the far stronger ensorcelments of Hoethan and Inanys. And even though she no longer possessed her precious Ginara Stone, the remembrance gave her courage. She must concentrate! Concentrate on him, on his ugly brutish face as it advanced towards her; use that to clear the mists from her mind.

She forced herself to stare myopically at him as he approached, trying hard to separate what was real from what was not: and slowly her sight began to clear. She could distinguish more details now; the room seemed to be stabilising, the areas of fogginess gradually retreating. But already Kovir was almost upon her; fists tight clenched, ready to give her a good drubbing in repayment for his fast-closing eye.

And then something seemed suddenly to release inside her – all her fear and loathing boiling out of her in a single instant; in one involuntary surge of fury and hatred, that had somehow congealed itself into an almost physical force deep within her – just as it had when she had unleashed the power of the *harrunor* amulet in Darien. And although this time the results were not so fearsome, they were equally effective: Kovir doubled up suddenly in his tracks, as if he had been struck hard in the belly by some invisible fist. For an instant he just stood there, grimacing up at her in silent agony; then he sank slowly to his knees and began to retch, bringing the contents of his stomach up on to the cold stone floor.

'What have you done to me?' he gasped between bouts of retching. 'Make it stop!'

But Keran was as unsure as he of exactly what she had done, and she knew of no way to undo it, or even to do the same thing again. Perhaps the *harrunor* amulet had opened up channels within her that had previously lain closed – but whatever the force she had somehow unleashed, it was something over which she had but scant control. As for Kovir, however, the effects did not seem to be too serious. They would just have to run their course.

'Keran! What in heaven's name is happening here?' The monk's voice made her spin about like a startled rabbit. Uhlendof and Leighor stood in the open doorway. They must have heard the commotion and followed her here.

'What is all this?' the monk demanded once more, striding across to the still-retching form of Kovir.

'It was him . . .' Keran stammered, strangely fearful and guilty, as if she had been caught at some forbidden childhood mischief. 'He attacked me . . .'

'Indeed!' Uhlendof cast a disbelieving eye down at the bleeding, retching form of the fallen apprentice boy, and then glowered back up at Keran. 'Then you seem to have had the better of the match, don't you, girl?' His tone was accusing and he stared at her without pity, almost as if he knew exactly what had taken place without the need to ask.

'Well, girl?' the monk demanded again, leaving her no time to think. 'What has truly happened here?'

'She is a witch!' Kovir gasped suddenly. His stomach having been relieved of its contents, he still retched profitlessly over the blotched flagstones; and it was all he could do to say as much as this. 'She . . . she has put a curse on me . . .'

'So!' Uhlendof spun back on her sharply. 'So this is the truth of it! Much as I have suspected since that first morning with the milk in the kitchens of Hallad's Keep! You remember that, do you not, lass? I feared then that you might have some blighted talent, some cursed predisposition towards the dark arts. And now, to my sorrow, I see that I was correct.'

'B . . . But . . .' Keran tried weakly to object, a wave of panicked confusion overtaking her. 'It is not dark . . . It is . . .' she was lost for words. How could she explain it to the raging monk? She could not satisfactorily explain it even to herself.

'It is entirely evil!' Uhlendof's voice was implacable. 'All such powers are the gifts only of the Dark One!'

'But what then of my staff?' Leighor asked, stepping forward. 'And the Stormwand of the giants?'

'They too are tainted,' the monk declared. 'If perhaps to a lesser extent. Some magicks bind more strongly than others. Some are more distant from their true creator. Yet all come ultimately from the same source.'

'Surely you do not truly believe that, priest?' Another voice came suddenly from behind them – the voice of Ariscel. 'Otherwise you would never have entered this place'

Both protagonists turned sharply to face the newcomer. He was standing in the shadow of a low arch that stood where Keran knew none had stood before. An archway that led through into a large underground chamber, dimly illumined by the glow of some small but fierce fire that burned within.

'All magicks are of evil provenance,' Uhlendof repeated sternly, his face seeming strangely dark and haunted now, half in shadow. 'The Tempter's lure: set to entrap ambitious fools!'

'In a way, Mallenian, perhaps you are right.' Ariscel advanced into the middle of the small dark chamber, paying no apparent heed to his choking apprentice on the floor. 'Indeed, all these forces, these magicks if you will, come ultimately from the Gods: Gods of good and Gods of ill. There are many dark magicks in the world, and one must be sure when one delves into such things that they come not from the Evil One, nor are constructed, however subtly, for his purposes. Yet there are many forces that yield much of great benefit. I have devoted a lifetime to their study, and I know.'

'No matter!' Uhlendof said swiftly. 'Some knowledge is better left unlearned! However bright-seeming these magicks may be, they are poisoned gifts, such as mortal man was never meant to wield. Ever have they done more harm than good, and the vanity of those who seek them out leads only to evil and destruction!'

Ariscel nodded impatiently, waiting for the monk's tirade to come to a natural halt before he spoke again. 'Indeed. Indeed. You would be surprised, were you to listen, how much I am in agreement with you. For those who enter foolishly into these things, the penalties are great. No magick, however small, is without price, and each has its dangers. See here!' He beckoned Leighor to come forward with his staff. 'This ashwood wand, of which you have just spoken. Some would term it a simple plaything, yet under the wrong circumstances it could be truly dangerous.'

'Why?' Leighor asked. 'What is it?'

'It is a Wand of Unveiling,' the Seer said at once. 'I do not know its provenance, yet it is a very rare and powerful thing. Its purpose is to lay bare any ensorcelment it touches and reveal the true nature of that which lies beneath . . .'

'Yes,' Leighor said slowly. 'That would account for much: the times that it worked, in Hirda's Garden and with the wall at Dom Udun Covarr; and even the times it did not, as with the bear . . .' He paused. 'Yet you said that its use bore a cost?'

Ariscel nodded. 'Aye, indeed. Such a staff is of use only in certain hands, perhaps those of one person in a hundred; one in a thousand, even. For into these it drains much of the force that it dissipates – either for good or ill.'

Leighor looked more than a little startled, almost letting the staff fall from his fingers. 'How will this have affected me?' he asked, appalled.

'I doubt in any major way,' Ariscel smiled. 'The wand is not of itself an evil thing, and you have not borne it long. Any effect will be very small. But take care. As I have said, these are not playthings, and must be used, if at all, only with the greatest caution. You know not what ensorcelment the staff may one day draw down upon you.'

'There!' Uhlendof nodded. 'Now you see the dangers of these things.'

'Aye,' Ariscel turned back to face Uhlendof. 'Yet despite all, there still remain many forces which are not of themselves evil. And with the proper motive and understanding they may be mastered to the cause of good: of protection, of healing, of foreseeing danger. How else are we to protect ourselves against those who use such arts for ill?'

New hope sprang within Keran's heart at the Seer's words, and she could not help but burst out: 'And will you help me to learn these arts, good Master Ariscel? To use them to the service of good?'

'No!' Uhlendof's furious negative echoed round the chamber. 'I shall not have this girl corrupted by your magicks! She may yet be spared the curse that lies within her.'

'Have no fear,' Ariscel shook his head. 'I shall not corrupt your charge. As you see,' he gave a perfunctory nod towards the groaning Kovir, 'I have apprentices enough for the present. Although she shows such talent I almost wish I could take her on.'

'Then why can you not?' Keran begged. 'I am willing to learn. I will do all that you say . . .'

Again Ariscel shook his head. 'It is not possible, lass. I have not the time now to take on new pupils; the days grow too dark and troubled to spare the long hours needed. Besides,' he cupped her chin in the palm of his hand, 'your gifts are of an uncommon sort; and my learning would profit you but little. No, your future now lies along other paths, ones that will not bring you back to cold Norndale for many a long year, if ever . . .'

But in what way are my gifts uncommon?' Keran asked. 'Can you not explain them to me?'

'No,' Ariscel smiled gently. 'They are elusive and nebulous, in some aspects surprisingly strong, in other, no less important ones, weak indeed. Yet there is an underlying shadow within them that worries me. Be careful, lass. In many ways your mentor is right to be wary. Yours are talents that could all too easily be misled into the purposes of evil. Beware!'

Leaving Keran to digest this, he turned sharply away to give Kovir a gentle prod with his boot.

'Up, you!' he ordered, his voice harsher now. 'You have croaked there long enough! Up and fetch a mop and bucket to clear this mess! You should be ashamed of yourself to be humbled so by an untrained maid!'

With a black look in Keran's direction, Kovir stumbled to his feet and fled the room, crashing heavily into Telsyan, Yeon and Zindur on their way in.

'What is all this?' Zindur demanded, staring after the bloodied apprentice. 'We heard great commotion and shouting.'

'I do not doubt it,' Ariscel said tartly. 'I should suppose that half the vale has by now. That lad shall be whipped!'

'You will not punish him on my account, surely?' Keran begged. 'For that will only make him hate me the more.'

'He shall have his punishment,' the Seer confirmed, frowning. 'That shall be his test. If he cannot quickly conquer his resentment, I shall have no further use for him. Such arts as I teach are far too dangerous to be entrusted to any who are slaves to their own ill-will.'

'But surely,' Keran chanced, the Seer's disturbing revelation still churning in her brain. 'There can be little harm in small, country magicks?'

Ariscel shook his head. 'The smallest of magicks holds as many dangers as the greatest, for both present the same basic choice.' He produced a scrap of parchment from his robe and held it out before him, between his finger and thumb. 'Watch!'

And even as he spoke the word, the parchment burst into flames, to be consumed in the space of a moment, the tiny, glowing embers blackening as they drifted to the floor. For a minute there was silence.

'You see,' Ariscel whispered through the still darkness, 'how easy it is to destroy a tiny scrap of parchment? Yet to create such a strip, even such a small thing as this, is entirely beyond my powers. That is the key. It is always so much easier to destroy than to create, to do evil than to do good. The weak will always choose the easier option, for it makes their power seem the greater. They will choose always to hurt and to destroy, and in so doing become ruined and corrupted. The choice is ever the same, at whatever level it is made; and the results the same – as you have seen this morning.'

'Aye,' Zindur broke in once more. 'What has been happening here?'

'A minor disagreement,' Uhlendof snapped. 'I shall tell you the details later, if you truly wish to hear them.'

'And what lies through there?' Yeon asked, pointing past Ariscel into the dull crimson glow of the chamber from which the Seer had emerged.

'That,' Ariscel sighed, 'is one of my workrooms, my forge; which I had not intended to show you at this time. But since you are all here, and wish to know all things, you might as well see. Come!' he waved them all forward impatiently. 'Come. You shall see, as you are so curious, the work I undertake for King Arminor.'

'How is it that we have never found this passage before?' Yeon asked as they bowed their heads to pass one by one beneath the stone arch. 'I am sure we have come past it many times before, and never noticed it.'

'Some things, perhaps, we do not notice,' Ariscel replied softly, 'until our attention is drawn to them.'

Leighor, being first to enter the inner chamber, was surprised to find how much larger it was than the small, dusty anteroom they had just left. For this in fact was no part of the house at all, but a natural chamber carved out of the mountain beneath, a low underground cavern with a small stony streamlet clattering through its centre and an arching roof hung with stalactites. The only light came from a squat furnace which stood close by the stream, its low, flickering flame barely penetrating the more distant reaches of the cavern. Two other figures lurked in the shadows behind it; one large and brawny – a typical villager – the other far shorter, but seeming just as powerfully built.

A door shut suddenly behind them, cutting off the last grey traces of daylight from the house beyond, and they were entirely alone; enclosed within the darkness of the chamber. For a moment Leighor felt something akin to panic; a dread of dark entombment here beneath the mountain. It was foolish, he knew. They had been far deeper in the vaults of the *maezgrull*. Yet here, because of the deep aura of unknown magic that surrounded them, he felt far more concern.

'You feel the *harrunor*?' Ariscel suddenly whispered behind him. 'Does its power frighten you?'

He nodded.

'You do well to be wary. The Mage Metal has the power to enslave the mightiest to its will: even raw it is yet dangerous.' Ariscel nodded towards the larger of the two who waited in the shadows. 'We shall proceed!'

At once the man bent to open a long metal box at his feet, revealing a dull, half-made sword that lay within. The blade seemed to glow faintly through the darkness with the unmistakable purple luminescence of *harrunor*. Yes. Leighor drew a sharp breath. It was made entirely of *harrunor*! Even quiescent in its leaden case, it threw out a tangible wall of power around it. An aura which seemed to affect all of his companions, stilling them into silence.

'A wondrous thing, is it not?' Ariscel whispered. 'Even only three parts complete. Wealth enough to furnish a score of castles. The greatest gift of the mines of Zumir.'

'Or their greatest curse!' Uhlendof hissed.

'In unwary hands perhaps,' Ariscel agreed. 'Even now it is yet dangerous, the power unchannelled, uncontrolled. It must still be melded, chained, forced to do our bidding. Made so that it cannot be corrupted. That is what we do now ... See!'

At his nod the two assistants combined to lift the sword; never touching the blade with their own hands, but using metal tongs to raise it first on to a high anvil that stood before the mouth of the furnace, and then to plunge it into the heart of the burning coals.

In the light of the furnace Leighor was able to see the smaller of the two clearly for the first time.

'A *mazgroll*!' he gasped.

'Hulgarung is no *mazgroll*.' Ariscel responded gently. 'Although you are correct inasmuch as he is one of the Hill Folk. Yet he is not of the *maezgrull* but the *ghrornan* race, who are more learned in the arts of metalcraft. Afni, my other helper, is the son of Guldor, the blacksmith from Darkrigg. But I do the village folk no dishonour to say that Hulgarung and others of his people have given me most help and counsel in my work.'

'And they help you freely?' Telsyan asked, his eyebrows raised.

'Aye; and why not?' It was the Hillman who spoke, his voice deep and guttural; startling the travellers as he took up the bellows and began to pump. 'Here there are yet a few quiet places where our folk may dwell in peace alongside the *U-Zumir*. For this, Arminor and his line are owed much; and we repay as we can.'

There was a silence, filled after a moment or two by the low voice of Ariscel. 'The *ghrornan* hold many ancient secrets still in their mountain strongholds. Without their help neither the sword nor the gauntlet could have been made.'

'The gauntlet?' Leighor questioned.

'Aye,' the Seer nodded. 'That is the other talisman I have wrought here from the *harrunor*, and which is now in Arminor's hand. But no more questions. The fire is hot enough. We begin!'

At once Hulgarung left off his pumping and came forward to help Afni draw forth the heated sword. Leighor gasped as the blade slid from the coals, for now it blazed with light: so intense and brilliant that it must surely outshine the stars themselves – and brighter yet, until its entire surface streamed with faery fire.

'How can such a small fire burn so hot?' Telsyan whispered.

Barely visible in the darkness behind them, Uhlendof snorted. 'That is no ordinary fire.'

Leighor shivered: he sensed it too. The scarlet flames gave out an aura of great magic that burned upward from the heart of the stone. The mixture of charcoals and dark woods within exuded sharp, aromatic odours which flowed gently through the stone chamber, although the woods themselves seemed hardly to be consumed at all. This was clearly a fire upon which many deep spells had been cast, and he doubted that it had been kindled by human hand.

Afni now held the sword steady upon the anvil, whilst Hulgarung – dripping with sweat now despite the bitter cold – took up his great black hammer and began to shape it; smiting the hot metal expertly with deep remorseless blows that echoed and resounded about the confined chamber. Every so often Afni would turn the blade so that each side might receive its proper attention from the Hillman's hammer. Yet throughout the lengthy working, the blade seemed neither to cool nor to lose one iota of its former brilliance.

When the Hillman seemed at last satisfied with his work, he stood back and nodded to Ariscel, who at once stepped forward.

At first the seer appeared to do little, only stretching his arms wide above the sword. Then he began to speak; uttering strange soft words: indecipherable, barely audible, beneath his breath. A few grains of a light yellow dust fell from his fingers on to the swordblade – hissing and flaming as they made brief contact with the hot metal. And then nothing but silence and stillness. Ariscel remained alone before the sword, his hands poised a foot or two above the blade, his face a mask of deep concentration.

For long minutes there was no movement. No sound but the laboured breathing of the two assistants in the darkness; and the travellers began to shift uneasily upon their feet, chafing at the penetrating cold.

But as Leighor's eyes slowly accustomed themselves to the strange quarter-light, he fancied that he saw a shimmering field of luminescent grey beginning slowly to form above the sword; hovering hazily, like a fragile curtain, in the motionless air. Slowly it grew; seeping outwards until it filled the entire space between Ariscel's outstretched fingers, rising in a shimmering arc of ghost-light whose apex wavered a foot or two above the seer's head. Leighor hardly dared breathe now for fear that he might in some way dissipate or destroy this fragile thing, this tenuous patina that now bathed the travellers' upturned faces in its light. Ariscel too was silent; neither speaking nor moving, entirely absorbed in his own ethereal creation.

And slowly the thin field of light began to alter, to swirl gently within itself, like smoke rising from a fire on a still day: wispy streams of nothingness coiling themselves into the strange, half-imagined shapes of birds, beasts and men; tall, dreamlike figures with gaunt, dark-lined features. The slow movement had an almost hypnotic effect upon those who watched, so that in the end they could not have truly said whether they saw anything at all in the smoky radiance, or whether all had been just imagining.

But then a great purple fire arose suddenly from out of the sword, to consume all before it; the silent flames burning red and gold, hungry and all-devouring. Yet so beautiful were they that Leighor somehow longed to reach out and touch them, to feel their warmth. And it was all he could do to prevent himself from being drawn forward involuntarily into the arc of fire. Yeon did in fact take one faltering step forward before Uhlendof hauled him urgently back with a sharp-hissed warning.

The flames appeared to take strength from the disturbance, burning still higher until even Ariscel seemed momentarily to flinch back from their ferocity. Yet he stood firm, the beads of perspiration streaming down his face and pouring from his unclad wrists. Then suddenly, as if a cold blast of wind had blundered through them, the flames arced and parted to reveal a hazy, trembling image in their midst; a seething picture painted in fiery hues of red and purple. Unlike the earlier shapings they had witnessed, this vision seemed to have substance, reality; as if it portrayed some actual landscape, some true time or place.

Leighor could make out what seemed to be a vast disordered army that marched across a limitless plain, bare of all habitations and inhabitants. Only blackened, smouldering ruins stood here to oppose the advance of that great army: lost towns and villages whose peoples were vanished and whose very memories would soon be forgotten. Starved jackals and other furtive creatures slank among the ruins, and dark storm-crows circled above.

Leighor shuddered, wishing now to draw back from this fearsome scene. But then – abruptly as the vision had arisen – it vanished, to be replaced by another: of horsemen questing blindly amongst barren hills, beneath dark, threatening skies. They seemed to search without hope, ragged and drawn, seeking some precious thing which they knew not whether they would ever find.

Again the flames rippled, and the vision changed, this time to a verdant valley which was now a battlefield, strewn with the tortured bodies of the dead and the dying. Hunched figures in grey rags scavenged among the bodies, and dark bat-things feasted.

As if in horror or despair Ariscel threw up his hands before his face. And this vision too quivered and was gone, to be replaced by no other. The Seer sighed deeply, even as the flames at last began to die. But they were not quenched entirely, seeming merely to shrink and concentrate themselves into a line of dark fire that hovered above the swordblade, as if fuelled by the white-hot metal itself.

Ariscel drew a rune in the air above the flames. And at once there came a bright explosion of light. Cold, white and blindingly painful: its sheer intensity forced the travellers to bow their heads and shield their eyes against it.

The light grew brighter yet, and still brighter; until the travellers feared they could bear it no longer. Then the whole brilliant circle of light cracked like a mirror, shattering into a thousand glittering fragments, which slowly faded and diminished as they drifted gently back down into the sword. They sparkled briefly, with a hundred shining colours; and then, like a spent firework, were gone. Now there was darkness; with only the low furnace and the dim glow of the cooling sword for illumination.

'It is finished for today.' Ariscel, like the sword, seemed now entirely extinguished. He turned to face the waiting company. 'The blade must cool, and I must rest.'

To Leighor, the Seer looked more worn and drained than he could ever have imagined – as if he had just endured several sleepless days and nights of some truly burdensome labour. Even so, the wonder of what he had seen was so great that he could not forbear from questioning him.

'These things we have seen,' he asked hurriedly, catching him by the sleeve. 'What is their meaning?'

Weakly Ariscel smiled. 'You have seen little, and most of that mere illusion. Our work here is long and untutored. Many days are wasted in exploring the dark within the metal. Perhaps this day we have cleansed it a little; but there is still much to be done.' He turned away.

'And the visions?' Leighor asked. 'Had they truth?'

'Perhaps.' The Seer shrugged distractedly. 'Some might say they are glimpses of things that have been, or are yet to come. Or mayhap they are but warnings of things that might occur should our endeavours fail. However, one must be wary of all one sees in the *harrunor* flame, for the metal twists and warps all it touches. Little may be trusted.'

Ariscel led them back up into the house, and then departed from them, not to be seen again that day or the next.

The days following were those that led up to the feast of Midwinter's Day, which fell roughly in the middle of the long month of Yearsend. This was the longest month of the year in the northern kingdoms, having 47 days in all; although in the south it was common to break the month in two to form Rallen and Zelve, with 24 and 23 days respectively. The final day of Yearsend was the last of the old year and a day of great celebration; although here in the north it was Midwinter's Day that occasioned the greater festivity, after the older style.

It was three weeks after Midwinter's Day when the long-awaited thaw finally came. The wind veered sharply round into the south a few days before the New Year and slowly the temperature rose. Daily the travellers looked south to Hythni's Pass for any sign of the dark streak across the mountainside that would proclaim the way safely open for the journey southward. But although the snows melted fast in the valley bottoms, the higher snows hung on tenaciously until the travellers began to despair of the pass ever clearing before the weather closed in once more.

'The snows will soon return,' the villagers told them darkly. 'A thaw like this so early in the winter is unnatural. No good will ever come of it.'

And the villagers' fears were to be confirmed far more swiftly than even they could have suspected.

The first the travellers knew of anything amiss was the long hoarse boom of a great mountain horn echoing through the midnight darkness from somewhere far up the valley. A sound abruptly cut short as the unknown sentry was silenced.

Leighor sat up sharply in his bed, his pulse racing. He guessed already what that dark sound must mean. The hurried clatter of feet along stairs and passageways beyond his chamber, and the sharp cries from without, served only to redouble his fears.

Hurriedly he dragged on his outer clothing, running out into the biting cold of the mountain night to find most of his companions already out before him. Ariscel stood in the open space before the house giving brisk orders to the groups of villagers who hurriedly assembled beneath with axes, bows and pitchforks.

'Make light!' His voice rose sharp above the whistle of the south wind as he pointed up the valley to thin columns of torchbearers already spreading out from the village. 'We must have light! That is most urgent! We must know where they are, and in what number.'

'Then it is true we are attacked?' Leighor said anxiously.

'Aye,' Uhlendof nodded. 'From the north. We know no more. Somehow Rievers have come over the pass.'

Leighor's eyes sought northward into the intense blackness at the head of the vale and he shuddered. This was where the hornblast had come from, yet he could see nothing at all. It was as if a dark curtain had been thrown across the vale, through which no light dared penetrate. Nor were there any sounds beside the sharp cries of villagers, borne upon the wind. Yet he could almost feel the deep malevolence that seeped down from those dark mountains. This was no false alarm, he was sure. He felt for the bow at his side, and knew fear.

'What can we do?' Zindur stepped forward to ask quickly. 'Where can we best help?'

'Men are needed on the line before the village,' the Seer told him at once. 'That must be held as long as possible. I will do what I can here. Only give me time!' Not pausing to see what the travellers decided, he turned sharply on his heel to re-enter the house.

'Well?' Telsyan asked.

'Do as he says,' Zindur grunted. 'If the line falls we will be of little use here.'

Taking burning brands from the house to light their way, the six began to run towards the makeshift line that had already been thrown across the valley a few hundred yards north of the village. Here a low ditch had been cut across the width of the vale in times past, and this now formed their sole defence against whatever lay in the darkness beyond.

There were several men Leighor recognised as they approached the makeshift trench, including Hulgarung the *ghrornan* metalsmith, Afni, and a number of Elfath's Wardens – although not the Wardenmaster himself.

'Choose yourselves a place in the line,' their apparent leader, a man called Menkurd, told them quickly, 'and ready your bows upon my order. Save your swords for later. If the fighting gets that close it will be a bloody night's work. We must take them at a distance if we can.' He looked at Keran for a moment. 'Women would do best to remain indoors.'

Keran shook her head. 'I shall stay with my friends.'

'As you wish.' The Warden shrugged and turned away.

There were now armed men positioned along the length of the great defensive ditch, a good half league from one side of the valley to the other; and torches burned everywhere, reminding Leighor incongruously of a procession of pilgrims he had once seen, making their way by night towards some distant shrine. Yet this was no band of pilgrims, as could be plainly told from the ranks of pikes and halberds, taut-strung bows and glinting pitchforks that swayed nervously in the unpractised hands of their bearers. The men seemed pitifully few; no more than one man to every three yards or so of trench, and Leighor noticed several women other than Keran amongst them. If the Rievers were come in any number the odds were poor indeed. And this was not Silentwater; there was nowhere else to run.

Beside him, Keran noticed a sudden movement in the darkness ahead, and cried out in alarm.

A dozen pairs of eyes followed her pointing finger. But Menkurd only smiled. 'Those are our own men, lass, a-lighting the beacons. The Rievers are not ready for us yet.'

And sure enough, small scarlet tongues of flame began suddenly to lick up from the feet of a line of bonfires – heretofore hidden – that had been laid a hundred paces or so in front of the main trench. The fires were too far apart to form any sort of barrier, and Leighor guessed that their main task must be to light the battleground for the archers. The steady light calmed his fears somewhat, for while those pyres burned they could not be taken entirely by surprise: they would have some warning before the onslaught came.

The fire-layers scurried back to their places in the line; and again there was silence and waiting. Some men hammered sharpened stakes in rows before the trench, but these were far too few to break any serious charge. And even if the dark had now been pushed back beyond the line of fires, it was just as deep and impenetrable as before. There could be a whole army out there, hidden in its depths – or else nothing at all.

'What hour is it?' Yeon whispered, his voice carrying clearly along the silent trench.

'I know not,' Zindur grunted. 'But dawn cannot be far away.'

'Three, four hours, at least.' Menkurd shook his head. 'There is little help there.'

And it seemed all of that time before the first of the attackers was sighted. The vision, strange and dreamlike, came almost as a relief after the long hours of waiting. A faint blur of movement in the dark, beyond pyres already beginning to burn low; a silent shifting of skeletal shadow-forms at the edges of their vision. Yet enough to bring everyone back to gut-wrenching wakefulness once more.

And then again nothing. But now every man stood ready; the last lingering hopes that the alarm might be false, or that the raiding party had fled back into the mountains, were gone. Every nerve was taut, every heart racing, waiting for the inevitable onslaught.

It came suddenly, with a loud high-pitched scream from somewhere far away to the right – quickly taken up by what sounded like ten thousand howling voices. And with a fearsome clashing of weapons upon shields, the brazen ranks of the enemy burst through the dying cordon of flame and were upon them. Draped in ragged white furs and bleached skins to blend them with the snows, they seemed true spawnings of a winter nightmare – as if the ice and snow themselves had taken on life, in a mockery of human form, to tear and rend with tooth and blade and claw.

For long moments the villagers stood frozen: warriors, farmers, men and women alike caught in a fatal spell of holding as the Rievers hurtled towards them. There was no visible leader, just one long line of screaming death-pale flesh. Gaunt, soulless Tarintarmen, their pale eyes burning red behind their war-markings; troglodytes and lumbering half-men from the deep bowels of the earth; and sly, ground-slinking goblins: charging as one in blood-hungry battle-frenzy. They seemed without number, utterly overwhelming. Surely that awesome onslaught must carry all before it . . .

And then a shout came up from Menkurd, echoed and re-echoed down the line. 'Let loose, men! Let fly your arrows!'

The first volley tore into the charging host at about seventy paces. Many fell, but far too few to make any impact on such a fearsome number. Sheer weight of attack must surely overwhelm the defenders within moments. Leighor struggled to operate his crossbow. But his injured arm was still unreliable and he could not tell whether his shaft struck home or not. Yet in that instant the whole charge seemed suddenly to fall apart; whole sections of the line keeling abruptly forward to be swallowed by the snow-clad earth, plummeting screaming into great black voids which opened up beneath them.

It took a few seconds for Leighor to realise what had happened; his confusion nearly as great as that of the enemy as they tumbled into the carefully camouflaged line of pits that had been set some fifty yards before the main trench, to swallow up just such a charge as this. Many survived, but these were the lucky ones who had chanced to fall upon the safe pathways between the pits; pathways which Menkurd's men must have used when they returned from lighting their pyres. A ragged cheer rose up from the village lines when the defenders saw what havoc their simple ruse had occasioned, their arrow fire now concentrating upon those few who were left.

Even so, some of the boldest of the first wave managed to reach the trench: gaunt-limbed Tarintarmen leaping the last line of stakes to fall upon the defenders with knives, flails and great hooked swords; bloody hand to hand combats breaking out wherever they broke through. But those who managed to get so far were few and quickly overcome; and for the moment there were none to follow after them.

Deep groans of dismay and howls of fury arose from out of the dark beyond the line of fires, where the main body of the attackers still lay in wait. Only the last fleeing goblins now scurried back into the shelter of the outer darkness, knives, clubs and other weapons left scattered in the snow behind them. The half-armoured body of a *Tarintar* captain was hauled from one of the trenches some yards to Leighor's right. And again there was stillness and silence – breached only by a dark grumbling from beyond the pyres, which must signify either debate or a passing of commands.

It was some time before the second attack came. And this time the Rievers advanced more slowly, coming forward in serried columns to cross the narrow bridges between the stake-pits two abreast, the front ranks bearing great wood and leather shields to deflect the arrows of the defenders. And now an answering hail of arrows arose from behind the Riever lines to spread death and confusion amongst the villagers, frustrating the aim of the Norndale archers and forcing them to break ranks and dive for cover. A flaming lance of purple fire lit up the night for an instant like day, to die amid the stench of smouldering flame and a terrible screaming from the centre of the village line.

Fearful cries rose now from many throats, and several of the defenders turned to flee. Menkurd barked furious commands, and suddenly Elfath too was behind them, striving desperately to bring some order back into the ragged line. Now gaunt, leatherwinged Haroodin swirled through the air above their heads taking refuge in the upper darkness, and descending, with shrill cries and raking claws, to spread further panic amongst the villagers.

'It is falling apart,' he heard Zindur mutter. 'If we do not steady ourselves quickly . . .' The rest was lost, as more screaming Riever archers came forward to take up positions behind the front line of shield bearers.

The enemy were so close now that Leighor could make out the individual faces, blank and expressionless behind their shields. And even as he watched, the numbers swelled. There were so many. Nothing the villagers could do would make any impression upon such a host. Men looked at one another nervously: Telsyan and Zindur, Yeon and Menkurd, Keran with her longbow, Uhlendof with his stout staff, grim-visaged villagers taking up halberds and pitchforks and spears. The rain of arrows shrank to a harmless spatter, as stocks ran short and men turned to more effective weapons.

Then suddenly, as if at some unvoiced command, the tide of Riever arrows also ceased; and the attackers stirred expectantly. There was a sharp cry from somewhere behind the Riever lines. Leighor tensed.

Yet there was no forward rush. No charge. In fact, if anything, the close-set ranks seemed to be losing their cohesion; breaking up amid an excited hubbub of dark mumbles and shrill cries. There was pointing – not towards the thin line of defenders, but somehow past them – and eyes rose, to fix upon something that floated above the villagers' heads.

Unable to restrain himself, Leighor chanced a brief look behind him; gasping with astonishment at what he saw. For, high upon the hillside behind them, the whole of Ariscel's house now shone with brilliant light. A blazing ball of fiery incandescence that seemed to have its core in the heart of the great tree itself – clinging to its bare branches and seeping outwards from its stripped crown.

Slowly, the orb of light parted company with both house and tree, rising – seemingly of its own volition – into the dark night air above. More eyes followed it now, villagers as well as Rievers. And it lit up the ground beneath it, climbing like a second moon into the coal black skies. Rolling ominously towards them, it was now a ball of living flame; too bright to look upon, too awesome to behold, from which both attacker and defender shrank away.

There was a sudden crash, as if of great thunder; and bolts of lightning began to descend with fire and fury upon the Riever ranks, striking terror and confusion into their number. As far as Leighor could see, the bolts appeared to do little real damage; yet their effect upon the morale of the attackers was devastating. The Rievers scattered before them: goblins fleeing in howling terror; Haroodin, Tarintarmen and Cavern Troglodytes, shorn of their garb of darkness, cowering away from the hated light. And even those men who ran with them were consumed with fear and awe – as most of the defenders would surely have been, had that fearsome orb been descending upon them.

A noisy crackle of *harrunor* flame tore up from the midst of the scattering throng to lance into the ball of fire. And then another. But neither to any effect; and there were no more. The Rievers stumbled and fell; biting, scratching, and falling over one another in their eagerness to escape. And with a loud roar the exultant villagers rose up from their lines to hunt down and pursue the remaining stragglers.

Leighor and the others remained, watching as the Riever companies broke asunder, fleeing up the vale beneath the still pursuing orb of light and thunder. And as the great fireball drifted thunderously northward, the darkness returned once more. But this time not so dark; for there was now a thin rim of light in the skies above the eastern ranges, where mighty Surangor, the Anvil Mountain, still slumbered beneath his heavy coat of snow.

 Dawn.

 The day would soon be here, and the dark night terror over.

Chapter Thirty
THE TESTING OF KING ARMINOR

Hythni's Pass proved a difficult climb. Even with so much of the snow taken by the mild south wind, there were still great drifts across the road that must be tunnelled through with the light, trekkers' spades that the villagers had given them. Once at the top of the pass, upon the high shoulder of Snaecoll, they could see back along the entire length of Norndale, to White Pass and the peaks beyond. Below them, Norndale turned sharply eastward, bearing its frozen river a league or so into the mountains before it came to a sudden halt against a towering wall of rock, to be swallowed up in a great black sump-hole that carried it who knew where beneath the mountains.

Darkrigg was barely visible now: no more than a few grey specks halfway along the broad depth of the valley. Leighor shivered. It was all too easy to imagine the valley already abandoned; left, like half a dozen others, bare and empty to await its fate. He felt the heavy weight of the new sword in its scabbard at his side, and looked away. Perhaps this dull grey sword of *harrunor* he carried might somehow turn things once more to their advantage. At any rate he hoped so; and that was one of the few hopes he still clung to.

In the end it had been no surprise when Ariscel had announced that he could no longer journey with them to Clanamel, and that they must bear the sword to Arminor in his stead.

'I am afraid that there is now far greater need of me here,' he had told them gravely. 'I had never expected the Curséd Ones to assail us here in such numbers, and for as long as this thaw lasts, they may return at any time. I cannot now go, and leave my people without defence. I may be an old man of fading powers, but what small skill I yet possess is of more use here than on the road to Clanamel.'

'Small skill?' Zindur objected. 'But what of the fireball?'

Ariscel had smiled. 'That, like most of my summonings, was a simple thing of little substance, the merest illusion; and if the Rievers had stood to face it they would have suffered little harm. Yet it served its purpose well, and there are other tricks that might prove as effective for a while. As long as I am useful here I cannot leave. Certainly not until Arminor sends fresh soldiers north to guard the pass – and that is partly in your hands, my friends; so Godspeed!'

Yeon had more than half expected to have the honour of bearing the great sword himself. And even Zindur, the warrior, or Telsyan, their leader, might have seemed more fitting. But no, the Seer had been firm.

'The sword is best fitted to your guardianship,' he had insisted, his cold grey eyes sharp and severe. 'You have been called upon this venture by chance, perhaps to some purpose that even you cannot now imagine. Mayhap in part this is the reason. Either way, I feel the sword belongs with you. It too bears much in its destiny of chance and caprice, and is to be handled at all times with great care. The sword is no weapon; it does not even have a good edge, for the metal is too soft to take one. It is best disguised by being worn in an ordinary scabbard, and is not to be used by you except in dire need.'

The Seer handed him a sealed letter. 'I had hoped soon to speak again with Arminor, but that is not to be. This letter explains much, including those properties and uses of the sword that I have so far been able to divine. Its uses are subtler than you may imagine, or than the king may desire; and it is best that I do not attempt to explain them to you now. Yet in emergency the sword may help you if it be drawn and held out before you. Normally I would have sent Hulgarung with you to give greater instruction to the king, but he too is now needed by his people, and must return to the high valleys.'

Leighor had at first been worried by this new commission, for he now knew something of the sword's power. Again, for some reason, he appeared to have been singled out from the others, and this troubled him. Coincidence and ill-fortune seemed to have dogged him continually over the four long years since his exile from Syrne. Had that solemn curse which had been pronounced upon him then, truly the power to affect his destiny? His rational mind rejected the notion, yet somewhere deep within him a nagging doubt still clung on.

He had tried to extract more information from the Seer on this subject and that of Erchoron's staff, but had not got very far. At the last, he had attempted to leave the staff behind, in Ariscel's keeping. But the Seer had refused his gift. 'It is yours, southron,' he had said as they departed, 'and it may yet prove of value to you in time to come. Keep it, and guard it well. But remember its dangers, keep it wrapped always in stout cloth, and use it only when you truly have to.'

With that he had taken his leave of them and turned away.

Leighor sighed again as they began the descent into the bare icy plateau beneath. Yet the weather seemed good indeed for this first day of the new year; and perhaps that was a fair omen for their journey. It was the first day of the month of *Ilter* of the Varroain year 785; the sun shone, a soft wind blew, and all appeared well with the world.

They camped that night in the cold, snowy wastes between the mountains, on the frozen banks of the stream that would later turn eastwards to form the Eld River that watered narrow Easterdale, a day's journey farther on to south and east. But their route did not lie that way; they were to continue upon a more westerly course, keeping to the high valleys and the twisting road that would eventually bring them through the towering heart of the Alisterlings, down into the broad vale of the River Irthing, at whose foot lay Clanamel.

In all, the journey took nine days. It was a safe if comfortless passage, in the main through high, barren valleys. They met with no other travellers until well into the sixth day, when their upland track finally coiled its way down to meet the young River Irthing at the head of its steep valley and they exchanged greetings with a solitary herdsman checking his pastures.

Over the next few days the Irthing grew steadily broader and deeper, its waters augmented by countless small streams and melting snows. A roaring torrent now, it plummeted over steep falls and raged through mountain gorges; until at last, its burden of ice all but gone, it slowed a little to meander through its own broad vale between the mountains. By the time the travellers came down to Clanamel the ground snows were almost gone, although they still kept hold upon the high mountains, which glowered down like frost-rimed giants upon the town beneath.

Clanamel itself was a fair city of wood and stone which stood upon the far bank of the Irthing, where the river turned eastward through a narrow gap between the mountains, to pass out on to the open plain. Because of this constriction of the Irthing valley the river here ran deep and strong; the region being named the Neck of Clanamel by its inhabitants. And the flatlands where the river finally emerged from the shadow of the mountains, were likewise termed the Lee; the Lee of Clanamel – a pleasant name, Leighor thought.

The town itself presented a cheering sight as the six travel-weary companions stepped finally on to the seven-arched bridge that led across the river into it. The yellow banners of Arminor flew from every tower that bestrode the broad stone walls, snapping taut in an icy breeze that swept down from the mountains. Smart-liveried guardsmen saluted at the gate, and many more soldiers were encamped both within and without the walls. Yet the city seemed pleasing and prosperous enough, with well-built houses of timber and stone, paved ways and large markets. After Darien, and to folk who had not seen a civilised city for many months, this seemed suddenly paradise.

But the people of Clanamel were nervous and unsettled, with many rumours of war. There were reports of a large force encamped upon the Lee of Clanamel, and tales of further armies gathering to the south. Many feared that these now intended to fall upon the city – and Arminor had done nothing to allay these fears by calling upon all healthy men to prepare themselves for battle.

It was thus that the travellers discovered that the king was no longer in residence in the city, but now abiding in his castle at Irun's Teeth, upon the southern flank of Mount Nektor, a further half-day's journey to the south. Only slightly disappointed, for they had feared to have missed the king altogether, the six found a fair looking inn and spent a comfortable night in the luxury of its soft feather beds before setting out the next morning on the winding road up into the mountains beyond the city.

The journey was long on foot, the River Irthing running along in parallel far beneath them; and it was early afternoon before they finally came upon King Arminor's fortress of Irun's Teeth.

As soon as he saw it, standing proud and invincible upon its high ridge, Leighor realised why this had been the king's choice. Mount Nektor stood at the southernmost edge of the Alisterlings; and from it spread broad vistas to south and west which lay hidden from Clanamel, a dozen leagues to the north in the cold embrace of the mountains. Overlooking the River Irthing as it poured out on to the plain, the castle commanded a magnificent view across sixty or seventy leagues of the undulating plains and rolling upland country of South Helietrim and northern Elerian. Across those brown lands, already bare of snow, all things could be seen. And there seemed indeed to be armies on the march.

'There must be ten thousand encamped there!' Yeon exclaimed, pointing to a mass of what must be tents and campfires alongside the River Irthing, perhaps a dozen leagues away and several thousand feet below.

'Surely not so many?' Telsyan objected. 'But my eyes are not so good as once they were. Can you make out the banners?'

Yeon shook his head, and then pointed suddenly away to the south. 'And there are more coming, look!'

The travellers followed his finger along the brown tracery of road that cut southward across the landscape. Upon it they could just make out hundreds of tiny dots, moving slowly towards the river. There were occasional sharp flashes of sunlight striking upon steel. As Leighor's eyes accustomed themselves to the distance, he began to make out more parties of soldiers and supplies approaching upon other roads: from south and east and west. His heart sank. 'If these be all enemies, then Arminor is truly in dire need.'

As they spoke, an armoured man rode down from the castle gates to give them challenge. 'What is your business here?' he demanded, staring coldly down at them from horseback. 'This is the king's demesne; and none are permitted to approach!'

'We seek audience of King Arminor,' Telsyan told him crisply.

'You?' He seemed amused. 'What do *you* desire of the king?'

'We bear messages of importance from the Sielders, from the Northlands, and also from Ariscel, the king's Seer, who has had to remain in Darkrigg to defend Norndale against onslaught by Rievers. They have few men and are in urgent need of aid.'

'Indeed?' the rider sniffed. 'Then they shall get little enough from us.' He nodded towards the south. 'As you can see, we have graver concerns of our own!'

Yet the name of Ariscel seemed to give him pause, and he nodded to the travellers to follow, turning reluctantly to canter back up to the castle gates.

Even so, it took a long wait and many persuasive entreaties before they were at last led up to the royal apartments, which overlooked the warmer, flatter lands to the south. Here on the slopes of Mount Nektor, however, winter still ruled, and a thick mantle of snow adorned the battlements and high balconies; croaking black ravens shivered as they clung to the outer walls.

The king's great chamber held few others beside themselves. A herald and two silent guardsmen waited close to the doorway, while three whispering courtiers stood in a huddled semicircle beneath the king's high seat.

Arminor himself was a large, strong-built man, partly run to fat; stern faced and dark eyed, with a full beard and dark, close-cropped hair which bore no hint of grey – although Leighor guessed the king must fast be approaching his sixtieth year.

Arminor acknowledged their obeisance curtly, seeming more preoccupied with a large map that lay across his knees.

'Well?' he demanded. 'What is this important message you bear from Ariscel? If he has found new troubles in the north, I can do nothing to help him. What passes here in the south must now be our first concern. When this business is done, then may we have the time and the resource to send good fighting men up into the north. Then, but not before. You may return with that message for Master Ariscel if you will. For now he must shift for himself. It will make a change.' He turned back to the map he had been studying. 'If that is all . . .'

'Nay, sire,' Telsyan took a step forward. 'That is not all. If you will permit, we have messages . . .' he produced Ariscel's letter and Uhlendof gave up the precious silver casket from Darien, 'and also the testament of Archbaron Eridar, Lord of the Sielders . . .'

'Eridar's testament?' Arminor showed new interest. 'I did not know such a thing existed. I had not even dared to hope.' He looked at Telsyan sharply. 'What is in it?'

'We do not know exactly, Sire,' the merchant passed letter and casket into the king's hands. 'But we have reason to believe that it may contain much of value and interest to your majesty.'

'Indeed.' Arminor examined the box closely, holding out his hand for a small knife with which to break the seals.

'These have not been tampered with?' he looked up sharply.

Telsyan shook his head, watching in silence as, with three brittle cracks, the seals parted; and the small box which they had journeyed so far and at such great cost to obtain flew open. Leighor craned his neck to see what lay within, glimpsing numerous small folded documents, all written in a tiny, cramped hand. Many bore official seals.

Arminor rifled through a few of them, his thick fingers unfolding them clumsily to read a few lines of each before passing on to the next – handing one or two on to a thin, grey-mantled man Leighor supposed must be his chief counsellor. After a few moments he set the box down and looked up at the travellers once more.

'You have done well to bring these things to me,' he said slowly. 'I have not time to study all these papers now, but there are items here that may prove useful indeed to our cause.' He snapped the casket shut once more. 'You have done well. Now, you look weary and in need of rest, Jorkath, my chamberlain,' he nodded to a portly official in dark robes who had appeared in the doorway, 'will attend to your needs. I may speak with you again of these things on the morrow.' He turned away, appearing to dismiss them.

Leighor was disappointed not to have been allowed a better look at the contents of the casket they had borne so far – so much so that he had all but forgotten the sword which had lain undrawn at his side these past ten days. Now, at last, he remembered.

'There is one thing more, sire,' he stepped forward.

'Yes' Arminor's voice bore a slight edge as he looked up again from his map.

'We have also brought a gift for you, from Ariscel: one that you were perhaps expecting. A sword.'

'A sword?' The king's eyebrows rose; and then the full import of what he was being proffered seemed to strike him. 'Ah! The *sword*. So he did not bring it himself. Where is it?'

Leighor stepped forward, kneeling to present it, his hands upon the hilt and the scabbard.

'Is this it?' Ariscel reached forward slowly, seemingly more than a little taken aback at the dull, plain grey of the hilt and the commonplace leather of the scabbard.

'It seems a poor thing,' the grey counsellor snorted. 'Much like the other. I fear that Master Ariscel wastes his time and your revenues upon these baubles.'

'Aye,' the king nodded. 'I fear, my lord Linede, that you may be right. Ariscel has promised much. At great cost in gold and in men I have supported him. And so far he has delivered little indeed for such sacrifice. A gauntlet that spits harmless flame, and now this oafish sword!' He turned irritably upon Leighor. 'What does this do? What wondrous properties does it posses, to repay its cost in gold and lives? Will it perhaps strike down my enemies in fire and thunder – as are reputed to do the dread amulets of the Curséd Ones? Or will it lend heart and courage to my armies, and make them eager for battle? . . . No? What then? Tell me: what is its purpose?'

Disconcerted by the sudden barrage directed at him, Leighor could only shake his head. 'I know not, Sire. Master Ariscel did not choose to share its secrets with us. He explains all in the letter.'

Linede snorted, his lip curling in contempt. 'I have no doubt it will be as useless as the other! It is no fit weapon for a king. Leave it for the Master at Arms to deal with.'

'No!' Leighor cried sharply, uncertain why he felt so strongly about the matter. 'I am sure this is a thing of greater worth than it appears. Ariscel, by his sorcery, saved us from certain defeat at the hands of the Rievers. He has placed similar trust in this weapon; which has been the focus of long labours over many months. At least take it as it was given. Read Ariscel's letter, and test it for yourself. It may not be as the amulets, yet it may still in some way prevail against them . . .'

'Indeed?' The idea seemed to appeal to Arminor, and he began to reach forward. Yet his fingers had not touched the hilt when the twin doors to the audience chamber burst suddenly open to admit a short, breathless figure in mud-stained travel clothes.

'Sire!' he strode hurriedly up to the royal presence and knelt. 'Urgent news! King Misan rides north to parley! He brings many great lords in his train, and will be here upon the morrow!'

'So!' Arminor rose at once, Leighor's sword for the moment forgotten. 'So Misan wishes now to parley? He brings his armies to my door, he lays waste my southern borderlands – and now he wishes welcome! The greatest coward, the greatest author of evils these poor lands have yet seen! What have I to say to such as he? If he wishes to parley, let him do it at the Diet in Tershelline – when the vote is decided!'

'It would be well if things were so simple, your majesty,' Linede said quickly. 'But you must remember that Misan has the right to demand audience. He is closest in blood to King Galdan, and until the election acts as regent in his stead. You must not defy him openly. He has the right to bring his soldiers where he will, and if he demands audience you must welcome him as your liege lord.'

'Never!' Arminor shook with fury. 'I shall not grovel to that bitch's whelp: that upstart, who lay still wet in his cradle when I was leading armies against the Riever tribes! If he wishes battle, then so be it! I shall not defer to him. I shall never bow before that craven coward!'

'I fear that this may be just the attitude he desires you to take, your majesty,' Uhlendof said quickly; 'that he may have excuse to settle the issue of the succession by force, whilst he possesses the advantage, and can call upon all the lords of the Varroain to take the field against you. That is no doubt why he brings so many of them with him now to witness your answer.'

Arminor shook his head. 'The lords will not unite against me. Most of them hate Misan far more than I, and will never follow him. And I fear not Misan's forces on their own. Yet I take your point, priest. Perhaps another tack is best. If Misan wishes to play games, then he shall learn that I too have games I can play. Games, mayhap, that shall not be much to his liking! Aye, let him come. Let them all come if they will: and we shall give them parley!

'We shall welcome them with all honour; with feasting and with songs. Then let Misan explain, before all assembled, why he brings his forces into the midst of my kingdom to threaten and make war upon his brother king! Come!' He strode from the hall. 'There is much to be made ready before the morrow. Much to be done! Tomorrow shall be a day long remembered in the annals of this land!'

In a moment he and his retinue had departed, gathering up the casket and its letters, but leaving Leighor's sword untouched. The southron attempted to call after them; but the messenger shook his head.

'Do not. He is distracted now. Let it wait upon a better time.'

Yeon watched the king depart, crestfallen. 'Is this the man who is to lead us?' he asked bitterly. 'The man who is to rouse the eastern lands against Misan and the power of the Amulet Lords? If so, then we have but small hope.'

'Aye,' Zindur nodded. 'He has told us nothing! Nothing of what lies within the casket. Nothing at all of this testament of Eridar's that we have borne south through so many dangers! We do not even know whether it does indeed hold the proxy of the Sielders!'

'I have little doubt that the proxy is there,' Telsyan said. 'I caught a glimpse of a document very much like it. And we can hardly expect Arminor to announce its presence here, in open court. Even so, I would dearly like to know whether that box holds anything that would help to clear our name and connect Lord Darvir with Eridar's murder. We shall have to speak with Arminor again. But I cannot deny that I too am a trifle disappointed in the man.'

'Few leaders are all that we expect of them,' Uhlendof said softly. 'Yet still we must follow and do our best to support and give counsel. Arminor may have his faults, but neither his deeds nor his purposes are those of evil; and he may yet save us from much worse.'

'Well spoken, stranger,' the messenger said suddenly, stepping forward. 'Arminor is an impatient man; quick to anger and slow to forget. Often he speaks in haste and has cause to regret his words later, but you will find no man of sounder heart or nobler purpose in all the Eleven Kingdoms.' He held out his hand. 'I am Paserian – although most call me simply Pace. One of the many who run errands for King Arminor when he has need of such services. I am pleased to meet you.'

The travellers introduced themselves, explaining a little of their mission south from Ariscel.

Pace nodded briskly. 'You had best keep the sword,' he said. 'Hold it close by you until the king receives it into his own hands. From what you have told me it sounds too valuable to leave in the hands of servants, and I do not think that we shall see the king again today.'

This proved true enough: and neither did he reappear the next morning; remaining closeted in his chambers until well past midday, and only emerging briefly then to direct the final arrangements in the great feasting hall before again retiring. All the while, the travellers were left very much to their own devices, with only Pace for company; and they had to content themselves with exploring the few open rooms of the castle, or staring down from the great south windows upon the armies assembling below. Yet even this activity was denied them at midday, when a rising mist enveloped the lowlands, cutting off all sight of the plains.

At the second hour of the afternoon all of this changed. Trumpets sounded suddenly from the upper parapets, their brazen notes echoing down through the cold stone to announce the arrival of King Misan at the outer gates. Immediately Pace hurried the travellers up to a dark minstrel gallery that overlooked the great hall, and from which they might have a clear view of all that passed beneath. They waited in silence.

Great yellow banners, bearing the black hammer and grey war-gryphon device of the kings of Helietrim, hung along the length of the hall, and an awning of cloth of gold was set in a great canopy above Arminor's throne. Motionless soldiers with gleaming halberds, attired in their elegant court liveries of yellow and crimson, lined the walls. And waiting before the throne stood Arminor's personal guard, their breastplates shining in the light of a hundred smoking torches. The king was certainly putting on a good show for his visitors.

Arminor himself entered moments later, accompanied by his heralds and his courtiers. Attired in ermine-trimmed robes of crimson and cloth of gold, he bore in his hand the jewelled sceptre of the kings of Helietrim, and upon his head an openwork crown set with diamonds. Taking his place beneath the canopy, two shieldbearers seated upon the steps beneath him, he awaited the arrival of King Misan.

A few minutes passed in almost surreal silence, with all below waiting motionless; like a fairground before the paying customers arrived.

And then, with a second flourish of trumpets, the great double doors at the hall's western end swung open to admit the Varroain lords, each preceded by his own personal standard. These entered one by one, to take their places in smaller canopied seats which had been set for that purpose around the edges of the hall. Watching from above, Leighor saw many arms and banners that he recognised, if few faces: the green and silver of Shulnharm, Margrave of Felldur; the brown bear of the kings of Holdar on its field of grey; the white and gold of the Knights of Imsild; and the sword and three dark peaks of distant Kalural and Zailim her king. He half expected to see the blue and gold of the Sielders, perhaps with Darvir in its train; but this was not to be. And, counting the varied banners, he reckoned that there were still perhaps more lords not present or represented here than those who were.

Last of all, to a salute of his own trumpeters and halberdiers, entered Misan. He was preceded by two banners; that of Petan – a black stallion upon a field of white – and the great purple banner of the High Kings of the Varroain with its white emblem of a hollow crown supported by eleven flaming swords.

Misan himself came as somewhat of a surprise. Leighor was not sure exactly what he had expected the High Regent to look like, but it was not this. For the man who temporarily occupied the throne of the High Kings of the Varroain was tall and fair, lean and finely built. He was indeed quite young: no more than forty. His face was pallid and clean-shaven, and might have looked handsome, were it not for the sharp, colourless eyes which flickered constantly from left to right like those of a hunter, taking in everything about them.

There was something dark and unsettling in those eyes, something that betrayed that their owner might halt at nothing to achieve whatever end happened to please him at any particular moment. Leighor had seen such eyes but once before – upon a madman held in chains in the airless cellars beneath the Hospitarion at Syrne – and even the distant memory sent a chill along his spine. Yet if Misan were insane, it was in no way obvious to those about him. In fact he held great presence for one so new to his title, the other nobles deferring to him naturally as he stood amongst them. Supremely confident in his shimmering robes of black – overlaid by the deep purple cloak of the High Kings of the Varroain – he bore no sign of rank upon his brow, but strode bare-headed into the chamber.

Arminor rose majestically from his throne. 'My noble lords, I bid you all welcome to this, my own small castle of Irun's Teeth. Here you are my honoured guests, and all I have is yours to command.'

'Greetings, Brother Arminor,' Misan replied, his voice sharp and strong, yet barely concealing a cutting edge of scorn. 'I am pleased to find that you welcome us so; for I had been given cause to fear otherwise . . .' He paused. 'Yet still do you seem to neglect the rightful honour and deference due to your overlord.'

'You are not High King yet, Misan,' Arminor growled. 'You only act the role until the electors decide – remember that.'

Leighor was pleased to note that there were many surreptitious nods of agreement from among the assembled nobles. But Uhlendof was less happy.

'Already he is letting the young one anger him,' he whispered. 'I like not the way this is going. Misan is too clever, by all accounts, to play at words to no purpose.'

'I may not yet be chosen,' Misan's voice remained soft, yet it carried to the far ends of the hall: 'yet for a while I am permitted these honours by right of kinship and stewardship. And therefore it is not my honour you demean by refusing obeisance, but the honour of the Varroain High Kingship itself!'

Arminor's face twitched nervously at the rebuke, and for a tense eternity he remained silent.

'Speak not to me of dishonour!' he exploded at last. 'or if you do, speak not of my dishonour, but your own! Why – I ask you openly before all assembled – why do you raise up vast armies against me, and bring them north to make war upon your brother king? Why do you come here to ravage and despoil my lands, and drive forth my people from their homes? Why – unless it be to gain by threats and bloodstrife that great prize which you know you cannot win in open conclave? You have gathered many noble lords here together to witness this meeting. Come now, tell us all: upon what grounds do you dare perpetrate such evils?'

Misan did not answer at once, but nodded slowly; as if seeking only to deepen the dense veil of silence that now hung over the great chamber. 'You ask me, my lord, why I have had need to act in such a wise? Yet surely these actions can come as no surprise to you? For have I not three times in as many months sent urgent messages north commanding you to appear at once before me in High Tershelline to answer certain grave charges? And each time has not my messenger been driven from your lands with violent words and sharp abuse?'

'Even if it were so,' Arminor answered. 'That were still no fit cause for such outrages as these. You have no right yet to command any to your will. Not unless the peril to these lands be grave, and the dangers pressing great. We are due in a month to meet at the Diet. That shall be soon enough for us to suffer your complaints and your vanities!'

'Nay!' Misan broke in angrily. 'Not soon enough! Not soon enough for the cause of justice. Not soon enough to answer the charges that I must bring against you! Aye! For the peril to these lands is indeed grave, and the dangers pressing. And it is you alone who are the cause – you, and your treasons!'

'Treasons?' Arminor laughed out loud. 'Treasons? What nonsense is this? Cease, lest you make this assembly a mummer-show for fools! Such accusations as these are unworthy even of you: the last vain throw of a wastrel, desperate to cling to the remnants of an imagined power! These charges are empty, and I defy them! Come! Before all present. Bring forth your proofs of these grave treasons. Bring forth your evidence – if there be any!'

Misan sniffed. 'There is evidence enough of these charges, you may have no fear. Sworn depositions made freely by your own servants, and held by me in Tershelline: plans, letters, and many other all too solid proofs of your foul treachery!' He strode forward. 'Would you hear the charges? They are numbered as follows: One, of making alliance with Rievers; of giving them safe haven in your kingdom in return for their aid in making war upon brother kings. Two, of joining with them in foul murder and the waylaying of travellers; of pillage and of theft. Third and last, of conspiring with them and sundry others to seize by force the crown of the High Kingdom itself! That, my lord, is why I am come with all these noble princes: to command you to return at once with us to Tershelline, and answer these accusations!'

Gasps of horror rose up from all corners of the chamber; and even Arminor stood temporarily dumbfounded.

'This is madness!' he said at last. 'Sheer madness! Are these truly the depths to which you now must sink in order to preserve your precious crown? I deny all your charges! They are trumped up nonsense! I swear now, before all assembled, that there is no grain of truth in them! Yet I would be fool indeed to subject myself to your judgement. To throw my fate into the hands of the one man with the most to gain from my ruin; simply because he has found a few rogues to set their hand to some pack of lies!'

'Nay, my lord,' Misan shook his head gravely. 'This is none of my doing, and it shall not be my judgement. Any trial of these matters will be before a jury of the noblest lords, freely chosen. You need have no fear of this, if you be truly innocent. Yet,' he turned suddenly to one side, that he might see also the faces of the watching nobles, 'yet there is one thing I must ask of you now, my lord: why is it that you permit Rievers and Tarintarmen to dwell unchallenged in the dales of northern Helietrim which are your ward? In Wastarldale, Forredale,

Morrimdale and so many others – that they may make war freely against the Varroain dominions! Why so, my lord? And why have these things been kept secret from all who should rightfully have knowledge of them, unless you yourself are in alliance with these bloody hordes?'

There fell a shocked hush upon the hall; and Leighor saw many, even of those lords who had previously seemed to take Arminor's part, looking upon him now with suspicion and horror.

Arminor too was visibly shaken. Clearly appalled that the news of his losses had emerged in this manner, for a moment he knew not what to say. 'I have no alliance with Rievers!' he mumbled at last. But his voice was a good deal less firm and self-assured than it had been. Horribly, it sounded that of an unmasked traitor – one who now tried desperately to save himself. 'We have suffered reverses recently. Great reverses – that is true enough. But our forces are small.'

'You seem to have many good men here,' Misan glanced around him at the lines of pikemen standing to attention about the hall, 'with few battle scars. And many thousands more assembled before Clanamel, by all reports. Perhaps these would be better used fighting Rievers in the north than kept here to threaten your brother nobles!'

There was a deep grunt of agreement from around the hall, and Uhlendof whispered, 'It goes badly.'

Yet suddenly Misan's manner seemed to alter; his voice softening, becoming subtle and persuasive. 'But truly I am not a vengeful man, and it grieves me to to be forced to treat with a brother monarch so. Mayhap, as you say, these accusations are false. And my noble lords, I am sure, wish also to give you every opportunity to answer these grievous charges. If your cause is just, then surely you cannot fear to set it before a jury of your peers? One made up of the very electors you claim are thronging to support you?

'Again I urge you, accept the judgement of these and other noble lords. It need not be termed a court, if you dislike that title. Let it be called a Concourse, a Great Assembly; anything you wish. All I beg is that you let these poisonous matters be tried openly, and quickly dispensed with.'

Leighor was surprised. After first attacking Arminor, apparently in order to destroy him before his fellow nobles, Misan now seemed to be doing his best to smooth Arminor's way to a face-saving compromise. There must be some trickery here, but he could not for the life of him think to what end.

'I do not ask you to accept now,' Misan continued smoothly. 'Take time to consult with your counsellors; to think it over. Then we shall speak again, alone; and see if some compromise cannot be reached. Can you not agree to that at least?'

Arminor, too, seemed nonplussed by this sudden change of tack; nervous of accepting the proffered compromise but unable to find any good reason for rejecting it. Eventually he nodded.

'Aye,' he grunted. 'I shall think further on the matter.'

'Good.' Misan smiled and turned back to the assembled nobles. 'You see, my friends, how easily the greatest differences may be resolved, if only we learn to compromise.'

Slowly now the assembly began to break up, and within minutes the hall was almost empty.

'Well, Misan certainly had to change his tack,' Yeon grinned, as the travellers too prepared to leave.

Telsyan shook his head. 'This I think has been as bad a day for Arminor as there has ever been these five and thirty years. He has lost much support this day, even among his friends; and I fear that Misan has forced him into some kind of trap, though I know not what.'

'But how did Misan learn of the occupation of the northern dales?' Leighor asked. 'He cannot have learnt it from Arminor!'

'There are many sources of information in a castle such as this,' Pace whispered. 'And Misan has spies everywhere. Arminor was foolish indeed to think he could keep such a secret for long – and now it has been revealed in the worst possible manner.'

'Aye,' Uhlendof nodded. 'Either way now, it goes badly for Arminor; for he must seem either traitor, or else a weakling who cannot hold his own lands secure, and tries to hide his failings.'

'But Misan can have no proof that Arminor is traitor,' Telsyan objected. 'None that will stand an hour's inspection, at least! By all the gods, we know he has no alliance with Rievers – as do all who overwintered in Norndale this year!'

Leighor frowned. 'Then why does Misan so insist upon an open trial? He cannot hold all the princes in his power, or he would have the election won already.'

'I am not sure,' Uhlendof answered. 'It would seem at first glance that Arminor has little to lose by accepting the judgement of the Diet. And if he refuses, Misan may then rightfully call upon all the princes of the Varroain to join in war against him. But then again, a treason charge is no light matter; and once Arminor has placed himself into Misan's hands, who knows what may happen?' He turned away. 'I would not like this choice to be mine . . .'

For the rest of the day the travellers were virtually prisoners in their cramped quarters low down in the belly of the castle, waiting while Arminor consulted in private with his supporters. What advice or promises of support he now received, none of them knew. It seemed that Arminor had few confidants, even amongst his own nobles, and little news leaked down to the lower tiers of the palace establishment of whatever transpired above. For everyone it was a time of imaginings and wild rumours, as nerves tautened and tempers flared. Several times, Telsyan attempted to find out what was happening. But however hard he pressed, he could get no farther than the stern-faced guards who stood watch upon all the corridors that led to the king's private quarters. The fate of all who dwelt within this castle; of Clanamel; of Helietrim, and perhaps of all the Varroain Realms; was being decided in small closeted meetings; and none of them could do anything at all to alter or influence the outcome.

'I would feel a deal more secure if Ariscel were here to advise the king,' Uhlendof said, surprisingly, as they sat together in one of the lower kitchens. 'I fear that Arminor may make a rash decision left to himself, and I see none of any merit here to advise him.'

It was then that Leighor had decided that he must speak with Arminor again at all costs. He had been entrusted with the grey sword, upon which Ariscel set so much store – and yet it still hung uselessly at his side in its battered leather scabbard. The sword had some great purpose, he knew; and it was his duty to see that it, and the letter Ariscel had included with it, did not lie forgotten at this time of crisis.

Using the confusion of the evening meal to cover his movements, he managed eventually to evade enough of the guards to get within striking distance of the royal apartments. To Leighor's surprise there was no guard upon the outer doors: which must mean that Arminor dined elsewhere – perhaps in one of the lesser halls with his nobles, or with Misan in the spacious apartments assigned to him. Yet this perhaps was to his advantage. For he could now gain entry to the king's apartments without need for the troublesome excuses and explanations that would otherwise have been required.

Checking cautiously to see that he was unobserved, he made for the doors and slipped into the darkened chamber beyond. The room seemed larger and more threatening now in its robes of darkness. And almost immediately there came the heavy tramp of soldiers' feet approaching from the corridor beyond.

At once the folly of his present course of action struck home. Were he to be discovered here, lurking in the darkness, he would almost certainly be taken for a spy – or even an assassin! He must hide himself quickly. Watch . . . see who this was . . . and await a more fortuitous moment to announce himself.

He had barely time to conceal himself behind a nearby alcove curtain, before the chamber doors flew open, and four liveried guardsmen marched into the room. Through the narrow gap in the curtain he could see only a small part of the room, but that was enough to tell that these men did not wear Arminor's uniform. Nor were their accents the normal warm burr of the Helietrim folk, but a more lilting westron twang.

Two others were with them, shadowy figures: one tall and fair, his voice only too familiar as he gave the soldiers orders to withdraw: Misan. The High Regent himself! The second was far shorter of stature, and hunched over a thin staff; a small, scuttling creature with lank hair and mud-streaked, silver-buckled shoes . . .

Leighor blinked, at first refusing to believe the evidence of his own eyes. Surely it could not be? It was impossible . . . They had left Inanys behind them, a thousand leagues to the north – outside Darien! Yet here he stood, as large as life, in the middle of the darkened audience chamber, alongside the High Regent of the Varroain. Inanys. It could be none other!

'Indeed, my lord,' the crookback's voice cut sibilantly across the chamber. 'I have done precisely as you commanded. Have I not always?'

'Aye, that: and much else besides!' Misan turned away. 'I warn you, Malencreyon; if you play some secret game of your own, or seek in any way now to betray me, you shall never make such a mistake again. Do you understand me?'

'As ever, noble lord,' Inanys bowed low. 'What could be clearer? But you treat me too harshly, master. Have I not journeyed half a thousand leagues into the cruel northron wastes at your command? Have I not struggled to this place by horse and on foot through winter mountains and bitter cold, facing wild beasts, Rievers and even worse? Would good Malencreyon do all these things to bring you such news as I now bear, were he not your most true and faithful servant?'

'Nay, crooked one,' Misan said coldly. 'I know you too well – well enough to see when you have something to hide. Perhaps you have never truly served me. Perhaps you would never even have returned unless you desired something of me. What is it?'

'Nay, master,' Inanys said swiftly. 'I have always been your servant. Listen. Here is proof . . .'

More whispered words now passed between them; but these, frustratingly, Leighor could not hear; and seconds later the crookback scurried from the room, leaving Misan to wait alone. It was several silent minutes before a door at the far end of the chamber at last creaked open to admit a second shadowed figure.

'Arminor!' Misan's voice rose sharply in greeting; but he did not move towards the king, nor did he hold out his hand.

'I am sorry I have been delayed,' Arminor grunted as he came fully into Leighor's field of vision. 'I hope that you have not—'

'Cease!' Misan cut through his apologies curtly. 'My time is precious, and I have none to waste upon such asinine prattle! Still less to spend cooling my heels in an empty chamber! If you have aught to say to me, then say it now; before even that little be gone.' His words were no longer smooth and persuasive as they had been in the open assembly. Now the scorn and contempt in them was open and unveiled; as if he spoke not to a fellow king but to a menial.

'Take not that tone with me!' Arminor bridled at once.

'I come here not to bandy words with you,' Misan's cold voice cut through the king's rising anger like a knife. 'You have had your time to think, and to consult with your accomplices. Now I await only your answer! Will you at once surrender yourself to me and come peaceably as my prisoner to Tershelline, or no?'

'Prisoner?' Arminor's voice deepened in outrage. 'You spoke not of prisoners before open assembly . . .'

'What do you think I spoke of?' Misan said with scorn. 'Do not pretend you were fool enough to have imagined otherwise.'

'Fool?' Arminor repeated. 'Aye, that is what I have been all along. Fool to have trusted your word; fool ever to have listened to your foul, serpent's tongue! The choice you offer is no choice at all! Either to go with you as prisoner to Tershelline, where your poisoners and assassins may do their work at their leisure; or else, what? War? is that what you truly desire?'

'You have the choice,' Misan said curtly. 'And now you must make it: the time grows short!'

'Then you know my answer. If there must be war, then so be it.'

'Aye,' Misan nodded. 'Ever have I known what answer you would give . . .' He turned sharply away, his purple cloak billowing out behind him in the fading light. 'I shall give the princes your answer, Arminor. I have bade them make ready to ride the moment I had it from you. So prepare yourself, Arminor, King of Helietrim, either to ride forth to give battle upon the Lee of Clanamel, or else to be proclaimed forever coward and traitor! Come out on to the plain, or hide yourself away in your deepest and most secret redoubt, as you will. Either way, the end will be the same!'

The twin doors swung open before him, and he was gone.

For a long time Arminor waited in the darkening chamber, and then with a sigh he seemed at last to come to some deep decision within himself, and strode purposefully from the hall.

Leighor remained where he was for several minutes more, wondering at all that he had seen and heard. And it was only when he had finally gathered the resolve to leave his hiding place that he remembered the dull grey sword that still hung, forgotten, at his side.

Chapter Thirty One
THE LEE OF CLANAMEL

Again Inanys had disappeared. As Leighor made his way back through the palace, he half expected to find him skulking in some dark corner nearby, or waiting for him in one of the long, gloomy passages. But of the crookback there was now no sign; and he told his story to the others in silence.

'So it is to be war,' Uhlendof sighed. 'Misan has worked his plans well; and for all our striving we have failed to deflect him from his course by so much as an iota. It is clear that he never intended a trial. This whole assembly has been but a charade to rally the princes behind him.'

'Some have remained,' Pace said softly. 'A few who have long taken Arminor's part, and will not desert him now. But I feel far fewer than he had hoped. Misan now has the power to destroy us: and even if we are not immediately defeated, I cannot see how we can not stop him becoming High King – and that was our main purpose.'

'Mayhap the lords will quickly tire of Misan's rule,' Yeon suggested, 'and turn against him.'

Uhlendof shook his head. 'Things may have come too far even for that. Once the lords who oppose Misan have been divided, they may be picked off one by one at his leisure. Of all Misan's enemies, Arminor is the strongest. If he falls, the others will have no core of strength to stand against him.'

'Then Arminor must not fall!' Telsyan slammed his fist hard against the table. 'We must go at once to the king and force him to hear us! We must make him take heed of Ariscel's warnings! Even if we be now at war with Misan; that does not mean that we have to meet him on his own terms! Now, at least, the king must see reason!'

But Pace shook his head. 'It is too late even for that. Arminor has already departed, and taken his chief counsellors and supporters back with him to the Neck of Clanamel, where he musters his armies.'

'Can we not follow him?'

'No, my lords. There are no more horses to be had. And besides, the king has given strict orders that you are to remain here with the sword until his return. He will speak with you then.'

Telsyan swore. Yet somehow Leighor was unsurprised. Events had been running fast out of their control ever since they had arrived at Irun's Teeth, and seemed to be heading remorselessly towards disaster. How it would come he knew not, but all his hopes of a successful ending to their enterprise had flown with the fateful departure of Misan this evening.

'And what of this tale of yours of the crookback?' Telsyan broke irritably into his thoughts. 'Are you sure it was Inanys you saw with King Misan?'

'As sure as that I see you now,' Leighor insisted. 'It was Inanys and none other.'

'Then it is true he is a spy!' Zindur snarled. 'I always thought as much. We were fools to let him journey even a single day with us!'

'Aye,' Telsyan nodded grimly. 'This news would explain much that happened on our travels. I always thought the crookback a black-hearted rogue, but never that he was Misan's creature! He must have been seeking Eridar's testament from the start. That was why he followed us. Thank the Gods we got it here in safety!'

'But he still knows enough to betray us,' Leighor said. 'He knows our names and our faces. He knows that we have gained Eridar's testament, if not yet what lies inside it. He has learnt of the Hillmen and the Stormgiants, and of many other secret enemies of Misan. Even without the testament, his treachery could destroy us all.'

'But how did Inanys know to follow us in the first place?' Uhlendof asked slowly. 'And how did he find us so soon after we left Ravenshald? Even Misan couldn't have learnt of Eridar's death in time to have sent him after us . . .'

'That is of no matter now!' Telsyan said sharply. 'The main facts stand, and we seem powerless to do anything about them.'

No one responded, and the travellers dispersed, each of them alone with his own gloomy thoughts.

Leighor toyed idly with the yellowing *Rudäis* pieces which had lain so long disused at the bottom of his pack, even attempting a reading; but the omens were uncertain and pessimistic, so he desisted, rejoining the others as they prepared to retire for the night.

The following day dawned clear and bright, and the travellers were cheered to see the sun once again shining upon the coiling river below and the distant Yimbrien hills far to the south. Birds sand merrily in the light south-eastern breeze, and even the snows upon the high balconies were slowly beginning to melt.

'What date is this?' Keran asked. 'For it seems to me that spring is come early this year.'

Uhlendof smiled. 'It is the thirteenth, the thirteenth day of *Ilter*, and none too early for spring to be showing his face in these parts. You have lived too long in the cold northlands, my girl, to know what a good spring is really like. Perhaps this year you shall see a real southland summer; and then you shall wonder where the sun has been hiding all these years!'

Leighor too smiled; yet if he could have then imagined what the summer of 785 held in store for all who now stood laughing in this warm, chamber, he might have wished that winter would endure for ever.

Their laughter was cut quickly short by a sharp cry from Yeon, who had gone to stand out upon the balcony. 'Here; look! There are men moving below!'

At once the travellers sped to the balcony to see for themselves. And sure enough, men were moving northward in long columns from camps along the river, and spreading out across the plain to form a long, armoured line between the waters of the Irthing and the steep base of the escarpment far below. Misan's army was on the move.

'Can they come up this way?' Telsyan asked urgently.

'No.' Pace shook his head. 'There are deep ravines below, loose rock and sharp scree. Not even a mountain goat could climb up into these peaks from the south. The only route lies through the Irthing gorge and the Neck of Clanamel.'

'Then what does Misan hope to achieve?' Uhlendof asked.

'He offers battle to Arminor,' Pace replied. 'Yet he must know that the king would be fool to ride out and do open battle upon the plain when he can hold out for many months in the shelter of the Neck of Clanamel. It must be that he intends only to close the way south. To show us that we are his prisoners here, confined within these mountains as his pleasure.'

Leighor stared down once more on to the open plain, wishing that he possessed some device to see the soldiers more clearly. They were much nearer now, having moved closer to the base of the mountains under cover of the previous day's fog. But they were still nearly a league away, and many thousand feet below.

Apart from the distance, however, the travellers had a perfect view of all that passed on the sweeping plain beneath, finding it unnerving, and at the same time strangely fascinating, to see the enemy so close at hand, and in such number. Leighor guessed that there must be at least twenty thousand troops assembling below; mounted and on foot. The banners of Elerian and Kalural, Holdar and Petan, Felldur and Coimbra, fluttered above long columns of soldiers in the clear morning air. And there were smaller, token companies from the farther provinces: from Selethir, Silgany and even the Sielders; along with the levies of many lesser lords, who led companies into battle beneath their own standards. Holdar and Kalural had provided archers by the hundred, while great ragged detachments of westron horsemen thundered across the open fields beneath the banner of Misan's own kingdom of Petan. Three glittering cohorts of the Knights of Imsild slowly took up positions to the east of the main line, beneath their pristine banners of white and gold.

'Look how many they are.' Pace shook his head. 'Three, at least, of those great lords below were firmly of Arminor's camp before yesterday's charade! Zailim of Kalural is one, Pirazzu of Coimbra, another. And there are many lords now under Misan's banner who formerly wavered. The High Regent's stratagems have gained him much!'

'Misan puts on a good show, sure enough,' Zindur snorted. 'But such an army is no use in a long siege. They are mostly peasants and levies, who will want to get back to their own farms for the planting. It will be breaking up within a month.'

'The Knights of Imsild are no farmers!' Yeon's voice shook with dismay at what he saw. 'Yet they should not be here at all! They are forbidden to take sides in the conflicts of the kings! It is against their oaths: against all honour!'

'Honour is a thing that is dying in this world I fear,' Telsyan grunted. 'And it dies fastest amongst those in whose charge it chiefly lies.'

Many faces began now to appear at windows and balconies across the southern rim of the castle, and within minutes it seemed that not a man or woman of all the household was at his post, but stood staring down upon the mighty host assembling below. Leighor wondered what the defences at the entrance to the Irthing gorge must be like, and how stout were the defenders. Perhaps Arminor stood there now, looking out at this same vast assemblage that arrayed itself upon the brown fields of the Lee of Clanamel. But this he had no way of telling, for high hills rose up to the east to block any view of the Irthing gorge at the point where the river flowed out on to the plain; and he had to content himself with imaginings.

The thin wail of battle-horns drifted up to them from the fields far below; and he could see that the whole line was now assembled and waiting in battle order, weapons glinting in the sun.

A party of mounted figures began to move slowly forward from the centre of the long line – which now stretched in a great curve from the banks of the Irthing to the near hills. And before these was borne the great purple banner of the High Kings of the Varroain.

'Misan!' Zindur hissed. 'What does he intend?'

And then there came a great sigh – or was it a groan? – from all who watched from the walls of Irun's Teeth, as another mounted party, preceded by many yellow banners, rode out of the shadow of the hills to face the first.

'Arminor!' Pace was appalled. 'What madness is this?'

'He may intend to fight,' Telsyan said. 'Misan challenged him openly to do battle upon the Lee of Clanamel or be forever labelled traitor and coward.'

'Surely Arminor would never fall for such a trick?' Zindur frowned. 'The challenge was but a ploy to provoke the king into some rash folly. He must know that our only hope is to remain within the shelter of the mountains until Misan's army starts to break up.'

Keran looked down upon the unfolding scene. 'Then why does he ride out now?'

'Perhaps only to parley once more,' Leighor suggested. 'He cannot mean to do battle . . .'

'Oh, but he does, my friends.' The voice of Linede, Arminor's chief counsellor, came as a shock to them all; and they spun about, startled, to face him.

'I thought you with the king!' Pace said quickly.

'I was, until this morning,' the other replied softly. There were five of Arminor's armed guards with him. 'The king has sent me to you to bear him the sword, Ariscel's sword . . .'

'He intends to do battle?' Telsyan gasped disbelievingly. 'To take the open field against such a force? But that is pure madness!'

'Perhaps not,' Linede answered. 'If we strike firm and fast, to drive their ranks asunder, a great victory may yet be won. Most of Misan's men are low-born levies, with no real interest in this fight; they will break soon enough. And many of those lords who now stand in line with Misan still support Arminor in their hearts, and will be loath to commit their forces against him.'

'But we cannot count on that!' Uhlendof broke in angrily. 'There is no need for anyone to take the field, when we have only to wait in safety behind our defences until Misan's army breaks up or deserts him.'

'To Arminor this is a matter of honour,' Linede smiled thinly. 'His honour has been impugned, he has been challenged to open combat; and he will fight.'

'You are his counsellor!' Uhlendof's voice cut sharply through the other's words. 'Counsel him! You must stop this!'

Linede shrugged. 'Perhaps it is better that we fight now, when we are strong and well-provisioned; than later, when hunger and dissension have done their work among us, and morale is low. Besides, as you can see, it is too late. The die is cast!'

'Then why do you desire the sword?' Zindur asked sharply. 'How can it now reach the king in time to alter matters?'

'Aye,' Pace nodded. 'By the fastest steed it is a four-hour ride to where the king lies! One must go back through the mountains to the River Irthing, and follow its gorge out through the Neck of Clanamel. There is no shorter way . . .'

'I do not question the king's commands!' Linede snapped brusquely. 'I obey them. Perhaps if I ride now, I may yet reach the king in time to aid him. I have already lingered here far too long!' He glanced behind him at the five waiting guardsmen, and then, turning back to the travellers, held out his hand for the sword. 'Give it to me quickly, and I shall ride!'

Leighor hesitated, not knowing quite why. This sudden change of attitude on Linede's part regarding the sword and its value seemed not the only suspicious thing about the High Counsellor's sudden appearance here, on the eve of an unnecessary battle: and he searched for some reason for delay.

'Good Master Ariscel bade me deliver this only into the king's hands,' he said at last, keeping a firm hold upon the sheathed blade at his side. 'I am sworn to that. Therefore if the blade is to go now to the king, I must accompany it.'

Linede shook his head. 'That is not possible. The king has ordered that you remain here until he returns; and that command must be obeyed. Give me the sword. I am the king's High Counsellor and act in his name. You will not be forsworn by giving the sword to me.' He advanced a step. 'I am Arminor's right hand: his hands are mine and mine his . . .'

'No!' Leighor took a hurried step back towards the balcony. 'I trust you not! The sword will never reach Arminor in your hands! Either I go with you – we all go with you – or not at all!'

Linede said nothing, but turned sharply to the soldiers behind him. He nodded. And at once all drew their swords to step forward and flank the grey-cloaked counsellor.

'Do not be foolish,' he glowered; 'or you may be given cause to regret your stubbornness.' He made a beckoning motion to Leighor with his left hand. 'The sword!'

'Nay,' said Zindur. 'I like this not!' And drawing his own great broadsword, he took a step forward to stand beside Leighor. 'The sword we shall take to the king ourselves, and *you* may remain behind.'

Immediately Telsyan, Yeon and Pace drew their weapons to stand alongside him, leaving only Keran and Uhlendof, weaponless, behind them.

'So this is the way of it?' Linede scowled. He took a quick step backward to stand behind the five guardsmen, and hissed, 'Take them!'

Yet the guards seemed at first hesitant to engage the four armed strangers and the bearer of the king's sword. And all appeared relieved, therefore, when Linede abruptly countermanded his order. 'No. Stand back! We want no alarm raised. There is a better way . . .'

Not removing his eyes from Leighor's face, the High Counsellor raised one hand to the jewelled gold brooch that pinned together the folds of his cloak. His fingers touched it. And the brooch seemed suddenly to shimmer, its colour slowly deepening and darkening; as if something bled upward from within the gold . . .

At once Leighor realised: the brooch was no brooch at all, but a gilded sham through which the inner core of *harrunor* now burned! And once that core was exposed, they would all most surely die! Linede was an Amulet Wielder, an agent of Misan – or else of the dark Mage Lords themselves – and that was why he so desired the sword!

The sword. Yes! Here at his side he bore thirty times more *harrunor* than lay in that tiny amulet. And what had Ariscel told them? In the time of greatest danger: only then to draw it forth . . .

His companions too had realised what was happening, and now threw themselves forward in a desperate attempt to halt the searing burst of Magefire that must surely follow. Yet even as they began to move, Leighor knew that they were too late.

Following the Seer's instructions now without conscious thought, he drew the long straight sword from its sheath, hardly daring to look at it as he held it out before him: pointed directly towards Linede and the pulsing amulet. And in that selfsame instant, Linede's brooch-amulet seemed suddenly to explode, erupting into a ball of cancerous purple flame that roared irresistibly towards him. It was too late.

At once all about him was engulfed in fire, his every sense overwhelmed in a holocaust of noise and searing flame. And for an instant he thought he was dying – or had already crossed that dread boundary without his conscious mind having absorbed the fact.

Yet he felt no pain; none of the feelings of dissolution of the body that he had imagined must precede oblivion. He could see nothing, but he could still feel the sword in his hand, somehow warm and comforting to the touch. And as his senses slowly cleared, he began to hear dry, choking coughs and the rising struggle of entangled limbs from the ground all around him – discovering to his surprise that he was the only person left standing in the whole of the chamber.

The sword before him glowed flaming white; as he had seen it but once before, in Ariscel's dark forge-room beneath the hills of Norndale. Startled, he dropped it at once from his hand – as if it had truly burned him – watching dumbstruck as it fell to the floor and its light slowly faded.

'Be careful with that sword, friend Leighor,' Uhlendof was on his feet behind him, brushing a thin coating of white dust from his habit. 'For it has just saved all our lives.'

'How so?' Leighor asked, perplexed, as he watched the rest of his companions struggle back to their feet behind him.

'In some way the sword turned Linede's flame,' Telsyan was the first to recover himself enough to answer Leighor's question; 'and sent it back upon itself to consume its own master.'

And sure enough, Linede lay quite still in the middle of the chamber, his eyes staring sightlessly up at the vaulted ceiling, an expression of mild astonishment upon his face. Yet where the amulet had once lain upon his chest, there was now only a blackened circle of ashes, perhaps a hand's breadth wide – but that circle ran deep, burning right through his clothing and the scorched skin, to reveal the blackened bones beneath.

The five guardsmen, who had been standing on either side of the High Counsellor when the blast had come, were now also beginning to recover. But not quickly enough to prevent themselves from being seized and bound by the travellers before they could offer any further resistance.

Leighor bent to retrieve the sword, even as Uhlendof turned to kneel beside the body of the former High Counsellor, running his fingers through the remnants of his clothing until at last he found a small packet of papers and a seal. The others gathered around him as he rose to study them.

'It is as I thought,' he nodded after a moment or so. 'Here lies the proxy vote of the Sielders; which is to go first to Arminor and second to any remaining candidate of his house. But there is nothing else of the testament here. The rest is probably already destroyed. Linede must have intended to take only this and the sword with him to Misan.'

'It seems that Arminor is surrounded by traitors,' Pace sighed, looking down at the five bound and gagged guardsmen on the floor.

'It seems so indeed,' Uhlendof nodded, turning to the seal which hung from his hand by its long ribbon. 'This, I fear, is Arminor's great seal. What mischief Linede might have made with this, I dread to imagine . . .'

'But what shall we do now?' Leighor asked. 'The noise will surely bring a dozen more guards upon us!'

'I think not,' Uhlendof said. 'The noise was not so great as you perhaps imagined. From where I stood there was but a brief roar, alike to distant thunder. I doubt if any beyond these chambers will have given it heed – and that is no bad thing, for now we know not who we may trust.'

'At least we may trust the king!' Telsyan said quickly. 'We must ride to him at once!' He turned to Pace. 'How may we get hold of some fast horses?'

'I fear it is too late for that . . .' Keran's voice came thinly from the balcony beyond, but there was a compelling edge to it that made the travellers turn.

'What is it?' Yeon asked, fear rising in his voice.

She pointed out towards the plain. 'The battle – it has begun.'

Only then did Leighor notice the dreadful silence that had fallen upon the castle walls, and the distant cries that rose and faded with the swirling breezes from below. He rushed to the window, reaching the balcony only seconds before the others, to look down aghast on to the plain beneath.

Much had changed since they had been surprised by Linede, perhaps only a half-hour before. Of the two parties of parleyers there was now no sign, and only two long lines of soldiers now faced each other across the empty fields.

No one spoke, for the situation, was clear enough. If there had been a parley, it was over, and both armies stood ready for battle. Yet Arminor's forces seemed small indeed compared to the host they now faced; less than half the number that stood against them. Barely ten thousand, Leighor guessed, and although they looked proud and fine indeed behind their bright banners, there were probably at least as many untrained levies among them as in Misan's far greater host. He had heard many songs and stories of small forces which had defeated greater ones, twice and even three times their number. But here, set out on the open plain before them, the odds seemed truly overwhelming; and the songs and stories to dwindle into mere boastings and romance-filled legends.

A few of the outlander lords still rode with Arminor, but Leighor's heart sank when he saw how few were the men behind their proud banners. Apart from the grey and yellow of Arminor's own troops, the only other force of any number – perhaps two thousand in all – stood waiting on the extreme western flank. The blue and orange banners were unfamiliar to him, and he asked whose troops they were.

'Those are the followers of Mathalas, lord of High Elerian,' Pace told him. 'He was very close to Galdan while he lived, and has long been an ally of Arminor. He must have brought his forces north in secret to join with the king. Mayhap that is why he was not at the assembly yesterday: he did not wish to reveal his hand too soon.'

'Aye, mayhap,' Zindur growled. 'And mayhap it is his presence now that had encouraged Arminor to take the field this day. Those troops would only be more mouths to feed during a long siege; and the king will want to use them while he can.'

'Even so, it is a desperate gamble,' Uhlendof muttered, half beneath his breath. 'He has been ill-advised, ill-advised indeed . . .' He shook his head.

And then a new sound drifted up from the valley below: a dull shuffling, a clatter of shields and swords, pikes and halberds, as the front ranks of Misan's infantry began to slow march forward. They attempted no charge, however, and with their lines intact they halted as suddenly as they had begun, some two hundred paces before the front rank of Arminor's army. Their pikes and halberds fell forward in unison, to break any sudden charge of the northron horse, and a line of archers ran forward to take shelter behind them. Through a dreamlike silence a thick cloud of arrows rose up from their bows to rain down upon Arminor's lines.

A shrill, distant cry rang out, and an answering hail of fire came back from the Helietrim lines – many men falling upon both sides before the armies ever met.

But now the centre of Arminor's line surged suddenly forward, like a great wave breaking upon dark sands; and the two armies were at once joined in bloody hand-to-hand conflict.

'It is a risky strategy Arminor tries,' Zindur noted dourly. 'He throws all his force at the centre, hoping to break a way through for his horse – but he leaves himself few reserves.'

Yet already Misan's lines buckled visibly, driven back by the sheer weight and ferocity of the Helietrim attack – and within moments they had burst asunder. A great cheer erupted from the throats of all who watched from the castle walls, as Misan's levies broke and scattered before the yellow banners of Helietrim, opening up a way for Arminor to lead his cavalry through into the heart of the enemy.

More men were already running forward to reinforce the broken line, but these were too late and too disorganised to hold; letting fall their weapons as they fled before Arminor's triumphant horse. And now the mounted lancers wheeled to tear into the unprepared reserves who waited on Misan's western flank. These were the men of Kalural and Holdar, who were here only under obligation, and had little real stomach for a fight.

Within minutes most of the Imperial front line was in full rout; only the powerful eastern flank, commanded by Misan himself, still held together. Yet this was still the strongest part of the High Regent's army, and contained the majority of his ablest and most seasoned troops.

'Arminor does well, the old fox,' Zindur nodded with approval now. 'If he can but collect his horse and get them back to his own lines, he will have done much; perhaps enough to end the battle well.'

Yet now all of Misan's reserve infantry poured suddenly forward to fall upon the tired remnant of the main Helietrim line. And with Arminor's horse committed to the forward attack, his footsoldiers were left to deal with the full weight of this second onslaught alone. But still their line held, although the fighting was bloody and their losses high.

The five companies of Misan's horse, however, did not join even in this attack, but still waited close by the river, on the far eastern corner of the battleplain. And somewhere amongst their number rode Misan himself.

'What does he wait for?' Telsyan said tensely, staring out at the close-ranked order of Misan's westron horsemen, and the Imsild Knights beside them. 'Why does he not commit his horse now, and have done?'

'Perhaps they wait to see how the battle will turn,' Yeon laughed, 'before they flee back to far Petan!'

'You may be right,' Zindur acknowledged. 'The Knights of Imsild will not wish to commit themselves until they are sure of the victory.'

The shrill cry of the Helietrim battle horns rang across the battlefield as Arminor's knights at last began to pull themselves together. They seemed to have taken few losses thus far, and still made a stirring sight as they rallied to their banners. However, they were now a good half league from their own embattled lines, and all but cut off from them. Only if Misan's horse remained unable or unwilling to intercept them could they hope to cut their way back without fearful loss.

Closer to hand the yellow battle ranks of the Helietrim yeomen still held firm. But looking directly beneath him, Leighor had a sudden shock; for the five columns of Mathalas' Elerian halberdiers, who held the right flank, seemed suddenly to be wavering. In fact it now appeared that they had ceased to fight at all, their weapons dropping from their hands as their lines fell apart before Misan's westron infantry like a rope of sand before the tide.

As if on this signal, the three gleaming cohorts of the Knights of Imsild, which had remained immobile throughout the battle, started abruptly forward, to take advantage of the newly created breach. And at once the two companies of westron riders, with Misan's personal banner at their head, turned westward to intercept Arminor's returning knights.

'What treachery is this?' Zindur bellowed.

'Mathalas's men have been in league with Misan all along!' Telsyan spat. 'The knights were waiting for this moment!'

And now a full twelve hundred of the Knights of Imsild, lances razor-sharp and banners flying, pressed through the narrow opening to fall upon the rear of Arminor's beleaguered army. Penned in now upon all sides, the tattered remnant of the Helietrim infantry were cut to pieces. Hundreds died in the first few minutes; falling beneath swords, lances and iron-shod hooves in a bloody mayhem of destruction. Without the aid of Arminor's cavalry, all were doomed.

But even as the cavalry tried to fight their way back across the brown fields towards them, they were met by Misan's fresh Petan horsemen, who rode hard in upon their right. These made no contact however, but halted at a hundred paces' distance to loose a withering volley of arrows into the Helietrim ranks. Yeon gasped as a staggering number of knights and horses fell beneath that first deadly barrage.

'The westron riders are goodly archers indeed,' Zindur grunted with professional detachment. 'Arminor will have to come to close quarters!'

But Leighor could see that already the tide of the battle had turned. Misan's forces now commanded most of the field, and even the levies that had been scattered by Arminor's first great charge now slowly gathered themselves together on the fringes of the plain.

Then, suddenly, a crackling river of silver flame burst forth from the centre of Arminor's milling cavalry to strike into the midst of the westron horsemen. For an instant Misan's ranks broke before it, men screamed, and horses reared in panic. But when the fire was not renewed, the riders rallied, and the westron ranks reformed.

Yet even now the Petan horsemen did not close, keeping their distance to fire volley on volley of deadly arrows into the clumsier northron horse. Many were the proud knights of Helietrim who fell to ignoble deaths that day, before ever they drew close enough to engage the enemy. Yet still there remained a dense cluster of yellow about the king's banner.

These last now rallied, and turned, lances lowered, to make a final great charge towards the centre of the westron horse and the great purple banner of Misan that rippled above. Now, at last, the westron arrows failed: and even the fleet plains horses were surely not swift enough to evade the thundering lances that bore remorselessly down upon them.

But then four bright flashes of intense purple light burst from beneath the great banners of Misan, to strike into the heart of the Helietrim charge – the swathes of yellow abruptly rent by a wall of crimson flame that cut through the mounted ranks like a dreadful scythe. And, to a terrible groan from all who watched on the castle walls, the last yellow banners fell, engulfed in a tower of fire that burned five, ten, twenty feet high, across the centre of the battle plain. Seconds later, the sound of four mighty thunderclaps echoed up along the high walls of Irun's Teeth.

'Arminor is fallen,' Pace said blankly. 'All is lost.'

Leighor stared down at the battlefield, unable to believe how quickly and how utterly all had changed. Bare minutes before it had seemed that Arminor was on the verge of a brilliant, audacious victory. And now the king was dead, and the last of his knights were being circled and cut down by the half-wild westron horsemen. Arminor's infantry fared no better, for the slaughter amongst their number had been great indeed, the last wounded remnants of the armies of Helietrim throwing down their banners and their weapons, and begging for quarter.

Still Leighor could not quite grasp the enormity of what he had just witnessed. 'Lost?' he shook his head. 'Arminor . . . ? All those men . . . ? What will happen now?'

Telsyan watched Misan's victorious forces reassembling in the growing shadow of the mountains far below, his face set. 'The way to Clanamel is thrown open. Misan will ride into Helietrim unopposed. What will happen then is anyone's guess. But any who have openly supported Arminor, whether in Helietrim or elsewhere, had best stay out of his hands. Misan is still too insecure upon his throne to be merciful.'

'Then is our cause entirely lost?' Keran demanded. 'Are we now all to be subject to Misan, and to the rule of the Mage Lords?'

'No!' Uhlendof shook his head defiantly. 'That cannot be! The amulets of power are displayed now openly for all to see. After this day's work their ownership can no longer be concealed! Their presence will divide those who bear them from those who do not. And there are many who will stand against the terror they will bring.'

'Who?' Leighor demanded.

'Here in the north, few,' Uhlendof acknowledged. 'Here the battle is lost. There may be a few skirmishes in the high mountain valleys, where some of Arminor's supporters may yet hold out for a while. But that cannot be for us . . .'

'Then where do you suggest we go?' Telsyan enquired. 'We must be long gone from this place before Misan gets here. This will be the first place he will turn – to seek out any who still oppose him!'

'We must go south,' Uhlendof said quickly.

'But why?' Leighor asked. 'Arminor is dead. Eridar's proxy is useless to us now . . . unless he has an heir!' He turned to Pace. 'Has he any such?'

'Arminor has no sons,' Pace answered slowly. 'But he is not the last of his house. It is little known, even amongst those closest to the king, but he has, I think, a cousin who dwells somewhere to the south. If that man still lives, he is Arminor's heir, and he will be heir also to Arminor's claim to the High Kingship of the Varroain.'

'Then it is settled,' Uhlendof said. 'Eridar's vote may still be of use, and we have a duty to go on. We must make first for Tershelline to see what support may be rallied there. And if again we fail, we must go farther south, to lands less beset by terror and war. Aye, south beyond the Isznells – as far as Syrne or Azila if needs be – until we find a place where men can rally, and a plan may be devised to defeat the perils that face us. We have the sword, we have the proxy of Eridar, we have the knowledge of what great evils will fall upon the world if Misan is allowed to gain a final victory. We must go on: and south is the only way!'

'South, through that battlefield?' Keran said in dismay.

'Aye,' Zindur nodded. 'if that be the only way. But if we are going, we must go quickly, before Misan's men come! See how they pour now through the Irthing Gorge! Come! We have but four hours to get clear away from here!'

HERE ENDS THE FIRST BOOK OF THE *AMULETS OF DARKNESS* CYCLE
THE SECOND BOOK WILL BE *THE TEARS OF GINARA*.

Appendix One
TIME

The calendar of the Eastern Realms of Osenkor has many regional variants in the lands both north and south of the Isznell Mountains. The most widely used forms are set out here.

DAYS OF THE WEEK

Sunday . . . . Named for Helior, the Sun God
Moonday . . . . Named for the Gods of Knowledge and Craft
Earthday . . . . Named for Ethimathé, the Earth Goddess
Midweeksday
Stormday . . . . Named for Arul, Lord of the Air
Fairday . . . . Named for Eldalis, Goddess of Harvest
Starday . . . . Named for Ginara, Goddess of Water

MONTHS OF THE YEAR

Northern Style		Southern Style	
Ilter	28 days	Ilter	28 days
Spring		*Spring*	
Vollining	36 days	Weone	36 days
Helery	26 days	Helerie	26 days
Oldar	32 days	Oldar	32 days
Summer		*Summer*	
Olvel	28 days	Olvel	28 days
Brannan	30 days	Selle	30 days
Bramall	22 days	Soselle	22 days
Autumn		*Autumn*	
Gurnithun	35 days	Guinde	35 days
Faestan	35 days	Faura	35 days
Vilvereem	28 days	Vilvereem	28 days
Winter		*Winter*	
Silstereem	20 days	Silstereem	20 days
Yearsend	47 days	Rallen	24 days
		Zelve	23 days

CALENDAR

There are two main calendars used by the men of the Eastern Realms:

The Varroain Calendar, dating from the birth of Terasil, first High King of the Varroain. Current year: 784

The Southern, or Samaran Calendar, dating from the foundation of the lost city of Surza. Current year: 3328

Appendix Two
RULERS OF THE NORTHERN REALMS OF OSENKOR ON THE 1ST DAY OF ILTER 785

Varroain Electors are marked with an asterisk*

RULERS OF THE ELEVEN KINGDOMS OF THE VARROAIN

Darvir . . . . Archbaron of the Sielders*
Shulnharm . . . . Margrave of Felldur*
Arminor . . . . King of Helietrim*
Misan . . . . King of Petan and Regent of Elerian*
Zailim . . . . King of Kalural*
Bey Varan . . . . Elector of Selethir*
Molurn . . . . Regent of Arethon*
Pirazzu . . . . Dorg of Coimbra*
Berund . . . . Dorg of Silgany*
Jaralm . . . . King of Holdar*

OTHER RULERS OWING FEALTY TO THE VARROAIN HIGH KING OR TO HIS SUBJECT PRINCES

Mehnok . . . . First King of Azila
Mathalas . . . . Dorge of High Elerian*
Nurambor . . . . Princips of Tershelline*
Nonbruneon . . . . Dorge of Low Elerian

NORTHERN RULERS NOT SUBJECT TO THE HIGH KING OF THE VARROAIN

Aguer . . . . King of Oleiyor
Ivo . . . . King of Scûn
Xhorlaq . . . . Great Khanain of Khiorim
Karadas-Ulgar . . . . King of High Ghorrunar
Enalkur . . . . Legendary Master of the North
Goromun . . . . Legendary Hillman King in the north
Numberless *maezgrull*, *ghrornan*, Riever and goblin chieftains

OTHER PERSONAGES OF NOTABLE RANK
Usialdun . . . . Grand Master of the Knights of Imsild*

Guniord . . . . Grand Master of the Durian Knights
Yranthred . . . . Prince of Petan, Brother to Misan
Jerunan . . . . Lord of Far Petan, Cousin to Misan
Eveor-Anka . . . . Commander of the Western Levies